FYODOR DOSTOYEVSKY was born in Moscow on October 30, 1821. He was educated in Moscow and at the School of Military Engineers in St. Petersburg, where he spent four years. In 1844 he resigned his Commission in the army to devote himself to literature. In 1846, he wrote his first novel, *Poor Folk;* it was an immediate critical and popular success. This was followed by short stories and a novel, *The Double.* While at work on *Netochka Nezvanova,* the twenty-seven-year-old author was arrested for belonging to a young socialist group. He was tried and condemned to death, but at the last moment his sentence was commuted to prison in Siberia. He spent four years in the penal settlement at Omsk; then he was released on the condition that he serve in the army. While in the army he fell in love with and married Marie Isaeva. In 1859 he was granted full amnesty and allowed to return to St. Petersburg. In the next few years he wrote his first full-length novels: *The Friend of the Family* (1859) and *The Insulted and the Injured* (1862). *Notes from Underground* (1864) was in many ways his most influential work of this period, containing the wellsprings of his mature philosophy: the hope of gaining salvation through degradation and suffering. At the end of this literary period, his wife died. Plagued by epilepsy, faced with financial ruin, he worked at superhuman speed to produce *The Gambler,* dictating the novel to eighteen-year-old Anna Grigorievna Snitkina. The manuscript was delivered to his publisher in time. During the next fourteen years, Dostoyevsky wrote his greatest works: *Crime and Punishment, The Idiot, The Possessed,* and *The Brothers Karamazov.* The latter book was published a year before his death on January 28, 1881.

COPYRIGHT © 1962 BY ANDREW R. MACANDREW

AFTERWORD COPYRIGHT © 1962 BY
THE NEW AMERICAN LIBRARY OF WORLD LITERATURE, INC.

Third Printing

SIGNET CLASSICS are published *in the United States*
by The New American Library, Inc., 1301 Avenue of
the Americas, New York, New York 10019,
in Canada by The New American Library of Canada
Limited, 295 King Street East, Toronto 2, Ontario,
in the United Kingdom by The New English Library
Limited, Barnard's Inn, Holborn, London, E.C. 1,
England

PRINTED IN THE UNITED STATES OF AMERICA

A NEW T...ION BY
ANDREW R. CANDREW

WITH AN AFTERWORD BY
MARC SLONIM

A SIGNET CLASSIC

PUBLISHED BY
THE NEW AMERICAN LIBRARY,
NEW YORK AND TORONTO
THE NEW ENGLISH LIBRARY LIMITED, LONDON

...sed

SIGNET CLASSICS CAREFULLY SELECTED, EDITED, AND PRINTED, PROVIDE A TREASURY OF THE WORLD'S ... WRITINGS IN HANDSOMELY DESIGNED VOLUMES.

Contents

Can't be helped, the track is covered.
Hopeless! We have lost our way.
Demons must have taken over,
Whirling, twisting us astray.

. . . .

Look at them! They're everywhere!
Hear the mournful tune they make!
What, a witch's wedding fare?
Or a goblin's gloomy wake?

> *(from "The Demons,"*
> *by Alexander Pushkin)*

And there was there a herd of many swine feeding on the mountain: and they besought him that he would suffer them to enter into them. And he suffered them.

Then went the devils out of the man, and entered into the swine: and the herd ran violently down a steep place into the lake and were choked.

When they that fed them saw what was done, they fled, and went and told it in the city and in the country.

Then they went out to see what was done; and came to Jesus, and found the man, out of whom the devils were departed, sitting at the feet of Jesus, clothed, and in his right mind: and they were afraid.

(Luke 8:32-37)

Part One

chapter 1

BY WAY OF AN INTRODUCTION: SOME BIOGRAPHICAL
DATA ON THE WORTHY STEPAN TROFIMOVICH VERKHOVENSKY

I

In approaching the recent, very strange events that occurred in our hitherto rather unremarkable town, I feel that I must start further back by supplying some facts about the life of the gifted and well-respected Stepan Trofimovich Verkhovensky. This may serve as an introduction to the story to come.

Let me begin by saying that Stepan Verkhovensky had always cut a rather special figure among us—in the civic sense, that is. He passionately loved his role—so much so, in fact, that I don't think he could have lived without it. But don't think that I mean to compare him with an actor—God forbid—I respect him too much for that. It may have been largely a matter of habit, or rather a constant and even praiseworthy tendency, ever since his childhood, to slip into a pleasant daydream about his taking a gallant civic stand. Thus, he greatly relished his idea of himself as a *persecuted* man—in fact, an *exile*. There is about these two words a certain traditional glamour that seduced him once and for all. As the years went by, by exalting this glamour he placed himself, in his own estimation, on a pedestal that greatly gratified his vanity.

In an eighteenth-century English satire, Gulliver, returning from the land of the Lilliputians, where the people were only a few inches tall, had become so used to thinking of himself as a giant that, back in London, he kept shouting at the carriages and people in the street to get out of his way so that he wouldn't crush them. They laughed at him and insulted him, and rude coachmen even lashed at him with their whips. But were they justified? What may not be done through habit? And it was habit that made Stepan Verkhovensky act as he did—and, after all, his behavior was milder and less offensive, for he was really a very nice man.

Although in the end he was completely forgotten, I think it should be said that he had had a certain reputation. There's no doubt that at one point—a very brief moment, to be sure—his name was mentioned almost in the same breath as those of Chaadayev, Belinsky, Granovsky, and Herzen. But Stepan Verkhovensky's active engagement ended almost as soon as it began, because of what he described as "a whirl of events." In fact, though, it turned out that there never had been any "whirl" or even any "events" to speak of. Only recently I learned for certain that Mr. Verkhovensky's reason for living in our province was not that he had been exiled from Petersburg and Moscow; nor was he ever under police surveillance as we had been led to believe. Such, then, is the power of auto-suggestion! Throughout his life, he himself sincerely believed that in certain government quarters they were very apprehensive of him, that his every step was watched, and that each of the three successive governors we had during twenty years had, on assuming his post, been warned about him by very highly placed, powerful people and consequently was full of misgivings on taking over the province. And if one of us had ever tried to persuade Mr. Verkhovensky that he really had nothing to fear, he'd certainly have taken it as an insult. Yet, at the same time, he was such an intelligent, gifted man, and his learning . . . well, it's true that there were no special academic achievements to his credit; in fact no achievements at all, I believe—but then, this is so often the case with our learned men in Russia.

When he returned from abroad in the late eighteen forties, he shone briefly as a university lecturer. Actually, he only had time to deliver a few lectures—on Arab culture, I believe. He also managed to defend a brilliant dissertation on the social and Hanseatic influence the little German town of Hanau might have had between 1413 and 1428 had it not been for certain special, rather cloudy circumstances. That dissertation was a clever, telling dig at the Slavophiles of the time and made him many enemies among them. Later, after he lost his position at the university, he succeeded in having published (just to show them whom they'd lost!) in some progressive monthly that often carried translations from Dickens and advocated the theories of George Sand, the beginning of some very profound study of, I believe, the underlying reasons for the extraordinarily high moral standards of some knights or other during a particular historical period, or something of that sort. In any case, he developed in it some subtle ideas of unbelievably high moral caliber. It was rumored later that continuation of the study had been forbidden by the authorities and even that the progressive magazine had suffered unpleasant consequences for having carried the first part. Well, it's very possible—all sorts of things happened at that time. In this particular case, however, it is more probable that nothing like that happened, that the author was simply too lazy to complete his research.

As to his lectures on Arab culture, they had to be discontinued because, at one point, someone—probably one of his reactionary enemies—wrote a letter to someone else informing him of certain matters. Whereupon someone asked him for certain explanations.

I can't vouch for it, but I have heard that at that time they discovered in Petersburg a monstrous, subversive organization of about thirteen members that had come close to blowing the regime sky-high. It was said that they were about to start translating Fourier himself! As chance would have it, the Moscow authorities just then seized a verse play that Stepan Verkhovensky had written six years earlier in Berlin, when he was still very young. The manuscript was being circulated from hand to hand and had already been read by two poetry lovers and one student.

That manuscript is lying on my desk in front of me now. I received it about a year ago from the author himself, who had only shortly before that recopied it in his own hand. It bears his signature and is bound in sumptuous red morocco.

I must say there's a lyrical quality about the play; perhaps it even shows some signs of talent. It's a little strange, but that's the way they wrote in the eighteen thirties. It would be difficult to tell you what it's all about, for to tell the truth, I can't make out a thing. It's some sort of allegory in lyrical-dramatic form that somehow reminds one of the second part of *Faust*. The action opens with a female chorus followed by a male chorus. Then there's a chorus of "occult" forces, and finally a chorus of human souls who haven't lived yet but would like to have a go at it. All these choruses sing something very obscure, mostly about a curse laid on someone or other. However, they handle the subject with delicate humor.

Suddenly the scene shifts and something called the Festival of Life takes place. Now everyone sings, including the insects. A tortoise arrives and says a few sacramental words in Latin. And, if I remember correctly, even a mineral (an inanimate object beyond all doubt) bursts into song at one point. In general, the lot of them hardly ever stop singing; when they do talk, it is only to exchange some vague invective—and even in this there's a hint of profound significance.

Then the scene shifts again. It's a wild, rocky spot, and among the rocks a civilized young man is out for a stroll. He keeps picking herbs and sucking them. When a fairy inquires why he is sucking them, he informs her that he feels an excess of life within him, that he's trying to forget himself and find forgetfulness in the juices of these herbs. But, he tells the fairy, his main wish is to rid himself of his brains—a wish that sounds quite superfluous. At this point, an incredibly handsome youth rides in on a black steed, followed by a huge crowd of people of all nationalities. The youth is Death, and all the people are thirsting for it.

Finally, in the closing scene, the Tower of Babel crops up. Some athletic-looking men are helping to complete its construction while singing a song of new hope. When they have completed the job the lord of something (Olympus, I believe) flees ignominiously, looking ridiculous, and mankind, having gained insight into things, takes over and immediately starts to live differently.

Anyway, this was the play that they thought dangerous. Last year I suggested to Mr. Verkhovensky that he have it published, for it is quite innocuous by our present standards. He spurned my suggestion with obvious displeasure. He didn't at all relish my calling his piece innocuous, and I think this accounts for his subsequent coolness toward me that lasted for two months.

And what do you think happened? At the very time I suggested that he have his play published here in Russia, it was printed abroad in a revolutionary anthology without his knowledge. Terribly scared, he scurried over to see the governor and wrote a noble letter of self-justification to Petersburg. He read it aloud to me twice, but never sent it off because he didn't know to whom to address it. He worried about it for a whole month. I'm certain, however, that in the secret recesses of his heart he was immensely flattered. He went to bed every night with a copy of the anthology that had been smuggled in to him, and during the day he kept it under his mattress. He didn't even allow the maid to make his bed during all that time. And, although he daily expected to receive a telegram from somewhere, he maintained a haughty, resolute expression. No telegram arrived. Eventually he forgave me too, which shows how kind he is and how unable to bear a grudge.

II

Of course, I'm not trying to say that he didn't suffer for his convictions at all. But I'm convinced that he could have gone on lecturing about his Arabs if he had only provided the necessary explanations. Instead, he let himself be carried away by his imagination and convinced himself that his academic career was shattered by a "whirl of events."

But, if you wish to know the real truth, the actual cause of the break in his career was a renewed offer, made in the most delicate terms by Varvara Petrovna Stavrogin, the wife of Lieutenant General Stavrogin and an extremely wealthy lady. She suggested he take upon himself, in the capacity of educational supervisor and friend, the education and intellectual development of her only son, for which she offered him, it goes without saying, fabulous remuneration. The offer had first been made when he was still in Berlin, after his first wife died. She was a native of our province, a frivolous girl whom he had married while still very young and impulsive. I believe he had a miserable time with that (it must be said) rather charming woman, partly because of financial restrictions and partly because of certain difficulties of a delicate nature.

She died in Paris, having been separated from him during the last three years of her life, leaving him a five-year-old son, "the fruit of our first, still unclouded happiness," as Mr. Verkhovensky once sadly put it in my presence.

The fruit of their happiness was immediately packed off to Russia and his education entrusted to some distant relative residing in a remote backwater.

That first time, Mr. Verkhovensky declined Mrs. Stavrogin's offer. Less than a year after his wife's death, for no particular reason he married an uncommunicative Berlin girl. However, this remarriage was not his only reason for declining the position as young Stavrogin's tutor: he was fascinated by the resounding fame of a certain professor and had his eye on an academic career for himself that he fancied would give him an opportunity to soar on eagle's wings.

So, with his wings already singed, he recalled the offer that even before had made him hesitate. Then the sudden death of his second wife less than a year after they were married decided him definitely. Let me say candidly: it was all made possible by Mrs. Stavrogin's warm understanding and classical friendship—if that adjective may be applied to friendship. He threw himself into the arms of that friendship and nestled there for twenty years. Now, although I say he "threw himself into the arms of . . ." let no one start imagining things: those arms must be understood in a highly moral sense. The most subtle, delicate link united these two remarkable people once and for all.

Stepan Verkhovensky also accepted the tutorship because the small estate he had inherited from his first wife was close to Skvoreshniki, the Stavrogins' magnificent estate near our town. Moreover, Mr. Verkhovensky felt that, in the quiet atmosphere of his study, undistracted by the immensity of the university load, he could devote himself to learned research and to enriching the treasure house of our national culture. No results of research actually materialized; what did materialize was the possibility of becoming, for the rest of his life—for over twenty years—the essence of reproach to his native land. As the poet put it:

> The essence of reproach you stand
> To your beloved native land,
> You liberal idealist.

Of course, the person the poet had in mind may perhaps have been entitled to stand in a reproachful pose for the rest of his life, boring though that might be. But Stepan Verkhovensky really only imitated such people, and besides, as standing took too much out of him, he often curled up on his side for a little rest. Still, he managed to remain the essence of reproach even in a recumbent position, and that was good enough for our province. You should have seen him when he sat down to a card table in our club. His whole person seemed to say:

"Ah, cards . . . Imagine me sitting down to play cards with you! I know it's most unsuitable. But whose fault is it? Who shattered my career? Ah, what is Russia coming to?"

And with an air of the utmost dignity, he'd play a heart.

As a matter of fact, he was very fond of cards, which fondness, especially later on, caused frequent and unpleasant squabbles with Mrs. Stavrogin, particularly since he constantly lost. But more of that later. In the meantime, let me only say that he was a highly sensitive man (in some ways, that is) and so was often depressed. During their twenty-year friendship, he had periods of what we called "social grief" two, three, or four times a year. Actually, they were simple fits of depression, but Mrs. Stavrogin liked to ascribe them to his suffering over social injustice. Later, in addition to his periods of "social grief," he slipped into periods of champagne drinking. But, with great tact, Mrs. Stavrogin tried to help him control this vulgar inclination. Yes, he needed a nurse of sorts, for he grew quite strange as time went by. Now and then, in the middle of a period of the most noble grief, he suddenly burst into laughter that was anything but refined. Occasionally, he even made humorous remarks about himself, and there was nothing Mrs. Stavrogin feared as much as a sense of humor. She was a woman classicist, a lady-protector-of-the-arts who acted only out of the loftiest considerations. The twenty-year influence of this lady upon her poor friend was decisive, so a few words about her personality may be pertinent.

III

There are strange friendships in which the two parties long to tear each other to pieces most of the time and yet cannot live without each other. Separation is unthinkable because the one who loses his temper and decides to break it up would probably die himself if he went through with it. I know for sure that on several occasions, after an intimate conflagration with Mrs. Stavrogin, Mr. Verkhovensky suddenly leaped up from the sofa where he was sitting and banged on the wall with his fists. And I don't mean that figuratively either. Once he even knocked down a good deal of plaster.

You may wonder how I can possibly know such an intimate detail. Well—suppose I witnessed it myself? Suppose Stepan

Verkhovensky himself often sobbed on my shoulder, painting his secret torments in the most lurid colors? And the things he told me on some occasions!

But, the day after sobbing like that, he was prepared to crucify himself for his ingratitude. He would hurry over to my place or summon me hastily just to tell me that Mrs. Stavrogin was an angel, the soul of tact and noble behavior, while he was just the opposite. And he not only confided in me, he often described everything to her in the most eloquent letters in which—above his full signature—he confessed, for instance, that only yesterday he had told an outsider that she kept him out of vanity, that she was envious of his talent, that she hated him and only concealed her hatred because she was afraid he would walk out on her and thereby compromise her literary reputation; that, finally, he loathed himself and had decided to die by his own hand and was only waiting for the word from her that would seal his fate—and so on. So you can imagine the pitch of hysteria this innocent, fifty-year-old babe could work himself up to! Once I read one of those letters; it was written after a quarrel between them that had started over some trivial matter and had become envenomed as it dragged on. I was horrified and begged him not to send it.

"Impossible . . . it's more honest this way . . . my duty . . . I'll die if I don't make a clean breast of everything—yes, everything!" he muttered as if delirious, and sent the letter.

And this is where the main difference between them lay— Mrs. Stavrogin never would have sent a letter like that. True, Mr. Verkhovensky was crazy about writing. He wrote to Mrs. Stavrogin even though they lived in the same house, and during his hysterical periods, he turned out two letters a day. I know for certain that she always read those letters very carefully, even when she received two on the same day. Then she folded them neatly, annotated and classified them, and filed them in a special drawer. Moreover, she did some soul searching over those messages herself.

But then, having left her friend wondering for the whole day, she met him and behaved as if nothing had happened. Gradually she trained him so well that he never raised the subject of a quarrel himself, but only glanced questioningly into her eyes. However, she never forgot anything, whereas he did— and too quickly at that. Often, on the very next day, encouraged by her polite composure, he laughed in the presence of strangers and even behaved with schoolboyish exuberance over the champagne. I can imagine the venomous looks she darted at him without his ever noticing. But then—perhaps a week, a month, or even six months later—he would recall by chance some expression from one of his letters and then the entire letter with all the circumstances that surrounded it, and he would suddenly be overwhelmed by shame. This tormented him so that he always ended by suffering violent stomach upsets. He usually suffered from these upsets after periods of nervous strain; they were a curious feature of his physical make-up.

Indeed, Mrs. Stavrogin must often have hated him. But he had become, above all, a sort of son for her—a creation, her own invention. And this Mr. Verkhovensky never suspected to the end of his life. Yes, he became the flesh of her flesh, and she held on to him, but not at all because she was envious of his talent, as he asserted. Ah, how insulting such assumptions must have seemed to her! She buried her unquenchable feeling for him under constant hatred, jealousy, and scorn. She protected him from every speck of dust, looked after him like a baby for twenty-two years, and spent sleepless nights when she sensed some threat to his reputation as poet, scholar, and fighter for social justice. She had invented him, and she was also the first to believe in her own invention. He was a bit like a part of her private daydream. Consequently, she made great demands upon him, almost making a slave of him.

Besides, she was incredibly unforgiving. Let me tell you a couple of anecdotes about that.

IV

Once, when rumors about emancipation of the serfs first started circulating and all Russia was rejoicing in anticipation of a moral regeneration, Mrs. Stavrogin received a visit from a baron from Petersburg, a man with the highest connections and very closely associated with the forthcoming reform. She valued such visits highly because, since the death of her husband, her links with high society had become weaker, destined, as they were, to break altogether in the end. The baron came to tea, staying for about an hour. She didn't invite anyone except Mr. Verkhovensky, who, she felt, would be a good showpiece for the baron. Apparently the baron had heard of him—unless he just pretended he had—but, anyway, he scarcely addressed him during tea. Of course, Stepan Verkhovensky felt he had to make a good impression, which should have been easy with his elegant manners. For, although he was, I believe, of humble origin, he had been brought up from earliest boyhood in a well-known Moscow family and spoke French like a native Parisian. He was present to help the baron realize from the first glance the sort of people with whom Mrs. Stavrogin surrounded herself even in her provincial isolation. However, it didn't quite pan out that way. When the baron confirmed the absolute authenticity of the rumors about the great reform, Mr. Verkhovensky allowed his enthusiasm to get the better of him, shouted "Hurrah!" and even gestured with his hand, intending to emphasize his exaltation. His exclamation wasn't loud and was quite elegant in a way. His outburst may even have been deliberate and the gesture carefully rehearsed before a mirror half an hour before the tea party. Still, something must have gone wrong, because the baron indulged in a very slight smile—although immediately afterward, with incredible politeness, he managed to slip in a phrase about the nation-wide delight, the lifting of all Russian hearts at news of the great event. Soon after this, he left, not forgetting to thrust two fingers into Mr. Verkhovensky's hand in parting. When they were back in the sitting room by themselves, Mrs. Stavrogin remained silent for three minutes, ostensibly trying to locate something on the table. Then she suddenly looked directly at Mr. Verkhovensky. She was very pale and her eyes flashed as she hissed at him:

"I'll never forgive you for this!"

The next day she behaved as if nothing had happened, and the incident seemed forgotten. Thirteen years later, however, she suddenly recalled it during one of their quarrels and reproached him for it. And she turned pale and her eyes flashed just as when she had reproached him thirteen years earlier.

Only twice during their entire relationship did she say to him, "I'll never forgive you for this!" The tea party with the baron was the second time. But the first time was also typical and so affected Mr. Verkhovensky's life that I believe it should also be told.

It happened in May 1855, when the news of General Stavrogin's death reached Skvoreshniki. That frivolous old man died of a stomach upset on the way to the Crimea, where he was to have joined units engaged in military operations. Mrs. Stavrogin, a widow now, went into full mourning. It must be said, however, that she cannot really have been very hard hit by her husband's death, for as a result of the complete incompatibility of their characters, they had been separated for over four years. She paid him a monthly allowance, for the general had only a hundred and fifty serfs, his army pay, a well-known name, and good connections, while she owned the Skvoreshniki estate and was the only daughter of a very rich contractor. Nevertheless, the suddenness of the news was a shock to her, and she retired into seclusion. It goes without saying that Mr. Verkhovensky remained constantly at her side.

May was in full swing. The long evenings were enchanting; the wild cherry was in flower. Every evening they met in the garden and sat till nightfall in the arbor, pouring out their thoughts and feelings. Those were very poetic moments. The change in her marital status somehow made Mrs. Stavrogin very talkative, and, one might say, she opened the recesses of her soul to her friend. This went on throughout several May evenings.

Then a strange thought suddenly occurred to Stepan Verkhovensky.

"Maybe," he wondered, "this inconsolable widow expects me to propose to her when the year of mourning is over?"

There's no doubt that this was a rather cynical thought, but then, the higher the stage of development a man reaches, the more prone he becomes to cynicism, if only because of the increasing complexity of his make-up.

He mulled over this thought for a while and came to the conclusion that it looked very much like it.

"Yes," he mused, "there's a huge fortune here, but . . ."

Indeed, Varvara Stavrogin could hardly be described as a beauty. She was tall and bony, and her complexion was yellow. Her face was immensely long, reminding one of a horse. Mr. Verkhovensky suffered growing misgivings and hesitations that even reduced him to tears once or twice (in general, he had a propensity for tears). Now, during their evening meetings in the garden, a faintly whimsical, sarcastic expression crept over his face; his bearing somehow became both smug and coy at the same time. These things happen to one involuntarily, and the more noble the person, the more it shows. It is hard to say, but possibly nothing to justify Stepan Verkhovensky's suspicions ever stirred in Varvara Stavrogin's heart. In any case, she would hardly be likely to wish to exchange the name Stavrogin for Verkhovensky, glorious though he may have made it. Perhaps it was simply a feminine play on her part, a display of unconscious female needs common to women under certain circumstances. I can't say for certain: to this day, woman's heart has never been explored to its depths.

Undoubtedly, it didn't take her long to decipher the queer expression on her friend's face, for she was as sensitive and observant as he was innocent. However, their evenings didn't change, and their conversations remained as exalted and lofty as before. Then, once, as night fell, they said good night, warmly pressing each other's hands at the door of the annex in the middle of the garden, into which Mr. Verkhovensky moved every summer from the huge Skvoreshniki house.

He had only just gone inside, and full of disturbing thoughts, he picked up a cigar. Before lighting it, he stopped wearily in front of an open window, looking distractedly at the light, cottony clouds gliding past the neat crescent moon. A sudden crackle made him start and turn. Varvara Stavrogin, whom he had left four minutes before, stood before him again. Her yellow face had turned almost blue; her lips were pressed tightly together and their corners quivered. For ten silent seconds her hard, merciless stare transfixed him; then she spat out in a quick whisper:

"I'll never forgive you for this!"

Ten years later, when Mr. Verkhovensky related this sad story to me in a subdued whisper behind locked doors, he swore that he had been so petrified that he neither saw nor heard Mrs. Stavrogin leave. And, since she never so much as hinted at what had happened and their relations continued just as before, he was inclined to think it had been a hallucination such as precedes illness, especially since he actually was ill for two weeks, thus, by chance, putting an end to their evening meetings in the garden.

But despite his hope that it had only been a hallucination, he kept expecting what may be termed an outcome to the affair. He couldn't believe that it had ended then and there. And so, at times, he must have felt strange looking at his lady friend.

V

She even decided what clothes he should wear to the end of his days. It was elegant and appropriate attire: a long black frock coat buttoned almost to the top and very well fitted; a soft, wide-brimmed felt hat (a straw one in summer); a white cravat with a full bow and loose ends; and a cane with a silver knob. She also made him wear his hair long and flowing onto his shoulders. His hair was dirty blond and had only recently started to go gray. He was clean-shaven.

It was said that in his youth Stepan Verkhovensky had been very handsome, and in my opinion, he was extremely impressive even in his older years. But then, is fifty-three really old? Yet, in his desire to pose as an old fighter for social justice, he certainly didn't try to look younger than his age. He even seemed to want to emphasize his advanced years. And so, tall and spare, with his long flowing hair and in that attire, he looked like some patriarch and even more like the engraving of the poet Kukolnikov that was reproduced in the 1830 edition of his works. He resembled that engraving when he sat on a garden bench in the summer with a lilac bush behind him, leaning with both hands on his cane, an open book next to him, musing poetically over the setting sun.

Speaking of books, let me note here that toward the end he read less and less—but that was only toward the very end of his life. He always read the numerous newspapers and magazines to which Mrs. Stavrogin subscribed. He was also interested in the latest developments in Russian literature, although on that point he maintained a dignified reserve. At one time he embarked with great enthusiasm upon a study of our home and foreign policies, but soon gave it up with a shrug. He also sometimes went into the garden carrying Tocqueville in his hand, but with a sentimental Paul de Kock novel concealed in his pocket. But all that is unimportant.

Now let me say, parenthetically, a few words about Kukolnikov's portrait too. Varvara Stavrogin had come across it when she was a little girl in an exclusive Moscow boarding school. She immediately fell in love with it, girls in boarding schools having a propensity for falling in love with anyone and anything, including their teachers—particularly teachers of penmanship and drawing. However, what concerns us here is not what sort of little girl Mrs. Stavrogin was but the fact that even at the age of fifty she still preserved that picture among her other intimate treasures. This may explain why she made Mr. Verkhovensky dress the way she did. But that, of course, is also immaterial.

During the first years of his stay at Mrs. Stavrogin's, Mr. Verkhovensky still intended to write a book. In fact, he was

about to start on it every day. But, in later years, he must have
forgotten whatever it was he had had in mind. More and more
frequently he said:

"I feel I'm ready to begin work. I have all the necessary
materials at hand, yet—somehow I can't get started."

And he lowered his head in despair.

Of course, the pangs of scholarly creation he suffered added
to his glamour in our eyes, although he himself thirsted for
something different.

"They've forgotten about me! No one needs me any more!"
he often exclaimed.

This despair became particularly intense toward the end
of the eighteen fifties, and Mrs. Stavrogin finally realized that
it was sincere. She couldn't bear the idea that her old friend
was forgotten and useless. To distract him and refurbish his
glory, she took him on a trip to Moscow, where she still had
a few elegant literary and learned acquaintances. But the
Moscow trip turned out to be rather unsatisfactory.

It was a strange time: something was in the air—something
very different from the old, settled calm; something quite unfamiliar that could nevertheless be scented all over the place,
even in Skvoreshniki. All kinds of rumors were reaching us.
The facts were, by and large, well known, but there were all
sorts of ideas surrounding those facts—indeed, an oversatura-
tion of ideas. And that was what was bewildering: it was hard
to accommodate oneself to those ideas or, indeed, grasp what
they actually meant. Mrs. Stavrogin, being a woman, persisted
in suspecting that there was something secret about them. She
started to read foreign newspapers and magazines that she
managed to obtain (although they were banned in Russia) as
well as all sorts of clandestine pamphlets and proclamations.
But she soon gave up, because they made her head spin. Then
she started to write letters. But she received few replies, and
even those she received were less and less intelligible as time
went by.

So she solemnly asked Mr. Verkhovensky to explain "all
those ideas" to her once and for all. When he was through,
however, his explanations left her eminently dissatisfied. His
views on the general commotion were exceedingly scornful.
Everything, in his opinion, boiled down to the fact that they
had forgotten him and that there was no room for him in
the new movement.

In the end, however, they remembered him. First in émigré

publications abroad that recalled his exile and martyrdom, then in Petersburg, where he was described as a former star of a famous old constellation and compared—for some obscure reason—with Radishchev. Then someone reported his death and promised to send in an obituary. After that, Mr. Verkhovensky was immediately resurrected and reappeared filled with new importance. All his scorn for the politicians of the day vanished, and he became frantically anxious to go to Petersburg, join the new movement, and show his mettle.

Mrs. Stavrogin regained her old faith and got busy. They decided to leave for Petersburg without further delay, find out everything for themselves, and if possible, give themselves ungrudgingly and unstintingly to the new cause. She declared, by the way, that she was willing to publish a new magazine and devote the rest of her life to it. Seeing how important all this was to her, Mr. Verkhovensky became even more overbearing, and Mrs. Stavrogin soon detected a patronizing tone in his dealings with her, a fact of which she made immediate note.

It must be said, however, that she also pursued another objective in going to Petersburg—namely, the renewal of her old connections. She had to try her best to remind society of her existence.

But the ostensible reason for her trip was to see her only son, who was just then graduating from a Petersburg boarding school.

VI

So they went to Petersburg and stayed there for almost the entire winter season. By Lent, however, their hopes had burst like an iridescent soap bubble. Their dreams were shattered, and the foggy confusion, instead of clearing, became thicker and more sickening.

In the first place, Mrs. Stavrogin didn't succeed in reestablishing her connections, except perhaps on a ridiculously small scale—and that at the cost of the most humiliating efforts. Offended, she plunged wholeheartedly into the service of the "new ideas" and began organizing political evenings at home. She invited all sorts of literary figures, who were immediately shepherded into her drawing room in droves. After that they started coming without being invited—one would bring along another. She had never seen such men of letters before; they were incredibly but quite openly vain, as though in being so vain they were performing some sort of function. Some, though by no means all, arrived drunk and then behaved as if there were something beautiful in drunkenness that they had discovered only yesterday. Indeed, they all seemed proud of something. Their faces proclaimed that they had just this minute discovered some terribly important secret. They swore at one another and admired themselves for doing so. It was difficult to find out what they had actually written, but they described themselves as critics, novelists, satirists, playwrights, and debunkers.

Mr. Verkhovensky managed to penetrate to their top layer, their ruling clique. He climbed an incredible distance to reach those who were actually at the controls, but they received him warmly. Of course, none of them had ever heard of him— they only gathered that he was for The Idea. And he maneuvered them so adroitly that, despite their exalted positions, he managed to get them to attend Mrs. Stavrogin's receptions once or twice. These men were very serious, polite, and well behaved, and the others seemed afraid of them. But apparently they didn't have too much time to spare. Two or three former literary lions with whom Mrs. Stavrogin had managed to maintain graceful relations also turned up. But, to her amazement, these genuine celebrities behaved sheepishly before the new rabble and shamefully tried to curry favor with them.

At first Mr. Verkhovensky was lucky. They used him as a sort of exhibit at literary gatherings. When he appeared for the first time on the dais at a public reading, he received a five-minute ovation. Even nine years later, the tears still sprang to his eyes when he remembered it—although those tears were due to artistic temperament rather than gratitude.

"I'd swear," he told me, although he insisted on secrecy, "I'd bet anything that none of that audience knew even the first thing about me!"

It is a terribly significant remark. On the one hand, it showed that he was intelligent and understood his position clearly, despite the state of exaltation he was then in. On the other hand, the fact that even nine years later he still couldn't think of it without trembling with resentment indicates that his intellect was not really so keen.

They insisted he sign two or three petitions protesting against something—he couldn't make out what. He signed. They also asked Mrs. Stavrogin to sign a protest against some "scandalous practice," and she did so.

Although most of the "new people" came to her house, they somehow felt obliged to look upon Mrs. Stavrogin sneeringly and with undisguised contempt. In moments of bitterness, Mr. Verkhovensky hinted to me that her jealousy of him dated from that time. She no doubt realized that she shouldn't associate with those people; nevertheless she received them very eagerly, with an almost hysterical, very feminine impatience. She obviously expected something from them. At her receptions she didn't say much, although she could have if she had chosen to. She preferred to listen.

They spoke of: abolition of censorship; the reform of spelling; substitution of the Roman alphabet for the Cyrillic; the recent exile of such-and-such; some scandal in the fashionable shopping center; the advantages of breaking up the Russian Empire into autonomous ethnic units united by freely accepted federal ties; abolition of the army and navy; the restoration to Poland of land up to the Dnieper; agrarian reform; abolition of inheritance, family, parental rights, and priests; women's rights; the scandalously luxurious mansion belonging to a certain Mr. Krayevsky, for which they couldn't forgive him; and so on.

Among these newcomers there were obviously a number of crooks. However, most of the others were honest, even good, people, although sometimes of astounding shades of opinion. Of course, the honest ones were much harder to understand than the obviously dishonest and the cynically rude, but it was impossible to tell who was using whom for what purpose.

When Mrs. Stavrogin revealed her intention of publishing a magazine, a new flood of people rushed to her receptions. But immediately many of them openly accused her of being a capitalist and exploiting labor. The rudeness of these accusations was only equaled by their complete unexpectedness.

Once the elderly General Drozdov, a friend and colleague of the late General Stavrogin's and a pleasant man in his way— we all knew him here—although very stubborn and irritable, a big eater, and an inveterate foe of atheism—once, at one of those receptions, he got into a heated argument with some famous youth.

"If you talk like that, you must be a general," the young man told him to clinch an argument, implying that he couldn't think of any more derogatory word than "general."

General Drozdov flew into a terrible rage.

"Yes sir, I am a general—a lieutenant general, to be precise, and I have served my tsar loyally, whereas you're nothing but a milksop and an atheist!"

An intolerable commotion followed, and the following day the incident was reported in the press. A petition was circulated protesting "the disgraceful attitude of Mrs. Stavrogin" in refusing to have the general thrown out there and then. There was also a cartoon in an illustrated magazine. It represented Mrs. Stavrogin, General Drozdov, and Mr. Verkhovensky beneath the caption: "Three Reactionary Bedfellows"; and under the cartoon there was a satirical verse written especially for the occasion by "a poet of the people."

I must note here that many generals do have a strange way of expressing themselves. For instance, they say things like "I've served *my* tsar . . ." as if they had a tsar of their own and not the same tsar as the rest of us, their common compatriots.

Remaining in Petersburg any longer was, of course, unthinkable. Besides, Mr. Verkhovensky finally proved a complete failure. He couldn't restrain himself and started defending the rights of Art. They laughed at him louder than ever. At the final gathering, he decided to touch them with his revolutionary eloquence, hoping to reach their hearts, figuring to gain their sympathy by mentioning his years "in exile." He accepted unquestioningly the uselessness, the ridiculous connotation of the notion "mother country"; he endorsed the theory that religion was harmful; but he declared loudly and proudly that he placed Pushkin's poems above shoes—very much so. They booed him so mercilessly that he dissolved into tears right there on the stage. Mrs. Stavrogin took him home more dead than alive.

"They treated me like an old nightcap," he kept moaning.

She sat with him the whole night, made him take sedative drops, and until daybreak kept whispering in his ear:

"You're still useful . . . you'll prove yourself yet . . . they'll still appreciate you . . . in some other place."

The next day, Mrs. Stavrogin received a visit from five men of letters, three of whom she'd never seen or heard of before. With very stern expressions on their faces, they informed her that they had studied the matter of her publication and had reached a decision. Mrs. Stavrogin had never asked anyone to study or decide anything about her projected publication. Their decision was that once she had founded the magazine, she should hand it over to them, together with the funds for running it, on a free, cooperative basis, and immediately retire to Skvoreshniki, taking with her Stepan Verkhovensky, who had become "definitely behind the times." Out of special consideration for her, they were willing to recognize her rights of ownership and send her one-sixth of the annual net profits—if there were any. And the most touching part of it all was that four of these five people were pursuing absolutely no gainful end in this transaction, but were acting only in the interest of the Cause.

"We left Petersburg in a complete daze," Mr. Verkhovensky told me. "I didn't understand any of it and kept muttering some nonsense to the rumble of the train:

> Bang, bing, kick 'em out,
> Kick 'em out, bang, bing . . .

"And on and on, all the way to Moscow. I only recovered when we reached Moscow—as if I expected to find things different in that city."

"Ah, my dear friends!" he sometimes exclaimed to us, inspired, "you have no idea how sad, how bitter one feels when a great idea to which you have devoted your life is taken over by inexperienced, clumsy hands that drag it out into the street and share it with other fools as stupid as themselves. Then you suddenly come across it in the flea market, unrecognizable, grimy, presented from a ridiculous angle, without sense of proportion, without harmony, used as a toy by stupid brats. Oh no, it was different in our time! That's not what we were trying to achieve. No, no, that's not at all what we were after! I don't recognize anything today. . . . But our time will come again and set a firm course and put an end to today's swerving. It must. Otherwise where will we wind up?"

VII

Immediately upon their return from Petersburg, Mrs. Stavrogin packed her friend off abroad "to recuperate a bit." Besides, she felt they had to have a little rest from each other. Mr. Verkhovensky left enthusiastically.

"I'll come back to life there," he declared. "I'll return to my studies there!"

But his very first letters from Berlin were of the usual tenor. "My heart is shattered," he wrote Mrs. Stavrogin. "I cannot forget! Here in Berlin, everything reminds me of the old days, the first joys and sufferings. Where is she? Where are they both today? Where are those two angelic women of whom I was never worthy? Where is my son, my dearly beloved son? And where am I, my former self, made of steel and unshakable as a rock? How is it that, today, someone called Andreyev, a bearded Russian-Orthodox fool, can break my whole life in two?" . . .

Now Mr. Verkhovensky had seen his son only twice in his life—when he was born, and recently in Petersburg, where the young man had just entered the university. Until then, as we mentioned, the boy had been brought up by some aunts (Mrs. Stavrogin provided for his upkeep) in a remote province far from Skvoreshniki. As to Andreyev, he was just an eccentric local shopkeeper who had taught himself archaeology and become a great collector of Russian antiques. He sometimes liked to challenge Mr. Verkhovensky's erudite statements and, even more so, his political beliefs. The shopkeeper, who looked very venerable with his white beard and silver-rimmed glasses, still owed Mr. Verkhovensky four hundred rubles for a few acres of timber he had bought from Mr. Verkhovensky's small estate near Skvoreshniki. Although Mrs. Stavrogin had supplied him with lavish funds for his trip, Mr. Verkhovensky had reckoned on those four hundred rubles to pay for some things he felt (probably secretly) he needed and he almost burst into tears when Andreyev asked him to wait another month. Actually, Andreyev was perfectly entitled to do this, since he had made the first payments almost six months in advance because Mr. Verkhovensky apparently had been in urgent need of money at that time too.

Mrs. Stavrogin eagerly read that first letter and underlined in pencil the words, "where are they both today?" Then she folded it, dated it, and locked it in her metal box. He was, of course, referring to his late wives.

The second letter from Berlin was a variation on the same theme.

"I am working twelve hours a day"—"I'd have settled for eleven," Mrs. Stavrogin muttered—"I am digging up material in the libraries, checking, comparing, copying passages, rush-

ing around, seeing various professors. I have renewed my acquaintance with the Dundasov family. Such nice people. Mrs.
Dundasov is still as lovely as ever. She sends you her regards.
Her young husband and three nephews are all here in Berlin.
I talk to the young people until dawn. We have parties here
that might be described as Athenian, but only, of course, in
the sense of being refined and intellectual and of high aesthetic
quality. Everything is so beautiful: there is a lot of music,
principally Spanish, and a great longing for the general regeneration of mankind. And there is the concept of eternal beauty,
the Sistine Madonna, the alternation of light and shadow, with
dark spots even on the sun! Ah, my dear, loyal, noble friend!
My heart is with you, and I am always yours and with you
alone *en tout pays* and even *dans le pays de Makar et ses veaux*
of which, you may remember, we so often spoke, shudderingly,
before we left Petersburg. The thought of it makes me smile
now. Once across the border I felt safe at last—a strange, new
sensation experienced for the first time in so many years
. . ." etc.

"What nonsense!" was Mrs. Stavrogin's verdict as she folded
this letter too. "If those Athenian evenings last until dawn,
how can he possibly spend twelve hours a day over his books?
Was he by any chance drunk when he wrote that? And how
does that Dundasov woman dare send me her regards? But,
after all, let him have his fling. . . ."

The sentence *dans le pays de Makar et ses veaux* stood for
the Russian saying "Where Makar never drove his sheep"—
i.e., Siberia. Mr. Verkhovensky was fond of translating all
sorts of Russian sayings into French in the most idiotic way.
Without doubt he could have translated them much better if
he'd wanted to, but he thought it witty to distort them like that.

However, his fling didn't last very long. He could not take
it for four full months and hurried back to Skvoreshniki. His
later letters were composed of tender outpourings to his much-
missed dearest friend; they were literally dampened with tears
of separation. Some people become attached to their homes
the way lap dogs do.

Their meeting was rapturous. But two days later, everything
was just as before—in fact, even duller than before.

"My dear man," Mr. Verkhovensky said to me a couple of
weeks later under a solemn oath of secrecy, "I must tell you,
I've discovered a terrible thing—terrible for me, that is. . . ."

Je suis un . . . nothing but a common hanger-on, *et rien de plus! Mais r-r-rien de plus!"*

VIII

Then things quieted down and remained quiet for almost nine years. The hysterical outbursts and sobbing on my shoulder that recurred at regular intervals didn't really disturb the calm atmosphere. I'm rather surprised that Mr. Verkhovensky didn't grow fat during that time. His nose turned a bit crimson and he himself grew even milder, but that was all. Gradually, he gathered a circle of friends around him, but— it must be said—it was always quite small. And although Mrs. Stavrogin had little to do with that circle, we all considered ourselves her protégés.

She had learned her lesson during her last stay in Petersburg and now definitely installed herself in our town. That is, she lived there in the winter and in the summer stayed on her nearby estate, Skvoreshniki. She never had so much weight and influence in our provincial society as during the last seven of those years—in fact, until our present governor was appointed. The former governor, our kindly, unforgettable Ivan Osipovich, was closely related to her, and once upon a time she had rendered him some important service. His wife trembled at the mere thought of displeasing Mrs. Stavrogin. So the adulation of our provincial society bordered at times on plain idolatry. Some of this glamour was, of course, reflected onto Stepan Verkhovensky. He was a member of the club and a stylish loser at cards, and was treated with general respect, although many thought him nothing but a "learned man."

Later, when Mrs. Stavrogin allowed him to live in a separate house, we felt freer. We gathered at his place twice a week and we enjoyed ourselves, especially when he was generous with the champagne. It came, by the way, from the shop of that fellow Andreyev whom we have already mentioned. Mrs. Stavrogin paid the bills every six months, and on those days Mr. Verkhovensky always had an upset stomach.

One of the earliest members of the circle was Liputin, a middle-aged official in the provincial administration, a great liberal with a reputation as an atheist in the town. He lived with his good-looking wife, who had brought him a handsome dowry and had three grown-up daughters. He kept his family terrorized and shut up at home; he was incredibly stingy and had managed to amass enough money to acquire a house and a bit of capital during his career as a public servant. He was a cantankerous character, and since he was also of modest station in life, he was little respected in the town and not even received in top society. He was, moreover, a notoriously malicious gossip, and at least twice had been chastised for his slanders—once by an officer and once by a landowner, the respected father of a family. But we liked his keen wit, his inquiring mind, and his talent for vicious jibes. Mrs. Stavrogin didn't like him, but he always managed to get around her.

Nor did she have much love for Shatov, who had joined our group only a year or so before. Shatov was a former university student who had been expelled from the university after some scandal. As a boy, he had been one of Mr. Verkhovensky's pupils. He was a serf by birth, the son of Mrs. Stavrogin's late valet, Pavel. She had done a lot for him, but now she disliked him because she considered him ungrateful and she couldn't forgive him for not coming straight to her when he was expelled from the university. As a matter of fact, he didn't even answer the letter she wrote him at the time; instead he sold himself to some enlightened merchant as tutor to his children. He accompanied the merchant's family abroad, performing the functions of a nurse rather than a tutor—but then, he was anxious to go abroad at the time. Just before they left on the trip, the merchant took on a governess for the children, an energetic Russian girl hired mostly because she was willing to accept such a modest salary. Within a couple of months, she was fired by the merchant for "free thinking." Shatov left and followed her to Geneva, where they were married. They lived together for about three weeks, then parted like free people, without obligations toward each other—although poverty was also a factor in their separation. After that, Shatov wandered about Europe by himself for a long time, living God knows how, polishing shoes in the street, working as a stevedore in seaports. Finally, about a year before, he had returned to his home town and gone to live with an old aunt, whom he buried a month later. Shatov had a sister called Dasha who had been brought up by Mrs. Stavrogin and whom that lady now liked very much and treated as an equal. But he had very little contact with her. Among us he was rather gloomy and taciturn, and when someone attacked his convictions he became morbidly irritated and unrestrained in his language.

"Tie Shatov up first, and then argue," Mr. Verkhovensky used to quip. But he was rather fond of him.

When abroad, Shatov radically altered his former socialist convictions and jumped to the other extreme. He was one of those Russian idealists who, once struck by some overwhelming idea, becomes obsessed by it, sometimes for the rest of his life. He cannot ever really grasp it, but he believes in it passionately, and his life becomes an uninterrupted series of agonizing pangs, as if he were half crushed by a heavy stone.

Physically, Shatov fitted his convictions very well: he was clumsy, towheaded, unkempt, short, big-shouldered, with blond, almost white, bushy eyebrows. His permanent frown and obstinately lowered eyes made him always look embarrassed about something. On his head one particular tuft of hair never flattened down but always stuck up like some plant. He was twenty-seven or twenty-eight.

"No wonder his wife deserted him," Mrs. Stavrogin said once, giving him a thorough looking over.

Shatov always tried to dress neatly despite his extreme poverty. He never asked Mrs. Stavrogin for help, managing as well as he could by doing odd jobs for the local merchants. At one point, he actually clerked in a grocery; at another, he was supposed to sail off on a river boat with a load of merchandise, but fell ill just before leaving. It is hard to imagine the poverty he could stand without even giving it a thought. After his sickness, Mrs. Stavrogin sent him a hundred rubles anonymously. He found out, however, who had sent the money, mulled over what he should do, decided to accept it, and went over to thank her. She received him with overwhelming warmth, but even on this occasion Shatov managed to disappoint her and disgrace himself: he stayed only five minutes and didn't say a word. He kept staring at the floor with a stupid, frozen smile; then, at the most interesting point in her speech, he suddenly rose without waiting for her to finish her sentence, nodded awkwardly without looking at her, and totally confused, stumbled against her expensive inlaid sewing table, which tipped over, fell, and broke. Finally, dead with shame, he rushed out.

Liputin often reproached him after that for having accepted the hundred rubles from that despotic woman, a former serf owner, and for not only accepting them but even trotting over there to thank her.

Shatov lived at the edge of town and kept very much to himself; he didn't like any of us to come and see him. But he came regularly to Mr. Verkhovensky's gatherings and borrowed books and newspapers from him.

There was another young man who came to our gatherings. He was a young local official called Virginsky. In some ways he was a bit like Shatov, although in others he seemed as different from him as it was possible to be. He was what is known as "a family man." He was a very sad young man (actually he was already past thirty) and well educated, although mostly self-taught. He was poor, married, and worked in a department of the local administration; he also supported his wife's aunt and sister. His wife and the other two ladies held the most progressive political views, which, however, they formulated rather crudely—an illustration of what Mr. Verkhovensky meant when he spoke on some occasions of "ideas that get caught up in the street." They took everything they read literally, and at a hint from progressive circles in the capital, they'd have tossed out of their windows everything they were advised to toss out. In our town, Mrs. Virginsky practiced as a midwife. Before her marriage, she had lived for a long time in Petersburg.

Virginsky himself was a man of exceptional purity of heart, and I have never come across a set of more passionately held convictions.

"Never, never will I give up these bright hopes!" he told me with shining eyes.

He always spoke of these "bright hopes" quietly, almost in a whisper, as if he were mentioning something secret.

He was quite tall, but very thin, and his shoulders were strikingly narrow. His hair had a reddish tinge and was growing thin. He took Mr. Verkhovensky's jibes at some of his opinions meekly, but when he answered him, he spoke very seriously, often leaving Mr. Verkhovensky speechless. Mr. Verkhovensky treated him kindly and paternally—as, for that matter, he treated us all.

"You're just a half-baked thinker," he teased Virginsky. "You're all the same! And, although I haven't noticed the same narrowness of outlook in you that I found *chez ces séminaristes* of Petersburg, I still maintain you're half-baked.

And Shatov is half-baked too, however well done he may imagine he is."

"And what about me?" Liputin asked him once.

"You're just a middle-of-the-roader; you'll always adapt yourself somehow to whatever may come."

Liputin resented this.

It was rumored and, alas, turned out to be true that, after less than a year of lawful wedlock, Mrs. Virginsky dismissed her husband, announcing that she preferred a certain Lebyatkin. The person in question later turned out to be a rather suspicious character and not the retired army captain he had posed as. He was only good at twirling his mustache, drinking, and talking the most cockeyed nonsense imaginable. He rather tactlessly moved right into the Virginsky household, welcoming the opportunity for free board. He slept there, ate there, and in the end, started treating the master of the house quite patronizingly. When told about his dismissal by his wife, Virginsky is supposed to have said:

"My dear, thus far I have only loved you; now I respect you."

But it is highly unlikely he ever made this statement so much in the style of ancient Rome. I've heard from other sources that he burst into tears.

Once, a couple of weeks after the dismissal, the whole "family" went to have tea with some friends outside town. Virginsky was rather exuberant and gay and took part in the dancing. Then, suddenly, without any provocation, he grabbed the gigantic Lebyatkin, who was dancing a solo, by his hair, bent him forward, and screaming and shouting, with the tears pouring down his cheeks, started pulling him around. The giant was so scared that he did nothing to defend himself and didn't even utter a sound while he was being dragged around. Later, however, he ardently resented the offense, as any honorable man would.

Virginsky spent the following night on his knees, begging his wife to forgive him. But she didn't, for he still refused to apologize to Lebyatkin. And on top of that, she accused him of shallowness of conviction and stupidity for kneeling while talking to a woman.

The retired captain vanished from our town soon afterward to reappear only very recently with his sister and a new set of objectives to which we'll come in time.

So it was no wonder that the wretched "family man" sought

refuge among us and needed our companionship. However, he never mentioned his family affairs in public. Only once, when the two of us were going home from Mr. Verkhovensky's place, did he say something vague about his unhappiness, but then he immediately seized my arm and said heatedly:

"Ah, it's nothing but a private matter that can in no way interfere with the common cause!"

Other people occasionally came to our meetings. There was a Jew named Lyamshin and a Captain Kartuzov. There was an open-minded old man, but he soon died. Once Liputin brought in an exiled Polish priest called Sloczewski, who was received as a matter of principle at first, but later on was no longer welcome.

IX

There was a time when it was said that our circle was a hotbed of freethinking, vice, and atheism, and this notion always lingered about us. But in actual fact we were just enjoying a pleasant, innocent Russian pastime—liberal blather. Liberal idealism and liberal idealists are possible only in Russia. Mr. Verkhovensky, like every witty man, needed an audience, and he also had to feel that he fulfilled a supreme duty by spreading ideas through words. Finally, he obviously needed someone to sip champagne with while exchanging a certain brand of pleasant Russian ideas about Russia, God in general, and the "Russian God" in particular, repeating for the hundredth time scandalous little jibes against the Russian authorities that everyone knew by heart. We didn't turn our noses up at local gossip, either, and often drew the most highly moral conclusions from it. We also frequently drifted into matters concerning mankind as a whole, discussing the future of Europe and the fate of man, forecasting dogmatically that Caesarism would reduce France to a second-rate power, a thing we were certain was imminent. The pope, we felt sure, would become just another cardinal in a unified Italy, and there wasn't the slightest doubt in our minds that this thousand-year-old matter would be settled with a snap of the fingers in our age of humanitarianism, industry, and railroads.

But then, idealistic Russian liberals had the same easy approach to everything.

Sometimes Mr. Verkhovensky spoke of art, and he spoke very well on the subject, although somewhat abstractly. At times he remembered the companions of his young days—all of them famous in the history of our movement—and he remembered them warmly and admiringly, but perhaps with a suggestion of envy. And if things became really unbearably boring, Lyamshin, the little Jewish post-office clerk, sat down at the piano and played, or gave imitations of a pig, a storm, a childbirth (including the infant's first cry), etc.—which was mostly why he was invited. And when we had had a lot to drink—which didn't happen very often—we were sufficiently moved to sing the *Marseillaise* together, with Lyamshin accompanying us on the piano. I can't guarantee that the result was very successful.

We enthusiastically celebrated February 18th, the day of the emancipation of the serfs, preparing for it long in advance by drinking innumerable toasts.

Long before Shatov and Virginsky joined us, when Mr. Verkhovensky was still living in Mrs. Stavrogin's house (it was some time before Emancipation), Mr. Verkhovensky had acquired the bad habit of muttering under his breath a well-known, although somewhat unconvincing, verse by some liberal ex-landowner:

> With their axes the peasants come walking,
> A terrible doom the land is stalking.

It went something like that, although I can't vouch for my accuracy.

Mrs. Stavrogin overheard him once, and shouting, "What stupid nonsense!" left the room in anger. Liputin, who happened to be present, remarked bitingly:

"Well, it would really be a shame if, in their joy, the peasants caused some unpleasantness to their former owners."

And he meaningfully drew his finger across his throat.

"Cher ami," Mr. Verkhovensky said good-humoredly, "take my word for it that this"—he imitated the gesture across the throat—"is no way to reform the landowners or help anyone else. We'll never manage to get things going if we lose our heads, although at times our heads do seem to be a positive hindrance."

I must say that many in our town expected something extraordinary to happen the day serfdom was abolished. Liputin and the so-called experts on people and the running of a state predicted it. Mr. Verkhovensky also seemed to share their opinion, and as the day approached, he begged Mrs. Stavrogin to send him abroad. In fact, he got cold feet. But the great day came and went and a few more days besides, and the haughty smile reappeared on Mr. Verkhovensky's lips. He formulated a few remarkable thoughts on the character of the Russian in general and the Russian peasant in particular.

"Being in a hurry as usual, we have been overanxious about our peasants. We have made them fashionable. A whole section of our literature has fussed about them as if they were some newly discovered precious stones. We've crowned their lice-infested heads with laurels, while in reality, in the past thousand years all we've got out of the Russian village is the Komarinsky Dance. Once a great Russian poet, who at the same time had some sense of humor, exclaimed, on seeing the great Rachel on the stage for the first time: 'I wouldn't exchange Rachel for a Russian peasant!' I'm prepared to go even further than that: I would give all the peasants in Russia for one Rachel. Let's face things soberly and stop mistaking our homemade grease for cleaning boots with *Le Bouquet de L'Impératrice* perfume."

Liputin readily agreed, but remarked that it was nevertheless necessary to pretend for the time being and praise the peasants in the interests of the Cause. He pointed out that even ladies of the highest society had shed hot tears over Grigorovich's story, "Anton the Sufferer," and some of them had even written from Paris to their estate managers back home, telling them that henceforth they were to treat the serfs as humanely as possible.

It was a rather unfortunate coincidence that, just after all those rumors started circulating about Anton Petrov, there was a certain misunderstanding in our province about ten miles from Skvoreshniki, and in the excitement they sent a detachment of soldiers this way. At that time Mr. Verkhovensky became so agitated that he gave us all a good scare. He ranted and raved at the club, saying that they hadn't sent enough soldiers and that we should wire for reinforcements; he rushed to the governor to assure him he had nothing to do with the whole business, insisting that they shouldn't try to accuse him of anything because of his old record and suggesting that the governor write immediately to whomever it might concern in the capital. Luckily, the whole incident soon blew over. Still, Mr. Verkhovensky's behavior struck me as very strange.

Three years later people started to discuss nationalism, and something called "public opinion" came into existence. That made Stepan Verkhovensky laugh.

"My friends," he lectured us, "if national consciousness has really come into existence among us, as we're told by the press, it is still attending some German elementary school and learning from a German textbook—learning by heart its eternal German lesson, and the German teacher can make it go down on its knees whenever he thinks fit. I have nothing against the German teacher. But I'm not so sure that this national feeling does exist today. I don't believe anything has come into existence; I think everything just goes on according to God's will—which should be good enough *pour notre Sainte Russie.* All these Pan-Slav and nationalist movements are really too old to be new. As a matter of fact, nationalism in this country has never been anything but a game for some gentlemen's club—and a Moscow club at that. Of course, I'm not talking of the times of Prince Igor. But finally, I say that its true origin is idleness. In our country everything comes from idleness, the good things as well. Everything comes from the cultured, refined idleness of our upper classes. I've been repeating this for thirty thousand years.

"Besides, we don't know how to live by our own labor. So why are they making all this fuss about some nascent 'public opinion'? What has happened? Did it fall suddenly from the sky? Can't they see that to have an opinion, people have to work themselves, have their own initiative, and have personal experience? No one gets anything for nothing. When we all work, we shall have our own opinions. And since we'll never go to work, those who work in our stead will make up our minds for us—the same old Europe, the same Germans, our teachers for two hundred years. Moreover, Russia is in too great a mess for us to disentangle it without the Germans and without going to work. For instance, I sounded the alarm and appealed to people to go to work. I devoted my life to that appeal and I believed in it, fool that I was! Now I don't believe any longer, but I keep pulling the rope of the alarm bell, and I'll go on ringing until the bell tolls my own requiem."

Alas, we went along with him. We applauded our teacher—and with what enthusiasm! But then, don't we still hear all around us the same "nice," "clever," old Russian nonsense?

Our teacher did believe in God.

"I don't know why everyone around here insists I'm an atheist," he said. "I believe in God—but let's make a distinction: I believe in God as a being that is conscious of Himself only through me. Of course, I cannot believe like my old maid, or like some gentleman who believes just in case, or like our dear Shatov . . . but no—Shatov doesn't really count. Shatov *forces* himself to believe, like a Moscow Slavophile. As to Christianity, well, despite all my respect for it, I'm not a Christian. I'm rather a pagan like the great Goethe or the ancient Greeks, if only because Christianity doesn't understand woman, a point that was so brilliantly developed by George Sand in one of her great novels. As for genuflections, fasts, and that sort of thing, I fail to understand what difference it can make to anyone whether or not I observe them. I can imagine how busy our local informers are, but I refuse to be a hypocrite. In 1847 Belinsky sent his well-publicized letter to Gogol from abroad, strongly reproaching him for believing in 'some sort of God.' *Entre nous soit dit,* I can imagine nothing funnier than Gogol—the Gogol of *that* time especially—reading that particular phrase and the letter in general! But disregarding the funny side of it, and since, after all, I agree in principle with that reproach, I'll simply say: there were real men at that time! Yes, they knew how to love their people, how to suffer for them. They were willing to sacrifice everything for the masses and at the same time managed to remain distinct from them, not trying to please them in everything. But you don't really expect Belinsky to try to find salvation in lean diets of vegetable oil, radishes, and peas during Lent!"

At this point Shatov intervened.

"Those fellows you mentioned never really loved the people; they never suffered for them or sacrificed anything for them, although to make themselves feel more noble they liked to think they did," he muttered gloomily, lowering his eyes and twisting impatiently in his chair.

"What? You say they didn't love the people?" Mr. Verkhovensky shouted in outraged tones. "You don't know what you're talking about! They loved the people! Most certainly!"

"They loved neither the people nor Russia!" Shatov yelled back, his eyes flashing. "It's impossible to love something you know nothing about, and they didn't know a damn thing about the Russian people! All of you, including yourself, and especially Belinsky, had just the most cursory glimpse of the Russian people. You can see that from his letter to Gogol alone. Belinsky is just like the fellow in Krylov's fable who, when he visited a menagerie, spent his time marveling at some French social insects and so managed to overlook the elephants. He began and ended with those bugs! Even so, I'd say Belinsky was cleverer than the lot of you. As to the rest of you, you've not only failed to look at the Russian masses, but treated them with scornful distaste, judging by the fact that by 'people' you've always understood the French people, and at that, only the people of Paris, and you're ashamed that the Russian people aren't like them. That's the truth! And a man who has no country has no God either. Rest assured that those who cease to understand the people of their own country and lose contact with them also lose the faith of their forefathers and become godless or indifferent. Yes, yes, it always proves true; that's why you and the lot of us today are either despicable atheists or indifferent, vicious human muck. Yes, Mr. Verkhovensky, you too. I make no exception of you! As a matter of fact, I was thinking of you when I said all that."

Having delivered his speech (a thing he did from time to time), Shatov as usual grabbed his cap and rushed to the door, convinced that now his friendship with Mr. Verkhovensky was finally ended.

But Mr. Verkhovensky always managed to stop him in time.

"All right, Shatov," he said good-humoredly, offering him his hand without rising from his armchair, "now, how about making up after that exchange of niceties?"

Awkward and self-conscious, Shatov hated sentimental effusions. Outwardly abrupt and uncouth, he was, I believe, secretly an extremely sensitive man, and although he often lost all sense of proportion, he himself was the first to suffer from it. So, after making some grunting noises over Mr. Verkhovensky's suggestion and shuffling his feet like a bear for a while, he suddenly grinned, put down his cap, and sat down— all without once raising his eyes from the floor. Of course, on these occasions, wine was brought in, and Mr. Verkhovensky proposed some appropriate toast, usually to one of the great social fighters of the past.

chapter 2

PRINCE HAL—MATCHMAKING

I

The other person in the world to whom Varvara Petrovna Stavrogin was as attached as to Mr. Verkhovensky was her only son, Nikolai Vsevolodovich Stavrogin. It was for him that Mr. Verkhovensky had been invited to come as tutor. Nikolai was eight at the time. His irresponsible father was already living apart from them, and the boy was entirely in his mother's care.

In fairness to Mr. Verkhovensky, it must be said that he knew how to gain the affection of his pupil. His secret was quite simple: he was a child himself. I wasn't around then, and since he always needed a confidant, he didn't hesitate to make a friend out of even such a small child, and as the boy grew, any gap that may have existed between them seemed to disappear. He repeatedly woke his ten- or eleven-year-old friend in the middle of the night and tearfully poured out his wounded sensibilities or even shared some family secret with him, which, of course, was quite unforgivable. Then they would sob in each other's arms.

The boy knew his mother loved him, but he didn't seem to feel very much for her. She didn't talk to him much and hardly ever prevented him from doing what he wanted, but somehow he felt the intensity with which she watched him, and that made him painfully ill at ease. In any case, Mrs. Stavrogin fully entrusted Mr. Verkhovensky with her son's education, as well as the building of his character.

We may assume that the tutor was to some extent responsible for upsetting his pupil's nerves, for when the boy was sent to boarding school at the age of fifteen, he was puny, pale, and strangely withdrawn. (Later, however, he was noted for his remarkably powerful physique. We may assume that the two friends' tears, when they sobbed in each other's arms at night, were not always caused by domestic intrigues. Mr. Verkhovensky had managed to touch the deepest-seated chords in the boy's heart, causing the first, still undefined, sensation of the undying, sacred longing that a superior soul, having once tasted, will never exchange for vulgar satisfaction. (There are even people who value that longing more than the most radical fulfillment, even when it is possible.)

Anyway, it seemed a good idea finally to separate the teacher and his pupil, even though it was rather late.

During his first two years at boarding school, young Stavrogin came home for the summer holidays. Then, when his mother and Mr. Verkhovensky went to stay in Petersburg, he sometimes attended their literary parties, looking and listening. He didn't talk much and was shy and quiet, as he had been before. He still treated Mr. Verkhovensky with tender affection, but was more reserved and obviously reluctant to discuss with him lofty matters or, for that matter, the past.

In compliance with his mother's wishes, after graduating from school he joined one of the most elegant Horse Guards regiments. However, he didn't go home to let his mother admire him in uniform as she suggested and wrote only seldom after that.

Mrs. Stavrogin sent her son all the money he wanted, despite the fact that, immediately after the emancipation of the serfs, her income was cut by about half. But then, it must be said, she had managed to accumulate a bit of capital and could probably afford it. She was very eager for her son to be a social success, and she was not disappointed. Where she had failed in renewing her connections, the rich young Guards officer succeeded easily. In fact, he established connections that she wouldn't have dared dream of. Everyone was delighted to receive him.

But strange rumors soon began to reach Mrs. Stavrogin. Her son apparently had suddenly plunged into the wildest dissipation. It was nothing like the usual drinking and gambling. The reports cited savage recklessness, people run down by his horses, and his unspeakably brutal behavior toward a lady of the highest society with whom he had an affair and whom he then insulted publicly. There was something obviously unnatural about it all. Apparently he had become a terrible bully and went around insulting people for the sheer joy of it. Mrs. Stavrogin was worried and depressed. Mr. Verkhovensky tried to assure her that it was just the growing pangs of a richly endowed and highly complex nature, that the stormy seas would calm down, and that her son's youth resembled Prince

Hal's, whose mad revels with Falstaff, Poins, and Mistress Quickly Shakespeare describes in *Henry IV, Part 1*.

Mrs. Stavrogin didn't just brush him aside with a "Rubbish, rubbish!" as she had tended to recently. On the contrary, she listened to him intently and asked him to tell her more about Shakespeare. Then she read the play herself. But Shakespeare's drama didn't reassure her—she couldn't find the least similarity between the two cases. Meanwhile, she eagerly awaited her son's reply to several letters of hers.

However, her questions were soon answered. She received the sinister news that her Prince Hal had been involved in two duels, one right after the other, in both of which he had been in the wrong. He had killed one of his opponents and maimed the other. He was court-martialed, reduced to the ranks, and transferred to an infantry regiment. Indeed, only special intercession from above saved him from a sterner sentence.

In 1863 he somehow managed to distinguish himself. They gave him a medal and promoted him to corporal. Then, in a surprisingly short time, they gave him back his commission.

During that whole period, Mrs. Stavrogin must have sent a hundred letters to the capital with pleas for special consideration. In this special instance she was willing to humble herself.

But, soon after he regained his commission, the young man suddenly resigned it and left the army. However, he did not return to Skvoreshniki; indeed, he ceased to write to his mother altogether. Later she found out circumspectly that he was back in Petersburg but he was never seen with his former acquaintances any more. He apparently was avoiding them. Finally, she discovered that he kept strange company, associating with the dregs of Petersburg; that he went around with penniless petty employees, drunks, and retired army officers who stooped to "dignified" begging in the street. It was said that he visited their filthy homes, spent days and nights in slums and God knows what grimy alleys; that he had let himself go, looked like a tramp, and apparently liked it that way.

He never asked his mother for money. He had inherited a small estate from his father that yielded a little income, for he had rented it to some German from Saxony. His mother at last succeeded in persuading him to come to see her, and Prince Hal appeared in our town. That was the first time I ever saw him.

He was a strikingly handsome man of about twenty-five, and

I must confess, he greatly impressed me. I expected to find a shabby tramp, debilitated by debauchery and reeking of vodka. But what I saw was the most elegant gentleman I'd ever met: he was dressed in the best of taste and behaved as only those accustomed to the most refined surroundings behave. And I was not the only one to be surprised—the whole town was, for everyone knew young Stavrogin's story, including details the knowledge of which was surprising. (And, even more surprising, a good half of these turned out to be correct.)

The new arrival immediately captured the attention of our local ladies. They split into two opposing groups: one adoring, the other crying for his blood. But all of them were fascinated by him. Some were attracted because they felt there was some mystery about him; others were positively thrilled by the thought that he was a killer. He also turned out to be rather well educated, even well informed. Of course, it didn't take much information to impress us, but he had enough to speak with competence on the great topics of the day, and what's more, he did so calmly, trying to make good sense. Curiously enough, from the first day of his arrival, we found him an extremely reasonable man.

He was elegant without affectation, not too talkative, very modest, and at the same time bold and self-reliant. There was no one like him around. Our local lions, full of envy, were pushed into the background.

I was also struck by his looks. His handsome head of black hair was somehow a bit too black, his light eyes were perhaps too steady, his complexion too smooth and delicate, and his cheeks too rosy and healthy; his teeth were like pearls and his lips like coral. This sounds like a strikingly beautiful face, but in reality it was repulsive rather than beautiful. His face reminded some people of a mask. There was also much talk about his great physical strength. He was of above-average height. His mother regarded him with pride, but also with constant worry. He spent six months with us. At first he was quiet, distant, and reserved. He attended social functions and rigidly adhered to etiquette. He was related to the governor through his father, and was received in the governor's mansion like one of the family.

Then the beast suddenly unsheathed his claws.

I must remark here that our former governor, dear old Ivan Osipovich, rather resembled an old woman—but a well-born old woman with good connections, which accounts for his remaining so long in office while always managing to dodge work and responsibility. His hospitality and amiability might have qualified him to be chairman of the local gentry association in the peaceful old days, but certainly not to be governor in our troubled times. People often said that it was Mrs. Stavrogin, not the governor, who ran our province. This, however, was nothing but a catty and absolutely unfounded remark. And indeed, too many people have exercised their wit on that subject. Actually, in recent years, Mrs. Stavrogin had deliberately withdrawn from among those in control and, despite her tremendous prestige in high society, she voluntarily remained within the strict limits she had set for herself. Instead of high politics, she had concentrated on running her estates and, within two or three years, had succeeded in raising her income almost to what it had been before Emancipation. Instead of making the romantic gestures of the past—such as the trip to Petersburg and the idea of founding a liberal magazine —she cut her expenses and started saving. She even decided to separate from Mr. Verkhovensky, allowing him to rent an apartment in another house, something that, under various pretexts, he had been asking her to let him do for a long time. Little by little, Mr. Verkhovensky started describing her as down-to-earth, referring to her facetiously as "my down-to-earth friend." Of course, he only indulged in jokes of this sort with great discretion and under suitable circumstances.

All of us who knew her well—and Mr. Verkhovensky better than any of us—understood that her son now represented her new hopes and even a new daydream of hers. Her great love for her son dated from the time of his success in Petersburg society and grew immensely when he was stripped of his commission and reduced to the ranks. But at the same time she seemed to be afraid of him and behaved rather slavishly toward him. She obviously feared something ill defined and mysterious, something she herself couldn't pinpoint. She often watched him discreetly and intently, trying to decipher and understand something. . . .

Then the beast unsheathed his claws.

II

Suddenly, without any provocation, our prince committed several unprecedented outrages, different from anything one would have imagined, not at all the usual run-of-the-mill things. These were completely inane, unprovoked, childish outbursts of spite. God knows what made him do what he did.

One of the most venerable members of our club, Mr. Gaganov, had the harmless habit, when excited, of adding the phrase, "Ah, no, I won't let them lead me by the nose!" to every sentence he uttered. What harm is there in that? Well once, as he made this remark to a group of important visitors, Stavrogin, who had been standing in a corner and had taken no part in the conversation, walked up to Mr. Gaganov and, suddenly thrusting out his hand, caught the old gentleman's nose between his index finger and thumb and pulled him along a few steps behind him.

He couldn't possibly have had a grudge against Mr. Gaganov, so it must have been simply an unforgivable schoolboy prank. Later, people who said they had observed his face while he was pulling his victim behind him agreed that it was almost dreamy, "as though he'd lost his mind." But that was recalled only much later. In the heat of the action it was not the first but the second moment that struck them, by which time he must certainly have regained his senses. In any case, he didn't seem in the least embarrassed. On the contrary, he smiled maliciously and looked highly amused, "without," as they put it, "the least sign of regret for what he'd done."

There was a great commotion, and they all crowded around him. Stavrogin turned his head, looking into the faces of those nearest him without uttering a word in answer to their shouting. Then he again seemed to slip into his dream—at least according to the accounts of witnesses—frowned, walked determinedly toward the affronted Mr. Gaganov, and muttered very quickly, with unconcealed irritation:

"Of course—you'll have to excuse me . . . I don't know why I suddenly felt such a terrible desire to do a stupid thing like that. . . ."

The casualness of his apology was in itself a fresh insult. The din redoubled. Stavrogin shrugged and walked out.

It was all very stupid, to say nothing of its outrageousness. It was—one could see from the first glance—a deliberate and calculated insult to our entire society. And, indeed, everyone took it as such. To start with, Stavrogin was expelled from the club. Then they decided to present a petition signed by all the members of the club to the governor, requesting him (without waiting for the affair to be heard in court) "to restrain this notorious bully, this dueling fiend, from the capital by the administrative measures at your disposal, thus safeguarding the public peace of the town from similar scandalous breaches." And they added innocently, "perhaps some law could be found that would also apply to Nikolai Stavrogin." The purpose of this remark was to needle the governor about his relations with Mrs. Stavrogin. And they amplified it further with great zest.

As luck would have it, the governor was away. He had gone to a neighboring town to attend the christening of the child of a pretty widow whose husband had died during her pregnancy. However, he was expected back soon. In the meantime, the victim of the outrage, the venerable Mr. Gaganov, was feted and acclaimed: everyone shook his hand and hugged him, and the whole town called on him to assure him of their sympathy and admiration. They even planned to give a subscription dinner in his honor, but finally gave up the idea on his own insistence. Perhaps it dawned on them at last that the man, after all, had had his nose pulled and that that was hardly a suitable occasion for celebration.

And yet, how had it actually happened? How could it have happened? It is remarkable that no one in town ascribed this absurd act to insanity. This indicates that they expected such acts from a Stavrogin in full possession of his faculties. I myself don't understand it to this day, despite the event that soon followed it and seemed to explain everything and satisfy everyone. Let me say only that, four years later, Stavrogin frowned and gave the following answer to my carefully worded question as to what had happened that time in the club:

"I was not very well then, of course."

But I don't want to anticipate.

I was also rather curious about the general outburst of hatred against the "bully, the dueling fiend from the capital." They insisted upon finding in his action a deliberate intent to insult our entire community. The man had succeeded in antagonizing everyone. But what did they really have against him? Until that incident he'd never had a quarrel with anyone and had been as polite as a young gentleman in a fashion plate would be if a fashion plate could talk. I'd say it was his pride that brought all that hatred down on him. Even the ladies who'd begun by adoring him now loathed him more than the men did.

It was a great blow to Mrs. Stavrogin. Later, however, she told Mr. Verkhovensky that she had felt it coming every day and had even somehow expected "something just like that."

It is remarkable for a mother to admit a thing like that. "Here goes!" she had thought with a shudder. The day after the scandal in the club, she broached the subject very carefully to her son, trembling despite her determination. She hadn't slept all night. In the morning she had hurried over to Mr. Verkhovensky's place to talk things over with him and there had burst into tears, something she never did unless she was alone. Now she wanted her son to say something to her, to have enough consideration for her to offer some sort of explanation. Nikolai Stavrogin, who was always polite and considerate to his mother, listened to her for some time with a frown, then without saying a word, got up, kissed her hand, and went out of the room.

That evening—deliberately it seemed—he caused a second scandal that, although less violent and shocking than the first, was sufficient to whip up a general clamor because of the already prevailing mood.

Just after the scene between mother and son, Liputin arrived to invite Stavrogin to a party he was giving to celebrate his wife's birthday. Mrs. Stavrogin had long noted with horror her son's predilection for such vulgar company, but she didn't dare say anything. Besides, he had made other acquaintances among the third-rate members of our community and even lower. Such, apparently, were his inclinations.

Stavrogin had not yet been to Liputin's house, although he had met him socially. He guessed that Liputin's invitation was connected with the scandal he'd caused in the club, that being a local liberal, Liputin was delighted by it and thought sincerely that that was the proper way to handle venerable club members and that it was all to the good. He laughed and promised to go.

There were many guests at the party, and they were a lively lot if not particularly distinguished. Liputin, vain and envious man that he was, spared no expense when he invited people to his house, although he only did so a couple of times a year.

This time, his usual star guest, Mr. Verkhovensky, couldn't attend because of illness. There was tea, refreshment, and vodka. There were three card tables going and while waiting for supper, the young people danced to a piano. Stavrogin danced a couple of times with Mrs. Liputin—an extremely pretty little woman who was dreadfully intimidated by him— then sat next to her, talking to her and making her laugh. Suddenly, noticing how pretty she looked when she laughed, he put his arm around her waist and, in front of the assembled guests, kissed her on the lips, lengthily and with obvious relish, three times in a row. The poor, frightened lady fainted. Stavrogin took his hat, walked over to the nonplused husband, muttered with obvious embarrassment, "Don't be angry," and left the room. Liputin ran after him, personally got his coat for him, and with effusive politeness saw him off downstairs.

The following day there was an amusing sequel to this relatively harmless incident, a sequel that brought Liputin some credit and that he managed to exploit to full advantage.

At ten in the morning, Liputin's servant, Agafya, presented herself at Mrs. Stavrogin's house. This saucy, red-cheeked woman of about thirty said she had a message from her master for Mr. Stavrogin and that she absolutely had to give it "to the gentleman in person." Despite a bad headache, Stavrogin came out. His mother happened to be present during the delivery of the message.

"The master ordered me first of all to convey his respects to you, inquire after your health," Agafya rattled off cheerfully, "and ask how you slept after last night's party and how you feel about it today."

Stavrogin grinned.

"Please give my regards to your master, Agafya, and tell him from me that he's the most intelligent man in this town."

"And to that my master told me to tell you that he doesn't need you to tell him that and he wishes he could return the compliment."

"Really? But how did he know what I'd say to you?"

"I'm sure I don't know, but when I was already on my way here, the master came hurrying after me, without his hat, and said, 'And if, in despair, he tells you to say to me that I'm the most intelligent man in this town, don't forget to tell him that I know it myself and wish I could say the same of him. . . .'"

III

Finally the explanation with the governor took place. Our nice, kindly Ivan Osipovich had been presented with the club members' angry petition immediately on his return to town. He realized he had to do something, but couldn't decide what. The hospitable old man seemed rather afraid of his young relative. Finally, he decided to try to persuade him to apologize to the man he had offended and to the club membership as a whole, and to do so in a manner that would satisfy the offended parties—even in writing if they demanded it. The governor also thought he might find tactful arguments that would convince Stavrogin to leave us and go, for instance, on an educational trip to Italy, say, or some other foreign country.

Previously Stavrogin had wandered unrestrainedly all over the house, like one of the family, but this time the governor received him in a reception room. At a table in a corner, Alyosha Telyatnikov, a well-mannered clerk who was more or less a member of the governor's household, was opening postal packages. In the adjoining room, sitting by the window, there was a big, heavy colonel with whom the governor had once served in the same regiment. He was there on a visit. He was reading the newspaper, *The Voice,* and of course paid no attention to what was going on in the next room. In fact, his back was turned to it.

The governor approached the subject circumspectly. He spoke very quietly, almost in a whisper. But he got all mixed up. Stavrogin's attitude was quite unfriendly. There was nothing about it that suggested a warm family feeling. He was pale; he looked down and frowned as if he were trying to suppress an acute pain.

"I know you have a kind and noble heart, Nikolai," the old man said, among other things. "You're a well-educated man and you've been in contact with the upper crust of society. . . . Yes, and until this happened, even here your behavior was above all reproach, which was a great comfort to your mother, who is so dear to all of us. . . . And now everything has taken such a strange and dangerous turn! Let me tell you, as an old family friend, as an old relative sincerely concerned for you, whose words should never be taken the wrong way. . . . Tell me, what is it that prompts you to perform such wild deeds—deeds that are unacceptable by any standard of behavior? What is the meaning of these acts that appear to be performed by someone in a state of delirium?"

Stavrogin listened, irritated and impatient. Suddenly a sly, sarcastic expression flashed across his face.

"Well, I suppose I may as well tell you what prompts me to do these things," he said gruffly, and looking quickly around, he leaned toward the governor's ear. The tactful Alyosha

Telyatnikov had discreetly moved his table a couple of paces further away. In the next room, the colonel coughed as he read *The Voice*. Poor Ivan Osipovich hastily and trustfully thrust his ear closer to Stavrogin, for he was a terribly curious man. And at that point, something quite unthinkable—although in other respects quite understandable—happened.

The governor suddenly realized that, instead of whispering some interesting secret into his ear, Stavrogin had caught it between his teeth and was biting the upper part of it quite hard. The old man trembled all over, and his breath failed him.

"Nikolai, what sort of a joke is this?" he moaned in a distraught voice.

Alyosha and the colonel couldn't make out what was happening; to the end, it looked to them as if the two men were whispering secrets to each other. However, the wild, desperate look on the governor's face worried them. They kept exchanging questioning glances: should they rush to his rescue or wait a bit longer? Stavrogin must have noticed this and he clamped harder on the ear.

"Nikolai, Nikolai . . ." the victim moaned again. "All right, you've had your joke—that's enough now. . . ."

Another moment and the poor old fellow would probably have died of fear, but his tormentor relented and let his ear go. However, the state of shock continued for a full minute after that, and later the old man had some sort of an attack.

Within half an hour, Nikolai Stavrogin was arrested and taken temporarily to the guardroom, where he was locked in a special cell with a special sentry posted at the door. It was a drastic step to take, but the mild governor was so enraged that he decided to do it whatever the consequences, including Mrs. Stavrogin's ire. To everyone's amazement, when she hurriedly and angrily rushed over to the governor's to demand an explanation, Mrs. Stavrogin was refused admittance. She returned home without even having left her carriage and hardly able to believe it herself.

Then at last all their questions were answered. At two in the morning, the prisoner, who had been very quiet until then and had even slept for a while, suddenly started stamping and pounding on the door with his fists. He wrenched the iron grating from the window—a feat requiring unnatural strength —broke the glass, and cut his hands. When the officer of the guard arrived with his men and the keys and ordered the cell unlocked so his men could overpower and tie up the maniac,

Nikolai Stavrogin turned out to be suffering from an acute attack of brain fever. So he was transported home to his mama. Everything was immediately clear. Our three doctors expressed the opinion that the patient might have been delirious for the three previous days and, although he had appeared to be acting consciously and even cunningly, was by no means in possession of his senses—which, indeed, seemed to fit the facts. Liputin, then, had been the first to stumble on the truth. The governor, being a very sensitive and tactful man, was confused. But it is interesting to note that he too had considered Stavrogin capable of any mad action while in his normal state. The club members were also embarrassed at having missed such an obvious explanation. There were, of course, some skeptics, but none of them made much of an impression.

Stavrogin stayed in bed for over two months. A famous Moscow doctor was summoned for consultation. The whole town paid their respects to Mrs. Stavrogin, and she forgave them. Nikolai recovered completely and accepted without objection his mother's suggestion to take a trip to Italy. She also managed to convince him to make a round of farewell visits and, if he could bear it, apologize to those he had offended. He eagerly agreed. Word spread in the club that he and Mr. Gaganov had had a long conversation in the latter's home that had left the offended party fully satisfied.

Driving around on these visits, Stavrogin was grave and unsmiling. Although everyone seemed to receive him with great sympathy, they felt rather awkward with him and were relieved at the thought that he was leaving for Italy. The governor actually shed a tear, but for some reason didn't dare embrace him even at their farewell meeting. However, some among us apparently continued to believe that he was a good-for-nothing who was simply pulling everyone's leg and that his sickness had nothing to do with it. He dropped in on Liputin too.

"Tell me," Stavrogin said, "how did you guess what I'd say about your intelligence and so provide Agafya with a ready answer?"

"Why," Liputin laughed, "of course, I consider you an intelligent man too, so I could predict your reaction."

"Still, it was a marvelous coincidence. Now tell me, does that mean that, in sending Agafya to me, you regarded me as reasonable and not a madman?"

"Yes, as the most intelligent, the sanest man. But I did pretend to believe you were a bit out of your mind. . . . Anyway, you yourself guessed what I thought very well—you even sent me a sort of certificate of wit by Agafya."

"Well, you're not quite right there. I really wasn't too well then," Stavrogin muttered, frowning. "But wait—do you really imagine that I could go around attacking people while in full possession of my senses? Why would I do such things?"

Liputin looked puzzled; he didn't know what to say. Stavrogin had turned slightly pale, or at least Liputin thought he had.

"In any case, you have a very amusing way of thinking," Stavrogin added. "As to Agafya, I gathered that you'd sent her over to abuse me."

"Well, you didn't expect me to challenge you to a duel, did you?"

"Ah, that's right, I've heard something about your disliking duels. . . ."

"Why should we adopt French customs in our country?" Liputin said rather unhappily.

"So you're a stickler for our Russian national ways?"

Liputin looked even unhappier.

"But what's that? What do I see here?" Stavrogin exclaimed, pointing at a book by Considerant lying open on the table. "Are you a follower of Fourier by any chance? That wouldn't surprise me at all. But isn't this a translation from the French?" Stavrogin laughed, drumming on the book with his fingers.

"No, it's not a translation from the French!" Liputin said, with undisguised irritation. "It's a translation from a worldwide human language, not only from the French. It's from the language of the world-wide socialist republic of harmony, and not just from the French. You understand?"

"There isn't any such language, damn you," Stavrogin said, laughing.

Sometimes a mere trifle strikes people and sticks in their minds for a long time. We'll return to Stavrogin later. Meanwhile, let me point out that, of all the impressions our town had made on him, the most striking was that of the insignificant figure of this petty local government official; this envious, coarse family despot; this mean usurer who locked up the candle ends and the leftovers from dinner and at the same time fiercely advocated God knows what "social harmony"; who spent nights in rapturous admiration over visions of the fantastic future Utopia that he believed was about to descend upon Russia and our province as surely as he believed in his own existence. And he believed that this Utopia was about to materialize in the very town where he had managed to accumulate enough funds to buy himself a house, where he had married his second wife for her dowry, and where there was not a man, including himself, within a hundred-mile radius who in the least resembled a member of the future world-wide harmonious socialist republic.

"God knows how such people get that way!" Stavrogin thought wonderingly every time he remembered that surprising follower of Fourier.

IV

Our prince traveled for over three years, so that they almost completely forgot about him in town. We heard from Mr. Verkhovensky that he'd been all over Europe and also visited Egypt and Jerusalem; that he'd later managed to attach himself to some learned expedition to Iceland and actually to visit that land. We were also told that he had spent a winter attending lectures in a German university. He only wrote to his mother once every six months, sometimes even less often, but she didn't seem to resent it. She humbly accepted her relations with her son as they were, although she missed her Nikolai and made up all sorts of daydreams about him. She never complained or shared her dreams with anyone. She had even become somewhat distant with Mr. Verkhovensky. She seemed to be making all sorts of secret plans, and grew stingier than ever, saving money with even greater zeal and becoming more and more irritated with Mr. Verkhovensky's losses at cards.

Finally, in April, she received a letter from Paris from her childhood friend Praskovia Drozdov, the general's wife. They hadn't seen each other or corresponded for over eight years, but now, suddenly, Mrs. Drozdov wrote that Nikolai had practically become a member of their household, that he had become a very close friend of her only daughter, Liza, and that he intended to accompany them to Verney-Montreux, in Switzerland that summer, despite the fact that in the family of Count K. (a very influential personage from Petersburg) he was also received like a son and had almost moved in on the count in Paris. Mrs. Drozdov's letter was brief and its point obvious, although she drew no conclusions from the above-mentioned facts. It didn't take Mrs. Stavrogin very long to decide what to do. Taking along her protégée, Dasha (Shatov's sister), she left for Paris by the middle of April and from there went to Switzerland. In July she was back by herself. She had left Dasha at the Drozdovs' who, she told us, were coming back to Russia by the end of August.

The Drozdovs also owned land in our part of the country, but General Drozdov (who was an old friend of Mrs. Stavrogin and a former army colleague of her husband) had found that his duties constantly prevented him from spending any time on his magnificent estate. Then, after the general's death, his disconsolate widow had gone abroad with her daughter and, while there, had decided to take a grape cure at Verney-Montreux during the second half of the summer. After that she intended to settle in our province permanently.

Mrs. Drozdov had a large town house that had stood empty and shuttered for many years. She was, in fact, a very wealthy woman. Like her childhood friend Varvara, Praskovia was the daughter of a rich government contractor and had received a big dowry when she married her first husband, Tishin. A retired cavalry captain, he was a gifted and intelligent man and very rich himself. When he died he left a substantial fortune to his daughter, Liza, who was then only seven. Now she was twenty-two, and a conservative estimate would have put her capital at two hundred thousand rubles—that is, without counting what would be left to her by her mother, who had no children by her second husband, Drozdov.

Varvara Stavrogin seemed very pleased with her trip. She felt she had reached a satisfactory agreement with her friend Praskovia Drozdov and as soon as she returned told Mr. Verkhovensky about it. Indeed, she chatted with him as she had not for a long time.

"Hurray!" Verkhovensky exclaimed, snapping his fingers.

He was very enthusiastic, especially since he had been feeling rather despondent during her absence. She had not even said good-by to him properly, nor had she confided any of her plans to "that old woman," fearing that his tongue would wag. She had been furious with him at the time because of a larger-than-usual gambling loss that he had just confessed to her. However, while still in Switzerland, she had felt she had been treating him roughly for some time. In fact, her sudden and mysterious departure had torn Mr. Verkhovensky's vulnerable heart, and to make things worse, he was suddenly beset with various other problems. First he was tormented by a financial difficulty of long standing that couldn't possibly be solved without Mrs. Stavrogin's intervention. Then, in May, our nice, meek Ivan Osipovich was replaced—and under rather unpleasant circumstances at that. And, while Mrs. Stavrogin was still away, the new governor, Andrei Antonovich von Lembke, took over. Immediately there was a noticeable change in everyone's attitude toward Mrs. Stavrogin and, naturally, toward Mr. Verkhovensky as well. At least he noticed some unpleasant and significant indications and was rather subdued by having to face everything alone. He knew from absolutely reliable sources that some of the ladies of our town intended to stop visiting Mrs. Stavrogin. The incumbent first lady, it was said, had a reputation for being very proud and haughty, but at least she was a real aristocrat, "unlike poor old Mrs. Stavrogin." Everyone seemed to have heard somehow that the new first lady and Mrs. Stavrogin had already met socially and had parted on decidedly unfriendly terms and that the mere mention of Mrs. von Lembke's name caused painful symptoms in Mrs. Stavrogin. But now, Mrs. Stavrogin's triumphant air and her scornful indifference to the ladies' opinions of her revived Mr. Verkhovensky's faltering spirits, and he immediately became gay and cheerful. He began to describe to her in gloating tones (in which she detected a certain obsequiousness toward herself) the arrival of the new governor in their town.

"I'm sure, *chère amie,* that you are already fully aware," he said in an affected voice, drawing out his vowels, "what a Russian administrator is like in general and, particularly, a newly promoted, newly baked we may say, Russian administrator. . . . But I don't suppose you'll grasp the meaning of what might be called 'administrative passion,' or what sort of animal it is."

"Administrative passion? No, I don't know what that is."

"Well . . . *vous savez, chez nous. . . . En un mot,* if you place some unspeakable nonentity anywhere, say in a wretched railroad-ticket office, the poor creature will start looking down on you as though he were Jupiter himself, as long as you want to buy a train ticket. Just *pour vous montrer son pouvoir.* And that's the type that attains to administrative passion. . . . *En un mot,* I read about some stupid sexton in one of our churches abroad—*mais c'est très curieux*—who kicked out of his church, and I mean literally turned out, a very nice English family—*des dames charmantes*—just before the beginning of the Lenten service—*vous savez ces chants et le livre de Job*—just because 'it ain't proper for them foreigners to wander around Russian churches except during proper visiting hours'. . . . The ladies almost fainted. . . . Well, that sexton was feeling his administrative passion to the full *et il a montré son pouvoir.* . . ."

"Make a short story of it if you can, my friend."

"Mr. von Lembke has left on a tour of the province now. *En un mot,* although he's a Russified German and Russian Orthodox, and even, to be fair, a handsome man, still in his forties—"

"How can you think he's handsome? He has bovine eyes."

"Yes, very much so, but I must concede to the opinion of our ladies—"

"Keep to the point, please. But, by the way, since when do you wear red ties?"

"That? . . . Just today—"

"And have you been exercising regularly? Do you go for a daily five-mile walk as the doctor ordered?"

"Not . . . not too regularly."

"I thought so! Even when I was in Switzerland, I knew you wouldn't do it," she said irritably. "From now on you'll walk not five miles but seven every day! It's incredible the way you've let yourself go—really unbelievable! You've not simply aged, you've grown quite senile in these past months. I was really struck by the sight of you when I first arrived, despite that red tie of yours. Ah, that tie, *quelle idée rouge!* And now tell me about von Lembke, if you really have something interesting to say. And please get it over with, for I'm very tired."

"*En un mot,* I was about to tell you that he is one of those men who've suddenly been entrusted with administrative power when they're in their forties, until which point they've been nonentities cooling their heels. Then, by finding themselves a brand-new wife or some other desperate measure . . . That is . . . he's out of town now . . . that is, I wanted to tell you that, they've been whispering things in his ear about me, that I'm a kind of perverter of youth, a provincial sower of the seeds of atheism. . . . And so he started making inquiries about me right away."

"Are you sure of what you're saying?"

"Yes, I've even taken some countermeasures. And when they went to him with talk about how you used to run the province, he dared to answer, 'Nothing of the sort will happen while I'm here.' "

"Is that what he said?"

"Yes—'Nothing of the sort will happen while I'm here.' And he said it with that arrogance of his. . . . And by the end of August we'll have the pleasure of seeing his wife. She's coming straight from Petersburg."

"No, from abroad. We met there."

"Vraiment?"

"In Paris *and* in Switzerland. She's related to the Drozdovs."

"She's related to them? What a wonderful coincidence! I've heard she's terribly ambitious and has very influential connections."

"Nonsense! Just very ordinary connections. She was a penniless old maid until she was forty-five. Then she hooked her von Lembke, and now, obviously, she's trying to push him ahead. They're schemers, both of them."

"They say she's two years older than he."

"Five years. Her mother wore out the seat of her skirts waiting to be received in my house in Moscow. She kept begging me to invite them to my receptions when the general was alive. And when she came, her daughter would sit all night with a great turquoise bow on her forehead, without ever being invited to dance. I'd feel sorry for her, and when two o'clock in the morning rolled around and she still didn't have a partner, I'd send her one. She was already twenty-five, but they dressed her in short dresses as though she were a little girl. It was positively awkward to invite them."

"I can see that bow now."

"I tell you, no sooner had I arrived than I stumbled upon an intrigue. You know—you've just read Praskovia Drozdov's letter—what could be clearer? And what did I find there? That fool Praskovia—she's always been a fool—looks at me questioningly as if to say 'What on earth have you come here for?' Can you imagine my surprise? I had a good look around and found that Lembke woman scheming away, and with her that nephew of old Drozdov—everything was clear! Oh, it took me no more than a blink of an eye to turn the tables on them and get Praskovia Drozdov back on my side. If they want to scheme, I'll show them what scheming is!"

"So you've succeeded in thwarting their plans. You're a real Bismarck!"

"I didn't have to be a Bismarck to detect falsehood and stupidity when I came across them. The Lembke woman is falsehood and the Drozdov woman stupidity. I don't think I've ever met a flabbier woman; she has swollen legs and, on top of that, a kind heart. What is more stupid than a kind-hearted fool?"

"A vicious fool, *ma bonne amie;* a vicious fool is even more stupid," Mr. Verkhovensky dissented bravely.

"Well, maybe you have a point there. I suppose you remember Liza?"

"Une charmante enfant!"

"Well, she's no longer an *enfant;* she's a woman, and a woman with plenty of character. She's high-spirited and quick-tempered, and I like the way she stands up to her silly, trusting mother. There was very nearly a real row about that nephew of old Drozdov's."

"Yes, but . . . he's really not related to Liza. . . . Unless he has views on her."

"You see, he's a young army officer and doesn't talk much—rather a modest young man, in fact. In all fairness, I must say that I don't think he ever approved of the whole intrigue. It was all the Lembke woman's idea. The nephew greatly admires Nikolai. So, of course, everything depends on Liza. Now, when I left, she was on the best terms with Nikolai, and he promised me he'd be back home in November. So it's the Lembke woman who's intriguing, and Praskovia is just blind. Can you imagine—she suddenly declared to me that all my suspicions were sheer fantasy! So I told her to her face that she was a fool. And I'm prepared to repeat it on the Day of Judgment. If it hadn't been for Nikolai's insistence that I leave things alone for the time being, I wouldn't have left without exposing that lying woman! She was trying to use Nikolai to get on the good side of Count K. She was actually trying to set the son against his mother! But Liza is on our side, and I've reached an agreement with Praskovia. Do you know, by the way, that the Lembke woman is related to Karmazinov?"

"What? Karmazinov is a relative of Mrs. von Lembke?"

"Certainly, a distant relation."

"You mean the novelist?"

"Well yes, the writer. What's the matter with you? What if he does regard himself as a great man? The swollen-headed creature! They will arrive here together; in the meantime, she's parading him around over there. I understand she intends to organize some kind of literary gatherings here, or something of the sort. He's coming here for a month to liquidate the last bit of some property he owned near here. I almost ran across him in Switzerland—without seeking it, believe me. However,

I hope that he'll be gracious enough to recognize me when we meet. In the old days he used to come to the house and write me letters. . . . Ah, I wish you dressed a bit better, Stepan—you get more slovenly every day. . . . Oh, the trouble you give me! What book are you reading now?"

"I—I—"

"I see—you're the same as ever: friends, drinking parties, the club, cards, and a reputation as an atheist. I don't like that reputation, Stepan. I don't like them referring to you as an atheist, especially not now. I didn't like it before either, because it was just empty chatter anyway. I suppose I was bound to say it finally."

"Mais, ma chère amie—"

"Listen to me now: as far as learning goes, of course, I'm nothing but an ignoramus compared to you. But when I was on my way back here from abroad, I kept thinking of you, and I came to one conclusion."

"What was that?"

"That we—you and I—really aren't the cleverest people on earth; that there are other people cleverer than we are."

"That's both witty and correct. There are people smarter than we, and they are therefore more likely to be right than we are. Therefore, we may have erred, right? *Mais, ma bonne amie,* let's assume I'm mistaken; don't I still have my eternal, supreme, human right to free thought? So, I have the right *not* to be a hypocrite and a bigot, even if it makes certain people hate me till they're blue in the face. *Et puis, comme on trouve toujours plus de moines que de raison* and since I fully go along with it—"

"What was that? What did you say?"

"I said *on trouve toujours plus de moines que de raison* and since I agree—"

"I'm sure you didn't make that up. You must have borrowed it somewhere."

"Blaise Pascal said it."

"I was sure it wasn't you. Why don't you ever say anything briefly and to the point yourself? You always drag everything out. I like his way of putting things much better than yours when you went on and on about administrative passion. . . ."

"Well, I must say I agree, my dear. But, in the first place, I'm no Pascal, and then, we Russians are incapable of saying anything in our native tongue. At least, we haven't said anything thus far."

"Hm . . . that may not be true at all. But you ought to write down and memorize phrases like that to use in conversation. . . . Ah, Stepan, to think that on my way here I longed to have a serious talk with you."

"*Chère, chère amie!*"

"Now, when all these Lembkes and Karmazinovs— Oh Lord, how far you've let yourself go! Ah, you make me so unhappy! I want those people to respect you, because they're not worth your little finger. But look at the way you behave! What can I show them? What will they see? Instead of standing like a living testament to our ideals and setting them an example, you surround yourself with all sorts of scum, acquire repulsive habits, and turn senile. You can't live without wine and cards; you read nothing but Paul de Kock's cheap French novels; you never write a word; and you waste all your time in idle chatter. Tell me, for instance, do you think becoming bosom pals with a disgusting creature like your Liputin is right?"

"Why do you call him *mine?* And why is he my *bosom pal?*" Mr. Verkhovensky protested meekly.

"Where is he now?" Mrs. Stavrogin asked sharply and sternly.

"He—he has the utmost respect for you. He's gone to Smolensk to receive a legacy left him by his mother."

"It looks to me as if all he does is receive money. And what about Shatov? Still the same?"

"Still bad-tempered and still a good man."

"I can't stand him. He's spiteful, and so full of himself."

"And how is Miss Shatov?"

"You mean Dasha? Why do you ask?" She looked at him with curiosity. "Well, she's fine. I left her with the Drozdovs. . . . And you know, when I was in Switzerland, I heard things about your son—bad things—"

"Ah, that's a stupid story. I wanted to tell you about it, my dear."

"All right, that'll do, Stepan; leave me in peace. I'm exhausted as it is. We'll have plenty of time to talk things over, especially the bad things. You splutter when you laugh, and that's really a sign of senility, you know! And how strangely you laugh these days. . . . Good God, what a lot of bad habits you've picked up! In your present condition, Karmazinov will never call on you, and that will make them happier than ever. You've finally revealed your true self for everyone to see. But

that's enough, enough. Can't you occasionally show me some
consideration at least and let me rest!"

Mr. Verkhovensky displayed his consideration for her and
left. But he left greatly perturbed.

V

Mr. Verkhovensky really had picked up some bad habits,
particularly lately. He had become noticeably more slovenly.
He drank more and had become more tearful and nervous and
rather hypersensitive to aesthetic values. His face had acquired
a peculiar knack of changing instantly from, say, a solemn,
inspired expression to a ridiculous and even idiotic one. He
couldn't bear to be left alone for a moment and constantly
craved distraction. He was always eager to hear any gossip and
the latest local anecdotes. And if no one went to see him for
a while, he walked disconsolately from room to room, stopped
by a window, chewed his lips, and ended by almost whimpering. He had forebodings, fearing that something inevitable was
going to strike him unexpectedly. He grew fearful and started
to attach great weight to his dreams.

All that day and the evening that followed he was very
despondent and agitated; he sent for me and talked to me
at great length, but all rather incoherently. (Mrs. Stavrogin
had known for a long time that he had no secrets from me.)
I got the impression that something special was worrying him
now—something that he couldn't quite formulate himself.
Formerly, when we were alone and he began to tell me his
troubles, a bottle had been brought in and things had soon
looked brighter. This time there was no wine, and he appeared
to suppress repeated impulses to send for it.

"And why is she so angry with me all the time?" he kept
complaining like a little child. "All men of genius, all those
who strive for progress in Russia have always been and always
will be gamblers and drunkards who burn up their talents in
alcohol . . . but I'm really not such a hopeless drunkard
and gambler. Then she reproaches me for not writing. Strange
idea! And why do I spend my days lying around? 'You,' she
tells me, 'must stand like a monument of reproach!' But,
entre nous soit dit, what's left for a man whose fate it is to

'stand as a monument of reproach' that's better than lying down? Doesn't she see that?"

I finally understood what was depressing him so much. That evening, he kept stopping by the mirror and looking into it. Once he turned his face from the mirror and said to me, "My dear fellow, I am a man who has let himself slip!" And indeed, until that very day, if there was one thing he had been sure of, amidst all those new ideas and views and Mrs. Stavrogin's changes of outlook, it was that he still possessed irresistible charms for her as a woman, not only because he was an exile and brilliant scholar but also because he was a handsome man. For twenty years he had harbored this flattering and reassuring conviction, and of all his convictions, it was probably the most painful for him to lose. Did he have a foreboding that night of the great trial he was to undergo soon afterward?

VI

Now I come to the rather amusing incident that marks the beginning of my story proper.

The Drozdovs came back at the very end of August. Their arrival, shortly before that of their relative, our new first lady, caused a great stir. But more of that later. For now I'll say only that Mrs. Drozdov, for whom Mrs. Stavrogin had so impatiently waited, brought unexpected trouble with her. Nikolai Stavrogin had left the Drozdovs as far back as July. He'd met Count K. and his family (including K.'s three daughters) on the Rhine and accompanied them to Petersburg.

"I could get nothing out of Liza," Mrs. Drozdov said. "You know how proud and stubborn she is. I could see for myself, though, that something had happened between her and Nikolai. I have no idea what caused it, but perhaps you can find out from Dasha. I think Liza was offended by something. And I must tell you, Varvara, I'm terribly glad to return your protégée. I'm not at all sorry to be rid of her."

This catty remark was uttered with a specially set face, and it was obvious that the "flabby" lady had prepared it in advance and was now relishing its effect. But Varvara Stavrogin was not a woman to be disconcerted by riddles and pinpricks. She sternly demanded more details. Mrs. Drozdov immediately changed her tone, and after a while burst into tears; she ended by protesting her deepest affection. This irritable but sentimental lady yearned for friendship just as Mr. Verkhovensky did, and her main complaint against her daughter Liza was that she was not a "real friend" to her.

Still, all Mrs. Stavrogin could gather for certain from the outpourings of friendship was that Liza and Nikolai had quarreled. But about the nature of the quarrel Mrs. Drozdov was obviously unable to enlighten her. As to her unpleasant remark about Dasha, the lady took it back, explaining that it had been made under the stress of irritation. But the main situation remained blurred and suspicious. According to Mrs. Drozdov, it had all started with "Liza's headstrong, sarcastic attitude," which "Nikolai, proud as he is—although very much in love with her—couldn't take, and returned in kind."

"And soon afterward," Praskovia Drozdov added, "we met a young man—a nephew of your Professor's, I believe. He had the same name. . . ."

Mrs. Drozdov could never remember the name Verkhovensky, so she always referred to Stepan as the Professor.

"Not his nephew, his son," Mrs. Stavrogin corrected her.

"All right, *son*; so much the better—what difference does it make? He's a young man like any other. He's very free and easy, but otherwise there's nothing special about him. Anyway, at that point, Liza did something she shouldn't have done: she started seeing a lot of that young man in order to make Nikolai jealous. I can't really blame her too much— it's a common feminine trick, and even rather charming, I think. But what do you suppose happened? Instead of being jealous, Nikolai became great friends with the young man himself, as though he either didn't see or didn't care. That made Liza furious. Well, then the young man left for somewhere or other (he seemed in a hurry, too), and Liza began to pick on Nikolai at every opportunity. She noticed that Nikolai spoke to Dasha sometimes; she threw genuine fits of rage that made my life impossible. I'm not supposed to get excited, you know—the doctors have warned me. And then I got so tired of that marvelous lake of theirs—besides, my teeth began to ache with rheumatism. . . . In fact, I've seen it in print—that the Lake of Geneva gives people tooth- aches; it's known for it. Then, on top of all that, Nikolai received a letter from the countess; he packed and left the same day. I must say they parted like good friends. Liza saw him off and was very gay and laughed a lot. But she was just pretending, I'm sure. As soon as he was gone, she grew quiet; she never mentioned him herself and never allowed me to. And I advise you too, Varvara, not to mention the subject in front of her—it would only make things worse. If you say nothing, she may want to talk about it, and you'll find out much more. I believe they'll make it up anyway if Nikolai comes back as he promised."

"I'll write to him immediately. If that's all there was, it was nothing. As for Dasha, I know her too well—it's all nonsense."

"I was wrong about Dasha, as I told you. They just talked—and not even in whispers. I was just so upset by everything. Anyway, Liza is as friendly with her as she was before."

That very day Mrs. Stavrogin wrote to her son Nikolai begging him to come back at least a month earlier than he had originally intended. But there was still much about the whole matter that she didn't understand. She turned it over in her head throughout the evening and during the night. Mrs. Drozdov's conclusions struck her as naïve and sentimental. "Praskovia was always sentimental even in boarding school," she reflected, "but a man like Nikolai isn't likely to fly from the sarcastic needling of a girl. There must be something more to it—if, indeed, there was any quarrel at all. There's that officer. . . . They've brought him along, and he lives in their house like one of the family. And why was she in such a hurry to take back her remarks about Dasha? I'm sure there is something she doesn't want me to know. . . ."

By morning Mrs. Stavrogin had a plan of action. It would solve at least one of the problems bothering her and was remarkable for its unexpectedness. I won't attempt to explain exactly what was in her mind when she conceived it, nor can I account for all its contradictory elements. I'll content myself with describing events just as they happened, and I decline all responsibility if they appear too incredible. I must, however, repeat that, by morning, she did not suspect Dasha of anything —if she ever had. She was much too sure of the girl. And then, she couldn't imagine her Nikolai falling for Dasha. In the morning, as Dasha was pouring tea, Mrs. Stavrogin studied her and muttered under her breath, "Nothing but nonsense!"

She noticed that Dasha looked tired, that she was even

quieter than usual and, in fact, rather listless. After breakfast, following a long-established habit, they sat down together to some needlework. Dasha was asked for a full account of her journey abroad, especially her impressions of the countryside, inhabitants, towns, customs, local arts, industries—indeed, everything she'd had time to notice. She was asked nothing about the Drozdovs or how she had got along with them. Dasha sat next to Mrs. Stavrogin, helped her with her embroidery, and answered everything in her rather weak, monotonous voice.

"Dasha!" Mrs. Stavrogin said suddenly. "Isn't there something special you'd like to tell me?"

Dasha stopped and glanced at Mrs. Stavrogin out of her pale eyes. "No, nothing," she replied.

"You're sure? You've nothing on your heart and conscience?"

"Nothing," Dasha said quietly, but there was a certain sullen determination in her tone.

"I was sure of it. I want you to know, Dasha, that I'll never have any misgivings about you. Now, sit tight and listen to what I have to say. Sit over there, on that chair. I want you to face me so I can see all of you. That's fine. Listen then: would you like to get married?"

Dasha gave her a long, questioning look, but she was not too surprised at the question.

"Wait. Don't answer. In the first place, there's a great difference in years, but I'm sure you realize how little that matters. You're a sensible girl, and you should be able to avoid the most glaring mistakes. And even so, he's still a handsome man. . . . Well, let me be direct with you—I have in mind Stepan Verkhovensky, for whom you've always shown so much respect. Well?"

Dasha's look became even more questioning, and this time there was surprise in it; she also blushed.

"Wait—say nothing; don't answer hurriedly! I've left you some money in my will, but still, think what'll happen to you, with or without money, if I die. They're certain to cheat you and take your money, and then you can say good-by to everything! But if you marry him, you'll be the wife of a famous man. Now, let's examine it from another angle: if I died tomorrow—although, of course, I've provided for him too— what would become of him? You see, I know I can fully rely upon you. Wait—let me finish. I'm fully aware that he's unreliable, ineffective, unfeeling, selfish, and afflicted with re-pulsive habits. But still, you ought to appreciate him because there are much worse men. You don't think I'd suggest some vicious brute just to get rid of you, do you? And the main reason why you should appreciate him is because I'm asking you to. Well, why do you sit there saying nothing?"

Dasha remained silent.

"Wait then—listen to me. He's nothing but an old woman, I know, but that's to your advantage, don't you see? He's a pathetic old woman, and there's certainly nothing about him to inspire love in a woman, except his helplessness. So try to love him for his helplessness. I'm sure you understand what I mean. You do understand, don't you?"

Dasha nodded.

"I never expected less from you. He'll love you because he has to—he must. He'll just have to adore you, Dasha!" Mrs. Stavrogin said in a strange, squeaky voice. "Anyway, knowing him, I have no doubt that he'll love you—and not only because he feels obliged. And remember, I'll be around. Don't worry, I'll always be around. He'll complain about you, spread all sorts of rumors, whisper nasty things about you to the first person he meets; he'll moan and whine unceasingly; he'll write letters to you from the next room—a couple of letters every day . . . but he won't be able to live without you, and that's what counts.

"You must make him obey you; if you can't, you're nothing but a fool. If he tells you he wants to hang himself, don't believe him—but keep your ear to the ground: anything may happen, and one day he may really end up hanging himself. His sort hang themselves not out of strength but out of weak-ness, so don't push him to the limit. That's the first rule in marriage. Remember, too, that he's a poet.

"Now listen to me, my girl, there's no greater happiness than self-sacrifice; besides, you'll render me a great service in this, and that's what's important. And don't think that what I've just said is a lot of rubbish. I know what I'm talking about. I'm looking after my interests; you look after yours, too. But I'm not forcing anything on you—it's whatever you say. Well, why do you sit there like that? Say something!"

"I don't really care, Mrs. Stavrogin. If there's no other way, I'll do it," Dasha said firmly.

"What do you mean 'no other way'? What are you trying to say?"

Mrs. Stavrogin glared at the girl. Dasha picked silently at the embroidery frame with her needle.

"You're a clever person, Dasha, but what you just said isn't very bright. It's true, of course, that I'm determined to marry you off, but it's not a question of there being 'no other way.' I've simply decided that it would be a good thing if you married and that the man should be none other than Mr. Verkhovensky. If he hadn't been here, I'd never have thought of marrying you off, although you're already twenty. . . . Well?"

"I'll do what you want, Mrs. Stavrogin."

"So, it's agreed, right? Wait—don't say anything—where are you going? I haven't finished yet. I'd left you fifteen thousand rubles in my will, but now you'll get them on your wedding day. Of that sum you'll give him eight—that is, not him but me, and I'll pay a debt he has for that amount. But I want him to know it's being paid with your money. So you'll have seven thousand left, and you must never give him a single ruble of it. Never. And never pay his debts, for if you do it once, there'll be no end to it. But, as I told you, I'll be around. You will receive a yearly allowance of twelve hundred rubles from me—fifteen hundred with all the extras—besides apartment and board, which I'll continue to supply as I have for him up to now. But you'll have to provide your own domestic help. As to the allowance, I'll pay you a lump sum once a year. You'll hold the purse strings, but I want you to be nice to him and let him receive his friends at home once a week. If they come more often, however, throw them out. But I'll see to that myself as long as I'm here. Now, if I die, your allowance will continue until his death—*his* death, do you hear?—because it is his allowance, not yours. As to you, besides the seven thousand—which you won't touch, if you're smart—I'll leave you another eight in my will. And that'll be all you'll get from me. I want to be sure that you realize that. Well, do you agree? Come, say something."

"But I've already answered."

"Remember, you're completely free. It will be just as you decide."

"Just tell me one thing, Mrs. Stavrogin. Has Mr. Verkhovensky said anything to you?"

"He has not. He knows nothing about it, but I promise you, he'll start talking soon enough!"

She got up very quickly, throwing her black shawl around her shoulders. Dasha blushed slightly and followed her movements with a perplexed look. Mrs. Stavrogin suddenly turned toward her, her face flushed with anger.

"You're a fool—a miserable little fool," she said, pouncing on Dasha like a hawk. "You're an ungrateful fool! Do you think that I would disgrace you? Do you? I tell you, he'll come crawling to you on his knees, feeling he's about to die of happiness! That's the way it will be arranged! You should know I wouldn't let anyone hurt you! Perhaps you think he'll marry you for the eight thousand—as if I were selling you. You're really an ungrateful little fool, just like the rest! All right now, get me my umbrella!"

And Mrs. Stavrogin hurried off on foot along the wet brick and plank sidewalks to Mr. Verkhovensky's place.

VII

Mrs. Stavrogin was telling the truth: she'd never have done anything to harm Dasha. Indeed, she felt she was being very generous toward the girl. Her indignation had been of the most noble and righteous nature when, as she wrapped herself in her shawl, she had caught Dasha's perplexed, distrustful gaze. She had sincerely liked Dasha ever since she was a child, and Mrs. Drozdov had been correct when she referred to the girl as Mrs. Stavrogin's "favorite." Mrs. Stavrogin had decided once and for all that Dasha was not at all like her brother, Ivan Shatov; that she was a quiet, gentle person capable of great sacrifices and very devoted to her, exceptionally modest, sensible, and above all, grateful. So far, Dasha seemed to have justified this estimation of her.

"There will be no mistakes in this child's life," Mrs. Stavrogin declared before Dasha was twelve. And with her propensity for clinging stubbornly to every plan, every fancy, every idea that attracted her, she immediately made up her mind to bring up Dasha like a daughter. She set aside a sum of money in the girl's name and engaged a governess for her, a Miss Criggs, who stayed with them until Dasha was sixteen. At that point she was abruptly dismissed for some unknown reason. After that, Dasha was educated by teachers from the town's secondary school who came to give her lessons at home. Among them was a real Frenchman who taught Dasha French, but he also, for some reason, was summarily dis-

missed. An elderly, impoverished, widowed gentlewoman also
came in to give her piano lessons.

Dasha's principal educator, however, was Stepan Verkhovensky. In fact, he "discovered" her. He started teaching
the quiet little girl before Mrs. Stavrogin even gave her a
thought. And, as I said before, children became extraordinarily
attached to him. Liza, Mrs. Drozdov's daughter, had also
been his pupil between the ages of eight and eleven (of
course, he taught her without remuneration—he'd never have
accepted money from the Drozdovs). But in that instance,
he had fallen in love with the charming child, and had created
all kinds of romantic tales for her about the land, the history
of mankind, and the organization of the world. His lectures
about primitive men and tribes were as enthralling as the
Arabian Nights. Liza, who listened ecstatically to his stories
while he was telling them, later, at home, imitated him very
amusingly. He found out about it and once surprised her during one of her performances. Terribly embarrassed, Liza threw
herself into his arms and burst into tears. Mr. Verkhovensky
also shed some exalted tears. But soon after that, Liza's
family moved to another town, leaving only Dasha.

When the schoolteachers started coming to give Dasha
lessons, Mr. Verkhovensky discontinued his studies with her
and gradually stopped paying any attention to the child. This
state of affairs prevailed for a long time. Then one day, when
she was seventeen, Mr. Verkhovensky suddenly noticed how
pretty Dasha had become. They were sitting at Mrs. Stavrogin's tea table. He spoke to her, was very favorably impressed by her answers, and immediately offered to give her
a comprehensive course in Russian literature. Mrs. Stavrogin thought it was a wonderful idea and thanked him. Dasha
was delighted. Mr. Verkhovensky began to prepare himself
specially for these lessons, and finally they began. He started
with the earliest period. The first lecture was fascinating.
Mrs. Stavrogin also attended it. When Mr. Verkhovensky
finished, he announced to his pupil that the next lecture would
be devoted to *The Lay of Igor's Host*. Abruptly Mrs. Stavrogin got up and said that there would be no more lectures.
He winced, but said nothing. Dasha flushed. And that was
that.

And now, three years later, Mrs. Stavrogin had come
up with her new idea.

Poor Mr. Verkhovensky, sitting all by himself, suspected

nothing. He felt rather sad and bored and kept glancing out of the window, hoping that one of his friends might turn up. But no one appeared. It was drizzling, and the air was growing raw; he thought they ought to have lighted a fire. He sighed. Suddenly he saw through the window a sight that startled him: Mrs. Stavrogin was coming his way. What could she want at this hour and in such weather? And why was she on foot and in such a hurry? He was so startled that he never thought of rushing for his coat and received her as he was, in his quilted pink smoking jacket.

"*Ma bonne amie!*" he exclaimed unconvincingly, moving forward to meet her.

"You're alone? Good! I can't stand your friends. Ugh! It's full of smoke in here. It really reeks! And look, it's past eleven, and you haven't even finished your breakfast! You enjoy living in such a mess, don't you? What are these scraps all over the floor? Nastasya, Nastasya!" she called out to the maid. "What's your Nastasya up to? Ah, there you are. Open those windows, my girl. And the doors too. I want them all opened wide; meanwhile, we'll go into the sitting room. I've come here on business, you know. And you, Nastasya, get busy. Sweep the room out properly for once!"

"The master always throws things all over the floor, ma'am," Nastasya whimpered shrilly.

"Then sweep up after him. Sweep fifteen times a day if you have to!"

They went into Mr. Verkhovensky's sitting room.

"What a poky sitting room you have," Mrs. Stavrogin said. "Now close the doors; I don't want her to hear. Ah, I must have this wallpaper changed. I'm sure I sent you the decorator with samples. Why haven't you chosen one? Sit down then and listen. Well—are you going to sit down or not? Where are you off to now? Where are you going?"

"I—I won't be a moment. . . ." Mr. Verkhovensky shouted back through the door. "Here—here I am."

"So you've changed your clothes." She looked him over, a sarcastic expression on her face. He had put his frock coat on over his pink smoking jacket. "Yes, that's certainly more fitting for what I have to tell you. Now, for heaven's sake, sit down!"

She gave it to him all at once, bluntly and convincingly. She hinted at the eight thousand rubles he needed so badly and mentioned the dowry. Mr. Verkhovensky's eyes nearly popped out. He started to tremble. He heard what she said, but it made no sense to him. He wanted to say something, but his voice failed him. He only knew that it would be as she had decided, that it was pointless to resist, and that for all practical purposes he was irrevocably married.

"*Mais, ma bonne amie,* it would be for the third time . . . and at my age . . . and she's only a child," he managed to say at last. "*Mais c'est une enfant!*"

"A child? She's twenty, remember. Will you kindly stop rolling your eyes? You're not on the stage. You're terribly clever and learned and all that, but you know nothing about life and you need a full-time nurse. If I die, what'll happen to you? She'll be a perfect nanny for you: she's modest, firm, and sensible. And, of course, I'll still be around for some time, for I hope I won't die this moment. She's a homebody and an angel of gentleness. This happy idea first occurred to me when I was in Switzerland. Don't you understand what it means, when I tell you myself that she's an angel of gentleness?" Mrs. Stavrogin suddenly shouted furiously. "You're living in a mess, and she'll introduce cleanliness and order here; everything will shine like a mirror. Do you really think that in presenting you with this treasure I should have to enumerate all the advantages you'll enjoy by accepting? Why, you should go down on your knees, you shallow, worthless creature!"

"But—I'm an old man."

"What's fifty-three? Fifty isn't the end of life; it's only half a life span. You're a handsome man—you know it very well. And you also know that she has great respect for you. If I died now, what would become of her? But married to you she'll be safe, and I'll feel reassured about her. You are a respected man; you have a name and a kind heart; you have an allowance that I consider it my duty to pay you. Perhaps you'll save her from all sorts of things; in any case, you'll be doing her an honor. You'll prepare her for life, mold her character, guide her views. So many young people are ruined nowadays because they're misguided! And in the meantime, your book will come out, and people will talk about you again."

"That's funny—I was thinking just recently of starting work on my *Tales from Spanish History,*" Mr. Verkhovensky said, gratified by Mrs. Stavrogin's adroit flattery.

"Well, there you are!"

"But—but what about her? Have you mentioned it to her?"

"Don't you worry about her. Anyway, that's none of your concern. Of course, you'll have to propose to her yourself—persuade her, beseech her, and all that sort of thing. But don't worry, I'll be around; I'll see that everything's all right. Besides, I know you're in love with her."

He felt dizzy; the room began to sway. He had a terrible thought that he couldn't push out of his mind.

"Excellente amie!" he gasped, trembling. "I could never . . . I never would have imagined you'd want to marry me off to another. . . ."

"You're not a young girl, Stepan. Only girls get 'married off,' remember that!" Mrs. Stavrogin said cuttingly.

"Well, maybe I didn't put it very well, but. . . ." He looked at her sheepishly.

"You certainly didn't!" she hissed at him scornfully. "Ah, good Lord, now he's going to faint! Nastasya, Nastasya! Get some water, quickly!"

But he didn't need the water. He recovered. Mrs. Stavrogin took her umbrella.

"I can see it's no use talking to you in your present state."

"Oui, oui, je suis incapable—"

"But by tomorrow you'll have had a rest and thought it over. Stay home, and if something happens, let me know—even if it's in the middle of the night. And don't bother to write me any letters—I won't read them. I'll come here tomorrow for a definite answer, and it'd better be a satisfactory one. Until then, try not to have any of your friends in; and I don't want to find this place in the disgusting mess in which it was this time. It's a real disgrace! Nastasya, come here!"

Needless to say, the next day he said yes. He couldn't help saying yes. There was a special circumstance that had to be taken into consideration. . . .

VIII

What we have referred to as Stepan Verkhovensky's estate—a fifty-soul affair by pre-Emancipation evaluation—didn't actually belong to him. The land (it adjoined Skvoreshniki) had been left by his first wife, and its rightful owner was their son,

Peter Stepanovich Verkhovensky. Stepan Verkhovensky had simply held the estate in trust for his heir, and when the son had come of age, he had given his father the power of attorney to go on running it. The arrangement was greatly to the young man's advantage: his father paid him an agreed sum of one thousand rubles a year while the actual income from the estate after the abolition of serfdom in 1861 was hardly half that. God knows how the figure had been arrived at; anyway, it was Mrs. Stavrogin who yearly made good on the thousand—Stepan Verkhovensky never actually contributed a single ruble. Indeed, he kept all the income from the estate for himself.

Furthermore, he drastically reduced its value by renting it out to some dealer and, without Mrs. Stavrogin's knowledge, selling for timber the woods that were its main asset. He sold the woods, bit by bit, for some time. The total value of the timber was at least eight thousand, but he got only five thousand for it. He went to such lengths because he lost heavily at cards in the club and didn't dare admit it to Mrs. Stavrogin. She almost gnashed her teeth with rage when she finally found out about it.

And now the son had announced that he was coming to sell his estate and had charged his father with carrying out the transaction. Because Mr. Verkhovensky senior had a generous and selfless nature, he felt guilty toward *ce cher enfant* (whom he'd last seen as a student in Petersburg). Originally the estate would have been worth thirteen to fourteen thousand, but now it probably wouldn't bring five. No doubt, from a strictly legal viewpoint, Mr. Verkhovensky could have invoked the power of attorney to justify his selling of the timber; he could also have claimed the right to deduct the difference between the annual one thousand rubles he had been sending his son and the actual income from the estate. But he was an honorable man, prone to noble gestures. He had conjured up a magnificent and dramatic scene and had decided to carry it through: when his Peter came, he would nobly lay out on the table the maximum sum possible—up to fifteen thousand, even—without saying a word about the money that he'd been sending the young man all the time. Then, shedding tears of affection, he'd press *ce cher fils* to his heart, closing all accounts between them.

Carefully and circumspectly he started to draw Mrs. Stavrogin into his dramatic plan. He even hinted that her participation would give their friendship and their ideals a specially noble luster; that it would show how generous the fathers of the past era were and, indeed, how noble their whole generation was compared with today's irresponsible young people who were going in for socialism. He said many other things besides.

Mrs. Stavrogin just let him talk. Then one day she announced that she was willing to pay the top price—that is, six, maybe even seven thousand (four would have been quite fair really, she said). She did not specifically mention the depreciation amounting to eight thousand rubles caused by the felling of the trees.

These talks took place about a month before the matchmaking. Mr. Verkhovensky was very worried and preoccupied about his son. At one time there had been some hope that the young man wouldn't turn up at all—of course, the father would have indignantly rejected use of the word "hope." Still, strange rumors about young Verkhovensky kept reaching us. After graduating from the university about six years before, he had apparently just loafed around Petersburg. Then we heard that he had been involved in the drafting of some seditious proclamation and was about to be tried. Then he turned up in Switzerland, in Geneva, and we feared he might have fled abroad.

"He's a great surprise to me," the embarrassed Mr. Verkhovensky told us at the time. "Peter, c'est une si pauvre tête! He's a kind, well-meaning boy, and awfully sensitive. I was so pleased when I met him in Petersburg because he was so different from the other young men of today. But c'est un pauvre sire tout de même. . . . And, let me tell you, the whole trouble stems from immaturity and sentimentality! It's not the practical aspects of socialism that fascinate them but its emotional appeal—its idealism—what we may call its mystical, religious aspect—its romanticism . . . and, on top of that, they just parrot others. But it puts me in a real fix: I have many enemies, and they are bound to ascribe it all to paternal influence. . . . Ah, my God, what times we live in! A boy like Peter among the revolutionary leaders! . . ."

Soon afterward, however, Peter Verkhovensky sent his father his exact address in Switzerland so his money could be sent there. That proved he had left the country legally. Now, having spent four years abroad, he was suddenly back in Russia and had informed his father of his forthcoming arrival in our town. That meant he had never really been in trouble with the authorities. On the contrary, it appeared that someone in a high position had taken an interest in him. His letter had been mailed from southern Russia where he was on some important errand, trying to organize something.

That was an excellent piece of news, but where would the father get the missing seven or eight thousand rubles to make up a decent *top* price for the son's estate? And suppose there was a lot of arguing, shouting, and even a legal action instead of the noble scene? Mr. Verkhovensky had a feeling that his sensitive Peter wouldn't meekly stand for a financial loss.

"I feel it," the older Verkhovensky once confided to me in a whisper, "because I've noticed that all these desperate socialists and communists are incredibly stingy, avaricious, and terribly eager to own things. One might even say the more ardent a socialist a man is, the stronger is his need to accumulate goods. Why? Does it stem from the emotional element in their socialism?"

I don't know whether or not there was any truth in Mr. Verkhovensky's observation. I only know that Peter had been informed that his father had sold the timber from his estate and about the other operations, and that Mr. Verkhovensky was aware that he knew it. And I had read some of Peter's letters to his father. He wrote very seldom—less than once a year—but recently, in announcing his impending arrival, he had written two letters, one immediately after the other. In general, these letters were no more than brief notes; but since their meeting in Petersburg, father and son had adopted an informal tone toward one another, in line with the *modern* trend, and now Peter's letters sounded rather like the instructions that, in the old days, an absentee landowner sent to the serfs whom he had entrusted with the management of his estate.

And now, suddenly and miraculously, Mrs. Stavrogin had offered Mr. Verkhovensky eight thousand rubles, clearly implying, however, that she wouldn't let him have it unless . . . So there was no question about it—Mr. Verkhovensky had to accept.

As soon as she left, he sent for me and locked the door behind me. Of course, he had his little cry, talked a lot and beautifully, often losing the thread of his thought, made an accidental pun with which he was very pleased, and later had a slight stomach upset. In brief, everything was as usual. At one point he produced a picture of his pretty German wife who had been dead for twenty years and, staring at it, moaned a few times, "Oh, will you ever forgive me?" Indeed, he seemed a bit bewildered. We had a few drinks in this crisis, and he soon fell into a blissful sleep.

In the morning he dressed with the utmost care, constantly preened himself before the mirror, and tied his cravat beautifully. He discreetly sprinkled perfume on his handkerchief, but when he caught sight of Mrs. Stavrogin through the window, he quickly took another handkerchief, hiding the scented one under a cushion.

"Good!" Mrs. Stavrogin said when he announced his consent. "In the first place, it shows fine determination and, in the second, you seem to have heeded the voice of reason, something you seldom do when it comes to your private affairs. Still, there's no need to rush things," she added, looking at the elaborate knot of his white cravat. "Say nothing for the time being, and I'll keep quiet too. It's your birthday soon, and I'll bring her over for tea. But no drinks, remember. I think I'd better take care of it all myself. You'll invite your friends—but beforehand we'll decide together which ones we want to come. If necessary, you'll have to talk with her the day before. But at your party we'll make no formal announcement, just drop a hint unofficially. And, a couple of weeks later, we'll have a quiet wedding—as quiet as possible, in fact. It might even be best if you both went away for a while right after the ceremony—to Moscow perhaps. I might come along too . . . but, in the meantime and above all—keep your mouth shut."

He was surprised. He even protested feebly that he didn't see how he could go through with it without talking it over with the bride-to-be, but Mrs. Stavrogin replied sharply:

"And what would be the point of that? It may still fall through."

"What do you mean?" he muttered, completely at a loss.

"Just what I say. I still have to decide. . . . Oh, all right, everything will go off just as I said, after all. I'll break the news to her myself. There's no need for you to interfere: everything necessary will be said and done. How can you help matters? Well, you can't, so please stay away from her, and don't write her any letters either. Don't make a sound, and I'll keep quiet too."

She firmly refused to explain further and left looking rather upset. She may have been a bit surprised at his eagerness to comply.

Alas, he still didn't understand his real situation, and he hadn't yet considered the matter from other angles. On the contrary, he had a new, conceited intonation in his voice and was obviously pleased with himself.

"I don't like it at all!" he kept repeating, stopping in front of me and spreading out his arms. "You know what? I think she's trying to make things so difficult for me that I will finally refuse. She knows even my patience has limits and I too may be finally driven to say no! She tells me to keep my mouth shut and not to communicate with my bride-to-be! But why then do I have to marry at all? Just because she's got the ridiculous idea into her head? But I am a responsible man and may not wish to submit to the fancies of a cranky woman! I have responsibilities toward my son and toward myself! Doesn't she realize that I'm sacrificing myself? Perhaps I'm willing to go through with it only because I'm tired of life and nothing matters to me any more. But if she keeps irritating me like this, it *will* matter to me—I'll resent it and I'll refuse! *Et enfin, le ridicule*. . . . What will they say in the club? What will Liputin say? And she says 'it may still fall through.' . . . What do you think of that? It really tops everything! It's really too much to stand! No, really—I'm a man with his back to the wall!"

And all the time there was something whimsically conceited, something playful in those self-pitying complaints. Later we had a few more drinks.

chapter 3

ANOTHER'S SINS

I

A week later things became rather involved.

It was, by the way, a very hectic week for me, for, being his closest confidant, I never left my poor betrothed friend. He was oppressed by shame more than anything else, and since that week there was no one except me before whom he could be ashamed, he was ashamed even before me. And the more secrets he revealed to me, the more ashamed he became and the more he resented me. In his morbidly suspicious state, he imagined that everyone in town already knew everything; he was afraid to appear in the club or even to see the friends of his own circle. He even took to going out for his daily exercise after nightfall, when it was dark.

Another week went by, and he still didn't know whether he was to be married or not. And he couldn't find out, hard though he tried. He still hadn't seen the bride-to-be—he wasn't even certain whether or not she was his bride-to-be. Indeed, he wasn't certain whether there was a single element of reality in the whole affair. And, for some reason, Mrs. Stavrogin wouldn't even receive him herself. She answered one of his early letters (and he wrote many more after it), asking him plainly to please leave her alone for she was very busy just then. She also informed him that she had many important things to tell him and was waiting till she had a free moment. He would just have to wait, and she would let him know when he could come and see her. Finally, she warned him that if he wrote to her again, she would simply send his letters back unopened, because his writing was nothing but a "silly, childish game." He showed me that note, and I read it myself.

However, this vexation and uncertainty were nothing compared to his main concern. This constantly obsessed him, causing him to grow thin and haggard. It was something of which he was so ashamed he wouldn't mention it, not even to me. Although he sent for me every day—he couldn't be without me for two hours, for my presence had become as indispensable to him as air or water—when I brought the subject up myself, he lied to me and tried, like a small boy, to divert my attention from it.

That rather offended me. Of course, since I knew him inside out, I guessed his great secret from the start. At the time, that secret rather discredited him in my eyes: I was still young then and was most indignant at the coarseness and ugliness of his suspicions. On the spur of the moment—perhaps I was getting rather bored with my role of confidant—I was perhaps too severe in my judgment of him. In my callousness, I wanted him to make a clean breast of it all, although I realized that some things are hard to admit. On his part, he saw through me too and realized how well I knew him and that I was furious with him. So then he was furious with me for being furious with him and seeing through him. My irritation could be called petty and silly, but it is very bad for real friends to be constantly together, face to face.

In a sense, he appraised certain aspects of his situation sensibly and was even rather subtle about certain points that he wasn't trying to hide.

"Don't imagine she has always been like that!" he'd say of Mrs. Stavrogin. "She was very different when we used to talk together. . . . Can you imagine—she could still keep up a conversation then! Would you believe me if I told you she once had some ideas of her own? Ah, she's quite changed now; she says that was nothing but old-fashioned chatter. She despises the past. Now she's always ill tempered and only concerned with her bookkeeping and accounting, and so unpleasant all the time. . . ."

"But why should she be unpleasant to you, since you're complying with her wishes?" I said.

"*Cher ami,*" he replied, giving me a subtle look, "if I hadn't complied, she'd have been frightfully, frightfully . . . but less so than now that I have complied."

He was very pleased with the way he had put it, and we emptied a nice bottle of wine that evening. But that was just one bright moment; the next day he was gloomier and more miserable than ever.

I was particularly irritated because he didn't dare call on the Drozdovs, who had just returned from abroad, although they were eager to renew their old acquaintance and kept inviting him. He spoke of Liza with an enthusiasm that I couldn't quite understand. Of course, he had been very attached to her when she was a child, but apart from that, he somehow firmly believed that near her he'd find immediate relief from all his sufferings and would even resolve his major problem. He expected to find some extraordinary creature in Liza, yet he couldn't make himself go to see her, though he was on the verge of going every day. As for me, I was longing to meet her myself, and Mr. Verkhovensky was the only person who could introduce me. I often saw her, wearing an elegant riding habit, passing along the street on a beautiful horse accompanied by a handsome young officer, her late stepfather's nephew. I was immensely impressed by her. Although my infatuation was ephemeral—I felt the hopelessness of it soon enough—it is easy to imagine how impatient I was with my old friend for his obstinate seclusion while it lasted.

First all our regular friends were warned that Mr. Verkhovensky was anxious to be left alone and couldn't receive anyone for some time. He originally wanted to send everyone a circular letter to that effect, but I dissuaded him and finally went to see each of them in turn and told them that Mrs. Stavrogin had commissioned the old man—that was the way we referred to him among ourselves—to put the correspondence of many years in order and that he had locked himself in to finish the job as soon as possible and that I was helping him. Liputin was the only one I didn't have time to see. I kept postponing my visit to him. As a matter of fact, I dreaded it. I knew that he wouldn't believe a single word of my story and that he would think there was a secret being kept only from him. I was sure that, as soon as I left him, he'd go tearing all over town prying and gossiping. But, while I was still thinking about it, I ran into him in the street. It turned out that he had already been informed by others whom I had warned. Surprisingly enough, he didn't inquire about Mr. Verkhovensky; instead, he interrupted me while I was apologizing to him for not having visited him and started talking about something very different. True, he had plenty to tell me. He was very agitated and was pleased to find someone to listen to him. He proceeded to tell me all the local news: the arrival of the new governor's wife, who was "so full of talk about the new ideas"; the opposition to her that had already formed in the club; how people were going around shouting about the new ideas and how everyone had become caught up in them; and so on. He talked without stopping for a good quarter of an hour and he was so entertaining that I couldn't tear myself away. I could never stand the man, but I must say he had a gift for making people listen to him, particularly when he was furious about something. In my opinion, he was a born spy. He always knew what was going on in town, especially if there was something scandalous about it, and it was surprising how nasty he could be about things that were obviously none of his concern. I've always felt that the main trait in his character was envy.

When later in the evening I reported my meeting with Liputin and our conversation to Mr. Verkhovensky, he suddenly became very agitated and asked me an inane question: "Does Liputin know?" I tried to explain to him that the man couldn't possibly know anything because there was no one who could have informed him. But Mr. Verkhovensky clung stubbornly to his suspicion.

"Take my word for it," he concluded unexpectedly, "he not only knows everything down to the minutest detail about *our* situation, he knows things that neither you nor I know, things that we may never find out about—or, if we do, it'll be too late!"

I made no comment, but there was a lot behind those words. After that Liputin's name didn't come up for five days. I felt that Mr. Verkhovensky was displeased with himself for baring his suspicions to me and saying too much.

II

One morning—it was seven or eight days after Mr. Verkhovensky had announced his willingness to marry—as I was hurrying over, at eleven o'clock, to join my grieving friend, I got involved in an adventure.

I met Karmazinov, "the great writer," as Liputin referred to him. I had read his books when I was a boy. His novels and short stories were very popular a generation ago and some still are today. As for me, I drank them in; they were the joy of my boyhood and youth. Later, my enthusiasm dampened somewhat. I liked the novels with a special message that he wrote later less than his early works, in which there was much real poetry. As to his latest stories, I didn't like them at all.

Generally speaking, if I must express my opinion on this delicate matter, these mediocre talents who are taken for near geniuses during their lifetimes vanish from people's minds as soon as they're dead; even while they're still alive, they are forgotten unbelievably quickly as soon as a new generation replaces the one in whose time they were active. It is as though the backdrop of a stage has been quickly changed. That certainly does not apply to the Pushkins, Gogols, Molières, Voltaires, nor to others who have something original to say. Mediocre talents usually write themselves dry as they grow older without even noticing it. And often a writer who has been credited with profound ideas and is expected profoundly to affect society's thinking displays, after a while, such shallowness and poverty in his central theme that people are not really sorry he has written himself dry so soon. But these white-haired old men don't notice it themselves and they become very angry. Toward the end of their careers their vanity reaches really amazing proportions. God knows what they finally imagine themselves—gods at least, I'd say.

Karmazinov, it has been said, valued his connections with high society and the powerful of this world more than his own soul. He could, it was said, be terribly nice, disarming in his simplicity, and irresistibly charming—if he needed you for some reason or if you had been recommended to him in the proper places. But if by chance some prince, countess, or anybody who could harm him came by, he considered it his sacred duty to forget about your very existence, before you had even left the room, as though you were a fly or a chip of wood. And what's more, he sincerely considered this to be very good tone. Despite his excellent control of his temper and his perfect knowledge of correct manners, his vanity is said to have verged on hysteria. He was quite unable to hide his literary conceit even among people who were not particularly concerned with literature. If someone chanced to display indifference toward his writings, he became painfully offended and tried to avenge himself.

About a year ago I read an article of his in a magazine. Written in a very pretentious tone, it was supposed to be poetic and full of psychological insight. In it he described the sinking of a ship somewhere off the coast of England and how he had himself seen people being saved and dead bodies being pulled from the sea. The whole rather long, wordy piece had but one purpose: to tell us about the author. One could read between the lines: "See—that's how I behaved. You don't have to see that sea, those crags, those splinters from the breaking vessel for yourself—I've just described it all with my powerful pen. Why are you staring at that drowned woman clutching a dead baby in her dead arms? Look at me! I couldn't stand the sight, so I turned away from it. Here—look at me standing with my back to it. Now I'm trying to turn my head again, but in horror I close my eyes. Don't you think it's all frightfully fascinating?"

When I told Mr. Verkhovensky what I thought of Karmazinov's article, he agreed with me.

When it was rumored that Karmazinov was coming to our town, I was naturally anxious to see him and, if possible, to make his acquaintance. I knew Mr. Verkhovensky would introduce me, since the two men had been friends at one time. But then I bumped into him on a street corner. I recognized him because a few days before he had been pointed out to me as he drove past in a carriage with the governor's wife.

He was shortish and looked like a prim, little old man, although he wasn't actually more than fifty-five at the time. His face was rosy, and thick, graying locks of hair that had escaped from under his top hat curled around his small, neat ears. His clean little face could not be described as handsome: his lips were thin, long, and slyly pursed; his nose was rather thick; and his intelligent eyes were small and sharp. He was dressed in a rather old-fashioned style. His cloak might have been worn in Italy or Switzerland at that time of year. But at least all the minor items of his attire—cuff links, stiff collar, buttons, tortoise-shell lorgnette on a thin black ribbon, and signet ring—were highly fashionable. I'd have bet anything that in summer this man wore light shoes fastened on the side with mother-of-pearl buttons. When I ran into him, he had just stopped at the edge of the sidewalk and was looking carefully around before venturing across the street. Noticing that I was staring at him, he asked me in a mellifluous, although slightly shrill, tone:

"Would you please tell me how I can get to Bykov Street?"

"Bykov Street!" I exclaimed in great excitement. "Why, it's just over there, the second turn on the left."

"Thank you so much!"

Damn it! It had all been so sudden, and I was afraid I must have seemed obsequious to him. He noticed this immediately and in a flash knew everything about me—that is, that I knew who he was, had read all his books, had admired him since my childhood, that I felt very subdued before him and looked up to him with humility. He smiled at me once more, nodded, and walked off in the direction I had indicated to him. Now, I don't really know why I turned back to follow him, why I caught up with him and then walked abreast of him ten steps or so until he stopped dead.

"Perhaps you could now tell me where the nearest cab stand is?" he called out to me. I didn't like his tone or his voice this time.

"Cab stand? The cabs usually wait on Cathedral Square."

And now I nearly scurried off to get him a cab, which, I suspect, was just what he expected me to do. Of course, I immediately came to my senses and stopped, but he'd noticed all right, for he was watching me with a nasty grin on his face. And at that juncture something happened that I'll never forget.

He suddenly dropped a small brown leather bag he was carrying in his left hand. Actually it was some sort of briefcase rather than a bag, or rather something resembling an old-fashioned lady's handbag. Anyway, whatever it was, I was about to rush to pick it up.

I am absolutely certain that I didn't pick it up, but I did, without a doubt, make the first movement. I couldn't possibly conceal it, and turned beet-red like an idiot. Sly man that he was, he immediately exploited the situation to his full advantage.

"Please don't bother—let me . . ." he said radiantly when he realized I wasn't really going to do it. He picked it up, as if forestalling me and, nodding again, went on his way, leaving me standing there like a fool. It couldn't have been worse if I'd really picked it up. For about five minutes I felt that I had been disgraced to the end of my days. But then, as I was approaching Mr. Verkhovensky's house, I burst out laughing. My meeting with the great man suddenly struck me as very funny, and I was sure Mr. Verkhovensky would be amused when I told him about it; indeed, I even thought I might act it out for his benefit.

III

But to my great surprise I found him very different from usual. True, he hurried forward to greet me eagerly and started listening to my story, but he looked so lost that I doubted whether he understood what I was talking about. However, as soon as I pronounced Karmazinov's name, he flew into a rage.

"Don't mention him to me! I don't want to hear a word about him!" he shouted, almost foaming at the mouth. "Here, look! Go on, read it yourself!"

He pulled a drawer open and tossed onto the table three sheets of paper scribbled over in pencil, all in Mrs. Stavrogin's handwriting. The first note was two days old, the second was dated from the previous day, and the third from that very day. He had received it only an hour before I arrived. All three concerned a trivial matter involving the lady's vanity and Karmazinov. Mrs. Stavrogin was apparently worried that Karmazinov might forget to call on her. Here is the first note, dated from two days before (there may have been one from three days before and even from five—who knows?):

If he at last decides to visit you today, please don't say a word about me. Not a hint. Don't bring up any subject that may remind him of me.

V.S.

Here is the second note:

If he finally decides to call on you this morning, the most dignified thing, I believe, would be not receive him at all. I don't know about you, but that's the way I feel.

V.S.

And here is the last note, dated that very day:

I am sure there is a cartload of rubbish strewn around your room and that the tobacco smoke rises a mile high. I am sending Maria and Fomushka over; they'll clean up the mess in half an hour. Don't get in their way while they're working; go and sit in the kitchen. I am sending you a Bokhara rug and a couple of Chinese vases. I meant to give them to you a long time ago. I'm also giving you my Teniers (temporarily). The vases can be placed on the window sill and the Teniers should be hung under Goethe's portrait— it will be more conspicuous there, and that corner is always bright in the mornings. If he comes, receive him with great courtesy, but try to talk about superficial things or on some erudite subject—and your tone should suggest that you only parted yesterday. Not one word about me. Maybe I'll drop in to see you in the evening.

V.S.

P.S. If he doesn't show up today, he won't come at all.

I read the notes and was a little surprised that he should worry about such a trifling matter. I looked at him inquiringly and noticed that, while I had been busy reading, he had changed his usual white tie for a red one. His hat and walking stick lay on the table. He himself was very pale. His hands were trembling.

"I'm not interested in all her worries!" he yelled, beside himself, in answer to my mute question. "*Je m'en fiche!* She has the cheek to make all that fuss about Karmazinov, and yet she has no time to answer my letters! Here, see—there's a letter of mine she returned unopened yesterday, It's on the desk over there, under that book, *L'Homme Qui Rit.* And what do I care whether she's worried about her darling son or not? *Je m'en fiche et je proclame ma liberté! Au diable le Karmazinov, au diable la Lembke!* I've stored her vases in the entry hall, hidden the Teniers in the closet, and demanded that she receive me immediately. Yes, that's right: I said *demanded!* I sent Nastasya over with an unsealed note written in pencil just like hers. I'm waiting now. I want to hear Dasha's intentions from her own mouth, and let Heaven be my witness—or at least you. You will be my witness, won't you, my friend? I don't want to be ashamed of anything; I don't want to lie; I don't want any mysteries about this business. I want to be told everything—told openly, honestly, and frankly, and perhaps I will yet amaze this generation with the gesture I make! . . . Well, my good sir, would you call me a vile schemer now?" he said, glaring at me as though I'd actually said something of the sort about him.

I insisted he take a drink of water. I'd never seen him in such a state before. While he was talking, he kept tearing across the room from corner to corner. Then he suddenly stopped and faced me in an extraordinary attitude.

"Do you really think," he said, looking me up and down with great disdain, "that I, Stepan Verkhovensky, cannot muster enough moral vigor to pick up my pack—my beggar's pack—hoist it on my weak shoulders, and walk out of here forever the first moment my dignity and independence demand it? It wouldn't be the first time—despite the sarcastic little smile I believe you indulged in just now, my good fellow —that Stepan Verkhovensky has opposed noble determination to tyranny, even if it is the tyranny of an insane woman— the most degrading, the cruelest tyranny of all. You don't think I'll find the strength to go and end my life as a tutor to the children of some merchant or die of starvation in a ditch! Answer me! Answer me immediately! Do you believe me or not?"

But I preferred to say nothing. I even pretended that I didn't wish to offend him by saying no but still couldn't make myself say yes. Something in his explosion offended me—oh, not personally, no—but I'll explain that later.

He turned even paler.

"I seem to bore you, Mr. Govorov." (That's my name.) "Perhaps you'd rather stop coming here altogether," he said in that tone of smoldering, white fury that usually precedes a deafening explosion.

I jumped up in alarm. At that moment Nastasya walked in and handed Mr. Verkhovensky a note. He glanced at it and tossed it across to me. It contained only two words scribbled in pencil by Mrs. Stavrogin: "Stay home."

Mr. Verkhovensky grabbed his hat and stick without a word and walked out of the room. I followed him mechanically. Suddenly voices and hurried footsteps resounded in the passage. He stopped as if struck by lightning.

"It's Liputin. . . . I'm lost!" he whispered, seizing me by the hand.

Just then, Liputin walked into the room.

IV

Why Liputin's arrival should signify his perdition, I had no idea and, in any case, I didn't attach any great importance to his words: I felt they were due to his shattered nerves.

Liputin's sudden appearance, however, suggested that he had gained the special privilege of entering this house whether visitors were welcome or not. Noticing the petrified Mr. Verkhovensky's blank stare, he immediately cried out:

"I have a visitor with me—a very special one—so I've taken the liberty of intruding upon you! Meet Alexei Kirilov, a brilliant construction engineer. And what's more, he knows your dear son Peter well and has a message from him for you. He's just arrived."

"The message—he's making that up," the newcomer said rudely. "Never was a message. But it's true I know Verkhovensky, and I even saw him near Kharkov just ten days ago."

Mr. Verkhovensky shook hands with them mechanically and motioned them to sit down. Thereupon he glanced at me, then at Liputin, and as if he had suddenly recovered his senses, hurriedly sat down too, without realizing he was still holding his hat and walking stick in his hand.

"I see," Liputin said, "that you were about to go out yourself, although I was told that you'd fallen ill with all that work."

"Yes, I'm ill . . . I thought a bit of fresh air would do me good," Mr. Verkhovensky said, tossing his hat and walking stick on the sofa and blushing.

In the meantime, I studied the visitor. He was quite young, twenty-seven or so, decently dressed, spare and wiry. He had dark hair, a pale, somewhat unwashed-looking complexion, and black lusterless eyes. He seemed dreamy and absent-minded and spoke abruptly and rather ungrammatically, arranging his words in peculiar sequences and getting mixed up when he had to cope with long sentences.

Liputin had noticed what a fright he'd caused Mr. Verkhovensky and was very pleased about it. He installed himself in a wicker chair that he pulled out into the middle of the room to be equidistant from Mr. Verkhovensky and the engineer, who were sitting on sofas at opposite sides of the room.

"I haven't seen Peter for a long time. . . . You met abroad, I suppose?" Mr. Verkhovensky muttered awkwardly.

"I knew him here and abroad."

"Mr. Kirilov has just returned home after four years' absence," Liputin chimed in. "He went abroad to specialize further in his profession, and he hopes to get a post here on the construction of the railroad bridge. He's waiting for an answer to his application now. He was introduced to Mrs. Drozdov and her daughter Elizaveta by the young Mr. Verkhovensky."

The engineer sat stiffly, listening with awkward impatience. He seemed to be furious about something.

"He knows Nikolai Stavrogin too," Liputin added.

"So you know Mr. Stavrogin," Mr. Verkhovensky said.

"I know that one too."

"I—I haven't seen my son Peter for a very long time . . . and I hardly feel entitled to call myself his father . . . yes, just as I said. Tell me, how was he? Why did he stay behind after you left?"

"Well, I just drove on, and that's all there is to it. . . . He'll manage to get here by himself." Kirilov again answered abruptly. He seemed really angry.

"So he's coming here! At last! You see—I haven't seen him for much too long a time. It has been too long. . . ."

Mr. Verkhovensky seemed to have become bogged down. "So now I'm waiting for my dear boy before whom I feel so guilty! What I mean to say is that, leaving him, in Petersburg, I . . . well, to cut the story short, I didn't think much of him, *quelque chose dans ce genre*. As a boy, you know, he was very sensitive and very . . . fearful. When he went to bed he said his prayers on his knees and made the sign of the cross over his pillow. He believed he might die during the night if he didn't. . . . *Je m'en souviens. Enfin*, he didn't have any aesthetic sense—no feeling for higher things, for anything universal—no germ of any great idea for the future . . . *c'etait comme un petit idiot*. But I think I'm getting all mixed up. Forgive me . . . you've found me in a state. . . ."

"Are you serious about him crossing his pillow?" the engineer asked with sudden interest.

"Yes, he did make the sign of the cross over his pillow."

"Just curious. Go on."

Mr. Verkhovensky looked questioningly at Liputin.

"I'm very grateful to you for coming to see me, but I must confess that, at this moment, I cannot. . . . May I ask you, however, where you're staying?"

"Filipov's house, on Nativity Street."

"That's the house where Shatov lives," I said unthinkingly.

"Yes, the very same house," Liputin cried cheerfully, "but Shatov lives upstairs in the attic, and Mr. Kirilov is staying in Captain Lebyatkin's apartment downstairs. But he knows Shatov and his wife—he saw a lot of them when they were abroad."

"Really? Do you know something about the hapless marriage *de ce pauvre ami* or about that woman?" Mr. Verkhovensky seemed carried away. "You're the first man I've ever met who knows her personally, and if—"

"Bunk!" Kirilov said, flushing heavily. "You really distort everything, Liputin. I never saw a lot of Shatov's wife. In fact, I only saw her once. Not too close, either. Why are you making all this up, Liputin?"

He turned sharply on the sofa and grabbed his hat, then tossed it away, settled down once again, and fixed his black eyes challengingly on Mr. Verkhovensky. I couldn't make out what it was that irritated him so much.

"I beg your pardon," Mr. Verkhovensky said solemnly. "I realize it's a delicate matter—"

"Nothing delicate about it—it's just a shameful mess. And

when I said 'bunk!' it wasn't addressed to you but to Liputin because he keeps adding things. I'm sorry if you took it as addressed to you. I know Shatov, but I don't know his wife. I know nothing about her!"

"I gathered that, and if I insisted, it was only because I am so fond of our poor friend, *notre irascible ami,* and have always taken a great interest in him. I feel he's changed his former opinions—which were perhaps immature, but nevertheless correct—a bit too radically. And the way he goes around shouting about Holy Mother Russia now—*notre sainte Russie*—I can only explain such an organic reversal—I must call it that—by some violent upheaval in his personal life, namely his unhappy marriage. I, who have studied my poor, dear Russia and know it like the back of my hand—I, who have devoted my life to the service of the Russian people, assure you that he knows nothing about the Russian masses. Furthermore—"

"Now, I—I know nothing about the Russian people or the masses, and I have no time to study them," Kirilov cut in impatiently and again twisted noisily on his sofa. Mr. Verkhovensky stopped in the middle of his sentence, gaping.

"But he does, he does study them!" Liputin interposed. "Mr. Kirilov is right now doing some interesting research on the causes of the increasing incidence of suicides in Russia and, in general, on the causes of an increase or decrease of suicides in a society. He has come, I understand, to remarkable conclusions."

Kirilov looked terribly agitated and muttered angrily,

"You have no right. . . . It's not really research. I won't bother with nonsense. I asked you confidentially just on the off-chance. It's not a study for publication, and you have no right . . ."

"Sorry. So I'm wrong to refer to your literary effort as research. Mr. Kirilov simply collects observations; he does not touch upon the essence of the matter or, as we might say, the moral aspect of it. Indeed, he denies there is any such thing as morality and he advocates the latest principle—total destruction in the name of the ultimate good. Mr. Kirilov has already demanded that more than one hundred million heads roll so that reason may be introduced in Europe, and that considerably exceeds the figure proposed at the last peace congress. In that sense, Alexei Kirilov is ahead of everyone."

Kirilov listened with a faintly scornful smile. After Liputin's comment, there was silence for about half a minute.

"What you just said, Liputin, is stupid," Kirilov said, finally, with a certain dignity. "You picked up the few points I happened to develop in front of you and twisted them to suit yourself. But you have no right, because I never talk about those things. I despise a lot of talk. If I find convincing reasons, it's enough. . . . You've acted stupidly. I'm not trying to reason about those points—they've been settled. I hate reasoning. I never want to reason. . . ."

"And perhaps that's very sensible of you," Mr. Verkhovensky couldn't resist adding.

"I apologize to you. I'm not quarreling with anyone present here," Kirilov muttered excitedly. "For four years I've seen very few people. For four years I've spoken very little and avoided everyone because of a certain purpose I had that is no one's business. Now Liputin has found out about it and it amuses him. I can see that, but I don't care. I am not offended. I'm just annoyed at the liberties he takes. . . . Now, if I don't explain myself, I don't want you to think it's because I'm afraid you may report me to the authorities. No, please—don't think that; you see, it's bunk in that sense."

No one had an answer to these words. We all simply exchanged glances. Even Liputin forgot to snigger.

"Gentlemen, I'm awfully sorry," Mr. Verkhovensky said, rising determinedly from the sofa, "but I am unwell and rather upset. You'll have to excuse me."

"Ah, you want us to go," Kirilov said, snatching up his cap. "I'm glad you reminded us, I'm very forgetful." He got up and, with a good-humored expression, walked over to Mr. Verkhovensky with outstretched hand. "I'm sorry you don't feel well and that I came."

"I wish you every success now that you have returned," Mr. Verkhovensky said, shaking his hand warmly and unhurriedly. "I understand from what you've told us that you've had to stay abroad for four years, avoiding people for your own reasons, and so you've forgotten Russia. You must look upon us stay-at-home Russians—just as we are bound to look upon you—with a certain surprise. *Mais cela passera.* There's only one point that remains unclear to me: you wish to build that railroad bridge for us, but at the same time you proclaim the principle of total destruction. They won't let you build any bridge."

"What was that? What did you say? Ah, that beats everything!" Kirilov seemed very surprised and suddenly dissolved in gay, clear laughter. For one moment his expression was altogether childlike, which I found suited him very much. Liputin rubbed his hands in delight at Mr. Verkhovensky's witty remark.

As for me, I was still wondering why Mr. Verkhovensky had been so frightened when he saw Liputin and why he'd exclaimed that all was lost.

V

We were standing in the doorway at that moment when hosts and visitors exchange their last amiabilities and then part happily.

"It's all because Mr. Kirilov is so gloomy today," Liputin remarked casually when he was already outside the room. "He had a quarrel earlier with Captain Lebyatkin over the captain's sister. The captain whips that fair, simple-minded sister of his, using a real Cossack whip. He does it every morning and every evening—twice a day, you see. So Mr. Kirilov has moved to a small cottage in the courtyard of the same house, because he wants to stay out of it. Well, good-by now."

"What—his sister? He whips her? You mean the sick one?" Mr. Verkhovensky stirred suddenly as if he'd just been lashed with a whip himself. "What sister? What Lebyatkin?"

He was again gripped by fear.

"Lebyatkin, the retired captain—although he once described himself merely as a retired lieutenant—"

"What do I care about his rank? Which sister? My God, did you really say Lebyatkin? But there used to be a Lebyatkin—"

"Sure, that's him. Remember, he stayed at Virginsky's?"

"But that fellow was caught with counterfeit bills, wasn't he?"

"Well, he's been back for three weeks now—and there's something peculiar about his reappearance."

"But he was such a vicious crook!"

"Why, you sound as though there were no other vicious crooks among us!" Liputin suddenly grinned, looking Mr. Verkhovensky up and down with his furtive, beady eyes.

"Ah, Lord, that's not what concerns me, although, of course, I fully agree with you as far as vicious crooks go. But what were you driving at, in bringing all that up? For I'm sure you were driving at something."

"It's not so very interesting. I can tell you that when Lebyatkin disappeared—because of those bills, we thought— he actually went looking for his sister, who apparently was hiding from him. Well, he found her and brought her back, and that's the whole story. But why do you look so frightened, Mr. Verkhovensky? I am simply repeating what he says himself when he's drunk; he'd never mention these things when he's sober. He's a highly irritable man and has what we might call a warrior's aesthetic feelings—but in bad taste, of course. As to his sister, she's not only mad but lame as well. She was seduced once upon a time, and since then, Captain Lebyatkin has received regular payments from the seducer to compensate him for his wounded honor. At least that's what he claims when he's drunk, but I believe he's just bragging. I know that that sort of thing is usually settled quite cheaply, whereas he's really come into big money all of a sudden. A couple of weeks ago he was walking around in rags, but recently I saw a whole roll of hundred-ruble bills in his hand. Now, his sister has some kind of fit every day. She screams and carries on, and he keeps her in line with his Cossack whip. A woman, he claims, must be taught respect. Well, I really don't understand how Shatov can go on living just above them. Mr. Kirilov couldn't stand more than three days of it. He knew them in Petersburg, but now he's moved into the cottage to be farther away."

"Is all that true?" Mr. Verkhovensky asked.

"You talk too much," Kirilov muttered angrily, turning toward Liputin.

"Mysteries and secrets!" Mr. Verkhovensky burst out. "Why all this secrecy all of a sudden?"

Kirilov frowned, blushed, shrugged, and started to walk away.

"Mr. Kirilov even tore the Cossack whip out of the captain's hand, broke it, and threw it out of the window. He was very angry," Liputin added.

"Why do you keep chattering like that, Liputin? It's very stupid," Kirilov said, turning back abruptly.

"Why be modest and hide a noble act? I mean *your* noble act, for I wasn't speaking of myself, of course."

"It's stupid and unnecessary. Lebyatkin is stupid, doesn't have a thought in his head, and is completely useless to the movement; in fact, he's harmful. Why do you go around bleating about all sorts of things? I'm leaving."

"What a pity!" Liputin cried with an angelic smile. "Otherwise, I would tell Mr. Verkhovensky another story that I'm sure would make him laugh. As a matter of fact, I came here specially to tell it to you, although I'm sure you must have heard it yourself. Well, I'll tell you some other time. Mr. Kirilov seems to be in a great hurry now . . . so good-by. It was something about Mrs. Stavrogin. She really made me laugh the day before yesterday—even sent for me specially. It's really too funny. Good-by now."

But now Mr. Verkhovensky grabbed him by the shoulders and pushed him back into the drawing room and into a chair. Liputin was a little alarmed.

"Why, of course," he began, looking up warily at Mr. Verkhovensky from his chair, "she summoned me suddenly and asked me confidentially whether I thought her son, Nikolai, was insane or not. Don't you find that strange?"

"You've gone completely out of your mind, Liputin," Mr. Verkhovensky muttered and then suddenly went wild with rage. "I knew very well, Liputin, that you'd come here specially to tell me some such filth—I'm surprised it's not worse!"

It immediately occurred to me that Liputin must know more about our secret than we would ever know ourselves.

"But, Mr. Verkhovensky—please, please . . ." Liputin muttered, looking very frightened.

"Stop it! And now start talking. Please, Mr. Kirilov, I'd be very pleased if you'd come back and witness all this. Please, I insist. Sit down, please. And you, Liputin—I want you to get straight down to business without beating about the bush."

"If I'd known you'd react like this, I'd never have started. I was sure, though, that you knew everything already from Mrs. Stavrogin herself."

"You were sure of nothing of the sort, and I told you to get down to business."

"All right, but, please—you must sit down yourself too. I'd feel awkward sitting here with you tearing around the room all the time. It doesn't seem right somehow."

Mr. Verkhovensky was on the point of exploding again, but controlled himself and slowly lowered himself into an armchair. Kirilov stared gloomily at his feet. Liputin seemed to be enjoying himself immensely as he watched them.

"All right, here goes . . . but you've mixed me up now, you know. . . ."

VI

"Suddenly, two days ago, she sent a servant over to my place with a message that she'd like to see me tomorrow at twelve. Well, the next day—yesterday, that is—I dropped everything and at noon sharp rang at her door. I was ushered straight into the drawing room, and not a minute later she came in, sat down, and invited me to sit down opposite her. I sat there unable to believe it all, for you know yourself how she's always treated me. And then she went directly to the point, without any formalities, as she always does.

" 'You must remember that about four years ago my son, who was not well at the time, did some strange things that puzzled everyone until they were explained. One of his strange acts concerned you personally. Later, after he had recovered, my son went to see you on my insistence. I also know that he had previously had some conversations with you. Now, tell me plainly and honestly how you . . .' At that point she hesitated a bit. 'How you found him then. . . . And what do you think of him in general? . . . What opinion did you form of him then, and what's your opinion of him today?'

"She stopped for perhaps as long as a minute and turned red. I was scared. And then she spoke again in a moving— no, that word doesn't fit her at all—let's say rather in a solemn voice:

" 'I want you to listen to me very carefully. I sent for you because I think you're an intelligent and observant man capable of perceiving things as they are.'—What do you say to those compliments, eh?—'You must of course remember,' she said, 'that you're talking to a mother. My son has had to go through much in his life and has suffered several hard blows. All that could have affected his mind. I am not, of course, implying that he might be insane; that's out of the question!' Ah, you should've heard how firmly and proudly she said that! 'But,' she went on, 'there might be something strange—some peculiar twist of thought—some predilection for certain views. . . .' Yes, those were her exact words, Mr.

Verkhovensky, and I admired the clever way she had put it. She certainly is a lady of great intelligence—'I for one,' she said, 'noticed that he was terribly tense all the time and subject to peculiar moods. But I'm his mother. . . . You're an outsider so you can form a much more objective opinion of him. I beseech you'—that's exactly what she said—'I beseech you to tell me the whole truth without trying to spare me; also, if you will always remember that this conversation is highly confidential, you may rest assured of my eternal gratitude and my willingness to show it at every opportunity.' Well, how does that strike you?"

"Well, I'm so flabbergasted that . . ." Mr. Verkhovensky muttered, "that I don't believe you."

"Can you imagine," Liputin resumed, as if he hadn't heard a thing, "how excited a man like me feels when such a question is asked him by someone so high and mighty and when he's furthermore requested to keep it confidential? Doesn't that indicate that something unexpected has happened to Mr. Stavrogin?"

"I know of nothing . . . I haven't seen Mrs. Stavrogin for several days now, but let me tell you . . ." Mr. Verkhovensky muttered, obviously finding it difficult to control his thinking, "let me tell you, Liputin, that if you were told something confidentially and are now discussing it publicly—"

"Absolutely confidentially! And may the Lord strike me down if—but, of course, it's all right to discuss it here among ourselves. There are no strangers present. Even Mr. Kirilov is no stranger. He—"

"Oh, I'm sure that the three of us will be very discreet. I wish, however, I could be as sure of you."

"But why do you say that? I have the greatest interest in keeping it all quiet since her gratitude depends on my discretion. But what I was coming to was a strange incident connected with all this—that is, more psychologically curious than strange. Last night, still affected by that conversation with Mrs. Stavrogin—and you can imagine that it did affect me—I asked Mr. Kirilov the following question:

" 'You have known Stavrogin both here and abroad,' I said. 'What do you think of him—that is, of his intelligence and abilities?' Well, Mr. Kirilov here answered in his usual laconic style and said Mr. Stavrogin is clever and sane. Then I inquired whether he hadn't by chance noticed a certain twist in his thinking or a certain peculiar way of seeing things—

what we might perhaps call aberrations of sorts. As you can see, I was repeating the question Mrs. Stavrogin had asked me. Well, Mr. Kirilov frowned, just as he's frowning now, thought for a second, then said, yes, there were things about Stavrogin that had struck him as peculiar. Now, I wish to draw your attention to the fact that if Mr. Kirilov found something peculiar, then it certainly must be peculiar."

"Is this true?" Mr. Verkhovensky asked Kirilov.

"I'd rather not talk about it," Kirilov said suddenly, lifting his head. His eyes flashed. "I challenge your right, Liputin—you have no right to bring me into it. I never expressed my opinion entirely. I used to know him in Petersburg, but that was a long time ago, and now, although I've met him again, I know very little about Nikolai Stavrogin. Please leave me out of it. It looks too much like gossip for my liking."

Liputin spread his hands wide, protesting his innocence.

"I'm a gossip? And why not a spy while you're at it? It's easy for you to criticize me, Kirilov, since you always try to keep out of things yourself. You may not believe me, Mr. Verkhovensky, but even that Captain Lebyatkin, who seems to be as stupid a man as could possibly exist—well, even he considers himself a victim of Mr. Stavrogin, although he's a great admirer of the gentleman's intelligence. 'The wisdom of that man,' he told me, 'amazes me. He's the wise serpent himself.' Those are his very words. So yesterday, still under the spell of the same conversation, I went over to ask him what he thought (that was after I'd talked to Mr. Kirilov about it). 'What do you think, Captain,' I asked him, 'about that wise serpent: is he sane or mad?' You would think someone had whacked him one from behind with a whip. He leaped up and exclaimed, 'Yes, yes—only that can't make any difference,' but he never said *what* difference or what he meant. Then he became very thoughtful—so thoughtful, in fact, that he sobered up. We were in Filipov's tavern. It took him perhaps half an hour to come to his senses, then he banged his fist on the table and shouted, 'Yes, sure, he's crazy! He's very smart, but I guess he's crazy too.' "

Mr. Verkhovensky seemed to be trying to figure something out.

"And how would Lebyatkin know?"

"Maybe Mr. Kirilov, who has called me a spy, can tell you. I'm not sure I'm a spy, but I'm sure Mr. Kirilov knows all about it and just isn't talking."

"I know nothing—or at least very little," Kirilov said irritably. "Go and make Lebyatkin drunk and find out. You even dragged me over here to find something out, to make me talk. So obviously you are a spy."

"I never paid for his drinks. He's not worth the money it would cost me—that's how much I value such secrets. It's he who's throwing the money around now; he, who only twelve days ago borrowed fifteen kopecks from me, now pays for champagne. You understand—it's him, not me! But you've given me a good idea, and I may in fact make him drunk and find out a lot of little secrets, you know—your little secrets," Liputin snapped back angrily.

Mr. Verkhovensky looked in bewilderment at the two men. They didn't seem to think anything of accusing each other in front of us. I decided that Liputin had brought Kirilov over because he wanted to draw him out in a conversation with a third person—that was a favorite trick of his.

"Mr. Kirilov knows Mr. Stavrogin very well," he went on spitefully, "but he's trying to conceal the fact. As to Captain Lebyatkin, he met Stavrogin even earlier, about five or six years ago, during what we might call the obscure period of Mr. Stavrogin's life, before he even thought of honoring us by coming here. Our prince, it appears, formed a rather strange set of acquaintances in Petersburg. I believe it was there that he met Mr. Kirilov too."

"Be careful, Liputin. Stavrogin will be here soon, and he knows how to take care of himself."

"Why should I worry? I'd be the first to say he's a man of the most refined, most exquisite intelligence. That's exactly what I said to his mother yesterday, to reassure her. 'But, of course,' I added, 'I can't vouch for his character.' Yesterday Lebyatkin also told me that he'd suffered because of Stavrogin's character. Ah, Mr. Verkhovensky, how can you accuse me of gossiping and spying when you yourself were anxious to draw all the information you could out of me and displayed such tremendous curiosity? Mrs. Stavrogin was much closer to the mark. 'I'm asking you,' she told me, 'because you were personally involved in an incident.' How can you suspect me of scheming when I swallowed an insult from his lordship in front of all my friends? After that, I should be entitled to take some interest in him without necessarily being a gossip. One day he shakes hands with you and the next, while enjoying your hospitality, he slaps your face in front of everyone—

because he happens to feel like it. It all comes from having too much money and nothing much to do! But, when there's a lady present, they're like roosters or butterflies, these rich landowners with their tiny cupid's wings, these demoniac lady-charmers! It's easy for you, Mr. Verkhovensky, hardened bachelor that you are, to call me a gossip because I say things about his lordship. But if you were to take a pretty young wife—for you're still a very handsome man, as you well know—you'd keep your door locked and even build barricades around your house to keep our prince out. And I'm sure that if Miss Lebyatkin, who gets those daily whippings from her brother, wasn't crazy and lame, she'd have been the object of his lordship's attentions too and that would explain how Lebyatkin's honor suffered at his hands, as the captain likes to put it. What stopped him, probably, was that it didn't appeal to his aesthetic sense. But even that's no guarantee. He picks them like berries, whichever kind suits his particular mood at the moment. How can you accuse me of gossiping! The whole town is shouting without waiting for me to start spreading rumors. I just agree with what they say about him, and there's nothing wrong with agreeing—or is there?"

"The whole town is shouting? What is it shouting about?"

"Well, I mean, Captain Lebyatkin shouts for the whole town to hear when he's drunk. It comes to the same thing. So what harm have I done? I only talk about it among friends —for, whatever you may say, I consider myself among friends here." He looked candidly at each of us in turn. "And now, listen to this: I've heard that his lordship sent three hundred rubles to Captain Lebyatkin from Switzerland by a very respectable young lady—an orphan, whom, by the way, I happen to know. Later, however, Lebyatkin was informed by another most respectable person whom I won't mention by name, but who is most trustworthy, that the original sum sent by Mr. Stavrogin was not three hundred but *one thousand* rubles. So now Lebyatkin goes around shouting that the respectable young lady shortchanged him by seven hundred rubles. He practically threatens to go to the police. In any case, he makes a lot of noise about it."

"How can you be so low—so despicably low!" Kirilov shouted, jumping up from his chair.

"And you—how can you say that, since the trustworthy person in question is none other than yourself? It was you who told Lebyatkin that Stavrogin had sent him a thousand

and not three hundred rubles. The captain himself volunteered that information when inebriated."

"It's—it's an unfortunate misunderstanding. There must be some mistake somewhere. It's all bunk, and you're being disgusting."

"I'm anxious myself to believe that it's all bunk and I'm sad because, whatever you may say, a respectable young lady is under suspicion—first of misappropriating seven hundred rubles and second of having been on intimate terms with Stavrogin. We all know that his lordship thinks nothing of disgracing a young girl or, for that matter, another man's wife, as he did that time at my house. And if he finds a kind-hearted man, he forces him to lend his well-respected name to cover up his own sins. That's what happened to me, for of course I'm referring to myself."

Mr. Verkhovensky rose from his seat. He was terribly pale.

"Watch yourself, Liputin, I warn you!"

"Don't believe him, don't believe him! There must be some mistake—Lebyatkin's always drunk," Kirilov muttered in great agitation. "It'll all be cleared up, but I can't stand any more of this; it's low and disgusting, and I've had enough of it—enough!" He rushed out of the room.

"Where are you going? Wait—I'm coming with you!" Liputin shouted, leaping up and darting off in pursuit of Kirilov.

VII

Mr. Verkhovensky stood thinking for a moment, glanced at me with unseeing eyes, took his hat and walking stick, and quietly left the room. I followed him. Passing the gate, he noticed that I was behind him and said:

"Ah, so you're here. Good. You can serve as a witness. *Vous m'accompagnerez, n'est-ce pas?*"

"You're not really going there, are you? Just think what a furor it may cause."

He stopped for a second and looked at me with a pathetic, helpless smile, full of shame and genuine despair and at the same time containing a strange exaltation. He whispered:

"But I can't marry to cover another man's sins, can I?"

I'd been waiting for him to say that. At last the unmentionable had been uttered after all those evasions and pretenses. I really exploded.

"How can anything so low, so filthy have occurred to an intelligent, generous man like you—and before Liputin's hints at that!"

He glanced at me without answering and walked on. I didn't want to be left behind. I wanted to tell Mrs. Stavrogin what I thought of it all. I'd have forgiven him if, in his old-womanish weakness, he'd simply believed Liputin, but he had thought of it long before; Liputin had merely confirmed his suspicions and poured oil on the flames. Mr. Verkhovensky hadn't hesitated to suspect the girl from the beginning, without any foundation whatsoever, not even Liputin's gossip. He had interpreted Mrs. Stavrogin's headstrong insistence as being motivated by desperate haste to cover up by marriage with a respectable man the misdeeds—so typical of a rich young gentleman—of her worthless son Nikolai! I badly wanted him to pay for that. He walked another hundred paces or so. Then he stopped.

"*O Dieu qui est si grand et si bon*! Oh, who can comfort me now?" he exclaimed.

"Let's go home, and I'll explain it all to you," I told him, turning him back by force.

"It's him!—it's you, Mr. Verkhovensky—certainly it's you!" said a fresh young voice that rang like music.

We hadn't seen her coming and now Liza was there, towering over us on her horse, with her constant riding companion behind her. She reined in her mount.

"Come here, come here quickly!" she called in a loud, joyful voice. "Look, I haven't seen you for twelve years and I recognized you immediately, and you . . . did you really not know me?"

Mr. Verkhovensky seized her outstretched hand, kissed it feelingly, and stared at her with a prayerful expression. He couldn't utter a word.

"He *did* recognize me and he's pleased to see me! Look, Maurice, he's delighted to see me again! Why, then, haven't you been to see us for two whole weeks? Aunt Varvara told us you were sick and couldn't be disturbed, but I knew she was lying. I was furious and said terrible things about you, but I wanted you to make the first move. That's why I didn't send you a message. But, my goodness, you haven't changed at all! Ah yes, I can see new wrinkles, plenty of them, around the eyes and on your cheeks. And your hair has gone quite gray. But your eyes themselves are still the same! And what about me—have I changed? Why don't you say something?"

I remembered at that moment being told that she'd been ill when she was taken away to Petersburg at the age of eleven and that, during her illness, she had kept crying and calling for Mr. Verkhovensky.

"You—I—" he murmured, his voice breaking with joy. "I just this moment said: 'Who can comfort me now?' and then I heard your voice. . . . It's a miracle and *je commence à croire*. . . ."

"*En Dieu? En Dieu qui est là-haut et qui est si grand et si bon?* You see, I still remember all your lessons by heart. You can't imagine, Maurice, the faith Mr. Verkhovensky instilled in me *en Dieu qui est si grand et si bon*! And do you remember how you told me about Columbus discovering America and everyone on board shouting, 'Land, land!' My nanny, Alyona, tells me that I went on shouting, 'Land, land!' in my sleep for weeks after that. And do you remember how you told me the story of Hamlet? And the way you described the transportation of the poor emigrants from Europe to America? And there wasn't a word of truth in it, Maurice— I found out later how they really transport the emigrants— but he lied so nicely, and it was so much better than the truth. Now, why are you staring like that at Maurice? He's the nicest and most reliable man in the whole world and you'll have to like him a bit, whether you want to or not, just as you'll have to like me! *Il fait tout ce que je veux*. But, tell me, my dear Mr. Verkhovensky, you must be feeling miserable again to actually shout out your need to be comforted in the middle of the street. You're unhappy, aren't you? Am I right?"

"This minute, I'm happy—"

"Is Aunt Varvara being nasty to you?" she went on, without heeding his answer. "Is she still the same spiteful, unfair but always irreplaceable aunt? Do you remember how you used to throw yourself into my arms in the garden and how I'd comfort you and cry myself? Come, don't mind Maurice; I've told him everything about you. If you felt like it, you could cry on his shoulder now, for as long as you wanted to, and he'd just stand still and never budge an inch from his post! Raise your hat a bit. Now take it off completely. Here, stand on tiptoe, stretch yourself: I want to kiss you on the forehead just as I did when we parted the last time. Look, there's a young girl admiring this scene from her window. Closer, closer! Ah, your hair's really turned white!"

She bent down in the saddle and kissed his forehead.

"I'm coming to pay you a visit. Right away. I know where you live and I'll be at your place in a few minutes. Since you're so mule-headed, I'll have to be the one to take the first step, but after that I'll take you to my place for the whole day. So hurry home and prepare to receive me."

And she galloped off, followed by her escort.

When we got back to his place, Mr. Verkhovensky sat down on his sofa and began to weep.

"*Dieu, Dieu!*" he kept muttering, "*enfin une minute de bonheur!*"

Within ten minutes Liza appeared, accompanied by her Maurice.

"*Vous et le bonheur, vous arrivez en même temps!*" Mr. Verkhovensky said, getting up to meet her.

"Here are some flowers for you. I just got them at Madame Chevalier's. She keeps flowers ready for birthdays throughout the winter. And now I want you to meet Maurice Drozdov. I wanted to bring you a cake, but he assured me that it wouldn't be in the Russian spirit."

Maurice was a thirty-three-year-old artillery captain. He was tall, handsome, and irreproachably correct. His looks were impressive, even severe at first glance, despite the great kindness of his expression that was obvious to anyone within a minute of making his acquaintance. At the same time, he was very reserved and not given to easy protestations of friendship. Later, many of our citizens said that he wasn't too bright, but that wasn't fair.

I won't bother to try to describe Liza Tishin's beauty. The town was buzzing about it, although many of our ladies dissented. A number of them already hated her, in the first place, for her pride—she and her mother still hadn't called on anyone. (The truth was that Mrs. Drozdov had not been feeling too well.) Their second reason for hating Liza was that she was a relative of the new first lady. The third reason was that she went around town on horseback. We'd never had any Amazons in our town before, so it was only natural for the appearance of a young lady on horseback before she'd even made her duty calls to be taken as a challenge to our society—despite the fact that it was generally known that she went riding on her doctor's advice, which incidentally caused quite a bit of conjecture on the state of her health. She really was not well. Her constant nervous tension was obvious at first glance. Alas, the poor girl was going through a very painful phase as we discovered later. Now, looking back, I don't think she was really as beautiful as she appeared to me then. Perhaps she wasn't even pretty. She was tall, slender, supple, and strong, but if her face was striking, it was because of its irregularity. She had a very thin face, slanting, almost Mongol eyes, high cheekbones, and a sallow complexion. But there was something irresistibly attractive in her face, and an uncanny power in those dark, slanting eyes. She seemed born to conquer and dominate. She looked proud, sometimes even arrogant, and I'm not sure that she'd ever succeeded in being kind. But she wanted desperately to be good and did violence to herself in her efforts to be kind. There were, no doubt, many noble aspirations in that generous nature, but everything in her seemed to be perpetually searching for a balance without ever finding it. As a result, she was always swirling in chaotic restlessness. Perhaps she was really too severe with herself for being unable to meet her own high demands.

She lowered herself onto a sofa and glanced around the room.

"Why at moments like this do I always feel so sad? Can you figure that out, you learned man? I've imagined, all this time, how happy I'd be when I met you again and how it would remind me of so many things . . . but now I don't feel happy at all, although I do still like you very much. . . . Ah, good Lord, look at that—he's still got my picture hanging on the wall! Let me look at it. I remember it very well now."

It was an excellent water-color miniature of Liza that Mrs. Drozdov had sent to Mr. Verkhovensky from Petersburg nine years earlier; it had hung on his wall ever since.

"Was I such a pretty child? It's hard to believe that that's my face."

She got up and, holding the picture next to her face, looked in the mirror.

"Here, quick! Take it away. No, don't hang it up again. I don't want to see it." She sat down on the sofa again. "One life ended and another began, then it ended too. Now a third has started, and so on and on without end. . . . All the loose ends seem to have been clipped off. See, I'm using overworked similes, but there's a lot of truth in them, you know!"

Smiling slightly, she looked at me. She'd cast two or three such glances at me already. Mr. Verkhovensky, in his excitement, had forgotten to introduce us.

"Why did you hang my portrait under those daggers? And why do you have so many daggers and sabers anyway? What are they for?"

And indeed, for some reason, he had two curved daggers hanging crossed on the wall and above them a genuine Circassian saber. As she asked about them, she looked at me so directly that I was about to answer, but stopped short. Mr. Verkhovensky at last remembered his omission and introduced us.

"I know all about you," she said to me. "I'm very pleased to meet you. My mother has heard a lot about you. I want you to meet Maurice Drozdov. He's a very nice man, believe me. You know, I've formed a rather funny idea of you, for I gather you're something like Mr. Verkhovensky's confidant, aren't you?"

I turned red.

"Oh, please forgive me, I used the wrong word. I didn't really mean 'funny,' but . . ." and she blushed too and looked rather embarrassed. "But why should you be ashamed of being nice? All right, we must be on our way, Maurice. And you, Mr. Verkhovensky, I'll be expecting you at our house in half an hour. My goodness, we've so much to talk about! From now on, I'm taking over as your confidant, and I want you to tell me everything, but everything!"

Mr. Verkhovensky was at once alarmed.

"Oh, don't mind Maurice—he knows everything anyway!"

"What exactly does he know? I don't understand."

"Why, what's the matter with you?" she cried in astonishment. "Then it's true that they're trying to keep it secret! So, that's why Aunt Varvara wouldn't let me see Dasha. She told me Dasha had a headache."

"But how—how did you find out?"

"Why, like everyone else. One doesn't have to be too smart to discover these things."

"Everyone else?"

"Well, what do you think? My mother found out from my

old nanny, Alyona, who got it from your Nastasya. And you told her yourself, didn't you? At least she says you did."

"I—I said something to her once," Mr. Verkhovensky muttered, blushing pitifully, "but I only hinted at it. . . . *J'étais si nerveux et malade et puis.* . . ."

She burst out laughing.

"I see—your regular confidant wasn't handy and Nastasya was, so that did it! Well, your Nastasya has a whole flock of cronies. . . . Ah, come on—suppose everyone does know about it? I think it's much better that way, anyhow. . . . So come over as soon as you can; we're dining early. Ah yes, I almost forgot," she said, sitting down again, "you must tell me—who is Shatov?"

"Shatov? Why, he's Dasha's brother."

"That much I know, of course. You really are funny," she said impatiently. "What I want to know is what sort of a man he is."

"Well, he's one of our local philosophizers, the nicest and quite the gruffest man you could find."

"I heard before that he was rather strange. But that's not what interests me. I understand he knows three foreign languages, including English, and that he can do literary work. If that's true, I have a lot of work for him. I need someone to help me out, and the sooner the better. Do you think he'll accept? He's been recommended to me."

"Oh, I'm sure he will, and you'll be doing *un bienfait*."

"It's not a question of philanthropy. I really need someone to help me."

"I know Shatov fairly well," I said, "and if you wish, I could go this minute and ask him."

"Then would you please ask him to come and see me at twelve tomorrow? That would be wonderful! Thanks so much! Well, are you ready, Maurice?"

They left. As I was leaving to go to Shatov's, Mr. Verkhovensky hurried after me, stopping me at the gate:

"*Mon ami,* please be here at ten or eleven tonight, when I come back. Ah, I am so sorry to be such a nuisance to you and everyone else!"

VIII

Shatov wasn't home. I went back a couple of hours later, but he was still out. Then, at around seven in the evening, I went over to his place for the third time. I'd decided that if I didn't find him home this time I'd leave a note. He still wasn't there and his place was locked. I would have asked Lebyatkin, who lived on the floor below, where Shatov was, but his apartment was also locked up and neither light nor sound came from inside. The whole house seemed deserted. As I passed Lebyatkin's door, I felt curious after the stories I'd heard about him. I finally decided I'd go back the first thing next morning, for I didn't think a note would be enough to convince Shatov, shy and stubborn as he was. I was already going through the gate, cursing my bad luck, when I bumped into Kirilov coming in. Actually, he recognized me first. He asked me who I was looking for, so I told him everything and also that I wanted to leave a note for Shatov.

"Come," he said, "I'll arrange everything for you."

I remembered Liputin saying that Kirilov had moved into a cottage in the courtyard of the house. The cottage was a little too big for one person, so he shared it with a deaf old peasant woman who kept the place for him. The landlord lived in a new house on another street, where he also had a tavern, and this woman, a remote relative of his, looked after his old house for him. The cottage was clean, although the wallpaper was grimy. The room we entered was filled with odd pieces of furniture of all shapes and sizes: two card tables, an alderwood chest of drawers, a large deal table that must've come from some peasant's house or a kitchen, a few chairs and a divan with wickerwork backs and leather cushions. In one corner of the room there was an icon under which the old woman had lit a lamp and on the walls hung two dim portraits, one of the late Tsar Nikolai I, for which he must have posed, to judge by the look of it, in the eighteen twenties, and the other of some priest.

We entered and Kirilov lit a candle. Then he produced an envelope, sealing wax, and a glass seal from his trunk, which stood in a corner and which he had still not unpacked.

"Seal your note and write the address on the envelope," he said.

I tried to tell him it wasn't necessary, but he insisted. I addressed the envelope and took my cap to go.

"Oh," he said, "I thought you'd like some tea. . . . I got some. Would you like a cup?"

I accepted and soon the old woman brought in the tea, that is, a large kettle of boiling water, a small teapot of very strong tea, two huge, crudely decorated, earthenware mugs, a fancy loaf, and a soup plate full of bits of loaf sugar.

"I love tea," Kirilov said. "At night, I walk up and down and drink tea. Until daybreak. Abroad it's not always easy to have tea at night."

"Do you go to bed at daybreak then?"

"Always . . . have for a long time. I don't eat much. Keep going on tea mostly. Liputin is sly. But he lacks patience."

I was rather surprised to find that he felt like talking. I thought I'd take advantage of the moment.

"I'm afraid our earlier meeting was rather unpleasant," I said.

He scowled.

"Bunk, sheer bunk. All caused by Lebyatkin's drunkenness. I didn't say anything to Liputin; I only explained a small matter and he got it all twisted. Liputin has plenty of imagination and was making a mountain out of nothing. Yesterday, I trusted him—"

"And today you trust me?" I laughed.

"But you know everything anyhow. Liputin now, he's either weak, impatient, harmful, or—envious."

That last adjective struck me.

"Of course," I said, "you suggest so many possibilities that one of them is bound to fit."

"They may all fit."

"Yes, that's true too. Liputin is a chaotic mixture. Is it true though that he was lying when he said you were going to write a dissertation or something?"

"Why should you think he was lying?" He scowled again and looked down.

I apologized and assured him I wasn't trying to pry into his private affairs. He reddened.

"It was the truth. I am writing. But what's the difference?" Then he smiled the same childlike smile I'd seen before. "But he invented all that stuff about the heads rolling—it was he who mentioned it to me in the first place. He doesn't understand very well. What I'm searching for is simply the reason why people don't dare kill themselves. That's all. But it doesn't make that much difference either."

"What do you mean—they don't dare? Aren't there enough suicides?"

"Very few."

"Do you really find that?"

He didn't answer but got up from the table and started walking up and down the room, absorbed in his thoughts.

"Well, what would you say prevents people from killing themselves?" I asked.

He looked at me blankly, as if he were trying to remember what we were talking about.

"I—I don't know enough about it yet. . . . There are two superstitions, though, that hold people back—two things, one very small and one very big, although the small one is very big too. . . ."

"What's the small one then?"

"The pain."

"The pain? Is it really that crucial in the case of suicide?"

"It's the first consideration. There are two kinds of suicides: those who kill themselves because of great sadness or anger and those who are insane—or whatever you want to call them; it doesn't make much difference—and do it suddenly. The latter don't think much about pain. They just do it suddenly and that's that. But those who have reasonable motives think a lot about pain."

"But are there people who have reasonable motives?"

"Plenty. And if there were no superstitions, there'd be even more. There'd be very many—everyone would."

"Everyone?"

He didn't answer.

"But aren't there ways to die painlessly?"

"Imagine a stone," he said, stopping in front of me, "say, the size of a house. It's hanging over your head. Well, would it hurt you if it fell on you?"

"A stone the size of a house? That's a very frightening idea."

"I'm not talking about fear. Would it hurt?"

"A thousand-ton mass of rock? No, of course not; it shouldn't hurt at all."

"But try standing under it while it's hanging there and you'll be very frightened that it'll hurt you. And the most learned doctor will also be afraid that it'll hurt. So everyone

real freedom

knows it doesn't hurt, but everyone is afraid it will."

"All right, what's the second consideration that holds people back?"

"The next world."

"You mean punishment?"

"That doesn't make much difference. The next world is enough."

"But aren't there enough atheists who don't believe in a next world?" He didn't answer, so I added, "Maybe you're judging by yourself."

"A man can't help judging by himself," he said, blushing. "Real freedom will come when it doesn't make any difference whether you live or not. That's the final goal."

"The goal? But what if no one wants to live then?"

"No one will," he said with assurance.

"Man fears death because he loves life," I said, "that's the way I see it and the way nature has ordained it."

"That's a base idea and in it lies the whole hoax!" His eyes flashed. "Life is pain, life is fear, and man is unhappy. Now everything is pain and fear. Now man loves life because he loves pain and fear. That's how it's been arranged. We are given life for fear and pain, and that's where the swindle lies. Today man is not a real man. One day there will be free, proud men to whom it will make no difference whether they live or not. That'll be the new man. He who conquers pain and fear will be a god himself. And the other God will disappear."

"Doesn't it follow then that, in your opinion, 'the other God' still exists today?"

"He doesn't exist, yet He exists. There's no pain in the stone itself, but there's pain in the fear of the stone. God is the pain of the fear of death. He who conquers pain and fear will be a god himself. Then there'll be a new life, a new man—a new everything. Then history will be divided into two parts: from the gorilla to the destruction of God and from the destruction of God to . . ."

"To the gorilla?"

"To the physical transformation of man and the earth. Man will be a god and he'll change physically and the whole world will change. Man's preoccupations will change; so will his thoughts and feelings. Don't you think man will change physically then?"

"If it becomes a matter of indifference to everyone whether

they live or not, they'll all kill themselves and that, of course, will make a physical difference."

"That'll make no difference. They'll kill deception, that's what they'll kill. He who wants to have supreme freedom must dare to kill himself. He who dares has broken the secret of deception. There's no freedom beyond that: that's all there is; beyond it there's nothing. He who dares to take his life is a god. Anyone can make it so that there will be no God or anything else. But no one has ever done it."

"But there have been millions of suicides."

"Yes, but all for the wrong reasons—all *with* fear and not *to kill* fear. He who kills himself just to kill fear will become a god immediately."

"He may not have much time, though."

"Makes no difference," Kirilov said with quiet pride— almost with scorn. "I'm sorry you find all this slightly amusing," he added after a moment.

"And I'm surprised to find that, although you were so irritable at Mr. Verkhovensky's, you're so aloof now, though you talk with great conviction."

"Over there? Over there it was funny," he said, smiling. "I don't like abusing people and I never laugh," he added sadly.

"Yes, your nights of tea drinking don't sound very gay."

I got up, picking up my cap.

"You don't think so?" He smiled with some surprise. "But why? No, I really don't know. . . ." He suddenly became confused. "I don't know what it's like for others, but I feel I can't go on like all the rest. . . . Others think of it and then immediately think of something else. But I can't start thinking of something else; I've got to keep thinking of the same thing. God has tormented me all my life," he concluded with sudden heat.

"But, tell me, why do you speak such awkward Russian? Can you really have forgotten it after five years abroad?"

"Don't I speak correctly? I don't know. No, it has nothing to do with going abroad. I've spoken this way all my life, because I don't care."

"Another question, perhaps even more indiscreet: I'm prepared to believe that you're reluctant to meet people and don't like to talk to them very much. Why, then, have you been so candid with me now?"

"With you? Why, over there, you sat so quietly—but what's

the difference? You look like my brother. Very much. Strikingly so." He went very red. "Dead for seven years. Older brother. Very, very much."

"I suppose he profoundly influenced your way of thinking?"

"N-no, he didn't talk much. Never said anything. I'll transmit your note."

He took a lantern to light my way to the gate and lock it after me.

"He's quite insane, no doubt about it," I decided. Then, at the gate, I had another encounter.

IX

Just as I lifted my foot to step over the high beam at the bottom of the gateway, a strong hand grabbed me by the front of my coat.

"Who goes there?" a powerful voice roared at me. "Friend or foe? Speak up!"

"He's a friend, a friend!" Liputin's voice squeaked in the dark. "It's Mr. Govorov, a well-bred gentleman with a classical education and connections in our highest society."

"I like him if he's . . . he's with society and class-ssical . . . ed-dication . . . that's the best. . . . My name's Ignat Lebyatkin, retired army captain, at the service of peace and of his friends . . . that's if they're loyal—the dogs! . . ."

Captain Lebyatkin, a big, heavy man, well over six feet tall, curly-haired, red-faced, and very drunk, could hardly stand straight and was having difficulty articulating. I had seen him from a distance before.

"Ah, he's here too!" he roared again, noticing Kirilov, who was still standing there with his lantern. Lebyatkin raised his fist, but immediately lowered it again.

"I forgive you for being so damned learned—me, Ignat Lebyatkin, the most educated of the lot!

> When that shell of love had burst
> And Ignat's breast was torn with pain,
> Sevastopol's armless hero cursed
> And wept in agony again.

"I didn't serve at the Siege of Sevastopol and didn't lose

an arm there; still—what poetry!" he said, thrusting his drunken face toward me.

"He's in a hurry, in a great hurry—he has to go home," Liputin said, trying to persuade him to let me go. "He'll tell Miss Tishin everything tomorrow."

"What? Liza?" Lebyatkin roared again. "Wait! Let me give you another version:

> As the star on her stallion twinkles by
> Surrounded by Amazon maidens wild,
> She smiles at me from her mount, oh my
> Aristocra-tic child!

"It's called, 'To the Star of the Amazon Maidens.' It's a hymn! You must understand it's a hymn if you're not an ass. Those good-for-nothings can't see it! Wait!" He seized my coat again as I tried to get past him through the gate. "Tell her I'm a knight—a knight of honor. As to that Dasha, she's nothing but a serf girl, and I'll break her in two with these two fingers. I won't let her—"

At that point I pushed him as hard as I could and he lost his balance and fell down while I dashed down the street. Liputin ran after me.

"Kirilov will pick him up. Do you know what I've just found out from him?" he chattered breathlessly. "You heard that verse, didn't you? Well, he's put that piece 'To the Star of the Amazons' in an envelope and he's sending it to Liza tomorrow, signed and all."

"I bet you talked him into it."

"You'd lose your bet!" Liputin guffawed. "He's in love with her, d'you hear? He's in love with her—like a tomcat. But, you know, it started with hatred. At first he hated her for going around on horseback; he practically swore aloud in the street when he saw her. And you should've heard the things he said about her! Only two days ago he let out a foul curse as she rode by; it was lucky she didn't hear it. And now, suddenly, he comes up with that verse! Can you imagine—he intends to propose to her! No, I'm serious! Really!"

"I'm surprised at you, Liputin! Whenever there's some silly, sordid business, one can be sure you've got a hand in it," I told him furiously.

"I think you're going a bit far, Mr. Govorov. Perhaps your

poor little heart is afraid of a potential rival. Could that be what's making you so angry?"

"What?" I roared, stopping dead.

"All right, but just to punish you I won't tell you another word! Wouldn't you like to know, though? For instance, I could tell you to start with that that idiot is no longer simply a retired captain but a local landowner, and a quite important one at that. Mr. Stavrogin, you might like to know, has given him his whole estate, which formerly had two hundred serfs on it. As God's my witness, I'm not making it up. I've only just learned about it myself from an unimpeachable source. But I won't say another word to you. Find out the rest for yourself! Good night!"

X

Mr. Verkhovensky was waiting impatiently for me. He'd been back for a whole hour and was on the verge of hysterics. At first, for five minutes or so, I was convinced he was drunk. But it wasn't that—his visit to the Drozdovs had simply left him completely befuddled.

"Mon ami, I feel completely lost. I love and respect Liza just as before; she's an angel . . . yes, as I said—just as before. . . . But, the two of them—I believe they only wanted to see me to drag some information out of me, and then, Godspeed! Yes, that's just the way it was."

"You ought to be ashamed of yourself!"

"My friend, I'm all alone now, completely on my own. *Enfin, c'est ridicule.* . . . That place is stuffed full of secrets too. They pounced on me with questions about pulled noses, bitten ears, and some Petersburg secrets too. They'd just found out about Stavrogin's exploits here four years ago. 'But you were here and saw it all—is it true that he's mad?' I don't even know what makes them think that and why Mrs. Drozdov should be so eager to believe Stavrogin's insane. But she really wants to! That Maurice Drozdov *est un brave homme tout de même,* but can she be doing it for his sake—and after she was the one to write first from Paris to *cette pauvre amie?* . . . *Enfin,* that Praskovia, as *cette chère amie* refers to her, is a type like Gogol's Mother Korobochka, but a wicked Korobochka—an immensely more aggressive and outrageous version of Korobochka."

"That would make her a monster, don't you think?"

"All right, maybe I'm exaggerating, but stop interrupting me. Everything's spinning round and round in my head. It seems they've definitely quarreled with Mrs. Stavrogin, although Liza kept saying 'Aunt Varvara this, Aunt Varvara that . . .' But Liza's rather sly, you know, and there's something hidden in that too. Ah, all those secrets! But the two women quarreled all right. It's true that her poor Aunt Varvara does go around bullying people, especially now, what with Mrs. von Lembke's lack of consideration for her, Karmazinov failing to visit her, and all society lacking in respect . . . and now, on top of all that, there's this talk about Nikolai's insanity, and then there's the business with Liputin, which I really don't understand . . . and the next thing I hear she's dabbing her forehead with vinegar and at that point we come pestering her with our letters and grievances. . . . Ah, how could I have caused her so much trouble at such a time! *Je suis un ingrat!* Look—I came back and found this letter from her. Read it, read it now! Ah, how could I be so ungrateful!"

He handed me the letter. Mrs. Stavrogin apparently regretted her morning note enjoining him to stay home. This message was quite polite, but still firm and terse. She wanted Mr. Verkhovensky to come over to her house on Sunday—that is, in two days—at noon sharp, and she advised him to bring one of his friends (my name was suggested in parentheses). She also promised to invite Shatov since he was Dasha's brother.

"You will receive her final answer," she wrote. "I trust it will satisfy you. Wasn't that the formality you were so insistent upon?"

"Note that irritated sentence about the formality at the end. Ah, the poor dear! My lifelong friend! I must confess that this sudden decision about my future has been weighing on me to some extent. I admit, I was still harboring a hope, but now, *tout est dit*. I realize it's all over. *C'est terrible.* Ah, I wish it didn't have to be all settled on Sunday. I wish things could remain just as they are: you'd come and see me and I—"

"I think you've been completely befuddled by Liputin's gossip and intriguing."

"My friend, you've just prodded another sore spot with your friendly finger. Your friendly fingers, by the way, are often merciless and sometimes clumsy too, if I may say so. But, believe it or not, I'd almost completely forgotten about all that gossip and muck. Well, actually, if I hadn't really forgotten, I did at least try, in my stupidity, to be happy all the time I was at Liza's. At least I tried to persuade myself I was happy. But now . . . now, when I think of that kind, generous woman, so patient with me despite my despicable behavior —well, perhaps not *really* so patient, but who am I to talk with my irresponsibility and bad character? I'm like a whimsical child, with all the selfishness of a child, but without its innocence. Why, Aunt Varvara, as Liza so elegantly calls her, has looked after me like a nurse for twenty years. And now, suddenly, after twenty years, the child has decided he wants to get married and starts nagging her: 'Come on, marry me off, hurry up, come on!' and sends her letter after letter while she's home with vinegar compresses on her head. Well, now he has achieved his aim: on Sunday he'll be an engaged man. Now, why did he have to insist; why did he write all those letters? Ah yes, I forgot: Liza said she adores Dasha, that she's *un ange*, but a rather secretive one! Both of them gave me advice, even Praskovia—well, no—Praskovia didn't really. . . . Ah, how much venom is concealed in that Gogolian character! Besides, strictly speaking, Liza didn't advise me either. 'Why do you have to marry? Aren't scholarly joys enough for you?' she said and laughed aloud. I forgave her that laughter because she was hurt herself. However, they told me that I couldn't manage without a woman around, that with old age approaching I needed someone to tuck me in and all that. . . . To tell the truth, sitting here with you these past days, I was beginning to feel myself that providence was sending me someone to tuck me in in the declining years of my stormy life . . . well, to do all sorts of things that have to be done. Look at the mess in this place; look at the papers and rubbish all over the floor! I told the maid to clean it up yesterday, but that book is still on the floor! *La pauvre amie* was angry because it's always so messy here. . . . Well, we won't be hearing her voice giving orders around here any more! *Vingt ans!* And I understand there have been anonymous letters claiming that Nikolai has sold Lebyatkin his estate. *C'est un monstre, et enfin* where does Lebyatkin come in? And Liza listening to every word. Ah, the way she takes it all in! I forgave her her laughter, seeing the expression on her face as she listened. And that Maurice, I wouldn't like to be in his shoes just now

—brave homme tout de même, although somewhat shy. But what do I care really?"

He fell silent. He looked tired and confused sitting there with his head lowered, staring at the floor. I took advantage of the interlude and told him of my adventures in the house where Shatov lived. I told him brutally and tersely that I thought Lebyatkin's sister, whom I'd never seen, might have been the victim of one of Stavrogin's whims at one time or another—during the obscure period of his life, as Liputin put it—and that there might very well be a reason for Lebyatkin to be receiving money from Stavrogin, and that was that. As to the gossip concerning Dasha, all that was completely unfounded and nothing but the fabrications of that despicable Liputin. That, at least, was what Kirilov hotly insisted, and he seemed to be trustworthy.

Mr. Verkhovensky heard my assurances with the expression of a man who could not be concerned less with it all. I then told him about my talk with Kirilov and added that Kirilov might very well be mad.

"No, he's not mad, but he's a person whose ability to think is very limited," Mr. Verkhovensky said listlessly, almost reluctantly. "People like him assume that nature and human society are different from what God has made them and from what they really are. There are many who go along with them, but not me. I met such people in Petersburg when I went there with *cette chère amie*—oh, how insulting I used to be to her! —but I wasn't impressed by their abuse or their praise. Nor will I be impressed now. *Mais parlons d'autre chose.* I think I have done something terrible. Yesterday I sent a letter to Dasha and now I curse myself for it!"

"What did you write to her?"

"Oh, my friend, please believe that I did it with the best intentions. I informed her that I had written five days previously to Stavrogin, also with the most honorable intentions."

"I see!" I shouted. "And what gave you the right to assume the existence of a link between them?"

"But, my friend, don't shout at me like that! Don't crush me completely! I'm crushed as it is, crushed like a cockroach. Yet, despite everything, I still believe that I've acted in the most honorable way open to me. Let's assume for a moment that something did happen in Switzerland, or began there. . . . Well then, I must ask them before I do anything—I don't

want to get in their way, to be an obstacle in their path. . . .
I did it with the best intentions."

"Ah, good Lord, you couldn't have done anything more stupid!"

"Stupid, stupid!" he caught me up eagerly. "You've never said anything more intelligent. It was stupid, but what can I do now? What's done is done. I'll go through with the marriage anyway, with or without another man's sins. Isn't that enough?"

"Here we go again!"

"You can no longer intimidate me with your shouting! You're facing a different Stepan Verkhovensky now. The old one is dead and buried. *Enfin, tout est dit.* And anyway, what right do you have to shout like that? and he's another romantic conquering yourself.' Now I'm willing to borrow that maxim from him. I'll conquer myself and marry. But what will I conquer after that, instead of the world? Oh, my friend, marriage is spiritual death for every proud soul, for all independence. Married life is nothing but a debauch. It will deprive me of my energy, of my courage to serve the cause. . . . Then there will be children. Not my children perhaps—I mean, certainly not my *child*. A wise man must never be afraid to face the truth.

"The other day Liputin was talking about keeping Nikolai out by erecting barricades. He's an idiot. A woman can deceive the all-seeing eye if she chooses. *Le bon Dieu,* when he created woman, was aware of all the dangers she'd present. . . . But I'm persuaded that she herself insisted He create her the way she is, with all those charms, for what man would be willing to court all that trouble for nothing? I suppose Nastasya wouldn't approve of my disrespectful talk, but *enfin tout est dit.*"

He wouldn't have been true to himself without the cheap, irreverent jokes that had been so much in vogue in his heyday. This particular one cheered him up a bit, but not for long.

"Oh, why can't Sunday be just blotted out!" he cried suddenly, in utter distress. "Can't we have one single Sundayless week? Why can't Providence cross one miserable Sunday off the calendar, if only to prove its power to the atheists? Ah, how I've loved her all these twenty years! But she never understood me."

"I don't understand either. Who are you talking about?"

"Twenty years, and she never understood! Isn't it cruel? And how can she think that I'm marrying from fear or for material considerations! Ah, she may be *cette* Aunt Varvara, but I've adored her alone among women for twenty years. She must learn that first or they'll have to drag me forcibly to that farcical wedding!"

It was the first time I had heard that confession, and it was rather forcefully expressed. I realized how deeply his aversion had struck him. "Now, it's all him—my poor boy! He is all to me! I wish he would come quickly. Ah, Peter, my son! I'm really unworthy to be called a father. . . . I've behaved more like a bloodthirsty tiger toward him, but . . . *laissez-moi, mon ami,* I feel like lying down for a little while. I must collect my thoughts. I feel so tired, so tired. And I think you should go to bed yourself. It's midnight, *voyez-vous.* . . ."

chapter 4

THE CRIPPLE

I

Shatov elected not to be stubborn and presented himself at Liza's house at noon as I had suggested in my note. We arrived almost simultaneously as I was also paying my first call on her that day. Liza, her mother, and Maurice were sitting in the large drawing room, arguing. Mrs. Drozdov wanted her daughter to play a particular waltz on the piano. Liza started playing, but her mother said that that wasn't the waltz she had asked for. Maurice innocently said he thought it was the right one, and that made Mrs. Drozdov burst into tears of fury. She didn't feel well and had great difficulty moving around. Her legs were swollen, and for several days she had done nothing but make scenes about every little thing, despite the fact that she was rather afraid of her daughter. They seemed quite pleased when we arrived. Liza flushed with pleasure, and, after thanking me for delivering her message to Shatov, went over to him, obviously full of curiosity.

Shatov had stopped awkwardly in the doorway. Liza thanked him for coming and led him over to her mother.

"This is Mr. Shatov, about whom I told you. And this is Mr. Govorov, a great friend of Mr. Verkhovensky's and my friend too. Maurice met him yesterday too."

"And which one is the professor?"

"There's no professor, Mama."

"That's not true; you told me yourself there would be a professor. This must be he." She motioned rather scornfully toward Shatov.

"I never told you I was expecting a professor today. Mr. Govorov works for the government and Mr. Shatov . . . is a former student."

"Well, student or professor, it really comes to about the same thing. Both have to do with the university. But then, whatever I say, you always say the opposite. But the one in Switzerland had a mustache and a small beard—"

"Mama's talking about Mr. Verkhovensky's son, Peter, whom she insists on calling a professor for some reason," Liza said and led Shatov off to the other end of the drawing room, where they sat down on a divan.

"When her legs swell up like that, she's always irritable," Liza whispered to Shatov, continuing to examine him with the utmost curiosity, especially his eternal tuft of unruly hair.

"Are you in the army?" asked the old woman, with whom Liza had heartlessly left me.

"No, I work for the government—"

"Mr. Govorov is a great friend of Mr. Verkhovensky," Liza immediately called out from the other side of the room.

"So you work for Mr. Verkhovensky. But he's a professor, isn't he?"

"Good heavens, Mama, you must dream of professors at night," Liza cried impatiently.

"I see too many of them as it is when I'm awake. But you must always contradict your mother. Now tell me, were you here four years ago when Nikolai Stavrogin was here?"

I told her I was.

"And there was an Englishman here with you, right?"

"No, there wasn't."

"So you see, there was no Englishman—it's all lies. Both Varvara and Verkhovensky are lying. They're all lying."

Liza laughed.

"That's because Aunt Varvara and Mr. Verkhovensky said yesterday that there was a resemblance between Nikolai and Shakespeare's Prince Hal," she explained. "Now Mother has proved them wrong by establishing that there was no Englishman here then."

"Since there was no Hal, there was no Englishman; Nikolai caused the trouble and played the fool all by himself."

"Mother's just teasing," Liza felt obliged to explain to Shatov. "She knows Shakespeare quite well. I read the whole of the first act of *Othello* aloud to her. But she doesn't feel well. Mama, it's striking twelve. Do you hear? Time to take your medicine."

"The doctor's here, ma'am," a maid announced from the doorway.

The old woman got up, calling to her lap dog, "Zimmie, Zimmie, come on, let's go!"

It was an old and nasty little beast and wouldn't listen to her. It scrambled under the divan on which Liza was sitting.

"So you don't want to come? All right, I don't want you either! Well, good-by," she said to me. "I don't remember your name. . . ."

"Anton Govorov."

"What's the difference? It goes in one ear and out the other. No, I don't need you to come with me. I was calling Zimmie, not you. I can still walk on my own, thank God, and tomorrow I intend to go out for a drive."

And she walked out rather angrily.

"Mr. Govorov, I'd like you to have a private chat with Maurice. I'm sure you'll both gain a lot by becoming better acquainted," Liza said with a friendly nod toward Maurice, who beamed under it. Having nothing better to do, I chatted with Maurice Drozdov.

II

To my surprise, Liza really had wanted to see Shatov about some strictly literary matter. I don't know why, but I had imagined that it was only a pretext. Maurice and I, realizing that Liza showed no sign of wanting to hide anything from us and was speaking quite loudly and distinctly, began to listen and soon we were invited to join her and Shatov in their conversation. It all boiled down to Liza's desire to write a book; she was trying to find an assistant because she lacked literary experience. I was surprised at the seriousness with which she started to explain her plan to Shatov. "She must be full of the new ideas," I thought. "She hasn't spent time in Switzerland for nothing." Shatov listened attentively, looking at the floor and showing no surprise that this worldly young woman should have such an unlikely ambition.

Her literary venture was to be along the following lines. Hundreds of national and local papers and journals are published throughout Russia and daily report thousands of events. As time passes, newspapers are either filed away, used for wrapping, or discarded as litter. Many of the events reported strike the public's imagination and are remembered for a while, but then they are forgotten. People sometimes like to look up such stories, but don't know where to start in this sea of newsprint unless they happen to know the place and date of the event that interests them. So, if the events of a whole year were summarized in one volume and classified according to a definite scheme, with an index and cross references indicating the dates, such a book would give a general idea of life in Russia during that particular year, even though, of course, only a very small sampling of events could be included.

"Instead of a sea of newsprint, there'd be a few bulky tomes, that's all," Shatov said.

Liza heatedly defended her project, though she found it difficult, from lack of habit, to put her ideas across. There would be only one volume, she assured Shatov, and that would not be as bulky as he imagined. And even if it were bulky, it would be manageable because the whole point behind her plan was the proper arrangement of the items. She'd never intended to pick up just anything and enter it. Official decrees, government policies, local legislation and regulations, although she felt they might be important, would still be left out. In general, much could be omitted and they could limit themselves to selecting news items that more or less expressed Russia's peculiar mental climate and the character of the Russian people at a given moment. Of course, anything could be used —odd incidents, fires, public subscriptions, good deeds, crimes, public pronouncements, reports on the flooding of certain rivers, perhaps, and yes, even certain government decrees too, as long as they were typical of the period in question. But the selection must be made with a view to shedding light on the general trends so that an over-all picture would be given. And finally, the almanac must be readable enough to hold the interest of the average reader—not to mention its value as a reference book. So, it would be what might be described as a reflection of the spiritual, cultural, and moral life of the country during an entire year.

"We want everyone to buy it; we want it to be an essential item on every desk!" Liza insisted. "But I do realize that its success depends entirely on the plan and that's why, Mr. Shatov, I've come to you."

She was very excited and despite her confused and incomplete explanations, Shatov got a fair idea of what she had in mind.

"That means the result won't be really impartial; there'll be a selection of items to fit a particular bias," he muttered.

"Certainly not. I don't want facts selected to fit preconceived ideas, nor do I want to have any preconceived ideas. The only bias I have is objectivity."

"Well, there's nothing so wrong about having a bias," Shatov said, stirring in his seat, "and anyway it's impossible to avoid being biased as long as there is any possibility of choice. The very selection of items constitutes advice on how they should be interpreted. But your idea doesn't sound bad."

"So you agree that a book along those lines is possible?" Liza asked hopefully.

"We'll have to see, to think it over. It's an immense undertaking, you understand. It's impossible to tell offhand. We need experience. And even when we've produced a volume, we'll still have everything to learn about how we should handle the materials. Perhaps, after many tries . . . One picks up ideas gradually. However, you may have something there."

Finally he raised his eyes from the floor and glanced at her. His eyes were shining. He was very interested.

"Did you think it up all by yourself?" he asked Liza in a shy but friendly tone.

"It was easy to think it up; the hard part will be to work out a way to organize the items," Liza said, all smiles. "I don't really understand it very well. I'm not awfully clever and I'm pursuing only what is obvious to me—"

"Pursuing?"

"You mean that's the wrong word for it?" she asked quickly.

"You can use it if you wish. I didn't mean a thing. . . ."

"While I was abroad, I thought there must be a way to make myself useful. Why should my money lie idle and why shouldn't I too contribute something to the common good? Then this idea occurred to me. I'd never given it a thought before and I was terribly pleased. I immediately realized I needed someone to help me. Of course, whoever helps me will be the copublisher. We'll go halves—the plan and the work will be yours and the original idea and the capital will be mine. Do you think the almanac will eventually be self-supporting?"

"If we plan it right, it should be."

"I'd better explain to you that I'm not principally interested in profits, but if the almanac sells, profits will be quite welcome."

"But what does that have to do with me?"

"Don't you understand? I am inviting you to become my partner—we'll share it, fifty-fifty. Just come up with a scheme."

"What makes you think I'm capable of coming up with something worth while?"

"Oh, I've heard a lot about you in various places. I know you're very intelligent and are . . . working for the cause and—and that you think a lot about things. Peter Verkhovensky spoke of you to me when I met him in Switzerland." And she added quickly: "And he's an awfully clever fellow, isn't he?"

Shatov glanced at her for a fraction of a second, his eyes immediately sliding away from her and returning to the floor.

"Nikolai Stavrogin also often mentioned you."

Shatov suddenly turned red.

"So here are the newspapers," Liza said hurriedly and thrust at him a bundle of papers tied with string, which she had prepared in advance. "I've tried to mark some items for selection. I've numbered them and—well, you'll see for yourself."

Shatov took the bundle.

"Take it home and have a look. Where do you live, by the way?"

"On Nativity Street, in Filipov's house."

"I know the house. I believe there's some kind of captain living there—Lebyatkin. He must be your neighbor," Liza said, again hurriedly.

Shatov sat for a whole minute without answering, staring

at the floor and holding the bundle of papers in his outstretched hand.

"You'd really better look for someone else to do the job. I
won't be any use," he muttered, very strangely lowering his
voice to a whisper toward the end.

Liza flushed.

"What job do you mean? Maurice, please get me that letter!"
she said.

I followed Maurice to the table.

"Have a look at it," she said to me in great agitation, un-
folding the letter. "Have you ever seen anything like it? Please,
read it aloud. I want Mr. Shatov to hear it too."

And, with considerable surprise, I read aloud the following
message:

"To the Perfect Maiden, Miss Elizaveta Tishin.
Dear ma'am,

Elizaveta my pet!
I've seen no sweeter lady yet,
And when in her saddle she rides by,
Letting her curls in the breezes fly,
Or when by her mother in church she kneels
And her pious flush to the world reveals,
I wish her my lawful wife, so dear,
And her and her mother beseech with a tear.

Composed by a little-educated man during an argument.

Dear Ma'am,

More than anything, I am sorry that I did not gloriously
sacrifice my arm at Sevastopol, in view of the fact that I
did not happen to be there at all. Instead, I served throughout the campaign in the supply corps, supplying lousy
victuals, which I consider a disgrace. You are an ancient god-
dess and me—I am nothing. Still, through you, I've sensed
eternity. Please consider the above poetry as just such and
nothing more because, whatever you may say, poetry is
nothing but nonsense and one can say things in it that, in
prose, would be considered insolent. Would the sun get mad
at an amoeba if it composed verses in the sun's honor from
the drop of water in which it lives among many other
amoebas (that is, if you look through a microscope)? Even
the humane society for the protection of animals in Petersburg, which consists of the best people and commiserates
profoundly with suffering dogs or horses, despises the meek

amoeba and fails to mention it at all because it still has very far to go when it comes to size. Me too—I have still to grow a lot and the thought of marriage may seem ridiculous, but I will soon be the owner of two hundred former serfs instead of a certain man-hater whom you despise. I could tell you many, many things and I am prepared to back them up with documents that might mean Siberia for someone. Do not spurn my proposal. Of course, what I mean by the letter from the amoeba is the above poem.

Your most humble servant,
I. Lebyatkin, Captain (Ret.)
At your service.

"This was written by a despicable creature; besides, he was drunk at the time!" I shouted, unable to control my indignation. "I know him!"

"I received it yesterday," Liza explained hurriedly. She was very red. "I gathered that it was from some local idiot, so I didn't show it to Mother, because I didn't want to irritate her still more. But if he continues, I really don't know what to do. Maurice wanted to go over and tell him to stop. Now, since I am considering you as my partner," she added, addressing herself to Shatov, "and since you happen to live in the same house, I thought I'd ask you what else I can expect from him."

"He's a nasty person and a drunkard," Shatov muttered reluctantly.

"And is he always that stupid?"

"Well, no—he's not completely stupid when he's sober."

"I knew a general who wrote poems exactly like that," I said, laughing.

"I'd say that the letter itself indicates that the man knew perfectly well what he was doing," remarked Maurice, who was usually so silent.

"I hear he lives with his sister," Liza asked.

"Yes."

"They say he bullies her terribly. Is that right?"

Shatov glanced at Liza again and scowled. He moved toward the door, muttering, "That's none of my business."

"Wait—wait a moment!" Liza cried in alarm. "Where are you going? There are many things we still have to discuss."

"What's there to discuss? I'll let you know tomorrow—"

"Why, we must discuss the most important thing—the printing press. Please believe me, I wasn't just talking. I'm serious about it," Liza assured him, growing more agitated. "Now, if we decide to go ahead with publication, where shall we have it printed? That's the most important question since we don't intend to go to Moscow and the local press is unsuitable for such an undertaking. I've been thinking for a long time of buying my own printing press, in your name, say. I know my mother wouldn't object as long as it was in your name."

"And what makes you think *I* know how to run a printing press?" Shatov asked gloomily.

"Why, back in Switzerland, Peter Verkhovensky suggested you for it. He told me you knew all about the business. He even wanted to give me a note of recommendation for you, but I forgot to take it."

Shatov's face, as I remember it now, fell. He stood there for a few seconds and then just walked out of the room. Liza was angry.

"Does he usually walk out on people like that?" she asked, turning toward me.

I shrugged. But at that moment, Shatov suddenly reappeared, walked over to the table, dropped his bundle of papers on it, and declared:

"I can't work with you. I have no time for it."

"But why? What's happened? What can have made you so angry?" Liza asked in a disappointed, cajoling tone.

The sound of her voice appeared to strike him somehow; he raised his eyes to hers for a few brief moments, as if he were trying to get a glimpse of what was going on inside her.

"All the same," he muttered almost inaudibly, "I don't want . . ."

And this time he really left.

Liza was dumfounded—abnormally so, it seemed to me.

"What an extraordinarily odd fellow," Maurice remarked loudly.

III

Of course, Shatov *was* strange, but there was much more to all this than met the eye. First, I couldn't believe that Liza was serious about that almanac. Then, there was that inane letter—clearly offering, however, to supply documented information. They hadn't discussed what that information might be but, instead, had spoken of something else. And, as far as the printing press was concerned, I felt that Shatov had walked out precisely because a printing press had been mentioned. That made me think that something must have happened here before my time—something I knew nothing about. So, I felt I wasn't wanted and that none of it was any concern of mine. Anyway, it was time for me to go: it was my first visit and it had lasted long enough. I got up to take my leave.

Liza seemed to have forgotten that I was in the room. She was standing in the same spot, near the table. Her head was lowered and she seemed to be intently examining a particular spot on the carpet.

"Ah, you're leaving too . . . good-by then," she murmured in her usual polite, friendly tone. "Please give my best regards to Mr. Verkhovensky and try to persuade him to come to see me very soon. Maurice, Mr. Govorov is leaving. And please forgive my mother for not coming out to say good-by to you. . . ."

I was already downstairs when a footman caught up with me.

"Sir, sir, Miss Elizaveta told me to ask you to come back, please."

"Miss Elizaveta?"

"Yes sir."

Liza received me not in the large drawing room where we'd been before but in a smaller room next to it. The door leading to the drawing room where Maurice was now alone was closed.

She smiled at me, but she was very pale. She was standing in the middle of the room and seemed to be struggling with herself. She hesitated. Suddenly, she seized me by the sleeve and led me over to the window.

"I want to see *her* immediately," she whispered, fixing on me the ardent, willful, impatient gaze that brooked no opposition. "I must see her with my own eyes, and I beg you to help me!"

She seemed frantic and at the same time thoroughly dejected.

"Who is it you wish to see, Miss Tishin?" I inquired apprehensively.

"That cripple—that Lebyatkin girl. . . . Is she really lame?"

I was astounded.

"I've never seen her, but I've heard that she's some sort of a cripple. I heard it only last night," I muttered hurriedly, speaking almost in a whisper as she had.

"I must see her. I want you to arrange it for today."

I was filled with immense pity for her.

"It's quite impossible. I really have no idea how to go about it," I said, trying to persuade her to be reasonable. "But I'll go and see Shatov."

"If you can't arrange it by tomorrow, I'll go over to her place myself. Maurice has refused to have anything to do with it; you're my only hope. There's no one else who can help me. I was very stupid with Shatov, but I'm sure you're a very kind and honorable man—and perhaps you like me a little. Please, arrange it for me—please!"

I very much wanted to help her in whatever way I could.

"Here's what I'll do," I said, after thinking the matter over for a moment. "I'll go over myself—I'm sure I'll be able to see her. I'll manage to see her, I promise, but you must allow me to let Shatov in on it."

"Tell him that I can't wait any longer, that I really need to see her, but explain to him that I didn't deceive him. Perhaps he left like that because he's so straight and honest and he suspected me of trying to deceive him. But I wasn't. I really intend to publish that almanac and to open a printing press—"

"Yes, he's very straightforward!" I agreed anxiously.

"But if you can't manage it for tomorrow, I really will go there myself. And I wouldn't care if everyone found out."

"I won't be able to come here tomorrow before three," I said, recovering my balance a bit.

"All right, at three o'clock. So, you *do* like me! I guessed as much yesterday at Mr. Verkhovensky's." She smiled and hastily shook my hand. She was in a hurry to rejoin Maurice in the drawing room.

I took my leave, worried about the promise I had made and unable to understand how I had become involved in it all. I saw her as a woman in real despair, who was not afraid to compromise herself by trusting a man she hardly knew. Her feminine smile and her noticing, even at our first meeting, how I felt about her tugged at my heart. I felt terribly sorry for her and that was enough! Her secrets had become sacred to me and if someone had tried to tell me about them, I believe I would have stopped my ears and refused to listen. Yet, I had a certain foreboding. . . .

And then, of course, I had no idea how I was going to arrange it—nor was I even sure now what I was actually trying to arrange. It was a meeting, but what sort of meeting? And how on earth could I bring them together? Shatov was my only hope, although I doubted, at that point, that he would co-operate. Still, I hurried over to his place.

IV

It was already past seven when I reached his house. To my surprise, he had visitors: Kirilov and a man called Shigalov, whom I knew slightly—he was Mrs. Virginsky's brother.

Shigalov must have been around our town for a couple of months or so at that time. I have no idea where he'd come from. All I know is that he'd had an article published in one of Petersburg's progressive magazines. Virginsky had once introduced us in the street and he'd struck me from the first as the gloomiest man with the most constant scowl I'd ever seen. Shigalov always seemed to be expecting the end of the world, and his was not one of those vague expectations based on some prophecy that might turn out to be wrong. No, he seemed absolutely certain that the end was coming, say, the next day at 11:25 A.M.

On this occasion, Shigalov and I didn't exchange a word; we simply shook hands like a couple of conspirators. What struck me most about him was his ears—they were incredibly large and thick and they protruded at an uncanny angle. His movements were awkward and ponderous. And where Liputin merely hoped that one day Utopia might be established in our province, this fellow was sure of the day and the hour when it would happen. I found him quite sinister and was exceedingly surprised to meet him at Shatov's, especially as Shatov wasn't too fond of visitors anyway.

I heard their voices while I was still on the stairs. They were all talking at once, apparently arguing, but as soon as I appeared, they fell silent. They had been standing up as they argued, but now they sat down, so I had to sit down too. An awkward silence followed and lasted for at least three minutes. Although I knew he recognized me, Shigalov pretended he didn't—not out of any hostility, I'm sure, but just like that, for no reason. Kirilov and I nodded to each other but didn't shake hands. Then Shigalov scowled at me sternly in the naïve belief that I would just get up and leave. At last Shatov rose from his chair; the other two also leaped up and left without saying good-by. When he was in the doorway Shigalov turned and threw out at Shatov:

"Remember, we're waiting for a full account from you."

"Like hell I'll give you an account! And you know what you can do with yourselves!" Shatov said and locked the door behind them.

"Slimy morons!" he said, glancing at me and smiling a peculiar, crooked smile.

Shatov looked furious. I was surprised to hear him volunteer that remark. Usually when I dropped in on him—which, by the way, I didn't do very often—he sat frowning for a long time, answered my questions reluctantly, and only toward the end came to life and talked freely. Then, when you left him, he scowled as if he were getting rid of a personal enemy.

"I had tea with that fellow Kirilov last night," I said. "He seems to be obsessed with atheism."

"Russian atheism's never been anything but playing with words," Shatov grumbled, getting up to light a new candle to replace the burnt-out end.

"No, this one doesn't look like just another phrasemaker to me. He can hardly talk at all, let alone play with words."

"Those people have nothing but paper schemes and blueprints in their heads—they're nothing but a bunch of flunkies," Shatov said quietly, installing himself in a chair in a corner of the room and leaning his elbows on his knees. "And there's hatred in it too," he added, after a minute-long silence. "I know they would be the first to suffer if somehow Russia changed, even if it were the change they want—if she became an infinitely wealthy and happy land. Then there wouldn't be anyone for them to hate, spit upon, and mock. They have nothing but animal hatred for Russia, and it has corroded their organisms. . . . And there are no tears hidden beneath their laughter! Never has a more hypocritical utterance been made in Russia than that one about tears concealed by laughter!" he said loudly, almost beside himself with fury.

"What are you talking about?" I said, laughing.

"And you're a 'moderate liberal,'" Shatov grunted. "You know," he added suddenly, "perhaps it was stupid of me to talk about their servility. You may say, 'You're a fine one to talk—you who were born a serf.'"

"I had no intention of saying anything of the sort, believe me!"

"Stop apologizing. I'm not afraid of what you might say. I was born of a flunky and now I've become a flunky myself, just like you. A Russian liberal is bound to be a flunky who goes around looking for someone whose boots he can polish."

"What boots? What sort of allegory is that?"

"It's not an allegory. I see it amuses you. True, Mr. Verkhovensky says that I'm lying under a rock, squashed but not quite crushed to death—just wriggling. That's a clever way of describing my state."

"Mr. Verkhovensky assures me that you have a phobia about the Germans," I laughed. "Still, I'd say we've managed to pick a thing or two from their pockets and put them in our own—"

"Yes, we took a quarter and paid them hundreds of rubles for it."

We remained silent for a while, then he said,

"And he—he caught that in America, lying on his side."

"Caught what? Who? What are you talking about?"

"Kirilov. He and I spent four months together in a hut, lying on the floor."

"Have you been to America?" I asked, surprised. "I've never heard you mention it before."

"There's nothing much to mention. Just over two years ago, three of us left as emigrants for the United States. We spent our last cash on the tickets. We went to get a firsthand taste of the life of an American worker and experience for ourselves what it is like to live under the worst social conditions. That was the object of our trip."

"Good Lord!" I laughed. "Wouldn't it have been better to go to some agricultural area in this country at harvest time, if it was really for personal experience? Why go all the way to America?"

"We hired ourselves out as hands to some boss. There were six Russians working for him—students, landowners straight from their estates, even army officers—and all of us with the same grand objective. Well, we worked, got soaked by rain and sweat, suffered, and exhausted ourselves; finally, Kirilov and I walked out. We got sick and couldn't take any more of it. When he paid us, our boss shortchanged us; instead of the thirty dollars we were each supposed to get, I received eight and Kirilov fifteen. And while we were there, we got beaten a few times. After that, we were unemployed and spent four months lying on the floor in that hut, he thinking of one thing and I of something else."

"Did your boss really beat you? In America? I can imagine you swearing at him!"

"Not at all. On the contrary, we immediately came to the conclusion, Kirilov and I, that compared to the Americans we Russians were just little children and to be their equal, a man had to be born in America or at least live among them for many years. And not only that—when, for instance, they charged us a dollar for something that was worth perhaps a penny, we paid enthusiastically. And we praised everything we found there—spiritualism, lynching, their makes of revolvers, and their hoboes. Once when we were riding somewhere in a train, a man put his hand in my pocket, took out my hairbrush, and started brushing his hair. Kirilov and I just looked at each other with a smile and decided that that was the thing to do. We greatly approved of it."

"It's strange the way Russians not only get all sorts of notions into their heads but even try to act upon them," I commented.

"Human blueprints," Shatov said.

"But still, they cross the ocean on an emigrants' ship and land in an unfamiliar place to experiment upon themselves, and so on. I must say, there's a certain noble determination in it. But how did you get out of there?"

"I wrote to somebody in Europe and he sent me a hundred rubles."

As was his habit, Shatov kept his head lowered while he talked, even when he became excited. Now, however, he suddenly raised it and said:

"You interested in the name of that man?"

"Who was it?"

"Nikolai Stavrogin."

He got up, went over to his desk, and started looking through the drawers for something. I remembered then that a rumor had circulated that Shatov's estranged wife had at one time had an affair with Stavrogin in Paris. That would've been about two years before, when Shatov was in America. If so, I wondered why he had come out with that name now.

"And I still haven't paid him back," he said, once again looking me intently in the eye. Then he sat down in his chair and asked me, in a completely different tone:

"I'm sure you've come to see me about something. What is it?"

I told him everything in the exact order in which it had happened. I explained to him that I had now come to my senses after making that promise on the spur of the moment, but that I gathered it was so terribly important to Liza that I was absolutely determined to help her, although I wasn't even sure exactly what I had promised to do. After that I solemnly repeated to him that she'd never had any intention of deceiving him, that it was just a misunderstanding, and that she'd been very depressed by his sudden departure.

He heard me out, listening to me very carefully.

"I may," he said, "have acted stupidly—I usually do. But if she didn't understand why I left, so much the better for her."

He got up, went to the door, opened it, and listened.

"Do you wish to see that person yourself?"

"Yes, but how could it be arranged?" I said, hopefully leaping up.

"Let's just go there while she's alone. But he'll give her a bad beating if he finds out we've been there. I often go there secretly. Earlier today I had a fight with him when he started on her."

"What?"

"I pulled him off her by his hair. He wanted to go for me, but somehow I frightened him off and that's how it ended. Now I'm afraid he'll come home drunk, remember what happened, and give her a bad beating for it."

We went hurriedly downstairs.

V

The door of the Lebyatkin apartment was not locked, so we just walked in. The whole apartment consisted of two small, mangy rooms with grimy walls from which dirty wallpaper hung in shreds. A few years before, these rooms had been used as a bar and restaurant; then the owner, Filipov, had transferred the business to his new house. The other rooms of the former bar were now locked, and these two rented to Lebyatkin. The first room was furnished entirely with plain benches and unpainted tables, except for one old armchair with an arm missing. In the second room there was a bed in one corner, covered with a cotton blanket. It belonged to Miss Lebyatkin. The captain himself would just fall asleep on the floor, often in whatever he happened to be wearing. The whole place was littered and there were puddles of some liquid all over the floor. In the middle of the floor in the first room there was a huge, soaking-wet floor rag and next to it, in the same puddle, an old, worn-out shoe. It was apparent that no one bothered with anything much around here, that the stoves were not lit, that the food was not prepared. I found out later from Shatov that they didn't even have a samovar. The captain had been completely penniless when he'd first arrived with his sister, and Liputin had been right when he'd said that at first he had gone begging from door to door. And now that he had unexpectedly come into money, he had started to drink very hard, had completely lost his head, and, of course, had no time to think about a decent place to live in.

Miss Lebyatkin, whom I wanted so badly to see, was sitting quietly on a bench by a plain kitchen table in the second room. She didn't make a sound when we opened the door, nor did she budge when we entered. Shatov told me that, because it didn't lock, their door had once remained wide open throughout the night.

In the dim light of a meager candle in an iron candlestick, I saw a woman of thirty or so, unhealthily thin and dressed in an old cotton dress that left her long, stringy neck uncovered. Her hair was thin, darkish, and rolled into a bun the size of a two-year-old child's fist on the nape of her neck. On the table, besides the candlestick, there were a small mirror, a battered pack of cards, an old worn songbook, and a bread roll from which a couple of bites had been taken. She gave us a cheerful look and I noticed that she used powder and rouge. She also obviously penciled her eyebrows, even though they were naturally long, fine, and dark. On her high, narrow forehead there were three deep furrows, quite distinct under the powder. She didn't get up or walk while we were there, but I knew she had a limp. I imagined that when she was a very young girl she may have been pretty. Even now, her quiet, gentle, gray eyes were remarkable and there was something dreamy and trusting in her cheerful gaze. This quiet cheerfulness was what surprised me most about her, after all the stories I'd heard about the Cossack whip and the brutalities of her brother. And, oddly enough, instead of the painful, even horrifying revulsion one usually feels in the presence of creatures who have been penalized by Providence, I somehow enjoyed looking at her from the very first minute, and if I felt anything later, it was pity and certainly not disgust.

"That's how she sits, for days on end, all alone, without moving. She looks into that mirror and lays out the cards," Shatov told me as we stopped near the door. "He doesn't even feed her, you know. The old woman from the cottage sometimes brings her something to eat out of pity. How can he leave her alone with a lighted candle?"

To my surprise, Shatov talked loudly, as if she weren't in the room.

"Hello, Shatsie!" Miss Lebyatkin said in a friendly tone.

"I've brought a visitor along, Maria," Shatov said.

"I'm very pleased to see him, but I don't seem to remember him. . . ." She examined me closely from behind the candle and then turned toward Shatov again. She appeared to have completely forgotten my existence and addressed him alone.

"I suppose you got bored with walking up and down in your attic?" she said, laughing and revealing two rows of magnificent teeth.

"Yes, I got bored and then I felt like paying you a visit."

Shatov pushed a bench toward the table, sat down, and motioned to me to do the same.

"I'm glad to have an opportunity to chat, too. But you're a funny fellow, Shatsie. You're just like a monk. When did you comb your hair last? Here, let me comb it." She took a comb out of her pocket. "I bet you haven't touched it since the last time I combed it for you, right?"

"I don't even have a comb," Shatov said, laughing.

"Are you serious? Then you can have mine. No, not this one—I have another; just remind me."

And she started combing his hair, looking very serious about it. She even made a part on one side. Then she leaned back, examined the result of her efforts, and put the comb back in her pocket.

"Know what, Shatsie? You're an intelligent man, I suppose, but you're bored with yourself. I don't understand you people. I can't understand how people can be bored. It's unhappiness, not boredom, really. But me—I enjoy myself."

"Do you enjoy yourself when your brother's around, too?"

"Are you referring to Lebyatkin? He's my servant. And it doesn't make the slightest difference to me whether he's around or not. I just call out to him, 'Lebyatkin, get me some water!' or 'Lebyatkin, bring me my shoes!' and he rushes off to do it. Sometimes, I can't help laughing, watching him."

"And it's exactly as she says." Shatov again spoke aloud,

disregarding the woman's presence. "She does treat him like a servant. I've heard her ordering him around myself, 'Lebyatkin, get me some water!' and laughing as she did it. There's a difference though: he doesn't really rush off to get it for her—he beats her instead. But she's not at all afraid of him. She has some sort of fit almost every day, and that mixes her up and makes her forget what's happened. Do you think, for instance, she remembers our walking in here? She may, but by now she has rearranged it all in her mind and takes us for very different people, although she does have some recollection that I'm Shatsie. And my talking loud like this doesn't matter, for she never listens to people unless they address her directly. Otherwise, she stops listening and plunges into her dreams. Yes, exactly—she plunges into them. She's an extraordinary daydreamer: she can remain sitting in the same place for eight hours, for days on end. You see that roll? She may have taken one bite of it since morning, and she won't finish it till tomorrow. Look, now she's started telling her fortune with the cards."

"Yes, Shatsie, I'm trying to tell my fortune, but it doesn't come out right," the woman said suddenly, having caught the words "telling her fortune." Then, without turning her head, she stretched out her left hand and took hold of the roll (she may have heard Shatov mention that, too), but after holding it for a while, she put it down without taking a bite. She had become absorbed in what she was saying.

"It always comes out the same with these cards: a journey, a villain, someone's perfidy, a deathbed, a letter from somewhere, some unexpected news—it's all nonsense, Shatsie, don't you think? If people can lie, why can't cards?" She suddenly mixed the cards up. "That's exactly what I told Sister Praskovia, who was a very nice person and used to come to see me in my cell whenever she had a moment and ask me to tell her fortune—in secret, of course, from the Mother Superior. And she wasn't the only one to come and ask me. They all came, moaning and groaning and shaking their heads and chattering, but I just laughed. 'And why should you expect to get that letter now, Sister Praskovia, after twelve years of waiting?' She had a daughter, you see, and that daughter got married and left for Turkey with her husband and was never heard of again. But the next day, I'm sitting in the Mother Superior's room—she was a former princess—and we're having tea with some visiting lady—a great dreamer, that one—

and also with a monk who'd been to Mount Athos—a funny little man, I thought. And, what do you think happened, Shatsie? That little monk had brought a letter for Sister Praskovia that very day, straight from Turkey! So much for the jack of diamonds—unexpected news, remember!

"Anyway, we're drinking our tea and that monk says to the Mother Superior:

" 'Above all, Reverend Mother,' he says to her, 'God has blessed your convent because there's a great treasure concealed within it.'

" 'What treasure?' the Mother Superior asks him.

" 'Why, the blessed Sister Elizaveta, of course.'

"And that saintly Sister Elizaveta had been living in a cage seven feet by five, set in a wall of the convent, for seventeen years, summer and winter, wearing just a coarse linen shift, and all she ever did all those seventeen years was poke a piece of straw or a twig in and out of her shift; she never spoke, never washed, and never combed her hair. In the winter, they passed a sheepskin coat into her cage and every day they gave her a crust of bread and a mug of water. The pilgrims stared, gasped, sighed, and left money.

" 'Talk of a treasure,' Mother Superior says to him, angrily. She disliked that Elizaveta terribly. 'Elizaveta sits there out of sheer spite, just because she's so mule-headed—it's all a sham.'

"I didn't like her saying that. I was thinking of becoming a recluse myself at the time.

" 'And in my opinion,' I says to them, 'God and nature are one and the same thing.'

" 'Well, I never . . .' they all said in one voice. The Mother Superior laughed and whispered for a while to the visiting lady. Then the lady called me over, put her arm around me, and gave me a pink ribbon. Would you like to see it, Shatsie?

"And then that little monk began lecturing me, but so nicely and humbly and cleverly, you know, and I sat there and listened to him.

" 'Do you understand?' he asks me.

" 'No,' I said, 'I don't understand a thing, and would you kindly leave me in peace.'

"And after that, Shatsie, they did leave me in peace all right.

"But then, one day as we were leaving the church, a lay

sister who was staying at the convent to atone for making prophecies said to me:

" 'Mother of God—what do you think that means?'

" 'She's the great Mother, the hope of the human race,' I said.

" 'You're right there,' she said to me. 'The Mother of God is our great mother earth, and there's great happiness for man in that. And in every earthly sorrow and in every earthly tear there's happiness for us. And once you've soaked the earth a foot deep with your tears, you'll rejoice in everything right away. And,' she said, 'you'll not have a single sorrow—not a single one. There is such a prophecy,' she told me.

"Those words touched me deep down inside and I began then, when I knelt down to pray, to kiss the earth, and every time I kissed it I wept. And let me tell you, Shatsie, there's nothing bad in those tears—and even if you have nothing to be sad about, the tears will pour from your eyes out of sheer joy. Sometimes I went to the lake shore: on one side there was our convent and on the other our pointed mountain—that's what they called it, the Pointed Mountain. I climbed that mountain, faced the east, and kissed the ground; and I cried and cried and didn't even know how long I stayed there crying or what was happening around me. Then I got up and turned around, and watched the sun setting, so big and velvety and so pretty. . . . Don't you like to watch the sun, Shatsie? It's so nice and so sad at the same time. Then I faced the east again and saw the shadow of our mountain stretching out far, far across the lake, straight as an arrow. It's slender— slender and maybe a mile long, reaching all the way to the island in the middle of the lake. It cut that island in half and as soon as it cut it all the way through, at that very moment, the sun finished setting and everything got dark all of a sudden. And then it got dark inside me too—I'm afraid of the dark, Shatsie—I remembered everything again . . . but most of all I cried about my baby. . . ."

"Did you have a baby, then?" Shatov asked. He had been listening very attentively, and now he nudged me with his elbow.

"Yes, yes, a tiny, rosy baby with teeny-weeny little nails, and what makes me even sadder is that I can't remember whether it was a boy or a girl. Sometimes I remember it as a boy, sometimes as a girl. And as soon as I had it, I wrapped it in cambric and lace right away, tied pink ribbons round it, stuck flowers in its blanket, got it ready, said a prayer over it, and unbaptized as it was, carried it off. I carried it through the forest. I was scared, very scared, and what made me cry most was that I'd had my baby and yet I didn't know whether I had a husband."

"But maybe there was one?" Shatov asked cautiously.

"You're really funny, Shatsie—the things you think up! All right, even if there was one, what's the good, since it's as though there wasn't one anyway. There's an easy riddle for you; try and solve it." She gave a little snort of laughter.

"Where did you take the baby then?"

"I took it to the pond," she sighed.

Shatov nudged me again.

"And suppose you didn't *really* have the baby? Suppose you simply dreamed it all up, huh?"

"That's a hard one, Shatsie," she said thoughtfully, without the slightest surprise. "I can't tell you anything about that. There may not have been one. But it's really an idle question, because I won't stop crying over it, anyway. No, I couldn't have dreamed it all up, could I?" Large tears glistened in her eyes. "Oh, Shatsie, Shatsie, is it true your wife ran away from you?" She cried suddenly, placing her hands on his shoulders and looking at him with deep sympathy. "Now, don't get angry, for heaven's sake; I'm sad about it myself. You know, Shatsie, I'll tell you about a dream I had: He came to me again, beckoned to me, and called out. 'Kitten,' he said, 'my little kitten, come out here to me, come!' And it was that 'kitten' that made me happiest. So he still loves me, I say to myself."

"Maybe he'll come someday when you're awake," Shatov mumbled.

"No, Shatsie, that's *really* a dream. He'll never come when I'm awake. Do you know the song?

> I have no need of your tower so tall,
> I'll shut myself in this small cell,
> And I'll live on here and save my soul,
> And I'll pray to God to save yours too.

Ah, Shatsie, Shatsie, my dear boy, why don't you ever ask me about anything?"

"Why should I? You wouldn't tell me anyway."

"Right, I won't tell you, I won't tell you. You can kill me, but I won't tell you," she said, quickly catching up his words.

"You can burn me, and I won't tell you; and they can do anything they like to me—I still won't tell them. They'll never know!"

"Well, so you see, everyone must mind his own business," Shatov said even more quietly.

"But if you asked me nicely, I might tell you!" she said eagerly. "Won't you try asking? Ask me. Insist, Shatsie, and I'll tell you everything. Convince me, Shatsie—make me want to tell you myself, Shatsie, Shatsie!"

But Shatov remained silent. No one spoke for a full minute. I looked at her. Tears were running down her powdered cheeks. Her hands were still on Shatov's shoulders, but she had forgotten about them and was no longer looking at him.

"Ah, what do I care about you, anyway," he said suddenly and pulled angrily at the bench I was sitting on. "Come on, get up," he said to me and put the bench back where it had been before.

"Don't want him to find out when he comes home. . . . It's time for us to go now."

"Ah, you're still talking about my servant!" the woman said, laughing suddenly. "You're afraid, eh? All right, good-by then, dear friends—but first listen to what I have to say. Yesterday that Kirilov fellow came in here with Filipov, the landlord, with that big red beard of his, just when my flunky was pouncing on me. So the landlord grabbed him like *that* and pushed him across the room. My flunky kept protesting, 'It's not my fault; I'm paying for another man's wrongdoing!' You should've seen how the rest of us laughed. I'm telling you, we just rolled around with laughter!"

"But Maria, I was here myself; it was me, not the Red Beard who pulled him off by his hair. The landlord came two days ago about a different matter. You've got it all mixed up."

"Wait—come to think of it, I guess I have mixed things up a bit. So you say it was you. You must be right, but why argue about it? What's the difference who pulls him off me?" She laughed.

"Let's get out of here now!" Shatov said, abruptly tugging at me. "I heard the gate creak. If he finds out we've been here, he'll beat her up."

And, indeed, before we'd reached the top of the stairs, we heard drunken shouting and swearing. We went into Shatov's room and he locked the door behind us.

"Better stay here for a few minutes if you don't want to cause a commotion. Hear him squealing like a pig? He must've tripped at the gate again. He does it every time and lands flat on his face."

Unfortunately, we didn't manage to avoid a commotion.

VI

Shatov stood by the locked door and listened. Suddenly I saw him jump back.

"He's coming this way," he whispered in a rage. "We probably won't be rid of him before midnight now."

Fists banged on the door.

"Shatov, Shatov, open up, it's me!" Lebyatkin was shouting. "Shatov, my friend,

> I have come to greet you, dear,
> To tell you that the sun is waking,
> And its yellow shafts so clear,
> Set the forest leaves a-quaking.
> I have come to tell you, dear,
> To announce I am awake. . . .
> Ah, God damn you, do you hear?
> Wide awake under the branches . . .

You know, branches just like those birch twigs they use for spanking—ha, ha, ha!

> Every birdie's craving for a drink.
> What drink would I like, d'you think?
> I don't care as long as I drink!

Anyway, damn your stupid curiosity! Say, Shatov, you have no idea how good it is to be alive!"

"Don't make a sound," Shatov whispered to me.

"Come on, open up! Can't you understand that there are more important things than brawling? There are moments for honorable gestures. Shatov, I'm a kind man. Please, Shatov —to hell with those proclamations, all right?"

Silence.

"Can't you understand, you stupid idiot, that I'm in love! I've bought myself a lover's frock coat. I paid fifteen rubles for it. A captain's love must have decorum. Let me in then!" he roared, savagely pounding on the door with his fists again.

"Get the hell out of here!" Shatov suddenly roared back at him.

"You—you—lousy serf! . . . and your sister's a serf too—and a lousy thief to boot!"

"And you—you *sold* your sister."

"You're lying! I'm not going to take any more dirt from everyone when I can end it all by telling. . . . Know what she is?"

"What is she?" Shatov said. Swayed by irresistible curiosity, he moved closer to the door.

"Can't you understand what I'm saying?"

"I'll understand when you've told me. What is she?"

"I'm not afraid to tell! I'm always prepared to say things out loud!"

"I don't believe you'd dare!" Shatov said, egging him on and motioning me to listen.

"You say I wouldn't dare?"

"That's right."

"I wouldn't dare?"

"Well, speak up then, if you're not afraid your master'll give you a thrashing. I know you're a coward, although you claim to be a captain!"

"I—I—she—she is . . ." Lebyatkin stuttered in a trembling voice.

"Well?" Shatov put his ear to the door.

There was no sound for at least half a minute. Then Lebyatkin cursed and, huffing and puffing like a samovar, withdrew downstairs.

"No use—he's too cunning to let it out even when he's drunk," Shatov said, moving away from the door.

"What's it all about?" I inquired.

Shatov shrugged, unlocked the door, opened it, and listened. He listened for a long time and even walked stealthily down a few steps. Finally he came back into his room.

"Couldn't hear a sound. He didn't touch her. Nothing. Guess he just fell down and went to sleep at once. I guess it's safe for you to go home now."

"But tell me, Shatov—what am I to make of all this?"

"Ah, that's up to you," he said in a weary, disgusted voice, sitting down at his desk.

I left. A single, rather incredible idea was gaining more

and more ground in my imagination. I thought of the coming day with anguish.

VII

The next day was the Sunday that was supposed to seal Mr. Verkhovensky's fate so irrevocably and is one of the key moments in my story. It was a day of the unexpected; a day of the denouement of many plots and the beginning of many future intrigues; a day of sudden explanations and thickening mysteries. In the morning I was supposed to accompany Mr. Verkhovensky to Mrs. Stavrogin's and at three in the afternoon I had to be at Liza's to tell her something, I wasn't sure what, and then to help her in something, what I wasn't sure either. It all ended in a way no one could have expected. Indeed, it was a day of most extraordinary coincidences.

When Mr. Verkhovensky and I arrived at Mrs. Stavrogin's at twelve sharp, she wasn't in: she hadn't yet returned from the cathedral. My poor friend, who was already in a very shaky state, was so depressed by this circumstance that he dropped listlessly into an easy chair in the drawing room. I offered him a glass of water, but although he was ashen and his hands were trembling, he declined my offer with dignity. I must note here that, for this occasion, he had dressed with special care, almost as though we were going to a ball. He wore a strikingly fine lawn shirt with his monogram embroidered on it, a white cravat, and a new hat and carried a pair of straw-colored gloves in his hand. There was a hint of perfume about him.

We had just sat down when a footman led in Shatov, who was obviously there by invitation. On seeing him, Mr. Verkhovensky got up and held out his hand, but Shatov gave us both a look, turned away, and installed himself in a far corner of the room, without even so much as nodding to us. Mr. Verkhovensky looked at me in dismay.

We sat there in dead silence for a few more minutes. Then Mr. Verkhovensky whispered something to me, but I didn't catch it, so, in a state of great agitation, he gave it up. The footman came in again, pretending to arrange something on the table, but actually to have a look at us. Suddenly Shatov asked him very loudly:

"Tell me, Alexei, do you know whether Dasha is out with Mrs. Stavrogin?"

"Madam went to church by herself. Miss Dasha is in her room upstairs. She doesn't feel well," the footman announced in dignified tones.

Mr. Verkhovensky again gave me such an appalled look that I started avoiding his eyes. Then I heard the rattle of a carriage outside and the house resounded with footsteps announcing the return of the mistress. We all got up, but again there was something unexpected: there were many footsteps approaching, indicating that Mrs. Stavrogin was not alone. This was strange because she herself had chosen this time for our visit. Then we heard a very rapid step, as though someone were running—and it couldn't possibly be Mrs. Stavrogin. But it was, and she burst into the room in a state of incredible excitement. Behind her, having fallen back because they were walking at a much slower pace, came Liza Tishin arm-in-arm with none other than Maria Lebyatkin. If I had seen it in a dream, I wouldn't have believed it!

To explain this bewildering development, we must go back an hour in time and report Mrs. Stavrogin's extraordinary experience in the cathedral.

To start with, almost the entire town was gathered in the cathedral, with our high society in the forefront. The new first lady was scheduled to make her first public appearance among us. I'll note here that there were already rumors that she was a freethinker and adhered to the "new way." The ladies had been warned that she was going to be frightfully elegantly dressed and were themselves resplendently attired. Only Mrs. Stavrogin wore her usual simple black dress, a color she had been wearing for the past four years. Arriving at the cathedral, she occupied her usual pew to the left in the first row and a liveried footman placed a velvet cushion before her for her to kneel on, just as he always did.

It was noticed, however, that all through the service she prayed with unusual fervor. Some even asserted later that there were tears in her eyes.

When the service was over, our parish priest, Father Pavel, delivered a solemn sermon. We thought highly of his sermons and always enjoyed them. We'd even tried to persuade him to have them published, but he could never make up his mind to do so. This sermon turned out to be exceptionally long.

It was while Father Pavel was delivering that long sermon of his that an old-fashioned horse cab drove up and a lady alighted from it. It was one of those cabs in which the passenger had to sit sideways and hold onto the coachman's belt for dear life, for the vehicle swayed like a blade of grass in the wind. There were still a few of them left in our town.

The cathedral entrance was cluttered with private carriages and also with police, so the cab stopped at the corner. The lady jumped down and gave the cabman four kopecks.

"Isn't that enough?" she said, as the cabman made a sour face. "That's all I possess," she added pitifully.

"Well, all right, you never know who you'll get," the coachman said with a helpless wave of the hand, looking at her with an expression that seemed to say, "It would be a sin to be nasty to someone like you." He thrust his leather purse back into his coat and, amid the laughter of the other cabbies, drove off.

Stares of curiosity and surprise accompanied the lady as she made her way toward the cathedral gate past carriages and flunkies who were waiting for their masters to come out of the cathedral. And her sudden appearance in the street among the ordinary people really was surprising. She was unhealthily thin, walked with a limp, wore too much powder and rouge, and had a long, thin neck that was altogether uncovered. Although it was a cold and windy late September day, she wore no coat or shawl but only a dark cotton dress. Her head was bare and her hair was rolled into a bun on the nape of her neck. The only decoration she wore was an artificial flower like those sold on Palm Sunday to decorate the angels; this was pinned to the right side of her bosom. The day before I'd noticed such a wax angel decorated with a wreath of paper flowers in the corner under the icon in Maria Lebyatkin's room. To complete the picture, she walked with her eyes modestly lowered, but at the same time she had a gay and playful smile on her face.

Had she arrived a few moments later, they probably wouldn't have let her into the cathedral. But she was just in time. She entered and made her way unobtrusively to the front.

Although the sermon was halfway through and the tightly packed congregation was listening to it in silence, with concentrated attention, a few people glanced with surprise and curiosity at the new arrival. She knelt at the altar rail, lowered her painted face, and remained in that position for a long time, apparently crying. However, when she rose from her knees and looked up, she appeared to have fully recovered and soon looked quite cheerful again. Gaily and with obvious pleasure, she let her eyes slide first over the faces of the congregation, then over the walls of the cathedral. She examined the faces of certain ladies with especial curiosity and even rose on tiptoe to get a better look at them. Twice she even giggled unexpectedly.

In the meantime, the sermon was concluded and the cross was carried out. The governor's wife was the first to move toward the cross, but before she reached it, she stopped, apparently to let Mrs. Stavrogin pass ahead of her. Mrs. Stavrogin walked straight past her, as though she weren't there. The dignified courtesy of the governor's wife no doubt contained a subtle snub to Mrs. Stavrogin. At least, that was the way everyone present felt—including Mrs. Stavrogin. But she walked on, apparently unaware of anyone's presence around her. She reached the cross, kissed it with an air of unshakable, regal dignity, and headed for the doors. The liveried footman cleared the way for her, although this wasn't really necessary, as people stepped out of her way anyway. But just before the door, her way was barred by a tight little knot of people. Mrs. Stavrogin halted, and at that moment the strange creature with the artificial flower elbowed her way through the crowd, hurried forward, and fell on her knees before Mrs. Stavrogin, who, being practically impervious to public displays of emotion, looked sternly and composedly at her.

At this point, let me explain as briefly as possible, that, although Mrs. Stavrogin had become rather thrifty—even stingy—during these past years, she occasionally spent liberally, especially for philanthropy. Indeed, she was a member of a philanthropic society in the capital. During a recent famine, she had sent a donation of five hundred rubles to the main office of the society in Petersburg, a fact that had become widely known around here. Recently (just before the appointment of the new governor), she had almost succeeded in organizing a ladies' committee for assistance to the town's poorest expectant mothers. Many people accused her of doing it all out of sheer vanity, but Mrs. Stavrogin's well-known impetuosity, combined with her determination, almost overcame all the obstacles in her way; the committee was on the point of being formed and the initial idea kept expanding in the exalted brain of its founder, who began to dream of launching another such committee in Moscow and gradually expanding its operations to all the provinces. But then there was the change of governor and everything was suspended. The new first lady, it was said, had also made a few unpleasant, but at the same time effective, comments on the impracticability of the project. Naturally, these remarks were brought to the attention of Mrs. Stavrogin in due course, with, of course, suitable juicy additions. And though God alone can penetrate a heart to its depths, I imagine that Mrs. Stavrogin now felt rather pleased at being stopped at the door of the cathedral. Knowing that in a moment the governor's wife, followed by the entire congregation, would pass by, she probably thought, "Let her see for herself how little I care what she thinks of me and how insensible I am to her cracks about my going in for philanthropy out of vanity. Let them all see how much their opinion matters to me!"

"What's this all about, my dear? What can I do for you?" Mrs. Stavrogin asked, looking intently at the kneeling figure.

The woman gave her a frightened, embarrassed look in which, however, there was also a sort of reverence. Then, suddenly, she giggled again.

"What does she want? Who is she?" Mrs. Stavrogin asked, sweeping a severe, questioning glance over the people around her. No one answered.

"Are you in distress? Do you need help?"

"I need—I came . . ." she said in a voice quivering with emotion—"I just came to kiss your hand." She giggled again.

Looking like a small child trying to cajole an adult into giving him something he wants, the woman leaned forward and tried to catch Mrs. Stavrogin's hand. But something apparently frightened her and she abruptly drew her hands back.

"Is that all you wish?"

Mrs. Stavrogin smiled compassionately. Then she quickly pulled her purse, with its mother-of-pearl clasp, out of a pocket, took a ten-ruble bill out of it, and handed it to the woman, who took it. Mrs. Stavrogin was very curious about her, apparently realizing she was no ordinary beggar.

"Look, she gave her a ten-ruble bill," someone in the crowd remarked.

"Please, your hand, please," the woman kept muttering, firmly holding in the fingers of her left hand the ten-ruble bill, which fluttered in the wind. Mrs. Stavrogin frowned slightly and, with an air of stern dignity, gave her hand to the poor creature, who kissed it with veneration. There was an exultant look in her grateful eyes now.

By this time the governor's wife had come up, followed by all our society ladies and our town's top officials. Whether she liked it or not, the first lady had to slow down and even come to a halt in the throng that had formed around Mrs. Stavrogin. Many of the others stopped too.

"You're trembling. You must be cold!" Mrs. Stavrogin said suddenly and, slipping off her cloak, which was caught in mid-air by the footman, she removed her black (and by no means cheap) shawl from her shoulders and, with her own hands, wrapped it around the bare neck of the kneeling woman, saying:

"Please, get up. Stand up, I beg you!"

The woman got up.

"Where do you live? Does anyone know where she lives?" Mrs. Stavrogin once again looked around impatiently. But all she saw were the familiar faces she met in society. Some of them were watching the scene with shocked disapproval, others with sly amusement, others again with an innocent longing for something scandalous to happen. Some were even beginning to laugh.

"I believe her name's Lebyatkin, ma'am," some kind soul finally volunteered. It was Andreyev, a well-respected, highly regarded merchant, with glasses, white beard, Russian shirt, and high hat—which he now held in his hand. "She lives in Filipov's house on Nativity Street."

"Lebyatkin? Filipov's house? Wait, I think I've heard something. . . . Thank you, Mr. Andreyev, but who is Lebyatkin?"

"He calls himself a captain and I must say he's not too well behaved. She's his sister, I'm sure. She must have escaped from the house," he said, giving Mrs. Stavrogin a significant look.

"Thank you, Mr. Andreyev. I understand what you mean. So, you are Miss Lebyatkin, my dear?"

"No, my name is not Lebyatkin."

"But Lebyatkin is your brother, isn't he?"

"Yes, Lebyatkin is my brother."

"Well, here's what we'll do, my dear. First you'll come home with me and then later I'll have you driven back to your family. Would you like to come?"

"Oh yes, I would!" Miss Lebyatkin cried, clapping her hands.

"Aunt Varvara, Aunt Varvara! May I come along too?" Liza's voice suddenly sounded out.

Liza had arrived at the cathedral with the governor's wife,

while her mother, following the doctor's orders, had gone for a drive in the carriage, taking Maurice along to keep her company. Now Liza suddenly left the governor's wife and darted toward Mrs. Stavrogin.

"Liza, my dear, you know very well I'm always happy to have you, but what would your mother say?" Mrs. Stavrogin began stiffly, but seeing Liza's extraordinary agitation, she suddenly stopped in confusion.

"I'm coming with you, Aunt. I must," Liza insisted, kissing her.

"But what's the matter with you, Liza?" the first lady said in an emphatically surprised tone.

"Ah, forgive me, my dear, *ma chère cousine,* I must go with Aunt Varvara." Liza turned quickly and, in a single movement, kissed her *chère cousine* twice. Mrs. von Lembke seemed surprised and not at all appreciative.

"And please tell *maman* to come over to Aunt Varvara's immediately. She told me this morning that she intended to drive over to your place—I forgot to warn you," Liza rattled on. "I'm sorry, Aunt, please forgive me. . . . Julie, *chère cousine* . . . I'm ready, Aunt Varvara!" Then, putting her mouth close to Mrs. Stavrogin's ear, Liza said in a breathless, desperate whisper, "If you don't take me with you, I'll run behind your carriage and I'll—I'll scream right now."

Fortunately nobody heard her. Mrs. Stavrogin stepped back a little and glared piercingly at the young girl. What she saw convinced her that she had to take Liza along.

"All right, let's put an end to this scene!" she said abruptly. "I'll be very glad if you come, Liza. That is," she added, in a deliberately loud voice, "if Mrs. von Lembke is willing to let you come with me." And she turned with an air of straightforwardness and dignity toward the first lady.

"Of course, of course—how could I stand in the way and deprive her of the pleasure," Julie von Lembke purred, "especially since I know what a willful, whimsical head she carries on those frail shoulders of hers." She smiled disarmingly.

"Thank you very much." Mrs. Stavrogin acknowledged her graciousness with a stately and dignified bow.

"And I am the more delighted," Mrs. von Lembke added almost rapturously, turning pink with agreeable excitement, "in that, besides the pleasure she will derive just from being in your home, Liza is moved now by the beautiful—I might even say, sublime—feeling of compassion. . . ." She glanced at

Maria Lebyatkin. "And what's more, on the very steps of the cathedral!"

"Such a feeling is all to your honor, madam," Mrs. Stavrogin said approvingly.

Mrs. von Lembke impulsively held out her hand and Mrs. Stavrogin, without hesitation, placed her fingers in it. The general effect on the audience was excellent: some faces beamed, ingratiating smiles appeared on others.

It suddenly became clear to everyone that it was not Mrs. von Lembke who had snubbed Mrs. Stavrogin by failing to call on her but Mrs. Stavrogin who had held her at arm's length, and that Mrs. von Lembke would have gone to Mrs. Stavrogin's house on foot had she been sure of being received when she got there. Mrs. Stavrogin's prestige rose immensely.

"Get in, dear," Mrs. Stavrogin said to Maria Lebyatkin, pointing to her carriage, which had driven up. Miss Lebyatkin joyfully limped forward to the carriage door, where a footman helped her in.

"Good heavens, how you limp!" Mrs. Stavrogin cried with obvious fright in her voice; she had turned pale.

Everyone noticed her turn pale, but no one understood why.

The carriage moved away. Mrs. Stavrogin's house was only a short distance from the cathedral. Later, Liza told me that during the whole ride, which lasted about three minutes, Miss Lebyatkin kept laughing hysterically and Mrs. Stavrogin sat in "some sort of a trance," as Liza put it.

chapter 5

THE WISE SERPENT

I

Mrs. Stavrogin rang the bell and let herself drop into an armchair by the window.

"Sit there, my dear," she said, motioning Maria Lebyatkin to a chair near a large round table in the middle of the room. Then, glancing at Mr. Verkhovensky, she asked: "What do you make of this, Stepan? Do you see this young woman here? What do you make of it?"

"I—I. . . ." Mr. Verkhovensky started to mutter, but he was interrupted by the entry of a footman.

"Bring me a cup of coffee, as quickly as possible. And don't have the horses unhitched; I'll be using the carriage."

"Mais chère et excellente amie, dans quelle inquiétude. . . ." Mr. Verkhovensky began in a dying voice.

"Ah! In French, in French! You can tell at once we're in high society!" Maria exclaimed delightedly, eager to sit in on a French conversation. Mrs. Stavrogin stared at her in near terror.

Everyone was silent, waiting for something to happen. Shatov kept his eyes on the ground. Mr. Verkhovensky was in a state of panic; he somehow felt responsible for what was happening. I noticed beads of perspiration on his temples. Liza sat in a corner, not far from Shatov. Her eyes kept darting from Mrs. Stavrogin to Maria and back. Her lips were twisted into an unpleasant grin that Mrs. Stavrogin fully noted. As for Maria Lebyatkin, she was thoroughly enjoying herself; without the slightest embarrassment, she inspected the rich drawing room, the furniture, the rugs, the paintings, the ceiling moldings, the large bronze crucifix in the corner, the porcelain lamp, and the albums and other small items on the round table.

"So you're here too, Shatsie!" she suddenly cried. "Imagine that. I've been looking at you for some time, but I kept saying to myself, 'It can't be he; how could he have got here?' " And she burst into happy laughter.

"So you know this woman?" Mrs. Stavrogin said, immediately turning toward him.

"Yes, I do," Shatov said between his teeth, shifting in his chair.

"What actually do you know? Please tell me quickly!"

"What do you mean?" Shatov smiled inappropriately. "You can see for yourself—"

"See what? Well—say something, for heaven's sake!"

"We just happen to live in the same house. She lives with her brother—some officer, I think."

"So?"

Shatov hesitated.

"So, there's n-nothing s-special t-to say!" he stammered and fell into an obstinate silence. His obstinacy even caused him to turn red.

"Well, there's obviously nothing to be got out of you," Mrs. Stavrogin said indignantly. She had guessed by now that everyone present knew something, but was avoiding her questions, trying to hide it from her.

The footman came in, bringing Mrs. Stavrogin's cup of coffee on a silver tray, but she motioned him toward Maria.

"Here, my dear, you looked so cold at the cathedral. Drink that; it will warm you."

"Merci," Maria said, taking the cup and immediately bursting into laughter because she had said *merci* to the footman. But when she felt Mrs. Stavrogin's glare on her, she put the cup down on the table.

"But, Auntie, you're not angry with me, are you?" she said quickly, in an incongruously playful tone.

"Wha-a-at?" Mrs. Stavrogin said, abruptly straightening herself up in her armchair. "I'm no aunt of yours! What do you mean by that?"

Maria, who hadn't expected such a violent reaction, stiffened in her chair and began to shiver all over convulsively, as though in a fit.

"I thought that was the proper way," she mumbled, looking at Mrs. Stavrogin with wide-open eyes. "That's what Liza calls you."

"And since when is she Liza to you?"

"But I heard you call her that yourself," Maria said a bit more cheerfully. "And then, I saw a beautiful girl who looked just like her in a dream," she said and giggled, apparently against her will.

Mrs. Stavrogin thought for a second, then calmed down somewhat. She even smiled at Maria's last remark. Maria, seeing her smile, got up and limped across the room to her.

"Here," she said, taking off the black shawl that Mrs. Stavrogin had given her at the cathedral. "Forgive me, I forgot to give it back to you."

"Please, put it back on and keep it. Sit down and drink your coffee. And please don't be afraid of me, my dear. Calm yourself; I'm beginning to understand you better now."

"Chère amie—" Mr. Verkhovensky again tried to say something.

"Oh, please, Stepan, I'm confused enough without you, so please spare me! Perhaps you could ring that bell—there, next to you. It rings in the maids' room."

A silence followed during which Mrs. Stavrogin's glance swept irritably over our faces. Then her favorite maid, Agasha, appeared in the doorway.

"Please get me the checkered shawl I bought in Geneva. And what is Miss Dasha doing?"

"She doesn't feel very well."

"Would you please ask her to come down? Tell her that I would be greatly obliged, even if she doesn't feel too well."

At that moment an unusual amount of noise came from the adjoining room once again: voices and footsteps. Then Mrs. Drozdov, out of breath and looking very irritated, appeared. She was leaning on Maurice's arm.

"Oh, my goodness, I hardly managed to get here! Liza, you're out of your mind! What are you trying to do to me?" she squeaked, investing that squeak of hers with all her accumulated irritation, as weak and irritable people usually do. "Ah, Varvara, I've come to fetch my daughter!"

Mrs. Stavrogin frowned at her, half rose to greet her, and hardly bothering to hide her own irritation, said,

"Hello, Praskovia. Please do me a favor and sit down. I was sure you'd come."

II

Her reception didn't surprise Mrs. Drozdov. Under the guise of friendship, Mrs. Stavrogin had always been rather domineering and scornful with her boarding-school friend. Besides, in this instance, the situation was special. Recently relations between the two houses had appeared on the verge of a complete break. To Mrs. Stavrogin the reasons for the increasing tension were unclear and therefore all the more irritating. But the main thing was that Mrs. Drozdov had begun to assume an overbearing attitude toward her. Of course, this greatly offended Mrs. Stavrogin, who was further irritated by certain strange, vague rumors that exasperated her by their very vagueness. Mrs. Stavrogin was a proud, straightforward woman with, so to speak, a propensity for frontal assault. More than anything, she hated sneak attacks and secret accusations, always preferring openly declared war.

Anyway, the two ladies hadn't seen each other for five days—in fact, since Mrs. Stavrogin had left "the Drozdov woman's" house confused and offended. I am sure that as she came into the drawing room now, Mrs. Drozdov was convinced that Mrs. Stavrogin would cringe before her. I could see it written all over her face. But apparently Mrs. Stavrogin was most aggressive and arrogant precisely when she suspected someone thought her beaten. On the other hand, Mrs. Drozdov, like so many weak people who are accustomed to accepting humiliation, displayed an extraordinary zest for attack at the first favorable opportunity. True, she wasn't feeling well just then and that made her excessively irritable. Let me add, finally, that the presence of the rest of us in the drawing room would not have prevented either of the childhood friends from letting herself go if it had come to an open clash: we were considered members of the household—even, in a way, dependents. I realized that then and there, with a certain alarm.

Mr. Verkhovensky, who had remained standing ever since Mrs. Stavrogin's arrival, sank limply into a chair when Mrs. Drozdov started squeaking. He tried desperately to catch my eye. Shatov shifted himself abruptly in his chair and mumbled something under his breath. I had the impression that he would have liked to get up and leave. Liza rose for a second, but slipped down into her armchair again without paying any visible attention to her mother's squeaking. It was not that she deliberately ignored her mother but rather that something else held her entire attention. She was now looking somewhere into space, almost absently, and had even ceased to take much notice of Maria Lebyatkin.

III

"May I sit here?" Mrs. Drozdov gasped, pointing out a chair close to the table and easing herself into it with Maurice's assistance. "I would never sit down in this house if it weren't for my wretched legs," she added in a breaking voice.

Mrs. Stavrogin lifted her head slightly, pressed her fingers to her right temple, and appeared to wince with pain (*tic douloureux*).

"Why do you say that, Praskovia? Why shouldn't you sit down in my house? Your late husband was always a dear friend of my husband's and you and I played with dolls together when we were little girls in boarding school."

Mrs. Drozdov waved her hands in protest.

"I knew that was coming!" she said. "You always bring boarding school up before you say wicked things to me. That's an old trick of yours—nothing but words. I won't hear any more about that boarding school of yours!"

"You sound in a very bad temper, Praskovia. Must be your legs. Here—have some coffee and relax."

"Listen here, Varvara, don't treat me like a little girl. And I don't want any coffee." She impatiently waved away the servant who was offering her a cup.

The others, by the way, also declined coffee, that is, everyone except me and Maurice. Mr. Verkhovensky, who had accepted a cup from the servant, put it untouched on the table. Miss Lebyatkin obviously longed to have a second cup and had even stretched out her hand to take one, but she had thought better of it and given up the idea with dignity, and now she was rather pleased with herself.

"You know, Praskovia," Mrs. Stavrogin said, smiling crookedly, "I'm sure you've been imagining things again and that's why you came here. You've lived your whole life by imagination alone. For instance, you were furious when I mentioned school; but do you remember that once you announced to the whole class that that hussar, Shablykin, had fallen in love with you and Madame Lefebure proved then and there that you were lying? But then, I know you weren't really lying; you had simply imagined it all—it made you feel better. All right, out with it now! What is it you're so displeased about? Speak up!"

"And you, Varvara, you fell in love with the priest who taught us Scripture. There's something for you to remember, since you don't seem ever to forget anything—ha-ha-ha. . . ."

She laughed biliously and lengthily, until finally her laughter turned into a cough.

"So you haven't forgotten the priest," Mrs. Stavrogin said with hatred, looking her straight in the eye. Her face had taken on a greenish tinge.

Mrs. Drozdov suddenly assumed an air of dignity.

"But I haven't come here to laugh my head off, Varvara. What I wish to know is—why did you have to mix my daughter up in your public displays? That's the object of my visit."

"What public display?" Mrs. Stavrogin said, straightening herself up threateningly.

"Mother, I would ask you, speaking for myself, to be a bit more careful what you say," Liza said, suddenly interfering.

"What did you say?" Mrs. Drozdov squeaked. She would have said more, but she fell silent before her daughter's glare.

"How can you talk of a public display, Mother! I came here with Julie von Lembke's permission, to find out more about this poor woman and try to help her."

"To find out about this poor woman," Mrs. Drozdov imitated Liza, bursting into sardonic laughter. "And do you think it fitting for you to get mixed up in that sort of 'story'? Ah, I've had enough of this bullying!" she exclaimed, turning angrily toward Mrs. Stavrogin. "I don't know whether it's true or not, but I've heard that you have the whole town dancing to your tune. Well then, the time has come for you to do some dancing of your own!"

Mrs. Stavrogin was sitting straight as an arrow ready to be fired from a bow. For ten seconds she glared at Mrs. Drozdov without budging.

"You can thank God, Praskovia, that we are among friends here, for you've said much too much today."

"Let me tell you that I'm not as afraid of society's opinion as some. I'm not like you, who pretend to be so proud, when all the time you're trembling over what they're saying about you. As to these people being friends, it's you who can consider yourself lucky that no stranger has overheard what's been said."

"Why, have you become wiser during this past week?"

"It's not that I've become wiser; it's just that the truth has become more generally known."

"What truth has become known? Listen, Praskovia, don't try to push me any further. I want you to tell me right now what you mean by the truth having become known. Explain, this very minute!"

"But there's the truth, sitting over there!" Mrs. Drozdov said, pointing suddenly at Maria Lebyatkin with the determination of despair that makes a person no longer care about consequences as long as his opponent is hurt. Maria, who had been observing Mrs. Drozdov all this time with gay curiosity, now dissolved in happy laughter at the sight of the finger pointed at her.

"My God, has everyone gone completely mad?" Mrs. Stavrogin cried. She turned very pale and leaned back in her chair. In fact, she was so pale that there was general consternation and Mr. Verkhovensky rushed toward her. I followed him across the room. Liza also got up, but she remained standing by her chair. But Mrs. Drozdov was more scared than any of us. She let out a short scream, struggled to her feet, and wailed:

"Varvara, dear, forgive my vicious stupidity! Go on, someone, get her some water at least!"

"Do me a favor, Praskovia, and stop whining. And you, Stepan, please get out of my way. No, I don't need any water," Mrs. Stavrogin said in a low but firm voice. Her lips were very pale.

"Varvara dear," Mrs. Drozdov went on, "I want to say— I know I was wrong to let out those careless words, but I want you to understand that I was exasperated by the anonymous letters some nasty, petty people had been peppering me with. . . . Well—why don't they write to you since the letters are about you? Why to me when I have a daughter? . . ."

Mrs. Stavrogin was looking at her speechlessly with wide-open eyes, listening in amazement. At that moment, a side door opened and Dasha appeared. She stopped and looked around, taken aback by the general agitation she found in the drawing room. She probably didn't notice Maria, of whose presence she hadn't been warned. Mr. Verkhovensky was the first to see Dasha. He made a sharp movement, blushed, and for some reason, announced loudly:

"Miss Dasha Shatov!"

All eyes turned toward her.

"So that's Dasha Shatov!" Maria Lebyatkin exclaimed unexpectedly. "Ah, Shatsie, your sister's not like you at all. I can't understand how my brother can refer to her as a serf girl."

Dasha, who had almost reached Mrs. Stavrogin's chair, was astonished at this exclamation. She turned toward the simpleminded woman and stared at her.

"Sit down, Dasha," Mrs. Stavrogin said with frightening composure. "Here, closer—here. You can see that woman just as well sitting down. Do you know her?"

"I've never seen her before," Dasha said quietly, then added, after a brief silence, "I suppose she must be Mr. Lebyatkin's sick sister."

"And I too, my dear—this is the first time I've seen you, although I've been wanting to meet you for so long. And now I see there's breeding in every one of your movements!" Maria cried enthusiastically. "As to what my servant goes around saying about you, it's unbelievable—how could a well-bred person like you take his money? For I know you're nice and good; I'm sure of it!" she concluded rapturously, waving her hand.

"Do you understand anything about this, Dasha?" Mrs. Stavrogin asked stiffly.

"I understand everything now."

"What's this about money?"

"That's the money Nikolai asked me to deliver to her brother, Mr. Lebyatkin, when we were in Switzerland."

There was a brief silence. Then Mrs. Stavrogin asked:

"Did Nikolai himself ask you to deliver the money to that man?"

"He was anxious for Mr. Lebyatkin to get the three hundred rubles. But since he only knew that Mr. Lebyatkin was due to come here, but not his address, he asked me to give him the money when he arrived."

"And what happened to it? Did it get lost? What does this woman mean?"

"Well, that I can't say. I've heard that Mr. Lebyatkin has been going around saying that I didn't give him all the money. But I don't understand what he's talking about: I sent him the three hundred rubles as I was asked."

Dasha seemed to have regained her composure. I must say, she was not the type to remain confused for long, whatever her inner turmoil may have been. Now she spoke unhurriedly, but without hesitation. Her original confusion had vanished and she didn't seem at all embarrassed. There wasn't the slightest suggestion about her that she might have felt in the least guilty about anything in this whole business.

Mrs. Stavrogin's eyes remained glued on her all the time she interrogated her, and when she finished, she deliberated for about half a minute.

"If," she then declared firmly, apparently addressing everyone, although her eyes were still on Dasha, "Nikolai asked you rather than anyone else, even me, to do that errand for him, he must have had good reasons for it. And since I have not been taken into the secret, I do not feel I have the right to pry further. However, the fact that you participated in this affair reassures me completely. I want you to realize that, Dasha. But I wish to add, my dear, that—in all innocence, of course—you have exposed yourself to unpleasantness by agreeing to have dealings with low characters. The libel spread by that man proves your mistake. But I'll have inquiries made about him and I assure you, I'll be able to give you adequate protection. And now, let's end the matter there."

"The best thing," Maria suddenly intervened, "would be to send him to the servants' quarters when he comes here. Let him play cards with the other flunkies there, while we sit here and sip our coffee. But I suppose we might send him a cup too, although I have nothing but contempt for him."

And she emphasized her contempt with a toss of her head.

"We'll put an end to that too," Mrs. Stavrogin said, having quietly heard Maria out. "Do ring that bell, Stepan."

Mr. Verkhovensky rang the bell, then suddenly stepped forward in great agitation, turned red, and said in a faltering, stammering voice:

"I too have—have heard the most disgusting story—I mean, libel—and—and it was with the greatest indignation—*enfin, c'est un homme perdu et quelque chose comme un forçat évadé.* . . ."

He broke off. Mrs. Stavrogin screwed up her eyes and scrutinized him from head to toe. The dignified footman, Alexei, came in.

"Have the carriage brought up," Mrs. Stavrogin ordered. "And you, Alexei, take Miss Lebyatkin home. She will direct you."

"Mr. Lebyatkin has been waiting downstairs for her for some time, ma'am, and he has asked me to announce him."

"That's impossible, Aunt Varvara!" Maurice said worriedly. Till then he hadn't said a word. "If I may say so, he's not a man whom one can receive. He is—he is . . . impossible."

"Tell him to wait," Mrs. Stavrogin said to Alexei, who then left the room.

"C'est un homme malhonnête et je crois même que c'est un forçat évadé ou quelque chose dans ce genre," Mr. Verkhovensky muttered again, turned red, and broke off.

"It's time we were going, Liza!" Mrs. Drozdov said with distaste. She rose, ready to leave. She now seemed to regret calling herself a fool in her recent fright. As she listened to Dasha, a haughty twist had appeared on her lips.

But what had struck me most since Dasha's arrival was Liza's face: her eyes now sparkled with unrestrained scorn and hatred.

"Wait a few more minutes, Praskovia, please," Mrs. Stavrogin said, stopping her with the same unnatural calm. "Do me a favor and sit down, for I would like to finish saying what I have to say and I know your legs ache. A while ago I lost my temper and said some unwarranted things to you. So, please, forgive me. I did a stupid thing and am the first to admit it now, for I believe in being fair. Of course, when you lost your temper, you mentioned some anonymous letters—but any anonymous message should be treated with contempt if only because it is unsigned. If you look at the matter differently, I don't envy you. In any case, I wouldn't have brought it up in your place; I wouldn't want to dirty my hands with it. However, you have dirtied yours and since you have brought up the subject, let me tell you that, six days ago, I also received a clownish anonymous letter. Some low character wrote that Nikolai has gone mad and that I must beware of some lame woman who, as the letter puts it—I remember it well—'will play a fatal part' in my life. Knowing that my son has many enemies around here, I sent for a man whom I knew to be a secret enemy of his—perhaps the most spiteful and despicable of them all—and after a talk with him, I was sure of the origin of those loathsome anonymous letters. Now, my poor Praskovia, if you have also been bothered, *through my fault*, by such despicable notes; if you have been 'peppered' with them, as you say—I am, of course, terribly sorry to have been the innocent cause of it. That's what I wished to explain to you. And now, I'm sorry to see that you're so tired out. Anyway, I have decided to *let in* that man whom Maurice says cannot be *received*, a word that doesn't really apply in this case. And I think that, for Liza especially, this will not be the proper place to be. Come here, Liza, let me kiss you once more."

Liza crossed the room and stood silently in front of Mrs. Stavrogin, who took her by the hands, kissed her, held her at a little distance from her, looked at her, made the sign of the cross over her, then pulled her back to her and kissed her again.

"Well, good-by, Liza," Mrs. Stavrogin said, and she sounded on the verge of tears, "and believe me, I'll always love you, whatever happens. God bless you! I have almost submitted gladly to His divine will."

She was on the point of saying something more, but she contained herself. Liza walked back toward the chair in which she had been sitting, still silent and deep in thought. Suddenly she stopped before her mother.

"I'm not going home yet, Mother. I'll stay a while longer

with Aunt Varvara," she said quietly, but with determination.

"Good gracious, what is this!" Praskovia wailed, helplessly wringing her hands.

But Liza didn't answer. She didn't seem to hear her. She simply resumed her seat and sat there staring somewhere into space again.

A proud, triumphant expression appeared on Mrs. Stavrogin's face.

"Maurice, I must ask you to do me a favor—go downstairs and have a look at that man and, if it's at all possible *to let him in,* bring him here."

Maurice bowed and went out. A minute later he returned with Lebyatkin.

IV

I have mentioned what Lebyatkin looked like: a tall, heavy, curly-haired fellow of about forty, with a ruddy, bloated face; cheeks that quivered with every movement of his head; small, beady, bloodshot eyes that sometimes had a sly look in them; side whiskers and mustache; and a rather too prominent, unpleasant-looking Adam's apple. But, oddly enough, that day he was wearing a frock coat and a clean shirt. It reminded me of one of Liputin's quips: "There are people on whom a clean shirt looks positively indecent."

The captain wore black gloves—that is, he held the right glove in his fleshy left hand, which was halfway encased in the unbuttoned left glove. In the same hand he also held a glossy top hat that, I'm sure, he was wearing for the first time. So the "lover's frock coat" about which he had shouted outside Shatov's door really did exist. Later I found out that both the frock coat and the shirt had been previously acquired on Liputin's advice. And there was little doubt that he had also driven up in a horse cab upon someone else's prompting and with someone else's help, for it would never have occurred to him to come here. Then too, he had to dress and get ready in some forty-five minutes, even assuming that he had found out about the scene at the cathedral at once. He wasn't drunk now, but he was in a state of hazy stupor typical of a man who has come to after days of heavy drinking. He looked as though, if someone had taken him by the shoulders and given him a couple of good shakes, he'd have become drunk again.

He entered the room quickly and tripped over the rug, which made Maria roll with laughter. He threw her a fierce look, turned briskly toward Mrs. Stavrogin, and took a few quick steps toward her.

"I have come here, ma'am—" he blared, as if talking into a megaphone.

"Please, my dear sir," Mrs. Stavrogin said, sitting up very erect, "sit down over there—that chair there, you see? I'm sure I will be able to hear you from there and, at the same time, I will be able to see you much better."

The captain stopped and stared blankly in front of him; then he obediently sat down on the chair by the door, to which Mrs. Stavrogin had pointed. His face expressed a mixture of hesitation, arrogance, and chronic resentment. It was obvious that he was frightened and that it was precisely his fear that offended his pride and made him resentful and capable of insolence. He was painfully aware of every movement of his big body and, as is usually the case under such circumstances, his main problem was his hands—he felt at every moment the futility of trying to find an appropriate place for them. At last he froze in his chair, clutching his hat and gloves, and fixed his blank stare on Mrs. Stavrogin's stern face. He may have wanted to look around the room, but thus far he hadn't dared. Maria probably found his awkward posture irresistibly funny and burst out laughing again, but he didn't budge. Meanwhile, Mrs. Stavrogin examined him mercilessly for a full minute.

"First of all, I would like you to tell me your name yourself," she said in measured, impressive tones.

"Captain Lebyatkin," he blared. "I've come, ma'am—" He started to rise, but she stopped him with a gesture.

"Wait! Is this poor person who has aroused my interest really your sister?"

"Yes, ma'am, she's my sister and she has slipped away from my supervision because she's in a condition . . ." He faltered and turned purple. "Please don't get me wrong, ma'am." He was becoming inextricably entangled. "A brother won't slander his sister. When I mentioned her condition, I didn't mean in the sense that it stained her reputation. . . . I wanted to say that lately—" He abruptly fell silent.

"Please, sir!" Mrs. Stavrogin said, throwing back her head.

"I mean that sort of condition!" he concluded, placing his index finger on his temple.

There was a brief pause.

"And has she suffered from it for long?" Mrs. Stavrogin asked in a drawling tone.

"I've come, ma'am, to thank you for the kindness you displayed toward her at the cathedral, to thank you in a brotherly, Russian way—"

"Brotherly!"

"Well, only in the sense that I am my sister's brother, ma'am, and also I would like to assure you," he went purple again and spoke faster, "that I'm not really as uncouth as I may look to you at first glance, in your drawing room. My sister and me—we're nothing, ma'am, compared to the luxury in which you live and which we see here. But I am a Lebyatkin, ma'am, and I'm proud of my reputation, so I've come to thank you and—and here's the money, ma'am!"

He brought out his wallet, pulled a wad of bills out of it, and started counting them with wild impatience. His fingers trembled. He was obviously very anxious to explain something, and indeed, an explanation was urgently needed. Finally, feeling that counting the bills like that was making him look foolish, he lost all control of his fingers: the bills stuck together, his fingers became all entangled, and to top everything, one green bill escaped and, zigzagging slowly, floated down to the carpet.

"Twenty rubles, ma'am!"

Lebyatkin leaped to his feet, holding up the bundle of bills, his face streaming with sweat in his agony. Then he caught sight of the bill on the floor, bent to pick it up, but felt that that would be too undignified, and shrugged.

"That's for your servants, ma'am, for your footman—for him to remember Miss Lebyatkin by."

"I can't allow that," Mrs. Stavrogin said hurriedly, with audible apprehension.

"In that case—"

He bent again and picked up the bill, turning purple. Then he crossed the room to Mrs. Stavrogin and held out the money to her.

"What is this?" she said, quite frightened now, and jerked back in her chair. Mr. Verkhovensky and Maurice took a step in her direction.

"Don't worry, don't worry—I'm not mad. I'm all right," Captain Lebyatkin tried eagerly to reassure everybody.

"I don't agree, my good sir; I think you're out of your mind."

"But, ma'am, I'm not at all what you think! Of course, I'm nothing but an insignificant cog. . . . Oh, madam, you live in palaces that are richly furnished, but the dwelling of my sister, Maria the Nameless, née Lebyatkin, is poor and miserable. We'll call her nameless, by the way, only *for the time being,* for God Himself won't allow her to remain that way forever! You gave her ten rubles, ma'am, and she took them, but she accepted them only because they were from you, ma'am, and I hope you appreciate that! Maria the Nameless would not have accepted money from anyone else, for that would have made her grandfather turn in his grave. He was a fighting officer killed on the field of honor in the Caucasus before the eyes of Yermilov himself. But from you, ma'am, she'd accept anything. However, each time she takes ten rubles with one hand, she'll hand you twenty with the other as a gift for one of your ladies' philanthropic committees in Moscow. For I know you yourself announced, ma'am, in the *Moscow News,* that you were conducting a local fund-raising drive and that anyone might contribute. . . ."

He suddenly ran out of breath. He had been breathing very hard as though performing some difficult athletic feat. What he had said about the philanthropic committee must've been prepared, probably also with Liputin's coaching. He was perspiring heavily and huge drops of sweat were visible on his temples. Mrs. Stavrogin glared at him piercingly.

"The subscription list is always available downstairs. It is with the hall porter and you can enter your subscription there if you wish to," she said sternly. "So I would appreciate it very much if, for the time being, you would stop waving your money around and put it in your pocket. That's better. Now, I'm very sorry, sir, that I made such a mistake about your sister and offered her charity as though she were a pauper when she's really so rich. However, there's still one thing that remains quite unclear to me: why should she accept charity from me alone, and never from anyone else? You insisted so on that point that I would like you to explain it to me precisely."

"That, ma'am, is a secret that will go to the grave—"

"But why?" Mrs. Stavrogin insisted, a little less firmly now.

"Ah, madam, madam! . . ."

He became grimly silent, placing his right hand on his heart. Mrs. Stavrogin waited, her eyes fixed on him.

"Madam," he roared suddenly, "please, madam, allow me to ask you one question—one single question, but let me ask it frankly, in the open, Russian way."

"By all means."

"Have you suffered in your life, ma'am?"

"Are you trying to tell me that you have suffered or are suffering through someone else's fault?"

"Here, ma'am, here!" he shouted, jumping up, probably without realizing it himself, and pounding his chest. "Here, in my heart, there has accumulated so much, so much bitterness that God Himself will be amazed when it all comes out on Judgment Day!"

"Hm, rather strongly put."

"Madam, if my language is full of resentment—"

"Please don't worry about that; I'll stop you if need be."

"May I ask another question, ma'am?"

"Go ahead, ask me another question."

"Can one die of excessive nobility of the soul alone?"

"I wouldn't know. I've never studied the matter."

"What! You say you never have?" he shouted with theatrical irony. "Well then, since it's like that,

Be still, oh heart bereft of hope!"

And he again pounded his chest extravagantly.

He started to pace the room. A common characteristic of people of this sort is their complete inability to keep their desires to themselves; on the contrary, they feel an irresistible urge to display them in all their messiness, as soon as they spring up in them. In polite society, such a person will always start timidly, but if you yield him a hair's width, he is sure to leap to the utmost insolence. Now Lebyatkin was excited. He walked up and down the room, waving his arms, paying no attention to the questions he was asked, chattering something about himself so fast that now and then he seemed to trip over his own tongue, and would abandon an unfinished sentence and skip to another one. True, he was probably not completely sober, for despite his much-publicized infatuation for Liza, he hadn't once looked at her, although she was sitting right there. But then, this is only an assumption on my part. Anyway, whether he was drunk or not, Mrs. Stavrogin

must have had a good reason for containing her repugnance
for such a character and listening to him. As to Mrs. Drozdov,
she trembled in terror, although I don't believe she understood
what was behind it all. Mr. Verkhovensky was trembling too,
but for the opposite reason: as usual, he was inclined to read
more into the situation than was actually there. Maurice stood
in the attitude of one who is ready to rush to protect anyone
who might require protection. Liza, who was very pale, stared
at the wild man with wide-open eyes. Shatov sat unbudging, in
his original position. But the strangest change had come over
Maria: she had not only stopped laughing but now looked
infinitely sad. She leaned her right arm on the table and
followed her orating brother with a long, sad gaze. Dasha
alone looked calm and composed.

"Stop talking in these absurd allegories," Mrs. Stavrogin
said at last, interrupting him angrily. "And you still haven't
answered my question, 'Why?' I'm waiting for your answer."

"I haven't answered that 'Why'? You're waiting for me to
tell you 'why'?" Lebyatkin said, winking. "But, ma'am, that
little word 'why' has been spilled all over the world since the
day of its creation; nature shouts it every minute at her
Creator and still hasn't received an answer after seven thousand years. So, do you really think, ma'am, that it would be
fair for Captain Lebyatkin alone to be made to answer that
question?"

"That's a lot of nonsense and has nothing to do with what
I asked!" Mrs. Stavrogin said, beginning to lose patience.
"That's some sort of allegory. I think, my good man, that you
are allowing yourself to use language that is altogether too
flowery—and I consider that impertinent."

"Madam," Lebyatkin went on, without paying any attention
to what she had said, "take me, for instance: I might possibly
have preferred to be christened Ernst, but in real life I must
answer to the vulgar name of Ignat. Maybe I would have
preferred to be called Prince de Montbart, yet I'm nothing
but Lebyatkin. That comes from the word *lebyad*—swan. Now
why is that? Well, ma'am, in my opinion—Russia is nothing
but a freak!"

"Is that the most specific thing you can say?"

"Oh no, I could recite you a poem called 'The Cockroach,'
ma'am—"

"What's that!"

"I'm not crazy yet, ma'am. I'm sure to go crazy one day

—absolutely sure—but not yet. Let me tell you, ma'am, that a friend of mine, one of the most distinguished people I've ever known, wrote a fable by Krylov called 'The Cockroach.' Now, may I recite it?"

"You want to recite one of Krylov's fables?"

"No, not Krylov's, my own fable—a fable of my own, personal composition! I want you to realize, ma'am, that I'm not so perverted and ignorant that I don't realize that our minister of education has unveiled a monument to him in the Summer Garden, that is designed mainly for recreation for people going through that period of life known as childhood. And, ma'am, you will find that at the bottom of this fable lies the answer to your question 'Why' written in letters of flame!"

"Go on, recite your fable then."

"Here goes, ma'am:

> A member of the cockroach brood
> A cockroach otherwise quite wise,
> Toppled into a jar of food,
> One terribly crowded with flies—"

"My heavens, what is this?" Mrs. Stavrogin cried.

"What? Well, when in the summer," the captain rattled on with impatient irritation, waving his arms fiercely, like an author interrupted while reading his work, "too many flies get into a jar, there occur cases of fly-cannibalism—any fool can see that. So don't interrupt. You'll see." He waved his arms even more fiercely. "Just listen and you'll learn. . . . So,

> The roach took up a lot of room,
> Indignant flies began to zoom.
> 'He's squashing us,' they cried aggrieved,
> 'Oh Jupiter!' They sighed and heaved.
>
> And as they cried thus in their rage
> Along comes Nikifor, the sage . . .

I'm afraid that's as far as I've got," the captain spluttered. "But never mind, I'll finish it in my own words. So this Nikifor picks up the jar and empties the whole mess—flies and cockroach and all—into a trough, which should've been done long before. But please note, ma'am—and I wish to make this crystal clear—the cockroach didn't protest! And that's the answer to your 'Why'," he roared triumphantly. "The cockroach does not protest! As to Nikifor—well, he symbolizes nature," he added hastily, pacing rapidly up and down the drawing room.

Mrs. Stavrogin became very angry.

"And what about the sum of money my son sent you and your claim that a part of it has been misappropriated by a member of my household?"

"Slander!" roared Lebyatkin, dramatically raising his right hand. "I never said so."

"No, it's not slander."

"Circumstances, ma'am, sometimes force a man to choose family disgrace over admitting the truth publicly. No, ma'am —Lebyatkin will never talk!"

He seemed dazzled. He was exultant; he felt his importance. He must have been having visions. He wanted to offend someone, to grind someone into the dirt, to display his power.

"Please ring the bell, Stepan," Mrs. Stavrogin said.

"Lebyatkin is cunning, ma'am." The captain winked at her with a nasty smile. "He's cunning, but he also has a weakness and that weakness is the old bottle of the hussars so celebrated by Denis Davydov. And, when he succumbs to that weakness of his, he occasionally sends off a letter in verse—a beauty, it's true, but one that, nevertheless, he would buy back later at the price of lifelong tears, because it ruins the feeling of the sublime. But the bird has been let out and it's impossible to catch it by the tail now. Well, it's also possible that, yielding to this weakness of his, Lebyatkin may have said things about a respectable young lady in his noble indignation over the insults he has suffered . . . and slanderers took advantage of it. But Lebyatkin is cunning, ma'am, and the vicious wolf who keeps pouring wine into his glass, waiting for him to stumble, is wasting his time, for Lebyatkin will never talk. Instead of the answer he's waiting for at the bottom of the bottle, all he'll find will be Lebyatkin's cunning! But that's enough, ma'am! Let me tell you that your palaces and domains could have been owned by the most noble person alive, but the cockroach will never protest! I want you to note this and acknowledge his great spirit!"

At that moment, the bell rang downstairs in the hall and almost immediately afterward Alexei appeared, responding somewhat belatedly to Mr. Verkhovensky's ring. The dignified old servant was considerably perturbed.

"Mister Nikolai has just arrived, ma'am, and he is coming up here this minute," he said in answer to Mrs. Stavrogin's questioning glance.

I well remember her face at that moment: first she went pale, but in the next instant her eyes suddenly sparkled. She sat up straight in her chair with an air of supreme determination. Indeed, we were all startled. Stavrogin's unexpected arrival—we hadn't expected him for another month yet—struck us not only because it was unexpected but also because of the strangeness of the moment. Even Lebyatkin stopped in the center of the drawing room and stood there like a post, gaping openmouthed at the door.

Soon the sound of rapidly approaching footsteps came from the large adjoining room. They were light, very quick footsteps and sounded almost as if the person were rolling along. Abruptly, someone rushed into the drawing room. It wasn't Stavrogin, but a completely strange young man.

V

I'll take the liberty of stopping here to sketch this unexpected intruder. He was twenty-seven, a little above average height, with thinning hair that he wore rather long and a pale, hardly noticeable mustache and beard. He was dressed neatly, even fashionably, but with no attempt at elegance. At first glance he looked a little hunched and stiff, but he wasn't really hunched and was even loose-limbed. He seemed eccentric, but later we all found his manners good and his conversation always to the point.

No one could say that he was bad-looking, yet nobody liked his looks. His head was elongated in the back and seemed compressed at the sides, making his face rather pointed. His forehead was high and narrow and his other features small and fine: a sharp nose and long, thin lips. He wore an expression of suffering that was actually due to the deep folds that ran down his cheeks and the wrinkles on his cheekbones. They gave him the look of a man convalescing after some serious illness. Nevertheless, he was in excellent health and quite strong, and in fact had never been sick.

He moved and walked hurriedly, even when he wasn't pressed for time. Nothing seemed to embarrass him ever and he remained the same man whatever the circumstances. He was greatly pleased with himself without being in the least aware of it.

He also spoke rapidly and hurriedly, but with assurance and without having to search for the right word. His thoughts were calmly formulated despite his hurried enunciation, and they had something precise and final about them that was very striking indeed. His articulation was remarkably clear —words poured out of him like small, even grains, carefully selected and always ready to serve. At first, the effect of this was pleasing, but after a while one began to feel uncomfortable over his too-perfect articulation and his smooth flow of ever-ready words. One began to imagine that the tongue in his mouth had something special about it, that it was very long and thin, very red, and exceptionally pointed, with a constantly flickering tip.

So this was the young man who now tore into the drawing room. To this day, I have the impression that he started talking in the adjoining room and came in talking. In a flash he was standing before Mrs. Stavrogin and prattling away smoothly,

". . . Imagine, Mrs. Stavrogin, when I got here, I felt certain he'd have been here for at least fifteen minutes, because he arrived in town about an hour and a half ago. We met at Kirilov's. Half an hour ago he left to come here, asking me to follow him in fifteen minutes—"

"But whom are you talking about? Who asked you to come here?"

"But Nikolai, of course. Is it really possible that you didn't know of his arrival until this second? But surely his luggage must have arrived earlier and I can't imagine why they didn't inform you. So I'm the first to announce it to you then? We could, of course, send someone to find him, but I'm quite certain he'll arrive himself any moment now, timing his appearance in accordance with certain expectations and, as far as I can judge, certain strategic considerations." At this point he glanced around the room, singling out Lebyatkin for special examination. "Ah, Miss Tishin!" he exclaimed, catching sight of Liza, and he flew over to her and caught the hand she offered him with a pleased smile. "I'm so glad to meet you almost immediately upon my arrival, and if I'm not mistaken, Mrs. Drozdov has also recognized the man she called 'the Professor' and is not as angry with him now as she was so often in Switzerland. But tell me, how are your legs, Mrs. Drozdov, and was your Swiss consultant right in prescribing the climate of your native land for them? I beg your pardon? . . . Hot compresses? That must be very soothing. Mrs. Stavrogin," he said, whirling around again, "I was so sorry that I just missed you abroad and couldn't pay my respects to you personally, especially as I had so many things to tell you. I did write to my old man, but it looks as though he, as usual—"

"Peter!" Mr. Verkhovensky cried, recovering from his stupor. He threw up his arms and rushed toward his son. *"Pierre, mon enfant!* And to think I didn't recognize you!" He hugged him, tears rolling down his cheeks.

"Come, come, don't be so dramatic; that's enough, enough. . . ." Peter muttered hurriedly, trying to free himself from the paternal embrace.

"I've always, always been guilty before you!"

"All right, that'll do for now. We'll get back to that later. I knew you'd kick up a fuss. Come on, get hold of yourself now!"

"But I haven't seen you for ten years!"

"So much the less reason for such an emotional demonstration."

"Mon enfant!"

"All right, all right, I know now that you love me, so you can keep your hands to yourself. You're embarrassing the others. Ah, here comes Nikolai—please, stop it now!"

Nikolai Stavrogin was now in the room: he'd come up quietly and halted for a moment in the doorway, calmly surveying the gathering.

I was struck by his appearance, just as I had been when I saw him for the first time four years before. I certainly hadn't forgotten him in the least, but there are faces that reveal something new every time one sees them, even if it happens to be the hundredth time. He was still as elegant and distinguished-looking as he had been four years before, and almost as youthful. His light smile still radiated a superficial amiability and the same self-assurance, and his eyes were still just as stern, thoughtful, and as it were, absent-minded. Indeed, in a sense, I felt as though I'd left him only the day before. However, there was one striking change I found in him: while before, even though he could have been described as strikingly handsome, his face had seemed somewhat like a mask (as some of our sharp-tongued ladies had put it); now, there could be no two opinions about his being incredibly handsome. But I can't say whether it was because he was rather paler and thinner or because some new thoughts were reflected in his look.

"Nikolai!" Mrs. Stavrogin cried, straightening her back, but not getting up from her armchair. "Stand still where you are for a second!" She stopped him with an imperious gesture.

But now, to account for the shocking question that followed her gesture—of which I never would have thought her capable—I must remind the reader what kind of a character Mrs. Stavrogin had always had and how extremely impulsive she was during moments of crisis. One must also take into consideration the fact that, despite her considerable strength of will, her quite adequate reasoning power, her common sense and business acumen, there were moments when she could act with complete abandon and, if I may say so, with a complete lack of restraint. One must also remember that the moment described here was one in which, as if by magic, the whole essence of her past and present life—and, perhaps, her future as well—was concentrated. I would also like to call attention to the anonymous letter that she had mentioned earlier to Mrs. Drozdov, which had obviously irritated her so much. She hadn't revealed the contents of this letter, but it may have contained the reason for her asking her son that terrible question:

"Tell me, Nikolai," she said, forming her words in a clear voice full of challenging, menacing overtones, "is it true that this poor, lame woman is your legal wife? Answer me before you move from the spot where you are standing now."

I remember that moment very clearly. He didn't bat an eye; he just looked closely at his mother. There wasn't the slightest change in his expression. Then he smiled slowly with a sort of condescending patience and, without answering, walked over to his mother's chair, took her hand, raised it to his lips, and kissed it. She didn't try to pull her hand away, for he affected her as irresistibly as ever; she simply kept staring at him. Her whole being turned into a question; everything about her seemed to say that, in another minute or so, she would collapse under this uncertainty.

But he remained silent. Having kissed his mother's hand,

he looked around the room once more and then unhurriedly crossed over to Maria. It is extremely difficult to describe people's faces at certain moments. I do remember, for instance, that Maria, half dead with fear, rose and stepped toward him with her hands clasped as if in prayer; but, at the same time, I remember the exaltation in her eyes—a mad, wild rapture that almost distorted her features out of all recognition. Rapture is a very difficult feeling to bear. Perhaps both fear and rapture were combined in her—anyway, I remember that I stepped hurriedly toward her, thinking that she was about to faint.

"You shouldn't have come here," Stavrogin said in a gentle, melodious voice, an extraordinary tenderness shining in his eyes. His tone and his every gesture denoted sincere, profound respect for her. The poor thing whispered to him breathlessly:

"And may I—now—may I kneel before you?"

"No, that's really out of the question," he said with such a dazzling smile that she also let out a happy little laugh. Then, speaking in the same melodious voice, he tried to persuade her as one persuades a child. He said:

"Remember, you are a young lady and, although I am a devoted friend, I'm still an outsider, being neither your husband nor your father nor your fiancé. So give me your arm and let's go. I will see you to the carriage and, if you'll allow me, I'll take you all the way home."

She listened to him attentively with lowered head.

"Let's go then," she said, sighing and giving him her arm.

But here, she had a minor accident. She must've turned a little carelessly or stepped on her weak, short leg, for she fell sideways against an armchair and, if it hadn't been there, she would have found herself stretched on the floor. Nikolai quickly caught her and, supporting her firmly, led her to the door. She was obviously very upset over her fall. She turned very red and looked embarrassed and ashamed. She kept her eyes on the ground and, limping heavily after Nikolai—almost hanging on his arm—she left the room without uttering a word. As they left, I saw that Liza had jumped up from her chair and was staring at them fixedly. She didn't take her eyes off them until they reached the door. Then she silently resumed her seat, but her face continued to twitch spasmodically as though she had touched some slimy creature.

During the scene between Nikolai Stavrogin and Maria Lebyatkin, we were all so silent that we could have heard a fly buzzing. But, as soon as they left, the silence was abruptly broken.

VI

Actually they exclaimed rather than talked. My recollection of the sequence of events is not too clear because of the general confusion. Stepan Verkhovensky exclaimed something in French and raised his hands to heaven, but Mrs. Stavrogin was too preoccupied with other things to pay much attention to him. Even Maurice haltingly muttered some comment. But the most excited of the lot was Peter Verkhovensky, who was trying heatedly to convince Mrs. Stavrogin of something, accompanying his arguments with wide, sweeping gestures. For some time I couldn't understand what he was saying. He kept rushing about the room, addressing himself to Mrs. Drozdov and Liza, and in his excitement, even shouting a few words at his father. Mrs. Stavrogin, her face flushed, stood up and shouted at Mrs. Drozdov:

"Did you hear? Did you hear what he told her?"

But Mrs. Drozdov couldn't answer her—she could only mutter something and shake her head. The poor woman had her own worries—Liza—and there was panic in her eyes as she looked at her daughter. And she didn't dare think of getting up to go home, as long as Liza didn't stand up and say she was ready to leave. Captain Lebyatkin, however, was mostly thinking of getting out of there. I had noticed that. He had been in a state of visible terror ever since Stavrogin had made his appearance. But Peter Verkhovensky had grabbed him by the arm and wouldn't let him go.

"It's indispensable—it's absolutely indispensable," he repeated, rattling off his smooth strings of words at Mrs. Stavrogin, trying to convince her of something. He was standing in front of her. She had resumed her seat and, I remember well, was listening to him with great eagerness now that he had finally managed to catch her attention. "It's indispensable," he was saying. "You must realize yourself, Mrs. Stavrogin, that there's a misunderstanding here. It may all look very queer, but it's really as obvious as a lighted candle and no more complicated than this finger of mine. Now, I know that no one has asked me to explain and that perhaps I look ridiculous, insisting on it. . . . But, in the first place, Nikolai attaches no significance to the business and, in the second, it's always difficult for a man to explain this sort of thing himself, so it's better left to a third person. Please believe me, Mrs. Stavrogin, Nikolai shouldn't be blamed in the least for not immediately answering your question directly, although he could have easily enough. I've known him since Petersburg. Besides, I should say that the whole incident, if anything, redounds to Nikolai's honor, if we must use that vague word 'honor' at all—"

"Are you trying to say that you witnessed some sort of incident that has resulted in this . . . this misunderstanding?"

"Yes, I was a witness and a participant," Peter said quickly.

"If you can assure me that it won't offend Nikolai's feelings—for I want you to know, he never, never conceals anything from me—and if you are certain that he would approve—"

"There's no doubt about it—he would approve. And that is why I consider it a great pleasure and privilege to tell you; I'm certain he would have asked me to do so himself."

It struck me as rather strange, this insistence on explaining other people's affairs by a man who'd appeared out of the blue. But he had caught Mrs. Stavrogin on his line and his hook had entered her most vulnerable spot. At that time, I still knew very little about the man or his schemes.

"I'm listening," Mrs. Stavrogin said with diffidence and reserve, painfully aware that she was indulging her curiosity.

"It's a short story—hardly a story at all, in fact," the smooth flow began, "although some author who had nothing better to do could blow it up into a whole novel. There's a rather curious twist to it. Mrs. Drozdov, and I'm certain Miss Tishin, will be interested in it, for there are a few features in it that, while they may not be really extraordinary, are certainly curious. Well, about five years ago, Nikolai Stavrogin met Lebyatkin—this very gentleman standing here openmouthed and, I believe, planning to make himself scarce at the first opportunity. Forgive me, Mrs. Stavrogin. . . . You! Mister-retired-supply-clerk—you see I remember you quite well —I wouldn't advise you to try to escape now! Both Nikolai and I are well aware of your activities here, for which you will have to account to us. Anyway, at that time, Nikolai called this man his Falstaff"—Peter decided an explanation was necessary here—"some ancient, grotesque character at whom everyone laughs and who accepts his position as long as he's given money. At that time, Nikolai was leading what I would describe as a *sarcastic* life in Petersburg—I can't find a better word for it, because he's incapable of utter despair and wasn't then pursuing any specific aims. This applies only to that particular period, Mrs. Stavrogin.

"Now, this Lebyatkin had a sister—the woman who was in this room just now—and they didn't have a corner of their own; they took shelter with anyone who would put them up. Lebyatkin hung around the shopping centers, always wearing an old uniform, stopped the better-dressed passers-by, and drank whatever they gave him. His sister subsisted like a little bird, mostly on fresh air. She helped to clean the tenement apartments where they spent their nights and sometimes received a few kopecks for her trouble. It was a sordid slum life and I'll skip the details. Nikolai had elected to live like that at that time out of sheer eccentricity. Again, Mrs. Stavrogin, I refer only to one particular period of his life and I've borrowed the word 'eccentricity' from Nikolai himself. He doesn't have many secrets from me. Miss Lebyatkin, who met Nikolai on various occasions, was struck by his looks. He was, so to speak, like a diamond against the grimy background of her life. I'm rather poor at describing human emotions, so I'll skip that and just say that she soon became an object of ridicule to nasty, petty people and grew very depressed. They'd always laughed at her there, but she'd never paid any attention to it previously. Even then she was a little touched, but not so much as now. There's reason to believe that when she was a little girl she acquired some sort of an education thanks to some benefactress. Nikolai never paid any attention to her; he spent most of his time with petty clerks, playing cards with a greasy pack, at a quarter of a kopeck a chip. But once a clerk was bullying her and Nikolai, without saying a word, grabbed him by the scruff of the neck and tossed him out of the second-floor window. There was no knightly indignation— the whole operation took place amid wild laughter and Nikolai laughed the most. And when it all ended without too much damage, they made it up and sat drinking punch together. But the oppressed, innocent victim didn't forget, and it resulted in her losing whatever scrap of sanity she had left.

"I repeat—I'm poor at describing feelings, but the main thing here is her dream, and Nikolai fed that dream of hers as though on purpose. Instead of laughing at her, he began treating Miss Lebyatkin with great respect and consideration. Kirilov, who was present once—he's a strange bird, that one, Mrs. Stavrogin, and an extremely outspoken man; he's here now and you may meet him someday—well, Kirilov, who usually doesn't say much, suddenly grew indignant and blurted out to Nikolai that he was ruining her completely by treating her like a countess. Well, Nikolai, who thought quite well of Kirilov, told him: 'Do you think I'm just making fun of her? No, reassure yourself, I really have great respect for her, because she's worth any of you.' And, you know, he said that in a very grave tone, although in twenty-three months he hadn't said much more than 'good evening' and 'good-by' to her. I was there and I remember that she ended by believing that she was sort of engaged to him and that the only reason he didn't elope with her was that he had too many enemies, that there'd be opposition from his family, and so on. It all ended when Nikolai had to go home. Before leaving, he arranged to pay her an allowance, a rather handsome one—three hundred rubles or more a year. So let's assume that, on his part, it was nothing but fooling, the whim of a man prematurely tired or even, as Kirilov puts it, the search for new sensations by an oversatiated man who tried to find out to what state he could reduce a poor cripple. 'You've deliberately picked on the most miserable wreck,' Kirilov said, 'scarred forever by beatings and abuse, and fully aware that the creature was dying of a laughable love for you, you've turned its wretched head completely, just to see what would come of it.'

"But how can a man be held particularly responsible for the delusions of a poor mad creature to whom he has hardly ever spoken more than a few words? Some things, Mrs. Stavrogin, are very difficult to discuss intelligently; in fact, they cannot be intelligently discussed at all. All right, let's assume that he acted eccentrically. So? That, then, is the worst that can be said. But still, people have managed to make a whole fuss about it. I happen to know, to some extent, what has been going on here."

He suddenly interrupted his narrative and was about to turn toward Lebyatkin when Mrs. Stavrogin stopped him with a gesture. She was in a state of extreme exaltation.

"Have you finished?" she asked him.

"Not quite. To give you a full picture, I would like, with your permission, to ask this gentleman a few questions. You will get a good idea of the whole situation, Mrs. Stavrogin."

"Wait—later, please. . . . Oh, I'm so glad that I listened to what you had to say!"

"And now you can see, Mrs. Stavrogin," Peter quickly added, "how difficult it would have been for Nikolai to convey all this to you in answer to your question, which was perhaps a bit too specific."

"Yes, much too specific."

"And don't you agree now that I had a point when I said that a third person could better explain that sort of thing than the person directly involved?"

"Yes, yes, certainly. However, you were wrong about one thing, and you're still wrong."

"Really? What's that?"

"The thing is . . . But why don't you sit down, Peter?"

"Oh, thank you. As a matter of fact, I do feel rather tired."

He quickly pulled a chair forward, turning it so as to have Mrs. Stavrogin on one side of him, Mrs. Drozdov on the other, and Lebyatkin, whom he kept watching, in front of him.

"Well, you were wrong in describing it as 'eccentricity.' "

"Ah, if that's the only—"

"No, no—wait," Mrs. Stavrogin stopped him. She appeared ready to launch upon a long and enthusiastic speech, and when Peter realized this he became all attention.

"No, it was something much nobler than mere eccentricity. I would even go so far as to call it saintliness! Here was a proud man who had been wounded early in life and had slipped into that phase you described so subtly as 'sarcastic.' . . . Well, he's really a Prince Hal, as your father once pointed out with such perspicacity. . . . That is, he would be just like Prince Hal if he weren't even more like Hamlet—at least that's my opinion."

"*Et vous avez raison!*" Stepan Verkhovensky agreed with feeling.

"Thank you, Stepan. I wish to thank you particularly for your unwavering faith in Nikolai and in his nobility and in the great things he will accomplish. Indeed, you have even sustained my faith in my moments of weakness."

"*Chère, chère . . .*" Mr. Verkhovensky took a step forward, but stopped abruptly. He must have realized that it might be unwise to interrupt her.

"And had my Nikolai always had near him," Mrs. Stavrogin went on in a tone almost of incantation, "a quiet Horatio, great in his humility—another beautiful phrase of yours, Stepan—he would perhaps long ago have escaped the sad, sudden demon of irony—another amazing expression of yours, Stepan—who has driven him to commit such strange acts during his life. But Nikolai never had either a Horatio or an Ophelia. All he had was a mother, and what can a mother do by herself under such circumstances? And you know, Peter, I believe I see now how a man like Nikolai could be attracted to slums, to the lower depths you have described. I can see so clearly now his 'sarcastic' attitude toward life (as you so aptly called it), his unquenchable thirst for contrasts, the grim, grimy background against which he stood out as a gleaming diamond—again, to use your comparison, Peter. And then he meets that downtrodden creature there, that cripple, that half-mad woman who, at the same time, perhaps has the most noble feelings. . . ."

"Hm, yes, that's possible."

"And, after all that, how can you fail to understand his refusal to join the others in making fun of her? Ah, you people! You can't see that by treating her 'like a countess' he is protecting her from bullies. (That Kirilov of yours, who seems to understand people so well—even he failed to understand Nikolai!) We may even say that it was precisely the fact that he stood out so that caused all the trouble: if the poor creature had lived in another environment, she wouldn't have woven such a mad dream. Only another woman can understand that, Peter, and it's a shame that you aren't—no, I don't mean it's a shame you aren't a woman, but I wish you were one for this once so you could understand!"

"You mean that the worse her circumstances, the better he would seem? I can certainly see that, Mrs. Stavrogin. It works a bit like religion: the worse off a man is, the more downtrodden, the poorer—the more stubbornly he clings to the idea that it will all be made up to him in paradise, especially with a hundred thousand priests busily working on his salvation, bolstering his beliefs, and making their living out of it. I'm sure I understand what you have in mind, Mrs. Stavrogin, rest assured."

"Well, that's not really exactly what I meant, but can you really contend that in order to kill this dream in that miserable organism"—I cannot explain why Mrs. Stavrogin used the word "organism"—"Nikolai should have started mocking and bullying her like those clerks? Do you really discount his great compassion, the exalted tremor that shook his entire being when he sternly answered Kirilov's reproaches: 'I am not making fun of her'? It is a noble, a saintly answer!"

"*Sublime*," Stepan Verkhovensky muttered.

"And I would like you to bear in mind that he's not so rich. What there is belongs to me and, at that time, he was taking practically nothing from me."

"I'm well aware of that—well aware, Mrs. Stavrogin," Peter said, moving impatiently in his chair.

"Oh, he has my character! I recognize myself in Nikolai. And I must make allowances for his youth, his impulsiveness. . . . And if we get to know each other more closely, Peter—and I sincerely hope we will, since I'm already so indebted to you—you may then be able to appreciate—"

"Yes, yes, believe me, I hope so too," Peter muttered rather abruptly.

"Then you may understand the impulse that in blind exaltation may be extended to a person unworthy of you in every respect, a person who cannot possibly understand you and who will make you suffer at every opportunity. . . . But despite all that, you still turn him into some sort of ideal, into your dream; you concentrate all your hopes on him and worship him all your life without knowing why. . . . Maybe it's just because he's unworthy of you. . . . Ah, I have suffered so much in the course of my life, Peter!"

Stepan Verkhovensky, with an expression of pain on his face, tried to catch my eye, but I managed to dodge his look.

". . . And not so long ago . . . Oh, how guilty I am toward Nikolai! But you wouldn't believe how much I have suffered from people—friends and enemies, and perhaps friends more than enemies. . . . When I received the first anonymous letter, Peter, you won't believe me, but I couldn't dismiss it with contempt! And now, I can't forgive myself for my weakness!"

"I've already heard a lot about those anonymous letters, and I'll trace them for you, rest assured," Peter said, coming to life.

"But you can't imagine all the intrigues that have been going on here! They've even started pestering poor Mrs. Drozdov! Now, what reason could they have for attacking her? Perhaps I was a bit hard on you today, dear Praskovia," she added, addressing Mrs. Drozdov in a generous gesture, but with a certain triumphant irony in her tone.

"Oh, forget it," Mrs. Drozdov said reluctantly. "I feel we should close the subject now—too much has been said as it is."

She gave Liza a timid look, but Liza's eyes were fixed on Peter.

"As to this poor girl who has lost everything except her heart, well, I intend to adopt her myself," Mrs. Stavrogin announced unexpectedly. "I consider it my sacred duty. From today on, I'm taking her under my protection."

"And, in a way, that would be a very good thing!" Peter declared, growing very alert. "Forgive me, but I haven't finished what I had to say. It's precisely protection that I had in mind. Can you imagine, Mrs. Stavrogin—as soon as Nikolai left (I'm picking up from the point where I left off), Lebyatkin here decided that it was his undisputed right to dispose of his sister's allowance in whatever way he thought fit, and he did indeed dispose of it. Now I don't know exactly what he did, but when Nikolai, who was abroad at the time, was informed of what was going on, he changed the arrangements. Again, I don't know any of the details—he will tell you himself—but I do know that the interested party was placed in some convent, where she was quite comfortable and under friendly supervision. See what I mean? But what do you think this Lebyatkin decides then? First he made frantic efforts to discover where his source of income—that is, his sister—was hidden. (He succeeded only quite recently.) Then he demanded her release from the convent, establishing some sort of a legal right to obtain it, and brought her straight here. Here, he doesn't feed her, beats her, bullies her, obtains a substantial sum from Nikolai through devious maneuvering, and immediately goes on a drunken binge. Then, instead of being grateful for this windfall, he arrogantly demands more money and threatens to bring Nikolai to court if, in the future, his sister's pension is not paid directly into his hands. Thus, he mistakes voluntary assistance for enforced payment. Can you imagine anything like it? Tell me, Mr. Lebyatkin, is *everything* I've just said correct or not?"

The captain, who had been silent until then, turned purple and took a couple of steps forward.

"You have treated me cruelly, sir," he said in one breath.

"Why cruelly? But wait—we can discuss cruelty and gentleness later; now, I would very much appreciate it if you'd answer my question: is *everything* I have said true or not? If there's something in it that isn't true in your opinion, you should point it out immediately."

Lebyatkin hesitated. This obviously annoyed Peter Verkhovensky; his face twitched with fury.

"Well, if you would like to make some correction," he said, giving Lebyatkin a meaningful glance, "go ahead. Don't keep us waiting."

"But you know very well, Mr. Verkhovensky, that I can do nothing of the sort."

"No, I don't know it. In fact, this is the first time I've heard that. Explain then. Why can't you say anything?"

Lebyatkin looked dumbly at the ground.

"Let me leave, Mr. Verkhovensky," he said firmly.

"Not before you have answered my first question: is *everything* I've said true or not?"

"It's true," Lebyatkin muttered in a wooden voice, raising his eyes to his tormentor. Big beads of perspiration had appeared on his temples.

"Is *everything* true?"

"Everything, sir."

"Now, do you wish to add anything? Perhaps you feel that we have been unfair to you—then say so, protest, make your dissatisfaction public."

"No, I have nothing to add."

"Have you or have you not recently made threats against Mr. Stavrogin?"

"It was—it was mostly due to liquor, sir." He raised his head. "Mr. Verkhovensky! If a man's family honor is lost and he himself is disgraced without having merited it, do you really feel that he's to blame?" he roared, suddenly forgetting himself as he had done earlier.

"But now, Mr. Lebyatkin, are you sober?" Peter Verkhovensky said, giving him a piercing look.

"Yes, I'm sober."

"In that case, what do you mean by family honor and unmerited disgrace?"

"I mean . . . I accused no one—I was just talking about myself. . . ." Lebyatkin mumbled, his resistance collapsing again.

"It sounded to me as if you'd resented what I said about you and your behavior. You are really too touchy, Mr. Lebyatkin, because I haven't said anything yet about your actual behavior. Perhaps I will come to it, but you must realize that I haven't said anything yet about your behavior in the *actual* sense."

Lebyatkin shuddered and stared wildly at Peter.

"I'm just coming back to my senses, sir."

"I see, and I woke you up?"

"Yes, you, Mr. Verkhovensky. For four years I've been asleep with a cloud hanging over me. Now, may I go, Mr. Verkhovensky?"

"Yes, you may go now, unless Mrs. Stavrogin would like to ask you herself. . . ."

But Mrs. Stavrogin just waved her hands: as far as she was concerned, he could leave.

Lebyatkin bowed, took a couple of steps toward the door, then suddenly stopped, put his hand on his heart, and seemed about to say something, but instead rushed away. In the doorway he almost butted into Nikolai Stavrogin, who stepped out of his way. The captain suddenly seemed to shrivel up and stood paralyzed, his eyes fixed on Nikolai's like a rabbit in front of a boa constrictor. Stavrogin waited for a moment, then pushing him slightly out of his way, entered the room.

VII

He looked calm and pleased. Perhaps something pleasant had happened to him of which we knew nothing as yet. But, whatever it was, he certainly seemed greatly pleased.

"Can you ever forgive me, Nikolai?" Mrs. Stavrogin asked him, unable to contain herself, as she rose to meet him.

But he just laughed.

"I see," he said in a light, good-humored tone, "you know everything now! And shall I tell you something? After I walked out of here, I said to myself that perhaps I should have told you some amusing little story instead of just leaving like that. But when I remembered that Peter had stayed behind, I knew I had nothing to worry about."

As he said that, he glanced cursorily around the drawing room.

"Peter has told us an old Petersburg story from the life of an eccentric," Mrs. Stavrogin chimed in elatedly, "of a wild and whimsical man whose behavior, however, was always noble and knightly—"

"Knightly? Would you really go as far as that?" Nikolai laughed. "But still, I'm very grateful to Peter and, in this instance, very appreciative of his eternal hastiness." At this point the eyes of the two men met for a split second. "But I think I should inform you, Mother, that Peter Verkhovensky is some sort of a universal peacemaker; peacemaking is his role, his forte, his disease, and I recommend him to you particularly in this capacity. I can guess what sort of things he's been rattling off here. His brain is a real filing cabinet, and when he tells something I always have the feeling that he is reading it off from his records. Note that, being a realist, he cannot lie since truth is more important to him than success—except for some rare instances when success is more important than truth." He was still looking around the room as he said this. "So you can see clearly, Mother, that I have nothing for which to forgive you, and if there's something mad about this whole affair it can be traced to me, which of course confirms my insanity. And we must, after all, keep up my local reputation."

And tenderly he put his arms around his mother.

"In any case it is now over and out in the open and we can let it rest," he added, a firm note in his voice. Mrs. Stavrogin caught that note, but her exaltation didn't evaporate; on the contrary, it increased.

"I didn't expect to see you for another month, Nikolai—"

"Of course, I'll explain to you what happened, but now I must . . ." and he crossed over toward Mrs. Drozdov.

But Mrs. Drozdov hardly bothered to turn her head toward him, despite the fact that she had appeared stunned when he had made his first appearance half an hour earlier. She now had other things to worry about: at the moment when Lebyatkin had stumbled into Nikolai in the doorway, Liza had begun to laugh—at first quietly and in spurts, but then more and more loudly, attracting more and more attention. Her face was flushed and the change from her earlier dejected state was very striking. While Stavrogin was talking to his mother, Liza twice beckoned to Maurice as if she wanted to whisper something in his ear, but when he bent toward her she exploded into loud laughter, and it was quite possible to imagine that she was laughing at poor Maurice. But to be fair, she seemed to be trying to control her laughter, pressing her handkerchief to her lips. Nikolai turned to greet her with the most innocent and disarming expression.

"You must excuse me," she said, speaking very rapidly. "You've met Maurice, of course. Ah, really, Maurice, how can one be so ridiculously tall!"

And she burst out laughing again. As for Maurice, he was certainly tall, but not at all ridiculously so.

"When did you arrive?" she mumbled, controlling another burst of laughter. She seemed a little ashamed of herself, but her eyes still flashed a wild, gay sparkle.

"A couple of hours ago, a bit more," Stavrogin said, looking at her closely. He was extremely courteous and polite to her, but it seemed to me that under this politeness he was rather indifferent, even bored.

"Where will you stay?"

"Right here."

Mrs. Stavrogin was watching Liza too and suddenly she stirred, went over to them, and asked her son:

"But where did you spend those two hours, Nikolai? The train comes in at ten, doesn't it?"

"I first dropped Peter off at Kirilov's, and as to Peter himself, I'd met him at Matveyevo—that's three stops before here. Then we traveled in the same car the rest of the way."

"I'd waited for Nikolai in Matveyevo since daybreak," Peter confirmed. "The rear cars of my train were derailed during the night. In fact, I almost broke both legs in the accident—"

"Broke both legs!" Liza cried. "Ah, Mother, and to think that last week we wanted to go to Matveyevo. Who knows, perhaps we would have broken our legs too."

"Good Lord!" Mrs. Drozdov crossed herself.

"But, Mother dear, please, you mustn't be too alarmed if I really break both my legs: it could happen to me any day. You say yourself that I ride too recklessly. Tell me, Maurice, will you help me to walk when I'm lame?" She began to laugh again. "If that happened, I'd never allow anyone but you to help me. You can count on that. All right, let's hope I break only one leg, but please say you'd consider it a lucky break for you."

"Why would it be lucky? To break a leg, lucky? . . ." Maurice frowned, seriously trying to understand what she meant.

"Well, then you, and you alone, would guide me, no one else!"

"Now Liza, even then it'd be you who led me," Maurice said even more seriously.

"Oh, my goodness, he's trying to make a play on words!" Liza cried, in pretended horror. "Listen, Maurice, don't you ever go in for that sort of thing. Really, how selfish can a man be? I'm sure you're just slandering yourself, Maurice, and I'm certain that, on the contrary, you'd tell me from morning to night that with a broken leg I was more fascinating than I'd ever been before! Oh, but it won't work because you're so incredibly tall and, with a broken leg, I'd be all shrunken and it wouldn't be so easy for you to support me. We wouldn't be much of a couple. . . ."

She broke into a long, painful fit of laughter. Her innuendos were transparent and her wit was blunt, but she obviously didn't care.

"Hysterics," Peter whispered in my ear. "We should get her a glass of water, quickly!"

He was right. In an instant everyone was fussing around her and she was given a drink of water. Liza had her arms around her mother's neck. She kissed her, cried on her shoulder, then leaned back, looking into Mrs. Drozdov's face, and went into another fit of laughter. Finally, her mother began to whimper and Mrs. Stavrogin led them both upstairs by the door through which Dasha had appeared earlier. But they didn't stay there long—four minutes at the most.

I will now try to retrace every detail of the closing moments of this memorable episode. I remember that when all the ladies had left, except Dasha who hadn't moved from her seat all this time, Stavrogin went around, shaking hands with each of us in turn, except Shatov, who remained seated in his corner with his head hanging even lower than before. The elder Verkhovensky tried to engage Stavrogin in some sort of witty exchange, but he quickly disengaged himself and moved toward Dasha. Before reaching her, however, he was overtaken by the younger Verkhovensky, who dragged him over to the window and started whispering something very important— that is, if one could judge by the gesticulations accompanying the whispering. Stavrogin, however, with a bored look, hardly seemed to be listening. He smiled his polite smile, then, toward the end, appeared to grow impatient and anxious to escape from Peter. He actually left the window as soon as the ladies returned. Mrs. Stavrogin installed Liza in the chair she had occupied, then insisted that they should stay for at least another ten minutes to give the girl time to recover, because she doubted that fresh air would be good for Liza's tense nerves. She was really fussing too much over Liza. She sat down next to her. Peter, who had been left by himself near the window, immediately joined them and engaged them in a cheerful conversation. At that moment Nikolai walked unhurriedly over to Dasha, who stirred, then leaped up, all pink and embarrassed.

"I believe I should congratulate you . . . or perhaps not yet?" he said with a rather strange frown.

Dasha said something, but I couldn't make out what.

"Forgive my indiscretion," he said, raising his voice a little, "but that's what I was told—in a special letter. Did you know that?"

"Yes, I knew that you had been specially informed."

"I hope I haven't done any harm in congratulating you," he laughed, "and if Mr. Verkhovensky—"

"Why? What are you being congratulated for, Miss Shatov?" Peter said, suddenly rushing over to them. "Ah, it's surely for that! Yes, your blush tells me I've guessed right. But then, what else can there be to congratulate beautiful and virtuous maidens for, and what congratulations make them blush most? So, if I've guessed, accept my congratulations too. And you must pay me—I've won our bet. Do you remember, in Switzerland, you bet me you would never marry? Ah yes, speaking of Switzerland, I almost forgot, although it was just about my main purpose in coming here . . ." He quickly turned toward his father and asked, "And you—when are *you* leaving for Switzerland?"

"Me? . . . Switzerland? . . ." Mr. Verkhovensky mumbled, quite bewildered.

'Why, aren't you going there? But you wrote to me that you were getting married, didn't you?"

"Peter!"

"Now why do you say 'Peter' like that? If you want to get married, I came hurrying to tell you that I have no objections—you wanted to know my reaction quickly," Peter started off in his smooth rattle. "On the other hand, if you need me to 'save' you as you wrote in the same letter, I'm willing to help you there too. Is it true, Mrs. Stavrogin, that he's about to get married?" Peter said, turning toward her. "I hope I'm not being indiscreet—he wrote me himself that the whole town knew about it, that everyone was congratulating him and that, to avoid it all, he goes out only after dark. I have that letter here in my pocket. But, believe me, Mrs. Stavrogin, I don't understand the first thing about my old man. Now, you tell me yourself, dear Papa: what do you want me to do—congratulate you or save you? You can't imagine how he writes—he's the happiest man on earth and then in the very next line he sounds the gloomiest notes of despair. In the first place he asks me to forgive him—well there, I suppose, he's being true to type. I can't avoid saying it: he has seen me twice in his life, and even then by accident, and suddenly, on getting married for the third time, he decides that he's failing in his parental duties and beseeches me from thousands of miles away to forgive him and not to be angry with him! 'Please don't be angry with me'—that's so typical of your generation. All right, I understand and I won't hold it against you, and so on. But the trouble is, I don't understand your main point. You talk in that letter about some sort of sins committed in Switzerland. You're marrying because of someone else's sins—I don't understand; I only know it has something to do with sins. The girl, he writes, is a pearl, a diamond, and he is, of course, 'unworthy' of her, but then, because of those sins, he's forced to go through with the wedding and make a trip to Switzerland and, therefore, he requests me to leave everything and rush to his rescue. Does that make any sense to you? But—from the expressions on your faces, I gather"—he turned completely around, holding the letter in his hand and smiling innocently— "that, as I so often do, I have made some sort of *gaffe*. . . . I'm too stupidly candid or perhaps, as Nikolai says, always in too much of a hurry. But I thought everyone here was a close friend—that is, a friend of yours, Father, because I'm really a stranger here and I realize that everyone knows something I don't know."

His eyes kept darting around the room.

"So, your father wrote to you that he was marrying because of another man's sins and asked you to come rushing to the rescue from Switzerland. Did he actually use those expressions?" Mrs. Stavrogin said, stepping up to him. Her face was all yellow and twisted; it twitched and her lips quivered.

"What I meant to say, you see," Peter said, looking alarmed, "is that, if there's something I didn't understand, then it's his fault for writing like that. Well, here's the letter. And you know, Mrs. Stavrogin, his letters are dreadfully long and they've been arriving in an uninterrupted stream, especially in the last couple of months. I must admit I couldn't be bothered to struggle through all of them. You must forgive me, Father, for admitting it so stupidly, but you will agree that, although you addressed those letters to me, they were intended rather for posterity and so you shouldn't really care whether I waded through them or not. . . . Ah, don't get offended. After all, you and I, we are close all right. But this particular letter, Mrs. Stavrogin, I read to the end. And I bet the sins he mentions—'someone else's sin'—are really his own peccadilloes—oh, most innocent, of course, but about which he has decided to raise a great furor with·overtones of self-immolation. Yes, precisely, the furor is for the sake of that self-immolating overtone.

"The true trouble, though, is financial—why not admit it, after all? He has, as you know, a weakness for a little game of cards. But perhaps I shouldn't have said that and I'm sorry. I do talk too much. But, I swear, Mrs. Stavrogin, he frightened the daylights out of me and, in a way, I was prepared to 'save' him. After all, he made me feel ashamed: what does he take me for? A heartless creditor holding a knife to his throat? He writes something about a dowry, but I'm beginning to wonder whether there's any truth to all this talk about marriage—do you really intend to marry, dear Papa? Perhaps it was all talk—an opportunity to display your literary style. Ah, Mrs. Stavrogin, I'm sure you must be blaming me now for my way of putting things, *my* style—"

"Not at all, not at all," Mrs. Stavrogin assured him with cold fury. "I can see you've been driven to the limit of your patience."

She was obviously listening with spiteful glee to Peter's "candid outbursts." And he was obviously putting on an act—a rather gross and unsubtle act, the purpose of which I didn't understand at the time.

"On the contrary," Mrs. Stavrogin said, "I'm extremely grateful to you for having spoken up. Without you, I would never have guessed. My eyes have been opened for the first time in twenty years. Now you, Nikolai—tell me what you meant when you said that you had also been specially informed: did Stepan Verkhovensky write to you too?"

"I received a very innocent . . . a very noble letter from him. . . ."

"I see that you have difficulty choosing your words, and that's enough for me! And you, Stepan, I would like to ask you an immense favor," she said, her eyes flashing. "Please leave us at once and never come back to this house again!"

We must remember that Mrs. Stavrogin had suffered a severe emotional crisis during the preceding hours and was still in a state of agitation. Of course, Mr. Verkhovensky had brought it on himself, but what struck me most then was the dignity with which he withstood his son's accusations and Mrs. Stavrogin's "curse" on him. He didn't once try to interrupt Peter or to justify himself. Where had this courage come from? All I know is that he had certainly been offended by the way his son had met him and, most of all, by the way he had reacted to his paternal embrace. In his eyes, at least, that was a deep and *real* grief. At the same time, it had suddenly and painfully dawned on him that he himself had acted despicably (he later frankly admitted that to me). Maybe he now reacted as he did because *genuine* grief can transform even the most irresponsible person into a strong and determined one, if only for a moment; also real suffering temporarily turns fools into wise men. If this is true, why couldn't a man like Stepan Verkhovensky change radically—even if only temporarily?

He bowed with dignity to Mrs. Stavrogin, without saying a word. And, indeed, what else could he have done? He was on the point of leaving, but could not resist the temptation to walk over to Dasha. She seemed to have anticipated his move, for, before he had time to say anything, she began to speak rapidly, in a dismayed tone, to forestall him:

"Please don't say anything, Mr. Verkhovensky," she said, looking at him with a pained expression and holding out her hand to him. "I want you to know that I respect you as much as ever and think just as highly of you . . . and please don't think badly of me either—I value your esteem immensely."

Mr. Verkhovensky bowed deeply to her.

"It's up to you, Dasha!" Mrs. Stavrogin said in a loud, cutting voice. "You know that in this whole business you've been free to act as you pleased and you still are—now and in the future."

"Oh my! I'm beginning to understand everything now!" Peter Verkhovensky exclaimed, slapping his forehead. "But that puts me in an awkward position! Please, you must forgive me, Miss Shatov. Ah, what have you done to me, you!" he said, turning toward his father.

"Peter, I don't think you should talk to me like that, my boy," Mr. Verkhovensky said very quietly.

"Please stop shouting!" Peter said, waving his hands at him. "Believe me, it's all your sick old nerves, and your shouting won't do them any good. Tell me rather why you didn't warn me. You should have realized from the beginning that I might let it out."

Mr. Verkhovensky looked intently at his son.

"You, Peter, who seem to be so well informed, did you really know nothing—had you heard nothing about what's been going on here?"

"What? Some people! It's not enough for them to be childish, they also have to be spiteful! Did you hear what he said, Mrs. Stavrogin?"

Everyone started to talk at once. And then something happened that no one could possibly have expected.

VIII

To begin with, let me say that, during the past couple of minutes, Liza had been urgently whispering to her mother and Maurice, who stood bent over her. She looked worried and determined at the same time. Then she got up, apparently anxious to leave, and started hurrying her mother, whom Maurice was helping up from her armchair. But apparently it was their fate to stay and witness the scene to the end.

Shatov, completely forgotten by everyone in his corner (not far from Liza), had apparently suddenly begun to wonder what he was doing sitting there. He got up from his chair and slowly crossed the room, walking straight toward Nikolai Stavrogin and keeping his eyes fixed on his face. Stavrogin, noticing him coming, smiled slightly, but his smile vanished as Shatov drew nearer.

When Shatov stopped, facing him silently and staring straight into his eyes, everyone's attention was caught and they fell silent. Peter seemed to be the last one to become aware of it. Liza and her mother stopped in the middle of the room. For five seconds no one moved. The look of haughty surprise on Stavrogin's face changed to one of anger. He knitted his brows. And then . . .

Suddenly Shatov swung his long and heavy arm, and his fist landed powerfully on Stavrogin's cheek. Stavrogin reeled violently. It was nothing like a conventional slap: Shatov didn't strike with the flat of his hand but with a tightly closed fist, and his fist was big and bony, covered with reddish hairs and freckles. Had the blow landed on Stavrogin's nose, it would have broken it. But it landed on his cheek, grazing the left corner of his upper lip and the upper teeth; blood began to stream.

I believe there was a scream. Perhaps it came from Mrs. Stavrogin; I can't say for sure. Then there was dead silence again. Actually the whole scene lasted only ten seconds at the most.

I wish to repeat here that Stavrogin was one of those people who do not know what fear is. In a duel he could remain completely relaxed while his opponent was taking aim at him and then shoot and kill with the most brutal indifference. If someone had slapped him, I don't believe he'd have even bothered to challenge the offender to a duel; he would have killed him on the spot—he was a man who could kill in cold blood, fully realizing what he was doing and not at all in a fit of fury. I don't think he had ever known those blinding moments of anger when one ceases to reason. Even in those moments of unbounded hatred that he sometimes experienced, he always retained complete control over himself; yet, with the full knowledge that killing a man except in a duel would mean forced labor for him, he would still have killed such an offender without the slightest hesitation.

I have watched Stavrogin closely for some time and, thanks to certain circumstances, I have learned a lot about him, so I know what I'm talking about. I suppose I could compare him with certain characters about whom legends still persist. There is the story, for instance, of the Decembrist Lunin. All his life he deliberately looked for danger. He so loved the sensation it gave him that it became a physical necessity for him. In his youth he fought duels over nothing, and when he was exiled to Siberia, he went bear hunting armed only with a knife. He also enjoyed tangling with runaway convicts in the Siberian forests—and they, let me say, are rather more dangerous than bears. Undoubtedly, such people know very well what fear is, otherwise they could lead much quieter lives and would have no physical need of the sensation of being in danger. What fascinates them, of course, is overcoming their fear. Lunin, even before he was exiled to Siberia, chose hunger and heavy physical labor rather than submit to his father's demands, which he found unfair. That indicates that he was not only eager to show his courage but found scope for struggle everywhere.

But, after all, many years have passed since then and the nervous, tormented, contradictory nature of our contemporaries is incompatible with the longing for strong, undivided sensations that filled the eager, restless characters of the good old days. Stavrogin probably would have despised Lunin and dismissed him as a boastful rooster who was really a coward at heart. Of course, he wouldn't have said so to his face. Stavrogin would probably have been just as successful as Lunin in killing a man in a duel or fighting a bear or a robber in the forest, but he would have done it without any sensation of joy, simply out of the unpleasant necessity to protect his life. And he would have done it with an air of boredom—with a lazy, indifferent expression on his face. And yet, in sheer wickedness, Stavrogin went further than Lunin and Lermontov too. He had more viciousness in him than both those men put together, but his viciousness was cold and controlled and, if it is possible to say so, *reasonable*—the most repulsive and dangerous variety there is. So let me repeat once more: I considered him then just as I consider him today (when everything is over) as the type of man who, if struck in the face or receiving a similar insult, would kill the offender then and there, without challenging him to a duel.

Yet something different and very strange happened in this case.

As soon as he had regained his balance, after almost being humiliatingly knocked down by the blow, and while the ignominious thud of that fist against his face was still in everyone's ears, he came back at Shatov and grabbed him by the shoulders with both hands. But almost immediately he let go of him and crossed his arms behind his back. Without saying a word, he glared at Shatov, his face turning paler and paler until it was as white as his shirt. But, strangely enough, all the fire seemed to go out of his eyes. Within ten seconds—and I'm certain I'm not imagining this—his look became completely calm. He was only frighteningly pale. Of course, I don't know what was going on inside him, but I think that, at that moment, Stavrogin was like a man forcing himself to hold on to a red-hot iron bar for ten seconds and managing to overcome the terrible pain, to prove his force of character to himself.

Shatov was the first to lower his eyes. He slowly turned away and walked out of the room, but his gait was not the same as it had been when he walked up to Stavrogin. He moved slowly, very clumsily, with his shoulders hunched and his head hanging, apparently debating something with himself. I believe he was muttering. Nevertheless, he picked his way carefully and managed to reach the door without butting into anything or upsetting any furniture. He opened the door just wide enough to get through and left the room almost sideways. The last I saw of him was the shock of unruly hair that always stood on end at the back of his head, clearly outlined in the doorway.

Then, before the general outcry, there rose a terrifying scream and I saw Liza seize her mother by the shoulder and Maurice by the hand and pull at them two or three times in an attempt to make them leave the room. Then she screamed again and fell full length on the floor, unconscious. I can still hear the back of her head bang against the carpet.

Part Two

chapter 1

NIGHT

I

Eight days went by. Now, as I write this, it's all over and things are pretty well known. But, at the time, we knew nothing and it's no wonder that much of it struck us as strange. Anyway, Mr. Verkhovensky and I kept to ourselves at first and watched developments apprehensively from a distance. However, I still went out occasionally and I shared with him whatever I learned. I believe that was all that kept him going.

Needless to say, all sorts of rumors spread through the town about that blow in the face, about Liza's fainting, and about the other things that happened that Sunday. However, it did seem strange that everything should have become known so quickly. Who was divulging it all? One would not have thought that any of the persons present had any need or advantage in disclosing what had happened. There had been no servants present. Lebyatkin alone might have blabbered, but rather from a lack of restraint than out of malice, for he left the room in a state of great fright, and fear destroys hatred for one's enemy. But Lebyatkin and his sister disappeared from Filipov's house the very next day. He must have moved somewhere in a hurry, for they seemed to vanish into thin air. Shatov, from whom I wanted to inquire about the whereabouts of Maria Lebyatkin, locked himself in his room, where he remained for the entire eight days, not even going out to do his odd jobs in town. He wouldn't let me in. I knocked on his door on Tuesday, but he didn't answer. I was sure from various indications that he was at home, so I knocked again. Then I heard him leap up—from his bed probably. He came over to the door and shouted at the top of his voice:

"Shatov isn't in."

So I left it at that.

Mr. Verkhovensky and I, although rather reluctant to acknowledge such a thought, yet, each prompting the other, came to the conclusion that the rumormonger could only be his son. However, in a conversation with his father a little later, Peter vehemently assured him that he had heard the story discussed all over town, especially at the club, and that every detail of it was known to the governor and his wife. The day after it all happened I came across Liputin and discovered that he knew everything down to the last word. This was remarkable; he was probably one of the first to find out.

Many ladies, among them the most elegant, were curious about "the mysterious cripple," as they referred to Maria Lebyatkin. Some of them were even anxious to meet Maria, which suggests that whoever was behind the Lebyatkins' disappearance had been well advised. But Liza Tishin's fainting was the most discussed topic. The entire upper crust was particularly interested in that, if only because it somehow involved the governor's wife, Julie von Lembke, to whom Liza was related and whose protégée she was. And what didn't they say! The mystery surrounding the whole affair and the fact that the Drozdovs' and the Stavrogins' houses were closed to visitors, intensified the gossip. It was rumored that Liza was in bed running a high temperature. The same thing was said of Stavrogin—with some additional unsavory details about a knocked-out tooth and a swollen cheek. It was even whispered in some dark corners that there was going to be a murder; that Stavrogin was not a man to endure such an insult; that he was out to kill Shatov, but was planning to do it secretly, as Corsican bandits do. This idea was very popular, although the majority of our upper-class young people listened to it with a great show of boredom and indifference—both, of course, affected.

In general, the old hostility toward Nikolai Stavrogin came clearly back into focus. Even the most solid citizens were anxious to impute some guilt to him, although they didn't know exactly for what. People whispered that he and Liza had had an affair in Switzerland and that he had completely ruined her reputation. Of course, cautious people contained themselves, but they still listened eagerly to all the talk.

Other things were also mentioned, but never in public. Some very strange things were discussed, although very seldom and only privately, and almost in secret. I only mention them here to warn the reader, because they will come up later as my narrative develops. Some people, screwing up their faces, said Nikolai Stavrogin had come for some special purpose; that, through Count K., he had made some high connections in Petersburg and, indeed, must be in touch with the authorities and was probably on some important secret assignment. And when some restrained and respectable citizens pointed out smilingly that the authorities were not likely to entrust a scandalous person like Stavrogin with official assignments, they were told that his link with the authorities was of a strictly confidential nature and that, under such circumstances, the less the agent looked like an official, the better it was. This sort of argument carried a good deal of weight, because we knew that in the capital they were quite interested in what happened in our town. I repeat—all these rumors sprang up only to disappear immediately upon Stavrogin's first public appearance. But I wish to note here that many of them were started by a few vague and abrupt remarks dropped in the club by Artemy Gaganov, a retired Guards' captain and important local landowner. He had just returned from Petersburg, where he had moved in high society, and he happened to be the son of the late Pavel Gaganov, the former committee member of the club who, slightly more than four years before, had had that run-in with Stavrogin and had suffered such a crude humiliation at his hands.

It soon also became common knowledge that the governor's wife had driven over to Mrs. Stavrogin's house on a special call, but had not been received because "Madam was not feeling well." Then it was learned that a few days after her attempt to visit Mrs. Stavrogin, Mrs. von Lembke had sent a messenger to inquire about her health. After that, she started to "justify" Mrs. Stavrogin, although of course only from a moral standpoint, that is, in the vaguest and most abstract way. At first she had listened so coldly and sternly to the nasty innuendoes about the Sunday incident that, for the next few days, people didn't bring them up in her presence. And this gave people the impression that the governor's wife knew all about the mystery, understanding its hidden meaning down to the minutest detail—and that she knew it not as an outsider but as someone directly involved. I should note that, by that time, Julie von Lembke was gaining the standing she had longed for among us and that she was already beginning to imagine herself surrounded by a court of admirers. A considerable faction in local high society had acknowledged her practical intelligence and tact—but we'll come to that later. Her patronage also partly accounted for Peter Verkhovensky's rapid social success, a thing that, at first, considerably puzzled his father.

Perhaps we both exaggerated somewhat. In the first place, within four days of his arrival, Peter made the acquaintance of everyone who was anyone in the town. He arrived on Sunday, and on Tuesday I saw him drive past in the carriage of Artemy Gaganov, a man who was proud, irritable, and haughty beneath his worldliness and with whom it was quite difficult to get along. Peter was also warmly welcomed in the governor's mansion and immediately found himself in the position of a young friend of the family. He was a constant guest at Mrs. von Lembke's dinner table. He had met her before, in Switzerland, but still there was something curious about his immediate success in the governor's house. After all, whether it was true or not, he was supposed to have been an active revolutionary abroad, contributed to certain foreign publications, and participated in certain congresses—facts that could easily have been checked from newspaper clippings. That, at least, is what I had been told by Alyosha Telyatnikov, now, alas, retired, who, at that time, during the tenure of the former governor, was himself a young favorite in the governor's mansion. One fact, however, was incontrovertible: this former revolutionary was treated in his homeland without any suspicion and, indeed, with outright enthusiasm. So perhaps there really was nothing against him after all. Once, Liputin whispered in my ear that he had heard somewhere, somehow, that Peter had confessed and had been pardoned after he had named the other persons involved and promised to work for tsar and country in the future. I repeated this malicious story to his father, who, although he was hardly in a state to think clearly, grew very thoughtful. Later it turned out that Peter had arrived with many letters of recommendation, one of which was addressed to the first lady and came from an incredibly important old Petersburg lady whose husband was one of the leading relics of Petersburg. The old lady in question, who happened to be Julie von Lembke's godmother,

mentioned in her letter that Count K. knew Peter well through
Nikolai Stavrogin and that he thought highly of him, "despite
his former errors." The governor's wife was anxious to maintain her scanty connections with Petersburg high society and
was very pleased to receive a letter from the important old
lady. But still, there was something more to it than that: she
had fallen into a familiar tone with Peter, which she also
imposed upon her husband, until the governor finally protested—but we'll come to that later. I will also set down for
the record that the great writer Karmazinov was very nice to
Peter and immediately invited him to his place. Such haste
on the part of a pompous, self-satisfied man like Karmazinov
wounded Stepan Verkhovensky's pride worst of all, but I had
my own explanation for it: in inviting a young nihilist to his
home, Karmazinov had his eye on the progressive young people in Moscow and Petersburg. The great novelist was kow-
towing to the new generation of revolutionaries, imagining, in
his ignorance, that they held the future of Russia in their
hands. He was ignominiously trying to flatter them, mostly
because they paid not the slightest attention to him.

II

Peter Verkhovensky dropped in on his father twice, both
times, alas, in my absence. He first came on Wednesday, that
is, four days after their first meeting, and even then it was
strictly on business. They had, by the way, settled their accounts over the estate, without anyone's knowing exactly
how. Mrs. Stavrogin took care of everything, putting up the
money and thus, of course, acquiring the land. Mr. Verkhovensky was merely informed by her footman, Alexei, that everything was settled and asked to sign something, which he did
silently and with dignity. Speaking of dignity, I must say that
I hardly recognized him during those days. He behaved as he
never had before; he was very silent and didn't write a single
letter to Mrs. Stavrogin after that Sunday, an abstention that
I felt verged on the miraculous. But, above all, he was eminently calm. He had seized upon some extraordinary notion,
and that gave him his composure—that was quite obvious.
Once he had got hold of that notion, he just sat waiting for
something. At first, however, he felt ill. On Monday, espe-

cially, he had a bad stomach upset. And then, he couldn't stand not knowing what was going on—although, when, leaving aside the facts, I tried to discuss the essence of the matter, he brushed aside my remarks with a wave of the hand and asked me to stop. His son's two visits affected him painfully, but they didn't weaken him. After each visit, he lay on the sofa, his head wrapped in a cloth soaked in vinegar. But, in the deeper sense, he remained calm.

Occasionally, however, he let me talk. There were times when I thought that his pleasant, mysterious firmness had left him and he seemed to be struggling against some new flood of temptations. Those moods didn't last, but I feel I must record them. I suspected he was longing to show his mettle, to leave his seclusion, to offer them a last battle.

"*Cher,* I'm certain I could have routed them!" he exclaimed on Thursday evening, after Peter's second visit, as he lay stretched out on the sofa with his head wrapped in a vinegar-soaked cloth. Until that moment, he hadn't exchanged a single word with me that day. "*Fils, fils cheri* and all that—I agree that such sentiments are strictly for chambermaids. And I don't blame him—I understand now. I didn't even provide him with food and drink. I packed him off from Berlin to the depths of Russia when he was still a baby—sent him off like a parcel. I know all that; I agree. So now he says, 'You never even looked after me—you just sent me off in the mail. And not content with that, you robbed me here, too.' 'But, you miserable wretch,' I shouted at him, 'all my life, the very thought of you has made my heart contract, even if I did send you off in the mail!' *Il rit.* But I admit it, I admit it—I did send him off," he concluded, almost raving.

"*Passons,*" he started again five minutes later. "I really don't understand Turgenev. That Bazarov of his is such a contrived character he couldn't possibly exist. They themselves were the first to repudiate him, declaring that he was like nothing on earth. Bazarov is a sort of murky mixture between Gogol's Nozdrev and Byron, *c'est le mot.* Just take a look at them: they turn somersaults and squeal with joy like puppies in the sun; they're happy; they're the conquerors. Byron indeed! They're just dull! They've the irritable vanity of cooks, a vulgar longing *de faire du bruit autour de son nom,* without realizing what *son nom.* . . . Ah, what a caricature he is! I tell him, 'Do you really, by any chance, wish to offer yourself as a substitute for Christ, just the way you are?' *Il rit. Il rit beaucoup, il*

rit trop. He has a strange kind of smile. I don't understand—
his mother didn't have a smile like that. *Il rit toujours.*"

Another silence followed.

"They're sly: everything on Sunday was planned in advance," he blurted out.

"There's no doubt about that!" I concurred enthusiastically,
pricking up my ears. "It was all prearranged and tacked together rather obviously—and, on top of that, they performed
rather poorly."

"Yes, of course, but what I meant was that they tacked it
together so obviously because they wanted it to be noticed by
. . . by those who were supposed to notice it. Do you understand?"

"No, I don't."

"*Tant mieux. Passons.* I'm terribly on edge today."

"Why did you have to argue with him at all, Mr. Verkhovensky?"

"I was trying to convert him. Oh yes, you may laugh. Poor
Varvara, she'll be hearing some things now! Ah, my friend,
would you believe it—I felt so patriotic the other day! But
then I've always been conscious of being a Russian. Besides,
a true Russian can't be any different from what we are, you
and I. *Il y a là dedans quelque chose d'aveugle et de louche.*"

"No doubt about that," I said.

"The truth, my friend, is always incredible; it becomes believable only when diluted with lies. And that's what people
have always done. Perhaps there's something here we don't
understand. Tell me, do you think there's something beyond
our understanding in their triumphant squealing? I wish there
was. Yes, I wish there was something in it."

I didn't answer, and he too remained silent for a long time.

"They say it's all French ideas," he began babbling again
after a while, sounding feverish, "but that's not true. It's
always been the same. Why blame French ideas? There's
nothing here but our congenital Russian inability to produce
an idea, our disgusting parasitism among nations. *Ils sont tout
simplement des paresseux,* and it has nothing to do with
French thought. Ah, the best thing for mankind would be
for all Russians to be annihilated. Oh, we were striving for
something different. I don't understand anything any more.
Can't you understand, I said to him, that if you push that
guillotine of yours into the foreground it is because nothing
is easier than lopping off heads and nothing is more difficult

than developing ideas. *Vous êtes des paresseux! Votre drapeau est une guenille, une impuissance!* Those carts or whatever they were, you know in

> The rattle of wagons bringing bread to men
> Is more use than the Sistine Madonna to them.

Or how does it go? . . . Some nonsense of that sort. But can't you see, I shouted at him, that man needs unhappiness just as much as he needs happiness! *Il rit.* You, he said, get a real kick out of making cracks like that while you stretch out your limbs (only he put it more disgustingly) on a velvet couch. And these familiar ways between us—it's all very well when father and son get along well, but as soon as they start berating each other . . ."

There was another minute-long pause. Then he got up.

"Do you know," he said, "I'm certain that this will end with a bang."

"It's already ended," I said.

"Vous ne comprenez pas. Passons. Usually things come to nothing in this world, but this will end in something, all right, I assure you!"

He walked up and down the room in a state of great excitement, then, when he reached the couch again, he collapsed onto it.

On Friday, Peter left on a trip, remaining away until Monday. I found out about this from Liputin, who also informed me that the Lebyatkins, brother and sister, were now living somewhere near Gorshechnoye, a village across the river.

"It was I who helped them move," Liputin said and then, leaving the subject of the Lebyatkins, he suddenly announced that Liza Tishin was going to marry her stepfather's nephew, Maurice Drozdov, and that, although it hadn't been announced publicly, they were engaged and the matter was settled.

The next day I saw Liza and Maurice out riding on horseback. It was the first time she had been out since her illness. Her eyes sparkled when she saw me; she laughed and gave me a friendly nod. I reported all this to Mr. Verkhovensky, but he only paid attention to the part concerning the Lebyatkins.

Now that I have described the mysterious events during

those eight days as they appeared to us who knew nothing at the time, I will present subsequent events with the advantage of hindsight, since everything was finally revealed and became common knowledge. I'll start on the eighth day after that Sunday—that is Monday evening a week later—because, on that evening, the beginnings of a new scandal occurred.

III

At seven in the evening, Nikolai Stavrogin was sitting alone in his study. He had always liked that room with its high ceiling, rugs, and rather heavy furniture from an earlier age. He sat on a couch in one corner, dressed to go out, but he seemed to have no intention of going anywhere. A lamp burned on the desk in front of him, its shade cutting off the light so that the corners on the far side of the large room were in darkness. He seemed to be deep in thought, absorbed and preoccupied. His face was drawn and tired. His cheek was indeed swollen, but the rumor that one of his teeth had been knocked out had been an exaggeration: it had only been loosened and now was firm in its socket again. The cut inside his upper lip had healed too. As to the swelling, it had lasted a whole week because Stavrogin had refused to see a doctor and have it lanced, waiting for it to go down by itself.

Neither would he let his mother come near him: she was allowed in only once a day for about one minute, and then only after dark. He didn't even receive Peter Verkhovensky, although Peter dropped in on Mrs. Stavrogin at least two or three times a day as long as he remained in town.

And then, on Monday, having returned in the morning from his three-day trip, having rushed all over town and then dined at Mrs. von Lembke's, Peter turned up in the evening at Mrs. Stavrogin's. She had been expecting him impatiently. He was informed that the ban had been lifted and Nikolai was receiving visitors. Mrs. Stavrogin herself accompanied the guest to the door of her son's study. She was anxious for the two men to have a talk, for Peter had promised to report the gist of the conversation to her. She knocked timidly on the door of the study and, receiving no answer, decided to open it a couple of inches.

"Nikolai," she said in a low, constrained voice, trying to catch sight of him through the crack in the door, "may I let Peter Verkhovensky in?"

"Of course you may!" Peter himself answered her in a loud, cheerful voice. He opened the door wider and stepped into the room.

Stavrogin hadn't heard the knock on the door and, although he had heard his mother's shy voice, he had had no time to answer it. On the desk in front of him was a letter he had just read and about which he had been thinking intensely. Peter's loud voice startled him; quickly he covered the letter with a paperweight he happened to have at hand. A corner of the letter and almost all the envelope stuck out from under it.

"I shouted like that to give you time," Peter said quickly, in a tone of remarkable innocence, hurrying over to the desk and staring at the paperweight.

"And, of course, you noticed that I was hiding a letter I had just received," Stavrogin said quietly, without moving.

"A letter? Ah, but why should that concern me?" Peter exclaimed. "But . . ." he whispered, indicating the door with his head. It was now closed tight.

"She never listens behind doors," Stavrogin said coldly.

"And even if she did, I'd have no objections," Peter said loudly and cheerfully, installing himself in an easy chair. "But tonight I want to have a little face-to-face talk with you, now that I've finally got to see you. First of all, how do you feel? You look fine to me. Perhaps you'll be able to appear tomorrow, hmmm?"

"Perhaps."

"Put their minds at rest at last and mine too!" Peter said, gesticulating wildly, but in a fond and jocular tone. "You've no idea what nonsense I've had to feed them all this time. Although I suppose you really do have some idea." He laughed.

"I don't have any very clear idea. I only heard from Mother that you were quite busy."

"Me? No, no, nothing special!" Peter cried as if defending himself from a grave accusation. "You know, I brought up Shatov's wife—that is, the rumors about your affair with her in Paris. That could, of course, explain what happened on that Sunday. You don't mind, do you?"

"I'm sure you've been giving your all."

"Just as I feared! Anyway, what do you mean by 'giving my all'? It sounds like a reproach. On the other hand, you seem willing to face things squarely. On the way, I was afraid you wouldn't be."

"I don't particularly feel like facing anything squarely," Stavrogin said, visibly irritated, but then he laughed.

"No, no, that's not what I have in mind. Make no mistake about that," Peter said, waving his hands, his words rattling like peas in a drum. He appeared pleased at his host's irritability. "I won't bother you with *our common* business now, considering your present state. I only came to talk about the Sunday incident, and only as much as is absolutely necessary, for it's impossible to let it go at that, after all. . . . I've come to offer a frank explanation that I probably need even more than you do. Maybe that does your pride good, but it's also the truth. From now on, I will always be completely frank with you."

"Haven't you been all along?"

"You know very well that I haven't—that I've sometimes twisted things around a bit. Now you're smiling; I'm glad, for it is a pretext for a frank explanation. I provoked that smile deliberately by using the phrase 'twisted things around.' I know you're angry at me for taking the liberty of presenting you with a distorted picture of the truth, but now I will follow it up with an explanation of my behavior. You see how open I've become! All right then, would you like to hear what I have to say?"

Stavrogin's expression, which had remained scornfully detached, even sarcastic, throughout his visitor's obvious attempts to irritate him with his carefully prepared, crudely naïve insolence, at last showed a trace of uneasy curiosity.

"Listen then," Peter began, wriggling more than ever, "when I came to this town about ten days ago, I had, of course, to adopt a certain role. Now, you may say, why not be oneself, right? But there's nothing more difficult than being oneself: no one believes you. I admit I thought of playing the fool because it is much easier to be a fool than to be oneself. But, on the other hand, a fool is an extreme and extremes provoke curiosity. So finally I decided definitely to be myself. Well, but what is my own character? It is the golden

mean: neither stupid nor intelligent, and rather ungifted—
furthermore, I've dropped from the moon, as the respectable
people here put it."

"That may all be quite right," Stavrogin said with a faint
smile.

"Ah, so you agree? Good! I thought that was your opinion
of me. Please don't worry, I'm not in the least offended. I
didn't say those things about myself to make you protest
politely and say, 'Oh no, you're really talented and intelligent'
—that sort of thing, you know. Ah, you're smiling again!
You've caught me out again: you wouldn't have said 'you're
intelligent.' So, all right—but I have to assume everything.
Passons, as my papa says, and also, parenthetically, forgive
my prolixity. That, by the way, is an example: I always talk
a lot—that is, I use a lot of words in a hurry, and the result
is not too brilliant. Now, why is that? It's because I don't
know how to talk—people who speak well use fewer words.
So, I lack talent. Isn't that right? But since this lack of talent
is a part of my nature, shouldn't I exploit it as best I can?
So, I exploit it. True, on my way here, I thought I'd try being
silent. But keeping quiet is a great talent, so it's beyond
my reach. And then, silence is always a little dangerous.
So I decided that the best course would be to talk—to talk
a lot, very fast, persuade, plead—and do it all in the most
untalented way and get all tangled up in my own arguments
in the end, so my audience would walk away from me
shrugging or rather spitting in disgust. In the final analysis I'd
have convinced them of my frankness, bored them to death,
and left them without any idea of what it was I was trying
to say—thus attaining all three of my objectives. Who, after
all that, would suspect me of plotting and conspiring? Any
one of them would have been personally offended with anyone who told them that I had some secret schemes. Furthermore, I can make them laugh occasionally and that presents
tremendous advantages. Now they'll forgive me anything if
only because the wise guy who published all those revolutionary pamphlets has turned out to be even more stupid than
they are themselves. Judging by your smile, you approve.
Am I right?"

Stavrogin, however, wasn't smiling at all; in fact, he was
frowning rather impatiently.

"What? Did you say it made no difference?" Peter went
rattling on again at great speed, although Stavrogin hadn't

said a word. "Please, please, I want to make it absolutely clear that I'm not here to compromise you by association with me. You know, you're terribly touchy today: I came here cheerfully with an open heart, but you've been trying to find something wrong with every word I've said. I promise I won't bring up any slippery subjects today. You have my word for it, and I subscribe to all your conditions in advance!"

Stavrogin maintained his stubborn silence.

"What? Did you say something? I believe I've blundered again: you never set any conditions and never will. All right, all right, I believe you; you can relax. I know myself that it's no use setting conditions for me, isn't that right? I'm talking for both of us now, I believe, but you'll have to forgive my lack of imagination. Remember, it all comes from my lack of talent. . . . You're laughing? Why, what's the matter?"

"Nothing," Stavrogin snorted, "I just remembered that I once said you were a rather mediocre person, but I don't believe you were present, so it must have been repeated to you. Now I would appreciate it very much if you would come quickly to the point."

"But I'm there already. To be precise, I'm on the subject of the Sunday incident. Now, what part was I playing on Sunday, would you say? Well, I think I impersonated a mediocrity in a hurry and captured everyone's attention by drowning them in my mediocre conversation. But they forgave me because, in the first place, I had landed from the moon—as they all seem to agree here—and in the second place because I told a nice little story and got you nicely off the hook. Doesn't that describe my role?"

"That is, you told the story in such a way as to leave doubt as to its veracity and to suggest that we were acting on a prearranged plan, whereas there was no such plan and I never asked you to do anything of the sort."

"Precisely, precisely!" Peter exclaimed delightedly, "I arranged it so everyone could see the strings behind it. But, surely you realize that I put on that show mainly for you, because I was trying to catch you off balance and compromise you. I wanted, above all, to find out how afraid you were."

"I wonder why you should be so frank with me now."

"Don't be angry, don't be angry; don't glare at me like that. You wonder why I'm being so frank with you? Well, just because everything's changed now—finished, over with and buried. My opinion of you has suddenly changed. The old methods are discarded: I'll never again compromise you by the old methods. From now on I'll use new ones."

"Change of tactics?"

"No tactics at all. From now on I leave it entirely up to you: if you wish, it's *yes*; if you don't, it's *no*. That's my new line. As to *our common concern*, I won't breathe a sound until you bring it up yourself. Does that make you laugh? I hope you enjoy laughing; I'd like to join you in it. But now I'm absolutely serious about what I've said, although it's quite obvious that only a man without talent can always be in so much of a hurry, isn't that right? Anyway, talented or not, I mean what I just said seriously."

And, indeed, he looked serious and spoke in a very different tone now. Stavrogin even thought he detected a strange emotion in his voice and gave him a curious look.

"So, you've changed your opinion of me?" he asked.

"I changed my opinion of you the instant you took your hands off Shatov's shoulders then—but that's enough, quite enough, and please don't ask me any more questions. I won't say anything more."

He jumped up, waving his hands as if to brush any possible questions away. But since none were forthcoming and he was in no special hurry to leave, he sank into the easy chair again.

"And, by the way, allow me to inform you parenthetically," he rattled on, as soon as he had resumed his seat, "that some of the citizens here are chattering away—something to the effect that you'll kill him. Lembke was on the point of alerting the police, but his wife protested. But that's enough of that. I just thought I'd let you know. And another thing: I moved the Lebyatkins across the river, you know, that same day. Did you receive my note with their address?"

"Yes."

"Well, I did that out of sincere zeal, rather than because of my mediocrity. If the result was not very brilliant, it was at least well meant."

"Well, I don't know—perhaps it was the proper thing to do," Stavrogin said thoughtfully. "Only please stop sending me notes."

"I had to send that one—"

"So Liputin knows?"

"Couldn't be helped. But you know yourself that he wouldn't dare—incidentally, it would be a good thing if we went to see

our people. I mean *them*, not *our* people, in case you wish
again to find fault with everything I say. Well, don't worry,
I didn't mean just now, but sometime. I'll let them know;
they'll meet some evening and we'll go over. They're waiting
with their mouths open, like little birds in a nest, for us to
arrive at the hotel. They're a hotheaded lot. They have their
books out and are preparing to start a debate. Virginsky the
cosmopolitan and Liputin the Fourierist with the talents of a
sleuth. That one is a valuable man in some respects but otherwise requires rough treatment. Then there's that long-eared
fellow who will expound his own system to us. And you know,
they're rather offended because I'm sort of neglecting them
and, as it were, cooling them off by pouring cold water over
them. Ha-ha! Really, we ought to go and see them."

"And you're trying to pass me off as some sort of leader
among them?" Stavrogin asked as casually as he could.

"By the way," Peter said quickly, trying to drown out the
question and acting as if he hadn't heard, "you know that
I've been seeing your mother up to three times a day and,
on those occasions, I've had to do plenty of talking."

"I can well imagine."

"You don't have to imagine anything. I simply assured her
that you had not the slightest intention of killing anyone and
said other sweet things. But what do you think of her knowing
the very next day that I'd taken Maria across the river? Was
it you who told her?"

"Never thought of telling her."

"I thought it couldn't be you. Who could it be then, I
wonder?"

"Liputin, for sure."

"N-no, not Liputin," Peter mumbled, frowning. "But I'll
find out who it was. It looks as though it might have been
Shatov. . . . But let's leave it for the moment, although it's
really very important. . . . By the way, I kept expecting your
mother to come out with the key question at any moment.
Ah yes, all this time she's looked so gloomy and sad, but
when I came today she was all smiles and sunshine. Why?"

"Because I promised her I'd go and ask Liza to marry me
in five days," Stavrogin said with unexpected frankness.

"Yes, of course—I see . . ." Peter muttered as if embarrassed. "There's some talk about her being engaged to
someone else, of course, but you're right—she'd come run-

ning to you right from the church if you whistled. I hope you don't mind my saying so?"

"I don't mind."

"I'm beginning to realize that it's extremely difficult to make you lose your temper today, and I'm becoming afraid of you. I'm very curious to know how you'll present yourself to them. I bet you've got a lot of tricks up your sleeve for the occasion. You don't mind my saying so?"

Stavrogin didn't bother to answer, which exasperated Peter even more.

"By the way, were you in earnest when you told your mother you'd propose to Liza?"

Stavrogin gave him a cold, scrutinizing look.

"Ah, I see, it was only to reassure her. Of course."

"And suppose I really meant it?" Stavrogin asked firmly.

"Why, in that case, God bless you, as they say on such occasions. It won't harm the Cause—note that I didn't say *our* Cause because I know you don't like the word 'our.' As for me, why, I'm at your service. You know that."

"So that's what you think?"

"I think nothing," Peter said hurriedly, with a laugh, "because I realize very well that you have thought out everything concerning your affairs in advance and, as I said, I'm at your service always and everywhere and under any circumstances—yes, any circumstances. You understand that, don't you?"

Stavrogin yawned.

"Ah, you must be tired of me!" Peter cried, suddenly jumping to his feet and seizing his brand-new homburg. He seemed about to leave, but then he didn't. He poured forth a stream of words, either standing in the middle of the room or pacing up and down it, occasionally slapping his knee with his hat for greater emphasis.

"I thought I might tell you something about the Lembkes that would amuse you," he announced cheerfully.

"No, some other time. How's Mrs. von Lembke by the way?"

"Ah, what an exquisite display of manners: you care about her just about as much as you care about an alley cat, nevertheless you feel duty-bound to inquire. I think it very praiseworthy. Well, I can assure you she's quite all right, regards you with a kind of awe, and has an almost superstitious expectation of great things from you. She doesn't mention Sunday's incident and is certain that you'll emerge with flying colors from it when you put in your first appearance. I tell you, she thinks you can do anything you want to do. You're more mysterious and romantic than ever, and that makes a very useful situation. They're all anxious for you to appear. When I left, the atmosphere was pretty hot and now it's even hotter. And, by the way, thanks again for that letter. They're all afraid of Count K. I think they take you for a secret government agent, and I encourage them to believe it. Hope you don't mind."

"Doesn't bother me."

"It will come in very useful later on. You see, they have their own ways here and I, of course, encourage that. Mrs. von Lembke in the first place, then Gaganov—that makes you laugh? But you know my line: I go around spinning inane yarns, but now and then I blurt out something intelligent that happens to be just what they're groping for. Then, as they flock around me, I begin to lie again. They give up on me: 'The fellow is quite able,' they say, 'but he's dropped from the moon.' Lembke invited me to join his administration to straighten me out. You know, I'm treating him horribly—that is, I'm discrediting him glaringly, but he just stares at me. His wife encourages me. And, Gaganov, by the way, is very angry with you. The other day, at his Dukhovo estate, he spoke of you in very deprecating terms. So, of course, I told him the whole truth—well, not the *whole* truth, of course, but still, the truth. I stayed at Dukhovo for an entire day. A fine estate and a beautiful house too."

"What—is he at Dukhovo now?" Stavrogin asked, suddenly stirring and jerking forward in his seat.

"No, he drove me to town himself this morning," Peter said, as though he hadn't noticed Stavrogin's sudden agitation. "Oh, I'm sorry, I've knocked something down—is it a book?" He bent down and picked up an illustrated luxury edition. *"Balzac's Women*—with pictures too, hm?" He opened it. "Never read it. You know, Lembke also writes novels."

"Really?" Stavrogin asked, sounding interested.

"He writes in Russian and it's a secret, although Mrs. von Lembke knows about it and approves. He's an old shoe, but he has a few tricks up his sleeve. They have worked it out very carefully: everything is strict, neat, and handled with great self-restraint. I wish we had something like that working for us."

"Sounds as though you admire the methods used by the government?"

"How can I help admiring them? Our government's methods are the only thing that is really natural to Russia and the only methods that can succeed here. All right, I won't," he cried suddenly. "That wasn't what I wanted to talk about. I won't say another word on that delicate subject. But I suppose I'd better go—you look positively green."

"I'm feverish."

"I can believe it. Why don't you stretch out? By the way, we have some members of the Skoptsi sect in our district. It must be curious to belong to a sect that goes in for castration, don't you think? But I'll tell you about it later. I have a funny little story for you, though. There's an infantry regiment stationed in the district. On Friday evening I was drinking with the officers. We have three friends among them, *vous comprenez?* We talked about atheism and you can be sure that God was badly demoted. They liked it; they squealed with joy. By the way, Shatov insists that if an uprising were started in Russia, it would have to begin with atheism. Maybe he's right. There was a gruff, white-haired old captain among them. He sat and sat in silence, but then he suddenly got up, stood in the middle of the room, and said aloud, but you know, as though he were talking to himself, 'If there were no God, how could I be a captain?' Then he picked up his cap, shrugged, and walked out."

"He expressed a quite logical proposition," Stavrogin said, yawning for the third time.

"You think so? I didn't understand and I meant to ask you. Well, what else is there? Ah, that Shpigulin factory is interesting. It employs five hundred workers, as you know. It's a hotbed of cholera and hasn't been cleaned for fifty years, and the workers are underpaid by the millionaire owners. I assure you, some of the workers have even heard about the International. What? That makes you smile? You'll see for yourself. Just give me the tiniest amount of time. I asked you for time before, but I must ask for some more, then—but I'm sorry, I won't, I won't; I didn't mean to speak about it. Don't frown, please. Good-by. Oh, how could I forget?" he said, coming back. "I was forgetting the most important thing: they've just informed me that our suitcase has arrived from Petersburg."

"What do you mean?" Stavrogin asked, looking at him without understanding.

"Why, the one with your clothes in it, of course—your frock coats, trousers, and underwear. Is it true that it's arrived?"

"Yes, they mentioned something about its arriving this morning."

"May I have it now?"

"Ask Alexei."

"All right, tomorrow. How about tomorrow? Because among your clothes, there's my coat, frock coat, and three pairs of trousers that were ordered at Charmer's on your recommendation, remember?"

"I heard that you were trying to pass yourself off as a dandy around here," Stavrogin said with a snort. "Is it true that you even intend to take riding lessons?"

Peter smiled crookedly.

"I'll tell you what," he said hurriedly, his voice quivering and faltering, "let's both avoid personal remarks once and for all. Of course, you're free to despise me as much as you like and to laugh to your heart's content, but I wish you would try to stop making personal remarks for the time being."

"All right, I won't say it again," Stavrogin said.

Peter smiled, slapped his knee with his hat, and shifted from one foot to the other. He seemed to have completely recovered his composure.

"Some people here even consider me your rival for Liza, so how can I help being interested in my appearance?" he said, laughing. "But I'd like to know where you get so much information. Hm, it's eight already—I must be on my way. I promised to drop in on your mother for a moment, but I think I'll skip it this time. And you, go to bed and cheer up. Outside it's dark and raining and the streets are not too safe at night, but I have a horse cab waiting for me. . . . Ah, by the way, somewhere around this town there's a convict, Fedka, roving about, who was formerly, believe it or not, a serf of mine. My dear papa shoved him into the army about fifteen years ago and the army even paid him for it. A very interesting character indeed."

"Have you—er—have you spoken to him?"

"I have. He's not hiding from me. He's prepared to do anything—for money, of course. But he has convictions too, although rather peculiar ones, I must say. Ah yes, again by the way, if you were serious earlier about you and Liza, let me state again that I'm also a man ready for anything, whatever it may be, and entirely at your service. . . . What are you doing? Why are you reaching for your stick? Oh, you weren't reaching for it. . . . Imagine—I thought you were reaching for that stick of yours."

Stavrogin wasn't reaching for anything. Nor did he say anything. He did get up, though, and his face twitched strangely.

"Also, if you feel something should be done about Mr. Gaganov," Peter suddenly blurted out, pointing directly at the paperweight, "I could, of course, arrange everything. In fact, I'm certain you couldn't manage without me."

Without waiting for an answer he quickly walked out of the room, but then his head reappeared in the crack of the door.

"I say that," he rattled off at full speed, "because Shatov, for instance, had no right to risk his life either, when he attacked you on Sunday."

IV

Perhaps Peter Verkhovensky thought that as soon as he was gone Stavrogin, left to himself, would start pounding the wall with his fists, and he certainly would have liked to see it. But, if so, he was deluding himself: Stavrogin remained completely calm. For two minutes or so he remained standing by his desk in the same position, apparently deep in thought. Then a cold, listless smile appeared on his lips. He installed himself unhurriedly on the couch where he had been sitting when Peter arrived and closed his eyes as though he were terribly tired. The corner of the letter still stuck out from under the paperweight, but he made no move to cover it. Soon he became completely unaware of his surroundings.

When Peter left without paying the promised visit to Mrs. Stavrogin, she was unable to resist going to her son's room, despite the unsuitability of the hour. She was at the end of her tether with so much worrying and somehow hoped that he would explain to her all the things she still couldn't understand. She knocked at the door and, receiving no answer, entered, as she had when bringing Peter to see him. Seeing Nikolai sitting immobile on his couch, she walked over to him, her heart beating. She was surprised that he should have dozed off like that, sitting upright and motionless, even breathing inaudibly. His face was pale and stern. It seemed frozen, the brows slightly knitted; he looked like a wax statue. She stood over him for maybe three minutes, hardly daring to breathe, and suddenly she was seized with panic. She tiptoed out of the room, stopping by the door to make the sign of the cross over him. She left unnoticed, carrying in her heart an even heavier sadness.

Nikolai slept for more than an hour, all that time remaining in a stupor. Not a muscle stirred in his face or body; his brow remained as sternly knitted as it had been when he sat down. Had his mother stayed for three minutes longer, she probably would have been unable to bear the depressing sight of this lethargic immobility and would have wakened him. But he was alone when he opened his eyes and, having opened them, he still didn't stir for another ten minutes. He appeared to be looking intently at some object in the corner of the room, although actually there was nothing there to attract his attention particularly.

Then the large wall clock struck the half-hour softly and dully. Stavrogin turned his head and glanced worriedly at it. At that moment the other door of the study opened and Alexei the footman walked in. In one hand he carried Nikolai's warm overcoat, scarf, and hat, while in the other he held a silver tray with a note on it.

"It's half past nine, sir," he announced in a quiet voice. He laid the clothes he had brought across a chair in one corner of the room, then held out to Stavrogin the tray with the note, which consisted of two lines written in pencil. Nikolai read them, took a pencil from the desk, wrote two words on the same piece of paper, and replaced it on the tray.

"Take it back as soon as I've left. Now I'll dress," he said, getting up from the couch.

Realizing that he was wearing only a light velvet jacket, he thought for a moment, then told Alexei to bring him the formal black coat he wore when paying official visits in the evening.

When he was dressed—overcoat, hat, and all—he locked the door through which his mother had come to visit him, took the letter he had tried to conceal under the paperweight, and walked silently out of the room, followed by Alexei. He followed a corridor that led to a narrow, stone back staircase. They went downstairs and entered a small room that gave directly onto the garden. In a corner there was an umbrella and a small lantern that had apparently been placed there for this occasion.

"It's been raining steadily and the streets are very muddy," the footman said, trying for the last time to dissuade his master from going out.

But the master opened the umbrella and, without answering, walked out into the damp, wet garden, which was dark as a cellar. The wind was howling and swaying the almost leafless trees; the narrow, sandy garden paths were soggy and slippery. Alexei was hatless and wore no overcoat. He held up the lantern, lighting the way about three paces ahead of him.

"Doesn't it make us too conspicuous?" Stavrogin asked suddenly.

"They can't see us from the windows, sir. And besides, everything has been thoroughly prepared," Alexei said in a quiet, even tone.

"Mother asleep?"

"Madam retired at nine exactly, as she's been doing recently, and there'll be no way for her to find anything out, sir. At what time shall I expect you back, sir?" he added, daring to ask a question.

"At one or half past—not later than two."

"Very good, sir."

They followed winding paths that they both knew by heart and reached a small gate in the corner of the stone wall surrounding the garden. It led to a small, narrow side street and was always locked. Alexei produced a key.

"Won't it creak?" Stavrogin inquired, alarmed again.

Alexei explained that he had oiled it himself the day before and again that day. He was soaking wet by now. He unlocked the gate and handed the key to Stavrogin.

"If you have decided to go far, sir, may I say that I would beware of people you may meet, especially in dark, deserted alleys, sir—especially across the river."

Alexei was unable to refrain from giving his young master this one additional warning. He had known Nikolai as a small boy, carried him in his arms, and was a responsible, serious-minded servant who had a taste for reading devout books.

"Don't worry, Alexei."

"God be with you, sir—but only if what you do is righteous."

"What?" Stavrogin stopped. He was already in the street.

Alexei firmly repeated his words. Formerly, he would never have dared to express himself to his master in such a way.

Stavrogin locked the gate, slipped the key into his pocket, and walked off along the narrow street, sinking about three inches into the mud with every step. At last he came out onto a long, paved street which, at that hour, was completely deserted. He knew the town like the back of his hand and realized that Nativity Street was still a long way away. It was after ten when he reached the locked gates of Filipov's old house. Since the Lebyatkins' departure, the lower floor had been unoccupied and the windows were now boarded up, but on the upper floor, in Shatov's room, there was a light. There was no bell, so Stavrogin began to pound on the gate with his hand. The window opened and Shatov looked out into the street. It must have been difficult for him to distinguish anything, for he peered into the darkness for a full minute.

"Is that you?" he asked suddenly.

"It's me," Stavrogin said.

Shatov closed the window, came downstairs, and unlocked the gate. Stavrogin stepped over the high plank at the bottom of the gate and, without saying a word, walked straight toward Kirilov's cottage.

V

The cottage doors were unlocked and, in fact, open. The passage and the first two rooms were dark, but a light shone in a third room, the one in which Kirilov lived and drank his tea. Laughter and peculiar exclamations came from there. Stavrogin walked toward the lighted room, but stopped in the doorway. There was tea on the table. An old woman, the landlord's relative, stood in the middle of the room. She wore nothing on her head and had a rabbit-fur jacket over her petticoat and a pair of old shoes on her bare feet. She held in her arms an eighteen-month-old child wearing nothing but a shirt, its little legs bare, its cheeks flushed, and its almost white hair ruffled. The child looked as if it had just been picked up from its cradle. It had probably been crying, for there were tears in its eyes, but it was now clapping its hands and laughing delightedly, although sobs could still be heard through its laughter. It was staring at Kirilov, who was bouncing a red rubber ball in front of it. The ball bounced to the ceiling and came down again and the child shouted, "Baw! baw!" Then Kirilov caught the "baw" and gave it to the child, who threw it with its little hands, trying to make it bounce too. Kirilov rushed to pick it up. Finally the "baw" rolled under a chest of drawers, the child shouted impatiently, "Baw, baw!" and Kirilov stretched out flat on the floor, trying to reach it with his hand. When Stavrogin walked into the room, the child caught sight of him and immediately began to bawl, clinging to the old woman, who at once took it away.

"Stavrogin?" Kirilov said, getting up from the floor with the ball in his hand. He didn't seem in the least surprised at the visit. "Have some tea." He scrambled to his feet.

"I wouldn't mind at all, especially if it's really hot. I'm soaking wet."

"It's hot, very hot," Kirilov assured him, sounding pleased. "Sit down. Don't mind the mud you track in. I'll wipe the floor with a wet cloth later."

Stavrogin sat down and emptied his cup almost at one gulp.

"Another cup?"

"No thanks."

Kirilov, who had been standing, immediately sat down in front of Stavrogin.

"How is it you came?"

"On business. Here, read this letter. It's from Gaganov. I told you about him in Petersburg, remember?"

Kirilov took the letter, read it, and looked expectantly at Stavrogin.

"As you know," Stavrogin began to explain, "I met him a month ago in Petersburg, for the first time in my life. We met three times in the presence of other people. Without being introduced to me or introducing himself, he managed to be very insolent. I told you that before, but there's something you still don't know: since he was leaving Petersburg before me, he sent me a letter, and although it was nothing like this one, it was quite shocking and very strange—if only because he didn't bother to explain why he had actually sent it to me. I immediately wrote back to him stating quite frankly that I assumed he resented that incident with his father in the club here four years ago and that I, for my part, was prepared to apologize to him in any manner he

cared to name because my action had been unintentional and
due to my illness at that time. I asked him to take that into
consideration. He didn't answer and left. And now I've met
him here and he is wild with rage. Some of his public statements about me have been reported to me: they are really
insulting and full of the most extraordinary accusations.
Finally, today, I received this letter—a letter such as probably
no one has ever received before—full of vulgar and offensive
phrases like 'you with your punched-in face.' So I have come
to you hoping that you won't refuse to be my second."

"You say no one has ever received such a letter," Kirilov
remarked, "but people write letters like that when they're in a
rage. Pushkin wrote one to Hekern. All right, I'll do it. Tell
me how to go about it."

Stavrogin explained that he wanted Kirilov to go the very
next day and that it was absolutely necessary to start by
offering to apologize once more and even offering to send a
second letter of explanation and apology—on condition, however, that, for his part, Gaganov promised to stop sending insulting letters. Stavrogin would then consider the letter he had
just received as never having been written.

"Too many concessions. He won't accept," Kirilov said.

"I came here, actually, to ask you whether you'd agree to
deliver those particular terms to him."

"I'll deliver them. That's your business. But he won't accept."

"I know that."

"He wants to fight. You'd better tell me how you want to
fight him."

"Well, I'd like to have it all over with tomorrow. You'll see
him around nine in the morning. He'll hear you out, refuse,
and put you in touch with his seconds, let's say, by eleven.
Now, you arrange with them for us to meet by one or two.
The weapons will, of course, be pistols and I would like you to
see to it that the barriers are ten paces apart and that we
start to approach each other at a signal. Each of us must
stop at the barrier, but may fire before, as he closes in. Well,
that's all, I believe."

"Ten paces between the barriers—that's very close," Kirilov
said.

"All right, make it twelve at the outside. You must realize
that he wants to fight seriously. Do you know how to load a
pistol?"

"I do. I have my own pistols. I'll give them my word that you've never practiced with them. His second will also give his word about his. Then there'll be two pairs of pistols: mine and his, and we'll toss to see which pair is to be used."

"Very good."

"Would you like to have a look at my pistols?"

"I suppose so."

Kirilov squatted down in a corner by his suitcase. He hadn't bothered to unpack it and just fished various items out of it as he needed them. He now pulled out from the bottom a palm-wood case lined with red velvet and produced from it a couple of beautiful and very costly pistols.

"I have everything: powder, bullets, cartridges. Wait—I also have a revolver."

He delved into his suitcase once more and emerged with another box containing a six-chambered American revolver.

"You have lots of guns and they're expensive too."

"Yes, extremely expensive."

Kirilov was almost penniless and, although he apparently never noticed his poverty, he seemed proud to display the costly arsenal that he must have acquired at great sacrifice.

"You're still determined to go through with it?" Stavrogin asked rather diffidently, after a brief silence.

"I am," Kirilov said curtly. By the tone of the question, he had realized immediately what Stavrogin had in mind.

There was another brief silence. Then Stavrogin asked even more cautiously, "When?"

Kirilov replaced the weapons in the suitcase and resumed his seat.

"It's not up to me, as you know. I'll do it when I'm told," he said abruptly, as if he disliked the question but at the same time was prepared to answer any other queries. His black lusterless eyes remained fixed on Stavrogin, and the expression on his face was calm and rather friendly.

"I can understand a man's shooting himself, of course," Stavrogin said, frowning slightly, after a three-minute silence. "I've thought of it myself sometimes. And I've often said to myself, 'Suppose I committed a crime?'—I mean something really disgraceful, unspeakable, ridiculous . . . something people would remember with disgust for a thousand years. And then I'd think, 'One shot in the temple and there'll be nothing left. So, what do I care about people and whether or not they'll loathe me for a thousand years?' Don't you agree?"

"You call that a new idea?" Kirilov said, after pondering for a while what Stavrogin had said.

"I—I didn't call it. . . . It's just that, when it occurred to me, I felt . . . it felt like a new thought."

"Felt a thought, did you?" Kirilov said. "That's good. There are many thoughts that have been there all the time but suddenly feel new. That's true. There are many things I see now as though for the first time."

"Let's say you've been living on the moon," Stavrogin interrupted him, anxious to work his thought through to the end, "and let's say you've done all those loathsome, ridiculous things there. Well, when you get here, you know that, back there, they'll keep laughing and spitting at the mention of your name for thousands of years to come, all over the moon. But now you're on earth and you look at the moon from here and why should you care what you did over there and whether your name has been disgraced on the moon for thousands of years?"

"Don't know. Never been to the moon," Kirilov said without any irony, just as a flat statement of fact.

"Whose child was that in here before?"

"The old woman's stepdaughter—I mean daughter-in-law—came here. Three days ago, with the child. She's sick, moans at night. It's very bad—her belly. When the mother goes to sleep, the old woman brings the child in here and I keep it quiet. With this ball. I bought the ball in Hamburg. I throw it and catch it—it strengthens the back. It's a girl."

"You like children?"

"Yes," Kirilov said, quite indifferently.

"So, you must like life too, then?"

"I like it, why?"

"And yet you intend to shoot yourself."

"So what? That has nothing to do with it. Life is one thing and the other thing is something else. Life exists, but there is no such thing as death."

"Have you come to believe in a future, eternal life then?"

"No, not in a future, eternal life, but in this present, eternal life. There are moments—you can reach moments—when time suddenly stops and becomes eternal."

"And you hope to reach such a moment?"

"I do."

"It's hardly likely in our time," Stavrogin said slowly and

thoughtfully, also without any irony. "In the Apocalypse, the angel promises that there'll be no more time."

"I know. There's a lot of truth in it; it's clear and precise. When man attains happiness, there will be no more time because there will be no need for it. It's a very true thought."

"Where will they hide time?"

"Nowhere. Time is not a thing, it's an idea. It will vanish from the mind."

"The old commonplaces of philosophy—always the same since the beginning of time," Stavrogin said with a mixture of sadness and disgust.

"The very same since the beginning of the ages! Yes, and there will be no others—ever!" Kirilov repeated. His eyes sparkled as though that thought proved his point.

"You sound very happy, Kirilov."

"Very happy," Kirilov said casually, as though answering the most everyday question.

"But only recently you seemed so worried and also angry with Liputin."

"Hm . . . I have nothing against anyone now. Then, I still didn't know I was happy. Have you ever looked at a leaf, the leaf of a tree?"

"I have."

"I saw one recently. It was yellow, with some green in it and a bit wilted at the edges. The wind was blowing it around. When I was ten, in the winter, I'd close my eyes and imagine a leaf—green, bright, with those little veins, and glistening in the sun. When I opened my eyes, I couldn't believe it possible because it was too beautiful. Then I'd close my eyes again."

"What is that, an allegory?"

"N-no, why? I meant no allegory, just a leaf. One leaf. It's beautiful, a leaf. Everything is good."

"Everything?"

"Everything. Man is unhappy because he doesn't know he's happy. That's the only reason. The man who discovers that will become happy that very minute. That stepdaughter will die, the little girl will remain—and everything is good. I've suddenly discovered that."

"So it's good, too, that people die of hunger and also that someone may abuse or rape that little girl?"

"It's good. And if someone breaks open that man's skull for the girl, that's good too. And if someone doesn't break his skull, it's equally good. Everything's good. If they only knew they were happy, they'd be happy, but as long as they don't, they're unhappy. And that's all there is to it."

"And when did you find out you were so happy?"

"Last week, on Tuesday. No—it was Wednesday. It was during the night between Tuesday and Wednesday."

"On what occasion?"

"I don't remember. I was just pacing the room. It's not important. I stopped the clock. It was two thirty-seven in the morning."

"Was that a symbolic gesture meaning that time must stop?"

Kirilov didn't answer the question. After a while, he said:

"They're bad because they don't know they're good. When they know it, they won't rape the little girl. They must find out that they're good, and then they'll be good to the last, the lot of them."

"So, since you've found out, you must be good now?"

"Right, I'm good."

"I must say I agree with that," Stavrogin said, frowning.

"He who succeeds in teaching men that they are all good will end the world."

"He who tried to teach that was crucified."

"He'll come and his name is man-god."

"God-man?"

"No, man-god—that's the great difference."

"I wonder now, was it you who lit that lamp before the icon?"

"It was I."

"So you've got religion finally?"

"The old woman likes to have the lamp lit . . . and today she had no time."

"But, I trust you've not yet started praying yourself?"

"I pray to everything. See that spider crawling there, on the wall? I look at it and I'm grateful to it because it crawls."

His eyes sparkled again. He looked straight into Stavrogin's face, firmly and unwaveringly. Stavrogin was frowning, watching him with distaste, but there was no sarcasm in his expression.

"I bet when I come over to see you next time, you'll be believing in God," he said, rising and picking up his hat.

"Why?" Kirilov said, also standing up.

"If you found out that you believed in God, you'd believe in Him, but since you still don't know, you don't believe yet," Stavrogin said with a snort.

"That's not right," Kirilov said. "You've twisted the thought. It's a drawing-room witticism. Remember the part you've played in my life, Stavrogin."

"Good-by, Kirilov."

"Come and see me again one night. When?"

"Why, you haven't forgotten about tomorrow, I hope?"

"Ah, I had. But don't worry, I won't oversleep. I'll be there at nine. I know how to wake up when I want to. I turn in and say to myself: seven, and I wake up at seven; if I say ten, it's ten sharp."

"Remarkable powers," Stavrogin said, looking at Kirilov's pale face.

"I'll come and unlock the gate for you."

"Don't bother, Shatov will do it."

"Shatov? Good. Good night then."

VI

The door of the empty house where Shatov lived was unlocked. Stavrogin entered and found himself in complete darkness. He was groping for the stairs when a door opened on the top landing and light shone out of it. Shatov had pushed the door of his room open without coming out himself. Stavrogin went up. From the doorway he saw Shatov standing expectantly in the corner of the room by the table.

"May I come in? I must see you on business," Stavrogin asked from outside.

"Come in and sit down. Lock the door. No, wait—I'll do it myself."

He locked the door, returned to the table, and sat down in front of Stavrogin. He had grown thinner during the past week and looked feverish.

"You've driven me out of my mind," he said in a half whisper, looking down. "Why didn't you come before?"

"Why were you so sure I'd come at all?"

"Wait—I was delirious—maybe I still am. Wait . . ."

He stood up and took something from the top of the three shelves of books. It was a revolver.

"I had a nightmare about you coming to kill me, so the next morning I spent the last of my money to buy this revolver from that good-for-nothing Lyamshin. I didn't want to let you get me. Then I came to my senses. . . . I have no ammunition. Since then it has been lying around on the shelf. Wait. . . ." He got up and was about to open the window.

"Don't throw it out," Stavrogin said. "Why should you? It cost money and, besides, tomorrow people will be going around saying there are guns lying around under Shatov's windows. Put it back. Fine. Now sit down. Tell me, why do you sound apologetic about thinking I'd kill you? You must understand—I haven't come here to make peace with you, but to have a talk, which is indispensable. Tell me, first of all—when you hit me, it wasn't because of my involvement with your wife, was it?"

"You know perfectly well that that wasn't the reason," Shatov said, staring down again.

"And, of course, not because you believe that stupid gossip about me and your sister?"

"No, no, of course not—that's idiotic! Dasha told me from the very beginning . . ." Shatov said impatiently, even stamping his foot.

"So I've guessed and you've guessed," Stavrogin said with detachment. "You're right—I've been lawfully married to Maria Lebyatkin for four and a half years, since Petersburg. That's why you hit me, wasn't it?"

Shatov looked at him silently in complete bewilderment.

"Yes—I guessed it, but I couldn't believe . . ." he muttered at last.

"Still, you struck me for it?"

Shatov flushed and mumbled almost incomprehensibly:

"I did it because of your degradation—for your lies! When I walked over to you it wasn't to punish you—I didn't know I'd hit you. . . . I did it because you've meant so much to me—I—"

"I understand, I understand. Spare yourself the trouble. It's too bad you're feverish. I have very important business to discuss."

"I've waited for you too long," Shatov said shivering, apparently on the point of jumping up from his chair. "Say what you have to say and then I'll speak too—later."

"What I have to say has nothing to do with all that," Stavrogin said, looking at him with curiosity. "Because of certain circumstances I had to come here at this very hour to warn you that you may be killed."

Shatov looked at him wildly.

"I'm aware that my life may be in danger," he said slowly, "but how did you know?"

"Because, like you, I'm a member of the society."

"You?"

"I can see by your eyes that you'd have expected anything of me but that," Stavrogin snorted. "But anyway you already knew that they were plotting against your life?"

"I never took it seriously and don't now, despite your warning, although who can be sure of anything with those morons!" Shatov suddenly shouted, furiously banging his fist on the table. "I'm not afraid of them! I'm through with them. That fellow came here four times to tell me that it was possible—but," he looked squarely at Stavrogin, "what do you know about it?"

"I assure you I'm not deceiving you," Stavrogin said rather coolly, sounding like a man who was merely discharging an obligation. "Are you trying to examine me by asking me what I know about it? Well, I know that you joined the society abroad two years ago under the old setup, just before your trip to America. I believe it was almost immediately after our last conversation about which you wrote to me so much from the United States. By the way, I hope you've forgiven me for not answering you by letter, except by—"

"By sending me money," Shatov said hurriedly. "Wait now." He pulled out a drawer and handed Stavrogin a rainbow-colored, hundred-ruble bill. "Here are the hundred rubles you sent me. I'd have perished there without you. It would've taken me a very long time to pay you back if it hadn't been for your mother: she gave me these hundred rubles after my sickness, when I was penniless. But go on, please." He was quite out of breath.

"In America, your views changed and when you got back to Switzerland you decided to resign. They ignored your request and instead ordered you to take charge of some printing press here in Russia and then hand it over to one of their people when he claimed it in their name. I'm not familiar with every detail of the assignment, but wouldn't you say that, on the whole, what I say is correct? As to you, you agreed to comply on condition—or simply hoping—that this would be the last thing they'd ask you to do and that after that you'd break with them altogether."

"That's all damned nonsense!" Shatov shouted at the top

of his voice. "I told them openly that I disagreed with them on everything! That's my right! I have a right to my conscience, to my own thoughts. I won't stand for it! There's no force that can make me!"

"You know, you'd better stop hollering like that," Stavrogin said seriously. "That Peter Verkhovensky is the sort of bird that might very well be eavesdropping on us directly or using someone else's ear. Even that drunkard Lebyatkin may have been instructed to keep his eye on you, just as you were ordered to keep yours on him, or would you say I'm wrong? You'd better tell me whether Verkhovensky has accepted your arguments now or not."

"He has. He said it was possible to leave the organization and that I was entitled—"

"Well then, let me tell you that he was lying to you. I know that even Kirilov, who is hardly connected with them any more, has been informing on you. Besides, they have lots of agents, many of whom don't even know they're working for the society. You've been watched all this time. And, by the way, Peter Verkhovensky came here mainly to settle this business about you and he has full authority to do so, that is, to have you liquidated at the first convenient moment, because you know too much and may decide to talk. I repeat, you can absolutely count on it. They are somehow convinced that you are a police spy and that, if you haven't informed on them yet, you're liable to at the first opportunity. Tell me now, is it really so?"

Stavrogin's matter-of-fact tone in asking him such a question made Shatov wince. His mouth twisted.

"Even if I were a spy, to whom would I report?" he said angrily. "No, leave me alone! Never mind me!" he shouted suddenly, coming back to his original idea that obviously preoccupied him much more than the news about his life's being in danger. "Tell me, Stavrogin, how could you—you of all people—get involved in this loathsome, stupid organization of flunkies? So you're a member of the society! Some achievement for Nikolai Stavrogin!"

He even clasped his hands despairingly, as though Stavrogin's membership in the organization were the most horrible disgrace that he could imagine.

"Forgive me for saying so," Stavrogin said with real surprise in his voice, "but you seem to consider me as some sort of sun and yourself as a bug in comparison. I could tell that even from your letter from America—"

"You know, you know very well—let's not talk about it at all!" Shatov cut him short. "If you can explain something about yourself, do so—something that would answer what I asked you," he added in a feverish voice.

"Of course. You want to know how I could get myself involved with such low, shady characters? Well, after what I've told you, I suppose I owe you a candid explanation. You see, strictly speaking, I have never belonged to the society and am more entitled than you to just walk out on them, since I never joined them in the first place. On the contrary, from the beginning, I told them that I was no comrade of theirs and that if I had helped them it was only accidentally and out of boredom. I only took a certain part in reorganizing the society, and that's all. But now I think they've decided it would be dangerous to let me go and have passed the death sentence on me too."

"With them it's always the death sentence, which is drawn up on an official document with seals and signed by three and a half men. . . . Do you really think they can carry it out?"

"There, you're partly right and partly wrong," Stavrogin said rather indifferently, almost lazily. "There's no doubt that they're a bit carried away by their imaginations and, like all small groups, tend to exaggerate their power and influence. But, if you ask me, the entire society is essentially one man— Peter Verkhovensky. He's too modest in claiming to be only an agent of the organization. But, in fairness, the group's ideology is no more stupid than that of other similar groups. They have links with the International; they have succeeded in creating a network of agents in Russia, and have even stumbled upon a quite original method—oh, only in theory, of course. As to their local plans, you must remember that the moves of the Russian branch of the International are so unaccountable and unexpected because everything seems worth trying in this country. And then, Verkhovensky is a determined character, you know."

"He's a bedbug, an ignoramus, and an idiot who understands nothing about Russia!" Shatov shouted furiously.

"You know him very little, although it's true that none of them understands very much about Russia. But then, who does? Even you and I don't understand so much more than they do. Besides, Verkhovensky is a fanatic."

"Verkhovensky a fanatic?"

"Certainly he is. There's a point at which he ceases to be a clown and becomes a maniac. I would like to remind you of one of your own statements—that one single man can be incredibly strong. Please don't dismiss him offhand like that; he's quite capable of pulling a trigger. They're convinced that I'm a spy too. Their organizational clumsiness makes them tend to see spies everywhere."

"But you're not afraid of them, of course?"

"N-no—not really. But, in your case, it's rather different. You really should keep in mind what I've told you. I don't think you should be offended at my telling you that danger threatens you from those fools. It has nothing to do with their intellectual prowess—they've annihilated better people than you and me. But it's quarter past eleven," he said, getting up and looking at his watch, "and I would like to ask you a question that has nothing to do with all this."

"Do! For God's sake, go ahead!" Shatov said, leaping up from his chair.

"What do you mean?" Stavrogin looked at him with surprise.

"Ask me—ask me that question, for God's sake!" Shatov repeated in extreme agitation. "But on condition that you allow me to ask you a question too. Please, please let me—I can't —go on, ask your question now!"

Stavrogin shrugged slightly and began:

"I understand that you've had some influence on Maria Lebyatkin here—that she liked seeing you and listening to you. Is that correct?"

"Yes . . . she did listen. . . ." Shatov said, embarrassed.

"One of these days I intend to announce publicly in this town that we are married."

"But is it possible?" Shatov whispered, almost horrified.

"Why? What do you mean by that? There are no difficulties. The witnesses to the marriage are present here. The marriage in Petersburg was fully legal and regular, and if it has remained a secret, it is because the witnesses to it—Peter Verkhovensky and Alexei Kirilov, as well as Lebyatkin himself, whom I'm now entitled to call my brother-in-law—have given me their word not to divulge it."

"That's not what I had in mind. You're so matter of fact!

But go on, please! And listen—you weren't forced to marry her, were you?"

"No, no one forced me to marry her," Stavrogin said, smiling at Shatov's belligerent impatience.

"Then why does she always talk about that child of hers?" Shatov said quickly, sounding feverish again.

"About a child? That's the first I've heard of it. She hasn't had a child—couldn't have had: Maria is a virgin."

"Ah, that's just what I thought! Listen now—"

"But what's come over you, Shatov?"

Shatov covered his face with his hands and turned away, then suddenly gripped Stavrogin by the shoulder.

"Do you know—do you have the least idea why you're doing all this and in the name of what you are willing to take punishment now?"

"That's a biting question and a clever one, but I have a surprise for you: yes, I do more or less know why I married her then and why I'm willing to accept *punishment now*, as you put it."

"Let's leave that for a moment—we'll come back to it— I want to speak about the most important thing: I've waited for you for two years."

"Is that so?"

"I've waited for you too long, thinking of you ceaselessly. You're the only man who could have—I wrote to you about that while I was still in America."

"I remember that long letter very well."

"Too long to read? I agree: six pages. No, wait—be quiet. Can't you give me another ten minutes of your time—but right now? I've waited for you too long!"

"I'll be glad to accommodate you. But I hope half an hour will satisfy you; that's all I can spare."

"That will do—on condition that you change your tone!" Shatov answered angrily. "But listen to me—I'm demanding when I should be imploring. Listen, do you understand what it means to demand when one is only in a position to implore?"

"I understand that it makes you feel you're soaring over commonplaces in pursuit of your higher ideals," Stavrogin said with a twisted smile. "And I'm sorry to see you're feverish."

"I implore you—I demand that you treat me with respect!" Shatov shouted at the top of his voice, "Not respect for me personally—to hell with that—but for the other thing. I only have time to say a few words about it. We're merely two creatures meeting in limitless space—for the last time in this world. Drop that tone and for once in your life talk like a human being! I'm not asking for my own sake but for yours. Don't you understand that you must forgive me for striking you in the face if only because it gave you the opportunity to take cognizance of your own immense strength? Ah, there it is again: that supercilious, elegant smile of yours. Ah, when will you understand! To hell with the young dandy in you! Understand, finally, that that is what I demand! Yes, I demand it—otherwise I won't talk, not for anything!"

His frenzy was making him completely delirious. Stavrogin frowned and appeared to grow more careful.

"Since, after all, I have agreed to stay here for half an hour when time is so precious to me," he said slowly and seriously, "you may rest assured that I'll listen to you at least with interest and—and I'm quite convinced that I'll hear much that's new to me."

He sat down.

"Sit down!" Shatov shouted, abruptly throwing himself into his chair too.

"I must remind you of what I was saying before, however," Stavrogin said, as though he had suddenly remembered something. "I was about to ask you a great favor concerning Maria, something that is very important—at any rate for her."

"Well?" Shatov said, screwing up his face with the expression of a man who has been interrupted at the most important point in his speech and glares at the interrupter although the meaning of the question hasn't yet reached him.

"You didn't give me a chance to finish my request," Stavrogin said with a smile.

"Ah, that's nothing—later . . ." Shatov brushed him aside with disgust, at last understanding Stavrogin's grievance. Then he went directly on to what interested him most.

VII

Shatov began almost threateningly, leaning forward in his chair, his eyes flashing, and his right hand raised in front of him with the index finger pointing upward. He himself appeared to be unaware of this.

"Do you know," he said, "which is the one and only God-bearing nation on earth, destined to regenerate and save the world in the name of the new God—the nation that alone holds the keys of life and the New Word? Do you know what the name of that nation is?"

"From the way you say it, I have no choice but to answer that it is the Russian nation, and the sooner I do so the better."

"Ah, you're already laughing—what a bunch!" Shatov said, catching fire again.

"Please, take it easy. I'm not laughing; in fact, I expected you to come out with something like that."

"*Something like that*? As if the very words were not familiar to you!"

"They're very familiar. I see only too well what you're driving at. Everything you've said, including the phrase 'God-bearing nation' itself, is simply the conclusion of a conversation we had just over two years ago, when we were abroad, shortly before your departure for the United States. At least, from what I can remember—"

"The phrase is yours and not mine at all. It is your own phrase and not the conclusion of some conversation we had. There was no conversation between us; there was a teacher *saying* great words and a disciple who had risen from the dead. You're the teacher and I'm the disciple."

"But if I remember correctly, after hearing my words you joined the society, and you only left for America considerably later."

"Yes—and I wrote to you about that from America. I wrote to you about everything. Yes, I couldn't tear myself from something that had stuck to me since my childhood like a bandage to a congealed wound without drawing blood. All the raptures of childhood, all the tears of hatred were there. . . . It's difficult to change gods. I didn't believe you then, because I didn't want to believe and I clung to that garbage dump. But the seed remained and grew. Tell me the truth: did you really not read all of my letter from America? Maybe you didn't read it at all?"

"I read three of the six pages: the first two and the last, and just scanned through the middle pages. However, I always meant to—"

"Ah, I don't care—to hell with it!" Shatov brushed him aside with his hand. "What depresses me now is that you don't believe what you yourself said then about the Russian people."

"I wasn't fooling you then any more than now," Stavrogin said in a tone that was hard to decipher. "I was trying to persuade you, but I was perhaps more interested in convincing myself than you."

"You weren't fooling! In America I lay on straw for three months next to that wretched Kirilov and then I found out that, at the same time—perhaps on the very same day— that you were sowing those ideas about God and Russia in me, you were poisoning Kirilov's mind, the wretched maniac. You implanted all sorts of lies and other drivel in his mind and brought him to the edge of insanity. Go and have a look at him now; go and admire your creation— though I know you've seen him already."

"In the first place, allow me to tell you that only a few moments ago Kirilov assured me that he was happy and good. Now, as to your assumption that it all happened at the same time, it is almost correct. But so what? I repeat, I wasn't deceiving either of you."

"Are you an atheist? You're an atheist now, aren't you?"

"I am."

"And then?"

"Then as much as I am now."

"It wasn't myself that I asked you to respect at the beginning of our conversation. A man of your intelligence should've understood that right away," Shatov muttered indignantly.

"I didn't get up and leave after the first word you said. I'm still sitting here quietly, listening to your questions and your shouting and trying to answer you, which shows that, so far, I haven't been lacking in respect for you."

Shatov waved his hands and interrupted him:

"Do you remember your own phrase: 'A Russian can't be godless. As soon as he becomes godless, he ceases to be Russian'? Remember?"

"What?" Stavrogin said, as though asking him to repeat what he had said.

"You ask what? Have you forgotten? But that is one of the most acute remarks you've ever made—it's a major characteristic of the Russian spirit that you divined. You couldn't possibly have forgotten it. Let me remind you further. You also said: 'One who is not Russian Orthodox cannot be a Russian.'"

"I suppose that's a Slavophile notion."

"No—today's Slavophiles reject it. Today, the people have grown too clever. But you went further—you believed that Roman Catholicism was no longer Christian. You maintained that Rome had proclaimed a Christ who had succumbed to the Devil's third temptation and that, by announcing to the world that Christ couldn't hold out on earth without an earthly kingdom, Catholicism had really proclaimed the Antichrist and thus was leading the Western world to perdition. You actually said that if France was suffering it was through the fault of Catholicism, because France had rejected the decaying Romish god, but had not found another to replace him. That's what you said then. I remember that conversation with you very clearly."

"If I believed it still, I'm sure I'd repeat it now. I wasn't lying when I spoke as a believer," Stavrogin said very seriously. "But I assure you that recalling my former beliefs like this leaves an unpleasant aftertaste in my mouth, so I'd appreciate it if you'd drop it. Could you manage that, do you think?"

"If you believed it still!" Shatov cried, entirely disregarding Stavrogin's request. "Wasn't it you who said that even if it was proved to you mathematically that the Truth was outside Christ, you would prefer to remain with Christ outside the Truth? Did you or didn't you say that?"

"Wait now. Let me ask you a question in my turn," Stavrogin said, raising his voice somewhat. "What, really, is the point of this impatient and hostile examination?"

"The examination is just about over and you'll never be bothered with it again as long as you live."

"You keep insisting that we're outside space and time—"

"Shut up!" Shatov shouted suddenly. "I know I'm stupid and awkward—and may my name be drowned in ridicule! Won't you allow me just to repeat the core of your former idea to you? Only a few words—only the conclusion!"

"If it's only the conclusion, go ahead—repeat it." Stavrogin was about to glance at his watch, but restrained himself.

Shatov again leaned forward in his chair and for a second raised his index finger once more.

"Not one single nation," he began, as though reciting, but at the same time glaring at Stavrogin, "has, as yet, based its life on reason and science, except for a few moments, and then out of sheer stupidity. In its very essence, socialism is godless—it proclaimed in its very first statement that it aims at an organization that does not presuppose God; that is, an organization based on the principles of reason and science exclusively. But reason and science have always performed, and still perform, only an auxiliary function in the life of peoples, and it will be like that till the end of time. Nations are formed and moved by some other force whose origin is unknown and unaccountable. That force is the unquenchable will to reach an end and, at the same time, the denial of that end. It is the force of an incessant and unwavering affirmation of life and a denial of death. It is the spirit of life, 'river of water of life' as the Scriptures call it, the drying up of which is threatened in the Apocalypse. Some philosophers claim it is based on an aesthetic, others on an ethical principle, but I call it simply the search for God. The objective of any nationalist movement in any people at any time is actually a search for God, for their own, national God—and it must, above all, be their own God— and belief in Him as the only true God. God's personality is a synthesis of the entire nation from the beginning of its existence to its end. Never have all nations—or even many of them—shared one common God; each of them has always had its own God. When gods become common, it is a sign that nations are doomed to disappear. When gods are shared, they die; and belief in them dies as the nations disappear. The more vital a people, the more individual and special its god. There has never yet existed a people without religion— that is, without a concept of good and evil. Each nation has its own concept of good and evil and its own native good and evil. When many nations begin to have common concepts of good and evil, those nations die out and then the difference between good and evil starts to fade and vanishes. Reason has never yet managed to define good and evil or even distinguish between them, if only approximately. On the contrary, reason has always mixed them up shamefully and miserably. As for science, its answers have always been based on brute force. This has been the special knack of pseudoscience, that terrible scourge of mankind, a scourge worse than plague, famine, and war, an evil that didn't exist until this century. Half-knowledge is a tyrant without precedent, one that has its own priests and slaves; a tyrant that is worshiped with unprecedented awe and adulation and before which science itself fawns and cringes. Well, those are all your own words, Stavrogin, except for the remarks about half-knowledge, which are my own. I happen to hate half-knowledge more than anything. But I haven't modified any of your thoughts or even changed a word of what you said."

"I doubt that those are my exact words," Stavrogin said cautiously. "You drank them in eagerly and just as eagerly distorted them without being aware of it. The fact that you boil God down to a mere national attribute—"

He suddenly became intensely observant, not so much of Shatov's words as of the man himself.

"So now I'm reducing God to a national attribute, am I?" Shatov shouted. "It's just the other way around; I'm raising the nation to God. And indeed, has it ever been otherwise? A people forms the body of its god. A nation is a nation only so long as it has its particular god and excludes as irreconcilable all other gods; so long as it believes that with the help of its god it will conquer and destroy all other gods. All great nations have so believed since the beginning of time—at least all who have left their mark as nations, who have led mankind. It is impossible to dismiss this fact. The Jews lived only to await the coming of the true God and they left the true God to the world. The Greeks worshiped nature and bequeathed their religion to the world—their philosophy and art. Rome deified the state and left the concept of the state as a legacy to the nations. France, during all her long history, has been nothing but the incarnation and elaboration of the concept of the Romish god and if she has now gone over to atheism—which they call socialism over there—it is only because even atheism is healthier than Roman Catholicism. If a great nation does not believe that it alone to the exclusion of any other possesses the sole truth, if it does not believe that it alone is destined to and can regenerate and save the rest of the world through the truth it holds, it immediately ceases to be a great nation and becomes merely an ethnographical designation. But there is only one truth and therefore only one people can possess it and, with it, the only true God, though other peoples may have their own particular gods, even great ones. Now, the only God-bearing nation is the Russian nation and—and do you really take me for such a fool, Stavrogin?" he suddenly screamed madly. "A fool who can't even tell the difference between the tired old platitudes from Moscow's Slavophile mills and the completely new word—the final, true, and *only* word of renewal and resurrection and—what the hell do I care if just now it strikes you as all very funny! And why should I care if you don't understand me, if you don't understand one word, one syllable of what I've said? Oh, right now, how I loathe your supercilious expression and your laughter!"

He leaped up from his chair. There was froth at the corners of his mouth.

"You have it all wrong, Shatov," Stavrogin said very quietly and seriously, without budging, "Your heated words have stirred very powerful memories in me. In your words I recognize my own mood of a couple of years ago and this time I won't tell you, as I did just now, that you have distorted my former ideas. In fact, I have the impression that they were, if anything, even stronger, more absolute, and I assure you for the third time that I would be very happy if I could agree to everything you've said now, down to the last word. However—"

"But you need a hare?"

"What?"

"I repeat one of your own disgusting expressions: 'Before you can cook a hare, you must catch it,'" Shatov said with a hostile laugh, and sat down again, "'and before believing in God you must first find a god.' That was one of your favorite sayings in Petersburg where you felt like Gogol's Nozdrev, who claimed he could catch hares by the hind legs."

"No, Nozdrev just boasted that he had already caught them. By the way, may I ask you something too? I feel I'm entitled to. Tell me, is your hare caught already or is it still roaming around?"

"Don't you dare ask it like that!" Shatov said, beginning to tremble suddenly. "Use other, different words."

"All right, I'll ask it differently, if you insist," Stavrogin said, looking at him sternly. "I wanted to find out whether or not you yourself believe in God."

"I believe in Russia and in the Russian Orthodox Church. . . . I believe in the body of Christ. . . . I believe that His new coming will take place in Russia. . . . I believe—I believe . . ." Shatov mumbled in ecstasy.

"But in God? Do you believe in God?"

"I—I *shall* believe in God."

Not a single muscle moved in Stavrogin's face. Shatov looked at him with blazing eyes, as though he wanted to set him on fire with his gaze.

"I never told you," Shatov said at last, "that I didn't

believe in God at all. I was only trying to say that I am nothing but a wretched bore for the time being—the time being. But who cares about me? It is you, not me, who matters. I'm nothing but a man without talent, and all I have to offer is my blood, like anyone else who has no talent. But the hell with my blood—I'm concerned with you. I've been waiting for you here for two years and for the past hour I've felt as though I were dancing naked before you. . . . You're the only one who could have raised that banner. . . ."

He didn't finish, but, as though in despair, put his elbows on the table and clutched his head in his hands.

"I wonder, hasn't it ever struck you as odd," Stavrogin said suddenly, "that everyone seems so anxious to force some banner upon me? Peter Verkhovensky is also convinced that I am the one to raise their banner, or, at least, words of his to that effect have been repeated to me. He's decided that I could be some sort of Stenka Razin for them, because of my 'uncanny talent for crime.' Those are supposed to be the actual words he used."

"What? Because of your 'uncanny talent for crime'?"

"Right."

"Hm," Shatov said with a fierce snort, "and is it true that in Petersburg you belonged to some secret society that practiced the most bestial sensuality? Is it true that you could have given some tips to the Marquis de Sade himself? Is it true that you used to entice children and abuse them? Speak up, man, and don't you dare lie to me!" he shouted, completely beside himself. "Nikolai Stavrogin may not lie to Shatov, who hit him in the face! Tell me the whole truth, and if what I've said is true I'll kill you here and now!"

"I did say those words, but I never harmed children," Stavrogin said. But he said it after a silence that had lasted too long. He had turned pale and his eyes glowed.

"But you did talk," Shatov went on imperiously, without taking his shining eyes from Stavrogin. "Is it true that you said that you could see no aesthetic difference between some voluptuous, bestial prank and a heroic feat such as even giving one's life for the good of mankind? Is it true that you found an equal beauty and an equal pleasure in those extremes?"

"It's impossible to answer just like that—I won't answer," Stavrogin muttered.

He could very well have risen and left, but he didn't,

"I don't know either why evil is ugly and good beautiful,

but I know why the distinction between good and evil becomes blurred in people like Stavrogin," Shatov, who was trembling all over, persisted. "Shall I tell you why you married that woman, so shamefully, so disgracefully? You did it precisely because the senselessness and the disgrace of it bordered on genius! Ah, you don't content yourself with teetering on the brink of the abyss—you plunge into it headfirst. You married her to satisfy your passion for cruelty, your passion for remorse; you went through with it for the mental sensuality. It was a deliberate laceration of the nerves. You couldn't resist making such a challenge to common sense! Think of it— Stavrogin and the half-witted, penniless, lopsided cripple! By the way, did you feel a voluptuous thrill when you took a bite out of the governor's ear? Did you, you good-for-nothing, loafing young gentleman?"

"You're a real psychologist," Stavrogin said, turning paler and paler, "although you're not quite right about my reasons for marrying. But who could possibly have supplied you with all that information?" He laughed constrainedly. "Could it have been Kirilov by any chance? But how could he? He took no part in—"

"Why have you turned so pale?"

"But what is it you want?" Stavrogin said, raising his voice at last. "I've been taking a lashing from you for at least half an hour. You might at least let me go civilly, unless you have good reason for treating me like this."

"Good reason?"

"Certainly. The least you could do now is explain what you're after. I've been waiting for it, but so far I've seen nothing but mad spite on your part. So now, please, will you unlock the gate for me?"

He stood up. Shatov rushed frantically toward him.

"Kiss the earth—drench it with your tears and ask for forgiveness!" he shouted, clutching Stavrogin by the shoulder.

"I didn't kill you, though, that day. . . . I drew my hands back . . ." Stavrogin said, looking down and appearing to be suffering great pain.

"Come on, spill the rest of it! You came to warn me of danger, you've allowed me to speak; tomorrow you will announce your marriage publicly. Do you think I can't see from your face that some new, dreadful idea is now taking hold of you? Stavrogin, why am I doomed to believe in you to the end? Do you think I could ever speak like this to anyone else? I'm usually very restrained, but I haven't hesitated to bare my soul before you, nor have I hesitated to caricature the great idea by putting it into words, since it was Stavrogin I was talking to. As though I'd be able to prevent myself from kissing the spots where your feet have trodden when you leave here. . . . I can't tear you out of my heart, Nikolai Stavrogin!"

"I'm sorry I can't love you in return, Shatov," Stavrogin said coolly.

"I know you can't; I know you're not lying. But listen, I can arrange everything: I'll catch the hare for you!"

Stavrogin said nothing.

"You're godless because you're a son of the idle rich, the last of the idle rich. You've lost the ability to distinguish good and evil because you've lost touch with the people of your own country. A new generation is on its way that is coming straight from the heart of the people and you won't recognize it—neither you, nor the Verkhovenskys, father and son, nor me, because I too, being the son of your flunky, come from the idle rich. Listen, Stavrogin, find God through labor. That is the essence of everything. Find God or you'll vanish without a trace like a rotten fungus. Find God through labor!"

"What sort of labor?"

"The work of a laborer, a peasant. Give up your possessions —ah, you laugh. Are you afraid that there's a trick in it somewhere, or what?"

Stavrogin was not laughing. "So you assume that God can be reached through labor, and especially the labor of a peasant?" he said thoughtfully, as though he had stumbled upon something new that was really worth thinking about. "By the way," he said, going off at a tangent, "speaking of possessions, you may be interested to know that I'm not at all rich and therefore have nothing much to give up. I'm hardly even in a position to provide for Maria's future. What I wanted to ask you was not to leave her if you can help it, because you are the only one who has some little influence upon her poor mind. I say that because who knows what may happen. . . ."

"All right, all right, about Maria . . ." Shatov said, brushing Stavrogin off with one hand; he held a candle in the other. "We'll see about her later—that goes without saying. But listen, go and see Tikhon."

"Who?"

"Tikhon. He's a former bishop. He's retired because of illness now. He lives just outside the town at the Efimovo Monastery of Our Lady."

"So?"

"Well, people come to see him from everywhere. I think you ought to go too. What would it cost you?"

"This is the first I ever heard of him. I've never yet had anything to do with people of that sort. Thank you, I suppose I'll go."

"This way." Shatov lighted Stavrogin downstairs. "Go on, then," he said, flinging the gate open.

"I won't come to see you any more. Shatov," Stavrogin said quietly, stepping out into the street.

The street was as dark as before and it was still raining.

chapter 2

NIGHT (CONTINUED)

I

He went along the entire length of Nativity Street. At the end of it the road started to go downhill. His boots squished in the mud. Suddenly, a broad, open misty space loomed up in front of him. It was the river.

The houses here were hovels and a maze of irregular twisting alleys replaced the street.

For a long while Stavrogin followed the fences, keeping close to the riverbank. He made his way easily, without even thinking about it. His thoughts were somewhere else altogether, until he realized with surprise that he was in the middle of our long pontoon bridge, which was all wet from the rain. It seemed deserted, so Stavrogin felt very strange when he suddenly heard a voice speaking familiarly in a tone that was rather pleasant despite its obsequiousness and exaggeratedly suave articulation, such as is affected by our over-genteel shopkeepers and their wavy-haired assistants.

"Might I, kind sir, avail myself of the shelter of your umbrella?"

And, indeed, a figure appeared and actually tried to join

Stavrogin under his umbrella, walking close to him, practically "rubbing elbows" with him, as the saying goes. Slowing his step, Stavrogin bent toward the man, trying to make him out in the darkness. He was rather on the small side and might have been some shopkeeper on a binge. His clothes were shabby and too light for the weather, and a cloth cap with a broken vizor sat precariously on his tousled, curly hair, which looked very dark. The fellow generally appeared to be very dark, swarthy, and wiry. His eyes were large and Stavrogin felt they must be shiny black with a yellow glint in them, like a gypsy's. He must have been forty or so and he didn't seem to be drunk.

"Do you know me?" Stavrogin asked.

"You are Mr. Stavrogin, sir. They pointed you out to me at the station the moment your train stopped that Sunday. And then, sir, I'd heard a great deal about you before that."

"From Peter Verkhovensky? Are you Fedka the convict, then?"

"I was actually christened Fedor, sir, and my name is Fedor Fedorovich. And may I inform you, sir, that my mother is still living in this part of the country and her back's getting more bent every day with praying to God for my salvation, so that her old age won't be wasted just lying around by the stove."

"You're an escaped convict, aren't you?"

"I decided to change my fate. I couldn't go all that time without my books, church bells, and good works—the sentence they gave me was too long."

"And what are you doing here?"

"I do my best, sir. I had an uncle who died last week in the local jail here. He used to be a counterfeiter. So to commemorate his passing, I threw a couple of dozen stones at the dogs—and thus far, that's the only thing I've had to do. Apart from that, Mr. Peter Verkhovensky has promised to get me a passport and, once I have that, I'll be able to go all over the country—so that's something I'm waiting for now. 'Because,' he said to me, 'my papa lost you at cards in that club of his and, personally, I find that inhumane and unfair.' And you, sir, how about letting me have three rubles to buy something to warm myself up?"

"So you were waiting for me here. I don't like that. Who sent you?"

"No one sent me. I simply knew about your kindness to

your fellow man. It's known to everyone anyway. You know how my kind lives: they give us either a handful of hay or a prod with the pitchfork. Last Friday I stuffed myself to the gills with meat pie, but the next day I didn't have a thing in my mouth and the day after I fasted and the one after that I skipped my meals. But I had plenty of water from the river, so maybe I'm breeding carp in my belly. So I wonder whether you wouldn't be so generous, sir. And besides, I have a lady friend waiting for me not too far from here, but she won't receive me unless I present myself with a few rubles."

"What did Peter Verkhovensky promise you on my behalf?"

"He didn't promise nothing firm, simply said that I might be useful to you, sir. But he didn't explain how, for young Mr. Verkhovensky is testing me to see how patient I can be, having no special confidence in me for the time being."

"Why is that?"

"Young Mr. Verkhovensky is an astrologer and he knows all about God's heavenly bodies, but he can make a mistake just like the rest of us. But you, sir—you're quite another matter, and I'm telling you the truth just as if you were the Lord God Almighty, because I've heard a lot about you, sir. When Mr. Verkhovensky decides that a man is a thief, to him he's a thief once and for all; then if he decides he's a fool—a fool he stays and that's what he is and nothing else. But, me, maybe on Tuesdays and Wednesdays I'm really nothing but a fool, but then on Thursdays I may be even smarter than he is himself. Today, for instance, he knows that I'm very impatient to get that passport because it's impossible to get along without such a document in Russia—so he's sure he's got hold of my soul. If I may say so, sir, it's easy for Mr. Verkhovensky to live in this world because he just imagines a man the way it suits him and then goes on living with him. Besides, he's really too stingy. And then he thinks that, without his permission, I won't dare to bother you, sir, but, honest to God, this is the fourth night in a row I've waited here for you, to show him that I can get along all right without him too. After all, I say to myself, it's better to bow to a jackboot than to a peasant's clog."

"And who told you I'd be crossing this bridge in the middle of the night?"

"That, I must admit, slipped out accidentally, mostly through Captain Lebyatkin's stupidity, because he has no idea how to stop himself talking too much. . . . So I'll take three rubles for the three boring nights I've spent here. And I'm even willing to forget about getting my clothes soaked."

"Well, here's the end of the bridge. I'm turning left and you're turning right. And listen to me, Fedor: I like people to understand what I say once and for all—I won't give you a single kopeck, and don't ever let me see you again, either on the bridge or anywhere else. I have no need for your services and never will have any need of them, and if you don't do as I say, I'll tie you up and hand you over to the police. Now —off with you!"

"Come, you could really give me something for my company. I've cheered you on your way a bit, haven't I?"

"Get going!"

"But do you know your way around here? There are all sorts of alleys and turns. I could guide you, because this here town is like the devil had been carrying it around in a basket and had shook it all out of shape."

"I warn you, I'll tie you up," Stavrogin said, turning toward him threateningly.

"Perhaps you'll think it over, sir. It's too easy to ill-treat the helpless."

"You sound a good deal too sure of yourself."

"I'm sure of you, sir, not really of myself."

"But I told you I didn't need you."

"But *I* need *you*, sir. So here's what we'll do: I'll wait for you here till you come back."

"I give you my word: if I see you again, I'll tie you up."

"Well, then I'll bring a belt for you to do it with, sir. And now, the best of luck to you for having sheltered a poor waif under your umbrella. For that alone, I'll be grateful to you to my dying day."

He fell back. Stavrogin reached his destination feeling very disturbed. This man who had come out of nowhere was too certain that he was indispensable to him and was too anxious to assert it. In general, he felt he was being treated rather offhandedly all around. But it was possible that Fedka was telling the truth and was trying to force his services on Stavrogin on his own initiative, without Peter Verkhovensky's knowledge. And that might turn out to be really most amusing.

II

Stavrogin's destination was a house at the very edge of town in a deserted alley between fenced-off vegetable gardens. It was a small wooden house, obviously newly built and not yet weatherboarded. The shutters on one of its windows had been deliberately left open and there was a lighted candle on the window ledge, evidently intended as a signal for the nighttime visitor they expected. When he was still about thirty yards away, Stavrogin discovered the tall figure of a man standing at the door of the house. Unable to wait, he must have come out to see whether anyone was coming down the road. Then Stavrogin heard his impatient but at the same time fearful voice:

"Is that you? Is that you, sir?"

"Yes," Stavrogin answered, but not until he had reached the door and was closing his umbrella.

"At last!" Lebyatkin said, beginning to fuss. "May I take your umbrella? It's so wet outside. I'll open it here in the corner. Please come in, please."

The door, standing wide open, led from the passage into a room that was lighted by two candles.

"If I hadn't had your word that you were coming, I would have given up hope."

"It's a quarter to one," Stavrogin said, glancing at his watch as he entered the room.

"But this rain—and it's a considerable distance—and I have no watch and all I can see from the windows is the vegetable gardens, so I was bound to get out of touch with what's going on in town. But, of course, I'm not complaining—I would never dare. I only mention it because I've been tortured all week by impatience to find out at last—"

"What?"

"To decide what will become of me, sir. Please come in."

He bowed low, indicating a chair by the table that stood in front of the sofa.

Stavrogin looked around. The room was very small and its ceiling was low. It was furnished with the bare essentials only: wooden chairs and a long wooden settee also completely new and without either cover or cushions, two limewood

247

tables, one by the sofa, the other in a corner, covered with a tablecloth and set with a number of dishes with a clean napkin spread over them. The whole room seemed spotlessly clean.

Lebyatkin had not been drunk for eight whole days, and his face looked bloated and yellowish. He seemed ill at ease and worried, but, at the same time, curious. He obviously didn't know what tone he should use to address Stavrogin or what behavior would be most advantageous.

"Here, as you can see, I live like the holy man Zosima. Abstinence, solitude, and poverty—the vow of a medieval knight."

"What makes you think that medieval knights made such vows?"

"Perhaps I've got it all wrong. I never received a proper education, alas! But, you know, Mr. Stavrogin, here I've mastered my shameful weakness for the first time—I haven't had a drink all this time—not a single drop! I feel I have my little corner though and for six days I've been experiencing the blessing of a clear conscience. Even the walls here smell of resin and remind me of Mother Nature. And what was I before?

> Homeless, at night the liquor I'd soak.
> Next day, tongue hanging, with thirst I'd choke.

As that poet of genius so strikingly expressed it. But you're soaked to the skin. Wouldn't you like some tea?"

"Please don't bother."

"The samovar has been boiling since seven o'clock, but I'm afraid it's gone out now—er—like everything in this world. They say even the sun will go out too, when the time comes. . . . But if you wish I'll get it going again. Agafya is still awake—"

"Tell me, is Maria—"

"She's here, right here. . . ." Lebyatkin whispered hurriedly. "Would you like to see her?" He pointed to the closed door leading to the adjoining room.

"Isn't she asleep?"

"Oh no, how could she be! She's been waiting for you all evening. As soon as she knew you were coming, she began making herself beautiful for you." Lebyatkin's face twisted slightly into a knowing, facetious smirk, but he hurriedly wiped it off.

"How is she, generally?" Stavrogin asked, frowning.

"Generally? Well, you know how it is yourself. . . ." Lebyatkin said with a regretful shrug. "Just now she's telling her fortune with the cards."

"All right, I'll see her later. First, I want to settle with you," Stavrogin said, sitting down in a chair.

Lebyatkin didn't dare sit down on the sofa. He hurriedly pulled up another chair and leaned forward trembling and full of awe, ready to listen to what Stavrogin had to say.

"What have you got under the napkin there?" Stavrogin asked, indicating the table in the corner.

"That?" Lebyatkin said, turning his head in that direction and sniggering ingratiatingly. "That's also part of your generosity—our housewarming, so to speak, and also, with due regard to the distance you've had to walk to get here and the fact that you must naturally be tired . . ."

He got up, reverently tiptoed over to the table and carefully pulled off the napkin. Under it there was a complete cold supper—ham, veal, sardines, cheese, a small green decanter, and a bottle of Bordeaux. Everything was laid out neatly, expertly, almost elegantly.

"Is this your effort?"

"Yes, sir. Since yesterday, I've been doing my best, so we could receive you decently. You know yourself that Maria isn't very concerned about that sort of thing. But, as I said, it is above all the result of your generosity. It's all yours, because you are the real master of this house, and I'm only, so to speak, in your employ, although I'm still a free man in spirit. Please leave me that last possession, sir!" he concluded self-pityingly.

"Hm . . . I wish you'd sit down again."

"Thank you, thank you, sir! I can be both grateful and independent at the same time, you know. Ah, Mr. Stavrogin, there's so much pent up in this heart of mine that I could hardly wait for your arrival! Now you're going to settle my life and the life of this poor creature and then—then I shall open my heart to you just as I used to do in the old days, four years ago. Why, you were kind enough to listen to me then and even to read my poems. I didn't mind their calling me your Falstaff, because you played such an important part in my life! But now, I'm in a state of dreadful apprehension and you are my only hope for guidance and advice—Peter Verkhovensky is treating me quite unspeakably."

Stavrogin observed him intently and listened to him with great curiosity. Although he had stopped drinking, Lebyatkin still didn't seem to be quite sober mentally. Habitual drunkards often tend to become permanently incoherent—dazed as it were—although they can still lie, cheat, and deceive as well as the next man when they feel it's necessary.

"I see you haven't changed at all in these four years, Captain," Stavrogin said in a slightly friendlier tone. "You seem to confirm the idea that the second part of a man's life consists of following the habits acquired during the first half."

"Those are words of great wisdom! You've solved the riddle of life!" Lebyatkin exclaimed, half theatrically, half sincerely, because he was a great lover of phrases. "Of all the things you've said, Mr. Stavrogin, what's most deeply engraved in my memory is what you uttered in Petersburg: 'It takes a great man to resist common sense.' I think that's really great!"

"Or a fool."

"All right, so a fool can do it too. But what I was trying to say was that all your life you've been coining those witty sayings while they— I would like to see Peter Verkhovensky or Liputin come out with anything like that, even once! Ah, Peter Verkhovensky has been so nasty to me!"

"But then you, Captain, haven't behaved so wonderfully either, I understand?"

"It's my drunkenness and, on top of that, the host of enemies I have! But now that's all past, and I will regenerate myself like the serpent. Do you know, Mr. Stavrogin, that I'm working on my will now? In fact I've already drafted it."

"That's interesting. What are you leaving and who will get what?"

"Our mother country, mankind, and the brotherhood of students! You know, I read in the newspaper about the life of an American. He left his huge fortune to build factories and to the real sciences, his skeleton to the students or to their academy over there, and his skin for a drum with a clause stating that the American national anthem should be beaten on it once a day and once a night. Alas, we Russians are but pygmies incapable of the flights of Americans' imagination! Russia is a freak of nature and not a product of the intellect. If I attempted to leave my skin to make a drum for, say, the Akmolinsk Regiment, in which I had the honor to serve, on condition that they beat the Russian national anthem on it daily, I'd be accused of liberalism and my skin would be banned. So, I'll content myself with the students. I do want to leave my skeleton to the academy of sciences though, but with the proviso that they stick a label on my skull with the words: 'A repentant freethinker.' So there!"

Lebyatkin spoke heatedly and there was no doubt that he sincerely admired the elegance of the American's will. He was also anxious to make Stavrogin, to whom he had at one time been a jester, laugh. But Stavrogin didn't even smile; on the contrary, he asked quite suspiciously:

"So you intend to make your will public while you're still living and receive money in advance?"

"Well, if I did, sir, what's wrong with that?" Lebyatkin said, closely watching Stavrogin's reactions. "Think what sort of a life I have! I've even stopped writing poems now and, you'll remember, there was a time when they amused even you. Remember, sitting before a nice bottle of something? But I've written my last, like Gogol wrote his *Last Story,* the one, you remember, in which he announced to all Russia that it had 'poured out of his breast in a song.' Well, I'm through too, and that's all there is to it."

"And what's this last poem of yours?"

"It's called 'If She Should Break a Leg.' "

"What?"

That was just what the captain had been waiting for. He loved his own poems, relishing them more than anything else in the world. But at the same time, being a confirmed ham, he also immensely enjoyed the fact that Stavrogin always laughed at his efforts. In fact, at times, he almost rolled around, holding his sides with laughter. Thus, Lebyatkin achieved two objectives at once: poetic satisfaction for himself and amusement for his master. But now he had another special and very delicate objective in mind: by reciting his poetry, the captain was trying to justify himself on a point about which he was particularly worried and somehow felt very guilty.

" 'If She Should Break a Leg'—I mean in a riding accident. It's just a fantasy, Mr. Stavrogin—raving, but the raving of a poet. Once, when I met a lady on horseback, I was quite struck by her and asked myself the following materialistic question: What would happen? That's in case, you know . . . The answer's obvious: all her admirers would scuttle off, all her suitors would make themselves scarce—*was ist das?*—

good-by my lass! The poet alone would remain faithful, his heart shattered within his breast. Mr. Stavrogin, remember, even a louse can fall in love; the laws of nature do not bar even it from love! But, for some reason, the riding lady took offense at the letter and at the poem. I've heard that even you were angry. Is that correct? I was so sad about it—I refused to believe it. After all, whom could I possibly hurt just by dreaming things up? Moreover, I swear that Liputin kept egging me on. 'Go on—send it,' he kept telling me. 'Every man has the right to free correspondence.' Well, so I sent it."

"I understand you offered her your hand?"

"It's all the work of my enemies—"

"Recite the poem," Stavrogin interrupted him sternly.

"It was raving, nothing but raving."

Nevertheless, Lebyatkin stood up straight and began:

> "The beauty of beauties a limb has broken,
> Always a charmer, now two times more,
> And he whose love was already bespoken,
> Now loves her twice as much as before."

"That'll do," Stavrogin said, stopping him with a wave of the hand.

"I dream of Petersburg; I dream of regeneration," Lebyatkin said as if there had never even been any mention of a poem. "You're my benefactor and I would like to know whether I may hope to be provided with money to make the trip. I've been waiting for you all this week like someone waiting for the sun!"

"Oh, well I hope you'll excuse me: I'm rather short now; and then, I really see no reason why I should give you money."

Stavrogin seemed to have grown suddenly angry. In a cutting tone he briefly enumerated all of Lebyatkin's misdeeds: drunkenness, lying, spending the money destined for his sister, threatening to reveal the truth, insolently accusing Dasha, and so on. The captain cringed, made gestures of protest, even tried to answer the charges, but each time Stavrogin stopped him peremptorily.

"And finally I would like to know," Stavrogin said at one point, "what you mean by what, in your letter, you call a *family disgrace?* Why should you consider it a disgrace that your sister is Stavrogin's legal wife?"

"But it's a secret, sir—a damning secret! I receive money from you and people ask me what the money's for. But I'm not allowed to answer and that harms my sister and the honor of my family."

The captain had raised his voice: he liked this topic—it was an old stand-by. Alas, he never suspected the blow that was in store for him this time! In a very casual tone, as if it concerned a routine household matter, Stavrogin informed him that one of these days, perhaps even tomorrow, he intended to announce his marriage "to the public, as well as to the police authorities" and that would settle the matter of "family honor" once and for all, as well as that of the payment of funds for Maria's subsistence. At first the captain just stared at him; his eyes almost popped out, and he did not quite understand. Stavrogin had to explain it to him further.

"But—but she's not quite right in the head."

"I'll take that into consideration."

"But what about your mother?"

"That's her affair."

"But will you take your wife to your house?"

"Maybe, but that has nothing to do with you."

"What do you mean, it has nothing to do with me?"

"You won't enter the house anyway."

"But I'm an in-law, aren't I?"

"People run from in-laws like you. And why should I go on supporting you? Can you tell me that?"

"Mr. Stavrogin, sir, I can't believe it! I'm sure you'll change your mind! It'd be like committing suicide! Think what they'll say here in society!"

"I don't give a damn about society here! Remember, I married your sister after I'd had too much to drink at a dinner— I bet a bottle of wine I'd go through with it. And now, I'll announce it publicly if it amuses me, do you understand?"

There was such irritation in Stavrogin's voice that, horrified, Lebyatkin began to believe him.

"But then, Mr. Stavrogin, what'll happen to me? What about me, Mr. Stavrogin? Aren't you just pulling my leg?"

"I am not."

"Well, I still don't believe you, whatever you say. Anyway, if you do it, I'll lodge a complaint."

"You're incredibly stupid, Captain."

"Maybe so, but what else can I do?" Lebyatkin muttered, completely at a loss. "Before, they used to put us up for the night in exchange for her cleaning the rooms, but what will happen to me now that you've taken everything away from me?"

"You told me you wanted to go to Petersburg and start a new life there. By the way, is it true, as I was told, that you intend to go there to inform on the others and thus obtain a pardon for yourself?"

The captain just gaped at him in silence.

"Listen to me now," Stavrogin said, leaning forward on the table, suddenly very businesslike. Until then, his tone had been rather ambiguous, so that Lebyatkin, to whom Stavrogin usually spoke as one speaks to a jester, was uncertain whether his master meant business or was just teasing him—whether he really intended to carry out his mad idea about the public announcement or was merely fooling him. But now he was so calm and convincing that a shudder ran down Lebyatkin's spine. "Listen to me, and you'd better tell me the truth, Lebyatkin! Have you already reported something or someone to the authorities, or haven't you? Have you managed to do something of the sort already, to send a letter to someone or something like that—something stupid?"

"N-no, er—I haven't done anything— Nor did I ever intend to," Lebyatkin mumbled, still staring at Stavrogin without moving.

"You're lying when you say you never intended to. When you asked me to send you to Petersburg it was precisely for that. Now, even if you haven't actually written a denunciation, are you sure you haven't talked to anyone? Don't lie now; I've heard something."

"When I was drunk—to Liputin. Liputin is a traitor. I opened my heart to him," the poor captain whispered.

"Opening one's heart is all very well, but it's dangerous to be a damned fool. If you had something on your mind you'd have done better to keep it to yourself—nowadays, clever people know how to hold their tongues."

"But, Mr. Stavrogin!" the captain said in a quivering voice. "Since you yourself weren't involved in their plotting, I didn't say anything against you—"

"I dare say you thought better of informing against your milk cow."

"Mr. Stavrogin, Mr. Stavrogin, please—let me explain. . . ."

And in complete despair, with tears in his eyes, Lebyatkin began hurriedly to describe his existence during the past four years. It was the stupid story of a fool who had become involved in something that didn't concern him, the gravity of which he couldn't appreciate, being constantly drunk and debauched. himself to be drawn into the "movement" just "to be now endly" and out of "solidarity with the body of university students," although he had never actually been a student himself; that, "knowing nothing about it," he had distributed leaflets, slipping them under doors, into mailboxes, into people's hats in the theaters, into the pockets of passers-by. Later, "they" started paying him because he was "so desperately hard up, Mr. Stavrogin, something incredible." So he was sent out and traveled through two districts "handing out all sorts of nonsense."

"Ah, Mr. Stavrogin," he cried emotionally, "what bothered me most was that it was strictly illegal—worse yet, unpatriotic! They printed stuff advising the peasant to take his pitchfork, go out in the morning poor, and return in the evening rich. Imagine that! It made me tremble with indignation, but I went on handing out that stuff. Sometimes they suddenly printed a few lines addressed to the whole of Russia that went something like this: 'Close the churches, do away with God, break up the family, abolish the rights of inheritance, grab your knives . . .' and I'm damned if I can remember what other nonsense they were supposed to do. Once I was caught with one of those proclamations by some army officers. They gave me a good walloping, but in the end they let me go, God bless 'em! And then, last year, I was almost caught handing counterfeit fifty-ruble bills made in France to Korovayev, but thank God, Korovayev drowned in a pond while he was drunk, just in time, and they couldn't pin anything on me. Then here, in Virginsky's house, I championed the freedom of the socialist wife. Last June, I was distributing leaflets again in one of the outlying districts here and I hear they're going to make me do it again. And now Peter Verkhovensky comes and announces that I'd better do what they tell me. In fact, he's been threatening me for a long time. You know yourself what he did to me that Sunday! I know I'm only a slave, a worm, and that's what makes me different from our great poet Derzhavin, but then you must understand how hard up I am financially, Mr. Stavrogin!"

Stavrogin heard him out to the end with considerable curiosity.

"Much of what you've told me, I'd never heard befor
said, "but then anything can happen to you." He st
thought for a while, then continued, "But ften now—
wish, you can tell them that Liputin was
simply wanted to scare me by threatening to repo th
you just assumed I must be compromised too and tha
the way to get more money out of me. Do you unde

"Mr. Stavrogin, sir, do you really think I'm in
danger? I was waiting for you to ask you that."

Stavrogin laughed.

"You can be sure they wouldn't let you go
even if I gave you the funds for the trip. But
I saw Maria." He got up.

"But what about Maria, sir?"

"I've already told you."

"Do you really mean it?"

"You still don't believe me, d

"Are you really going to
shoe?"

"We'll see about that

"If you wish, I'll g
thing that's not for

"That's a good

"Your umb
brella?" Leb

"Anyb

"Ah
the m

Hi
wa

r his hand.

His kind tone had its effect; her fear vanished, although
she kept glancing at him timidly, as though trying to understand something. She gave him her hand shyly and at last a
hesitant smile appeared on her lips.

"Oh, Prince, good evening," she whispered with a strange
look in her eyes.

"You must have had a bad dream," he said with an even
warmer and brighter smile.

"How did you know I was dreaming about *it?*"

She suddenly began to tremble again, recoiling from him and lifting her hand as if to defend herself, apparently ready to cry.

"Come, pull yourself together. You know you have nothing to fear now. Why, you don't recognize me, Maria!" Stavrogin said, trying to calm her, but it was no longer so easy. She kept staring at him silently, in the same painful bewilderment, her poor sick head full of tormenting thoughts as she strove to understand something. She kept lowering her eyes, then raising them again and shooting at him quick, intent glances that seemed to take in everything about him. Finally, she made up her mind and, although still not really reassured, said to him:

"Please sit down here, so I can have a better look at you later."

Her voice was almost firm and she clearly had something new in mind.

"But don't worry, I won't look at you now—I'll look down. But you mustn't look at me either until I ask you to. Well, sit down then!" she said, a note of impatience in her voice.

The new feeling seemed to be taking possession of her more and more. Stavrogin sat down and waited. The silence lasted for some time.

"Hm . . . it's all very strange," she muttered at last in a tone that sounded almost disgusted, "of course I'm upset by those horrible dreams, but still, why did you have to appear in that form in my dream?"

"All right, but let's leave your dream for the moment," he said, turning toward her despite her request. For a split second his earlier expression seemed to flash in his eyes. He realized that although she was longing to look at him, she was forcing herself to keep looking down.

"Listen, Prince," she said, suddenly raising her voice, "listen now!"

"What is all this comedy?" he said impatiently. "Why do you turn away and avoid looking at me? What's it all about?"

But she didn't even seem to hear him.

"Listen, Prince," she repeated again in a firm voice, an unpleasantly fussy expression on her face. "When you told me in the carriage on Sunday that our marriage would be publicly announced, I was afraid it would be the end of our secret. Since then I've been thinking about it all the time and I see now that I won't be up to it. I suppose I could manage to dress decently and be a possible hostess, for it's really no great feat to have people for tea, especially if you have servants. But still, how would it look to others? That Sunday, I noticed a lot in that house. There was that pretty young lady who kept looking at me, especially after you came in. For it *was* you who came in then, wasn't it? Her mother is nothing but a ridiculous little old society lady. And my Lebyatkin, he also gave quite a performance! I only stopped myself from laughing by looking at the ceiling: there are beautiful patterns on that ceiling over there. *His* mother should be a mother superior; although she gave me this shawl, I'm still afraid of her. I'm sure all those people got a strange impression of me, and I don't blame them: how could they accept me as one of them? Of course, a countess needs only moral qualities—no need for her to be a good housewife with all the servants she has under her. And, yes, she needs some sort of refined ways, too, to receive foreign travelers. Nevertheless, on that Sunday, they found me quite hopeless. Except for Dasha. She's an angel. But I'm terribly afraid that they might hurt *his* feelings by some careless remark about me."

"Don't be afraid and stop worrying," Stavrogin said, his mouth twisting.

"But then, I wouldn't mind too much even if *he* was a bit ashamed of me, for there'll always be more pity than shame in him. He can judge each man for what he is, and he knows that they have more claim to pity than I do."

"It sounds as though you resent them a great deal, Maria."

"Who? Me? No!" She laughed frankly. "I wasn't offended in the least. I looked at the lot of you and saw you were all angry at one another and quarreling, and I said to myself, 'There are people who get together and don't know how to have a good time and enjoy themselves. So much wealth and so little happiness!' I found it all very shocking. But now, I don't think I'm sorry for anyone but myself."

"I understand you have a bad time with your brother when I'm not here."

"Who told you that? Nonsense! It's much worse now: I have horrible dreams now and they're horrible because you've arrived. Anyway, I would like to know why you have come. Will you kindly tell me?"

"Tell me, would you like to go back to the convent?"

"I had a feeling they'd offer to let me go back to the convent! There's nothing so wonderful about that convent of yours, you know. Why should I go back there now? What would I take there? I'm all alone now and it's too late for me to begin a third life."

"You seem to be very angry about something. Perhaps you're afraid I don't love you any more."

"You're the least of my worries. What worries me is that I myself may fall very much out of love with someone."

She laughed scornfully.

"I must have displeased *him* extraordinarily," she suddenly added, as if talking to herself. "Only I can't think what I did wrong, and that will haunt me as long as I live. I've lived for five full years afraid that I was guilty of something before *him*. I've prayed and prayed and kept thinking of my great guilt before him. And then it turned out that it was true."

"That what was true?"

"I'm afraid that perhaps there's something on *his* part," she went on, either not hearing or ignoring his question. "Again, how could he get involved with such a third-rate crowd? The countess would have gladly torn me to pieces, although she did invite me to ride next to her in her carriage. They're all against me. It is possible that *he* is too? Is it possible he has betrayed me?" Her lips and chin began to tremble. "Listen, have you read about Grishka Otrepyev, the pretender, the false tsar, whom they anathematized in seven cathedrals?"

Stavrogin didn't answer.

"You know, I think I will turn and look at you now," she said, apparently having made up her mind suddenly. "Look at me too and please look very closely. I want to be really sure at last."

"I've been looking at you all this time."

"Hm . . ." she said, examining him intently, "you've put on a lot of weight."

She was about to say something else, but suddenly terror again distorted her features and she reeled back, raising her arm as if to ward off a blow.

"What's the matter with you, anyway?" Stavrogin cried, almost beside himself with irritation.

Her fright lasted only an instant, and her face twisted into a strange, suspicious, and unpleasant smile.

"Please, Prince, rise and come in!" she suddenly said in a firm and determined tone.

"Come in? Where am I supposed to come in to?"

"For five years, all I have done is imagine the way *he* would come in. Get up and go into the other room. I'll sit here as though I weren't waiting for anything. I'll be holding a book. At that moment you'll enter, returning from a five-year journey. I want to see what it will feel like."

Stavrogin gnashed his teeth and muttered something under his breath.

"That'll do!" he said, slapping the table with the flat of his hand. "I would like you to listen to what I have to say now, Maria, and I would appreciate it if you'd give me all your attention. After all, you're not completely mad!" he blurted out in his impatience. "Tomorrow, I will announce that we are married. But you may rest assured, you'll never have to live in palaces. Would you like to spend your life with me? Then it will be very far from here, in the mountains, in Switzerland. There's a certain spot there. . . . Now, I promise you I'll never abandon you and never have you shut up in a lunatic asylum. I have enough money to live on without depending on anyone. You will have a maid and you won't have to do any housework. You will have anything you wish as long as I can possibly get it for you. You will be free to practice your religion, to come and go as you wish, to do whatever you like—I won't touch you. I'll always be there, in that spot, with you. If you so choose, I won't say a word to you as long as I live; if you wish, you may tell me your stories every evening, as you did in Petersburg. But then, you must be prepared to spend all your life in that same place and it's a bleak spot, I warn you. Well, is that what you want? It's up to you to decide. Are you sure you won't be sorry one day and torment me with your tears and curses?"

She heard him with obvious interest and, after he had finished, remained silent for a long time.

"It sounds quite incredible to me," she said at last, and there were both sarcasm and revulsion in her tone. "I might go on living forty years like that in those mountains of yours." She laughed.

"All right, suppose we do live there for forty years?" Stavrogin said, frowning.

"Well, there's nothing in the world that could make me agree to go there."

"You won't come, even with me?"

"Why? Who do you think you are to imagine that I'd

go with you? Sit with you for forty years on a mountain? Just fancy that! I must say, people have become very patient nowadays! No, I can't believe that my falcon has turned into an old owl. . . . That's not the way my prince is!" she concluded, proudly raising her head.

He suddenly got an idea.

"Why do you call me 'Prince'—whom do you take me for?" he asked her quickly.

"Aren't you a prince?"

"I have never been anything of the sort."

"You admit to my face, just like that, that you're not a prince?"

"As I said, I've never been a prince."

"Good God," she said, clasping her hands, "I expected anything from *his* enemies, but never such insolence—never! Is he alive?" she asked threateningly, advancing on Stavrogin. "Or have you killed him? Admit it!"

"Whom do you take me for?" he said, jumping up from the chair, his face distorted; but nothing could frighten her now. She sounded victorious.

"Who knows who you are or where you come from! But in my heart, deep down, I felt that some scheming was going on! And that's why I wondered: what does that blind old owl want with me? No, my good man, you're a very poor actor— even worse than my Lebyatkin is. Give my regards to the countess and tell her to find someone a little better than you to send to me next time. Tell me, did she hire you? Has she given you a job in her kitchen to reward you? I see through all of you with all your tricks, you know!"

He seized her by the arm just above the elbow, but she kept laughing in his face.

"You do look a lot like him. You might even be related to him. Ah, they're smart all right, those people! The only difference is that my man is a handsome falcon and a prince, while you are an owl and a shopkeeper! My man, if he fancies, will bow down to God, and if he doesn't fancy— he won't; but you, you're the fellow who got slapped around by Shatsie—ah, dear, nice Shatsie!—my Lebyatkin told me all about it. And what were you so scared of then? I saw how mean your face was when I stumbled and you held me up, and I felt as though a worm had crawled into my heart. 'This isn't he!' I said to myself. 'It can't be! My falcon would never be ashamed of me in front of a society girl!' Ah, my

God, my only happiness in these five long years has been the thought that my falcon lived somewhere there, beyond the mountains, and flew around and looked at the sun. Tell me, you fraud—how much did you earn for impersonating him? Did it bring you good money? I wouldn't have paid you a kopeck for your work, ha-ha-ha!"

"Ah, the idiot!" Stavrogin muttered, still holding her by the arm.

"Take your hands off me, you fraud!" she shouted imperiously. "I'm my prince's wife, and I'm not afraid of your knife!"

"Knife!"

"Yes, knife! You have a knife in your pocket. You thought I was asleep when you came in, but I saw you take out your knife!"

"What are you talking about, you miserable wretch? What sort of nonsense have you dreamed up?" he said, pushing her off so violently that she banged her head and shoulders painfully against the settee.

He turned away and rushed toward the door, but she jumped up and ran after him, limping and hopping. She was already out of the house before Lebyatkin stopped her, and she managed to cry out into the darkness after Stavrogin:

"You false pretender, Grishka Otrepyev—anathema on you!"

IV

"A knife, a knife!" he repeated with tireless rage, striding through mud and puddles, without paying any attention to where he was going. Now and then he felt like laughing, loudly and madly, but for some reason he suppressed his laughter. He only came to his senses on the bridge, at the very spot where he had met Fedka the runaway convict on his way to Maria's. Fedka was there now, and as soon as Stavrogin came into sight, he removed his cap, bared his teeth in a wide grin, and began quickly chattering about something. For a while Stavrogin just walked on, completely ignoring the tramp, who again had latched onto him. But then he suddenly realized that he had completely forgotten about Fedka, although he had been repeating the word "knife" under his breath. He grabbed the tramp by the scruff of the neck and, with the force of all his pent-up rage, lifted him off his feet and hurled him violently against the planking of the bridge. For an instant Fedka seemed ready to fight back, but he realized that, faced with such an opponent, who moreover had caught him completely unawares, he was no more than a wisp of straw, so he relaxed and gave up all pretence of resistance. Pinned down on his knees, his arms twisted behind his back, the sly tramp awaited calmly what was to come next, without seeming in the least worried about it.

And he was right. Stavrogin, using his left hand, had already removed his woolen scarf to tie the prisoner's hands behind his back when he suddenly changed his mind and pushed Fedka away. Fedka was up on his feet at once and a broad knife he carried in his boot flashed in his hand.

"Put that knife away at once!" Stavrogin ordered him, and sure enough, the knife vanished as quickly as it had appeared.

Then Stavrogin, without saying anything more, casually resumed his way. But the stubborn thug kept following him, although instead of chattering he now trailed respectfully a whole step behind. Thus they crossed the bridge and reached the opposite bank of the river, where they turned left. They entered a long deserted alley that was a shorter way to the center of the town than Nativity Street, the road Stavrogin had taken on his outward journey.

"Is it true, as they say, that you robbed a church around here a few days ago?" Stavrogin asked unexpectedly.

"Well, at first I thought I'd do a bit of praying," the tramp answered calmly and politely, as if nothing had happened a few minutes before. There was a certain dignity in his tone and his previous familiarity had vanished. He sounded like a businesslike man who had been slighted, but who knew how to forgive a slight.

"And when the good Lord led me there," he went on, "I found great plenty, so I decided to help myself, because poor homeless people like me can't do without some help from somewhere. And believe me, sir, it was a total loss to me because the good Lord punished me for my sins—I got only twelve rubles for the censer, the pyx, and the deacon's strap. And I gave Saint Nicholas' chin piece away for nothing: I thought it was solid silver, but they insisted it was only silver-plated."

"And while you were at it, you slit the watchman's throat, didn't you?"

"You see, sir, actually that watchman and I were in it together. But then the morning after, we got into a little argument by the river over which of us should carry the bag. I sinned there, I admit, but it made it easier for him."

"All right, go on knifing people, go on robbing."

"That's word for word what Mr. Verkhovensky said to me, because he's exceedingly stingy and tough when it comes to helping out a fellow man. And, on top of that, he says he doesn't give a kopeck for the Creator who made us all out of a handful of earth. He claims that it was nature created us all down to the last beast, and he can't see that it's impossible to live without helping one another. When you try to make him see it, he just stares at you like a cow at a windmill—really something amazing. Now, please believe me, that Captain Lebyatkin—to whom you've just paid a visit—well, when he still lived in Filipov's house, he often left his door wide open all night while he lay dead drunk on the floor with money just pouring out of his pockets. I saw that with my own eyes, sir, because, as you must understand, people like me can't do without help in life."

"You saw it with your own eyes? Did you drop in on him at night, then?"

"Maybe I did, sir, but no one knows about it."

"Why didn't you slit his throat?"

"I made some calculations, sir, and I restrained myself. I calculated that I could always figure on relieving him of a hundred and fifty rubles or so. Why should I do a thing like that when I'm fairly sure to get maybe fifteen hundred rubles if I wait long enough? Because that Captain Lebyatkin—I heard it from him with my own ears when he was drunk—was relying heavily upon your assistance. In fact, there isn't a tavern or a dive around here where he didn't explain everything to everyone present when he was in the state I mentioned, sir. So, having heard it repeated from several sources, I also decided to place all my hopes upon Your Honor. I feel the same about you, sir, as I would about my own father or my brother, and I will never say anything about you to Peter Verkhovensky or to any living soul. So what do you say, Your Honor, will you be kind enough to let me have those three rubles? You'd set my mind at rest, sir, by giving me an answer, sir, because in my position, as I told you, one can't do without a helping hand."

Stavrogin laughed loudly. He took out his purse in which he had maybe fifty rubles in small denominations and threw Fedka a bill. Then he threw him another, and another, and a fourth. Fedka jumped around, trying to catch them as they fell. The bills were dropping into the mud. Fedka exclaimed "Ah-ah-ah!" as he snatched at them. Finally, Stavrogin tossed the whole roll of bills at him and, still laughing, walked off. This time Fedka didn't follow him. He remained behind, kneeling in the mud and searching for the scattered bills that were sinking in puddles or being carried off by the wind. For a full hour his fitful cries of "Ah-ah-ah!" rose in the darkness.

chapter 3

THE DUEL

I

The duel took place the next day at two in the afternoon. Artemy Gaganov's insistence on fighting expedited the issue. He couldn't understand his opponent's conduct and was livid with rage. He had been insulting Stavrogin with impunity for a whole month without even making him lose his temper. The challenge had to come from Stavrogin because Gaganov had no real excuse for issuing one. He was somehow ashamed openly to acknowledge the true reason for his hatred of Stavrogin—the four-year-old family insult. He felt himself that he couldn't possibly give that as a reason for a challenge in view of the humble apologies Stavrogin had twice offered him. He had decided that Stavrogin was a shameless coward who, incredibly enough, had done nothing when Shatov had punched him in the face. So he had decided to send him the extraordinarily rude letter that had finally forced Stavrogin to challenge him.

Once the letter was sent off, Gaganov became feverishly impatient: one minute he expected the challenge; the next, he despaired that it would ever come. In case the letter was effective, he got himself a second—Maurice Drozdov, a school friend of his and a man whom he regarded very highly. So, when Kirilov presented himself with his message the next morning at ten, he found that everything had already been prepared for the eventuality. All of Stavrogin's apologies and unheard-of concessions were dismissed offhandedly. Drozdov, who had learned the details only the night before, listened openmouthed to Stavrogin's incredible proposals and was about to insist on a reconciliation. But realizing that Gaganov, who had guessed his intention, had started shaking with rage, he swallowed hard and said nothing. If he hadn't promised his friend to be his second, he would have left then and there. Now he felt he would have to let things take their course and could only hope that he might be of some help.

Kirilov then delivered the challenge. All of Stavrogin's conditions were immediately accepted without the slightest objection. Gaganov only insisted on an addition, but a rather ferocious one: if nothing decisive resulted from the first exchange of shots, they would repeat the whole procedure again, and if again nothing happened, they would try it for a third time. Kirilov frowned and objected to the propriety of a third exchange, but Gaganov wouldn't budge and Kirilov agreed, stipulating, however, that "three times is fine, but a fourth is ruled out." That, they accepted.

The encounter was set for two in the afternoon in a small wood near Brykov, between Skvoreshniki, on the one side, and the Shpigulin plant on the other. The rain that had been falling since the day before had stopped, but it was damp, wet, and windy. Low, tattered clouds sailed rapidly across the cold sky; the heavy rustling of their branches seemed to roll from one treetop to the next and the roots creaked. It was a very gloomy day indeed.

Gaganov and Drozdov drove up in a smart open carriage drawn by a pair of horses. Gaganov held the reins himself. They were accompanied by a footman. Stavrogin and Kirilov followed them almost within the minute. They arrived on horseback, and they were also accompanied by a mounted servant. Kirilov, who had never ridden a horse before, sat up in the saddle fearless and straightbacked, holding the heavy case containing the pistols (which he wouldn't entrust to the servant) in his right hand and the reins in his left. In his inexperience, he kept tugging at the reins, which made the horse constantly jerk its head from side to side and tend to rear. This, however, didn't seem to worry Kirilov in the least.

Gaganov, a morbidly suspicious man who was ready to see an offense in everything, took the arrival of the riders as a fresh, deliberate insult; he felt that his opponents were so cocksure that they hadn't even considered the possibility that they might need a carriage. He alighted from his open carriage green with rage. He noticed his hands were trembling and immediately confided this to Drozdov. He didn't even acknowledge Stavrogin's bow, but simply turned away. The seconds drew lots to decide which pistols to use. The lot fell to Kirilov's. They measured the distance between the barriers and told the opponents to take up their positions. The servants were ordered to move the carriage and the horses three hundred paces back. The pistols were loaded and handed to the opponents.

It is a pity that there is no time to dwell on details here. However, a few comments are necessary. Maurice Drozdov looked sad and worried, but Kirilov was completely calm, apparently unconcerned, very precise about the minutest details of his duties, but without any exaggerated fuss and also without much curiosity about the fatal issue that was now so imminent. Stavrogin was paler than usual and dressed rather lightly for the season: he wore a light coat and a white fur hat. He looked very tired, frowned occasionally, and made no effort to conceal his bad mood. But the most remarkable of them all was Gaganov, so a few special words should be devoted to him.

II

We have not yet had an opportunity to describe his appearance. He was a big, tall man, white-skinned and well fed, in fact, on the fat side. He was thirty-three, with blond, slightly thinning hair and rather handsome features. He had resigned his commission with the rank of colonel and if he had elected to remain in the army and had succeeded in rising to general's rank, he would probably have acquired an even greater impressiveness and dignity. Perhaps he would have turned out to be a fine fighting general.

In describing the man, we cannot ignore the fact that his reason for resigning his army commission was the obsessive thought of the disgrace to his family of the insult inflicted upon his father four years earlier by Stavrogin. He had felt that it would be dishonest on his part to remain in the service and that he was disgracing his regiment and his brother officers by his very presence, although, of course, none of them knew about the incident. It is true, though, that he had considered resigning even before that, for a very different reason, but he had hesitated. Strange as it may sound, his original impulse to get out of the army had been caused by the manifesto of February 19 proclaiming the emancipation of the serfs. Artemy Gaganov was one of the richest landowners of the province. He did not stand to lose very much by the manifesto and was perfectly capable of understanding its humanitarian aspect —and almost capable of understanding its advantages to the country's economy—but somehow he took the emancipation of the peasants as a direct, personal slight. This was something unconscious, but the less he could explain it, the more it tormented him. However, until his father's death, he did not dare to do anything drastic about it. Meanwhile, in Petersburg he became known to many remarkable personages, with whom he carefully kept in touch, for the "respectability" of his thinking. He was a man given to brooding and secretiveness. He belonged to those now rare members of the Russian gentry who are excessively proud of and much too serious about the length and purity of their lineage. At the same time, however, he violently disapproved of Russia's past and viewed most Russian traditions as fit for a pigsty. In his childhood, in the elegant military school in which he was proud to have started and ended his education, he had acquired certain romantic notions: he had developed a liking for the concept of castles and chivalry in all its operatic aspects. The thought that in the days of the ancient Kingdom of Muscovy the tsar could, if he so decided, inflict corporal punishment upon a Russian nobleman, made him almost weep with shame, and comparison of such ways with those of foreign lands made him blush. This stern, rigid man, who understood the army so well and performed his duties so punctiliously, was really a dreamer. Some people felt he had the makings of an eloquent orator, but, if he had, he had never done anything about it publicly during his thirty-three years.

He behaved with haughty arrogance even in the select

Petersburg circles he frequented, and coming across Stavrogin there, when he had just returned from abroad, he was almost beside himself with rage.

Now, standing at the barrier, he was in a state of indescribable agitation. He was terrified that, somehow, the duel might be stopped; the very thought of a delay sent shivers down his spine. He looked up with a horrified expression when, instead of giving the signal for the duel to start, Kirilov suddenly addressed the combatants. But it was only a matter of form, as the speaker himself stated:

"Just a matter of form—routine. Now that the pistols are loaded and in your hands and I must give the signal, I ask you for the last time—perhaps you'd like to make it up. It's my duty as a second to ask this."

Maurice Drozdov, who seemed to have deliberately refrained from uttering a word since the day before, because he felt guilty at having lacked the firmness to stand up for what he felt was right, suddenly and energetically backed up Kirilov's routine suggestion.

"I fully subscribe to Kirilov's words. The notion that a reconciliation at the barrier is impossible is nonsense worthy only of the French. And anyway, I don't understand what this duel is all about. I've been wanting to say so for a long time. I mean, apologies have been offered, haven't they?"

He had turned very red, for he seldom spoke for so long or with such heat.

"Once more, I'm prepared to repeat my offer to make all possible apologies," Stavrogin said with what sounded like excessive haste.

"How can such a thing be tolerated!" Gaganov shouted furiously, addressing his second and stamping his foot with rage. "If you are my second and not my enemy, Maurice, I would like you to explain to this man"—he pointed at Stavrogin with his pistol—"that the concessions he's offering me are nothing but fresh insults. I don't seem to be able to do anything to offend him! He wouldn't even find it disgraceful to walk away from the barrier! What does he take me for, I ask you—you who are supposed to be my second! You're doing this deliberately to make me miss!" he shouted, spluttering and stamping his foot again.

"That's that, then," Kirilov shouted loudly. "Please wait for my signal. One . . . two . . . three!"

At the word "three," the opponents started walking toward

each other. Gaganov raised his pistol immediately and fired at the fifth or sixth step. For a second he marked time, then, realizing that he had missed, quickly walked the rest of the way to the barrier. Stavrogin walked up to the barrier too and raised his pistol. However, he raised it obviously much too high and fired without taking aim. Then he took out his handkerchief and wrapped it around the little finger of his right hand. Only then did the others realize that Gaganov hadn't missed altogether: his bullet had nicked the finger, grazing it without damaging the bone. Kirilov immediately declared that if the parties were still dissatisfied, the duel must go on.

"I declare," Gaganov said, addressing his second, Drozdov, "that this man deliberately fired in the air." He again pointed at Stavrogin with his pistol. "This is adding a new insult. He is trying to make the duel impossible."

"I'm entitled to shoot any way I please so long as I conform to the agreed rules," Stavrogin said firmly.

"No, he isn't! He isn't! Explain to him!" Gaganov shouted.

"I fully agree with Mr. Stavrogin's statement," Kirilov declared.

"Why is he sparing me? I despise his generosity! I spit on it! I—"

"I give you my word I had no intention of offending you," Stavrogin said impatiently. "I fired in the air because I don't feel like killing anyone—you or anyone else. It's none of your business. You were right, though, that I do not consider myself offended and I'm awfully sorry that it should exasperate you so. However, I won't let anyone deprive me of my right."

"Well, if he's so reluctant to spill blood, ask him why he challenged me to a duel in the first place?" Gaganov yelled hoarsely, again addressing Drozdov exclusively.

"What else could he do?" Kirilov interposed. "You wouldn't listen to reason, so what other means were there to get rid of you?"

Drozdov, who had weighed the situation with painful care, suddenly said:

"I must admit I don't see how the duel can go on when one of the parties declares that he will only fire in the air. For obvious reasons—"

"But I didn't say that I would fire in the air every time!" Stavrogin cried, losing patience. "You have no means of knowing what I have in mind or where I intend to aim next time. I don't in the least wish to interfere with the normal course of the duel."

"If that's the case, the duel may continue," Drozdov told Gaganov.

"Take up your positions, gentlemen!" Kirilov ordered.

They approached the barriers once more and again Gaganov missed and again Stavrogin fired over his opponent's head. Actually, it could have been argued that Stavrogin was taking proper aim had he refused later to admit that he had missed deliberately. He didn't point his pistol at a cloud or the top of a tree but actually aimed at Gaganov's head, only raising his aim a few feet above it at the moment he fired. And, indeed, his second shot was lower and more plausible than the first, although nowhere near enough to convince Gaganov.

"Again!" He gnashed his teeth. "But I don't give a damn! I have been challenged and I'm going to take advantage of my rights! I demand a third try at any cost!"

"You're fully entitled to it!" Kirilov said cuttingly.

Drozdov said nothing. They took up their positions for the third time. This time Gaganov walked the whole way up to the barrier and took aim at his opponent twelve paces away. His hands were trembling so much that he could not fire accurately. Stavrogin stood with his pistol lowered, waiting without moving for him to fire.

"Too long! You're taking aim too long!" Kirilov shouted. "Fire! Go on, fire!"

Gaganov fired and this time Stavrogin's white fur hat flew into the air. The shot turned out to be pretty accurate: the hat was shot through very low above the head—another quarter of an inch and all would have been over. Kirilov picked the hat up and handed it to Stavrogin.

"Fire! Don't keep your opponent waiting!" Drozdov shouted, in a state of extreme agitation. Stavrogin, absorbed in examining his hat, seemed to have forgotten all about shooting. Stavrogin started, looked at Gaganov, and, this time, without making the slightest pretense of trying to aim at him, turned away and fired into a clump of trees.

The duel was over. Gaganov stood there completely crushed. Drozdov walked over and started to say something to him, but Gaganov seemed unable to understand. On leaving, Kirilov removed his hat and nodded to Drozdov. But Stavrogin disregarded all formalities: after he fired into the trees, he didn't even bother to look at his opponent, who was still standing at

the barrier. He silently handed the pistol to Kirilov and walked
off toward the horses. He looked angry and didn't say a word.
Neither did Kirilov. They mounted their horses and set off
at a gallop.

III

"Why don't you say something?" Stavrogin called out impatiently to Kirilov as they neared the Stavrogin house.

"What do you want?" Kirilov said, almost slipping off his
horse as it reared.

"I didn't intend to, but I've offended that idiot again,"
Stavrogin said, containing his outburst of ill temper.

"You certainly did," Kirilov said sharply. "Besides, he's
no idiot."

"I did everything I could, though."

"That's not true."

"What else could I have done?"

"Not challenge him."

"Maybe you think I ought to let him slap me around too?"

"Yes, let him slap you."

"I cease to understand," Stavrogin said, irritated. "Why
should people expect things of me they don't expect of others?
Why should I stand things that no one else would and take
upon myself burdens that no one else would bear?"

"I thought you were looking for burdens."

"Me?"

"Yes."

"You've noticed that?"

"I have."

"It's so obvious?"

"It is."

For a moment they remained silent. Stavrogin looked very
worried.

"I didn't fire at him because I didn't want to kill. That's all
there is to it, I assure you," he said hurriedly, in a worried
tone, as if trying to justify himself.

"You shouldn't have offended him in the first place."

"What should I have done, then?"

"You'd better have killed him."

"Are you sorry I didn't?"

"I'm sorry about nothing. I thought you really wanted to kill him. You don't know what you're searching for."

"I'm searching for a burden." Stavrogin laughed.

"If you didn't want blood spilled, why did you give him the opportunity to kill you?"

"If I hadn't challenged him, he would've killed me anyway, without a duel."

"That's none of your business. Maybe he wouldn't have."

"He might have contented himself with slapping me—is that what you mean?"

"That's none of your concern—just bear your burden. Otherwise there's no merit in it."

"What do I care whether there is merit in it or not. I'm not looking for approval."

"I thought you were," Kirilov said with icy coldness.

They reached Stavrogin's house.

"Would you like to come in?"

"No. Good-by." Kirilov got off the horse and took his case under his arm.

"At least you're not angry with me?" Stavrogin said, offering him his hand.

"Not at all." Kirilov had to retrace a few steps to take the hand offered him. "Sacrifice is easy to me because it's my nature; it's harder for you because you're different. You shouldn't feel too ashamed of it, just a little."

"I know I'm not really a strong man, but I don't pretend to be strong—"

"And you shouldn't. You aren't strong. Come and have tea with me sometime."

Stavrogin entered his house quite overcome.

IV

Inside, Alexei the footman informed him that Mrs. Stavrogin, exceedingly pleased that her son had gone out for his first ride after his week-long indisposition, had ordered her carriage and driven out "for a breath of fresh air, as Madam always did, although during the past week Madam has forgotten what fresh air feels like."

"Did Miss Dasha accompany her?" Stavrogin asked, impatiently interrupting the old man. He frowned noticeably when he was told that Dasha "couldn't accompany Madam because she is not feeling well and is now in her room."

"Listen, old man," Stavrogin said, as though he had suddenly come to a decision. "Keep an eye on her all the time, and if she tries to see me, stop her. Tell her that I can't see her, at least for the next few days, that I myself ask her, please, to wait, and that I'll let her know when I can. Do you understand?"

"Very good, sir," Alexei said, looking down sadly.

"Don't do anything, though, until you're sure she's really coming to see me."

"Rest assured, sir, I understand very well. Miss Dasha has always addressed herself to me whenever she has wished to visit you, sir."

"I know that. Still, don't do anything unless you're sure she wants to see me. Now, I would appreciate it if you would get me some tea, and as quickly as possible."

No sooner had the old man left than the door of Stavrogin's study opened again and Dasha appeared in the doorway. She was pale, but looked calm.

"Where have you come from?" Stavrogin cried.

"I was outside, waiting for him to leave. I heard what you told him about me and, when he came out, I hid myself around the corner on the right. He never saw me."

"I've been thinking of breaking off with you, Dasha—for the present. I couldn't see you last night despite your note. I wanted to write to you myself, but I don't know how to write," he added with annoyance, almost with disgust.

"I myself thought we should break off. Mrs. Stavrogin is getting quite suspicious about us."

"Let her."

"We ought not to worry her. And now—until the end comes . . ."

"So you're still expecting the end to come?"

"Yes, I'm sure of it," she said.

"Nothing ever ends in this world."

"There will be an end to this; and when it comes, you'll call me and I'll come. And now, good-by until then."

"And what will the end be like?" Stavrogin said, smiling bitterly.

"You weren't wounded? And you didn't kill him?" she asked without answering his question.

"The whole thing was so stupid. No, don't worry, I didn't

kill anyone. Anyway, you'll hear all about it from everyone around. I don't feel very well right now."

"All right, I'm going. There won't be any announcement of the marriage today, will there?"

"No, not today, nor tomorrow either. I don't know about the day after tomorrow—perhaps we'll all be dead by then. That would be the best thing that could happen. Leave me, leave me alone, now."

"You won't drive another person to her doom—I mean that insane woman?"

"No, I won't destroy either of the insane women, but I'm sure to spell the doom of the sane one—that's how vicious and disgusting I am. You know, Dasha, I really believe I'll call you at the very end of ends, just as you suggested, and that, despite your sanity, you'll come to me. Tell me, why are you destroying yourself?"

"I know that in the end I will remain alone with you and I am waiting for that."

"And suppose I never call you in the end; suppose I desert you?"

"That's impossible. You'll call me all right."

"That implies great contempt for me."

"You know very well that there is much besides contempt."

"But—the way you put it—there still is contempt?"

"I didn't express myself properly. As God's my witness, I hope with all my heart that you won't need me."

"Whichever way you put it, it comes to the same thing. I, too, wish I would not drag you to your perdition."

"There's nothing you can ever do that will cause my perdition, and you know it better than anyone else," Dasha said quickly and firmly. "If I don't go with you, I'll become a nurse, and care for the sick, or go around selling Bibles. I've made up my mind. I don't want to marry anyone; I don't want to go on living in houses like this one; I don't want any of that—but you know all about it."

"No, I've never been able to find out what you actually wanted. Sometimes I think you've taken a fancy to me like an elderly nurse to some patient in her ward or, even better, like one of those God-fearing little old ladies who are forever going to one funeral after another and who take a fancy to some particularly charming corpse that is rather prettier than the others. Well, why are you looking at me like that?"

"Are you very ill?" Dasha asked with deep sympathy, looking at him with strange intensity. "Ah, good Lord, and he claims he doesn't need me!"

"Listen, Dasha, I've been haunted by spirits all the time recently; one smallish fiend came to me on the bridge and kept offering to slit Lebyatkin's and Maria's throats for me and release me from legal matrimony without leaving any loose ends behind. He asked me for three rubles in advance, although he made it perfectly clear that the whole operation would cost at least fifteen hundred. Some calculating demon, he was—a real bookkeeper, I'm telling you!"

"Are you so sure it was a spirit?"

"I'm not sure at all! In fact, I know it was only Fedka the convict, the runaway from Siberia. But that's not the point. Guess what I did. I gave him all the money I had in my wallet and now he's convinced that it was the advance he asked for!"

"You met him at night then and he made you that offer? Can't you see that they've completely entangled you in their nets?"

"Well, let them. You know, though," he added with an unpleasant, irritated smile, "I can see by your eyes that there's a question that keeps buzzing in your head all the time."

Dasha seemed frightened.

"I have no question," she said with alarm, as if trying to stifle the question within her, "nor do I have any doubts. You'd better keep quiet!"

"Does that mean that you're certain I won't turn to Fedka?"

"Ah, why must you torment me so!"

"All right, all right, forgive me my poor joke—I must be becoming contaminated by their bad manners. You know, ever since last night I've felt as though I were about to burst out laughing and go on laughing and laughing without stopping for a long time. I feel loaded with laughter. . . . Sh-sh-sh, Mother's back. I heard her carriage creaking as it stopped."

Dasha seized his hand.

"May God save you from your demon and—and call me, call me soon!"

"Ah, what kind of a demon is he? He's really just a small, repulsive, pimply abortion of a demon with a cold in the nose. He's one of those failures—but Dasha, isn't there something you would like to say but don't dare?"

She looked at him reproachfully, then turned toward the door.

"Listen!" he shouted after her, his face twisted into a

malicious grin. "If—well, you understand—*if* I did go to him and *if*—well, in a word, *if* . . . and if after that I called you, would you still come to me?"

She left without turning her head, covering her face with her hands.

"She'll come even *if* . . ." he whispered, having thought for a while, and an expression of disgust and contempt appeared on his features. "Just a nurse! Hm . . . but maybe that's what I need."

chapter 4

GENERAL ANTICIPATION

I

Details of the duel spread rapidly all over the town and the way society took Stavrogin's side was truly remarkable. Many of his former enemies now declared themselves his friends. The main reason behind this dramatic reversal of public opinion was a striking statement made by a person who until then had never voiced an opinion and whose views, therefore, impressed the overwhelming majority of our citizens all the more.

On the day after the duel, everyone who counted in the town was at the head landowner's house on the occasion of his wife's birthday. The star of the party was Julie von Lembke, who arrived in the company of a radiantly beautiful and happy Liza, which, of course, immediately aroused the suspicion of the ladies. There was no doubt any more about her engagement to Maurice Drozdov. In answer to a jocular question from a retired but still influential general (of whom more later), Liza herself had answered directly that she was engaged. But, for some reason, none of the ladies present wanted to believe in this engagement. They all stubbornly assumed that there was some family mystery behind it, something secret that had happened in Switzerland, in which, they insisted for some reason, Mrs. von Lembke had played a part.

It would be hard to explain why these rumors, or rather fancies, were so persistent or why there was this insistence on the local first lady's having a part in it. Now, as soon as she came in, all eyes turned toward her filled with expectation.

It must be noted also that, because the duel was so recent and because of certain circumstances surrounding it, it was still mentioned with considerable diffidence and in hushed tones. Moreover, nobody knew yet what position the authorities would take. As far as was known, neither of the duelists had been bothered so far. It was, for instance, public knowledge that on the morning after the duel Gaganov had left for his Dukhovo estate without interference. So everyone was waiting impatiently for someone else to bring the subject up first and open the floodgates to the general impatience. In this their main hope lay in the above-mentioned retired general, a hope that, as it turned out, was justified.

This general was one of the most solid members of the town's club. He was not one of the richest of the local landowners, but he had original ideas, was an old-style lady killer, and was fond of boldly stating in public what others had in mind but didn't dare mention above a whisper. This was his main role at our society gatherings. And he had a special way of lisping and drawling his words, a habit he had probably picked up from Russians who had traveled abroad or from landowners who had once been rich but had been ruined by the emancipation of the serfs and for whom elegance of speech was an indication of their standing. Stepan Verkhovensky once quipped that the more thoroughly a landowner had been ruined, the more sweetly he lisped and the more he drawled. He, of course, was not aware of his own noticeable drawl and lisp.

The general spoke knowingly on the subject not only because he was remotely related to Gaganov—although there was a quarrel and even a legal action between them—but also because, in his youth, he had himself been involved in two duels, for one of which he had even had to serve a stretch as a simple private in the Caucasus. Someone mentioned that Mrs. Stavrogin had driven out again after her son's illness, commenting on the excellent matching of the four gray horses that pulled her carriage (which were from the Stavrogins' own stud) rather than on her personally. Suddenly the general declared that he had come across "young Stavrogin" on horseback that day. Everyone immediately fell silent. The general smacked his lips and, twisting a gold snuffbox (obviously a gift from some august person) in his fingers, announced unexpectedly:

"I'm really sorry I wasn't here a few years ago—I mean, I was in Karlsbad at the time. . . . I'm, er—I'm very interested in that young man—I heard so much about him when I came back that time. Hmm. Now, is there any truth in the story that he's insane? Some people claimed so then. Then, recently, I heard that some student insulted him in front of some female relatives of his and that he crawled under the table. And now Stepan Sysotsky has just told me that Stavrogin fought a duel with that fellow Gaganov. Seems he challenged him with the sole objective of offering his forehead as a target to an enraged man, just in order to be left alone by him. Hm . . . that's a throwback to the traditions of the Guards in the eighteen twenties. Does he have any friends around here with whom he maintains relations?"

The general stopped talking as though waiting for an answer. The gates for the expression of public opinion were unlocked.

"What could be simpler!" the governor's wife said suddenly and loudly, irritated by the fact that all eyes, as if following a command, had suddenly turned toward her. "Is it really so surprising that Stavrogin fought Gaganov, but did nothing about the student? After all, he couldn't challenge a former serf of his to a duel, could he?"

These were weighty words offering a simple and obvious explanation that somehow had never occurred to anyone, words that had tremendous consequences! Everything indicative of gossip and scandal was immediately relegated to the background, and this new aspect was brought to the fore. The outlines of a new face appeared—the face of a man who had been misunderstood by everyone, a man adhering very strictly to social standards. Receiving a deadly insult from a student, that is, an educated, independent man, he disregards that insult because it came from a former serf. Elegant society is shocked and disgusted by a man who has been slapped with impunity, but he despises their opinion because he knows that they do not truly understand the standards of behavior, although they are quick to express their opinions about them.

"Yes, and here we are discussing correct behavior!" remarked one old gentleman member of the club to another in a noble burst of self-castigation.

"True, true, my dear sir," the other agreed enthusiastically. "One can never predict what young people will do next."

"But the question here is not one of young people in general," a third venerable club member objected. "Here we are concerned with not just *a* young man but with the most brilliant specimen of the young set. That's the way to look at it."

"Yes, we needed someone like that around here. We were running out of real gentlemen."

The crux of the matter was that the new glamorous personality, who had now shown his mettle, was also a member of one of the oldest families and one of the richest landowners in the province, and so could not help being a real asset in public life. I have already mentioned in passing the mood of the local landowners.

Some people were quite ecstatic.

"He not only did not challenge that student to a duel, he even forced himself to take his hands off him. That's something worth noticing, sir," someone pointed out.

"Nor did he drag him through our new courts!"

"Despite the fact that he could've got at least fifteen rubles in damages for a personal insult to a born gentleman, ha-ha-ha!"

"No, let me tell you something about those new courts!" another man butted in, in a frenzy. "If someone gets caught red-handed stealing or embezzling, the best thing he can do is to run home and kill his mother. They'll immediately acquit him and the ladies in the public gallery will wave their handkerchiefs at him! Believe me, it's the truth!"

"Very true, very true!"

Of course, they couldn't do without recalling some old stories. They remembered Stavrogin's connections with Count K., whose severe personal disapproval of the latest reforms was well known. He was famous for his extensive activities, although he had slowed down somewhat recently. And now, suddenly, the public became convinced that Stavrogin was engaged to one of the count's daughters, although there was really no basis for starting such a rumor. As to mysterious Swiss adventures and Liza Tishin, even the ladies ceased to mention them. Let us add also that Mrs. Drozdov and her daughter had by this time paid all the visits expected of them. Liza was now considered just another young lady "showing off" her strained nerves. Now her fainting on the day of Stavrogin's arrival was laid to the student's ugly aggression. People even began to dismiss as commonplace, incidents for which the day before they had been seeking the most fantastic explanations. And they completely forgot that a certain cripple had been involved in the story—even found it too embarrassing to remember it. "Anyway, even if there'd been a hundred cripples in his life, so what? Weren't we all young once?" Many commented upon Stavrogin's respectful treatment of his mother and searched for other virtues to ascribe to him. They spoke favorably of the good education he had acquired in the four years he had spent in German universities. Gaganov's behavior was declared absolutely unforgivable and Mrs. von Lembke was now definitely credited with uncanny insight.

So, when Stavrogin himself made his appearance, he encountered a general mood of naïve seriousness. Realizing from the way everyone looked at him that great things were expected of him, he immediately lapsed into a profound silence, which satisfied his audience infinitely better than if he had saturated them with his conversation. In short, he could do no wrong—he was in fashion. In provincial society, once a person has appeared in society he can never hide again, and Stavrogin once again started to perform all his social duties with refinement and perfection. Certainly they didn't acclaim him as an amusing and cheerful guest. "This man has suffered enough in his life," they said. "He's not like other people and has good reason to be so pensive and quiet." Even his pride and the air of supercilious inaccessibility that had brought him so much hatred four years before were now considered impressive and attractive.

Mrs. Stavrogin was triumphant, although she may have been sad about the broken plans for her son's marriage with Liza. Family pride, of course, had a large part in her attitude. But the strangest thing of all was that Mrs. Stavrogin had become convinced that her Nikolai really was engaged to a daughter of Count K., although she, like everyone else, had simply succumbed to the wild rumors circulating and had never dared to check it directly with her son. Only once or twice, unable to restrain herself, had she discreetly reproached him for his lack of openness with his mother. Nikolai had smiled, but had remained silent, and to her his silence meant confirmation. But, nevertheless, she never forgot about the lame woman. The thought of her lay like a heavy stone on her heart. It was a nightmare that conjured up strange visions and premonitions that became intertwined somehow with her dreams about the count's daughter. But we shall come back to that. It goes without saying that Mrs. Stavrogin regained the respect and extreme courtesy she had formerly received in society, but now she took little advantage of it and drove out only very seldom.

However, she paid a solemn visit to the governor's wife, for obviously the first lady's words at the party touched and entranced her more than anyone's. They removed a great deal of the oppression that had been weighing on the poor woman since that unfortunate Sunday. "I misunderstood her!" she said with characteristic impulsiveness, and to Mrs. von Lembke herself she simply declared that she'd come to *thank* her. Mrs. von Lembke was highly flattered, but maintained her detachment and reserve. By then she had become extremely conscious of her worth. In fact, she may have had a rather exaggerated idea of it. For instance, she declared in the middle of the conversation that she had never heard anything of Stepan Verkhovensky's activities or, for that matter, of his reputation for learning.

"Of course, I receive his son Peter—I'm very fond of him. He's a very impulsive young man, but he's still young and, I must say, he's very well informed. Anyway, he's not just a retired old critic."

Mrs. Stavrogin hastened to straighten her out on that point: Stepan Verkhovensky had never been a critic. On the contrary, she explained, he had always lived in her house. But he was famous because of certain circumstances connected with his earlier career "that are too well known to the world to need repeating." Later, he had become known for his "works on Spanish history," and now he intended to write about contemporary German universities and, she thought, about the Dresden Madonna. Clearly, Mrs. Stavrogin refused to desert Stepan Verkhovensky before Julie von Lembke's scorn.

"The Dresden Madonna? Surely you mean the Sistine Madonna? My dear Mrs. Stavrogin, I must confess I sat in front of that painting for two full hours once and I left rather disappointed; I couldn't make anything of it and I really wondered what all the fuss was about. Karmazinov, too, says it is rather hard to understand. Nowadays, no one finds anything so remarkable about it, neither the Russians nor the English. I'd say it has been overpublicized by the older generation."

"So, I gather there's a new fashion now."

"Well, I'm convinced that we shouldn't just dismiss the opinions of the young. People simply brand them as Communists, but I think we must treat them with understanding and appreciation. Lately I've been reading everything—the newspapers, all the proclamations of communes, and all about the natural sciences. I subscribe to everything. For we must understand, mustn't we, the society we live in and with whom we have to deal. One cannot live all one's life shut up in the ivory tower of one's own fantasy. I thought a lot about it and decided to be nice to the young people and thus prevent them from going over the brink. Believe me, Mrs. Stavrogin, only we who belong to the best society can keep them from plunging into the abyss into which they are being pushed by these silly, intolerant old men. Still I'm very glad to hear all about Mr. Verkhovensky. It gives me an idea: we could use him at our literary gatherings. I'm organizing a day-long entertainment to be paid for by subscription, the proceeds to go to needy governesses from our province. They are scattered all over Russia and there are six of them in this district alone. In addition, there are two women telegraphists, two university students, and many others who would like to follow a career but can't afford the training. The lot of the Russian woman is terrible, Mrs. Stavrogin, my dear! The question is under study in our universities and has even come up before the Council of State. In this strange country of ours, everything is possible and I think we can guide this great public cause along the proper path only by kindness and the direct participation of all society. Ah, do we really have so many people of great character among us? There are many, of course, but they are scattered all over the place. So let us close our ranks and grow stronger. In short, I will start with a literary matinee followed by a light lunch; then there will be an intermission, and later in the evening a ball. We thought of starting the evening with *tableaux vivants,* but that would have been too expensive, so we decided to offer a couple of quadrilles in costumes and masks, representing the best-known literary movements. Mr. Karmazinov gave me that amusing idea. He is a tremendous help to me. And you know, he is going to read his latest piece for the occasion—no one has read or heard it yet. It is his latest and last literary piece, his farewell to the public. It is a charming little work called *Merci.* He finds the French title more amusing and also more subtle. In fact, I suggested that type of title to him. I suppose Mr. Verkhovensky could also read us something if it's not too long or too learned. I believe his son Peter and someone else also want to read something. Peter will stop over at your place and give you the program, or if you'll permit me, I'll drive over myself."

"I hope you won't object to my putting my name down on your subscription list. And I will pass your request on to Mr. Verkhovensky and insist myself that he accept."

Mrs. Stavrogin returned home completely conquered by Mrs. von Lembke and, God knows why, terribly angry with Stepan Verkhovensky, who, poor man, had been sitting home all this time and knew nothing about all these developments.

"I find her absolutely irresistible and really cannot understand how I ever could have been so wrong about her!" she told her son and Peter Verkhovensky, who had dropped in to see them that evening.

"Still, you should make peace with the old man—he's in rather a bad way," Peter said. "You might as well have relegated him to the kitchen. Yesterday, when he met you driving out in your carriage, he greeted you, but you turned away. But you know, we'll make an important man of him yet. In fact, I have something in mind for him and I believe he can still be useful."

"Oh, he'll be reading something at the gathering."

"I wasn't talking about that. I was going to see him today anyway, so would you like me to tell him?"

"If you wish, although I'm not sure how you'll be able to arrange it," she said hesitatingly. "I wanted to have a talk with him myself. I wanted to fix a day and a place where we could meet." She frowned.

"But why bother making a date just to tell him that? Why can't I just tell him?"

"I suppose you can tell him. But still, tell him that I want him to come to my place and that I'll let him know when. Tell him I'll do so without fail."

Peter ran off with a wide grin on his face. As far as I can remember, he was being particularly nasty at that time and vented his irritation on almost anyone. Curiously enough, people forgave him for it. In general, everyone seemed to feel that he should be regarded in a special way. I must note here that he was very angry about Stavrogin's duel. It had taken him completely by surprise and he had turned very green when he first heard about it. Perhaps it was mostly a blow to his vanity:

he heard about it only on the following day, when everyone else already knew about it.

"But you had no right to fight that duel," he whispered to Stavrogin, when he came across him in the club, on the fifth day after it had occurred.

Remarkably enough, that was the first time the two had met in those five days, despite the fact that Peter had been paying almost daily visits to Mrs. Stavrogin.

Stavrogin passed by him without stopping, looking at him absently, as if he had no idea what Peter was talking about. He was making his way across the large ballroom toward the bar.

"And then you went to see Shatov too. And you intend to make your marriage with Maria Lebyatkin public," Peter whispered, hurrying after Stavrogin and unthinkingly grasping his shoulder.

Suddenly Stavrogin shook off his hand and turned on him with a threatening frown. Peter stared at him, his lips stretching into a strange, long, thin smile. Stavrogin walked on.

II

Peter went straight from Mrs. Stavrogin's to his father's, impatient to vent his spite on the old man. He wanted to get even with him for an offense of which I had no idea at the time. During their last meeting, namely on Thursday of the previous week, Mr. Verkhovensky had chased Peter out of his house with a stick, after an argument that he himself had initiated. Mr. Verkhovensky had concealed the fact from me at the time, but now, as Peter rushed into the room with his usual arrogant grin, his eyes darting around all the corners with such unpleasant inquisitiveness, Mr. Verkhovensky motioned me unobtrusively not to leave. So I had the opportunity to witness this meeting from beginning to end, and I found out how they really felt toward each other.

Mr. Verkhovensky was stretched out on a sofa. He had grown thin and yellow since the previous Thursday. Peter sat down on the sofa next to him, casually tucking his feet under him and taking up more space than respect for his father dictated. Mr. Verkhovensky made room for him with dignity and without saying a word.

An open book lay on the table. It was Chernyshevsky's novel *What Is to Be Done?* Alas, I must here admit a strange small weakness of my friend's—the notion that he must come out of his retirement to offer a final battle. It was getting hold of him more and more. I gathered that he was *studying* this novel so that, in the event of a future clash with the "squealing demons," as he called them, he would know their tricks and arguments in advance, straight from their own textbook, and so be able to thwart and refute them before *her*. Oh, what torments that book caused him! At times he couldn't stand it any longer, threw it aside, and paced the room almost in a frenzy.

"I admit that Chernyshevsky's fundamental idea is right," he told me once breathlessly, "but that only makes it more horrible! It's our own idea—we were the first to plant it, to nurture it. Besides, what new contribution could they possibly have made? And, good Lord, just look how it's expressed! It is so incredibly distorted and twisted around!" he shouted, rapping the book with his fingers. "You don't really imagine, do you, that that's what we were striving for? Who would ever recognize our original idea in that?"

"I see you're enlightening yourself!" Peter said with a smirk, picking the book up from the table and looking at the title. "It's high time. I'll bring you something even better if you wish."

Mr. Verkhovensky let this pass, sticking to his dignified silence.

Peter then quickly explained the object of his visit. Mr. Verkhovensky was obviously dumfounded and listened to his son with a mixture of alarm and growing indignation.

"And so this Mrs. von Lembke really thinks that I'll go and read some piece of mine at her house? Just like that?"

"You don't get it. She doesn't really need you at all. She's just being nice to you to get on the right side of Mrs. Stavrogin. Anyway, it goes without saying that you won't dare balk. Besides, you're longing to do it." Peter grinned unpleasantly. "You old-timers are all so hellishly ambitious. But listen, try not to bore them to death. What do you have? Spanish history, I understand. You'd better let me have a look at it two or three days beforehand, otherwise I'm afraid you'll put everyone to sleep."

These remarks were too crude and too obviously deliberate; Peter was rather clumsily suggesting that there was no other way of communicating with his father, that he was incapable of understanding more refined language and more subtle concepts. So Mr. Verkhovensky continued firmly to ignore his insults. Peter's news, however, had made a shattering impression upon him.

"And it was *she, she herself,* who asked *you* to tell me all this?"

"As a matter of fact, she wanted to fix a day and a place for a mutual explanation; the leftovers of your sentimental goings-on, I suppose. You have been flirting with her for the past twenty years and that's given her some very peculiar ways of doing things. But you needn't worry: now she herself says every minute that she has finally seen 'through you.' I told her to her face that all that tender friendship of yours was nothing but a mutual outpouring of slops. She told me quite a bit, and I must say, I was shocked to find that you've been just like a flunky to her all this time. It even made me blush for you, you know."

"So I've been her flunky, have I?" Mr. Verkhovensky said, unable to restrain himself any longer.

"Worse than that—you've been a hanger-on, that is, a voluntary flunky. You were too lazy to work, but you were fond of money. Well, all that has dawned on her at last. You should hear the terrible things she says about you now. Ah, those letters you wrote her really made me laugh, although I was also disgusted and ashamed. It's incredible how perverted you are—there's something so corrupting in begging and you are a striking example of it."

"So she showed you my letters."

"All of them. But how could I possibly read them all? Brrr— what a lot of paper you've wasted! I'd say there are about two thousand of those letters. And you know, old man, there was a moment when she was prepared to marry you. You were really stupid to miss the opportunity! I mean from your point of view—for it would certainly have been better than being offered the chance to 'marry another man's sins,' as you are now, just because she's taken it into her head and because she can pay you for it."

"Pay me! She told you she was paying me?" Mr. Verkhovensky cried out in pain.

"What do you expect? I tried to defend you, and money, after all, is the only excuse you can have. She understood very well that you, like everyone else, needed money and that, from that point of view, you were probably justified. I made it as clear to her as twice two is four that you were deriving mutual advantage from each other, she being a capitalist and you her resident sentimental jester. As a matter of fact, she doesn't even resent your doing all those things for money, although you did milk her like a cow. What she's angry about is that for twenty years you've hoodwinked her with your high-sounding pretenses, made her lie to people all that time. She, of course, will never admit that she lied, but you can be sure that she'll make you pay double for it. I wonder how you can have failed to see that one day you were bound to pay for it all? You weren't *that* stupid, after all. Yesterday, I advised her to send you to an old-people's home. Oh, don't worry —one for gentlefolk, of course; nothing that would hurt your feelings. As a matter of fact, I believe that's just what she will do. Now, do you remember the last letter you sent me, when I was in Kharkov Province three weeks ago?"

"You didn't show that to her, did you?" Mr. Verkhovensky cried, horrified.

"I certainly did! As a matter of fact, it was the first thing I did. That was the letter in which you informed me that she was exploiting you because she was jealous of your talent; it also contained that story about 'another man's sins.' My, what sensitivity you have, old man! I almost split my sides laughing! By the way, your letters are incredibly boring and your style is atrocious. I often left them unread and I believe I still have an unopened one somewhere. I'll send it to you tomorrow. But that last letter of yours was really perfect! Ah, you should have heard me laugh!"

"You monster! You freak!" Mr. Verkhovensky shouted.

"Damn it all, it's impossible to talk to you. Tell me, are you offended again, as you were last Thursday?"

Mr. Verkhovensky drew himself up threateningly.

"How dare you talk to me like that?"

"Like what? You mean in plain language?"

"Tell me, you freak—are you really my son, or aren't you?"

"You're in a much better position than I to answer that one. Although, of course, every man has a tendency to delude himself under such circumstances—"

"Shut up!" Mr. Verkhovensky said, shaking all over.

"Now you see, you're shouting at me and insulting me as you did last Thursday, when you even raised your stick to me. But I did find that document; indeed, I found it that very day.

Just out of curiosity, I spent the whole evening going through my luggage looking for it. It's true, of course, that it's nothing definite—just a note written by my mother to that Polish fellow, you know. But then, if we consider her character and—"

"One more word and I'll slap your face!"

"What a man!" Peter said, suddenly addressing me. "You realize this has been going on between us ever since last Thursday. I'm delighted that you're present and will be able to judge for yourself. Now he's furious because I spoke about my mother that way. But didn't he bring it up first? In Petersburg, when I was still a schoolboy, he woke me up at night and threw his arms around me, crying like an old woman. That was when he told me all those stories about my mother. He was the original source of my information, you know."

"Ah, but I was referring to purely spiritual matters then. You understood nothing of what I said!"

"But all the same, you must admit that what you did was more degrading than anything you can pin on me. Personally, I don't care. I'm thinking of how it must look to you. As far as I'm concerned, don't worry, I don't blame my mother: if it was the Pole, so it was the Pole and if it was you, so it was you. It's not my fault that the two of you got into such a stupid mess in Berlin at that time, and, from what I know of you, I can't imagine your acting any more intelligently. You really are a ridiculous bunch and I can't understand what difference it can make to you whether or not I'm your son. Listen"—Peter turned to me again—"he has never spent a ruble on me. He never set eyes on me until I was sixteen, and then he robbed me. And now he goes around shouting that his heart has been bleeding for me and puts on a show for my benefit, like a comedian. I guess he forgets that I'm not Mrs. Stavrogin."

He got up and took his hat.

"I curse you! I lay my father's curse upon you from now on!" Mr. Verkhovensky said, stretching his hand out toward his son. He was as pale as death.

"Ah, the inanities this man is liable to come out with!" Peter cried, this time in genuine surprise. "Well, the best of luck to you, Papa, for I don't expect to come to see you again. Let me have that literary piece of yours as soon as possible. And try to fill it with less nonsense and more fact.

Yes, facts, facts, and more facts—and, above all, keep it short. Good-by now."

III

Actually, Peter Verkhovensky had certain plans in which he wanted to use his father. I believe he wanted to drive him to despair and then involve him in a certain scandal, for special reasons that I shall discuss later. He was full of such schemes and calculations, most of them really fantastic. And, besides his father, he had, as it turned out, several other victims picked out. Among these, the one on whom he based his greatest hopes was none other than Governor von Lembke himself.

Andrei Antonovich von Lembke belonged to that strong and favored tribe of a few hundred thousand that, in Russia, forms a firmly knit alliance without perhaps realizing it themselves. It is not a planned, deliberately organized association, of course, but a spontaneous tribal union that needs no explicit agreements and is morally obligatory. Every member can count on the full support of any and all members of the tribe, and owes the same to them, wherever and under whatever circumstances it is demanded. Andrei von Lembke had the honor of being educated in one of those Russian establishments to which the scions of the wealthier and better-connected families are sent. Upon graduation from such establishments, students are almost immediately appointed to fairly important positions in government service. One of von Lembke's uncles was a mere lieutenant colonel in the Army Engineers, another was a baker, but he had still managed to get into one such select establishment and meet many members of the above-mentioned tribe there. He was a cheerful companion and a dull student, and was generally liked by his schoolmates. When, in the higher classes, many of the young men—mostly Russians—had learned to discourse on the important problems of the day, Andrei von Lembke was still absorbed in innocent, schoolboy pranks. He amused everyone with tricks that were none too clever, although sometimes they were rather cynical. But then, that was exactly what he had set out to do. Sometimes, when asked a question by the teacher, he blew his nose in such an outlandish way that the whole class, including the teacher, burst out laughing; in the dormitory, he posed in obscene *tableaux vivants* that were greeted by uproarious applause. He performed—and quite well at that—the overture from *Fra Diavolo* using his nose as a musical instrument. He also distinguished himself by his deliberate slovenliness, which for some reason he considered very witty. During his senior year he even started writing verse—in Russian, because his knowledge of his own tribal German was highly ungrammatical, as was that of many members of the tribe in Russia.

This partiality for versification drew von Lembke close to a gloomy, unhappy-looking classmate, the son of some poor general of Russian stock who, for some reason, was considered, in the school, as Russia's future literary glory. This fellow took a patronizing interest in him.

But three years after leaving the school, the gloomy future luminary—who had given up a government job to devote himself entirely to literature and, as a result, was going around with holes in his shoes and a ragged, threadbare overcoat in the late fall, his teeth chattering with cold—by chance ran into his former protégé by Anichkin's Bridge. And what do you think? At first he didn't even recognize von Lembke: he stopped and gaped at him in amazement. He saw in front of him an irreproachably dressed young gentleman, with magnificently trimmed, reddish side whiskers, a pince-nez, patent-leather shoes, immaculate butter-colored gloves, a warm, comfortable overcoat, and brief case under his arm. Von Lembke was nice to his friend—he gave him his address and invited him to drop in on him "one of these evenings."

His former classmate did call on him, probably mostly out of spite. The hall porter stopped him in the vestibule (which was not very elegant, although it did have a red felt carpet) and asked him what he wanted. He walked up to the top floor and pulled the bell, which rang loudly. Instead of the luxury he had expected, the visitor found his classmate occupying a small, shabby-looking room. Part of it was screened off by a dark green curtain and the upholstery of the ramshackle furniture was also dark green, as were the curtains on the high, narrow windows. The house actually belonged to a very distant relative of von Lembke's, a civil servant of general's rank who was his patron.

Von Lembke received the visitor warmly and was serious and tactful. They talked about literature, but well within conventional bounds. A servant in a white tie served them weak tea with small, dry cookies. Out of sheer spite, the visitor asked for some soda water. He obtained it, but with some delay, for von Lembke had to recall the servant and repeat the order before he finally brought it, a circumstance that seemed to embarrass him. However, he then suggested himself that his guest might like to have something to eat and seemed quite relieved when the visitor declined and finally left.

Actually, von Lembke was just setting out on his career and was still sponging on a highly placed member of his Germanic tribe.

At that time, he was sighing after his protector's fifth daughter, and the feeling seemed to be reciprocated. When, however, it came time to marry her off, Amalia was given away to some old German manufacturer, a friend of the bride's old father. Lembke didn't waste too much time shedding tears but made himself a cardboard theater instead. The curtain went up, the actors gesticulated, the public sat in the boxes, the fiddlers in the orchestra moved their bows across their fiddles, the conductor waved his baton, and in the front rows elegant gentleman and Guards officers clapped their hands. Everything was made of cardboard and entirely conceived and executed by Lembke himself, who spent over six months on the project.

Lembke's patron organized a special "intimate" reception to show the toy theater. It was attended by all his five daughters, including the newly wed Amalia with her German manufacturer, as well as many other *fraus* and *fräuleins* with their German escorts. They all examined and admired the model theater; then they danced. Lembke was very pleased and soon recovered completely from his unhappy love.

As the years went by, his career advanced. He continued to work for the government and always managed to land himself good jobs under chiefs who were uniformly his compatriots, so that finally he attained a rather high rank for his age. Sometime before this, he had decided to marry, so he looked around for someone suitable. Once, without his superiors' knowledge, he sent a novel to a publisher, who, however, declined to publish it. To make up for that, he built an entire railroad station out of cardboard and it turned out to be quite a success: passengers, carrying their luggage, left the building accompanied by their children and their dogs and boarded the train. Conductors and other attendants walked among them. A bell rang, a flag was waved, and the train started. That clever toy took him about a year to complete. But, when he was through with it, he was still unmarried. He had a wide circle of acquaintances, mostly among his own tribe, but he also, of course, moved among people of native stock, chiefly in the course of his duties.

When he was almost thirty-nine, he finally came into some money. His uncle the baker died and left him thirteen thousand rubles. All he needed now was a good, safe post. Despite his relatively exalted position in the service, Lembke was deep down a very modest man who would have been perfectly contented with some unimportant job that would have afforded him sufficient independence, such as superintendent of lumber purchases for the government or something cozy and comfortable like that. He would have been happy to hold such a post till the end of his life. But then, instead of some Gretchen or Ernestine, Julie appeared on the scene. Von Lembke immediately rose a full rung in his career, and the modest hard-working official suddenly discovered that he too might have a spark of ambition.

By pre-Emancipation standards, Julie owned an estate with two hundred serfs and, what's more, she had very important connections. Von Lembke himself was a handsome man, while she was already in her forties. It is interesting to note that he actually fell in love with her. It happened gradually, after the realization had come over him that they were engaged. On the morning of their wedding day he even sent her some verses. She enjoyed it all very much, including the piece of poetry—to be past forty is no joke. Soon afterward he was promoted, decorated, and then appointed governor of our province.

Before they came our way, Mrs. von Lembke carefully prepared her husband. She thought he had a few assets working for him: he knew how to enter a room, how to look dignified, and how to listen with an understanding expression without saying anything; he had learned how to assume several impressive attitudes, was capable of making a public address, had, indeed, a few odds and ends of ideas, and had even mastered some of the indispensable catchwords of liberalism. But even so, she was afraid he had become too placid and that, after his long and arduous pursuit of a career, his only real longing was for peace and rest. While she tried to pour some of her own brimming ambition into him, he suddenly started building a cardboard Lutheran church with a pastor coming out to preach his sermon to a congregation listening with piously clasped hands (except for one lady wiping away her tears with a handkerchief and an old man blowing his nose). A tiny organ—specially ordered in Switzerland, notwithstanding the expense—played an appropriate tune. Mrs. von Lembke showed alarm when she found out about her husband's creation, and she immediately locked it up in a trunk she kept in her room. To make up for this, she allowed him to write a novel, but insisted that it should be kept absolutely secret. And after that, she depended only upon herself to achieve her ambitions.

But the trouble with that was that she was really a frivolous lady with an inadequate sense of proportion. She had been an old maid much too long. More and more new ideas cropped up in her ambitious and somewhat overstimulated mind. She had grandiose plans, was determined to run the province herself, longed to have an immediate following, and so had to choose a political trend to follow. At first Lembke was a little overawed by his new post, but he soon realized, with his civil servant's instinct, that there was actually nothing for him to fear in the governorship. And indeed, the first two or three months passed very satisfactorily. Then Peter Verkhovensky appeared on the scene and strange things began to happen.

From the beginning, the younger Verkhovensky assumed a very offhand manner with the governor, but Julie von Lembke, who was usually so sensitive when it came to her husband's position and prestige, either refused to notice this or at least considered it unimportant. Peter became a favorite of hers and he ate, drank, and almost lived in her house. The governor fought back: he addressed him as "young man" in front of people and patted him condescendingly on the back, but that didn't seem to make the slightest impression on the fellow. Peter seemed to be laughing in his face, even when he was apparently serious, and he said the strangest things to him in front of other people. Once, on returning home, the governor found the young man asleep on the couch in his study, although he had not been invited. Peter explained that he had dropped in on him and, not finding him at home, had "at least had a good sleep." Lembke was offended and complained to the first lady, who laughed aloud and remarked pointedly that it was his own fault if he couldn't command the respect of "that boy"; Peter never indulged in undue familiarities with her; and besides, she found the young man "naïve and refreshing, although of course he doesn't belong in society." The governor continued to pout for a while. She made them make peace. Peter Verkhovensky didn't really apologize; he made some crude joke that at another time might have been taken for a fresh insult, but was now accepted as a sign of regret. Lembke's weak position where Peter was concerned was due to a blunder he had committed when they first met—he had told him about his novel. Thinking that he was dealing with an ardent, romantically inclined young man and being starved for an audience, Lembke had, early in their acquaintance, read two chapters of his literary creation aloud to him. Peter listened without concealing his boredom; he yawned rudely and didn't utter a word of praise. Then, before he left, he asked Lembke to lend him the manuscript so he could read it quietly and at leisure and form an opinion of it. The governor consented. Since then, Peter had failed to return the manuscript, although he came to the house daily, and when he was asked about it, he just laughed. Finally, he announced that he had lost it in the street the same day he had borrowed it. When Mrs. von Lembke found out about all this, she was extremely angry with her husband.

"I hope at least you haven't told him about that cardboard toy temple of yours?" she cried, almost in panic.

That made von Lembke think, and thinking was bad for him—definitely not recommended by his doctors. In addition to the trouble that had turned up in the province—of which more later—there was a special matter that was breaking his heart. It had nothing to do with his pride in his position as a government servant of executive rank. When he married, Mr. von Lembke had never even considered the possibility of family quarrels and disagreements. Such things had never entered his dreams about his Gretchens and Ernestines. He didn't feel he could stand family scenes. But Julie had been very direct with him:

"You can't be angry with him, if only because you are much more reasonable than he is and stand incomparably higher on the social ladder. There are many remnants of his former freethinking ways in this boy, and I think this is just a schoolboy prank. However, he can't be changed just like that—he needs patient handling. We must understand the importance of our young people. Through patience and kindness, I am successfully preventing them from plunging over the brink."

"But he comes up with such damned nonsense," von Lembke protested. "How can I tolerate it when, in my presence, he declares that the government is deliberately filling people with vodka to stupefy them and thus prevent them from revolting! Just imagine how it looks to other people when I have to listen to that sort of thing!"

Lembke was thinking of a recent talk he had had with Peter. In a naïve attempt to dampen the fellow's liberalism, the governor had shown him his private collection of all kinds of Russian proclamations printed abroad. He had been collecting them since 1859, not simply out of a collecting mania but rather out of an edifying curiosity. Guessing his intention, Peter said rudely that one line in any of those proclamations had more sense in it than there was in all the government files— "and that doesn't exclude those of your office either."

Lembke winced.

"But it's a bit early," he said almost apologetically, "a bit early for us—"

"No, it's not too early. The fact that you're afraid shows that it isn't too early."

"But, look, here's an appeal to destroy churches—"

"And why not? You, for instance, are an intelligent man and you don't believe. But you know very well that you need religion to keep people asleep. The truth is better than lies, you know."

"I agree, I agree—I'm in full agreement with you, but still, it's much too early for this country," the governor repeated, screwing up his face.

"But what kind of government servant are you, agreeing that churches should be razed to the ground and saying that you are willing to march on Petersburg, making it only a question of timing?"

Lembke resented being caught out so stupidly.

"That wasn't what I meant; that wasn't what I said," he said, getting further and further involved in the argument and becoming irritated by the slight to his self-respect. "You're still young and ignorant of our methods. You are quite wrong. You see, you call us government servants. That's right. Independent officials—that's right, too. But hold on a minute—how do you expect us to act? We act on our own responsibility and, as a result, we serve society as much as you do. The difference is that we are trying to hold together what you are trying to undermine. Without us the whole thing would fall apart. We aren't your enemies. By no means. We say to you, 'Go ahead, fight for progress—even go on undermining all the old ways that must be changed—but we shall hold you within the necessary bounds and save you from yourselves, because without us you would simply undermine Russia and make it look like heaven knows what, and our duty is to preserve a presentable appearance for our country to the outside world.' You must understand that we and you are mutually indispensable, just as the Whigs and Tories are mutually indispensable in England. Well then, so we are the Tories and you're the Whigs—that's the way I see it."

Von Lembke had grown positively enthusiastic. Ever since his days in Petersburg, he had been fond of speaking as an intelligent, liberal man, and since this conversation was private, he could really let himself go. Peter was silent and unusually serious. This whetted the governor's oratorical appetite even further.

"Do you know," he went on, pacing up and down his study, "that I, who am 'the master of the province,' have too many duties, and consequently cannot carry out any of them; on the other hand, I can tell you just as truthfully that there's nothing for me to do here. The secret reason for this is that everything depends on the views of the central authorities. Well then, let the central authorities, say, for political reasons or to appease popular unrest, decide to switch to a republican form of government and, say, simultaneously strengthen the power of the governors—we, the governors, would accept their republic— and not only a republic but anything they might come up with. I, at least, feel I'm ready. . . . Well, in a word, let the central authorities send me a telegram commanding me to show *une activité dévorante* and I'll give them that mad activity. I told them straight to their faces: 'Gentlemen,' I told them, 'if you wish to have a flourishing administration in the province, all you have to do is increase the gubernatorial powers.' You see, all establishments, administrative or judiciary, must lead a so to speak dual existence—that is, on the one hand, it is indispensable that they exist (I agree that they should) and, on the other, that they do not exist—depending on what the central authorities have in mind. If it turns out that these establishments are needed, they will be right here at hand. If the need for them passes, no one will find them in my province. That's the way I visualize their *activité dévorante*—but there can be none of it unless they increase gubernatorial powers. We are talking here just between the two of us, and I can tell you that I have requested Petersburg for authorization for a special sentry at the governor's mansion. I'm waiting for their answer now."

"You really need two sentries."

"Why two?"

Lembke, who had been pacing the room, stopped in front of Peter.

"I don't think one would be enough to make people respect you."

The governor's face twitched.

"You really allow yourself to say God knows what, Verkhovensky. You take advantage of my kindness. You keep making unpleasant digs and trying to play the part of a rough diamond."

"Ah, whatever you say," Peter mumbled, "you're preparing the way for us and working for our victory."

"What do you mean by *us* and what victory are you talking about?" Lembke inquired, gaping at him in surprise. But Peter never answered that question.

When she heard the report of this conversation, the governor's wife was extremely displeased.

"But you didn't really expect me to talk sharply to your favorite, especially in a private conversation?" Lembke said, defending himself. "Of course, I may have talked too much, although I meant well really."

"Too well, indeed. I had no idea you had that collection of proclamations. I would like to see them, please."

"The trouble is . . . he asked me to lend them to him—for one day."

"And you gave them to him! The same old story! What a thing to do!"

"I'll send someone to his place to pick them up right away."

"He won't give them back."

"I'll demand them!" von Lembke cried indignantly, jumping to his feet. "Who is he anyway that I should be so careful with him? And what does he take me for, imagining that I'll let him get away with that?"

"Sit down and take it easy," his wife said, calming him. "And now, let me answer your first question: he came to me with very strong recommendations. He is obviously an able man and sometimes he says very intelligent things.

Karmazinov assures me that he has connections everywhere and has a tremendous influence on the younger generation in the capital. Now, if through him I succeed in grouping them around me, I'll save them from perdition and point out a new road for their ambitions. He is devoted to me from the bottom of his heart and always listens to my advice."

"Certainly, but while we're being so nice to them, God knows what they may do. Of course, it's just a rumor," he said in self-defense, "but I heard that seditious leaflets have appeared in yet another of our districts."

"Ah that! Back in the summer, rumors about that were circulating, along with all that talk about the proclamations and counterfeit bills. But I have yet to see a single one of them. Who told you anyway?"

"I got it from von Blum."

"Ah, him! Please, don't even mention his name in my presence."

Furious, Julie von Lembke was struck dumb for a full minute. Von Blum was a government clerk whom she loathed. But we'll dwell more on that later.

"And please stop worrying about Verkhovensky," she concluded their conversation. "If he were up to any tricks around here, he wouldn't speak to you the way he does—the way he speaks to everyone. I'm not afraid of a loud talker like him and, besides, I assure you, if something were to happen, I'd be the first to find out and it would be through him. He is fanatically—yes, fanatically—devoted to me."

I must remark here, in anticipation of later events, that if it hadn't been for Julie von Lembke's vanity and conceit, petty, vicious people wouldn't have been able to get away with as much as they did in our province. Much can be laid to her door.

chapter 5

PREPARING FOR THE GALA

I

The date of Julie von Lembke's gala for the benefit of needy governesses had been fixed several times, only to be repeatedly postponed. Meanwhile, Peter Verkhovensky bustled around her, and Lyamshin, the petty government clerk who had sometimes visited the elder Verkhovensky and who now found favor in the governor's house because he played the piano, ran errands for her. Also helping Mrs. von Lembke in her preparations was Liputin, whom she was grooming as chief editor of a future independent local newspaper. A few ladies, married and unmarried, also buzzed around her in their eagerness to help, and even Karmazinov himself, although he did not actually buzz around her, often repeated aloud that he had a pleasant surprise for everyone when the literary quadrille began.

There were plenty of subscribers and donors, including all select society; even the nonselect were welcomed as long as they brought cash. Mrs. von Lembke explained this position by declaring that mixing of the classes had to be tolerated now and then, for "otherwise how could *they* be enlightened?"

So the unofficial organizing committee resolved that the gala reception would be held in a democratic spirit.

The great response from subscribers brought in an unexpected amount of cash and gave the organizers all sorts of wonderful ideas; this was the reason for the constant postponements. They were still undecided where the grand ball at the end of the program should be held—in the huge mansion of the head landowner, placed at the first lady's disposal by his wife, or at Mrs. Stavrogin's Skvoreshniki estate. Skvoreshniki was, of course, rather far from town, but many members of the committee felt that, for some reason, people would feel more at ease there. Mrs. Stavrogin was anxious for them to decide on her place and it was strange to see this proud lady now almost cringing before the governor's wife. She was probably very pleased that, for her part, Julie von Lembke almost humbled herself before Nikolai Stavrogin, lavishing more attention on him than on anyone else. I must repeat here that Peter had been going around trying to impress on everyone in the governor's mansion that Stavrogin was a man with the most mysterious connections in a most mysterious world and that he was certainly in town on some mysterious mission.

People were in a strange mood at that time. Especially among the ladies there was a trend toward frivolity, and it was by no means gradual. It was as though a few extremely unconventional notions had been set floating in the air. There was a kind of exaggerated gaiety, something loose, something that left a rather unpleasant impression upon me. An unrestrained attitude was the fashion. Later, when it was all over, this was attributed to Julie von Lembke, but I doubt that the blame was all hers. In fact, at first, most people praised the new first lady for bringing local society together and making life much more exciting. There were a few scandalous incidents, but Mrs. von Lembke cannot be held responsible for them; indeed, at the time, people were simply amused and laughed over them—no one protested. A considerable faction, it is true, with their own views about what was happening, held aloof from it all, but even they didn't grumble. In fact, they smiled.

I remember that, at that time, a fairly large circle centered around Julie von Lembke's drawing room came into existence spontaneously. This circle included several very attractive ladies, and the young people of the group organized picnics and dances and sometimes paraded through the town in real cavalcades—carriages, riders, and all. They were always looking for some shocking adventure and often they contrived incidents just to have something amusing to tell later. Pranks and practical jokes became fashionable, though some of these tricks were really in questionable taste. They treated our town as if it were a city of imbeciles. The people called them the Jeerers or the Tormentors because they stopped at practically nothing.

Once, for instance, the wife of a lieutenant from the local regiment, a brunette who was young and pretty, although a bit prematurely aged by her husband's rough treatment, thoughtlessly sat down to a whist game in which the stakes were high, hoping to win enough money for a coat. Instead she wound up losing fifteen rubles. Afraid to tell her husband, and not having the money to settle her debt, she recovered some of the boldness she had had in her youth and decided to borrow the sum, then and there, from the son of the mayor, a boy who was already dissolute despite his youth and who happened to be at the party. The nasty youth refused; furthermore, he went to the poor lady's husband and told him very loudly what had happened. The lieutenant, who, it is true, did have to make both ends meet on his army pay alone, took his wife home and there had the time of his life, despite her shrieks, wails, and pleas for mercy.

This revolting story only gave rise to laughter all over town.

And then, although the lieutenant's wife did not belong to the circle around Julie von Lembke, one of the ladies of the "cavalcade," a lively and eccentric woman, who happened to know her, went to call on the poor girl and then simply took her to her own house without more ado. There the playful young people received her with open arms, loaded her with presents, and kept her prisoner for four days. She lived at the eccentric lady's, rode all over town with the young crowd, and attended their parties at night. They all advised her to lodge a complaint against her husband and promised her that they would be witnesses for her in court. The husband didn't dare protest. Finally, the poor thing realized that she was courting trouble, became frightened, and on the fourth evening managed to evade the vigilance of her protectors and return to her husband. It is impossible to say what happened between the pair, but the shutters of the low wooden house in which the lieutenant lived remained shut for two whole weeks. Mrs. von Lembke admonished the naughty youngsters when she found out what had happened. She was particularly displeased with the eccentric young lady, although the lieutenant's wife had been brought to the governor's mansion and introduced to her personally on the very first day of her abduction. However, the whole incident was soon forgotten.

Another time, a minor government employee from another district married the daughter of a colleague of his from our town, a seventeen-year-old beauty known to everyone around here. Then it suddenly became known that, on the very first night after the wedding, the groom had treated the beauty rather impolitely, avenging thereby a slight she had inflicted upon him. Lyamshin, who had been practically a witness to it all, because he had got drunk at the wedding and had spent the night in the house, hurried around spreading these interesting tidings the next morning. Immediately a group of ten was formed. They all mounted horses. A few, like Peter Verkhovensky and Liputin, who, despite his graying hair, regularly participated in the wild escapades of the young set, had to hire Cossack horses for the occasion.

When the newlyweds appeared in a carriage to pay their calls on the day after the wedding—a custom in our town that was obligatory whatever the circumstances—the riders surrounded their carriage and escorted them throughout the whole morning, laughing and jeering. True, they didn't follow the couple inside the houses they visited; they waited for them outside without dismounting. They also refrained from actually insulting the bride or the groom directly. Nevertheless, it ended in a row. It became the talk of the town and, of course, everyone found it hilarious. But not so the governor. He was angry and had another heated scene with his wife, who was also displeased and considered, at one point, refusing to receive the wild set in her house. However, a day later, she forgave them, swayed by Peter's arguments and also by a few calming words from Karmazinov. He, as a matter of fact, had found the joke rather witty.

"It's in keeping with our way," he said, "and at least these young people displayed considerable character and boldness. While you're being so indignant, the rest of the town is just laughing."

At that time, a woman who went from door to door selling Bibles made her appearance in our town. She seemed a respectable woman, although she was obviously of the commercial class. People started talking about her because a curious item about women who went around selling Bibles had recently appeared in the Moscow and Petersburg papers. Again, that rogue Lyamshin got busy. With the assistance of a former divinity student who was hanging around town waiting for a teaching vacancy in a local school, Lyamshin filled the woman's bag with a collection of foreign pornographic photographs while feigning an interest in buying some Bibles from her. The pornographic material had been especially provided by a respectable old gentleman who wore a distinguished order around his neck and who, as he put it, liked "healthy laughter and cheerful jokes"; he will remain unnamed here.

Later, in the shopping arcade, when the poor woman dipped into her bag for the sacred books, the dirty pictures fell out and were scattered all over the place. People started to laugh, to protest, then to swear. A fight broke out and the police arrived. The woman was locked up and only in the evening, as a result of the indignant protests of Maurice Drozdov, who had discovered the details behind this disgusting episode, was she released and escorted out of town.

This time, Mrs. von Lembke did throw Lyamshin out of her house. But, that same evening, a bunch of the young people brought him back to the governor's mansion, announcing that he had composed a new piano piece and insisting that she hear it. The piece was really quite amusing; it was entitled the

"Franco-Prussian War" and opened with the martial strains of the "Marseillaise":

Qu'un sang impur abreuve nos sillons!

There was a grandiose challenge in it, an exaltation over future victories. Then suddenly, along with the majestic measures of the French national anthem—somewhere beneath it, in some corner, but still very close—sounded the vulgar strains of "Mein Lieber Augustin." The "Marseillaise" failed to notice it and reached its glorious climax, but "Augustin" gained strength and became more and more arrogant; then its rhythm suddenly blended with that of the "Marseillaise." The anthem, finally noticing "Augustin," seemed to grow angry. It tried to throw it off, to chase it away like an obtrusive fly, but "Mein Lieber Augustin" held on firmly, gay, self-confident, insolent, and self-satisfied. And then, suddenly, the "Marseillaise" started sounding silly. It could no longer hide the fact that it was irritated and offended and turned into a wail of tearful indignation, its arms stretched out to Providence:

Pas un pouce de notre terrain, pas une pierre de nos forteresses!

But, by now, it was forced to sing in the rhythm of:

Ach mein lieber Augustin, Augustin du!

The "Marseillaise" tune slipped in the most ridiculous way into that of "Augustin," finally yielding and dying out. Only from time to time did the measures of *qu'un sang impur* break through, only to be drowned out immediately by the syrupy little waltz. Then the "Marseillaise" became completely subdued, as though Jules Favre were sobbing desperately on Bismarck's chest and abandoning everything, but everything, to him. And now "Augustin" turned fierce. It let out hoarse growls that suggested great quantities of gulped-down beer and boundless self-admiration and a demand for billions of francs, fragrant cigars, sparkling champagne, and hostages. And, as "Augustin" turned into a bloodcurdling roar, the "Franco-Prussian War" came to an end.

The company gathered in the governor's mansion applauded, and the governor's wife shrugged, smiled, and asked:

"How can I chase that impossible creature away after this?"

And so peace was made, for the "impossible creature" did have talent of sorts. Once Mr. Verkhovensky tried to convince me that the lowest, most despicable characters can have outstanding artistic talent and that there is no connection between the two things. However, there was a rumor that Lyamshin had stolen that piece from some modest young man from out of town, who remained anonymous, but that was only a passing remark. This miserable fellow, who had turned up regularly at Mr. Verkhovensky's parties for several years, where, on demand, he had impersonated all sorts of little Jews and acted such scenes as the confession of a deaf peasant woman or a childbirth, was now making hilariously funny sketches of Mr. Verkhovensky himself at Mrs. von Lembke's, presenting them as "A Liberal of the Eighteen Forties." With everyone roaring with laughter, expelling him was out of the question—he had become much too useful for that. Moreover, he fawned slavishly upon Peter Verkhovensky, who by that time had acquired an uncannily strong influence over Mrs. von Lembke.

I would not bother to dwell so long on this character if it were not for a shocking incident in which, I was assured, he took part and which I cannot leave out of my narrative.

One morning, the news of an ugly and revolting sacrilege spread all over the town. The old Church of the Nativity of Our Lady, a well-known historic building in our ancient town, stands near the entrance to the vast market place. There was a large icon of the Virgin set into the wall behind a grating near the gate of the churchyard. One night the grating was ripped out, the glass smashed, and some pearls and precious stones stolen from the crown and setting of the icon—although, I must say, I don't know whether they were really precious. But the most shocking part of it was that a senseless, vicious sacrilege was added to the theft: it was rumored that a live mouse had been found behind the broken glass of the icon. It is pretty certain now, four months later, that the crime was perpetrated by Fedka the convict, but for some reason people insist that Lyamshin also had a hand in it. At the time, no one suspected Lyamshin of having anything to do with it, but now everyone seems certain that it was he who put the mouse there. I remember that our authorities didn't know what to do. A crowd milled around the scene of the crime all that day, although it wasn't a really huge crowd—I'd say a hundred persons were on hand, some coming, some going. As they arrived, people crossed themselves and kissed the icon; many seemed eager to make contributions to make good the damage to the icon. Soon a collection plate was produced with a monk to hold it. And not until about three in the afternoon did it occur to the authorities that they could forbid people to loiter there and make them move along after they had been given their chance to pray a little and to make their contributions.

The incident made a most ominous impression upon Governor von Lembke. I've been told that Mrs. von Lembke explained later that, after that sinister morning, she noticed a strange dejection in her husband that lasted until he left our province two months later for reasons of health, a dejection that I believe is still with him in his Swiss retirement where he is recuperating after his brief tenure in our province.

I remember arriving at the market square somewhat before one in the afternoon. The crowd was silent and the people looked sullen. A fat, pale-faced merchant drove up in a hackney cab, got out, bowed to the icon, kissed it, slipped a ruble into the collection plate and, grunting, got back into his carriage and drove off. Then a coach arrived with two local ladies accompanied by two of our playboys (one of whom was a very old boy at that). The two men alighted from the carriage and pushed their way toward the icon, elbowing people out of their way rather offhandedly. Neither removed his hat, and one of them slipped his pince-nez on his nose. There was a subdued, but clearly hostile murmur from the crowd. The fellow with the pince-nez took out a purse that was tightly stuffed with folding money, fished out a copper, and tossed it into the collection plate. Then the two men, laughing and talking loudly to each other, turned to walk back to the coach.

During this incident, Liza and Maurice Drozdov arrived on horseback. Liza jumped off her horse and threw the reins to her companion, whom she asked to remain mounted. It so happened that she was very close to the icon when the copper was tossed into the plate. She turned red with indignation, removed her round riding hat and her gloves, got down on her knees on the dirty sidewalk, and reverently bowed her head to the ground three times. Then she took out her purse, but finding there was only some small change in it, she removed her diamond earrings and put them in the plate.

"Is it all right? Will these do for the setting?" she asked the monk agitatedly.

"It's all right," the monk said. "Any contribution is welcome."

The people around remained silent, and it was impossible to tell whether they approved or disapproved.

Liza got back onto her horse and galloped off in her begrimed riding habit.

II

Two days after this, I saw Liza with a large party driving somewhere in one of three carriages surrounded by gentlemen on horseback. She stopped the carriage she was riding in, beckoned to me, and when I went over, insisted that I join them. They made room for me in the carriage and she introduced me to the elegant ladies sharing it with her, then explained that they were off on a very interesting expedition. She kept laughing all the time and seemed rather exaggeratedly gay. In general, lately, her gaiety had often verged on exuberance.

The destination of the expedition was indeed far away. They were going across the river to visit the lodge of the house of a merchant named Sevostyanov, where our local simple saintly soul and prophet, Semyon Yakovlevich, lived. He had lived there in peace and contentment for the past ten years and his renown had spread well beyond the boundaries of our province, reaching even Moscow and Petersburg. People came to see him from all over the country, hoping to receive some prophetic message from him; they paid him their respects and brought him gifts. Some of the gifts were very substantial, and unless the saintly man himself immediately decided what to do with them, they were scrupulously turned over to the church for good works, most of them going to the Monastery of Our Lady in our province. For this reason, a monk from the monastery was constantly on duty at Semyon Yakovlevich's.

Everyone in the party was looking forward to a great deal

of fun. Of them all, only Lyamshin had ever seen Semyon. He claimed that he had been to see him once before, on which occasion the saintly man had ordered Lyamshin chased away with brooms and had himself personally hurled two large boiled potatoes at him. Among the riders I noticed Peter Verkhovensky, again sitting rather awkwardly on a hired Cossack horse. Nikolai Stavrogin was there too; he never missed any public amusement and now, although he was mostly silent, he had, as always, the right composed but amused expression.

When the party passed the inn on its way to the bridge, someone suddenly announced that the body of a man who had shot himself had been discovered that day in a room there and that the police were about to arrive to investigate the death. Immediately someone suggested that we stop and have a look at the suicide. The suggestion met with general approval —the ladies had never seen a suicide before. I remember one of them saying, "I'm so bored with everything that I can't afford to be too fussy about entertainment—anything will do as long as it's amusing."

Very few of the party preferred to wait outside. The rest crowded into the dirty corridor of the inn and, to my surprise, I saw that Liza was among them. The room where the man had shot himself was opened and, of course, no one dared to stop us from entering. The suicide turned out to be not much more than a boy, nineteen at the most, and a very handsome boy at that, with thick blond hair, a regular, oval face, and a magnificent open forehead. Now that the stiffness of death had set in, his face looked like carved marble. On the table by the bed was a scribbled note in which he asked that no one be blamed for his death, and stated that he was shooting himself because he had "squandered" four hundred rubles. There were three grammatical mistakes in the four lines of the note.

A fat landowner, who was staying in the same inn on his own business and who apparently was a neighbor of the dead boy's, was there, moaning and sighing. From what the landowner said, we gathered that the boy had been sent to town from his village by his widowed mother, his sisters, and his aunts to make some purchases for his oldest sister's wedding. They had entrusted him with those four hundred rubles, which represented years and years of saving, trembling at the mere thought that he might lose them, showering him with admonitions, and sending him on his way with countless prayers and signs of the cross. During his visit to our town he was supposed to stay at his cousin's. Until then, he had always been a quiet, trustworthy boy.

When he had arrived in town three days before, the boy had never even gone to his cousin's. He had stayed at the inn, and the first thing he had done was go to the club, seeking some back-room card game with high stakes. But it so happened that there was no game going that night. So the boy went back to the inn—it was already past midnight—and ordered champagne and Havana cigars and later a supper of six or seven courses. But the champagne made him drunk and the cigars made him sick, so he didn't even touch the supper; instead, he went to bed almost unconscious. Next morning he woke up as fresh as a rosy apple and immediately drove to a gypsy caravan that had pitched camp across the river and that he had heard about the night before in the club. He hadn't returned to the inn for two days, in fact, until the day before, at five in the afternoon. He arrived drunk, went straight to bed, and slept until ten at night. When he awoke, he demanded a cutlet, a bottle of Château d'Yquem, some grapes, paper, pen, and ink. No one noticed anything special about him: he seemed calm, quiet, and friendly. He must have shot himself around midnight, although strangely enough no one heard the shot and they only found out what had happened that day, when he failed to answer their knocking and they broke down his door. The bottle of Château d'Yquem was half empty and about half the grapes were left. The shot had been fired from a small, double-barreled revolver straight into the heart. There was very little blood. The weapon had fallen from his hand onto the carpet. The youth himself was half reclining on the sofa. Death must have been almost instantaneous. There was no trace of suffering in the boy's expression: it looked serene and full of the joy of living.

We gazed at him with great curiosity. In general, there is always something exhilarating in another man's misfortune—and that is true whoever you may be. The ladies were silent, but their companions attempted to show that they retained their wit and composure under any circumstances. One remarked that the boy had taken the wisest course open to him; another suggested that, although it had lasted only a moment, the boy must have had the time of his life. Someone suddenly wondered aloud why people had suddenly taken to hanging and shooting themselves so often around here. Had we suddenly been uprooted, he wanted to know, or had the ground sud-

denly started slipping from under our feet? The others glared
disapprovingly at the philosopher. Lyamshin, who had assumed his role as the clown, took a grape from the plate and
one or two gentlemen laughingly followed his example.
Another, trying to top this, was about to help himself to some
Château d'Yquem, but at that moment the police inspector
arrived and asked them to "clear the room." And, as everyone
had had enough by then, no one protested, although Lyamshin
began pestering the inspector about something. After this stop-
over, the party resumed its trip in a mood almost twice as gay
and cheerful as before.

We arrived at Semyon Yakovlevich's at one. The gate of the
merchant's large yard stood wide open and anyone was free
to enter the lodge where the saintly man lived. We were told
that Semyon was eating, but that we could go in. And we did—
all of us. The simple-minded, saintly man received his visitors
in a rather large, three-windowed room that was divided into
two halves by a waist-high wooden barrier stretching from wall
to wall. Ordinary visitors were separated from him by the
barrier, a few lucky ones were admitted to his half through a
special door in it. He sometimes invited these fortunate people
to sit down on leather-covered armchairs or a couch, while he
himself always presided in a shabby, antique Voltaire chair.

Semyon Yakovlevich was a rather big, pale, bloated man of
fifty-five or so, with thinning fair hair surrounding a bald
patch; he was shaven, his right cheek was swollen, and his
mouth looked slightly twisted. There was a large wart near his
left nostril. His small, narrow eyes were sleepy, calm, and self-
assured. He wore a German-style black frock coat, but had
no waistcoat or tie. His shirt was very coarse, but white and
quite clean. His feet were probably sore, for he wore slippers.
I remembered hearing that he had once been in government
service and had even held a substantial position.

He had just finished eating a bowl of fish soup and was starting on his second course—boiled potatoes in their jackets with
salt. I understand he never ate anything else. He drank a lot of
tea, of which he was very fond. Three servants, paid by the
merchant, attended him: one wore a frock coat, another looked
like a factory hand, and the third like a verger. There was also
a very lively boy of sixteen or so, as well as the monk in
charge of the collection plate, who seemed rather unsuitably
fat. On one of the tables a huge samovar was bubbling and
beside it stood a tray with perhaps as many as two dozen

glasses on it. On another table lay the gifts brought by visitors: some loaves of sugar, a few pounds of tea, a pair of embroidered slippers, a silk kerchief, a length of cloth, a piece of linen, and so on. Almost all the money offerings went into the monk's collection plate.

The room was crowded. There were perhaps a dozen visitors. Two of them had been admitted to Semyon's half of the room: a little, white-haired old man, a pilgrim from among the "simple" people, and a smallish dried-out monk, who had apparently come from far away and who sat there quietly with his eyes cast down. The other visitors, on the near side of the partition, were also mostly "simple folk," except for a fat merchant who had come from a provincial center—a bearded man who wore a Russian shirt and was reputed to be worth a hundred thousand rubles—an impoverished, middle-aged gentlewoman, and a landowner. Each person present was hoping that Semyon would speak to him, but no one dared address him first. About four of them were kneeling, of whom the one who attracted the most attention was the landowner, a big man of forty-five or so. He had been kneeling right by the partition for over an hour, waiting ecstatically for the saintly man to address him. But Semyon seemed quite unaware of his presence.

Our ladies gathered by the partition, giggling and exchanging lively remarks in whispers. The other visitors, both those kneeling and the rest, had been pushed back or were screened from Semyon's view, except for the landowner, who remained in the front row stubbornly holding onto the partition with both hands. Amused and keenly curious eyes were fixed on Semyon Yakovlevich, some of them from behind lorgnettes, pince-nez, and even opera glasses. Semyon, for his part, lazily sized them up with his sleepy little eyes.

"Ah, what lovelies!" he exclaimed in his low, hoarse voice. We all laughed. What could he possibly mean by that exclamation? Semyon, however, did not elaborate, but plunged into silence again, concentrating on chewing his potatoes. When he had finished with them, he wiped his mouth with a napkin and a servant brought him tea.

Usually he invited some of his visitors to partake in this tea drinking by pointing at the lucky ones. His choice was unpredictable. Sometimes, passing over the rich and powerful, he ordered that tea be offered to some peasant or a ragged old woman; sometimes, ignoring the poor and downtrodden, tea was sent only to some rich, fat merchant. And then, tea wasn't served in the same way to everyone: some received theirs already sweetened, others received their lump of sugar separately, and others had to drink it without any sugar. On this occasion, the elect were the little monk (already sweetened tea) and the old pilgrim (tea without sugar). For some reason, the fat monk in charge of the collection plate was passed over that day, although until then he had regularly had his daily glass.

"Semyon Yakovlevich, please say something to me! I've been longing to meet you for so long," said the elegant lady who earlier in the carriage had stated that she wasn't fussy about the sort of entertainment, as long as it was amusing.

Semyon didn't even look at her. The kneeling landowner sighed deeply, like a huge bellows.

"Sweet tea!" Semyon said suddenly, pointing at the merchant reputed to be worth a hundred thousand rubles.

The merchant stepped forward and stood next to the landowner.

"More sugar for him!" Semyon ordered, and when another lump was added to the already sweetened tea, he ordered again, "Give him more! And still more!"

They sugared his tea for a third and a fourth time, after which the merchant began sheepishly to sip his syrup.

The people around murmured and began crossing themselves.

"Semyon Yakovlevich, sir!" the mournful but strident voice of the impoverished gentlewoman resounded suddenly. She had been pushed into the background by our crowd. "I have been waiting a full hour for your blessing. Guide me, poor, wretched woman that I am, please!"

"Ask her," Semyon said to the servant who looked like a verger.

The servant walked up to the partition.

"Have you done what Semyon Yakovlevich told you last time?" he asked the gentlewoman—who was a widow—in a quiet, even voice.

"How could I, Semyon Yakovlevich?" she wailed. "Those cannibals are taking me to court—me, their own mother. They've even threatened to start criminal proceedings against me!"

"Give it to her!" Semyon ordered, pointing to a sugar loaf. The boy leaped to the table, grabbed the loaf of sugar and handed it to the woman.

"Ah, sir, you are so kind! That's really too much for me!" she tried to protest.

"More! More!" Semyon ordered.

Another loaf was given to her.

"More, more!"

A third and a fourth loaf were given to the widow, who was now entirely surrounded by sugar. The monk on duty from the local monastery sighed: all that sugar could have taken the road to the monastery, as it did on other days.

"But what am I supposed to do with all this sugar? I'm all alone and there's enough here to make me sick—unless there's some prophecy in this—"

"Of course it's a prophecy," someone in the crowd said.

"Give her another pound," Semyon decided.

There was one loaf of sugar left on the table, but Semyon had said one pound, and that's what they gave her.

"Lord, oh Lord!" the people muttered. "There's certainly some prophecy in this!"

"First sweeten your heart with love and charity and only after that come complaining against your own children, the flesh of your flesh—that's the prophecy, I dare say," the fat monk interpreted in a quiet but self-satisfied tone. He was still irritated at not having been offered tea.

The gentlewoman went for him angrily. "How can you say such a thing, Brother," she rasped. "They dragged me into the flames by a rope when the Vershinin house caught fire. Then they slipped a dead cat into my trunk. I tell you, they're capable of anything—"

"Out! Out!" Semyon suddenly shouted, waving his hands.

The verger and the boy hurried through the partition. The verger took the widow's arm. She calmed down and left with him without resisting, only glancing back at the sugar loaves that the boy was carrying behind them.

"Take one back!" Semyon ordered the servant who looked like a factory hand and who had stayed by him. The man rushed after them and soon the three servants and one loaf of sugar were back. The widow left with the three other loaves.

"Semyon Yakovlevich!" a voice called from behind. "I had a dream. I dreamed of a jackdaw who took off from water and flew straight into fire. What does that mean, Semyon Yakovlevich?"

"Cold weather coming," Semyon interpreted.

"But Semyon Yakovlevich, you still haven't answered me

and I'm so fascinated by you!" the elegant lady from my carriage tried again.

"Ask him!" Semyon said, pointing at the kneeling landlord
and ignoring the lady.

The fat monk attached to the collection plate, to whom
the order was addressed, got up and walked slowly and with
dignity toward the kneeling figure.

"What wrong have you done? Have you been ordered to do
something?"

"I mustn't fight; I must not give rein to my hands," the landowner said in a hoarse voice.

"Have you obeyed?"

"I couldn't. My own strength gets the better of me."

"Out, out with him! Chase him with the broom! The broom!"
Semyon shouted, waving his hands.

Without waiting for the penance, the landowner leaped up
and rushed out.

"He has left a gold coin behind," the monk announced,
picking up a half-imperial from the floor.

"Give it to him!" Semyon said, pointing to the fat, rich
merchant. The man reputed to possess a hundred thousand
rubles didn't dare refuse.

"Gold attracts gold," the monk from the monastery couldn't
refrain from quipping.

"Sweet tea for that one over there!" Semyon suddenly ordered, pointing to Maurice Drozdov.

A servant poured the tea and took it by mistake to the
dandy wearing the pince-nez.

"No, no—to the long-legged one, there!" Semyon corrected
him.

Maurice bowed rather stiffly, in military fashion, took the
glass, and started sipping the tea. I cannot explain why, but
our entire group was practically convulsed with laughter.

"Maurice," Liza suddenly said to him, "that gentleman who
was kneeling over there has left. Go and kneel in his place."

Maurice looked at her nonplused.

"Please, Maurice, you'd be doing me a great favor. Listen,"
she insisted with strange heat, "you must. I absolutely want
to see what you'd look like kneeling there. If you refuse, don't
ever come to see me again. I demand that you go down on
your knees now!"

I have no idea what she was after, but she made her demand
insistently and imperiously, as if she were in a trance. As we

shall see later, Maurice himself explained such whims, which had become more frequent recently, as outbursts of blind hatred for him. There was no real spite in it—he knew that she really thought well of him and liked him, but there were moments when she was overcome by unconscious fits of hatred that she couldn't control.

Silently, he handed his glass to an old woman who stood behind him, opened the door of the partition, and without having been invited, stepped into Semyon's private half of the room and went down on his knees in the middle of it, in full sight of everybody. I believe that, simple, sensitive man that he was, he was shocked by Liza's humiliating him in front of us all. Perhaps he thought that she would be ashamed herself when she witnessed the humiliation she had thrust on him. Of course, no one but he would have risked such a naïve method to try to change a woman. Now, he knelt there with a grave and dignified expression on his face, long, ungainly, and ridiculous. But none of us laughed. The unexpected incident produced a painful impression on us all. We all looked at Liza.

"Anoint, anoint him!" Semyon Yakovlevich muttered.

Liza went suddenly pale. She let out a cry and rushed through the partition. A short, hysterical scene followed. She caught Maurice by the elbow and started pulling him up with both hands.

"Get up, get up!" she screamed, beside herself. "How dare you kneel here! Get up immediately!"

Maurice rose from his knees. She squeezed his arm above the elbow with both hands and looked intently into his face. There was fear in her eyes.

"Ah, what lovelies!" Semyon Yakovlevich said again.

Finally she dragged Maurice back to our side of the partition. A stir passed through all our group. The lady from our carriage, probably wishing to dispel the embarrassing atmosphere, addressed Semyon for the third time and, in a shrill voice, asked him with a playful smile:

"Well, Semyon Yakovlevich, can't you really prophesy something for me too? I was so hoping you would!"

"I'll let you have something in your ——!" Semyon said, turning suddenly on her and using an unprintable expression. He articulated every word with deadly precision. Our ladies let out shocked cries and rushed toward the door. The gentlemen burst into stentorian laughter.

And that was the end of our expedition to the saintly half-wit.

But another, rather mysterious incident is supposed to have occurred at this juncture, and it is actually because of it that I have dwelled so lengthily on this trip.

They say that when everyone rushed toward the door, Liza, supported by Drozdov, suddenly found herself face to face with Stavrogin in the doorway. I must say here that, since her fainting spell on that Sunday, she and Stavrogin hadn't exchanged a word, although they had come across each other on several occasions. I saw them almost butt into each other, and it seemed to me that they stopped for an instant and looked at each other strangely. However, I couldn't see very well with so many people tearing about. Some witnesses insisted that when Liza came close to Stavrogin, she raised her hand to the level of his face and would probably have struck him if he hadn't at that moment turned away from her. Maybe his expression irritated her; maybe she resented his smile after the scene with Drozdov. I admit that I myself saw nothing, but others insisted they did, although everyone certainly could not possibly have seen it in that melee. However, some may have. Anyway, I didn't believe it at the time. I do remember, though, that Stavrogin was rather pale throughout our trip back.

III

On the same day—in fact, possibly at the same time—a meeting took place between Mrs. Stavrogin and Mr. Verkhovensky. She had decided to see him a long time before and had informed her former friend of that fact, but somehow she had kept postponing it until then. They met at Skvoreshniki. Mrs. Stavrogin arrived at her country house in a bustle. The day before it had finally been decided that the reception was to be held in the head landowner's house, but the quick-witted Mrs. Stavrogin had immediately realized that nothing could prevent her from giving her own special party at Skvoreshniki afterward and inviting the whole town. Then they could decide for themselves which was the better house and who received with better taste and organized a better ball. Indeed, she was

almost unrecognizable these days. She seemed to have under-
gone a metamorphosis, from the unapproachable "supreme"
lady, as Mr. Verkhovensky described her, to just another
whimsical society woman. But this may have been only a superficial impression.

When she arrived at the empty country house, she inspected the rooms, accompanied by her faithful old footman
Alexei and by Foma, a specialist in interior decoration and,
in general, a man of experience. They discussed what furniture
and paintings should be brought from the town house, where
these things should be placed, what flowers should be brought
from the hothouse and how they should be arranged, where
to hang the curtains, where the bar should be, whether there
should be only one or two buffets, and so on.

And, suddenly, in the middle of all these worries and pre-
occupations, she decided to send the carriage for Mr. Verkhovensky.

Mr. Verkhovensky, who had been warned long before of
the forthcoming meeting, had been expecting something like
this every day, so he was ready for the sudden invitation. On
getting into the carriage he crossed himself, because, for him,
this was the moment of decision. He found his former friend
in the main drawing room, sitting on a small couch in a recess.
Before her stood a small marble table and, pencil in hand, she
was jotting down something on a sheet of paper. Foma was
measuring the windows and the height of the gallery, and Mrs.
Stavrogin was taking down the figures and making notes in
the margins. Without stopping her writing, she nodded in Mr.
Verkhovensky's direction, and when he muttered some form of
greeting she hurriedly proffered him her hand and, without
looking up, pointed to a spot next to her, inviting him to sit
down.

"I sat there for about five minutes, trying to control my
feelings," he told me later. "The woman I saw was not the one
I'd known for twenty years. I felt that everything had come to
an end and this conviction lent me a strength that rather surprised her. I swear, she was really amazed at my stoicism in
this final hour."

Suddenly she put down her pencil on the marble table and
turned to him.

"We have business to discuss," she said. "No doubt you have
prepared all sorts of high-sounding words and dramatic

phrases, but I think we'll do better by getting straight down to business, don't you agree?"

He winced. She was really in a hurry to set the tone of their talk, he thought, wondering what was coming next.

"Wait, keep quiet; give me a chance to say what I have to say and then you may—although I really wonder what you can possibly have to say," she added, speaking very quickly. "The twelve hundred rubles of your allowance, as long as you live—I consider that my sacred duty. . . . Although, why is it my sacred duty? Let's simply call it an agreement, all right? That's much more realistic. If you wish, you can have it in writing. In case of my death, special arrangements have been made. But at present, above and beyond that figure, I provide you with a house, a servant, and your maintenance in general. In terms of cash, that amounts to, say, fifteen hundred, wouldn't you say? Well, I'll add to that another three hundred, making a grand total of around three thousand rubles. Would three thousand a year satisfy you? It seems to me it should be quite adequate. In case of an extreme emergency, I could even let you have more. So, take the money, send me back my people, and go and live by yourself in Moscow, Petersburg, here—wherever you wish, only not with me. Do you understand?"

"Not so long ago," Mr. Verkhovensky said slowly, with sad precision, "another demand, just as unexpected and insistent, was made to me through these same lips. I humbled myself and agreed to hop around like a fool to please you. Yes, I dare say, just like *un petit Cossaque du Don qui saute sur sa propre tombe*. And now—"

"Stop! You're impossibly long-winded, Stepan. You didn't actually dance, but you came to see me in a new cravat, a new shirt, new gloves, and with your hair carefully slicked down and pomaded, and reeking of perfume. I tell you, you were anxious to get married yourself. It was easy to see that from the expression on your face—a quite unseemly expression, I might add. If I didn't comment on it at the time, it was simply because I didn't want to offend you, believe me. But, as I say, you were anxious to get married—extremely anxious, despite all the low things you were saying about me and your fiancée. But this is different and I don't see why you should drag some Don Cossack dancing on his tomb into it. I don't understand what you can mean by it. I certainly don't want you to die. Please, go on living as long as possible; I will be very pleased."

"In a home for old people?"

"Why in an old-people's home? They don't accept people with a yearly income of three thousand rubles. Oh, yes, I remember now," she said, laughing impatiently, "I remember, your son Peter once made a crack about a home for old people. Well, I must say, there's one particular establishment of that sort that we might keep in mind. Very respectable gentlemen live there, including several colonels; I understand a general is even considering entering it. If you wished to retire there with your income, you could really find peace, security, contentment, and be waited on hand and foot. You could devote yourself to your scholarly research; in any case, you'd always find a ready game of whist."

"*Passons.*"

"*Passons?*" Mrs. Stavrogin said with irritation. "All right, in that case, that's all. You've been warned: from now on we live quite separately."

"And that's that? That's all that's left, after twenty years together? Is this your last farewell?"

"You're incorrigibly addicted to exclamations, Stepan. It's no longer the fashion. People talk coarsely now, but at least to the point. And then, why do you keep bringing up those twenty years? It was really nothing but twenty years of self-admiration. Every letter you wrote to me during that time was actually addressed to posterity, not to me. You are a stylist, not a friend. Friendship is just a pretty word and ours was nothing but a mutual outpouring of slops."

"Good God, how you pick up other people's words! It sounds as though you'd deliberately learned them by heart. Ah, they've managed to put their livery on you too. You, too, are rejoicing and greeting the sun! Ah, *chère, chère,* what a mess of pottage you've sold your freedom for!"

"I'm no parrot, repeating other people's phrases," Mrs. Stavrogin said, seething with rage. "I assure you, I have amassed plenty of words of my own. What have you done for me in these twenty years? You haven't even read the books I sent you—they'd have remained uncut if I hadn't had them rebound by my bookbinder. What books did you recommend to me when, during the early years, I asked for your guidance? Nothing but Kapfig and more Kapfig. You were even jealous of my education and you did your best to prevent me from acquiring any general culture. And yet, it's at you that everyone laughs. I admit that I myself have never considered you anything but a literary critic. But, on our way to Petersburg,

I told you I intended to publish a magazine and devote my life to it, and you gave me a sarcastic look and immediately became impossibly overbearing."

"It wasn't that, not at all; we were simply afraid of persecution at the time."

"No, it was exactly as I say. There was absolutely nothing for you, at least, to fear in Petersburg. And do you remember later, in February, when we received that warning, you came and demanded that I immediately write a letter declaring that you had nothing to do with the magazine and that the young people were coming to see me not you, that you were simply my son's tutor who still lived in my house because I owed you some of your fees? Do you really not remember? Yes, you've had an outstanding career all along, I must say."

"That was only a moment of weakness, a moment when I entrusted myself entirely to you!" he exclaimed, pained. "But do you really think we must end it all because of such little things? Is there really nothing left between us now, after all these long, long years?"

"You are so horribly calculating—you want to make me feel that I am still in your debt. When you returned from your trip abroad, you looked down on me and wouldn't let me say a word. Then, when I went abroad myself and tried to share with you the impression made upon me by the Madonna, you didn't listen to me; you smiled superciliously into your cravat as if I couldn't appreciate these things as much as you."

"No, you're wrong, you must be wrong, *j'ai oublié*—"

"No, I'm right—it was just as I say. Besides, nothing really entitled you to feel so superior because all the things you were supposed to be and to have done were nothing but nonsense—pure invention. Today, no one admires that Madonna any more, except for some moldy old men. There's nothing to her—that's been proved."

"It's been proved, has it?"

"She's of no use whatsoever. This jar here is useful because we can put water in it; this pencil is useful because you can write anything you wish with it. But what is she? Just a female face—and much less successful than a real face that nature has created. Now try, for example, to draw an apple and then put a real apple next to it. Which one will you take? I'm sure you won't make a mistake. And that's what all your theories amount to the moment the first ray shed by free investigation exposes them to the light."

"Is that so?"

"You're being sarcastic, as I can see by your smile. Now what, for instance, did you tell me about charity? And yet, the pleasure one derives from charity is the pleasure of pride— the pleasure of a rich man taking advantage of his wealth and power and comparing his own importance with the insignificance of the pauper. Well, charity corrupts both the giver and the receiver; furthermore, it doesn't do any good because it only perpetuates poverty. The lazy, those who are unwilling to work, crowd around those who give money away just as gamblers crowd around the green baize—with the hope of getting something for nothing. But the miserable coppers that are tossed to them are not enough to satisfy one hundredth of the people's needs. How much have you given out in alms during your lifetime? A score of coins, if that? Try to think. Try to remember—when was the last time you gave something? Two years ago? Maybe even four? In fact, you just make a lot of noise and make things worse. Charity ought to be forbidden in a modern society. Under the new organization, there won't be any poor."

"Oh, what an avalanche of ready-made phrases! I see you have even come down to the 'new organization.' Poor woman! God help you!"

"Yes, Stepan, I've come down to it, as you put it. You were very careful to conceal from me all these new ideas that by now are familiar to everyone. And you hid them from me out of sheer jealousy, to maintain your authority. Today, even a woman like that Julie von Lembke has about a hundred-mile start on me. But my eyes have been opened. You know, I used to defend you because everybody—yes, everybody—said deprecating things about you."

"That'll do!" he said, rising from his seat. "And now, I suppose, all that's left for me to do is wish that one day you may repent of your words."

"Sit down a minute, Stepan. I have something else to ask you. You have been invited to read at that literary matinee, haven't you? It was arranged through me. Tell me, what exactly do you intend to read?"

"What do I intend to read? Well, precisely about that queen of queens, that ideal of mankind, the Sistine Madonna, who in your opinion is not worth as much as a jar or a pencil."

"So your subject won't be history?" Mrs. Stavrogin said, bitterly disappointed. "But they won't even listen to you. Ah, you're really obsessed by your Sistine Madonna! Now, tell me, what pleasure will you get from putting all those people to sleep? Please believe me, Stepan—what I'm saying now is for your own good. It would be very different if you picked out some short but amusing medieval anecdote from Spanish history. You know, something that happened at court—or, better still, if you selected one incident and filled it out with some *ad lib* stories and witticisms. Their court was so magnificent and they had so many gorgeous ladies and mysterious poisonings. Karmazinov even said it would be difficult not to make something interesting out of Spanish history."

"Now it's Karmazinov—that fool who has written himself dry—who's looking for a subject for me!"

"Karmazinov has an almost statesmanlike insight. I see you've become very insolent, Stepan!"

"Your Karmazinov is a spiteful old woman who wrote himself dry long ago. Ah, *chère, chère,* since when have you become so enslaved by them?"

"I can't stand him myself because of the airs he puts on, but I must respect his great intelligence. I repeat, I've defended you as well and as vigorously as I could. And, really, why should you insist on being boring and ridiculous? Why not come out on the stage with the benign smile suited to a representative of a past epoch and tell them two or three little anecdotes with your inimitable wit, the way you alone know how to tell them? And, although you may be an old man, although you may belong to another age, although you may have lost touch with them—you can acknowledge it yourself with a smile in your introduction and they'll all see what a nice, kind, witty old wreck you really are. In brief, you'll show them that you're an old-fashioned man, but progressive enough to see all the ugliness of certain ideas you yourself used to profess. Please, as a special favor, do as I ask."

"That's enough, *chère,* don't ask any more of me; I can't— I will read them a piece on the Madonna that will raise a storm that will crush either them or me."

"It will certainly be you who is crushed."

"Well, I suppose then that such is my fate. I will tell them about that low slave—that perverted, stinking flunky who was the first to climb a ladder with scissors in his hand to slash the divine image of the human ideal in the name of equality, envy, and digestion. Let my curse thunder forth, and then— then—"

"Then? The lunatic asylum?"

"Possibly. But whatever the outcome, whether I'm defeated or victorious, that same night I'll take my beggar's pack—I'll leave all my belongings behind, all your gifts and allowances and promises of future blessings—and leave on foot to end my life as a tutor in some merchant's family or die of hunger in a ditch by the road. I have spoken; *alea jacta est!*"

He rose again.

"I was sure of it!" Mrs. Stavrogin cried, her eyes flashing. She also rose to her feet. "I've known for years that your only aim in life was to disgrace me and my house with your slander! What do you mean—a tutor at a merchant's or dying in a ditch? It's all nothing but sheer spite and slander—nothing else!"

"You have always despised me, but I will end like a knight loyal to his lady because your opinion is what matters to me most of all. From this moment on I'll accept nothing from you and shall revere you unrewarded."

"That all sounds rather stupid."

"You've never respected me. I may have had a thousand weaknesses. Yes, I ate your food. (I'm talking now in the language of the Nihilists.) But eating has never been the supreme motivation of my acts. It just happened—I'm not very sure how. But I always thought that there was something more important between us than food and I've never, never been a vile calculator! So now I'm going to put things straight. I'm setting out late in the season; it's late fall, mist hangs over the fields, the road is covered with the hoarfrost of old age, and the wind howls to remind me of the grave that is my destination—but I'll set out on my way,

> Full of love so pure and noble,
> Faithful to his sweetest dream.

Oh, good-by, my dreams! Twenty years! *Alea jacta est!*"

His face was sprinkled with tears that had suddenly gushed from his eyes. He picked up his hat.

"I don't know Latin," Mrs. Stavrogin said, trying to control herself.

Who knows, perhaps she too felt like crying, but her indignation and the impulse she was acting under got the better of it.

"I only know that that's all just a silly game. You will never be able to carry out these threats that fill you with such self-admiration. You will never go anywhere, nor work for a merchant—you'll end your days on my hands, after living quietly on your allowance and receiving your good-for-nothing friends at home on Tuesdays. Good-by, Stepan."

"*Alea jacta est*—the die is cast!"

He bowed deeply to her and left. He returned home half dead from emotional exhaustion.

chapter 6

Peter Verkhovensky Gets Busy

I

The date of the gala was fixed definitely. As it drew nearer, Governor von Lembke grew more sad and retiring. He was full of all sorts of sinister forebodings, which worried his wife very much. Indeed, things weren't going as well as they should have. Lembke's mild and kindly predecessor had handed the province over to him in rather a poor state: there was a threat of a cholera epidemic now; in some places there was a high incidence of plague; fires had ravaged towns and villages throughout the summer, and more and more stupid rumors about arson were circulating. The incidence of robbery and violence had doubled. Still, all this would have been manageable if there hadn't been other things to disturb the governor, who until then had been a happy man.

What worried his wife most was that every day he turned quiet and more strangely secretive. What could he possibly want to hide from her? True, he seldom contradicted her and, for the most part, fully complied with her wishes. On her insistence, he had enforced two or three measures aimed at the strengthening of gubernatorial powers, which were rather shaky legally. With the same aim in view, a few really serious transgressions had been condoned and people who should have been sent to prison or to Siberia had been, on her insistence, promoted and rewarded. And then, some queries and complaints were systematically ignored. All this came to light later. Lembke signed everything he was asked to sign and never questioned the part his wife played in the performance of his duties. But he was liable to suddenly kick up a row over "mere trifles," and this always took his wife by surprise. It was obvious, though, that those moments of rebellion were a compensation for the long days of compliance. Despite all her subtlety and intuition, Mrs. von Lembke couldn't understand this delicate need in her husband's noble character. Besides, she had too many other things on her mind to be bothered trying, and that caused a great deal of misunderstanding.

Certain things are none of my concern here and, anyway, I don't feel qualified to discuss them. It is none of my business to comment upon administrative shortcomings and, indeed, I will eliminate this whole aspect of the situation from my narrative. When I set out to record these events I had another objective in mind. Besides, the present investigation in our province, now being conducted by the central government, is sure to bring many facts to light, if we will just wait a bit. Some explanations, however, cannot be avoided.

But to return to Mrs. von Lembke. The poor lady, with whom I greatly sympathize, could have attained everything she wanted so badly (glory and all that) without going to such lengths and without getting involved in violent and eccentric movements, the way she did from the very moment of her arrival. But, whether it was the fault of too much romanticism or of the sad and repeated failures of her early years, when her luck suddenly changed she felt somehow that she was some sort of chosen creature, almost an anointed one, upon whom "a tongue of flame" had descended. And it was precisely in that tongue of flame that all the trouble lay, since it was not, after all, a chignon that sits comfortably on any woman's head. But it would have been quite hopeless to make a woman see that.

So, anyone who encouraged her illusion was assured of her favor, and people vied with each other in encouraging it. In no time, the poor lady became the target of all sorts of people trying to influence her, while fancying herself as a highly original thinker. Many charlatans feathered their nests during her husband's brief tenure by taking advantage of her naïveté. And what a tangle she got herself into, all the while deluding herself that she was acting independently! She favored many conflicting interests and ideas: the big landed estates, because of the aristocratic aura she saw in them; the gubernatorial authority, which she strove to strengthen; the new, democratic local institution; the new order of the future; free-thinking; and all sorts of socialist notions. She was fascinated both by the severe elegance of an aristocratic drawing room and by the coarse vulgarity of the young people around her, who behaved in her house almost as if they were in a local dive. She longed to bring about general happiness, to reconcile the irreconcilable, or, to put it more accurately, to unite everyone and everything in the common adoration of her person. She had her favorites, of course. She became very fond of Peter Verkhovensky, who used the most unabashed flattery on her. But he also interested her for a very different reason, a very incongruous one that perfectly characterized the poor lady: she hoped that he would reveal to her a conspiracy to overthrow the existing regime. Unlikely as that may sound, it was just as I say. She was somehow convinced that a plot against the government was being hatched in our province just at that time, and Peter, by an alternation of silences and hints, encouraged her in that strange notion. She imagined he was connected with all the revolutionary elements active throughout Russia, but that, at the same time, he adored her and was totally devoted to her. Uncovering the plot, gratitude from Petersburg, a spectacular career for her to follow, her influence on the young generation through "kindness," which would keep them from "going overboard"—all that managed to coexist somehow in her confused, dreamy head. Why, hadn't she already conquered and saved Peter himself? She was, for some reason, quite certain of that. And she would save the others too. None of them would perish. She would rescue them all. She would handle each case individually; report them, and then explain their motivations—act in the interests of higher justice. Then, perhaps, history, and maybe the whole Russian liberal movement, would bless her name. And, at the same time, the plot would be thwarted. Why, her way had all the advantages!

However, the governor had to be made a little more cheerful for the forthcoming gala reception. He had to be distracted and reassured. For this purpose, she sent Peter to have a talk with him, hoping he would know how to relieve her husband's gloom. She may even have hoped that Peter could do this by giving him some tips straight from the horse's mouth. She had implicit trust in Peter's know-how.

Peter hadn't been in the governor's office for a long time, and now he swept in on him at a moment when the patient was in a most delicate state.

II

Von Lembke proved quite unable to handle one particular contingency. A short time before, in the district in which Peter had been having such a good time, a second lieutenant had been reprimanded in front of his men by his immediate superior. The second lieutenant, who had recently arrived from Petersburg to join the regiment, was still a very young man. He was silent, sullen, and forbidding-looking, although rather short, fat, and red-cheeked. Unable to bear the reprimand, he suddenly flung himself at his senior officer with an unearthly scream that shook the whole company. He savagely lowered his head, hit the officer with all his might, and sank his teeth into his shoulder so violently that he could hardly be dragged off. There was no doubt that the man had gone mad. Indeed, his behavior during the past few weeks had been very peculiar. He had thrown two icons belonging to his landlady out of the house in which he was billeted, chopping one of them to pieces with an ax; then, in his bedroom, he had placed on three lecterns the works of Vogt, Moleschot, and Buechner and had lit a taper before each of them. Judging by the number of books found in his room, he was well read. If he had had fifty thousand francs, he perhaps would have sailed off to the Marquesas Islands, like the "cadet" Mr. Herzen describes with such a light touch in his book. When he was arrested, a collection of the most violent and wildly subversive leaflets was found in his pockets and in his billet.

I think that political leaflets as such are a trivial matter and nothing to worry about. We've seen so many of them! Besides, these particular leaflets were not new: identical handbills, I was told later, were found in another province, and Liputin, who had been traveling through still another province, assured me that he had come across the same leaflets there. But what struck the governor was the fact that the manager of Shpigulin's plant had at the very same time handed over to the police two or three bundles of leaflets identical to those found on the lieutenant. They had been planted at the factory during the night. The whole affair was really unimportant. The bundles hadn't even been opened, so none of the workers could have had a chance to read them. But still, it made Governor von Lembke ponder. He viewed it all in an unpleasantly complicated light.

This was an early feature of what became known as the "Shpigulin incident," which caused quite a stir around here. Distorted versions of it appeared in even the Petersburg newspapers. About three weeks earlier, a Shpigulin factory worker had come down with Asian cholera and died. Then more cases of the disease broke out among the factory workers. People in our town became panicky, for the epidemic seemed to be moving our way from the neighboring province. I must note that all the necessary precautions had been taken to meet the emergency, but somehow the plant belonging to the Shpigulins, a millionaire family with very high connections, had been overlooked. And now people claimed indignantly that the plant, and especially the workers' quarters attached to it, were a center of infection because they were so dirty that even if there hadn't been any cholera around, it would have started there anyway. Appropriate measures were decided on immediately and the governor firmly demanded that they be carried out forthwith. The factory was cleaned up within three weeks, but then—no one knows exactly why—the Shpigulins closed it down. One of the Shpigulin brothers was already living permanently in Petersburg and now, after the authorities ordered the place cleaned up, the other brother left for Moscow. The manager paid off the workers and, as we discovered later, swindled them mercilessly. The workers protested, demanded to be paid the wages due them, and naïvely went to the police, but all rather quietly and without undue agitation. And it was just at this juncture that the leaflets had been discovered and brought to Governor von Lembke by the manager.

Peter now rushed into the governor's study unannounced; he was, after all, a close friend, and besides, he was on an errand from the governor's own wife. At the sight of Peter, Lembke frowned and came to a halt by his desk in an attitude of hostile expectation. Until then he had been pacing the room, discussing some private business with his subordinate, Blum, a clumsy, taciturn German whom he had brought along with him from Petersburg despite his wife's protests. When Peter came in, Blum stepped back toward the door, but didn't leave the room. Peter even had the impression that he exchanged a significant glance with his superior.

"Aha, so I caught you napping, you secretive statesman!" Peter shouted, roaring with laughter and slapping his open hand down on a leaflet that lay on the desk. "One more for your collection, right?"

Lembke flushed and his face twitched.

"Leave that alone!" he shouted, trembling with fury. "At once! And don't you ever again dare—"

"What's the matter with you? Are you angry with me?"

"May I inform you, my good man, that from now on I do not intend to put up with your *sans façon,* and I'd like you to remember—"

"Well, I'll be damned! He really means it!"

"Shut up!" Lembke shouted, stamping his foot on the carpet. "And don't you dare . . ."

God knows how it would have ended if it hadn't been for a circumstance of which Peter (and even the first lady) was apparently completely unaware. The wretched governor had reached such a state of collapse that he had secretly begun to suspect his wife's relations with Peter. When he was alone, especially at night, he spent some unpleasant moments brooding on this subject.

"I simply imagined," Peter said, "that if a man reads you his novel until past midnight for two nights in a row and wants to know your opinion of it, he is beyond such superficial formalities. Mrs. von Lembke receives me like an intimate and now you . . . How can I help getting lost?" he asked, with something that sounded almost like dignity. "Here, by the way, is your novel."

He placed on the desk a large, heavy, rolled manuscript wrapped in blue paper.

Lembke blushed and laughed sheepishly.

"Where did you find it?" he asked carefully, but was unable to control a surge of joy, hard though he tried.

"Imagine—rolled up as it is, it had rolled under a chest of drawers. They only found it the day before yesterday when they were scrubbing the floor. Ah, you gave me a lot of trouble with it!"

Lembke lowered his eyes, a severe expression on his face.

"I haven't slept for two nights in a row because of you," Peter announced. "Once they'd found it, I read it throughout those two nights, since I have no time during the day. Anyway,

I can't say your novel is to my taste; that's not the way I see things. Not that I really care—I have never gone in for literary criticism. Still, I couldn't put the manuscript down, although I didn't agree with its ideas. The fourth and fifth chapters are— are—well, I'm damned if I can describe them! You've stuffed so much humor into them that I literally rolled around with laughter. I must say you have a knack of ridiculing things *sans que cela paraisse*. Of course, in chapters nine and ten, that stuff about love (which is not my field) is rather effective. And I almost shed a tear reading your Igrenev's letter—I must say you've got a subtle portrayal there. You know, that letter is very moving, although, at the same time, you manage to show his hypocritical side, right? Did I get it? But the ending! I must admit I felt like giving you a good beating for that. What are you trying to tell us there? Why, it's the same old worship of a happy family life—breeding children, acquiring capital, and living happily ever after. And your ability to charm your reader—even I, as I said, couldn't put the book down—only makes it worse. The average reader is stupid and I would have thought it was the duty of intelligent people to make him see things as they really are. But I suppose I've said enough. Good-by now. Next time, don't be so unfriendly. I wanted to tell you a couple of things that I thought might be useful to you, but you're so strange today—"

While Peter was talking, Lembke had taken his novel, locked it in an oak bookcase, and made a discreet sign to his assistant to leave them. Blum, with his long, mournful face, had disappeared.

"I'm not 'so strange,' " Lembke muttered, now frowning, but no longer sounding angry. He sat down at his desk. "It's simply that I have a lot of worries. Sit down and let's hear that couple of useful things you say you have to tell me. I haven't seen you for a long time, Peter—but please, don't burst in on me in that style of yours again; it's quite embarrassing sometimes when I'm occupied with—"

"I have the same style for everybody—"

"I know, I know and I'm sure there's no harm intended. Still, there are times when one has other worries. But sit down."

Peter immediately sprawled out on the couch. A moment later he tucked his feet up under him.

III

"What worries do you have? Not this nonsense, surely?" Peter said, nodding toward the leaflet. "I can get you as many of those as you wish. I came across plenty of them back in Kharkov Province—"

"You mean when you were there?"

"When else? Surely not when I wasn't there. There's one with a vignette, a small ax, on top. Allow me." He took a leaflet and examined it. "Yes, sure, here it is—the ax, see? It's exactly the same."

"Yes, I see the ax."

"So? Are you frightened of an ax?"

"No, it's not the ax, and I'm not frightened of anything, but there are certain circumstances. You see—"

"What circumstances? The fact that they found those leaflets at the Shpigulin plant? Ha-ha-ha! Listen, take my word for it, the workers at that factory will soon be composing leaflets themselves."

"What do you mean?" Lembke glared at him.

"Just that. You'd better watch out, Governor. You're much too softhearted; you write novels and all that, but what's needed here are the old-fashioned methods."

"What old-fashioned methods? What are you driving at? I ordered the factory cleaned, and cleaned it was."

"And now there's a mutiny among the workers. They need a good flogging, the lot of them, and that's all."

"Mutiny? What rot! I ordered the place cleaned up and it was."

"Ah, Governor, you're such a softhearted man!"

Lembke felt offended again, but he forced himself to keep talking to Peter in the hope of learning something from him. "In the first place," he said, "I'm not as softhearted as you think—and in the second—"

"Aha! Here's another old acquaintance!" Peter interrupted him, swooping down on a leaflet lying under a paperweight. It had been printed abroad and was in verse. "Well now, this one's called 'A Noble Heart' and I can recite it for you by heart too! Yes, this is it—that old noble heart whose acquaintance I made while I was still abroad. Where did you dig up this one?"

"You say you saw it when you were abroad?" Lembke asked,

sounding worried.

"Sure, a full four months ago, maybe even five."

"You seem to have seen so many things abroad," Lembke remarked, giving him a subtle look.

But Peter, ignoring the governor's remark, unfolded the leaflet and read it aloud:

"A Noble Heart

He had no claim to noble birth,
Grew up with those who till the earth,
And persecution was his fate,
By tsar and nobles full of hate.
Suffering he steeled his heart to meet,
Though they might punish, torture, beat,
His voice will ring to eternity:
Liberty, equality, fraternity!

And as rebellion broke out,
He escaped to foreign lands,
From the rack, the chain, the knout,
From the bloodstained torturers' hands.
The suffering masses all were bent,
On rising from Smolensk to Tashkent.
Closing their ranks along the line,
They waited for his rebel's sign.

They considered his arrival,
Tantamount to their survival,
Spelling the end of the regime,
So their lives they could redeem.
Land must be owned in common; search
To find some new and better ways;
Abolish family, marriage, church,
Those vestiges of the bad old days!"

"I bet you got it from that officer, didn't you?" Peter said.

"So you know that officer too?"

"Sure I do. We spent two whole days drinking together. He was trying hard to drink himself insane."

"Maybe he didn't go insane."

"What makes you say that—because he started biting people?"

"But wait. If you saw the poem abroad and then you found it in the hands of that officer——"

"Sounds mysterious to you, doesn't it? I see you're trying to examine me, Governor. Well, let me tell you," Peter started in a very important tone, "that whatever I saw and did abroad, I reported and explained to qualified persons upon my return, and those explanations must have been satisfactory, or I would not have been able to honor this town with my presence. So I consider my case closed and I don't feel I owe any further explanations to anyone. And my case is closed not because I'm an informer but because I had no choice. Those who gave me letters of recommendation to Mrs. von Lembke had all the information and in the light of it decided that I was an honorable man. But to hell with all that; I came here to tell you something very important and I'm glad that you sent that chimney sweep of yours out of the room. This is very important to me, Governor—I have a very special request to make of you."

"A request? Go ahead, please. I must admit I'm rather curious to hear what it can be. And again, I repeat, you're a constant puzzle to me."

The governor was a little worried. Peter crossed his legs.

"In Petersburg," he began, "I was very frank about many things. But about others, such as this, for instance"—he banged his finger on the "Noble Heart"—"I said nothing, mainly because it wasn't worth mentioning, but also because I only answered the questions they asked me. I don't like to anticipate them in such cases. That, in my opinion, is the main difference between a low informer and an honest man who is simply forced by circumstances—but that's neither here nor there. Now, however, when those fools—when, as I see, it's all come out and is already in your hands and, as I realize, could never have escaped your attention, because you have a very sharp eye and know how to keep people guessing about your next move—well, those fools still persist and . . . well, Governor, I've come to ask you to save one such fool. He may even be insane, but I want to intercede for him because of his youth and the hardships he has suffered and because I know what humanitarian principles you have. For I'm sure your humanitarianism goes beyond novels and manifests itself in real life as well." He suddenly and impatiently finished his speech on that note of crude sarcasm.

In fact, Peter sounded like a clumsy, straightforward, tactless man overflowing with humanitarian feelings and suffering from excessive sensitivity. But, above all, he seemed an obviously limited man, a point that Lembke immediately noted with some subtlety. He had suspected it for a long time and particularly during the past week as, alone in his study at night, he had brooded about Peter, trying to understand the unaccountable fancy Julie seemed to have taken to him.

"For whom are you pleading, then? What does all this mean?" the governor inquired in a statesmanlike tone, trying to conceal his curiosity.

"He is—he is— Damn it, I can't help trusting you! It's not my fault if I consider you the most honorable and, what's more important, the most perspicacious—I mean a man who can best understand—well, damn it . . ."

It sounded as though Peter's emotions had overcome him.

"You must understand, after all," Peter went on, "that in naming him, I am delivering him into your hands, sort of betraying him. Isn't that right?"

"But how can I guess whom you mean if you don't make up your mind to tell me?"

"Ah, that's just it! You come along and practically knock people out with your logic! Well, hell, here goes: that fellow, that 'noble heart,' is none other than Shatov. Well, there you are."

"Shatov? What do you mean, it's Shatov?"

"Shatov is the 'noble heart' mentioned in that leaflet. He lives here. He's a former serf. He's the one who punched Stavrogin in the face—"

"Yes, I know about that," Lembke said, screwing up his eyes. "But, excuse me, I don't understand what the charges against him are and even less what your request is actually all about?"

"Why, I'm asking you to save him. Don't you understand? I've known him for eight years and I used to be his friend," Peter said with growing agitation. "Anyway, I don't have to account to you for my earlier life." He waved his hand in despair. "There's nothing to the whole thing. It involves three and a half men here and, all told, counting those abroad, ten at the most. But, in this case, I was relying on your humanitarianism and intelligence. You'll understand the case and put it in its true perspective as the stupid dream of a confused man hatched by a long life of misery—remember that—and not as some extraordinary conspiracy or what have you against the regime!"

He sounded almost out of breath.

"Hm, I may conclude, then, that Shatov is responsible for the pamphlets with the ax," the governor announced, almost majestically. "But then, may I ask how he could manage, if he were the only one involved, to distribute them here, in the neighboring provinces, and even as far away as Kharkov? And, even more important, where could he have got them from?"

"But I told you, there seem to be, at the most, say five people involved in it; or ten if you wish, at the outside. How can I know for sure?"

"You don't know?"

"How the hell should I know?"

"Why, you know that Shatov is one of the conspirators all right."

"Oh well!" Peter shrugged helplessly as if giving up in the face of the governor's uncanny insight. "Listen then, I'll tell you everything. I know nothing about the leaflets. I mean not a damn thing. Hell, do you understand what I mean?—nothing! Well, of course, there's that second lieutenant, and someone else, and then Shatov, and somebody else again, and that's probably all—nothing but human junk, see? But it's for Shatov that I've come to intercede, because he wrote that poem and had it printed abroad himself. I know that for sure. As to the leaflets, I know nothing."

"If it's his verse, the leaflets must be his too. But I would like to know what reasons you have for suspecting Mr. Shatov. What are they?"

Looking now like a man who had definitely been driven beyond all patience, Peter pulled out his wallet and produced a scrap of paper from it.

"Here are the reasons!" he shouted, tossing the note on the table.

The note, as it turned out, had been written about six months previously and was very brief. It read: "Impossible for me to print 'Noble Heart' here. That or anything else. Have it printed abroad. (Signed:) Ivan Shatov."

Lembke looked intently at Peter. Julie had been right when she remarked that Peter had a bovine look, especially at certain times.

"It means," Peter said hurriedly, "that Shatov wrote these verses six months ago, but couldn't arrange to print them here on a secret printing press and therefore wanted them printed abroad. Seems rather obvious, doesn't it?"

"Yes, quite obvious. But whom did he ask to print it?

That's not so obvious, or is it?" Lembke asked, guffawing with subtle irony.

"But Kirilov, of course, since the note is addressed to him while he was abroad. Didn't you know? I'm rather offended that you pretend you know nothing when you've really known everything about that poem all along! How else could it be here, on your desk? But, in that case, why are you inflicting all this upon me?"

He nervously mopped his brow with his handkerchief.

"I may have heard something or other," Lembke parried adroitly, "but who is this man Kirilov that you mentioned?"

"You know, he's that engineer who arrived recently—the one who was Stavrogin's second at the duel. He's some sort of maniac, a madman. That lieutenant of yours may have had a fit of madness, but this Kirilov is completely insane; I can vouch for that. Ah, Governor, if the authorities had any real idea what kind of people these are, they wouldn't have the heart to hurt them. If anything, they ought to be locked up in an institution—the lot of them, I tell you, and I came across plenty of them back in Switzerland at all their congresses."

"They direct the movement in this country from there?"

"Who the hell directs what! Three and a half organizers! Why, just looking at them makes one fall asleep out of sheer boredom. And what's this movement in this country you're talking about? The leaflets perhaps? So, whom have they managed to recruit? Second lieutenants suffering from delirium tremens and two students! Now, you're a smart man, so let me ask you this question: why can't they get any solid, respectable citizens? Why do they only get immature students of twenty-one or twenty-two at the most? And, even so, how many of them do they have? There are millions of bloodhounds out looking for these subversives; and how many have they found? Seven men. I tell you, they just put you to sleep."

Lembke listened to him attentively, but the expression on his face said: "You'll have to come up with something better than that!"

"But excuse me," he said. "You claim that this note was addressed abroad. But I don't see any address here. What makes you say it was addressed to Mr. Kirilov, and abroad, and also that—that it really was written by Mr. Shatov?"

"All you have to do is get a sample of Shatov's handwrit-

"I don't want, of course, to pry into something that doesn't concern me. But it seems to me that, up to now, you've expressed yourself in a very different vein here—for instance, about Christianity, social institutions, and finally, the regime—"

"Suppose I have said certain things—so what? I still say them, but I don't think those ideas should be carried out the way those fools want to. What's the use of biting your superior officer's shoulder? Didn't you yourself agree with me, only objecting that it was too early to go through with it yet?"

"It wasn't actually the things you mentioned that I agreed with when I said it was too early."

"Ha-ha, I see you like to hang your every word on a peg and label it! You're such a careful, diplomatic man!" Peter said in a tone that was suddenly gay. "Listen, my dear Governor, I had to get to know you; that's why I spoke to you that way. I get to know many people by that approach, not only you. Perhaps I was trying to appraise your character."

"Why should my character concern you so much?"

"How should I know why?" Peter said laughingly. "You see, my dear Mr. von Lembke, you are very clever, but it hasn't yet come to *that* and I'm sure it never will. Do you understand? Perhaps you do. Although I may have given certain explanations in certain quarters when I returned from abroad, I see no reason why a man who holds certain sincere convictions shouldn't act in accordance with them. However, no one *there* ever asked me to investigate your character, nor do I have any such missions for *them*. Please try to grasp this: I could very well have given those two names *there*, while making my original explanations, instead of mentioning them to you. If I were guided by considerations of financial or other advantage, then of course I'd be acting stupidly now, because they will be grateful to you rather than me. Anyway, I'm doing it all for Shatov's sake," Peter said in a noble tone, "for him alone, in the name of our former friendship. Of course, when you finally write to *them*, you could, I suppose, put in a word of praise for my efforts, if you felt like it—I certainly wouldn't sue you for it, he-he-he! Well, adieu for now. I've overstayed my welcome, I'm sure, and talked too much," he added pleasantly, getting up.

"On the contrary, on the contrary, I'm very glad we've been able to clear up a few things," Lembke said, also get-

ting up and smiling pleasantly, apparently at Peter's concluding words. "I'm very grateful for the service you're willing
to render us and you may rest assured that, as far as mentioning your zeal goes—"

"Six days—the main thing is those six days during which
you mustn't move. That's what I want most of all!"

"All right."

"I can't tie your hands, of course, nor would I dare to pre-
sume anything of the sort. You'll have to keep your eye on
them, but please, don't scare them before it's time—I rely on
your intelligence and experience in that. I'm sure you have
plenty of bloodhounds and retrievers all over the place, ha-ha!"
Peter blurted out cheerfully.

"Not really," the governor demurred good-humoredly.
"Young people somehow like to imagine that the authorities
have so many bloodhounds. . . . But let me ask you something
else: if, as you say, that Kirilov, who was Stavrogin's second
at his duel, is involved, then, Stavrogin too—"

"Stavrogin what?"

"I mean if they're such close friends?"

"No, no, no! You've got it all wrong, smart though you
are. In fact, I'm surprised at you. Why, I thought you knew
something about it all. No, Stavrogin is quite the opposite—
in fact, completely the opposite— *Avis au lecteur,* to whom
it may concern!"

"Really? I have difficulty believing that," Lembke said, in-
credulously. "My wife told me that, according to certain information she'd received from Petersburg, he's a man with
what we might call instructions—"

"I know nothing, nothing, nothing. *Adieu. Avis au lecteur!*" Peter said, clearly refusing to discuss the point any
further and darting toward the door of the governor's study.

"Wait, Peter, wait a minute—I have another small matter
I'd like to talk to you about. I won't keep you any longer after
that."

He produced an envelope from a drawer of the desk.

"Here's an item that belongs in the same category. By showing it to you, I'm proving the great trust I have in you. Here
it is, sir; what do you think of it?"

The envelope contained a strange anonymous letter addressed to the governor, which he had received the day before.
To his intense annoyance, Peter Verkhovensky read the following:

YOUR EXCELLENCY:

For your rank entitles you to be thus addressed. Hereby, I wish to inform you of the existence of plots against high government officials and against our country. For that's the direction in which things are going. I have been distributing these things for many years. Godlessness is a cause too. An uprising is being hatched. There are thousands of leaflets and a hundred people will run wherever they're told by them, with their tongues hanging out, unless the authorities lay their hands on them. Because those leaflets promise so many good things and people are stupid and then there is vodka. The people searching for those responsible will get hurt too. I wish well to both sides and that's why I have repented. In view of my circumstances, I am only willing to inform to save my country and the Church if I get a pardon for myself from the Secret Police by telegraph. Let others answer for it. Leave a lighted candle in the window at the entrance to your porter's lodge at seven o'clock. When I see it, I will believe you and come and kiss the hand of the authorities, who are so generously handing me a pension, for how otherwise would I subsist? But you—you will not regret it and you will receive a high decoration. We must proceed discreetly though. Otherwise they will wring my neck.

I remain Your Excellency's desperate servant, a repentant freethinker who falls at your feet—

INCOGNITO

The governor explained that the letter had been left in the porter's lodge when no one was around the day before.

"So what do *you* make of it?" Peter asked almost rudely.

"I think it's a joke."

"I think you're right. It's not easy to put one over on you, I see."

"I think so mostly because it's really too stupid."

"And have you received any other anonymous messages?"

"Yes, two."

"Were they in the same style? In the same handwriting?"

"Different styles and different handwriting."

"But were they trying to be funny, like this one?"

"Yes, they tried to be funny, but actually were rather nauseating."

"Well since, as you say, you've had others, this must be the same sort of thing."

"The main feature of these messages is their stupidity.

Those others are educated men—they wouldn't write like that."

"Certainly. Of course not."

"But suppose this one really wants to give us some information?"

"It's quite impossible," Peter said drily, cutting him off. "What can it mean—a telegram from the secret police and his pension? It's obviously a joke at your expense."

"Yes, I suppose you're right," Lembke said shamefacedly.

"I'll tell you what—let me keep that letter for a while. I'm sure I can find out who sent it. Even before I find the others."

"All right, keep it," Lembke agreed, although with some hesitation.

"Have you shown it to anyone?"

"No, of course not. Why should I?"

"What about Mrs. von Lembke?"

"What are you talking about? God forbid! Above all, don't show it to her!" the governor cried in alarm. "It would give her a real shock—and she'd be terribly angry with me."

"Yes, she'd blame you first and say that you must have asked for it if people write that sort of thing to you. I know the way women reason. Well, good-by for now. I may bring you the author of this in two or three days. But, above all, remember our agreement."

IV

Peter Verkhovensky may not have been a stupid man, but Fedka the convict was right about him when he said that "he first invents himself a man and then lives with him." Thus, leaving Lembke, he felt absolutely certain that the governor would keep quiet for at least six days, a delay that Peter needed. But he was deceiving himself, and his mistake lay in having created a Governor von Lembke in his own imagination who was nothing but a simple-minded fool.

Like any other morbidly suspicious person, Lembke always first became exultant whenever an uncertainty was dispelled. He felt that the situation had taken a good turn, despite the complications and bother that it involved for him. At least the old suspicions that had plagued him had proved completely unfounded. And then he had been feeling so tired lately, so hopelessly exhausted, that he naturally longed for peace. But alas, new misgivings began to assail him. His long stretch in Petersburg had left an ineradicable mark on him. He knew a lot about the "new generation," being familiar, in his official capacity, with the secret files on them and also being a curious man and a collector of their leaflets. However, he had never been able to make heads or tails of them. And now, he felt like a babe in the woods. An inner voice told him that there was something incongruous and unreal in Peter's words. "But," he argued with it, "who the hell can tell what they may do, this 'new generation,' or what goes on among them?"

And, as though specially to irritate him further, Blum's head appeared in the crack of the door. All the time Peter had been there, Blum had remained close by.

This Blum was a remote relative of Lembke's, a fact that the governor always very carefully concealed. I must apologize, but I feel that, though he may be unimportant, a few words should be said here about Blum. He was one of that strange species of German "failures," who are "failures" not because they are particularly stupid but for some unknown reasons. German "failures" are no mythological creatures—they really exist, even in Russia, and form a species all by themselves. Lembke had always displayed the most touching concern for Blum and, whenever he could and in the measure of his own success, had always appointed his relative to the best possible subordinate post; but in none of these did Blum have any luck. Either his post was abolished or some new, unfriendly superior was placed over him—once, he had almost landed in criminal court with another official.

He was conscientious, but often needlessly so, and in a gloomy way that only harmed him. He was tall, stooping, red-haired, mournful, and actually rather sensitive. And, for all his zeal, he was often as stubborn as a mule; and, when he took an unyielding position, he usually chose the wrong object and the wrong moment. He, his wife, and their numerous children were all fanatically devoted to his benefactor. Aside from von Lembke, no one had ever liked him. Mrs. von Lembke had taken an immediate dislike to him, but had never been able to overcome her husband's insistence on keeping him around. This had been the subject of their first marital quarrel, and it had occurred very early—in fact, during their honeymoon, when Blum, until then carefully kept hidden from her, had appeared on the scene. Julie had been shocked by the thought that Blum was related to her husband, secret though that kinship was. Although Lembke beseeched her, with hands clasped as in prayer, telling her emotionally the sad story of Blum's life and of their friendship since childhood, Julie felt it was an ineradicable disgrace and used every stratagem, including fainting fits, to cause a break between the two men. But Lembke remained unshakable and declared that he would not send Blum away. She was greatly surprised at his stand and finally had to yield and allow her husband to keep him. It was agreed, however, that the fact that Blum was related to Lembke would be an even more jealously guarded secret (as if that were possible) than before and that even his first name would never be used because, like Lembke, he was called Andrei—in fact, worse still, he was Andrei Antonovich, just like the governor. In our town, Blum made no friends except a German pharmacist, never visited anyone, and as everywhere else, settled down to a parsimonious and solitary life. For a long time he had been aware of Lembke's secret literary ventures. More often than not, he volunteered for secret reading sessions, listening to Lembke's novel sometimes for six hours at a stretch, sitting stiffly, sweating, trying hard not to doze off, smiling. Then, back home with his long, thin wife, he bemoaned his benefactor's unfortunate weakness for literature.

Now, as Blum came in, Lembke gave him a long-suffering look.

"I'd like to ask you, Blum, to leave me alone." He spoke quickly in a worried tone, afraid that Blum might try to resume the conversation that had been interrupted by Peter's arrival.

"Still, I'm convinced it could be arranged most tactfully and discreetly, without any publicity. You have all the necessary authority to do it," Blum insisted, respectfully but stubbornly, stooping as he took a few short steps toward Lembke.

"You know, Blum, you're so loyal to me that I can never look at you without fear."

"You always like to say clever things like that, then later you feel you have nothing to worry about and go to sleep. But, in the long run, you only harm yourself that way."

"You know, Blum, I've just come to the conclusion that we've been wrong about it all along."

"What makes you think so? What that corrupt young man said to you, a man of whom you yourself are so suspicious?

He has conquered you by saying flattering things about your literary talents."

"You don't understand the first thing about it. Your plan is idiotic, I tell you. We'll find nothing and we'll only provoke a storm of protest. Then we'll become a public laughingstock. And then there's Julie—"

"I'm convinced that we will find just what we're looking for," Blum said, putting his right hand on his heart. "We shall make a surprise search, in the small hours of the morning, keeping strictly to the letter of the law and using the utmost discretion. Such young men as Lyamshin and Telyatnikov seem positive that we'll find everything we want. They've been there themselves often enough. No one is too well disposed toward Mr. Stepan Verkhovensky. Mrs. Stavrogin has obviously turned her back on him, and every honest man—if there are any hiding somewhere in this coarse, vulgar town—is certain that the source of godlessness and social subversion is hidden there. All the forbidden books are stored there—Ryleyev's *Thoughts*, the complete works of Herzen, everything. I have an approximate list, in case it's needed—"

"Ah, you're really very naïve, my poor Blum. Everyone has those books."

"And there are plenty of leaflets and manifestoes there too," Blum continued, disregarding Lembke's interruption. "In the end, I'm sure we'll find out who's producing the leaflets here. The young Verkhovensky looks very, very suspect to me."

"You're all mixed up between the father and the son, Blum. They don't get along together at all, you know; the son laughs openly in his father's face."

"They're just putting it on."

"Blum, you must've sworn to drive me mad! Just think for a moment: whatever one may say, he's quite a personality around here. He's a former professor, a man with a name; he'll kick up a fuss, people will make a laughingstock of us, and we'll miss everything we're after. And then, think what Julie will say."

But Blum wasn't listening. He stubbornly pursued his notion.

"He was just an assistant professor and only held the rank of collegiate assessor when he retired from government service," he said, hitting his chest with his fist. "He has never received any awards of distinction and was dismissed from the service on suspicion of subversive activities against the regime. And then, he used to be under special secret surveillance and

I'm sure he still is. So, in view of the unrest prevailing these days, you are duty-bound to act. You're letting an opportunity of distinguishing yourself go by and sheltering the true culprit."

"Julie!" the governor shouted suddenly, hearing his wife's voice in the next room. "Get out of here, Blum!"

Blum winced, but didn't give up.

"Allow me, allow me!" he urged the governor, pressing his hands even harder against his chest.

"Go away, go away!" Lembke muttered through clenched teeth. "Do as you please. We'll see about it later—oh, good God!"

The heavy drapery before the door parted and Mrs. von Lembke appeared. She stopped majestically, measuring Blum with a haughty, scornful glance, as though even his presence there was an insult to her. Blum bowed respectfully to her and silently, still respectfully bent, tiptoed toward the door, his arms held a little away from his body.

Whether Blum took Lembke's last slightly hysterical remark at its face value—that is, as authorizing him to do as he pleased—or whether he pretended to do so for the good of his benefactor, confident that he could guarantee the final success of his plan, this conversation, as we shall see, had the most unexpected consequences, which caused a great deal of laughter, received considerable publicity, provoked Mrs. von Lembke's wrath, and completely befuddled the governor, throwing him into the most lamentable state of indecision precisely at the critical moment.

V

Peter had a very strenuous day. From the governor's mansion, he hurried off to Nativity Street, but passing through Bykov Street on his way, he had to go by the house where Karmazinov was staying. He suddenly grinned, snorted, and went in. He had himself announced and the servant came back to say,

"The master is expecting you, sir."

That made Peter rather curious: he had never promised to come and see Karmazinov.

But it was true that the great author was expecting him. Indeed, he had expected him the day before and even the day before that. Four days before, Karmazinov had handed Peter the manuscript of his piece, entitled *Merci,* which he intended to read at the literary gathering being organized by the governor's wife. Karmazinov had been guided by sheer courtesy and was certain that his gesture would flatter the young man, giving him a chance, as it did, to acquaint himself with this literary chef d'oeuvre before anyone else. Peter had noticed for some time that this vain man, who had been spoiled by success and was so insultingly inaccessible to the nonelect, this man of "almost statesmanlike wisdom," was plainly trying to ingratiate himself with him—sometimes, all too obviously. Peter had apparently guessed that, even if the great man didn't hold him to be the actual leader of the entire secret revolutionary movement, he had at least assumed that he was one of those initiated into all the secrets of the Russian movement and had an unquestionable influence upon the younger generation. The state of "the most brilliant mind in Russia" interested Peter, but for certain reasons of his own he had thus far avoided any intimate conversations with him.

The great writer was staying at his sister's—the wife of a court chamberlain and local landowner. Both she and her husband greatly admired their illustrious kin, but now, to their regret, they were both out of town, visiting Moscow, so the house was being run by an old lady, a poor relation of the chamberlain's, who ordinarily had charge of the housekeeping. As soon as Karmazinov had arrived, everyone in the house had started walking on tiptoe. The old lady sent off almost daily reports to Moscow about how the great man had slept and what he had eaten; once she even sent a wire reporting that, after a gala dinner at the mayor's, Mr. Karmazinov had had to take a spoonful of a certain medicine. She only dared to enter his room on very exceptional occasions. He, on his part, was polite to her, although his tone was rather dry and he only addressed her when he needed something.

When Peter came in, the famous man was eating his midmorning beef cutlet with half a glass of red wine. On each of his previous visits, Peter had found him eating that midmorning cutlet; it had always been devoured in his presence without Karmazinov's making a gesture to offer him some. After the cutlet, a servant wearing a frock coat and gloves and walking on noiseless soles brought him a tiny cup of coffee.

"A-ah!" Karmazinov said in a delighted voice. He wiped

his mouth with a napkin, jumped up, and hurried forward to exchange kisses with his guest—a gesture Russians tend to make if they are really famous.

But, knowing from previous experience that Karmazinov, although he initiated this kissing ceremony, actually only offered his cheek to be kissed, Peter presented him with his own cheek. So the two cheeks met. Karmazinov, pretending not to notice this maneuver, sat down on the couch and pleasantly pointed to an armchair in front of him for Peter, in which Peter immediately sprawled.

"You won't be wanting any lunch, of course?" Karmazinov said, departing this time from his habit, but in a way that suggested a polite refusal.

Peter, of course, immediately said that he'd very much like to have something to eat. A shadow of offended surprise passed over the features of his host. But it lasted only a moment. He nervously rang for the footman and, despite all his polish, there was a note of shrill irritation in his voice as he ordered the servant to serve lunch for one more.

"What would you like, a cutlet or a cup of coffee?" Karmazinov inquired.

"Both—cutlet and coffee—and, of course, I'd like some wine. I'm quite hungry," Peter said, attentively examining his host's attire.

Mr. Karmazinov was wearing some sort of indoor quilted jacket with small mother-of-pearl buttons. It was rather too short and stretched incongruously across his small, rotund belly, but then there are many different tastes. A woolen plaid wrap covered his knees and trailed on the floor, although the room was quite warm.

"You sick or something?" Peter asked.

"No, I'm not sick, but I'm afraid I could easily become ill in this climate," the writer replied shrilly, but carefully molding each word and lisping aristocratically. "I was expecting you yesterday."

"Why? I never promised I'd come."

"No, of course you didn't, but then you have my manuscript. Have you read it?"

"Manuscript? What manuscript?"

Karmazinov was terribly surprised.

"But you've brought it with you? You have it here with you?" he said, suddenly becoming so alarmed that he even stopped eating, staring questioningly at Peter.

"Ah, you mean that *Bonjour* thing, is that it?"

"*Merci*—"

"All right, *Merci*. No, I'd forgotten all about it. I haven't looked at it. I've been too busy. It doesn't seem to be in any of my pockets here; must've left it on my desk. But don't worry, I'm sure we'll find it."

"No, I think I'd rather send someone to your place, in case it gets lost—or someone might steal it."

"Who on earth would want to steal it! And what's the panic anyway? Mrs. von Lembke says you always have several copies of your works, one abroad at a lawyer's, one in Petersburg, one in Moscow, and one in the safe at your bank. Isn't that so?"

"But, as you know, Moscow could also burn down and my manuscript with it. No, I'd better send someone to your place right away."

"Hold on, here it is!" Peter exclaimed suddenly, producing a bundle of sheets from the back pocket of his trousers. "Sorry, it's a bit crumpled. Imagine that, ever since I took it from you, it's been right there in my back pocket along with my handkerchief. I completely forgot about it."

Karmazinov eagerly seized the manuscript, looked it over with great concern, counted the sheets, then put it reverently next to him on a small round table where he could keep an eye on it all the time.

"You don't seem to be a very avid reader," he hissed, unable to restrain himself any longer.

"No, not very."

"And, in the way of modern Russian literature, do you read anything at all?"

"In the way of modern Russian literature? Wait, I think I have read something . . . something called *The Way* or *On the Way* or *The Parting of the Ways*—I can't recall exactly. I read it a long time ago, maybe five years. I have no time for reading."

A brief silence followed.

"When I arrived here," Karmazinov said, after a while, "I assured everyone that you were an extremely intelligent person and now, I believe, everyone is quite taken with you."

"Thanks."

Lunch was brought in. Peter pounced on the cutlet with great zest, ate it up, gulped the wine, and started to sip his coffee.

Karmazinov, finishing off the last bit of his cutlet and the last sip of his wine, observed Peter out of the corner of his eye, thinking, "This ignoramus must have understood my sarcasm very well. And I'm sure he read my manuscript eagerly enough—he just lied to give himself airs. But perhaps he isn't just pretending, perhaps he's really that stupid. But I like my geniuses on the stupid side and perhaps he really is some sort of a genius. Damn him, anyway!"

The writer got up and started to pace up and down the room to promote digestion. He did this after every meal.

"Will you be staying around here long?" Peter asked him.

"Actually, I came here to sell the estate—everything depends on that."

"Oh, you didn't come because they were expecting an epidemic in France after the war, then?"

"N-no—that wasn't exactly the reason," Karmazinov said; he gracefully molded his phrases as he paced the room and each time he turned, gave a little kick with his right foot. "Although I really firmly intend to live as long as possible," he said, snorting with a trace of venom. "There's something in the Russian upper classes that wears out very quickly, in every respect. But I wish to wear out as slowly as possible, and that's why I'm going to live abroad for good. The climate is better there and the stone buildings are healthier and everything is more solid. I think Europe will last long enough—for my lifetime, at least. Don't you think so?"

"How do you expect me to know?"

"Hm. If Babylon really collapsed there, it would be a great collapse indeed. I do agree with you on that point, although, as I said, I'm sure it will last at least through my lifetime. In Russia, on the other hand, there isn't even anything to speak of to collapse. Holy Russia is less capable of offering resistance to anything than any other place. The ignorant masses still manage to subsist on the Russian god, but according to the latest reports, that god is no longer reliable and he is hardly able to hold his own against agrarian reform. To say the least, he has become very shaky. And now, the railroads and you people—well, I've altogether ceased to believe in the Russian god now."

"And what about the European god?"

"I believe in no god. I have been slandered before the young generation of this country. I have sympathized with almost every one of its movements. I have seen the leaflets that are being circulated here. Many people are surprised by them because of their wording, nevertheless they are impressed, without even realizing it, by the potency of the message they carry. We've all been slipping for a long time, feeling that there's nothing to hold on to. I, for one, am convinced that that mysterious propaganda will succeed because Russia is *par excellence* the one place in the world where anything imaginable can happen without meeting the least resistance. I understand very well why wealthy Russians have been rushing abroad and why every year this exodus increases. They are just following their instincts. When the ship sinks, the rats are the first to leave. Holy Russia is a poor, wooden, and—and dangerous country. She's a country of vain beggars in the upper crust, with the majority of the people stowed away in ramshackle wooden huts. Russia would welcome any way out as soon as it was shown her. Those in power are still trying to resist, but all they can do is brandish a bludgeon in the dark and bring it down on the heads of their own supporters. Everything here is doomed. Russia, as it is, has no future. I have become a foreigner and I'm proud of it."

"But you started to say something about those leaflets; I'd like to know what you really think of them."

"Everyone is frightened by them; therefore they must be potent. They expose deceit and prove that there's nothing in this country that one can lean on or rely upon. They speak up while everyone around remains silent. The strongest point in them—despite their wording and style—is their ability to face things as they are. This ability to face the truth belongs exclusively to Russia's young generation. In Europe, they aren't quite that bold yet; there are stone structures there and people have something to hold on to. As far as I can see or judge, the gist of the Russian revolutionary idea is its denial of the concept of honor. I admire the straight and fearless way they express that. They wouldn't understand it yet in Europe, but in Russia that's just what people will pounce on. To a Russian, honor is nothing but a load to carry; it has been useless throughout our history. The Russian people would enthusiastically follow a man who promised them the right to act dishonorably. Myself, I belong to the older generation and I must admit I still stand for honor. But that's nothing more than a habit with me. I just prefer the old style perhaps simply out of cowardice—one must live out one's life somehow, after all."

He suddenly interrupted himself, thinking, "But here I am talking and talking while he sits watching and says nothing. He came here in the hope that I'd ask him a direct question. Well, I'll ask him one."

But Peter then blurted out unexpectedly, "Mrs. von Lembke has asked me to find out from you, by hook or by crook, what kind of surprise you're preparing for the ball, the day after tomorrow."

"Yes indeed," Karmazinov said with a dignified air, "I have something that should really surprise them. But I won't give away my secret."

Peter didn't insist.

"You must know a fellow named Shatov living here?" the great writer said then. "Imagine—I still haven't had a chance to meet him."

"A nice fellow. But why do you ask?"

"Oh, nothing special, but he seems to go around saying all sorts of things. Wasn't it he who punched Stavrogin in the face?"

"That was he all right."

"And what do you think of Stavrogin?"

"I don't know—seems to be just another playboy," Peter mumbled.

Lately, Stavrogin had apparently been cutting him and so Karmazinov had taken a violent dislike to him.

"If what the leaflets advocate was ever realized," Karmazinov said with a smirk, "I suppose that playboy would be one of the first to be strung up on a branch."

"Maybe before that," Peter said suddenly.

"Serve him right," Karmazinov said, no longer laughing; his tone was rather too serious.

"You said that once before, you know, and I told him you did."

"Did you really tell him?" Karmazinov said, laughing.

"And shall I tell you what he said? He said that while he might be strung up on a branch, a flogging would be enough for you—not just a token flogging, but one that really hurt, the way peasants are flogged."

Peter rose and picked up his hat. On parting, Karmazinov held out both hands to him.

"And if everything that's planned came about," he suddenly squeaked, a syrupy note in his shrill voice and still holding Peter's hands in his own, "when would you say it would be?"

"How on earth should I know?" Peter said rather rudely.

For a moment they looked into each other's eyes in silence. "Roughly? Approximately?" Karmazinov squeaked, his tone sweeter than ever.

"You have plenty of time to sell your estate and to get the hell out of here," Peter said even more rudely. They looked at one another intently and in silence for a full minute.

"It'll begin in May and everything will be over by October," Peter announced briskly.

"Thank you, thank you most sincerely!" Karmazinov said in a fervent voice, pressing both Peter's hands.

Back in the street, Peter thought, "You still have plenty of time to desert the ship, you old rat! Well, well, well, if even this man with his 'almost statesmanlike wisdom' asks so confidently about the exact day and hour and thanks me so humbly for the information, how can we doubt ourselves after that?" He grinned. "He's really not that stupid, but since he's just an emigrating rat, he won't go and inform on me. His type never does."

And he darted off to Filipov's house on Nativity Street.

VI

Peter first went to see Kirilov, whom he found alone, standing in the middle of the room. He was doing exercises; his legs were wide apart and he was waving his arms above his head peculiarly. There was a rubber ball on the floor and the remnants of his breakfast tea were on the table. Peter stood in the doorway for a full minute, watching him.

"I see you're taking good care of your health," he said loudly and cheerfully, stepping into the room. "Ah, what a nice ball you've got here! It bounces beautifully! Do you use it in your exercises too?"

"Yes, it's good for the health too," Kirilov muttered drily, putting on his jacket. "Sit down."

"I've only dropped in for a minute, but I suppose I may just as well sit down. It's all very fine to be thinking of your health, but I've come to remind you of our agreement. The time is drawing near in a certain sense," he announced, twisting awkwardly in his chair.

"What agreement?"

"What do you mean, asking me that?" Peter asked worriedly. He looked almost frightened.

"It was no agreement. There's no obligation on my part. Your mistake."

"Listen, what's going on, after all?" Peter said, jumping up thoroughly perturbed.

"I do just as I like."

"Which is?"

"Just what it was before."

"But what am I supposed to understand by that? Does it mean that you still intend to go through with it?"

"It certainly means that. Only there was never any agreement and I owe you nothing. There was nothing involved but my free will and there's nothing but my free will in it now."

Kirilov gave these explanations drily, with an air of disgust.

"That's fine with me; let it be your will, as long as it doesn't change," Peter said, resuming his seat, apparently satisfied. "You're just quibbling about words; I've noticed that you've been irritable all the time lately and that's why I've avoided coming to see you. But, to tell you the truth, I'm certain you won't change that mind of yours."

"I dislike you very much, but you can rest assured I won't change it. However, I don't recognize any obligation on my part."

"But wait a minute," Peter said, becoming worried again. "We ought to settle the matter once and for all—it demands precision and you keep jolting me. Do you mind if I say something?"

"Go ahead."

Kirilov stared into a corner.

"You decided long ago to throw away your life—I mean, the idea occurred to you. Have I put it correctly? Is there any mistake?"

"I still have the same intention."

"Very good, and I want to point out here that no one forced you into it."

"Certainly not. What you say is stupid."

"All right, I admit I expressed myself stupidly. It would be very stupid to force someone to do it. Now let me continue: you were a member of the Movement under the old organization and you confessed your plans to one of the members—"

"I confessed nothing—I simply told him."

"Fine. It would really be ridiculous to confess that sort of thing. What sort of confession would it be? So, you simply told him."

"No, it isn't fine, because you're cackling too much. I owe you no explanations and you're incapable of understanding my ideas anyway. I wish to deprive myself of life because the idea has occurred to me, because I don't want to have the fear of death, because—because—that isn't any of your business! What does it all have to do with you? Want some tea? It's cold. Here, I'll get you another glass."

Peter had actually grabbed the teapot and was looking for an empty glass. Kirilov went to the cupboard and brought a clean one.

"I've just had lunch at Karmazinov's," Peter remarked. "Then I listened to him talking, and that threw me into a sweat and I ran all the way here, which made me sweat some more—so now, I'm very thirsty."

"Drink. Cold tea's good for that."

Kirilov sat down in his chair again and fixed his eyes on a corner.

"They decided in the Movement that I could be useful," he went on, in the same tone, "by killing myself. So, when you stir up trouble here and the police begin looking for you, I'll suddenly shoot myself, leaving a note saying that it was I who did it all; then they'll leave you alone for at least a year."

"Even a few days would be important, even a single day would help."

"All right. So, with that in mind they asked me to wait if I didn't mind and I said—fine, I'm willing to wait for a moment suitable to the Movement, because it makes no difference to me."

"Yes, but remember, you promised that when you drafted that last letter of yours you'd consult me and that when you came to Russia you'd place yourself at my—well, yes, at my disposal. Oh, of course, I mean only concerning that particular business—in everything else you are, of course, perfectly free," Peter added almost amiably.

"I promised nothing. I accepted because I don't care."

"Very good, very good. I have not the least intention of imposing upon your privacy or your pride—"

"It has nothing to do with pride."

"But remember, they collected a hundred and twenty thalers for your fare, so you did accept money after all."

"Nothing of the sort," Kirilov said, flushing angrily. "One doesn't get paid for that sort of thing."

"Some do."

"You're lying. As I had promised in my letter, I paid you back—you personally. A hundred and twenty thalers—and that sum must have been sent there, unless you yourself failed to send it."

"All right, all right, I don't deny that. I did send the money on. The main thing is that you haven't changed your ideas."

"I haven't. Whenever you come and tell me the time has come, I'll do it. Is it going to be soon?"

"A few days more. But remember, we compose the note together, that very night."

"Night or day, I don't care. You said I was to assume responsibility for the leaflets?"

"Right, and something else too."

"I won't assume responsibility for everything."

"What won't you assume it for?" Peter said, worried once again.

"Anything I don't feel like. But that's enough. I don't wish to talk about it any more."

Peter forced himself to change the subject.

"All right, something else: will you come to see us tonight? It's Virginsky's birthday and we'll use that as a pretext to get together."

"I don't want to come."

"Please come—you really ought to; we must impress them with our numbers and our personalities—there's something fatal about your personality."

"Really?" Kirilov laughed. "All right then, I'll come over, but not because of my personality. What time?"

"As early as possible. Be there by half past six if you can. And you know, if you wish, you can come in and sit down and not say a word, however many people are there. But don't forget to bring a pencil and some paper with you."

"What for?"

"Well, since it can't make any difference to you, do it as a special favor to me. Sit there, without exchanging a word with anyone and, from time to time, pretend to take a note or two—you can doodle or something."

"What nonsense! What's the point of that?"

"But it makes no difference to you! You keep saying that nothing makes any difference."

"But still, why all that?"

"Well, an inspector in our Movement has stayed behind in Moscow, and I've been telling them around here that he might pay us a visit. So they'll take you for the inspector and, since you've already been here for three weeks, they'll really get a shock."

"Tricks—you have no inspector in Moscow either."

"Suppose there isn't one, what the hell? What do you care? Remember, you're a member of the Movement yourself."

"Tell them I'm the inspector and I'll sit and say nothing, but I don't want pencil and paper."

"But why not?"

"I just don't."

Peter was furious. His face even took on a greenish tinge. But he controlled himself and picked up his hat.

"And is *he* here?" he asked suddenly in a hushed tone.

"Yes."

"That's good. I'll get him out of here soon, you needn't worry."

"I'm not worried. He only spends the nights here. The old woman is in the hospital and her daughter-in-law is dead; I've been alone for two days now. I showed him the spot in the fence where the board can be removed and that's where he gets through; no one sees him come in."

"I'll take him off your hands very soon."

"He tells me he has plenty of places where he could spend the nights."

"He's lying. They're looking for him and here, for the time being at least, he's safe. But do you talk with him?"

"Yes, we talk all night. He doesn't think much of you. I read the Apocalypse to him and we have tea. He listens—very attentively in fact—all night."

"But, damn it, you'll convert him to Christianity."

"He's a Christian anyway. And you needn't worry, he'll slit that throat for you. Whom do you want him to kill for you, anyway?"

"No, that's not what I intend to use him for. I have other plans for him. By the way, does Shatov know about Fedka?"

"I don't talk to Shatov or even see him."

"Are you angry with each other?"

"No, we aren't angry; we just look the other way when we meet. We spent too long lying next to each other in America."

"I'm going over to see him now."

"That's your affair."

"Later, Stavrogin and I may drop in on you too, at around ten, after we've seen Shatov."

"All right, come along."

"I have to have an important talk with him. Listen, won't you give me your ball? What use can you have for it now? I'd like to use it for exercise too. I'll gladly pay you for it."

"No need for that. Take it."

Peter picked up the ball and shoved it in his back pocket.

"But you'll get nothing against Stavrogin out of me," Kirilov muttered as he let his visitor out. Peter looked at him in surprise, but said nothing.

Kirilov's last remark embarrassed Peter considerably. He didn't have time to digest it walking upstairs to Shatov's room; he only managed to change his bilious expression to a pleasant grin.

Shatov was at home. He wasn't feeling well and was lying on his bed, although fully dressed.

"Oh, I'm so sorry!" Peter shouted, while he was still by the door. "Nothing serious, I hope?"

The pleasant expression slipped from his face and a suggestion of hatred flashed in his eyes.

"It's nothing," Shatov cried, jumping up nervously. "I just have a slight headache."

He seemed bewildered by this sudden visit.

"I've come to see you about a business that makes no allowances for sickness," Peter said quickly, in a peremptory tone. "May I sit down?" he added, sitting down. "And you too sit down on your bed. That's right. Tonight many of us will meet at Virginsky's, ostensibly on the occasion of his birthday. There won't be any outsiders. The necessary steps have been taken to see to that. I'll come with Nikolai Stavrogin. Knowing your present mood, of course, I wouldn't drag you there—I mean that I wouldn't inflict it upon you, and not that we're afraid you might inform on us. But it so happens that your presence there is indispensable. You will meet people there who will decide how you can resign from the Movement and to whom you can turn over the assignments entrusted to you. We shall do it very discreetly—I'll install you in a corner and, since there'll be a lot of people, most of them won't be aware of anything. I admit I've had to argue a lot on your behalf, but I think I've managed to bring them around now, on condition, of course, that you turn over the press and all the papers. After that, you'll be free to go wherever you fancy."

Shatov listened to him with an angry frown. He no longer felt in the least bewildered or afraid.

"I recognize no obligation on my part to account to any of your damn morons," he said cuttingly, "and I don't have to ask anyone's permission to go wherever I damn well please."

"That's not quite true. Much had been entrusted to you and you had no right to break off just like that. And finally, you've never stated your intentions clearly; consequently, you've put them in an equivocal position."

"As soon as I arrived I declared my position clearly by letter."

"No, not clearly," Peter said, calmly pursuing his argument. "For instance, I sent you that poem, 'A Noble Heart,' to be printed and told you to store the copies here in your place until we asked for them. That and the two other leaflets. Well, you returned it all to me with an ambiguous, meaningless letter."

"I plainly refused to print the things."

"No, not plainly at all. You wrote you *couldn't,* but never explained *why* you couldn't. *I cannot* doesn't mean *I refuse.* It could have been assumed that outside causes prevented you and that was how your note was interpreted. And since there was no indication in it that you intended to break with the Movement, the Movement might have entrusted you with something again and thus compromised its safety. There are people here who contend that you were simply trying to induce them to give you an important assignment and then were going to inform on the Movement. I defended you as hard as I could and showed them your scribbled, two-line answer as a document proving your innocence. But now, having reread those two lines again and again, I must admit that they're misleading."

"You've kept that note so carefully all this time?"

"Certainly, I have it even now."

"All right. What the hell do I care!" Shatov shouted furiously. "So let your morons think I've informed on them. I don't give a damn! I'd like very much to see what you can do about it."

"You will be among the first to hang when the revolution triumphs."

"You mean when you have taken over the government and control Russia?"

"It's nothing to laugh at. I repeat once more: I stood up for you. Whatever you think, I still advise you to come to Virginsky's today. Why waste so many words on false pride? Why not part good friends? You realize that, in any case, you must return the printing press, the type, and the old papers. Well, that'll be the subject of the discussion."

"All right, I'll be there," Shatov growled, lowering his head in hesitation.

Peter, without moving, observed him out of the corner of his eye.

"Will Stavrogin be there too?" Shatov inquired suddenly, raising his head.

"Certainly he'll be there."

"Ha!"

There was a brief silence during which Shatov kept snorting with a disgusted expression on his face.

"And what about that wretched poem of yours—the one I refused to print? Has somebody finally printed it?"

"Yes."

"Is it to assure schoolboys that Herzen himself wrote it in your scrapbook?"

"Yes, Herzen in person."

They remained silent now for about three minutes, after which Shatov got up from his bed.

"Get out of here, you," he said. "I don't wish to be in the same room with you."

"I'm going," Peter said lightly, immediately getting to his feet. "One more thing, though: I believe Kirilov is all alone in his cottage, since the old servant woman isn't there."

"Yes, he's all alone. But get out—I can't stand your presence in this room any longer."

Peter reached the street full of pleasant thoughts: "Well, you're really in a fine mood now and tonight your mood will be even better! That was just the way I wanted you today—I could not have hoped for anything better. The Russian god himself seems to be helping me!"

VII

Peter must have been very active and very successful that day, because there was a wide, complacent grin on his face when at six sharp that evening he arrived at Stavrogin's house. However, they didn't let him in to see Stavrogin right away. Stavrogin, he was told, was locked in his study with Maurice Drozdov. This piece of news immediately alarmed him, and he installed himself by the door to Stavrogin's study to wait for the visitor's departure. He didn't have to wait long. Peter heard a loud noise and a very sharp, resounding voice; then the door opened and an extremely pale Maurice Drozdov emerged. He passed by Peter without seeing him, and Peter immediately darted into the study.

I cannot avoid dwelling on this brief encounter between the two "rivals." It was indeed brief, and although it seemed impossible under the circumstances, it still occurred.

Here's what happened. Nikolai Stavrogin was dozing on the couch in his study after dinner when the footman Alexei came in and announced the unexpected visitor. Hearing his name, Stavrogin leaped up from the couch, unable to believe his servant. But soon a smile of haughty triumph twisted his lips, although the incredulous, surprised expression had not left his eyes. Drozdov, when he came in, was apparently struck by Stavrogin's smile and expression; at least, he suddenly stopped in the middle of the room, unsure whether to advance or turn around and leave. While his visitor hesitated, Stavrogin managed to change his expression and step toward him with an unsmiling and astonished air. Drozdov did not take the hand that was offered him, but awkwardly took hold of a chair, pulled it toward him, and sat down without waiting to be invited. Stavrogin sat down on the couch, half facing and half sideways to his visitor, and waited.

"If you can do it, marry Liza Tishin," Drozdov suddenly blurted out, and it was impossible to tell from his intonation whether this was a plea, a piece of advice, a concession, or a command.

Stavrogin remained silent. But that, apparently, was all Drozdov had to say to him. He waited for a reply, his eyes fixed on Stavrogin.

"If I'm not mistaken—and I'm certain I'm not—Miss Tishin is already engaged to you," Stavrogin said finally.

"She is engaged to me," Drozdov confirmed firmly and clearly.

"Have you quarreled, then? Forgive me for asking, Drozdov."

"No, she likes me and respects me, she says, and her opinion is the most precious thing in the world to me."

"I'm sure of that."

"But you know very well that even on her wedding day, even in church, at the altar, she would walk out on me and on everyone else, if you called her."

"Even from the altar?"

"Yes—and after the altar."

"Aren't you mistaken?"

"No. Under her intense hatred for you, full-blooded and violent, I see the sparks of love at every moment—and of madness. Yes, the most sincere, full-blooded, violent love, and madness! And, on the contrary, under the love she has for me, which is also sincere, constant hatred smolders—a great, terrible hatred! Before I saw it for myself, I could never have imagined that such metamorphoses could exist."

"But still, I am surprised that you should come here like this, to dispose of Liza's life. Unless she's authorized you to do so?"

Maurice Drozdov frowned and, for a minute, lowered his head.

"That's nothing but words on your part," he said suddenly. "They are vengeful and triumphant words, for I'm sure you can fill in what I haven't said. But is there really room for petty vanity here? Aren't you satisfied as it is? Do we really have to cross the *t*'s and dot the *i*'s? All right, I'll dot them for you, if you really need my utter humiliation: I have no right and she couldn't have authorized me to come here. Miss Tishin knows nothing about it, and her fiancé has lost the last traces of sanity and should be locked up in a madhouse—and, to top it all, he has come himself to report that fact to you. In the whole world, you're the only person who can make her happy —I can only make her unhappy. You pursue her and torment her, but for some reason you don't want to marry her. If this is the lovers' quarrel that you had abroad, if sacrificing me can help put an end to it—go ahead, sacrifice me. As things are, she's too unhappy and I can't stand it. My words constitute neither permission nor an order, so they can't possibly offend you. If you wanted to take my place beside her at the altar, you wouldn't need my permission, so there was no need for me to come to you on this crazy errand. Anyway, after what I've done now, marriage between her and me is out of the question. I couldn't possibly lead her to the altar after acting so basely, for being here and telling all these things to you—perhaps her most implacable enemy—seems to me a villainy such as I'll never live down."

"Would you shoot yourself during the wedding service, at the altar?"

"No, later, much later. Why should I stain her bridal gown with my blood? But I might not even shoot myself at all, then or later."

"Perhaps you're just saying that to set my mind at rest?"

"Your mind? What difference can a little blood more or less make to you?"

Drozdov turned very pale and his eyes flashed. For a minute or so, they lapsed into silence.

"Forgive me the questions I asked you," Stavrogin said, breaking the silence. "I know I had no right to ask some of them. One question, however, I am fully entitled to put to you: tell me, what makes you believe that I feel that way about Liza? I mean that seriously. You are so sure of it that you were able to come to me and—and risk making me this offer."

"What?" Drozdov cried with a start. "Didn't you care for her? Don't you still? Do you really not intend to do anything about it?"

"As a general rule, I never discuss my feelings for a woman with a third person—in fact, with anyone other than the woman concerned. You must forgive me—I suppose it's an organic peculiarity of mine. However, I will tell you the truth about everything else: I am already married, so it would be impossible for me to marry or even, as you put it, to 'do something about it.' "

Drozdov was so amazed that he fell back in his chair and for some time stared at Stavrogin speechlessly.

"I must say I never, never expected that," he muttered. "That day you said you weren't married and—and I believed . . ."

He was growing paler and paler, turning completely ashen. Suddenly he slammed his fist on the table as hard as he could.

"If, after this admission, you don't leave Miss Tishin alone, and if she's unhappy through any fault of yours—I'll kill you with a stick like a stray dog and leave you to rot in a ditch!"

He leaped up and rushed out of the room.

Peter, who darted in as soon as Drozdov was out of the way, found Stavrogin in a different mood from what he had expected.

"Ah, it's you!" Stavrogin said, laughing loudly, laughing apparently at the figure of Peter, who appeared to have sprung up out of nowhere, obviously breathless with curiosity. "Were you eavesdropping? Wait—what have you come about? Ah yes, I remember, we have to go and meet 'our friends!' Let's go; there's nothing I'd like better just now—a very good idea of yours!"

Stavrogin took his hat and the two men immediately left the house.

"So the mere fact that you're about to meet 'our friends' makes you laugh?" Peter rattled off cheerfully, trying to keep level with his companion on the brick sidewalk, although he was often forced to step down into the mud because Stavrogin apparently didn't even notice that, by walking in the middle, he was occupying the entire sidewalk.

"It doesn't make me laugh at all," Stavrogin answered loudly and cheerfully. "As a matter of fact, I am convinced that they're a most solemn crowd."

" 'Dismal morons,' as you once described them."

"Well, there's nothing funnier than certain dismal morons."

"You mean Maurice Drozdov, don't you? I bet he came to concede his fiancée to you. Am I right? I kind of advised him to do that—indirectly, of course, as you can well imagine. Anyway, if he doesn't turn her over to us on his own, we'll take her from him ourselves, right?"

Peter, of course, knew what he was risking in getting himself involved in such complications, but then, when he was excited, he was prepared to risk anything rather than remain in ignorance. Stavrogin just laughed.

"So you still intend to help me?" he asked.

"If you call on me. But there's a best way of achieving things, you know."

"I know your way."

"No, you don't really. It's still a secret. But, remember, secrets cost money."

"I know how much it costs too," Stavrogin growled under his breath, but then controlled himself and fell silent.

"How much? What did you say?" Peter became alarmed.

"I said to hell with you and your secrets. You'd better tell me whom you'll have there. I know we're going to a birthday party, but I want to know who will actually be there."

"Oh, the whole damn lot of them—even Kirilov."

"Are all of them members of cells?"

"God, you're really in a hurry! We have yet to form one proper cell around here."

"How did you manage to distribute so many leaflets then?"

"Where we're going now, there will only be four cell members. The others are spying on one another in expectation, and vying with each other in coming to me with information. Very reliable people. They are material that still needs to be organized and sorted out. But you wrote the charter yourself, so I don't suppose there's any need to explain these things to you."

"What is it, then? Is it hard going? Any snags?"

"It's going better than it has any right to. Let me make you laugh: the first thing to produce a great effect is a dress uniform. There's nothing stronger than uniforms. So I'm deliberately inventing ranks and functions. I now have general secretaries, secret emissaries, treasurers, chairmen, registrars, and their deputies. It's all taking very well; it's been a great success. The second thing, of course, is sentimental claptrap. As you know, in this country, socialism mostly propagates itself through sentimentality. But in that lies trouble too, because we're bound to stumble against second lieutenants who bite and the like. Then come the unmitigated crooks. They, certainly, are very nice people and are often a great asset to the Movement, but they need constant supervision and that takes up a lot of our time. And finally, the main force, the cement holding the whole structure together, is shame about their own personal opinions. Yes, that's a real force! And who worked on it? Who managed to leave them completely blank, without a single one of their personal opinions left? Now they're ashamed of anything they may think for themselves."

"But if it's all as you say, why do you drive yourself so hard?"

"Why, if a fellow's just lying around, gaping at everything, you can't help grabbing him! Don't you really believe that we can succeed? I suppose you do have faith, but the trouble with you is that you don't want it badly enough. Yes, we can succeed using fellows just like that. I assure you, they'll jump into water and even into fire if I reproach them simply for not being really liberal. Fools reproach me for having deceived everyone here with talk about a 'central committee' and innumerable 'chains of command.' You yourself once took me to task for it, but I don't think it's a swindle. Why, the central committee is you and me, and we'll soon have as many chains of command and branches and cells as we wish."

"But what human muck!"

"That's the material we need; we'll make use of them, all right."

"And what about me? Do you still need me?"

"You're the leader, the force; I'm only at your side, a sort of secretary. We'll

> Board our ship
> With oars of oak
> And sails of silk
> And at the helm,
> Fair Liza—

or however the song goes—"

"Ha-ha, you're stuck!" Stavrogin roared with laughter. "Let me tell you a better fairy tale. Here you are, going around calculating something on your fingers and forming cells from some unknown forces. That's all nothing but bureaucracy and sentimentality, nothing but good cement. There's something better than that: convince any four members of a cell to kill the fifth, assuring them that he's about to inform on them, and lo and behold, they'll be linked to you forever by the blood spilled. They'll become your slaves and won't dare ask you for accounts or rise against you. What do you say? Ha-ha-ha!"

Peter thought, "I'll make you eat those words, and no later than tonight. You're going too far after all."

That was what Peter was thinking, or at least something along those lines, as they arrived at Virginsky's house.

"I suppose you're going to try to pass me off as some member of the Movement, from abroad, some inspector from the International or something like that," Stavrogin asked suddenly.

"No, you won't be an inspector; you'll be a founding member from abroad who is in on the most important secrets. That's your role. I suppose you'll make a speech?"

"Where did you get that idea?"

Stavrogin was so surprised that he stopped by a lamppost. Peter met his stare calmly and arrogantly. Stavrogin spat and walked on.

"But *you* will speak, won't you?" he suddenly asked Peter.

"No, I guess I'd rather listen to you."

"Damn you, you've really given me a good idea."

"What?" Peter said, starting with alarm.

"I think, after all, I will make a speech there, and after that I'll give you a beating—and believe me, it'll be a good one."

"Ah, by the way, earlier today I told Karmazinov that you had said he ought to be flogged and flogged painfully, the way a peasant is flogged."

"But I never said that. Ha-ha-ha!"

"Never mind that. *Se non è vero.*"

"Well, thanks anyway, my sincere thanks."

"Shall I tell you what Karmazinov told me? He said that, essentially, our teaching is the denial of honor and that the easiest way to attract the Russian man is to promise him the right of dishonor."

"Excellent words, golden words!" Stavrogin said. "He hits the nail right on the head. The right of dishonor. They'll all come rushing to us and there'll be none left on the other side. But tell me the truth, Verkhovensky—you're working for the secret police, aren't you?"

"If you really thought so, you wouldn't have asked me. No, for the moment, I'm not from the secret police. But that's enough for now—we've arrived. Come, put on an appropriate expression, Stavrogin. I always do when I appear among them. Try to look as grim as possible—that's all there is to it. Nothing else is required. It's really very simple."

chapter 7

AMONG FRIENDS

I

Virginsky lived on Ant Street in his own—that is, his wife's —house. It was a wooden, one-story structure and the Virginskys were its only occupants. About fifteen guests had gathered there on the occasion of the host's birthday, but the party didn't look at all like what one would expect a provincial birthday party to look like. From the beginning of their life together, the Virginskys had decided it was stupid to invite guests on their birthdays and that a birthday was not an occasion to celebrate anyway. In a few years they had managed thoroughly to isolate themselves from social life. He, although he was an able man in many ways, was generally considered a solitary crank, and an arrogant one at that. As for Mrs. Virginsky, she was a midwife by training and that alone placed her rather low on the social ladder, lower even than the priest's wife, despite her husband's respectable official rank. However, she lacked the humility that should have gone with her humble station. And, on top of that, after her affair with that crook Lebyatkin—an affair that had been shockingly open as a matter of "principle"—even the most broad-minded of our ladies had turned their backs on her with unconcealed scorn. Mrs. Virginsky, however, took it all as if that was just what she wanted, and it is worth noting that those same ladies called on her—Arina Virginsky—whenever they were in need of a midwife, in preference to three other local ladies who practiced that profession. She even received calls from estates outside town, to attend the wives of landowners, so great was the trust they had in her competence, her luck, and her sure hands in critical moments. Finally, she confined her practice to the richest patients, because she loved money passionately. Once she realized her power, she abandoned all restraints on her temperament. Apparently, during the performance of her duties in the most distinguished houses, she liked to scare nervous ladies in labor with her incredible, nihilistic forgetfulness of all the rules of decency or by jeering at "all that's holy" at the very moments when "holy" things might be the most useful. Our local doctor, Rozanov, positively assured us that once, when a certain woman, writhing in the pangs of childbirth, began to implore the Lord for help, Arina Virginsky delivered herself of a freethinking phrase that acted upon the patient like a pistol shot, thus stimulating, through fright, a quick delivery. But Nihilist though she was, Mrs. Virginsky did not turn up her nose at social prejudices, even the most old-fashioned ones, as long as she felt they were to her advantage. She would never, for instance, miss the christening of a child she had helped to deliver, and on these occasions, she always appeared in a green silk dress with a train, with her hair specially curled, although at any other time she seemed to take special delight in appearing in public in the most slovenly attire. And although, to the great embarrassment of the officiating priest, she always assumed a scornful air during the christening ceremony itself, she invariably managed to be the one to hand the champagne around (that was why she dressed up and came in the first place) and heaven help a guest who having taken a glass, forgot to put money on the tray for her "good works."

The guests gathered at the Virginskys' that evening (almost all men) were a motley lot. There were no drinks and no card games. In the middle of the fair-sized living room, which was papered in very faded blue, two dining tables had been pushed together. They were covered with an extra-large tablecloth that was not too clean, and on it stood two big, hissing samovars. A huge tray holding twenty-five glasses and a basket of sliced, unbuttered French bread, such as one would expect to find in a boys' or girls' boarding school, stood at the end of the table. The tea was poured by Arina Virginsky's thirty-year-old, unmarried sister, a taciturn and venomous virgin, with no eyebrows, who nevertheless shared her sister's modern ideas and who inspired fear in Virginsky himself in his domestic life.

Altogether, there were three ladies in the family—Mrs. Virginsky, her browless sister, and Virginsky's own sister. Mrs. Virginsky, the mistress of the house, was about twenty-seven, rather disheveled but of quite imposing good looks. She wore an everyday woolen dress of greenish color and sat looking at the guests with shining eyes that seemed to say, "See, there's nothing in the world I'm afraid of!" Virginsky's sister, who had just arrived from Petersburg, was a rather well-fed, short, compact, red-cheeked, rotund university student and a nihilist. She sat next to her sister-in-law. Still wearing her traveling clothes and clutching some sort of a bundle on her lap, she examined the guests with her impatient, darting eyes. Virginsky himself wasn't feeling too well, but he appeared anyway and sat in an armchair by the table. The guests were seated on straight chairs around the table, stiff and dignified—it was evident that they were waiting for an official meeting to open. The atmosphere of general expectation was quite obvious, although, while waiting, they conducted rather loud and extraneous conversations. When Stavrogin and Verkhovensky appeared, a dead silence fell.

I suppose, though, that at this point I should explain a few things to make the situation more understandable.

I'm sure that each of these people had come to the meeting in the hope of hearing something interesting, something of which they had been given an idea beforehand. They represented the flower of the reddest liberalism in our ancient town and had been carefully hand-picked by Virginsky for this "conference." Let me note also that among them there were some—but only a few—who had never before been in his house. Of course, most of the guests had no very clear idea why they had been summoned, although they all thought that Peter Verkhovensky was an emissary from abroad with special powers. That notion had somehow caught on immediately and naturally was flattering to them. On the other hand, among the group there were a few who had received definite instructions. Peter had managed to form a Five in our town and yet another Five, consisting of army officers stationed in our district, along the lines of a cell he had previously formed in Moscow. They say that he also had a Five in Kharkov Province. Now the five members of our local cell were sitting at the table, but they managed to look so unconcerned and commonplace that no one could tell who they were. Since it is now no longer a mystery, I can say that they were Liputin, to start with, then Virginsky himself, then Mrs. Virginsky's brother, the long-eared Shigalov, Lyamshin, and one Tolkachenko, a strange man of forty or so who was famous for his profound knowledge of people, especially of swindlers and criminals, and who spent his time going from one dive to another (and not only in the course of his research on people). He stood out among us because of his badly cut clothes, his heavy laborer's boots, the sly look in his half-closed eyes, and the rather complicated colloquial expressions he used. Lyamshin had brought this man to Stepan Verkhovensky's gatherings once or twice, but he had failed to make an impression there. He usually turned up in our town when he was unemployed because he could get employment with the railroad here.

These five would-be statesmen had joined this first cell in the unshakable belief that theirs was only one among hundreds and thousands of similar Fives scattered throughout Russia, all controlled by some vast, mysterious central organization that maintained close contact with the European and worldwide revolutionary movements. Unfortunately, however, even at that time, signs of disaffection were beginning to appear among them. The fact of the matter was that, although they had been waiting for Peter's coming, which had been announced to them first by Tolkachenko and then by Shigalov; although they expected him to perform miracles; although they had immediately and unquestioningly agreed to form the cell as soon as Peter had suggested it to them—as soon as they did so, they seemed to become full of resentment, perhaps precisely because of the eagerness with which they had agreed to it. Of course, their main reason for agreeing had been the fear that they might later be reproached for not daring to join; but still, they felt Peter Verkhovensky should have rewarded them for their generous gesture by revealing something really important to them.

But Verkhovensky had never even thought of satisfying this legitimate curiosity and hadn't told them anything special. In general, he had treated them very roughly and rather disdainfully. That irritated them, and cell member Shigalov was already trying to stir up the others to ask Peter for an "official account"—but, of course, not now, at Virginsky's, because there were too many outsiders present.

Speaking of outsiders, I suspect that the above-mentioned members of the first Five suspected that among the guests gathered at Virginsky's that evening there were members of other Fives organized locally by Verkhovensky and belonging to the same mysterious organization. So, the assembled guests were suspicious of one another and each of them tried to impress the others by his attitude. This imbued the gathering with a confused, mysterious, and, at the same time, somewhat romantic air. There were, however, some persons who were above suspicion, such as an army major, a close relative of Virginsky's who had arrived, quite innocently, without being invited and couldn't possibly be turned away. Virginsky wasn't worried about him because the major, although he didn't sympathize with their political ideas, "would never think of informing" on them since, despite his stupidity, he enjoyed being among extreme liberals and liked listening to them talk. Moreover, he had been compromised once in his youth—whole bundles of Herzen's periodical *The Bell* and reams of subversive leaflets had passed through his hands, and although he had been too afraid even to unwrap them, he would have considered a refusal to distribute them as outright cowardice. To this day there are many Russians like that.

As to the remaining guests, they either belonged to that

bilious type full of frustrated romantic aspirations and pride,
or to the type filled with the first impulse of generous youth.
There were two or three schoolteachers, of whom one was
past forty-five and lame, a very venomous and remarkably vain
man, and also two or three officers. One of these, a young
artillery officer, a silent boy who had only recently been grad-
uated from a military academy and who hadn't yet had time
to make any acquaintances in our town, now suddenly found
himself at Virginsky's holding a pencil and notebook in his
hands. He kept jotting down notes and hardly said a word
to anyone. Everyone noticed this, but for some reason they
all tried to pretend they hadn't. Also present was the former
divinity student who had helped Lyamshin smuggle the pornographic pictures into the bag of the woman who sold Bibles.
He was a big fellow, overbearing but careful, with a reproachful smile combined with an expression of the utmost
satisfaction with his own perfection written all over his face.
For some reason, the son of the mayor was also there—that
wayward, corrupted boy I mentioned before in the sad story
of the second lieutenant's wife. He remained silent the entire
evening. Finally, there was a hotheaded, tousled, eighteen-
year-old schoolboy who wore a gloomy, offended expression,
apparently suffering over being eighteen. This baby, we found
out later to our amazement, was the head of an independent
subversive group that had been formed among the senior
class of the local school.

I have not mentioned Shatov, who had installed himself at
a far corner of the table. His chair was slightly out of line
with the other chairs. He looked down, maintained a grim
silence, and refused both tea and bread. He never once put
down his cap but held it in his hand all the time, as though
he wanted to make it obvious that he was no guest but was
there strictly on business and intended to get out as soon as
he was through. Not far from him sat Kirilov, who was also
very silent, but who instead of looking at the ground like
Shatov, examined in turn all those who spoke. He regarded
them with his black, lusterless eyes, listening to them in
silence and without the slightest surprise or emotion. Some
guests, who had never seen him before, stole sidelong glances
at him.

I can't say whether Mrs. Virginsky herself even knew of
the existence of the Five. I imagine she did—probably through
her husband. But Virginsky's student sister was certainly un-

aware of anything. As a matter of fact, she had her own pre-occupations: she intended to stay with her brother for a couple of days only, after which she planned to go farther, traveling from one university town to another to "share in the sufferings of poor students and urge them to protest." She carried with her a few hundred copies of a lithographed manifesto, I believe of her own composition. It is interesting to note that the schoolboy conceived a deadly hatred for her from the very first glance and that she responded to him in kind, although until then they had been completely unaware of each other's existence. The major was her uncle and this was the first time they had met in ten years. When Stavrogin and Verkhovensky walked in, her cheeks were as red as cranberries because a moment before she had had a frightful row with her uncle that had been triggered by his views on the emancipation of women.

II

Verkhovensky sprawled in his chair at the head of the table with emphatic lack of regard for the assembled company. He had hardly said hello to anyone and now looked around him with an air of haughty disdain.

Stavrogin, however, bowed politely to everyone.

Although all these people had been waiting for the two of them to appear, every one of them now pretended, as though by common agreement, that they had hardly noticed their arrival. Mrs. Virginsky turned toward Stavrogin and asked him rather gruffly:

"Want some tea, Stavrogin?"

"Yes, please."

"Give Stavrogin some tea," she said to her sister, who was pouring it. "And what about you, Verkhovensky?"

"Sure I do. Anyway, what's the idea of asking guests whether they want tea? And put some more cream in mine this time. Somehow one always gets some unspeakable concoction in this house instead of tea, even at an anniversary or a christening—"

"Why, you mean to say even *you* recognize christenings?" the girl student laughed suddenly. "We were just discussing it."

"That's old stuff," the schoolboy grunted from the opposite end of the table.

"What's old stuff? Trying to overcome superstitions is old stuff? I'm afraid it's still very topical, to our great shame," the girl immediately responded to his challenge, leaning forward in her chair. "Anyway, I say there are no harmless superstitions."

"All I meant to say," the schoolboy said, becoming terribly agitated, "was that, although superstitions do, of course, belong to the past and must be done away with, a silly superstition like christening has been dealt with long ago and everyone knows that it's stupid, so it's not worth wasting one's time on and people's wits could be put to better use on more important subjects—"

"You go on and on and it's impossible to make out what you're trying to say," the girl student shouted angrily.

"I thought everyone was entitled to express his opinion, and if I wish to express mine, I have just as much—"

"No one is trying to deprive you of your right to speak!" Now it was the mistress of the house who sharply interrupted the boy. "You're simply being asked not to chatter like that because no one can understand what you're talking about."

"I'm afraid I must object—I am not being treated with due courtesy inasmuch as I'm not being given an opportunity to finish my thought. It's not a lack of ideas, but rather that I have too many of them . . ." the schoolboy muttered, almost despairing and getting completely mixed up.

"Well, if you don't know how to express yourself, just shut up!" the girl student fired at him.

The boy jumped up from his chair.

"I simply wished to state," he shouted, burning with shame and not daring to look around him, "that you started all this just to display your wit, as soon as Mr. Stavrogin came in! And that's the truth!"

"That's a dirty, unfair thing to say and it shows that you're still at an inferior stage of mental development. And, from now on, I don't wish you to address me," the girl rattled off at full speed.

"Stavrogin," the mistress of the house said, "before you came in, they were arguing their heads off about family rights. This man here," she nodded in the direction of the major, "was defending them. Of course, I haven't the slightest intention of bothering you with old rubbish like that which has long since been settled, but I would still like to know where all those family rights and duties came from—I mean, was it in the form of the superstitions that have come down to us? Well, that's my question: what's your opinion on the subject?"

"What do you mean, where did they come from?"

"Why, just as we know, for instance, that the superstition about God comes from thunder and lightning!" the girl student burst out again, her eyes all but leaping out of her head and flying at Stavrogin. "Today, it's well known that, in their fear of thunder and lightning, primitive men defied the unseen enemy because they felt helpless before him. But where did the superstition about the family originate? Where does the notion of 'family' come from?"

"It's not quite the same thing," Mrs. Virginsky said, trying to restrain her sister-in-law.

"I'm afraid that an answer to that question would be rather indiscreet," Stavrogin said.

"What do you mean?" the girl student said, bending forward in surprise.

Titters came from the group of teachers which were immediately echoed at the other end of the table by Lyamshin, the schoolboy, and, after a brief interval, by the major, who laughed hoarsely.

"You should write vaudeville sketches!" Mrs. Virginsky said to Stavrogin.

"A remark like that doesn't do you any credit, whatever your name is," the student declared, quite indignant now.

"Next time don't jump at people like that," her uncle the major said to her. "Remember, you're a young lady and should know how to behave. You see what happens when you insist on sitting down on a needle."

"I would appreciate it if you would also keep quiet and abstain from addressing me with such familiarity. And please spare me all your repulsive metaphors. I don't remember meeting you before, and I don't recognize you as a relative of mine."

"But I happen to be your uncle, and I carried you in my arms when you were a baby!"

"I don't care who or what you may have carried in your arms. I never asked you to carry me around, Mister Bad-Mannered Army Officer, so I must assume you did it for your own pleasure. And again, I must remind you that I won't tolerate your using that familiar tone with me!"

"That's the way they all are!" the major said, banging his fist on the table and apparently addressing Stavrogin, who sat across the table from him. "I must say, I'm interested in liberalism and contemporary problems and I like to listen to intelligent discussions, but I do wish it could be confined to men. I don't care to hear that sort of thing from these modern women! No sirree, that's something I really can't stand! Stop wriggling, you!" he shouted at the girl student, who was bouncing about in her chair, "I'm also entitled to have my say! I've been slighted, remember!"

"You only prevent others from talking—you have nothing to say yourself," the lady of the house muttered indignantly.

"No, I think I'll say what I have on my mind, this time," the major said heatedly. "I'm counting on you, Mr. Stavrogin, because you've just come in, although I don't have the honor of knowing you. I say that, without men, they'd perish like a bunch of flies. All that stuff about the emancipation of women shows nothing but a lack of originality. I assure you that the whole furor was invented for them by men who, in a moment of aberration, called that trouble down on themselves. I just thank God I'm not married. Women haven't the slightest ability to be original: they can't even invent a new design for their embroidery—even for that they call on men. Here, for instance, look at her: I carried her in my arms when she was a baby, I danced the mazurka with her when she was ten, and now, when she arrived, I naturally rushed up to give her a big hug, and then the second thing she tells me is that there's no God! Well, I wouldn't mind it so much if it had been the third thing she said, but she had to blurt it out as soon as she'd said hello! All right, I can see that there may be intelligent people who don't believe in God—they arrive at that point by thinking it out and all. But she's just a brat. What do you understand about God? I bet some fellow student taught you that stuff. If he had taught you to light sanctuary lamps before icons, you'd have done that just as zealously."

"You're a liar and a spiteful man. I have already demonstrated the inconsistency of your views to you," the girl said scornfully, as if it were beneath her dignity to talk to such a person. "I told you that, in catechism class, we were all taught that if you honor your father and mother, you'll live long and become rich. That comes in the Ten Commandments. Now, if God finds it necessary to offer people rewards for love, such a God must be considered immoral. That's how I proved my point to you and I didn't just blurt it out as soon as I'd said hello—I simply said it because you made a claim on me. Now whose fault is it if you're so stupid that you still can't understand? That makes you feel bad and then you get furious and that explains the behavior of all your generation."

"Silly goose!" the major said.

"And you're a moron!"

"Go on, insult me."

"But just a minute, Major," Liputin squeaked from the other end of the table. "I'm sure you told me yourself that you didn't believe in God."

"And suppose I did? It's a different matter for me. I, perhaps, do believe in God, although not completely. But, even if I don't quite believe, I'd still never go around saying that God ought to be shot. When I was still serving in the Hussars I often used to wonder about God. In all the songs a Hussar drinks and has a great time and all that. But, believe me, even then, although I may have actually drunk a lot, I often jumped up from my bed at night and stood in my socks, crossing myself before the icon and beseeching God to give me faith, because even then I couldn't prevent myself from worrying about whether or not God existed. Yes, I had a rough time of it. In the morning, of course, one got distracted and faith vanished as it were. Yes, in general, I've noticed that in daylight faith seems to decrease—"

"Do you have a pack of cards by any chance?" Verkhovensky asked the mistress of the house, yawning quite openly.

"I'm in full sympathy with your question," the girl student cried, growing crimson with indignation at the major.

"Precious time is being wasted on stupid talk," Mrs. Virginsky broke in, looking reproachfully at her husband.

The girl student drew herself up.

"I wanted to inform the meeting about the suffering of the students and about their protest. Now, since time has been wasted on idle and immoral discussion—"

"There isn't any such thing as moral or immoral!" the schoolboy said, unable to restrain himself once the girl student had opened her mouth.

"I'm well aware of that, Mister Schoolboy, and knew it long before they taught you about it."

"But I claim," the boy rejoined fiercely, "that you're nothing but a brat and that you don't have to tell us things we know already just because you happen to have come from Petersburg. As to the Commandment 'Honor thy father and mother,' which you misquoted, everyone in Russia has known it's immoral ever since Belinsky explained that it was."

"Will this nonsense never end?" Mrs. Virginsky said in a determined tone to her husband. Being the mistress of the house, she felt personally ashamed at the silliness of the arguments, particularly since she'd noticed a few smiles and bewildered glances exchanged between the last two arrivals.

"Ladies and gentlemen!" Virginsky said suddenly, raising his voice. "If any one of you wishes to speak about something that is more closely connected with the business at hand, or if he has some declaration to make, I suggest he proceed without further delay."

"I'd like, if I may, to ask one question," said the lame teacher, who till then had sat in dignified silence. "I would like to know whether the lot of us gathered here constitute a business meeting or whether we're just a bunch of ordinary mortals come to visit friends? I ask this mostly as a matter of form but also to dispel any possible misconceptions."

This sly question produced its effect. Glances were exchanged, each one expecting the other to answer. Finally, however, everyone somehow wound up staring at Verkhovensky and Stavrogin.

"I suggest we simply take a vote on the question of whether or not we are an official meeting," Mrs. Virginsky said.

"I second the motion," Liputin said, "although it is somewhat vaguely worded."

"I second it too," "Me too . . ." several voices were heard.

"Yes, I think it would contribute to a more orderly procedure," Virginsky said in approval.

"Then let's vote!" the mistress of the house declared. "You, Lyamshin, please go and sit down at the piano; you'll be able to cast your vote from there when the balloting begins."

"What, again?" Lyamshin protested. "Haven't I thumped it often enough for you, as it is?"

"I earnestly request you to sit down and play. Unless you no longer wish to be useful to the Cause."

"But I promise you, Mrs. Virginsky, no one is eavesdropping. It's sheer imagination on your part. And with these high windows, who could understand what's going on here, even if he tried to listen in?"

"We can't understand it ourselves," someone grumbled.

"But we must always take every possible precaution. I'm

thinking of possible spies," she explained, turning to Ver-khovensky. "They'll think we really are having a birthday party when they hear the piano."

"Ah, damn it!" Lyamshin swore. He sat down at the piano and played a waltz, almost banging the keys with his fists.

"Those who wish this gathering to be an official meeting, raise your right hands," Mrs. Virginsky sang out.

Some raised their right hands; others didn't. There were also some who, after raising them at first, at once put them down again.

"Oh hell, I don't understand a damn thing!" an army officer cried.

"Neither do I," another said.

"I do!" someone else announced. "If it's *aye*, you raise your hand."

"But what does *aye* mean?"

"It means we're having an official meeting."

"No, this isn't an official meeting."

"I voted for an official meeting!" the schoolboy shouted, addressing Mrs. Virginsky.

"So, why didn't you raise your hand?"

"I was watching you and since you didn't raise yours, I didn't raise mine."

"Very stupid of you: I didn't raise mine because I proposed the motion. Ladies and gentlemen, I suggest we start all over again: this time, those for the meeting, sit quiet and don't raise your hands; those against—raise your right hands."

"Those against?" the schoolboy asked.

"Why, you must be doing it on purpose!" Mrs. Virginsky shouted angrily.

"Now, just a minute, ma'am—are those who want this to be a meeting or those who don't supposed to raise their right hands? Let's have it clear now!" two or three voices rose in protest.

"Those who do *not* want it."

"That's plain enough, but what are they supposed to do, raise them or not raise them?" one of the officers cried in despair.

"Ah, it doesn't look as if we're quite ripe for a constitution yet!" the major remarked.

"Please, Mr. Lyamshin, take it easy. The way you bang, we can't hear a word of what's going on," the lame teacher pleaded.

"I assure you, Mrs. Virginsky, no one is trying to eaves-drop!" Lyamshin said, jumping up from his stool. "Anyway, I don't want to play all the time. I came here as a guest, not a drummer!"

"Ladies and gentlemen," Virginsky suggested, "just speak up now: are we a meeting or aren't we?"

"We are! We are!" came from all sides.

"All right then, there's no need to vote on it. Enough of that! Are you all satisfied or does someone feel we should still vote?"

"No need, no need, we understand!"

"Perhaps someone among you doesn't wish this to be a meeting?"

"No, no, we all want a meeting!"

"But what does it mean, a meeting?" someone inquired, but he received no reply.

"We must elect a chairman!" voices came from all directions.

"The master of the house, of course—Virginsky!"

"Well, if that is your wish, ladies and gentlemen," the elected chairman began, "I will repeat my original proposal: if there's anyone here who has something to say more closely connected with the business at hand, let him do so without any further waste of time."

A general silence followed during which all eyes gradually wound up focused expectantly on Verkhovensky and Stavrogin again.

"Don't you have a statement to make, Verkhovensky?" the mistress of the house asked point-blank.

"No, none at all," he answered, stretching in his chair and yawning. "Unless . . . wait—I think I would like a glass of brandy."

"And how about you, Stavrogin?"

"No thank you, really, I don't drink."

"I didn't mean about the brandy. I was asking you whether you wanted to speak?"

"About what? No, I don't."

"They'll bring you some brandy," Mrs. Virginsky told Verkhovensky.

The girl student stood up. She had made several previous attempts to be recognized.

"I have come here to report on the sufferings among underprivileged students and on ways to rouse them to protest, all over the country—"

But she stopped short. At the opposite end of the table, another speaker had materialized and all eyes turned toward him. The long-eared Shigalov, looking gloomy and morose, slowly got to his feet, and with a sad expression placed a voluminous, closely written notebook on the table. He stood there in complete silence. Many looked with surprise at the notebook. Liputin, Virginsky, and the lame teacher, however, seemed very pleased about something.

"I'd like to address the meeting," Shigalov said mournfully but firmly.

"You have the floor," Virginsky said, authorizing him to speak.

The speaker sat down, remained silent another half minute, then said in a grave voice: "Ladies and gentlemen—"

"Here's that brandy!" Mrs. Virginsky's sister, who had been pouring the tea, announced in a scornful and disgusted tone. She brought a bottle and a glass that she carried between her fingers without tray or saucer and put them in front of Verkhovensky.

The interrupted orator looked around with offended dignity.

"Never mind, go on. I wasn't listening anyway," Verkhovensky shouted, pouring brandy into his glass.

"Ladies and gentlemen," Shigalov started again, "I request your attention and, as you will see later, I ask for your assistance in a matter of prime importance. But, first of all, I must say a few words to introduce my main point."

"Say, Mrs. Virginsky, do you have a pair of scissors by any chance?" Peter Verkhovensky asked suddenly.

"What do you want scissors for?" she asked, looking at him pop-eyed.

"I forgot to cut my nails. I've been meaning to do it for three days," Verkhovensky said, examining his long, rather dirty nails with detachment.

Mrs. Virginsky flushed with anger, but Miss Virginsky, the student, seemed to enjoy Peter's interruption.

"I believe I saw them over there on the window sill," she announced.

She got up, found the scissors, and brought them to Peter, who took them without even looking at her and started working on his nails. Mrs. Virginsky thought there must be a reason for Peter's action and suddenly became ashamed of her first reaction. The members of the meeting exchanged glances in silence. The lame teacher watched Verkhovensky spitefully and enviously. Shigalov went on with his speech.

"Having devoted all my energies to a study of the social organization that will supersede the present one in the future society, I have come to the conclusion that all those who have devised social systems, from antiquity down to this very year, have been nothing but dreamers, writers of fairy tales, and fools who have contradicted themselves because they have understood nothing about the natural sciences or about that strange animal called man. Plato, Rousseau, Fourier, aluminum pillars—all that may be fit for sparrows, but certainly not for human society. But we need to know what the future organization of society will be, especially now that we are about to go over to action—so we won't have to think any more about it. I therefore wish to propose my own system of world organization. It is all in here!" he announced, slapping the notebook in front of him. "I had hoped it would be possible to present my book to this meeting in abbreviated form, but I realize now that I will have to add many more oral explanations, so I estimate that a comprehensive presentation will take at least ten evening sessions, one for each chapter of my work." (Some laughter from the audience.) "Furthermore, I must warn you that my system is not yet complete." (More laughter.) "I have become entangled in my own data and my conclusions directly contradict my original premises. I started out with the idea of unrestricted freedom and I have arrived at unrestricted despotism. I must add, however, that any solution of the social problem other than mine is impossible."

The laughter grew louder and louder, but it was the young, the obviously less indoctrinated ones, who laughed the most. Mrs. Virginsky, Liputin, and the lame teacher looked rather annoyed.

"But if you yourself have failed to develop an acceptable system and even despair of arriving at one, what then are *we* supposed to do?" one of the officers inquired cautiously.

"Well, you have a good point there, Mr. Officer," Shigalov answered cuttingly, "and you're right to use the word 'despair.' Yes, I was in despair, but that doesn't alter the fact that what is written in this book cannot be changed and that no one will ever find a way out. So, I invite all those gathered here to devote ten evenings to the study of my book and, afterward, to express their opinions on the subject. Now, if the meeting refuses to listen to me, we'd better speak up here and now: let the men go back to serving the state and the women return to their kitchens, because if they don't accept my book, they'll never find any other solution. There is none! If they miss the opportunity I am offering them, they will only hurt themselves, because they are bound to have to face the facts later."

"So everything boils down to Shigalov's despair," Lyamshin concluded, "and thus the outstanding question is whether Shigalov should or should not despair."

"Shigalov's despair is a private matter," the schoolboy declared.

"I propose we take a vote on whether Shigalov's despair has a bearing upon the state of our common cause and whether we should spend so many evenings listening to him or not," an officer said cheerfully.

"Well, I don't think that's quite the point," the lame teacher finally managed to put in, speaking with a sort of sarcastic grin that made it very difficult to tell whether or not he was serious. "I would like to suggest, ladies and gentlemen, that perhaps Mr. Shigalov is taking his problem a little too much to heart and is, besides, too modest. I know his book. He offers as a final social solution the division of mankind into two uneven categories. One-tenth will be granted individual freedom and full rights over the remaining nine-tenths, who will lose their individuality and become something like a herd of cattle. Gradually, through unlimited obedience and a series of mutations, they will attain a state of primeval innocence, something akin to the original paradise on earth, although, of course, they'll have to work. The procedure Mr. Shigalov suggests, which would deprive nine-tenths of mankind of their free will and transform them into a herd through re-education of entire generations, is very interesting; it is based on data gathered from the natural sciences and is very logical. We may disagree with some of his conclusions, but we must give the author's intelligence and vast knowledge their due. It's really a shame that his stipulation that we should devote ten evenings to his theories is impractical, for otherwise I'm sure we would have heard many very interesting ideas."

"You're not serious, are you?" Mrs. Virginsky asked the lame teacher with a certain alarm. "So this man, not knowing what to do with people, turns nine-tenths of them into slaves! I have suspected for a long time that he might come up with something like that!"

"You are talking about your brother, remember," the lame teacher reminded her.

"Who cares about family relationships! You're not trying to pull my leg by any chance, are you?"

"And those people will have to work for the nobles and obey them as if they were gods—that's real degradation!" the girl student said.

"What I'm offering is not degradation but paradise on earth," Shigalov said peremptorily. "Anyway, there's no other solution," he concluded.

"But, instead of your paradise on earth," Lyamshin shouted, "I'd grab those nine-tenths of mankind and blow them sky-high, leaving only the well-educated tenth, who would then live happily ever after in accordance with scientific method."

"Only a clown would say such a thing!" the girl student cried, flushing.

"He's a clown all right, but he's a useful clown," Mrs. Virginsky whispered in her ear.

"Perhaps yours would indeed be the best solution to the problem!" Shigalov said, turning excitedly toward Lyamshin. "You don't even know how important what you've just said is, Mr. Funny Man. But since your proposal is impractical, we must content ourselves with what you call paradise on earth."

"What bunk!" Verkhovensky couldn't help muttering, although he went on cutting his nails and showed no signs of concern.

"Why is it bunk?" the lame teacher said, pouncing on him as if a word from Peter was all he had been waiting for. "Why bunk? In a way, Mr. Shigalov is a fanatic of humanitarianism; but then, think of Fourier, Cabet, and even Proudhon himself —they provide plenty of incredible and tyrannical solutions to the problem. Mr. Shigalov's approach may even be more realistic than theirs. I assure you, when one reads his book, it is impossible not to agree with certain things he says. Perhaps less than any other, can he be accused of being unrealistic; his paradise on earth is almost the true thing: an idyl, the loss of which—if it ever existed—mankind keeps bemoaning."

"Damn it, I could've bet I'd get involved in an argument," Verkhovensky muttered again.

"And let me tell you, sir," the lame teacher continued, becoming more and more agitated, "that to think about and discuss the future social structure is almost a compulsion among our contemporaries. It was Herzen's sole concern all his life.

As to Belinsky, I know for certain that he spent entire evenings debating the future social organization with his friends and deciding in advance the smallest of its, so to speak, domestic arrangements."

"Some even go nuts," the major suddenly remarked.

"Still, I say there's a greater possibility of arriving at something by talking it over than by just sitting and taking on dictatorial airs," Liputin hissed, apparently at last plucking up enough courage to start his attack.

"When I said bunk, I wasn't talking about Shigalov," Verkhovensky mumbled. "What I meant," he added, raising his eyes slightly from his nails, "was that, in my opinion, all those books, all those Fouriers, Cabets, and this stuff of Shigalov's too, and the business about human rights—it's all a kind of fiction, and you can write hundreds of thousands of such fictions if you feel like it. It's nothing but an aesthetic pastime. I can well understand that you people get bored in this lousy little town, so you go for any scrap of paper as long as there's something written on it."

"Just a minute, sir, just a minute," the lame teacher stopped him, fidgeting in his chair. "I concede that we're only small-town folk and, for that alone, deserve to be pitied—still, we feel pretty sure that nothing has yet happened in the world that we could've missed completely. Now, for instance, we've been told—through the intermediary of foreign-made leaflets —to close our ranks and form cells for the sole purpose of total destruction because, it's contended, there's no longer any cure for the world and the only way is the radical measure of chopping off a hundred million heads. Then, after thus easing our burden, we will be able to leap over the ditch with much less trouble. There's no doubt that it's a very bright idea, but I submit it's just as unrealistic as Mr. Shigalov's theories to which you referred with such contempt just now."

"Well, I didn't come here to debate," Verkhovensky said, muttering some strong expression under his breath. Apparently unaware that he had blundered, he drew the candle closer to him better to see the progress he was making with his nails.

"It's a pity you didn't come here to debate, and it's also a pity that you're so entirely preoccupied with your toilet now."

"Why should my toilet bother you?"

"Chopping off a hundred million heads is as difficult as reforming the world through propaganda—in fact, even more difficult, particularly if we're dealing with Russia," Liputin risked once more.

"Russia's their main hope, though," an officer remarked.

"Yes, we've heard about Russia's being their main hope," the lame teacher said, throwing himself into the fray again. "We know that a mysterious finger is pointing at our beautiful land as the country best fitted to perform the great task. Just one thing: I'd personally feel I'd be getting something out of a gradual solution of the problem through propaganda—at least it'd give me a pretext to chat a bit and then I might be rewarded by the government for my efforts in trying to enlighten the masses and promote social progress. But what would I personally get out of a quick solution with a hundred million heads rolling? If I started spreading that kind of propaganda, they might even cut my tongue out for me."

"They will certainly cut yours out," Verkhovensky said.

"Well then, you can see for yourself that, under the most favorable circumstances, that sort of butchery couldn't be completed in less than fifty or, at the very least, say, thirty years. After all, people are not sheep; they won't let themselves be butchered just like that. Wouldn't it be better to pick up one's belongings and emigrate somewhere across the ocean, to some quiet islands, and there close your eyes to everything and live in peace? Believe me"—he tapped his finger meaningfully on the table—"the only result of your sort of propaganda will be emigration—nothing else!"

He looked very pleased as he finished his speech. Liputin was smiling perfidiously. Virginsky had been listening to the discussion with a mournful expression. All the rest had followed the argument with the utmost attention, particularly the ladies and the officers. They had all seen very clearly that the advocate of chopping off a hundred million heads had been backed against the wall, and they were waiting to see how he would react.

"I must say, you put it very well," Verkhovensky said, sounding even more indifferent, even more bored than before. "It's a good idea for them to emigrate. But still, if, despite all the obvious disadvantages that you predict, more and more people volunteer to fight for the Cause, I suppose we can manage all right without you. You see, my good man, we have a new religion to replace the old one; that's why we have so many volunteers and are able to operate on a grand scale. But go ahead and emigrate! I would, however, advise

Dresden rather than those remote, peaceful islands in the ocean, because, in the first place, Dresden is a city that has never had an epidemic, and a civilized person like you is sure to be afraid of death; in the second place, it is near the Russian border, and you would be able to receive your income quickly from your beloved mother country; and in the third place, Dresden possesses many so-called art treasures, and you must be a man with aesthetic tastes, for if I remember correctly, you were formerly a teacher of literature; and finally, Dresden contains its own pocket Switzerland that would provide inspiration for your poetic vagaries, because I'm sure you're quite handy at composing verse; in short, Dresden is a sort of treasure store in a tobacco pouch!"

There was a general stir, especially among the army officers. In another moment, everyone would have been talking at the same time. But the lame teacher rose irritably to the bait.

"No, we may yet decide not to abandon the common cause just like that. You mustn't reckon on it, sir. . . ."

"Would you be willing to become a member of a Five then, if I offered it to you?" Verkhovensky barked out, putting the scissors down on the table.

A shudder seemed to pass through everyone in the assembly: the mystery man apparently had come out into the open at last; he'd even publicly mentioned the word Five.

"An honorable man doesn't shrink from work for the common cause," the lame teacher said, trying to wriggle out of it, "but—"

"No sir, try to do without any *buts*," Verkhovensky interrupted him sharply and imperiously. "I declare, ladies and gentlemen, that I must have a plain answer. I understand very well that in coming here and in having asked you to meet in this place, I owe you some explanation," he said, thus making another surprise announcement, "but I can't explain anything until I know the nature of your opinions. Skipping discussion —because we surely don't want to have another thirty years of tongue-wagging such as we've had for the past thirty years— I ask you what you prefer: do you want the slow solution of writing social novels and preordaining human destiny bureaucratically on paper for thousands of years in advance, while the tyrants, meanwhile, snatch the juicy morsels that were destined for your mouths; or are you for a quick solution, whatever it may consist of, which will finally enable men to organize their society themselves, not just on paper but in real life? Some people shout about those hundred million heads that must roll, although, after all, that may be nothing but a metaphor. Anyway, why should we shrink from it when we think that, within a hundred years or so, tyranny is bound to devour not one hundred million but five hundred million? Note also that an incurable patient cannot be cured, whatever you prescribe for him on paper. On the contrary, if we delay much longer, he will be so pestiferous that he'll end up by infecting us and all the fresh forces that, today, we can still rely upon, so that, in the end, everything will fail. I fully agree that it's extremely pleasant to wag one's tongue eloquently and expostulate about liberalism, whereas action in its behalf may hurt. Well, anyway, I'm not good at speaking. I've come here to inform you of a few things, so I would ask this worthy company not to vote, really, but simply to tell me what you prefer—to keep plodding through this quagmire at a snail's pace, or to go across it full steam ahead, as quickly as possible."

"I'm for going full steam ahead!" the schoolboy shouted rapturously.

"Me too," Lyamshin chimed in.

"There's no question about what one should choose," an officer muttered, and his statement was approved by another officer and by someone else. Verkhovensky's announcement that he had some communications to make had really struck home; they were hoping he would make them then and there.

"I can see, ladies and gentlemen, that your answer is in the spirit of the proclamation," Peter said, looking around the assembly.

"Yes, yes, all of us!" most voices confirmed.

"I admit I would have preferred the humanitarian solution," the major said, "but since it's the way everyone else feels, I guess I'll go along too."

"So, it appears you're not against it either?" Verkhovensky said to the lame teacher.

"I'm not actually," the lame man muttered, blushing, "but if I agree with the rest, at this time, it's only not to upset the unanimity—"

"So that's the way you are! First, you argue for months for the sake of exercising your liberal eloquence and then you vote along with the rest! But, wait—I suggest that every one of you first think again whether he's really prepared for whatever may come."

For what were they supposed to be prepared? It was a vague question, but how intriguing!

"Of course we're all prepared," people declared on all sides, although many sidelong glances were cast around.

"But maybe you'll be angry with yourselves later for accepting so quickly. That's what always happens with you people."

They grew agitated in various ways. The lame teacher pounced on Verkhovensky again.

"I wish to point out to you, however, that answers to such questions are, as a rule, subject to certain conditions. Even if we have consented, you must still keep in mind that a question asked in such a strange way—"

"What strange way?"

"Not in the way such questions are usually asked."

"Please explain what you mean. And, by the way, I was sure you'd be the first to feel resentful because you'd accepted too readily."

"You have squeezed this declaration of our readiness for immediate action out of us, but what right did you have to act this way? Who authorized you to ask us such questions?"

"You should have worried about that a bit earlier. Why did you answer? Now, after you've accepted, it suddenly occurs to you."

"But, in my opinion, the casual frankness of your main question suggests that you really had neither the authority nor the right to ask it and did so just to satisfy your own curiosity."

"What are you driving at?" Verkhovensky cried, apparently alarmed.

"What I'm driving at is this—new members are recruited in secret and not publicly, before a gathering of twenty unknown people!" the lame teacher barked. Getting this off his chest had put him into a real turmoil.

Verkhovensky, pretending alarm, looked over the company.

"Ladies and gentlemen, I consider it my duty to inform you that this is all bunk. Our talk has led us too far afield. I haven't recruited anyone yet and no one has the right to say that I am recruiting—we were simply discussing opinions. Isn't that right? But whether it's right or not, your attitude worries me," he said, once again turning toward the lame teacher. "I never imagined that such innocent matters had to be discussed only in private here. But perhaps you're afraid that someone here may inform on the rest? Is it really possible that there might be an informer among us now?"

There was a general commotion as everyone talked at once.

"If there were an informer here," Verkhovensky went on, "I've compromised myself more than any of you, so I suggest you answer the following question—that's if you wish to answer it—I leave it up to you entirely."

"What question? What is it?"

"It's a question that will make it clear whether there is any point in our remaining together or whether we should immediately take our hats and each go his own way."

"Well, what's the question?"

"If each of us knew that plans for a political murder were afoot, would he, foreseeing all the consequences of it, go and inform, or would he stay quietly at home ready to face the consequences come what might? Opinions on this subject may differ and the answer to my question will tell us whether we should part or remain together—and I don't mean for tonight only. So allow me to address the question to you first." Peter turned toward the lame man.

"Why must I be the first?"

"Because it was you who started it all. And please, don't try to dodge it. Your agility won't help you here. However, it's really up to you to answer or not."

"I hope you'll excuse me if I say that your question is really rather insulting."

"Couldn't you be a bit more precise?"

"I've never been a stool pigeon yet, my good sir," the teacher said, wriggling more than ever.

"Please be more explicit—you're holding us up."

The lame teacher became so irritated that he stopped answering his tormentor and simply glared at him from under his glasses.

"Yes or no? Would you inform or not?" Verkhovensky shouted.

"I certainly *wouldn't* inform!" the teacher shouted even louder.

"And no one would inform! Of course not, no one would!" many voices shouted.

"Allow me to address you now, Major. Would you inform or not?" Verkhovensky went on. "And I want you to note that I have deliberately picked you this time."

"I wouldn't inform, sir."

"But suppose you knew that someone intended to kill and rob someone else, some ordinary mortal; you would turn him in, wouldn't you?"

"Certainly, but in that case it would be a matter of civic duty, whereas before we were dealing with political denunciation. I've never yet been a stool pigeon, sir."

"None of us has ever been a stool pigeon," voices rose again. "It's just a waste of time to ask such a question. We all have the same answer for you: there aren't any stoolies among us."

"Why is this man getting up?" the girl student cried suddenly in surprise.

"That's Shatov," Mrs. Virginsky told her. "Why have you risen, Shatov?"

Shatov was standing up. He had his cap in his hand and was looking straight at Verkhovensky. He apparently wanted to say something to him, but hesitated. His face was pale and angry, but he controlled himself and without saying a word walked across the room toward the door.

"Shatov, don't you realize that it's to your disadvantage to act like this," Verkhovensky shouted after him, hinting at something.

"But then it's to your advantage, you low schemer—you traitor!" Shatov shouted at him from the doorway. Then he left.

Considerable agitation followed and many voices rose.

"So you see, that tested him!" someone said.

"It did come in handy!" a voice agreed.

"Isn't it too late now, though?"

"Who invited him?" "Why was he received?" "Who is this Shatov?" "Will he inform on us or not?" Questions poured in from all sides.

"If he really were an informer, he'd have kept quiet, but it looked as if he couldn't care less—he just walked out."

"And here's Stavrogin getting up too. Stavrogin hasn't answered the question either!" the student called out.

Stavrogin really had stood up and, at the opposite end of of the table, Kirilov had risen too.

"Just a moment, Mr. Stavrogin," the mistress of the house said, addressing him sharply. "All of us here have answered that question, and here you're leaving without saying anything. Well?"

"I see no need to answer it," Stavrogin mumbled.

"But we have compromised ourselves, and you haven't!" some shouted.

"And what do I care if you have?" Stavrogin laughed, but his eyes were flashing.

"What do you mean?" voices cried, and several men leaped up from their seats.

"Wait, gentlemen, wait!" the lame teacher screamed. "Remember that Mr. Verkhovensky himself didn't answer the question—he only asked it."

The remark had a spectacular effect. Stavrogin laughed unrestrainedly at the lame man's words and left, followed by Kirilov. Verkhovensky followed them into the hall.

"What are you doing to me?" he muttered, grabbing Stavrogin's hand and gripping it as hard as he could in his own. Without saying a word, Stavrogin broke his grip.

"Be at Kirilov's. I'll come there. I must absolutely, absolutely—"

"There's absolutely no necessity as far as I'm concerned," Stavrogin cut him sharply.

"Stavrogin will be there," Kirilov said to settle matters. "Stavrogin, it is necessary for you to be there. You'll see why when we get there."

And they left.

chapter 8

THE FAIRY-TALE PRINCE

They left. Peter Verkhovensky was about to rush back into the "assembly room" to quell the disorder there, but apparently decided it wasn't worth bothering with; he dropped it and within two minutes was in the street, hurrying after Stavrogin and Kirilov. Suddenly he remembered a short cut to Filipov's house and, floundering in the mud, he made his way through a narrow alley, reaching the house just as the two men were going through the gate.

"So you're here already?" Kirilov said. "That's fine, come in."

"Why did you tell me you lived alone?" Stavrogin asked as they passed a boiling samovar in the corridor.

"You'll see whom I live with. Come in," Kirilov said.

As soon as they were inside, Peter took from his pocket the anonymous letter von Lembke had shown him and placed it in front of Stavrogin on the table. The three sat down. Stavrogin read the letter in silence.

"So?" he asked.

"That animal will do just as he says here," Verkhovensky exclaimed, "and since he is under your control, you must tell us what to do about him. I assure you, he may go and see Lembke tomorrow."

"Let him go."

"Why? Especially since we have ways of stopping him."

"You're mistaken: he's not under my control. Anyway, I'm in no danger. You're the only one that's threatened."

"No, you too."

"I don't think so."

"But others may not spare you. Don't you understand that? Listen, Stavrogin, you're just talking. Are you really so reluctant to part with your money?"

"So you need money?"

"Yes, we absolutely have to have two thousand rubles— fifteen hundred at the very least. Let me have that sum tomorrow or even tonight, and I promise I'll send him off to Petersburg by tomorrow evening, which is exactly what he wants. And, if you wish, his sister will leave with him."

He sounded completely at a loss somehow and spoke recklessly without weighing his words. Stavrogin watched him with curiosity.

"There's no reason for me to send her away."

"Perhaps you'd even prefer her to stay around?" Verkhovensky asked, smiling sarcastically.

"Perhaps."

"So, will you give me the money or not?" Verkhovensky shouted, glaring at Stavrogin impatiently and full of hatred.

Stavrogin looked him over gravely and said:

"I will not."

"Watch out, Stavrogin! Either you know something or you've already done something about it yourself! You're not serious, I'm sure."

Peter's face twisted, the corners of his lips quivered, and

he suddenly dissolved into senseless laughter that seemed quite incompatible with his personality.

"Why, I know you received some money from your father," Stavrogin said calmly. "My mother paid you six—or was it eight?—thousand rubles for your father. So you can pay the fifteen hundred out of your own money. I'm tired of footing bills for others; I've given out so much money, it's beginning to annoy me." He laughed himself at his own words.

"Ah, I see, you choose to joke!"

Stavrogin got up. Verkhovensky immediately leaped up too and leaned with his back against the door, barring the exit. Stavrogin was about to push him out of his way and leave, but suddenly stopped himself.

"I won't let you have Shatov," he said.

Verkhovensky started. They glared at each other.

"I told you before why you need Shatov's blood," Stavrogin said, his eyes flashing. "You want it to cement your cells. You succeeded very cleverly in making Shatov leave just now because you knew perfectly well that he wasn't going to promise not to inform—he would consider it too degrading. But what do you want from me now? Why me? You've been pestering me almost since the first moment you returned from abroad. The explanations for your behavior that you've offered so far are sheer raving nonsense. And yet you suggest that I hand fifteen hundred rubles over to Lebyatkin, thus giving Fedka a reason to cut his throat. I know you think that I would also like to have my wife killed into the bargain. Then, once I am bound to you by that crime, you figure you'll have me in your power. But what do you need that power for? What the hell do you intend to do with power over me? Now, once and for all, have a good look at me and tell me—do I look like your man? You'd better leave me alone."

"Has Fedka been to see you on his own?" Verkhovensky asked breathlessly.

"Yes, he has, and his price is fifteen hundred. But perhaps you'd rather he confirmed it himself—there he is." Stavrogin pointed.

Peter quickly turned in that direction. In the doorway a new figure emerged from the darkness. Fedka still wore his sheepskin coat, but he no longer had his cap on: he was at home. He stood there, a grin uncovering his even white teeth. His black eyes with their yellowish glint darted cautiously around the room, observing the three gentlemen. There was something he couldn't figure out and since it was Kirilov who had brought him there, Fedka kept turning to him questioningly. He remained standing in the doorway, refusing to step into the room.

"You probably arranged to have him here to listen to our bargain and even to see the money, isn't that right?" Stavrogin said, and without waiting for an answer, he walked out of the house.

Verkhovensky, almost beside himself, caught up with him at the yard gate.

"Stop! Don't move!" Verkhovensky screamed, grabbing Stavrogin by the elbow. Stavrogin tried to brush him off, but Peter held on tightly. That infuriated Stavrogin. He seized Verkhovensky by the hair with his left hand, picked him off his feet, hurled him to the ground, and walked on. But before he had gone more than about thirty paces, Peter caught up with him again.

"Let's make it up, let's make it up," Peter whispered haltingly.

Stavrogin shrugged without stopping or turning his head.

"Listen, would you like me to bring Liza to you? Tomorrow, if you wish! No? You don't want me to? Tell me what you want and I'll do it. Listen, you can have Shatov, do you hear?"

"So it was true that you'd decided to kill him?"

"But what do you want with Shatov? What?" Verkhovensky went on in a breathless rattle, running ahead of Stavrogin, then turning and seizing him by the elbow, apparently hardly aware of what he was doing. "Listen, I'll yield Shatov to you, as long as you're willing to make it up with me. It's a high price, but I'm willing to pay it. Just let's make it up!"

At last Stavrogin looked at him. He was dumfounded. This was not the man he knew—his look was different, his voice was not the same as usual, not what it had been in Kirilov's house just a few minutes before; he had the impression he was dealing with someone else. The tone was different too: Peter Verkhovensky was begging. Here was a man who had lost all control of himself, a man from whom his most treasured possession had been taken away.

"What's the matter with you, anyway?" Stavrogin cried.

But Peter kept trotting alongside him without answering, staring at him with the same beseeching yet relentless look.

"Let's make it up!" he whispered again. "Listen, I have a

knife hidden in my boot just like Fedka, but I'm still willing to make it up with you."

"But what the hell do you want from me, anyway?" Stavrogin exploded in a mixture of anger and indignation. "What's the big mystery? Do you need me as a talisman or what?"

"Listen, we'll create political unrest," Peter muttered, as though in delirium. "Don't you believe we can do it? We can cause such a mess that everything will go flying to hell. Karmazinov is right: there's nothing to hold on to. Karmazinov is very smart. Only ten cells like that throughout Russia and no one will be able to touch me."

"You mean cells made up of the same sort of idiots?" Stavrogin couldn't help remarking.

"Ah, I wish you were a little less clever yourself, Stavrogin. You'd be much better off if you were more stupid! Although, you know, you're not really so intelligent that I should wish that on you. You're scared. You don't believe; you're staggered by the great scope of it all. And why are they idiots? They're not really that idiotic. Nowadays, you know, no one thinks things out for himself and there's a terrible dearth of originality. Virginsky is a man of tremendous integrity; he has ten times as much of it as the likes of you and me. But then, it's true, who cares? Liputin is a crook, but he has his good points— every crook has his good points. Lyamshin, now, has no good points at all, but to make up for it, I have him completely under my control. Well, a few more cells like that and I'll have enough ready money and documents wherever I go. Well, isn't that alone good enough? And also places to hide out, so they could just go on looking for me. Suppose they uproot one group, there'll still be the others. Yes, we will start unrest. Don't you really believe that we two are quite enough?"

"Take Shigalov as your partner and leave me in peace."

"Shigalov is a genius! Do you know, he's a genius in the same sense that Fourier is, only bolder and stronger than Fourier. I'll take him in hand. He's the man who invented 'equality.'"

"Something special must have happened to him," Stavrogin thought, giving Peter another look. "He's feverish and raving." They walked on without stopping.

"He's got everything so well arranged in his notebook," Verkhovensky went on. "He has a great spy system. In his system, each member of the movement watches all the others and has to report to them. Each belongs to all and all belong to each. All are slaves and equal in their slavery. In the first place, there is a lowering of the level of education, science, and arts. The highest level of science and art is accessible only to those with the greatest abilities. Those with the greatest ability have always taken over power and become tyrants. The most gifted men cannot help being tyrants and they have always perverted others more than they have been useful to them; so they are ostracized or put to death. They cut out Cicero's tongue, gouge out Copernicus' eyes; they throw stones at Shakespeare—that's Shigalov's system for you! The slaves must be equal: without tyranny there has never yet been freedom or equality, but in the herd there is equality and that's what Shigalov teaches. Ha-ha-ha, you look surprised? Well, I'm all for Shigalov!"

Stavrogin quickened his pace, wanting to get home as fast as possible. "If he's drunk, where could he have got drunk?" flashed in his mind. "Could it possibly be that brandy?"

"Listen, Stavrogin, leveling the mountain is a good idea and there's nothing ridiculous about it. I'm all for Shigalov! No need for education—we've had enough learning as it is. Even without it we have enough material to last us a thousand years. All we have to do is organize obedience—that's the weak point in this world of ours. The thirst for knowledge is an aristocratic thirst. No sooner do we have a family and experience love than we begin to desire to own things. We shall kill that desire; we shall spread drunkenness, gossip, information on others; we shall strangle every genius in infancy. Everything must be reduced to the common denominator of complete equality. 'We've learned our trade; we're honest and we need nothing more'—that's the English workers' latest declaration. 'Only the indispensable is indispensable'—that will be the motto of our globe from now on. But they need to be shaken up too and we, the rulers, will also take care of that. Because slaves must always have rulers. There'll be total obedience and total depersonalization, but Shigalov decrees that they must be shaken up and suddenly made to devour one another once every thirty years—within certain boundaries, of course—just to prevent them from getting too bored. Boredom is an aristocratic feeling, and under Shigalov's system there will be no room for the masses to desire anything. Desire and suffering are for us— the slaves will have only Shigalov's system."

"So you're placing yourself outside the system?" Stavrogin asked, despite himself.

"Yes, and you too. And you know what—I thought I'd hand the world over to the pope. I'd like him to come out barefoot and show himself to the masses: 'Here, see what they've done to me!' And everyone would follow him, even the armies. So the pope will be on top, us around him, and below us, society organized along Shigalov's lines. All that's needed is for the International to come to terms with the pope, which is bound to happen. Of course the old fogy will accept immediately, for there's no other way out for him, ha-ha-ha! Do you think all I've said is so stupid—do you? No, tell me, is it stupid or not?"

"It is rather," Stavrogin muttered impatiently.

"Rather stupid? Listen, I'll drop the pope! And to hell with Shigalov! What we really need is something topical, something exciting rather than this system of Shigalov's. Shigalov's theory is too much like a trinket. It's an ideal; it's for the future. Shigalov is a jeweler and he's stupid, as are all lovers of mankind. What's needed is hard, crude work, and Shigalov despises rough work. Listen to me: in the West they'll have the pope and we—we will have you!"

"Leave me alone. You're drunk," Stavrogin muttered and quickened his pace.

"Stavrogin, you're an extraordinarily handsome man!" Peter cried in what might have been rapture. "Do you have any idea how handsome you are? What is most valuable about you is that sometimes you don't seem to realize it at all. Ah, I have made a thorough study of you: I've often observed you when you weren't looking, you know. There's even a certain sincerity about you, and some naïveté. Yes, yes, I know it! But it must hurt you—you must really suffer from that sincerity of yours. I love beauty. I'm a nihilist, but why shouldn't I love beauty? As if nihilists couldn't love beautiful things! Nihilists can't love idols, though, but me—I love idols and you're my idol! You never insult anyone and yet they all hate you; you treat everyone as your equal and yet they're all afraid of you—and that's good. No one will ever walk up to you and pat you on the shoulder: you're an aristocrat. An aristocrat who goes in for democracy is irresistible. You think nothing of sacrificing your own or someone else's life. You're just what I need. I don't know anyone like that except you. You are the leader, the sun, and I'm your worm—"

And he suddenly kissed Stavrogin's hand. A cold shiver ran down Nikolai's back; he pulled his hand away in horror. They stopped.

"He's mad," Stavrogin whispered, horrified.

"Maybe—maybe I'm raving," Peter rattled on, "but it was I who devised the first step. Shigalov could never have invented the first step. There are many Shigalovs, but there's only one man in Russia who devised the first step and who knows how to make it. And that man is me. Why do you look at me like that? I need you. Without you, I'm a zero, a fly in a glass jar, a bottled thought, a Columbus without America."

Stavrogin stood still, looking intently into Peter's mad eyes.

"Listen, first we'll start unrest," Verkhovensky said in a terrible hurry, tugging constantly at Stavrogin's left sleeve. "As I told you, we are penetrating deep into the masses themselves. Do you know that, even now, we are terribly strong? We have people other than those who cut throats, set places on fire, go in for classical assassinations, and go around biting people. Those people only get in the way. Without discipline, what they do can have no sense for me. In reality, I'm a crook and not a socialist, ha-ha-ha! I have them all at hand already: we have the teacher who makes the children entrusted to his care laugh at their God and at their families; we have the lawyer defending the well-educated murderer because he has reached a higher stage of development than his victims and couldn't get hold of their money without killing them; the schoolboys who, to experience a strong sensation, kill a peasant, are also with us; the juries who acquit criminals are all working for us; the prosecutor torn by his anguished fear of not being liberal enough does us a service. Ah, we have so many high government officials with us, and so many literary figures who don't even know it themselves! On the other hand, the obedience of schoolboys and little fools has reached the high-water mark; the educators' gall bladders have ruptured and everywhere people's vanity and appetites have reached unheard-of proportions. Have you any idea how much we can do with ready-made ideas alone? When I was leaving for abroad, the rage of the day was Littré's theory that crime is insanity; today, it is no longer insanity but the soundest common sense—indeed, almost a sacred duty or at least a noble gesture of protest. How, they say, can an educated killer help killing if he needs money? The Russian god has already capitulated to cheap liquor: the people are drunk, the children are drunk, the churches are empty, and in the courts of justice the alternative is between two hundred lashes and a bucketful of vodka. And those are only the first tender shoots. Just give the new generation time to mature! It's really a shame we haven't time to wait, otherwise we'd let them get even drunker! Ah, what a pity no such thing as the proletariat really exists! But it will come into existence; we are moving toward it!"

"It's also a pity that we've grown so stupid," Stavrogin mumbled, resuming his way.

"Listen, I saw with my own eyes a six-year-old child leading his drunken mother home by the hand while she kept abusing him in the foulest language. Do you think I'm happy about that? When we have them all under our control, I suppose we'll cure them—and if need be, we'll chase them out into the wilderness for forty years. But now, we must have one or two generations of debauchery, of unheard-of, degrading vice that turns a man into a repulsive, abject, cruel, selfish bug! Yes, that's what we need now! And we must have nice, fresh blood handy, to get them accustomed to it. Why do you laugh? I'm not contradicting myself—I'm only contradicting Shigalov and the philanthropists. I'm a crook and not a socialist! Ha-ha-ha! It's a shame though that we don't have much time. I promised Karmazinov to begin in May and to finish by October. Too soon? Ha-ha! Let me tell you something, Stavrogin: the Russian people have never been cynical, although they have always used the foulest language when they swear; and, do you know, our downtrodden serfs had more self-respect than, say, Karmazinov? The serfs were flogged, but they stuck to their gods and he didn't."

"Well, Verkhovensky, this is the first time I've heard you say such things and I must say I'm surprised," Stavrogin said. "So, you're really not a socialist at all but just a man thirsting for political power—"

"I'm a crook, a crook! Are you worried about who I am? All right, let me tell you who I am—I was coming to it anyway. You know, I meant it when I kissed your hand—but I want other people to believe in you too, to believe that we know what we're after while the others are just swinging in the dark and knocking down their own men. Ah, if only we had more time—but we don't. We shall proclaim destruction because—because, once again, the idea is so attractive for some reason! And anyway, we need some exercise. We shall set towns on fire, we shall create myths, and for that, any lousy cell will be useful to us. In those Fives I'll find you volunteers who'll be prepared to assassinate anyone and will thank you for sending them to do it. So we'll start unrest, and there'll be havoc everywhere—havoc such as the world has never before witnessed. Russia will be shrouded in mist and the earth will weep for its old gods—and it is then that we shall use him—"

"Who?"

"The fairy-tale prince."

"What?"

"The fairy-tale prince—you!"

Stavrogin thought for a moment.

"You mean as a pretender?" he asked in great surprise, looking at the madman. "Ha! So that's what your plan really is!"

"We shall say that he's in hiding," Verkhovensky said in a low, passionate whisper, sounding really drunk. "Do you know what the phrase 'he is in hiding' means? It means that he'll appear one day. We shall launch a legend that is even better than the one the sect of the Castrates has: he exists, but no one has ever seen him. Ah, what a marvelous legend we could let loose on them! The main point is that a new authority is coming and that's just what they'll be longing and crying for. What use can we have for socialism? It destroys the old authority without replacing it. But we will have authority— authority such as the world has never before heard of. All we'll need then will be a lever to lift the earth, and since we have it, we'll lift it!"

"So you were seriously counting on me?" Stavrogin snorted maliciously.

"Why do you laugh? And why do you sound so nasty? Remember, I'm like a child now, and you can scare me to death with a mere grin. Listen, I won't show you to anyone, not anyone. That's the way it must be. He exists, but no one has ever seen him because he's in hiding. You know, though, we might show you to one in, say, a hundred thousand; then the rumor will spread all over the earth: 'He has been seen,' 'They saw him!' The leader of the sect of the Flagellants, Ivan Filipovich, was seen by some 'with their own eyes,' as he ascended into heaven in his golden chariot. And you're much better than Ivan Filipovich. You're a beautiful, proud young god who seeks nothing for himself, but stays in hiding with a halo of sacrifice around his head. The main thing is to create a legend—after that, all you have to do is look at them and they'll be conquered. 'He,' they'll be saying, 'is in hiding now and he'll bring us the New Truth.' And, in the meantime, we'll pass a couple of judgments of Solomon here. Our cells, our Fives, of course, don't need any newspapers. If we grant only one petition out of ten thousand, they'll all come to us with petitions. In every corner of the country, every peasant will know that there's a hollow tree where petitions can be deposited. And the earth will resound with cries that 'A new and true justice is on the way!' And a storm will rise and the old edifice will collapse and then we'll decide how to put a strong, permanent stone structure in its place. For the first time! And we'll be the only ones to build it—us and no one else!"

"Sheer insanity!" Stavrogin said.

"Why, why don't you want it? Are you afraid? But I latched onto you because I thought you feared nothing. Have I miscalculated? But then, I am still a Columbus without an America and is a Columbus without an America supposed to make any sense?"

Stavrogin remained silent until they reached his house, where he stopped in front of the door.

"Listen," Peter said, reaching up toward Stavrogin's ear, "I'll arrange it for you without money. I'll get rid of Maria by tomorrow if you wish—and I'll bring you Liza tomorrow too, and I don't need any money for that either. Would you like to have Liza tomorrow?"

"He must be really out of his mind," Stavrogin said and smiled as the door of his house opened.

"Stavrogin, so America is ours?" Verkhovensky cried, seizing his arm once more.

"What for?" Stavrogin asked seriously.

"So, you just don't feel like it! I might have known it!" Verkhovensky shouted in a fit of mad fury. "You're lying, you miserable, lecherous, perverted son of the rich! I don't believe you! I know you've a wolf's appetite! But I want you to understand that your bill has run too high as it is and I can't afford to give you up! There's no one in the world to put in your place. I invented you while I was still abroad—invented you while actually looking at you. If I hadn't been looking at you from my corner, nothing of this sort would ever have occurred to me!"

Without answering, Stavrogin started up the steps.

"I give you one day, Stavrogin," Peter Verkhovensky shouted

after him. "All right, I give you two—three days. I can't give
you more than three days. And then you must give me your
answer!"

chapter 9

AT TIKHON'S (STAVROGIN'S CONFESSION)

[In Dostoyevsky's original version of *The Possessed*, this chapter, "At Tikhon's," which is generally referred to as "Stavrogin's Confession," came between the chapters entitled "The
Fairy-Tale Prince" and "A Search at Stepan Verkhovensky's."
Dostoyevsky's publisher, however, refused to print it, feeling that it was too shocking and would compromise the
author. Dostoyevsky agreed, so this chapter was never included in the novel during the author's lifetime. Now, it is
often published at the end of the book as an explanatory
supplement shedding some light on the behavior of one of
the central characters, Stavrogin. In this translation, however, the chapter is given in its proper place, in the belief
that this will enable the reader to follow the development
of the narrative as Dostoyevsky conceived it in the first
place.—A. MACA.]

I

Stavrogin didn't sleep that night. He sat on the couch with
his eyes fixed blankly most of the time on one spot in a corner
near a chest of drawers. His lamp burned all night. He finally
dozed off at seven in the morning, still in a sitting position, and
when he was wakened by the presence in the room of Alexei,
who, following a well-established routine, had come in with his
morning cup of coffee at half past nine sharp, Stavrogin
opened his eyes and seemed rather annoyed to find that he had
slept so long and that it was already so late. He gulped down
his coffee, dressed, and left the house in a hurry without answering Alexei's cautious query as to whether the master had
any further orders for him. In the street, he walked with
lowered eyes, deep in thought, raising his head only briefly and
at intervals and revealing, at those moments, a vague but intense anxiety. At a street corner not far from his house, a
group of fifty or more working men passed in front of him.
The men walked solemnly, almost in silence, and in orderly

formation. As he waited near a store for them to pass, he heard someone say that they were the workers from Shpigulin's factory. Stavrogin hardly paid any attention to them. By half past ten he was approaching the gate of the Efimovo Monastery of Our Lady, on the outskirts of town, near the river. At this point, he seemed suddenly to remember something alarming and bothersome. He stopped, fumbled nervously for something in his side pocket, then grinned. He passed through the gate and asked the first lay brother he saw where he could find Bishop Tikhon, who was living in retirement in the monastery. The lay brother bowed several times, then turned and led the way. At the entrance to a long, two-story wing of the monastery, Stavrogin was passed on to a fat, self-important, gray-haired monk who led him down a long, narrow corridor. The monk also bowed repeatedly; however, being unable, because of his corpulence, to make deep bows, he contented himself with jerking his head up and down. He kept motioning to Stavrogin to follow him, although this was unnecessary, for Stavrogin was close behind him anyway. The fat monk asked all sorts of questions, bringing the Father Archimandrite into his talk, and when Stavrogin didn't answer, he became more and more deferential. They obviously knew who he was, Stavrogin realized, although he couldn't remember ever coming here since his childhood. When they reached the door at the very end of the corridor, the monk opened it unhesitatingly and asked a novice, who immediately appeared in the doorway, whether it was all right to go in; then, without even waiting for a reply, he threw the door wide open and, bowing his head, suggested that the "esteemed visitor" step in. After being thanked for his efforts, the monk puffed hurriedly off as though pursued by someone.

Stavrogin entered a rather small room and, almost at the same moment, a man appeared in the doorway leading to the room beyond. He was a tall, thin man of about fifty-five; he was dressed in a simple cassock and looked rather sickly. There was a vague smile on his face and his whole expression was strange and rather shy. This was Tikhon, of whom Stavrogin had first heard from Shatov and about whom he had managed to pick up some further scraps of information since then.

That information was varied and contradictory, the only common element being that both those who loved Tikhon and those who hated him (and there were some) seemed to be holding something back. Those who didn't like him probably held back out of contempt for him; while his admirers, even the most ardent of them, seemed to do this out of a sense of discretion, as though they wanted to conceal something, some weakness—as though they were even afraid that Tikhon might be branded as simple-minded. Stavrogin had found out that Tikhon had already been living in the monastery for six years and that he received visits from the humblest peasants as well as the most famous people. Even in Petersburg he had had an ardent following of men—and an even more devoted following of women. On the other hand, Stavrogin had also heard from a venerable and respected member of our town's club the verdict "that Tikhon is almost insane, and there's no doubt about it—he must drink." I'll anticipate here a little and declare, on my own responsibility, that that is sheer nonsense and that Tikhon simply suffered from acute rheumatism in his legs and had some kind of recurring nervous fits. Stavrogin also had learned that the retired bishop had failed to instill the respect due him in the monastery. This, he had been told, was either because of his weak character or because of his absent-mindedness, an unforgivable trait in one of his rank and position. It was even rumored that the Father Archimandrite, a stern disciplinarian in the performance of his duties as Father Superior of the monastery and a man famous for his religious erudition, harbored a secret hostility toward Tikhon, condemning (not to his face and only by implication, of course) his casual attitude toward life and viewing it as almost a manifestation of heresy. The monks, too, treated the sick bishop rather familiarly, if not really disrespectfully. The rooms that made up Tikhon's retreat were rather strangely furnished. Alongside heavy, clumsy old furniture covered with worn leather, there were two or three costly and graceful items: a gorgeous easy chair, a big superbly finished desk, a delicately carved bookcase, little tables, book stands, and so on—all gifts, of course. An expensive Bokhara carpet and several mats were on the floor. There were engravings of "worldly" and mythological subjects, and in a corner not far from them was a large stand glittering with gold-and-silver-mounted icons, one of which was very ancient and contained relics. His library, it was said, was a motley and incompatible collection: next to the works of the great servants of God and the Christian saints, there were plays, novels, "and perhaps even worse."

After a rather awkward exchange of greetings, uttered hurriedly and indistinctly, Tikhon ushered his visitor into the other cell, which he used as his study. Still rather hurriedly, he invited Stavrogin to sit on a settee while he himself took a wicker chair at the desk nearby. To his own surprise, Stavrogin felt strangely at a loss, as though he were absolutely determined to do something special that was indispensable but rather beyond his power. For a minute, he looked around the study, but obviously did not register what he saw; he seemed to be deep in thought, but he probably could not have said what he was thinking about. The stillness brought him back to his senses, and then he noticed that Tikhon's eyes were lowered and that he was rather incongruously smiling. This angered and shocked Stavrogin, and he felt like getting up and walking out; the man must be drunk, he thought. But, at that moment, Tikhon suddenly raised his eyes and looked at him so firmly, with such insight and such an uncanny, enigmatic expression that Stavrogin almost winced and immediately appraised the situation quite differently: Tikhon knew why he'd come to see him; he had been warned (although who in the world could have known why Stavrogin had come?), and if he didn't speak first, it was only out of consideration for his, Stavrogin's, feelings and out of fear of humiliating him.

"Have we met before?" Stavrogin began abruptly. "Did I introduce myself when I came in? You must forgive me, I'm so terribly absent-minded——"

"No, you didn't introduce yourself, but I've had the pleasure of seeing you once before, here in the monastery—just by chance—about four years ago."

Now Tikhon spoke smoothly and unhurriedly, in a soft voice, clearly molding his words.

"I didn't come here four years ago," Stavrogin replied with quite unwarranted snappishness. "The last time I came here was when I was a boy—you weren't here then."

"Couldn't you have forgotten?" Tikhon asked guardedly, reluctant to insist.

"No, I couldn't—it would be ridiculous to forget something like that," Stavrogin said. Unlike Tikhon, he insisted in his denial and the fervor with which he did so seemed disproportionate. "Possibly," he went on, "you've heard about me and then imagined you'd seen me, and that's what confused you."

Tikhon said nothing. Stavrogin noticed that a twitch—a

symptom of chronic nervous exhaustion—passed across his face every now and then.

"Perhaps you're not feeling too well today," Stavrogin said. "Maybe I'd better leave." He started to rise.

"Yes, I've had an acute pain in my legs today, and yesterday too, and I haven't been able to sleep much at night—"

Tikhon stopped, noticing that his visitor was suddenly immersed in a strange dreaminess. A two-minute silence followed.

"Why were you watching me?" Stavrogin suddenly asked with alarm and suspicion.

"Looking at you, I was reminded of your mother's face. Although there's little physical likeness between you, there's much inner, spiritual resemblance."

"There's no resemblance of any sort, especially no spiritual resemblance—absolutely none, believe me!" Stavrogin said, again reacting with unnecessary heat. "You're saying that just to make me feel—just because you're sorry for me now," he blurted out. "But—but then, does my mother come to see you?"

"She does."

"I had no idea. She never told me. Does she come often?"

"At least once a month."

"I had absolutely no idea. Never suspected anything of the sort. Never. And she must've told you, of course, that I'm insane?" he blurted out again.

"No, not that you're insane, although I've heard that said by others."

"You must have a wonderful memory if you can remember such unimportant details. And have you heard about my face being slapped?"

"I've heard something about it."

"You must have heard everything there is to hear. You seem to have plenty of time to listen to all sorts of stories. And you've surely heard about the duel?"

"I have."

"I see there's no need for newspapers around here. But tell me, has Shatov spoken to you about me?"

"No, he hasn't. In fact, although I've known him for a long time, he hasn't been to see me lately."

"Hm. What's that map you have there? Isn't it a map of the last war? What do you want with that?"

"I like to follow the description of the campaign on the map. It's most interesting."

"What book is that? Ah yes, I know, it gives quite a good description of the operations. Still, I must say, it's rather inappropriate reading for a man like you."

He took the book and gave it a curious glance. It was an adequate description of the last war, although its chief merit was literary rather than military. Stavrogin twisted the book in his hands for a moment, then put it down with sudden impatience.

"I really have no idea why I came here in the first place," he said with distaste, looking Tikhon straight in the eye as though challenging him to answer.

"You seem a little out of sorts too."

"Yes, a little."

And then, briefly and so abruptly that many words were almost unintelligible, he told Tikhon that he was subject to strange hallucinations, especially at night; that he seemed to see or feel close to him some evil creature, mocking and "rational," which took on a variety of personalities and characters, but which he knew was always the same creature— "and it always makes me furious."

His revelations were wild and incoherent and might indeed have come from a madman. And yet, Stavrogin spoke with uncharacteristic simplicity and with greater sincerity than ever before in his life, as though his former self had suddenly been completely superseded. He was not at all ashamed of the fear with which he spoke of the apparitions that haunted him. But this state lasted only for a moment and disappeared just as suddenly as it had come.

"It's all nonsense," he said self-consciously and with irritation, becoming himself again. "I'll see a doctor about it."

"I think you ought to," Tikhon said approvingly.

"Why, you sound as though you knew all about it. Have you come across others with hallucinations like mine?"

"I have come across some, but very few. I remember clearly only one case similar to yours—a former army officer . . . after he had lost his wife—they were very close. I only know the other case by hearsay. Eventually they both took a cure abroad. Have you been suffering from it long?"

"A year or so, but it's really nothing. I'll see a doctor. Anyway, it's just a lot of nonsense. It's myself in various forms—nothing else. But my adding that last phrase may lead you to believe that I'm really not so sure about whether it's just myself and not the Devil."

Tikhon looked at him questioningly.

"And you actually see him?" he asked, thus apparently discarding any doubt about it's being a hallucination. "Do you actually see a figure or something of the sort?"

"It strikes me as odd that you should insist so on that point since I've already told you—yes, I see him," Stavrogin said, getting angry once again and sounding more and more irritated as he spoke. "Of course I see him, just as clearly as I see you. Sometimes, though, I see him without being sure that I do—and yet, I do see him. And sometimes I don't know what the truth is—whether it's him or me. None of it makes any sense. But why should it be so difficult for you to assume that it's the Devil!" he added, breaking into loud laughter and switching abruptly to a sarcastic tone. "Surely, it would be more in keeping with your trade, don't you think?"

"It sounds more like an illness, although—"

"Although what?"

"Demons do exist, though different people conceive them differently."

"Now you've lowered your eyes," Stavrogin broke in irritatedly, with a sarcastic snort, "because you're ashamed for me because I believe in the Devil; and you think that, while pretending I don't believe in him, I'm slyly trying to find out from you whether he really does exist or not."

Tikhon smiled quizzically.

"So let me tell you to start with," Stavrogin went on, "that there's nothing I'm ashamed of! And now, to make up for my bluntness, I'll declare openly and unblushingly that I *do* believe in the Devil; that I believe canonically in a personal, not an allegorical devil. And I would also like to assure you that I don't wish to extract any secrets from anyone. Well, I suppose that covers it."

He let out a nervous, unnatural laugh. Tikhon looked at him with curiosity, but there was also shyness and gentleness in his eyes.

"Do you believe in God?" Stavrogin asked him unexpectedly.

"I do."

"Well then, you know, they say if you have faith and command a mountain to move, it'll move—but excuse me, I'm talking nonsense. Still, I'm rather curious: could you move a mountain or not?"

"If God so commanded, I could," Tikhon said quietly and again lowered his eyes.

"No, that would be like God moving it Himself. I want to know whether you—you personally—could move it, as a reward for believing in God."

"Maybe I wouldn't be able to move it."

"You say 'maybe'? Well, that's still not bad, ha-ha! But I see you're not quite sure?"

"I still have doubts because my faith in God is imperfect."

"What—you? You don't have complete faith either? I never would have suspected it, looking at you!"

Stavrogin looked at Tikhon with genuine surprise; the sarcastic tone of his earlier questions had vanished.

"Yes—perhaps my faith isn't really perfect."

"But still, you do believe that, say, with the help of God, you could move the mountain. That's quite an achievement in itself. At least it shows that you want to believe. And I also see that you take that stuff about the mountain literally. That's also a lot in itself. A very sound rule. I've noticed that our leading Levites incline strongly toward Lutheranism and are prepared to seek natural explanations for miracles. It is better than answering like that archbishop, '*Très peu*'—although, to render him justice, it was spoken under threat of the sword. You too are a Christian, aren't you?"

Stavrogin was talking very fast and his words fell, now grave, now mocking.

"Let me not be ashamed of Thy cross, O Lord," Tikhon said with strange passion, almost in a whisper, and lowered his head once more.

"Tell me now, is it possible to believe in the Devil without believing in God?" Stavrogin asked, laughing.

"Very possible indeed—happens all the time," Tikhon said, raising his eyes and smiling.

"And I'll bet you consider that sort of belief more worthy of respect than complete disbelief?" Stavrogin said, laughing loudly.

"No, on the contrary, I feel that absolute atheism is more worthy of respect than worldly indifference," Tikhon said in a light and cheerful tone, but at the same time darting a worried look at his visitor.

"I see—so that's how you feel. You know, you really puzzle me."

"Whatever you say, a complete atheist still stands on the next-to-the-top rung of the ladder of perfect faith. He may take that last step; and he may not—who knows? But the indifferent, they certainly have no faith, only an ugly fear—and only the more sensitive of them have that."

"Hm. Have you read Revelations?"

"I have."

"Do you remember where it says 'And unto the Angel of the church of the Laodiceans write. . . .' ?"

"I do."

"Do you have it here?" Stavrogin became strangely agitated; his eyes searched Tikhon's desk for the book. "I'd like to read you that passage. Do you have it?"

"I know the passage by heart," Tikhon said.

"You do? Recite it then."

Stavrogin cast his eyes downward, placed the palms of his hands on his knees, and prepared to listen. Tikhon recited the passage without omitting a word:

" 'And unto the Angel of the church of the Laodiceans write: These things saith the Amen, the faithful and true witness, the beginning of the creation of God; I know thy works, that thou art neither cold nor hot; I would thou wert cold or hot. So then because thou art lukewarm, and neither cold nor hot, I will spew thee out of my mouth. Because thou sayest, I am rich, and increased with goods and have need of nothing; and knowest not that thou art wretched, and miserable, and poor, and blind, and naked—' "

"That's enough," Stavrogin said, interrupting him. "You know, I like you very much—"

"I like you too," Tikhon said very quietly.

Stavrogin fell silent and became dreamy, as he had before. It was a state that came over him in waves—this was the third time. Indeed, when he told Tikhon he liked him, he was almost in this state—at least, his saying it had come as a surprise to himself. A minute went by.

"Don't be angry," Tikhon whispered, touching Stravogin's elbow very lightly with his finger and looking very embarrassed.

Stavrogin started and frowned angrily.

"How could you know I was about to get angry?" he asked quickly. And as Tikhon tried to say something, Stavrogin interrupted him with strange agitation, "Just what made you think that I was about to burst out? Yes, I was furious and—all right—and it was because I'd said I liked you. You're right, but you're an unabashed cynic; you have a very low opinion of human nature. Another person wouldn't necessarily have become furious with you—but it's me and not someone else you're dealing with now. Anyway, you're a sort of saintly village idiot and a crank."

He was becoming more and more irritated and certainly was not mincing his words.

"Listen," he went on, "I don't like spies and psychologists, at any rate, those who pry into my soul. I need no one; I can manage very well on my own. Unless you imagine, by any chance, that I'm afraid of you?" Raising his voice, he glared at Tikhon challengingly. "Perhaps you think I've come here to reveal some 'shocking' secret to you and are waiting to hear it with all your monkish curiosity? Let me tell you that I won't tell you a thing; I won't reveal any secrets at all, because I have absolutely no need of you! Besides, there's no mystery except in your imagination."

Tikhon looked at him hard.

"It surprises you that the Lamb prefers a cold man to a lukewarm one," he said. "You don't want to be *just* lukewarm. I have a feeling that you intend to do something extraordinary, something horrible perhaps. Please, don't torture yourself; tell me—"

"You're certain that I came here with something?"

"I guessed it," Tikhon whispered, casting down his eyes.

Stavrogin was rather pale; his hands trembled slightly. For some seconds he stared silently into space, hesitating. Finally, out of his side pocket, he produced some printed sheets and put them on the desk.

"These sheets are meant for circulation," he said in a breaking voice. "If just one man reads them and understands them, I won't conceal them from anyone any longer. I've decided that. You—I don't really need you at all, because that's the way I've decided myself. But read it—don't say anything before you've read it through and then tell me everything you think."

"But, do you really want me to read it?"

"Go ahead, I'm not worried."

"I can't make it out without my glasses, the print is so fine. It must've been printed abroad."

"Here are your glasses."

Stavrogin handed them to him and leaned back on the settee. Without glancing at him, Tikhon began to read.

II

The printing was certainly foreign. There were three small sheets of ordinary letter paper, covered closely with print and clipped together. They must have been produced by some clandestine Russian printing press abroad and, at first glance, looked very much like a political pamphlet. The heading read: "From Stavrogin."

I incorporate this document verbatim into this chronicle. I have only taken the liberty of correcting the numerous misspellings, which rather surprised me since the author was, after all, an educated, even a widely read man—relatively speaking. However, I've made no changes in the syntax, although it isn't always correct either. Whatever else, it is obvious that the author is no man of letters.

I'll indulge now in one remark, although I will be anticipating. In my opinion, this is a morbid document—the work of the demon who had taken possession of this man. It gives the impression of a man in acute pain tossing about in his bed, trying desperately to find a position in which he will obtain relief, if only for a moment. Or perhaps not even to relieve his pain but only to replace his former state briefly by any other one. At such a point it is obviously impossible to worry about whether one's position is elegant or reasonable. The fundamental idea of the document is a grim, naked need for punishment, for a cross, for public execution. And yet that need for a cross appears in a man who doesn't believe in the cross—which is "quite an idea in itself," as Stepan Verkhovensky once put it, although he had something else in mind.

On the other hand, the document, although it sounds like a reckless and violent outburst, was written with a definite purpose. The author claims that he simply had to write it, that he was forced to—and this seems quite likely. He would gladly have avoided this painful task if he could have—but, being forced to do it, he seized the opportunity to make another violent outburst. Yes, the patient tosses in bed, trying only to replace one agony by another; similarly, it seemed to the author that challenging society would be a less painful position, so he threw down his gauntlet before it.

And indeed, the very existence of such a document fore-

casts a new, unexpected, and irreverent challenge to society.
The author's only desire was to come to grips with an enemy
quickly.

And who knows, perhaps his intention to make those sheets
public was the equivalent of biting the old governor's ear all
over again, although in a different way? I don't know why this
should occur to me now, after so much else has become clear.
I don't wish either to establish the authenticity of the document or, indeed, to claim that it is a false confession, a piece
of sheer fabrication. The truth, most likely, lies somewhere
between the two.

Anyway, I've run too far ahead; it would be more sensible
to turn to the document itself. This is what Tikhon read:

From Stavrogin.
I, Nikolai Stavrogin, retired army officer, lived in Petersburg in 186–, wallowing in vice from which I derived no
pleasure. For some time I rented three lodgings. The one
I actually lived in was a furnished room with service and
board. Maria Lebyatkin, who is now my lawful wife, lived
in the same house then. The other two lodgings were rented
by the month and I used them for my love affairs. In one of
them I used to receive a certain lady who happened to be in
love with me and, in the other, her maid. For some time, I
toyed with the notion of making the two run into each other.
I wanted the lady and the girl to meet at my place. Knowing
them both, I anticipated deriving great fun from playing
such a stupid trick on them.

In the course of carefully setting up this encounter, I
found myself forced to go more often than before to my
lodging on Pea Street, which was the one where I used to
meet the maid. I had only one room there, which I rented
from a lower-class family on the fourth floor. They themselves occupied the adjoining small room, in which they felt
so crowded that they kept their door ajar all the time. And
that suited me fine. The husband, who had a beard and wore
a long coat, worked in some office and was away from morning to night. The wife, a woman of around forty, used to
cut up old clothes and make new ones out of them and she,
too, often had to leave the house in order to deliver her
work. I stayed alone at home with their daughter, who
looked altogether like a child. She was called Matryosha.
Her mother loved her, although she often beat her and
kept nagging at her, as that type of woman does. This

little girl waited on me and tidied up my room. I declare I have forgotten the number of that house. Now, having made inquiries, I have found out that the house in question has been demolished and where there used to be two or three old houses now stands a new and very big one. I have forgotten the last name of those people, if I ever really knew it. The woman was called Stepaniada; I haven't the faintest notion what the man's name was. I can't say what happened to him. I suppose if I wanted to find them and had inquiries made by the Petersburg police, they could certainly be traced. The apartment gave onto a corner of the inside courtyard. The house was pale blue.

One day I missed my penknife, which I didn't need at all and which had just been lying around. I mentioned this to my landlady without its ever occurring to me that she would thrash her daughter for it. But it so happened that the woman had just finished bawling the child out because she already suspected her of having taken a scrap of cloth to make a dress for her doll. In fact, she had even pulled her hair. When the piece of cloth was finally discovered under the tablecloth, the little girl just looked at her mother in silence, without a word of reproach for having been unjustly punished. I noticed that—the child deliberately didn't speak. I remember it so clearly because it was the first time I had looked into the girl's face—until then, it had merely flashed past my eyes without my noticing it. She was fair-haired and freckled and there was nothing particular about her face— it was simply the face of a very quiet little girl. The mother was irritated because she didn't complain. And then the matter of my missing penknife came up. The woman was furious because she had punished the child unjustly before. She tore some twigs from the broom and in my presence whipped the girl until she was covered with welts, although she was already in her twelfth year. Perhaps because I was there, Matryosha didn't cry. She only gasped strangely at every blow and then continued to gasp like that for a whole hour after the woman was through with her.

When the beating was over, I found my penknife on my bed, on the blanket. Without saying a word to anyone, I slipped it into my waistcoat pocket, went out, and threw it away in a distant street. I immediately realized I had done something despicable, but at the same time I felt a pleasurable sensation which burned me like hot iron and with which I became very much preoccupied. I must note here that I had experienced all sorts of evil desires before and that

I had pursued them to the point of unreasonableness or, to be more exact, with obstinate recklessness, but never to the point of losing control over myself. Even when a sensation reached the point of incandescence I felt in full control of myself and could even stop it if I chose, although I very seldom did choose to stop. At this point I declare that I don't wish to avoid any responsibility for my crimes, either because of environment or of sickness.

After crying for two days, the little girl became even quieter. I am certain, though, that she bore no grudge against me and, at the most, felt ashamed at having been punished in my presence like that. But, submissive child that she was, she blamed even her shame on no one but herself. This is very important for an understanding of what happened.

After that, I spent three days in my main lodgings. Many people nested in the small tenement rooms in that house, which reeked most unpleasantly of food. They were mostly petty officials, either unemployed or holding the lowest positions, prospective country doctors waiting to leave for their villages, and an assortment of Poles. All of them cringed before me. I remember the lot of them well. In this bedlam, I kept very much to myself—that is, as far as the other lodgers were concerned, because I was surrounded by my own friends, who were terribly devoted to me and loved me dearly for my purse. We behaved very badly and the other lodgers were rather afraid of us and treated us with considerable respect, despite the stupid pranks and nasty tricks—sometimes quite unforgivable ones—that we played on them. Let me say here that I wouldn't have minded at all if they had packed me off to Siberia then. I could have hanged myself out of sheer boredom, and if I didn't, it was because I was still hoping for something, as I had hoped all my life. I remember that I was then seriously preoccupied with theology. It distracted me a little but afterward things became even more boring. As to my political views, I just felt I'd have liked to put gunpowder under the four corners of the world and blow the whole thing sky-high—if it had only been worth the trouble. But even if I had done it, I would have done it without malice, simply out of boredom.

I'm really no socialist. I prefer to think I had some sort of a sickness. Once I jokingly asked Doctor Dobrolubov, who was starving with his family in a small tenement, whether he knew of any drops to induce civic zeal in a man, and he said: "No, nothing to induce civic zeal, but I think I could prescribe you something for criminal zeal," and he looked very pleased with himself, although he was completely penniless and had a pregnant wife and two little girls to provide for. Here, however, I must remark that if people weren't always too pleased with themselves, no one would be willing to go on living.

So I stayed there for three days and then returned to my Pea Street lodging. The mother was getting ready to leave with her sewing and the father was out as usual. Matryosha was left alone. The windows that gave onto the courtyard were open. Many tradesmen lived in the house, and songs and the pounding of hammers came from every floor throughout the day. I had been in for over an hour and, all that time, Matryosha had sat on a stool in her family's small room. She had her back turned to me and I could see she was sewing something. Finally she began to hum a tune, very, very quietly, as she did sometimes. I took out my watch. It was two o'clock. My heart began to pound wildly. I got up and walked over to her. They had a lot of geraniums in their window and now, in the sun, the flowers looked very bright. Quietly, I sat down next to her. She gave a great start and jumped up. I took her hand, kissed it, pulled her back down onto her stool, and looked into her eyes. My kissing her hand made her laugh, the way a baby laughs, but that only lasted one second, and then she leaped up again, so frightened now that her whole face twitched convulsively. She stared at me with horrified, unblinking eyes and her lips began to quiver. She didn't cry out, though. Again I kissed her hand and then sat her on my knee. She jerked back and suddenly smiled, a sort of shameful, strangely twisted smile, her whole face flushed with shame. I kept whispering something in her ear and laughing. Finally something very peculiar happened. I'll never forget it and, at the time, it took me completely by surprise. The little girl suddenly flung her arms around my neck and started kissing me desperately, her face expressing perfect rapture.

I stood up, shocked that a little thing like her should behave like that. I felt pity for her and it angered me—

That was the end of the sheet and the sentence broke off suddenly. I must mention here that there were actually five sheets.* Tikhon had one of them and the other four were still in Stavrogin's hands. When Tikhon looked at him question-

* The fact that the three sheets mentioned at the beginning of the chapter have here become five is presumably due to the existence of two versions of the confession. See footnote, p. 421.—A. MacA.

ingly, Stavrogin, who had been waiting for him to look up, handed him the continuation.

"But there's something missing here," Tikhon said, looking at the sheet. "Yes, look—you've given me the sheet numbered 'three.' I need the second one."

"Yes, I know, but for the time being the second sheet is still held by the censor," Stavrogin answered quickly, grinning awkwardly. He had been sitting motionless all the time, watching Tikhon read with feverish eyes. "You'll get it later, when you've earned it," he added with unconvincing casualness. He laughed, but he looked pitiful.

"At the point we've reached, I wonder if it makes much difference whether or not I skip the second sheet," Tikhon remarked.

"What do you mean it makes no difference? What makes you say that?" Stavrogin said with sudden heat, leaning forward. "It does make a difference! I see you're terribly keen to suspect the most disgusting things, just like all monks. Monks would make the best police investigators, I think."

Tikhon watched him in silence.

"Don't start imagining things now," Stavrogin said. "It wasn't really my fault that the little girl was silly enough to misunderstand me. Nothing happened—nothing at all!"

"Well, thank God," Tikhon murmured and crossed himself.

"It would take too long to explain everything. There was a sort of—of psychological misunderstanding in it."

He suddenly blushed and his face reflected feelings of disgust, sadness, and despair. They didn't talk or look at each other after that for more than a minute.

"You know, I think you should read it, after all," Stavrogin said, unthinkingly wiping with his fingers the cold sweat that was trickling from his brow. "And I think it'd be better if you didn't look at me at all. I feel now as if I were in a dream— and—and—don't push me to the limit of my patience," he added in a whisper.

Tikhon quickly turned his eyes away from Stavrogin, took the third sheet and, without stopping again, read to the end. There were no more interruptions in the sheets Stavrogin had handed him. Sheet number three, however, began in the middle of a sentence. Here is exactly how it went:

. . . through a moment of real, although not too intense, fear.* I felt really cheerful that morning and very kindly

---

* For the beginning of this sentence see last paragraph of the note

toward all of them, and my whole gang was very appreciative of that. But I walked out on them and went over to Pea Street. I met her when I was still downstairs in the hallway. She was returning from the grocer's, where they had sent her to get some chicory, and when she saw me, she darted upstairs in a great fright. It was more horror than fright, a numb, petrifying horror that she felt. By the time I got upstairs, the landlady had already slapped the girl for having rushed in like that and that concealed the real reason for the child's panic. And so, for now, there was nothing to worry about. The girl hid somewhere, staying out of sight all the time I was there. I spent an hour or so in my room, then left.

But toward evening, the fear came back to me, and this time it was much stronger. The worst of it was that I was frightened and I knew it. Ah, I can't think of anything more absurd or more degrading! I've never known fear, either before or after that—never! But that time I was scared all right—I was literally shaking with fear. I was acutely aware of it and appallingly humiliated. If it had been permissible I would have killed myself, but I felt I was unworthy of death. Though, in truth, that's not the reason why I didn't kill myself—it was also out of fear that I didn't do it. People kill themselves out of fear, but they also remain alive out of fear. A man begins by not daring to kill himself and then the whole business becomes impossible. Besides,

---

below. In an earlier, more explicit version, there is no mention of the missing sheet of the confession; instead there is the following passage, which seems essential to dispel any doubts about what happened and should follow the sentence ending "her face expressing perfect rapture."

"When it was all over, she seemed at a loss and I did nothing to make her feel better. I felt no tenderness for her any more. There was a shy little smile on her face, but I thought she looked stupid. She looked more and more lost and, finally, covered her face with her hands and stood motionless in the corner, facing the wall. I was afraid she would again become terror-stricken, so, without saying a word, I left.

"I believe that what had happened struck her in retrospect as an abomination; the thought of it must have revolted her. Although she must have been exposed to foul language and all sorts of conversations ever since she was a baby, I am convinced that she herself was totally innocent in those things. For, certainly, it appeared to her, after it was over, that she had committed an unspeakable crime, that she had guilty of a mortal sin, that, indeed, she had 'killed God.'"

When Tikhon resumes his reading "in the middle of a sentence," the suppressed beginning of that sentence reads: "That night, at a bar, I got involved in a brawl for which, as I said earlier, I was longing. In the morning I woke up in my lodgings, to which Lebyatkin had brought me, and my first thought was: had she told about it or not? I went through . . ."—A. MacA.

that night, sitting in my tenement, I felt great hatred for her and decided to kill her.

With that intention in mind, I hurried to Pea Street at dawn. All the way there, I was thinking how I'd insult her and then kill her. What made me hate her most was the thought of her smile; it generated scorn combined with a feeling of morbid disgust in me. What could she possibly have imagined, flinging her arms around my neck like that! But when I reached the Fontanka Embankment I felt awful. And, on top of that, I became aware of a new, horrible feeling. I returned home and lay down on my bed, shivering, so overcome by fear that I didn't even hate the girl any more. I no longer felt like killing and that was what I had realized on the Fontanka Embankment. I understood then for the first time in my life that fear, if it is only strong enough, completely kills hatred and even all desire for revenge.

I awoke around noon feeling quite well. I was rather ashamed of my thoughts of the day before, of wanting to kill her. That put me into a foul mood. Despite my revulsion, I had to go to Pea Street. I recall clearly that I was longing to pick a quarrel with someone, but a really serious one. When I got to my Pea Street lodging, I found that Nina, the maid, had been waiting for me there for an hour. She'd come on her own initiative and was rather apprehensive lest I be angry at her visit. She always came like that. I didn't really like her, but this time I was terribly pleased to see her, which delighted her. She was rather pretty, yet self-effacing at the same time, and she had the sort of manners that the lower-middle classes appreciate so much. My landlady thought the world of her. I found the two of them sitting and having a cup of coffee together, with the landlady obviously enjoying the nice chat they were having. I also caught a glimpse of Matryosha in a corner of the adjoining room: she was standing still and looking sulkily at her mother and the visitor. She didn't run away or hide herself when I came in, as she had done the other day, and that came to me as a great surprise. It also struck me that she looked very thin and drawn and must be feverish. I was warm and friendly with Nina throughout her entire visit and she left in a happy mood. I left the house at the same time as she did and, for the next two days, stayed away from Pea Street. I was fed up with the place. And yet I missed it.

So, finally, I decided to finish it all. The best thing was to leave Petersburg. That's how far I had gone! But when

I went to Pea Street to tell them I was giving up my lodging,
I found the woman greatly grieved and alarmed: Matryosha
had been ill for three days and was delirious for the third
night in a row. Naturally I immediately inquired what she
was raving about. (We were talking in whispers in my
room.) The woman told me that the child was raving about
"real horrible things. I, she says, have killed God." I offered
to call a doctor and pay for the visit, but the woman refused.

"With God's help she'll get better by herself. Anyway, she
doesn't stay in bed all the time. She even went down to the
grocer's earlier today."

I decided to see Matryosha alone and, since the landlady
mentioned that she had to be on the other side of the city
at five, I decided to return later.

I had no idea, though, why I wanted to be there or what I
intended to do.

I had something to eat in a tavern and at exactly five-
fifteen was back. As usual, I used my key. She was alone
at home, lying behind the screen on her mother's bed. I saw
her peeking out at me, but I pretended I hadn't noticed a
thing. The windows were open. It was warm, even hot. I
paced my room for a while, then sat down on the couch.
I remember clearly every moment of it. I don't know why,
but I decidedly enjoyed keeping Matryosha in suspense by
not saying anything to her. I waited for a full hour. Suddenly she leaped up from the bed behind the screen. I heard
the thud her feet made on the floor when she jumped off the
bed, then her hurried steps. The next thing I knew, she was
standing in my doorway. I was in such a mean mood, it
pleased me that she'd made the first move. Ah, it was all so
despicable on my part and, indeed, very humiliating.

She stood there looking at me in silence. Since I'd last
had a close look at her, she had really grown very thin. Her
face seemed to have shrunk and now her head must have
been on fire. Her eyes had grown larger and were staring at
me with what struck me at the time as dumb curiosity. I
sat without moving, staring back at her. Then I suddenly
felt that hatred stirring in me again.

It seemed to me that Matryosha was no longer at all
frightened of me, and I thought she might very well be
delirious. But she wasn't. She suddenly began shaking her
head the way simple, common people do to mark their disapproval of you. Then, incongruously, she raised her little
fist and shook it at me threateningly from where she stood.
At first her gesture struck me as funny, but after a while

I couldn't stand it any more. I got up and took a step toward her. There was an expression of despair on her face that was quite unimaginable in a child. She kept shaking her head reproachfully and threatening me with her fist. I spoke to her then, softly and kindly, because I was afraid of her, but I soon realized she didn't hear me and that frightened me even more.

All of a sudden, she covered her face with both hands as she had that other time, walked toward the window, and stood there with her back to me. I also turned away from her and sat down by the window. I still don't understand what I was waiting for or why I didn't leave then and there. For, apparently, I really was waiting for something. Perhaps I would have sat there for a while, then got up and killed her, just to put an end to everything in my despair.

But soon I heard her hurried footsteps again. She went out onto the wooden landing leading to the staircase. I got up and ran to my door; I was just in time to catch sight of her entering the tiny chicken coop of a storeroom next to the lavatory. I sat down by the window and once more the thought of death occurred to me. To this day, I can't understand why that was the first thing that came into my head. Apparently there must have been something that led up to it. I couldn't really believe the thought that had just flashed through my head, but—I remember it all very clearly and also how my heart was pounding.

A minute later I glanced at my watch, taking note of the exact time. Why I needed to note the time so precisely, I really don't know—all I can say is that I was anxious to register everything. So I remember every detail and can see it all as though it were happening before my eyes. It was getting late. A fly kept buzzing and settling on my face. I caught it, held it for a moment between my fingers, then let it out of the window. A cart drove noisily into the courtyard below. For some time a tailor had been singing very loudly, sitting at his window, which faced onto the corner of the courtyard. I could see him at his work. It then occurred to me that, since no one had seen me coming in when I entered the courtyard and walked upstairs, I obviously should remain and leave unseen, so I pushed my chair farther away from the window so the tenants of the house shouldn't see me. Oh, how despicable I was! I picked up a book, but dropped it almost at once. Then I began watching a tiny red spider on a geranium leaf and I dozed off. I remember everything down to the last moment.

I suddenly took out my watch. Twenty minutes had passed since she had left the room. I decided to wait exactly fifteen minutes more. I imposed that interval upon myself. It also occurred to me that she might have returned to the room while I had been asleep. But it was impossible: there was a dead silence and I could hear the hum of every tiny fly. My heart started beating again. I took out my watch: there were still another three minutes to go. I forced myself to sit them out, although my heart was pounding painfully.

Then I stood up, put on my hat, buttoned my overcoat, and looked around the room to see whether there were any signs that I had been there. I moved the chair closer to the window, where it had been before. After that I quietly opened the door, locked it behind me with my key, and went to the little storeroom. Its door was closed but not locked. Although I knew it wasn't locked, I stood on tiptoe and peeked through a chink at the top, instead of opening it. And, at that very second, as I was raising myself on tiptoe, I remembered that before, sitting by the window and watching the red spider, I'd visualized myself, just as I passed out, rising on tiptoe to bring my eye to the level of that chink. I mention this small detail to prove that I was quite lucid and that, therefore, I cannot be held to have been of unsound mind or irresponsible for my actions.

I peered through the chink. It was a long time before I could make out anything because it was dark in there, although not completely dark. But, finally, I saw everything there was to be seen.

Then I decided to leave, and I walked down the stairs. I met no one—there was no one who later would be able to point a finger at me. Three hours later, my cronies and I were sitting at my place in our shirt sleeves, sipping tea and playing cards with a greasy old pack. Then Lebyatkin recited some poetry, others told stories. It so happened that, for once, our conversation was quite witty and intelligent and not nearly as flat and stupid as usual. Kirilov was there too. Although there was a bottle of rum on the table, no one besides Lebyatkin touched it. Prokhor Malov remarked that "when Stavrogin hasn't got the blues and is in a good mood, we all feel cheerful and sound more intelligent." I remember his saying that; it shows that I was cheerful and not at all dejected, and that I said some rather clever things. But I remember perfectly that I knew even then that I was a low and loathsome coward to have such a feeling of relief and that I would never regain my self-respect, not in this life, nor after my death—never. And what's more, I felt that the Jewish saying that "one's own stench doesn't bother one" applied to me. I say this because, although I felt I was loathsome, it didn't bother me too much or make me feel particularly ashamed.

It was then, while sipping my tea and chatting with them about something or other, that, for the first time in my life, I formulated to myself in so many words the idea that I neither know nor feel what evil is. It wasn't simply that I had lost the feeling of good and evil, but that I felt there was no such thing as good and evil (I liked that); that it was all a convention; that I could be free of all convention; but that if I ever attained that freedom, I'd be lost. That was the first time I realized it and formulated it, just then— drinking tea, laughing and telling them something, I don't even remember what. Old commonplaces sometimes strike people as completely new even when they are over fifty.

But I kept expecting something to happen. And something did. Around eleven o'clock the little daughter of the janitor of the Pea Street house came over to tell me that Matryosha had hanged herself. I went over there and was relieved to find that the landlady herself couldn't tell exactly why she had sent the girl to me. Naturally, she was wailing and whimpering, as that sort of woman does on such occasions. There were the curious and, of course, the police. I stayed around for a while and then left.

They hardly bothered me at all, asking only the usual questions. And I told them nothing except that the little girl had been ill and delirious and that I had offered to pay for a doctor. They asked me something about my lost penknife and I told them that the mother had given the child a spanking over it, but that there had been nothing special about it. They never found out about my visit that evening. And that was the end of it.

I stayed away from Pea Street for a whole week after that and then went over to give up my lodging. The landlady was still whimpering, although she had started fiddling with her rags again and sewing.

"It was over that penknife of yours that I was unfair to her," she said without any particular reproach, although, apparently, she had been saving it up to tell me when I came.

I settled with her for what I owed her and told her I was leaving, pretending that it was because I couldn't very well continue receiving Nina there after what had happened.

She said once again how much she admired Nina and, as I was leaving, I gave her five rubles above what I owed her for the rent.

The main trouble was that I found life so boring it drove me mad. I'm sure I would have forgotten the Pea Street incident and the danger that I had escaped if I hadn't kept angrily remembering for some time the circumstances that had accompanied it. I took out my spite on whomever I could. It was then that I decided—but for no special reason at all—to cripple my life and make the most loathsome mess of it that I possibly could. For a year before that, I had been thinking of suicide, but now I decided to do better than that.

Once, looking at Maria Lebyatkin, the lame woman who did some part-time cleaning in the tenements and who wasn't mad then, only an exalted idiot, secretly and desperately in love with me (my companions had nosed out her secret)—I decided to marry her. The idea of Stavrogin's marrying such a creature set my nerves a-tingle. There couldn't be anything more freakish. It only makes any sense at all if one remembers that it happened just at that particular period of my life. In any case, I didn't really marry simply because I had made a bet for a bottle of wine after a good dinner.

It happened at a time when I still couldn't possibly know —and that's the main thing. The witnesses to my marriage were Kirilov; Peter Verkhovensky, who was then working for the government in Petersburg; her brother, Lebyatkin; and Prokhor Malov, who has since died. No one else ever found out, for they were sworn to silence. I've always felt there was something vile about keeping it secret—I wanted to make my marriage public. Nevertheless, it has remained a secret to this day, when I am finally disclosing it.

After the wedding, I left for my mother's country estate, to take my mind off it all. In our town, I left behind me the impression that I was insane—an impression that still persists and that harms me, as I will explain later. From this town I went abroad, where I stayed for four years.

I was in the East, visited the monastery on Mount Athos, attended services there that lasted eight hours; I went to Egypt, lived in Switzerland, even traveled all the way to Iceland, and then attended the University of Göttingen for a whole year. During the last year of my absence, I became closely acquainted with a Russian family living in Paris, and while in Switzerland, I became quite friendly with two Russian girls staying there. A couple of years ago, passing a stationery store in Frankfurt, I saw, among other post cards, the picture of a small girl, very richly dressed. She reminded me of Matryosha. I bought it and when I returned to my hotel I placed it on the mantelpiece. I left it there without moving it and without as much as glancing at it, and when I left Frankfurt I forgot to take it with me.

I mention that to prove again how clear my recollections are and with what detachment I can view them. I could reject them wholesale at will. Reminiscing has always bored me and I have never felt nostalgic for the past as many people do, especially since I loathe my past, like everything else connected with me. As to Matryosha, I even forgot her picture on that hotel mantelpiece.

About a year ago, in the spring, I was traveling through Germany and absent-mindedly missed the station where I was supposed to change trains and went on in the wrong direction. I got out at the next stop. It was between two and three in the afternoon. The weather was fine. It was a tiny German town and, since I had to wait there until eleven at night for my train, I went to the hotel. I was rather pleased with my adventure as I was in no particular hurry to get anywhere. The hotel turned out to be small and wretched, but it stood among trees and was surrounded by flowerbeds. They gave me a very small room. I ordered some food, ate with considerable appetite, since I had been traveling throughout the preceding night, and fell sound asleep at around four.

I had a very strange dream such as I'd never had before. As a rule, my dreams are either stupid or frightening. In the Dresden art gallery there's a painting by Claude Lorraine listed in the catalogue, I believe, as "Acis and Galatea" but which, for some reason, I've always referred to as "The Golden Age." I had seen it many times, the last time three days earlier, when I had passed through Dresden. I even went to the gallery specially to see it and, indeed, perhaps it was to see it that I had stopped over in Dresden in the first place. Well, it was that picture that I saw in my dream—not as a picture but as a sort of reality.

Actually I'm not even too certain what it was I dreamed about. I was in a corner of the Greek archipelago—yes, and time had slipped back over three thousand years. I remember the gentle blue waves, the islands and the rocks, the luxuriant shore line, the magic panorama on the horizon, the beckoning, setting sun—it is impossible to put it into words. This was the cradle of European civilization—the thought filled my heart with love. It was a paradise on earth, where gods descended from heaven and fraternized with men. This was the corner of the earth where the first mythological stories were enacted. Ah, and the people who inhabited that land were so beautiful! They awoke innocent and went to sleep at night in innocence. Their woods and glades were filled with cheerful songs; the unspent energy of their youthful vigor went into love and simple joys, and I felt all that, visualizing, as it were, all their great three-thousand-year destiny of which they had no inkling. My heart danced with joy at these thoughts. Ah, I was so happy because my heart danced like that and because, at last, I loved! The sun flooded the islands and the sea, rejoicing at the sight of its beautiful children. Oh, a wonderful dream, a noble delusion! It was the most improbable ideal, but an ideal for which men have striven desperately throughout the ages and for which they have given their lives; an ideal for which they have sacrificed everything, for which they have longed and pined and in the name of which their prophets have been crucified and murdered; an ideal without which men wouldn't want to live and could not even die. And I seemed to live through all that in my dream. I repeat, I don't really know what I dreamed—what I know is that I had that feeling in my dream. However, when I woke up, the cliffs and the sea and the slanting rays of the sun seemed to be still before my eyes, which, for the very first time in my life, were filled with tears. I remember those tears because I was happy and quite unashamed of them. A feeling of still unexperienced happiness rushed into my heart, making it ache.

The day was already declining and the slanting rays of the setting sun pierced through the foliage of the flowers in my window and spread out in my small room. I hastily closed my eyes, hoping to recapture the vanished dream, but then, suddenly, in the middle of the bright light I saw a tiny dot. Gradually the dot assumed a shape and then I clearly recognized the tiny red spider that I had seen on the geranium leaf. At that time too, just as now, the slanting rays of the sun had been pouring in. I felt as though something had stabbed me and I sat up in my bed. And then it happened— I saw before me . . . (No, not really of course—ah, if only she had been real—if only I could have seen her in the flesh just once after that time—only for a second—if only I could tell her how . . .) Well, I saw Matryosha with her drawn features and feverish eyes and, just as she had that time, she stood in my doorway, shaking her head reprovingly and threatening me with her little fist. Ah, the pitiful despair of that helpless creature with its immature brain threatening me (oh God, what could she possibly do to me!), but, of course, blaming only herself.

I had never experienced anything like it before. I remained sitting like that until night. I didn't stir and had no idea of the time. Now I would like to explain clearly what happened. Was it what they call remorse or a feeling of guilt? I can't answer that even today. But I know that I can't bear to see that figure, and precisely when it stands in the doorway— yes, and just at that moment, not a second earlier or later, just when she shook her head and threatened me with her tiny raised fist. Now her gesture and the threat in it were no longer comic but terrifying. I pitied her and my pity extended into madness, and I would have given my body to be torn to pieces if only it could be undone. It is not my crime that obsesses me; it is not even that I regret her dying so deeply. What I cannot stand is that moment, and since then I have relived it almost every day, and I know perfectly well that I am doomed. It is that vision that I cannot bear, just as I couldn't bear it even then, although I didn't know it. And this apparition doesn't come to me by itself—I call it forth and I can't help doing so, although it makes life impossible for me. Ah, if only I could see her when I am awake, even if it was nothing but a hallucination! I wish she would look at me with her big feverish eyes, just as they were then, that she would see—but it is just a stupid idea, and nothing of the sort will ever happen!

Why do none of my other recollections stir such emotions in me? I'm sure that many of them would be found even more criminal in the eyes of men. In my present state, the other memories arouse only hatred in me and, before, I simply used to push them somewhere into the background and thus obtain an artificial peace of mind.

After it happened, I roamed all over the world for a year, trying to keep my mind occupied. And yet, I also know that, even now, I could keep Matryosha away if I chose to do so. I am in complete possession of my will just as before. But that's the snag: I've never wanted to keep her out and I never will. And so it will go on until I go insane.

Two months later, in Switzerland, probably as an antidote produced by my organism's defense mechanism, I experienced a fit of passion—one of those frenetic outbursts such as I used to have before. I felt an irresistible temptation to commit another crime—bigamy in this instance, since I was already married. But I followed the advice of another girl to whom I had admitted my intention and fled. I had told her almost everything, including the fact that I didn't love the other girl but only desired her, that indeed I'd never be able to love anyone and that there was nothing but desire, as far as I was concerned.

Besides, that new crime wouldn't have freed me from Matryosha at all.

And so I decided to have three hundred copies of these sheets printed and bring them back to Russia. When the time comes, I'll send them to the authorities, to the police, and to the newspapers, with a request that they be made public, and also to people I have known personally in Petersburg and in Russia in general. At the same time, a translation will appear abroad. Well, even if it doesn't make sense, I'll still have the sheets published. I realize that I may not be bothered legally or, anyway, very little, since I am the only witness against myself, there being no complainant and no evidence to speak of. Finally, there is that persistent rumor about my being insane of which my family will certainly try to take advantage to stop any possible legal prosecution. I mention this in passing, just to establish the fact that now I am in full command of my senses and have a good grasp of the situation. But there will still be those who know everything. They will stare at me and I will look at them. I want everyone to stare at me, although I don't know whether it will really make it any easier for me. It is my last resort.

Once again, if the records of the Petersburg police are searched thoroughly enough, I'm sure something will crop up. I'm certain some people must remember the house— it was sky-blue. As for me, I don't intend to go anywhere and for some time—a year or two—I'll be at my mother's Skvoreshniki estate. If summoned, I will go wherever I'm wanted.

(Signed:) NIKOLAI STAVROGIN

III

It took Tikhon about an hour to read the sheets. He read slowly, perhaps rereading some passages. Ever since the matter of the missing sheet had come up, Stavrogin had sat silent and motionless, leaning back in the corner of the settee. He appeared to be waiting for something.

Tikhon removed his glasses, waited a while, then looked hesitantly at his visitor. Stavrogin started and leaned forward quickly.

"I forgot to warn you," he said abruptly, "that it would be quite pointless for you to try to dissuade me. I'm determined to go through with it. It will be published."

He blushed and lapsed into silence.

"You didn't forget. You warned me of that before I began reading."

There was a suspicion of irritation in Tikhon's tone now. The document had obviously produced a strong effect upon him. The Christian in him was shocked, and he was not a man who was always able to control himself. It was not for nothing that he was considered in the monastery as a man who could not handle himself too well in public. So now, despite all his Christian meekness, indignation was obvious in his tone.

"Whatever you may say," Stavrogin went on gruffly and without noticing the change in Tikhon's tone, "however strong your arguments are, they won't change anything: I won't give up my plan. And don't interpret this as a clumsy, or, if you wish, shrewd, invitation to you to start dissuading me and begging me not to do it," he concluded with a crooked smile.

"I couldn't possibly try to dissuade you or beg you to give up your plans. Your idea is noble and it reflects the true spirit of Christianity. Repentance can go no further than the courageous choice of self-inflicted punishment that you are contemplating, if only—"

"If only what?"

"If it really *is* repentance and really a Christian thought."

"Hairsplitting," Stavrogin muttered absently.

He got up and started pacing the room, apparently unaware of what he was doing.

"You sound as if you were trying to give the impression of being coarser than you are deep down in your heart," Tikhon said, becoming more outspoken.

" 'Give the impression'? I wasn't trying to give any sort of impression. I wasn't putting on an act. Anyway, what do you mean by 'coarser'?" He blushed and that made him angry. "I know that everything in there," he said, nodding toward the sheets, "is the miserable, filthy, crawling truth, but let the very depravity of it serve to strengthen—"

He broke off, apparently ashamed to go on, as though he considered it degrading to try to explain. But at the same time he was submitting with visible pain to some unconscious need to stay there in order to explain. It is worth noting that nothing more was said by either of them concerning Stavrogin's removal of one sheet of the confession.

Now Stavrogin stopped near the desk, picked up a small ivory crucifix, and started twisting it around in his fingers. Suddenly he snapped it in two. That brought him back to himself and he gave Tikhon a bewildered look. Then his upper lip began to quiver as though someone had slighted him, and there was proud defiance in his eyes.

"I did think you'd say *something* to me—that was why I came," he said in a hushed tone, appearing to make a violent effort to control himself and throwing the two halves of the crucifix to the desk.

Tikhon quickly lowered his eyes.

"This document came straight from a mortally wounded heart, am I right?" he asked insistently, almost with heat. "Yes, it is a penance and your natural need for it has overcome you. The suffering of the creature you wronged has so shattered you that it has brought home to you the problem of life and death, so there is still a hope that you are now on the great, still untrodden path of calling disgrace and universal scorn down upon yourself. And you have asked the whole Church to judge you, although you do not believe in the Church—do I understand you correctly? But even now, you hate and despise all those who will read your confession and are challenging them to battle—"

"Who, me? Challenging them to battle?"

"Why, since you aren't ashamed to admit your crime, should you be ashamed of your repentance?"

"Who says I'm ashamed?"

"You're ashamed and afraid."

"Afraid of what?" Stavrogin grinned nervously and his upper lip started quivering again.

"Let them stare at me, you said, but you—how will you look at them? You want hatred from them so you can answer them with an even greater hatred. Certain passages of your narrative are emphasized by the way you present them: you seem to admire your attitude and use every detail to impress the reader with how insensitive and shameless you are, although, as a matter of fact, you may not be so at all. On the other hand, low passions and idleness do make one insensitive and stupid."

"Stupidity is no vice," Stavrogin snorted, growing pale.

"It can be sometimes," Tikhon went on with stern passion. "Hurt and tormented though you are by the vision of the girl in the doorway, it appears from your document that you still can't decide what your main crime is or of what you should be most ashamed—the callousness of your act of violence or the cowardice you manifested on that occasion. At one point you even try to convince the reader that the child's threatening you with her fist no longer impressed you as ridiculous, but as terrifying. What I want to know is, how could the girl's shaking her fist have seemed funny to you, even for a second—because it did, I know it did."

Tikhon stopped. He had spoken like a man giving free rein to his emotions.

"Go on, go on," Stavrogin urged him. "You sound irritated; I like irritated monks—let yourself go. That's the way I like a monk to be. But let me ask you something. Here we've been talking for more than ten minutes since you read those," he nodded at the sheets, "and although you're angry, I haven't yet seen any sign of scorn or revulsion in you. You can't be too fussy, for you're talking to me as though I were your equal."

He added the last words, "as though I were your equal," very softly; they seemed to have slipped from his tongue by themselves, almost without his being aware of them. Tikhon looked at him intently.

"You surprise me," Tikhon said after a pause, "and since I know you are sincere now, I must tell you that as a matter of fact I *am* guilty of those feelings—I *did* feel revolted by you and I was rude to you, but you, in your longing for self-punishment, didn't even notice it, although you did notice my impatience, which you called irritation. But you yourself feel that you merit incomparably greater scorn, and your remark about my speaking to you like an equal, although involuntary, was admirable. I won't hide anything from you: I was horrified to see your great, unused powers had been so deliberately turned toward filth. Apparently men cannot with impunity become alien in their own land. There is one torture devised for those who have torn themselves away from their native soil —it is boredom and the inability to do anything, try as they may to keep busy. But a Christian accepts responsibility whatever his environment. God has not grudged you intelligence— you are capable of answering the question, 'Am I or am I not responsible for my actions?' Therefore, there is no doubt that you are responsible. 'Temptation cannot but enter the world, but woe unto him through whom temptation cometh.' As to your transgression itself, well, many commit similar ones, but go on living in peace with their consciences and even consider such things the inevitable errors of youth. There are also old men with the smell of the grave already about them who likewise still go on sinning, playfully shrugging off their responsibility and reassuring themselves. The world is full of such horrors. You, at least, have felt the full depth of your transgressions, and that's a very rare occurrence."

"It sounds as though those sheets have instilled respect for me in you," Stavrogin said, smiling wryly. "No, Reverend Father Tikhon, I understand now why they say you're not fit to be a spiritual guide." He went on smiling more and more artificially and inappropriately. "They strongly disapprove of you around here. They say that as soon as you perceive something sincere and humble in a sinner, you become enthusiastic, begin apologizing and repenting, and humble yourself before him."

"I won't answer you directly, but I'll readily admit that I don't have a way with people. I've always felt it was a great shortcoming in me," Tikhon said with a deep sigh, and he sounded so simple and unaffected that Stavrogin looked at him with a smile. "As to those," he added, glancing at the sheets, "there is not and cannot be any worse crime than what you did to that little girl."

"Let's stop comparing and measuring things," Stavrogin said after a brief silence, and there was a slight annoyance in his tone. "Perhaps I don't really suffer so much as that suggests— perhaps I even made up much of it against myself," he concluded unexpectedly.

Tikhon said nothing. Stavrogin, deep in thought, his head lowered, paced the room.

"Tell me," Tikhon asked suddenly, "that girl with whom you broke off that affair in Switzerland—where is she now?"

"She's here in town."

Another silence followed.

"I may have slandered myself a lot," Stavrogin repeated insistently. "I don't even know to what extent myself. But even if I do defy people with the crudeness of my presentation, as you pointed out, so what? That's as it should be. They deserve it."

"In other words it is easier for you to hate them than to accept their pity?"

"Yes, you're right. I'm not accustomed to being so outspoken, but since I've begun—I mean with you—well, let me tell you that I despise them all as much as I despise myself or, as a matter of fact, more—infinitely more. Not one of them is fit to sit in judgment over me. I wrote that nonsense just because I fancied—out of sheer cynicism. Perhaps I exaggerated or even made it all up in a moment of tense emotion." He broke off angrily and turned red once more because he had said something against his will. He stretched out his hand, picked up a piece of the broken crucifix from the desk, and turned his back on Tikhon.

"Answer one question. Tell me just as though you were talking to yourself in the darkness of the night," Tikhon said in an exalted voice. "If someone forgave you for that"—he pointed at the sheets—"not one of those whom you fear or respect but some anonymous stranger, on whom you'll never set eyes; if then, reading your terrible confession, he forgave you silently, without saying a word to anyone—tell me, would the knowledge of it make you feel better or wouldn't it make any difference? And if it is too hard on your pride to answer that question aloud, don't speak—just think the answer."

"I'd feel better," Stavrogin said in a very low voice, "if you forgave me—much better," he added in a whisper, his back still turned to Tikhon.

"I'll forgive you, if you'll forgive me too."

"Forgive you for what?" Stavrogin turned and faced him. "What wrong have you done me? Ah, I see, that's just your monastic formula. Ugly humility. May I tell you that I find all those old, monastic formulas of yours very inelegant? Do you really find them so graceful yourself?" He snorted with irritation. "But what am I doing here anyway? Ah," he said suddenly, glancing at the crucifix he had broken. "I did that— how much did that thing cost? Would twenty-five rubles do?"

"Don't worry about it," Tikhon said.

"Perhaps fifty? Why shouldn't I pay for it? There's no reason why you should forgive me the damage I've caused. Here's fifty rubles." Stavrogin took the money out and put it on the desk. "Well, if you don't want to take it for yourself," he said with growing irritation, "take it for your poor, for your church, for—listen, I'll tell you the truth: I want you to forgive me, and after you, another, and then a third perhaps, but as to the rest—let them hate me!"

His eyes sparkled.

"You couldn't bear universal pity with humility, could you?"

"No, I couldn't. I don't want universal pity and anyway, there's no such thing as universal pity, so it's just an idle question. Listen, I don't want to wait; I'll make the thing public. And don't you try to get around me. I can't wait any more—I can't!" he added, beside himself.

"I'm afraid for you," Tikhon said, really sounding almost frightened.

"You're afraid I won't be able to stand it? To stand their hatred?"

"Not only their hatred."

"What else then?"

"Well—their laughter," Tikhon whispered as though squeezing the words out of himself with a great effort.

He had been unable to restrain himself and had said something that he himself knew would have better remained unsaid.

Stavrogin was taken aback. He looked at Tikhon anxiously.

"I knew it!" he said. "So you find me a comic character after reading my confession. Please don't look so embarrassed —I expected as much."

Tikhon was really embarrassed and hurriedly tried to explain what he had meant, which of course only made matters worse.

"Such undertakings require serenity—even for suffering one needs supreme spiritual detachment. But nowadays one doesn't find serenity of mind; people argue and argue and fail to understand one another just as they did when the Tower of Babel collapsed."

"I've heard all that before and I find it boring. It has been said over and over again, thousands of times," Stavrogin said, interrupting him.

"But you won't even attain your goal," Tikhon said, going straight to the point. "Legally, of course, you're unassailable. And that's the first thing they'll tell you, with a smirk. They'll wonder what you're after—for who will understand the real purpose of your confession? Indeed, people will obstinately refuse to understand it because they'll view such an unusual penance with alarm and avenge themselves on anyone who wishes to suffer it, for the world revels in its own filth and will make a laughingstock out of anyone who tries to clean it up, because ridicule is the quickest way to kill—"

"Be more specific; say everything you have on your mind," Stavrogin said, urging him on.

"At first, of course, they'll express their horror, but it will be more feigned than sincere, more for the sake of appearances. I'm not talking about the pure hearts, for they will be truly horrified, but silently so, and then—also in silence—they will accuse themselves. But no one will know about them, just because of their silence. But the rest, the worldly people who are only afraid of things that threaten their individual interests—it is they who, after their first surprise and a display of sham horror, will hastily burst out laughing. They will also be curious about the madman—because they'll be convinced you're mad. Not quite mad enough to be irresponsible, perhaps, but mad enough to permit them to laugh at you. Do you think you will be able to stand it? Won't your heart be filled with a hatred that will inevitably lead you to damnation? That's what I'm so afraid of."

"But look at you yourself! I must say, I'm surprised at the low opinion you have of men—you talk of them with such disgust," Stavrogin said rather spitefully.

"Well, you know, I was actually judging mostly by myself when I spoke of others!" Tikhon exclaimed.

"Ah, really? Then it's possible there's something in my misfortune that amuses you?"

"Who knows? There may be."

"All right then, in that case I'd like you to point out to me exactly where I sound ridiculous in my confession. I know myself where I'm ludicrous, but I want you to put your finger on it for me. And please be cynical about it, because you *are* a great cynic. You saintly people are all great cynics, the lot of you! You yourselves don't realize how much you despise people! Please answer me in all sincerity, and let me tell you: you're a very peculiar man yourself!"

"To begin with, in the eyes of the world, your intention to do this great penance is ridiculous in itself. There is something ludicrous about it, something contrived—not to mention its loose and vague form, as though you were stammering out of fear and weakness. Oh, don't doubt your eventual triumph!" he cried out suddenly, almost in rapture. "Even in that form you will triumph," he pointed at the sheets, "as long as you sincerely accept their spitting at you and trampling upon you

—if you can endure it! The most degrading cross has always produced the greatest glory and force, as long as the humility of the martyrdom is sincere. But do you have that humility? What you need is not a challenge but infinite humility and humiliation! You mustn't despise those who judge you, but believe in them sincerely, as in a great church; then you will triumph over them and turn them toward you by your example, and you will be united in love—ah, if only you could endure it!"

"Now show me what, in your opinion, is most ridiculous in those sheets."

"Why? Why do you keep worrying about its ridiculousness? Why do you have this morbid obsession?" Tikhon said, with pain, shaking his head.

"Whatever it is, I want you to put your finger on it."

"The ugliness will doom it," Tikhon whispered, lowering his eyes.

"Ugliness? What ugliness?"

"The ugliness of your crime. All crimes are ugly in their essence, but the more blood there is in them, the more horrible they are—the more, if I may say so, they are picaresque; but there are utterly shameful, degrading crimes which are not even mitigated by their horror—"

Tikhon didn't complete his thought.

"Does that mean that you feel I must have looked especially ludicrous when I kissed the little girl's hand and—and was so frightened after that, well, and all the rest of it? I see. I see what you mean very well. And so you think I won't be able to take it?"

Tikhon remained silent. Stavrogin's face was pale and distorted.

"Now I can also guess why you asked me about that young lady in Switzerland," Stavrogin said very quietly, almost to himself.

"You're not ready for the test, not prepared for it," Tikhon said.

"I would like you to understand that I am mainly concerned with forgiving myself," Stavrogin said, gloomy exaltation in his eyes. "Here's my confession; here's the whole truth —all the rest is nothing but lies. I know that only then will that apparition disappear. That's why I'm looking for infinite suffering for myself. So don't frighten me, or I shall go to my perdition full of spite," he added, and again it appeared that these last words had slipped from his tongue by themselves, against his will. Tikhon was so surprised at them that he rose from his seat.

"If you really believe that, then you can forgive yourself, and if you are willing to pursue that forgiveness through suffering in this world, then you do have complete faith!" he exclaimed rapturously. "But how could you say that you didn't believe in God?"

Stavrogin didn't answer.

"God will forgive you for not believing, for you do worship the Holy Ghost without knowing it."

"There's no forgiveness for me," Stavrogin said grimly. "It says in your book here that there's no greater crime than to offend 'one of these little ones,' and there can be none!"

He pointed to the Bible.

"As to that, I have good news for you," Tikhon said with gentle emotion. "Christ will forgive you too, if you succeed in forgiving yourself—no, wait, don't listen to me; I was blaspheming: even if you don't attain peace with yourself and fail to forgive yourself, He will still forgive you for your intention and for your great suffering, for there are no words and no human thoughts that can express all the purposes of the Lamb 'until His ways are revealed unto us.' Who can embrace Him, the unbound, and grasp Him the ungraspable?"

The corners of his lips started twitching and again a slight spasm passed over his face. For a while he tried to gain control of himself, but, failing, lowered his eyes.

Stravrogin took his hat from the settee.

"I'll come back sometime," he said in an exhausted voice, "and then we—I have enjoyed talking to you tremendously and I do appreciate . . . the way you feel. Believe me, I do understand why some people like you so. Please pray for me to the One whom you love so much."

"Are you leaving already?" Tikhon stood up quickly, looking surprised that Stavrogin should be going. "And I wanted . . ." he muttered with apparent embarrassment, "I wanted to ask you for a kind of favor—but I really don't know how to put it now—"

"Please do, I'd be happy to," Stavrogin said, sitting down and still holding his hat in his hand.

Tikhon looked at the hat, at the worldly, detached way this man, who five minutes before had been so tormented and agitated, was now sitting and granting him an extra five minutes to state his business. He became even more embarrassed.

"Well, all my request consists of is that—well, since you have already confessed—well, you realize, Nikolai—I believe that's your Christian name, isn't it?—that if you publicize those sheets, you will ruin all your prospects, in the sense of a career and all the rest—"

"What career?" Stavrogin said, grimacing with distaste.

"Why do you have to spoil it? Why do you have to be so intractable?" Tikhon said, almost beseechingly, obviously conscious of his own clumsiness. A painful look came over Stavrogin's face.

"I told you before and I say again: nothing you may say will change anything. And, in general, all this conversation is becoming unbearable."

He stirred impatiently in his seat.

"You didn't understand me. Hear me out and don't get angry. You know what I think: your martyrdom, if it were really inspired by humility, would be a great Christian act provided you could endure it and go through with it. And even if you failed to go through with it, God would still take your original sacrifice into account. Everything will be taken into account—not a word, not a movement of the spirit, not a thought, even a vague one, will be lost. But I would like to suggest another idea to you, an even greater one—something great beyond all shadow of doubt."

Stavrogin remained silent.

"You are longing for martyrdom and self-sacrifice: well, overcome that desire too—put away those sheets and your intention to publish them and then, I am certain, you will overcome everything. You'll conquer your pride and put your demon to flight. You'll end up the winner and gain your freedom."

His eyes sparkled; his hands were clasped as if in prayer.

"You take it all so tragically and attach such exaggerated importance to it. Still, rest assured that I greatly appreciate your concern," Stavrogin said politely, but with a hint of distaste. "I see that you are absolutely determined to trap me—oh, of course, with the best intentions, out of sheer kindness and concern for your fellow man. You would like me to come to my senses reasonably, without any acrobatics and publications—to settle down and perhaps wind up as a member of the local club who visits this monastery on holidays. Am I wrong? On the other hand, being a psychologist and a cynic, you know that that's what will happen anyway and that all there is left to do now is to plead with me insistently enough to allow me to save face, because it's what I want myself. I would bet that you were thinking of my mother too, of her peace. . . ."

"I wanted to suggest a different penance instead of that one!" Tikhon went on ardently, completely ignoring Stavrogin's words. "I know an old man—not here, but not too far away. He's a hermit, an ascetic, and his Christian insight is so great that you and I couldn't even follow his thought. I will beg him and he will allow me to tell him about you. Do I have your permission? Go and serve as a novice under him. Go for five years, for seven—for as long as you yourself feel is necessary. Take a vow and, through that great sacrifice, you will find everything you are longing for on earth, even things you do not expect to find, for you can't even imagine now all that you will gain!"

Stavrogin heard him out with a serious expression. His pale cheeks reddened.

"Are you suggesting that I become a monk in that monastery?"

"You don't have to enter a monastery; you don't have to enter an order. Just become a novice—a secret novice. You could even do it while living in the world."

"Ah, forget it, Father Tikhon," Stavrogin interrupted with distaste and got up. Tikhon got up too. "What's the matter with you now?" Stavrogin shouted suddenly, looking at Tikhon with anxiety.

Tikhon stood before him, his palms pressed together, and a painful convulsion, apparently caused by a great fright, twisted his face for a second.

"What's the matter, what's the matter?" Stavrogin repeated, hurrying over to support him, for he thought Tikhon was about to collapse.

"I can see—I can see just as if it were real," Tikhon chanted in a heartbreaking voice, his features reflecting immense grief. "Never before have you stood so close to a new and even more heinous crime than at this very moment. Ah, you poor, wretched young man!"

"Take hold of yourself, please," Stavrogin said, now really worried for him and trying to reassure him. "Perhaps I'll postpone it for a while—reconsider it. You may be right. I won't circulate these sheets. Please, calm yourself."

"Now, not after the publication, but before it, perhaps a day, perhaps an hour before you take the great step, you will plunge into a new crime as a way out and you'll commit it solely to avoid the publication of these sheets upon which you now insist."

Stavrogin was actually shaking with anger, and there was something of fear in it too.

"You damned psychologist!" he said, abruptly ending his visit and stalking furiously out of the cell without turning his head.

chapter 10

A SEARCH AT STEPAN VERKHOVENSKY'S

At this time, an incident occurred that greatly surprised me and shocked Stepan Verkhovensky to the core. At eight in the morning his maid came running over to my place to announce that her master had been "raided." At first I couldn't understand what had happened; I gathered only that some officials had come to Mr. Verkhovensky's house and confiscated his papers, which had been tied up in a bundle and taken away in a wheelbarrow by a soldier.

I found Stepan Verkhovensky in an extraordinary state of mind: although he was understandably indignant and agitated, there was also an unmistakable elation in the way he looked at me. A samovar was boiling in the middle of the table and next to it stood a glass of tea, apparently untouched and forgotten. Mr. Verkhovensky was walking aimlessly around, now circling the table, now drifting into the corners of the room, obviously unaware of his movements. He wore a red flannel shirt, as he often did at home, but upon seeing me, hastily donned his waistcoat and jacket, something he had never bothered to do before.

"*Enfin, un ami!*" he cried, seizing me warmly by the hand and drawing in a deep breath. "You're the only person I've sent for," he said. "No one else knows anything about it. I must tell Nastasya to lock the door and let no one in, except *them*, of course, as you can well understand. You do understand?"

He looked at me worriedly as though waiting for a reply. Of course, I started questioning him and managed to make out from his rather disconnected answers, which were full of interruptions and irrelevancies, that, at seven in the morning, an official of the province administration had unexpectedly come to see him.

"I'm sorry, I've forgotten his name. He doesn't come from this part of the country; I believe Lembke brought him along with him, *il y a quelque chose de bête et d'allemand dans sa physionomie. Il s'appelle* Rosenthal. . . ."

"It wouldn't be Blum, by any chance?"

"That's right, that's his name—Blum. *Vous le connaissez?* There's something obtuse and self-satisfied in his face that otherwise looks stiff and severe. A typical police employee, one who's accustomed to carrying out orders—I know the kind. I was still in bed when he came and said he'd like to have a look at my books and manuscripts—yes, *je m'en souviens*, those were the words he used: 'have a look.' He didn't arrest me; he just took the books—*il se tenait à distance*—and when he started explaining the purpose of his visit, he looked as if he expected me to pounce on him at any moment and start flailing. . . . *Tous ces gens du bas étage sont comme ça* when they're dealing with a gentleman. Of course, I immediately understood what was going on: *voilà vingt ans que je m'y prépare!* I unlocked all the drawers and handed him all the keys. Yes, I handed everything over to him—myself! *J'étais digne et calme.* Of the books, he took the foreign editions of Herzen's works, the bound copies of *The Bell* magazine, four copies of my poem, *et enfin tout ça.* Then he also took my papers and letters and *quelques unes de mes ébauches histori-ques et politiques.* All that he took away. Nastasya says that the soldier loaded it onto a wheelbarrow and covered it up with an apron. *Oui, c'est cela*, an apron!"

None of it made any sense. What could it all mean? I fired more questions at him: Had Blum been alone? In whose name had he searched the house? What right did he have? What explanations had he given?

"He was alone, *bien seul*, although I believe someone was waiting in the passage. *Oui, je m'en souviens, et puis.* Ah, yes, I believe there was someone else as well, and there was also the janitor at the gate outside. You'd better ask Nastasya; she can tell you much more about it than I can. *J'étais surexcité, voyez-vous, il parlait, il parlait . . . un tas de choses. . . .* Although, as a matter of fact, he didn't say much—it was I who talked all the time. I told him about my life—oh, of course, only the one aspect of it with which he was concerned—*J'étais surexcité mais digne, je vous assure.* I'm afraid, though, I couldn't help bursting into tears. Ah, they'd borrowed that wheelbarrow from the store on the corner."

"Good Lord, how could they do such a thing! But for heaven's sake, Mr. Verkhovensky, be more precise—otherwise it sounds as though you were telling me about a dream you had."

"But I feel as if I were in a dream, *cher. Savez-vous,* I heard him pronounce the name Telyatnikov, and I believe that that was the fellow who was hiding in the passage. Yes, I remember him suggesting that they call the prosecutor, Dmitri Mitrich, who, by the way, still owes me fifteen rubles from a game of whist. *Enfin,* I couldn't understand very well what they wanted, but I outsmarted them. What would I want with Dmitri Mitrich anyway? So I started pleading with him to keep the whole thing secret. I believe I pleaded very, very hotly and I'm afraid I may have lacked a little dignity there, *comment croyez-vous?* Well, finally he accepted. He even said he himself had insisted that it was much better to keep the whole thing quiet because actually he'd only come to have a look around, *et rien de plus,* and nothing, nothing else, and what would it look like if they found nothing and nothing came of it? So, in the end, we parted on the best of terms *et je suis tout à fait content.*"

"But wait a minute—he wanted to adhere to the usual procedure, which offers you the proper legal protection in such a case, and you yourself insisted on being deprived of it!"

"No, I'd rather have it this way, without any protection. What do I want a public scandal for? Let everything be as friendly as possible, at least for the time being. If they get to know about it, my enemies in this town, you know . . . *et puis,* what good would the prosecutor do, *ce cochon de notre procureur, qui deux fois m'a manqué de politesse et qu'on a rossé à plaisir l'autre année chez cette charmante et belle* Natalia Pavlovna *quand il se cacha dans son boudoir. Et puis, mon ami,* don't argue with me and don't discourage me completely, because there's nothing more painful for a man who is unhappy and in trouble than to have his friends come and point out to him that he was wrong here and there and then.

Sit down and have some tea. I must say, though, I'm quite exhausted—I wonder whether I shouldn't lie down a bit and put a vinegar compress on my head. What do you think?"

"Yes, and some ice too. You're terribly upset. You're pale and your hands are shaking. Stretch out and lie quiet for a while."

He hesitated about stretching out, but I insisted. Nastasya brought a bottle of vinegar, I poured some onto a towel and put it on his forehead. Then Nastasya climbed up on a chair and lit the little lamp before an icon. I was rather surprised, for I had never seen that icon before nor had I ever noticed a sanctuary lamp in Mr. Verkhovensky's house.

"It was my idea," Mr. Verkhovensky said, giving me a sly look. "Just after they left. When they come to arrest you and find such things in your room, it impresses them—and, then, they're bound to report what they see to their superiors."

When she was through lighting the lamp, Nastasya started to go out, then stopped in the doorway, looking tearfully at her master, the palm of her right hand pressed against her cheek.

"*Éloignez-la* under some pretext," he asked me, discreetly jerking his head toward the poor woman. "I can't stand this Russian pity, *ça m'embête.*"

But she left herself. I noticed that he kept squinting at the door and listening for any noises from the passage.

"I must be ready," he said, giving me a meaningful look. "They may come and take me at any moment, and then, pfft! I'll have vanished into thin air."

"What are you talking about? Who wants to take you away?"

"*Voyez-vous, mon cher*, I asked him point-blank as he was leaving what they intended to do about me."

"You might as well have inquired what part of Siberia they were going to send you to," I said irritatedly.

"That was exactly what I had in mind, when I asked him that, but he left without answering. You see, for clothes, underwear, and especially warm things, you're at their mercy. They may tell you themselves what they want you to take along, or they may send you off in just an army greatcoat. But I've hidden thirty-five rubles here, in the slit inside this waistcoat pocket. Feel it," he whispered, squinting furtively at the door through which Nastasya had disappeared. "I don't think they'll take the waistcoat from me and then, to mislead them, I've left seven rubles in my purse as though that were all I had on

me. It includes some change and there are some more coppers on the table, so I think they'll think that's all I have on
hand. I must take my precautions—God alone can tell where
I'll have to spend the coming night."

I felt helpless before such insane ideas. Obviously, they had
no authority either to search or to arrest him as he had suggested, and I was sure he was all mixed up. It is true that
this happened before the new liberal legislation had been
passed, but it is also true that they'd offered him the protection of whatever legal guarantees there were at the time, a
protection he himself had insisted on rejecting, to "outsmart"
them. Of course, not so very long ago, a governor had emergency powers at his disposal. But how could an emergency
be invoked in this case? I felt completely at a loss.

"There must've been instructions from Petersburg behind
it," Mr. Verkhovensky suddenly blurted out.

"A special wire from Petersburg about you? Why? Because
you happen to own a volume of Herzen and because of that
poem of yours? You must be completely out of your mind!
What's there to arrest you for?"

I was really angry now. He grinned and I could see he
was offended, not because of my impatient tone but rather
because I had said that he had done nothing for which they
could arrest him.

"Who can tell, nowadays, what one may be arrested for?"
he muttered mysteriously.

A wild, incongruous thought occurred to me.

"Mr. Verkhovensky, my dear fellow—remember I'm your
friend—tell me confidentially: do you, by any chance, belong
to some secret society? Do you or don't you?"

To my complete amazement, he wasn't too sure about that
either: he wasn't sure whether he belonged to a secret group
or not.

"It depends what's meant by that, *voyez-vous*—"

" 'What's meant by that'?"

"You see, when a man belongs with all his heart to progress,
who can vouch for him one way or the other? One may be
under the impression that one doesn't belong to any group and
then, lo and behold, you find that you do belong to something."

"How is that possible? It's either yes or no!"

"*Cela date de* Petersburg, when she and I wanted to launch
that magazine. That's the origin of it all. We gave them
the slip then and they forgot about us. But now, they've sud-

denly remembered again. Ah, can't you really understand, *cher*," he cried in a pained voice, "that they intend to pick us up and dispatch us to Siberia to finish our days there, if they don't entomb us in a dungeon and forget us."

And suddenly he burst into tears. Hot tears rolled and rolled out of his eyes, and he covered his face with his red silk scarf and sobbed convulsively for about five minutes. I was shocked. This man, who for twenty years had prophesied and preached to us, whom we regarded as our patriarch and teacher, who had always behaved with such regal airs among us and whom we admired from the bottom of our hearts— he was now crying like a little boy caught doing something naughty and waiting for his teacher to come back with the cane he had gone to fetch. I was immensely sorry for him. He apparently felt as certain that they were going to pack him off to Siberia as he was of my presence there next to him; he really expected them to come and take him away that very morning, at any minute. And all because of Herzen and that poor poem of his! Such a failure to grasp the realities was at once endearing and repugnant.

Finally he stopped sobbing, got up from the sofa, and again started pacing the room while he talked to me, although he stopped repeatedly to look out of the window and to listen to any possible creaking in the passage. Our conversation was still disconnected, and all my efforts to calm and reassure him bounced off him like so many peas off a wall. He hardly listened to what I said, although he desperately needed my reassurances; indeed, the whole point of his ceaseless chatter was to extract them from me. I saw now that he couldn't have managed without me and that he wasn't going to let me leave him. So I stayed and we spent two hours talking like that. Among other things, he told me that Blum had taken two leaflets he had found away with him.

"What d'you mean, leaflets?" I cried in an inadvertently horrified tone. "Surely you're not—"

"Ah, they slipped ten of them under my door," he said with irritation. (His tone kept switching from whimpering humility to arrogant irritability.) "Anyway, I had already disposed of eight so Blum only got his hands on two." Suddenly he turned red with indignation. "But are you lumping me together with those people, by any chance? Do you really believe for one moment that I have anything to do with those crooks, those good-for-nothings, with that lovable son of mine, *avec ces esprits forts de la lâcheté?* Ah, for heaven's sake!"

"Well, I only hope there hasn't been a mix-up somewhere—but no, how could they!" I said.

"Savez-vous," he burst out again, "I'll kick up a row there. Oh, please, don't leave me, I can't stay by myself! *Ma carrière est finie aujourd'hui, je le sens.* I feel I may suddenly start biting people, you know, just like that second lieutenant."

He gave me a strange look, full of fright, but at the same time full of a longing to frighten me too. He seemed to grow more and more irritated as time went by and the police wagon didn't come for him. He seemed actually furious about it. Suddenly Nastasya, who had come out of the kitchen into the passage for some reason, butted into the coat stand and it fell with a thud. Mr. Verkhovensky stood rooted to the ground. I saw he was trembling all over. Then, when he realized what had happened, he literally screamed at Nastasya and, stamping his feet, chased her back into her kitchen. A minute later, he told me in a tone full of despair:

"This is the end of me, *cher!*" He sat down next to me and looked at me intently. His look was overflowing with self-pity. "Understand, *cher,* it's not Siberia that I'm afraid of, I swear, *je vous jure!* I'm afraid of something else——" Tears spurted from his eyes.

I gathered that he was about to tell me something very important, something that, up to now, he hadn't been able to bring himself to admit.

"I'm afraid of disgracing myself," he said mysteriously.

"What do you mean, disgracing yourself? Come, mark my words, Mr. Verkhovensky, everything will be cleared up no later than today. They're bound to see that they were wrong and you were right!"

"What makes you so sure they'll pardon me?"

"Who's talking about 'pardoning'? You haven't done anything to be pardoned for!"

"Qu'en savez-vous? What do you know about it? All my life has been devoted to—ah, *cher,* they're sure to remember it. And then," he added unexpectedly, "even if they find nothing against me, *so much the worse!*"

"Why would it be worse?"

"Yes, worse."

"I don't follow you."

"Ah, my friend, let them send me to Siberia or to Archangel

if they must; let them deprive me of my civic rights and all that—let me perish, if I must. But I'm afraid of something else; I'm afraid—"

Again he was whispering; he looked terrified, oppressed by a terrible secret.

"Well, tell me, what is it you're so afraid of?"

"Flogging," he said, looking at me helplessly.

"Flogging? Who's going to flog you? Why? Where?" I shouted, thinking he had gone mad.

"Where? Well, wherever it's done—"

"And where's that?"

"Ah, *cher*, we all know how it happens: suddenly the floor opens under your feet and you're lowered. . . . I'm sure you know as well as I do."

"Fairy tales!" I cried, guessing what it was all about. "Old wives' tales! Do you really still believe in all that?"

"Fairy tales? But they didn't just spring up from nowhere, those fairy tales as you call them. People who get flogged don't go around boasting about it afterward. I've gone all over the whole thing thousands of times in my imagination."

"But why should they flog you? Why, you haven't done a thing!"

"That makes it even worse—they'll see I haven't done a thing and they'll flog me."

"And you're sure that they'll take you to Petersburg for that?"

"My friend, as I said before, I regret nothing, *ma carrière est finie*. Since the day she said farewell to me in Skvoreshniki, I've cared nothing for my life. But, oh, what shame, what ignominy if she finds out! Ah, *que dira-t-elle*, when she finds out?"

"She won't find out anything because nothing will happen to you. I feel as though I have never really known you—that's how much you've surprised me today."

"My dear friend, I want you to understand that it's really not fear of the thing itself. Suppose they did actually pardon me and bring me back here without doing anything—well, it would still be the end: *elle me soupçonnera toute sa vie*, she'd think they'd done it to me—me, the poet, the thinker—the man whom she'd admired for twenty-two years!"

"It would never even occur to her."

"It's sure to occur to her," he whispered with deep conviction. "She and I spoke of it in Petersburg, during Lent, just before we left; we were so frightened then. She'd suspect all her life that it had happened and how could I convince her that it hadn't? For that matter, I couldn't even convince anyone here in this town. *Et puis, les femmes* . . . She'd be glad. Of course, she'd be grieved, very deeply and sincerely, being a loyal friend of mine, but deep down she'd be pleased. It'd give her ammunition against me for the rest of her life. Ah, this is the end of my life! After twenty years of perfect happiness with her, this is what I've come to!" And he covered his face with his hands.

"Listen," I said to him, "wouldn't it be best to inform Mrs. Stavrogin of what's happened?"

"God forbid!" he cried, leaping up. "Never! Not under any pretext, after what was said at our parting in Skvoreshniki—never!"

His eyes flashed.

We remained there, I believe, for an hour or more, waiting vaguely for something to happen. He stretched himself out on the sofa and closed his eyes, remaining in that position for a full twenty minutes without uttering a word; I thought he'd fallen asleep or even fainted. Suddenly he jumped to his feet, tore the vinegar-soaked towel from his head, rushed over to the mirror, and tied his tie with trembling hands. Then, in a stentorian voice, he summoned Nastasya and ordered her to bring him his overcoat, his cane, and his new hat.

"I can't stand it any longer," he said in a gasping voice. "I'm going there myself."

"Where?" I cried, also leaping up.

"I'm going to see Lembke. I must, I must, *cher*—it's my duty; I'm a citizen and a man, not a chip of wood, and I intend to have my rights respected. For twenty years I've failed to see to it that my rights were respected. I've been guilty of criminal neglect there. But now, I intend to stand on my rights! I'll make him explain everything: if he has received a telegram concerning me, he must tell me all about it. He has no right to torture me like this. If he has to arrest me, let him go ahead and arrest me!"

He was stamping his feet and shouting now in a shrill, squeaky voice.

"This time I agree with you," I said as calmly as I could, although I was really worried about him. "It will make you feel much better than sitting here and waiting in your present state of anguish. But I really think you ought to pull yourself together: you look like God knows what and you certainly shouldn't go there in such a state. *Il faut être digne et calme avec* Lembke. And I must say, just now, you look very much as though you could throw yourself on someone and bite him."

"I'm betraying myself; I'm walking straight into the lion's mouth."

"I'm coming with you."

"I expected no less of you and I accept your sacrifice, the sacrifice of a loyal friend. But you're coming only as far as the door of the house. You mustn't compromise yourself any further by associating with me. *O, croyez-moi, je serai calme!* I feel that, at this minute, I am *à la hauteur de tout ce qu'il y a de plus sacré!*"

"I may very well step in there with you, too," I interrupted him. "Yesterday that fellow Vysotsky came to tell me, on behalf of that stupid organizing committee of theirs, that they hoped I'd come to their gala party and act as an usher or whatever they call it—you know, one of the young gentlemen who are supposed to supervise the refreshments, take care of the ladies, make the guests comfortable, and wear a red and white rosette in their lapels. I intended to get out of it, but now I wonder whether I shouldn't use the invitation as a pretext for getting myself admitted to the house and having a good talk with Mrs. von Lembke herself. So we'll go in together."

He listened to me, nodding constantly, but I don't think he took in a word. We were standing by the door now.

"Cher," he said, pointing to the sanctuary lamp under the icon, "I never went in for that sort of thing much, but all right—so be it!" He crossed himself and added, *"Allons!"*

I had hoped that he'd feel better outside, that the fresh air would calm him; that he'd go back home, go to bed, and have a good rest.

But it didn't work out that way. As we were walking along the street, we became involved in an incident that decided Mr. Verkhovensky irrevocably. Yes, I must confess, the energy my poor, dear friend displayed that morning came as a complete surprise to me.

chapter 11

FREEBOOTERS—A FATAL MORNING

I

The incident that occurred on our way to the governor's was really quite extraordinary. I'd better describe it as it unfolded. About an hour before Mr. Verkhovensky and I stepped out into the street, a procession of seventy or more workers from the Shpigulin factory had paraded through the town, watched with curiosity by many people. The men had marched in a quiet, orderly fashion. Later, some people claimed that these seventy men had been elected from among the factory's nine hundred workers to complain to the governor (the owners being absent) about the manager, who had shamelessly cheated them, a fact that had now been established beyond any doubt. Others maintained that the seventy men were not representative of the nine hundred workers at all, because the workers would never have elected so many to form a delegation; that they were simply a batch of the most disgruntled individuals concerned only with their own business and that, therefore, there was no question of an organized revolt. A third group maintained heatedly that the seventy men were not merely rebellious workers but—much worse than that—political revolutionaries; that the group was made up of the most rabid of them, who could only have been brought to this state of political frenzy by subversive literature. In a word, whether or not there was some hidden influence or incitement exerted has never been made plain.

Now, my personal opinion, for whatever it is worth, is that no subversive literature was involved in it at all and that, even if the workers had come across some, and even if they'd read it, they certainly wouldn't have understood a word, because the authors of that sort of thing write so obscurely that it's hard to tell what they mean. And since the workers really were being defrauded at the factory and the police authorities to whom they had complained seemed uninterested in their plight, what could have been more natural than for them to try to address themselves to the governor himself, and, if possible, even to present a written petition to him, throwing themselves at his feet as before Providence and trusting to his sense of justice? I don't think there was any need here for revolt or for a representative delegation, because the procedure is an ancient and historical one—the Russian people have always liked to talk directly to the "big boss," even if simply for the pleasure of it, regardless of what the results of such talks are likely to be.

So I am convinced that if Peter Verkhovensky, Liputin, and even Fedka did go among the workers (and there are concrete indications that they did) to talk to them, they can't have contacted more than two or three men—say, five at the outside—and even that was just an experiment, and they must soon have realized that nothing would come of it. As to a revolt—even if the factory hands had understood any part of the propaganda aimed at them, the chances are that they'd have stopped listening soon enough because it would have sounded inappropriate and inane to them. However, Fedka was another matter. He seems to have been somewhat more successful than Peter. It has been established beyond doubt now that Fedka and two factory hands were involved in starting a fire that broke out three days later in our town. Three other workers were caught in the district three months afterward and convicted of arson. But even if Fedka did manage to draw some workers into direct action, it was only those five, and nothing of the sort can be imputed to any of the other workers at the factory.

Whatever the case may be, the workers arrived quietly and stood in an orderly formation in the small square facing the governor's residence. I'm told they removed their caps as soon as they found themselves in the vicinity of the ruler of the province, although the governor wasn't even home at the time. The police authorities arrived on the scene, first in the persons of individual policemen, then in a whole detachment. Of course, they ordered the demonstrators to disperse. But the workers just stood there stubbornly like a flock of sheep driven against a wall, and declared flatly that they'd come to see the big boss in person. The artificial barking of the policemen ceased and was superseded by quiet deliberations, mysterious whisperings, and some ominously knitted eyebrows on the part of the police authorities in charge. The police chief finally decided to wait for the return of Governor von Lembke himself. It is a pure fabrication that Lembke drove up at full speed in a troika and plunged into the fray before he had even set foot on the ground. It is true, though, that he liked to drive at breakneck speed in his yellow-backed carriage and, as the horses, drunk with speed, became more and more frantic, he liked to draw himself up to his full height, holding onto a strap he had had attached to the carriage for that purpose and stretching his free arm out before him like a figure on a monument. He would survey the town thus, to the great delight of the local shopkeepers.

But in this instance he did not plunge into the fray, although, of course, it was impossible for him to refrain from using a strong expression as he alighted from the carriage; but, even then, he only did so with an eye to his popularity.

And the stories about the summoning of soldiers with fixed bayonets and about telegrams asking for reinforcements of Cossacks and artillery are even further from the truth. They are nothing but fairy tales, and no one believes them today. It is also completely untrue that firemen sprayed the crowd with water. That legend started because the police commissioner, under the pressure of excitement, shouted at the crowd that none of them would get away with it and they'd all "look like a lot of drowned rats by the time they got home." But the Moscow and Petersburg papers reported firemen drenching the crowd.

The most accurate account, I believe, is the one that says a police cordon was immediately thrown around the petitioners and a special messenger dispatched in a police carriage toward Skvoreshniki, in which direction the governor had driven out half an hour before.

But still it remains a mystery to me how an ordinary group of seventy petitioners with nothing particularly unusual about them could be transformed, just like that, in the blink of an eye, into an uprising threatening the very foundations of our society. Why did Lembke himself immediately assume this when he arrived with the messenger twenty minutes later? My private opinion is that it was in the interests of the above-mentioned police commissioner (a great pal of the factory manager's) to present the crowd to the governor in that light and thus avoid an investigation of the matter.

And it was the governor himself who gave him the idea. In the couple of days preceding this the two men had secretly conferred twice, and although these conferences were conducted in rather vague terms, the police commissioner had been left with the definite impression that the governor was stubbornly clinging to the idea that the political pamphlets were having an effect and that he would be very disappointed if the rumors of a subversive plot turned out to be sheer nonsense.

"I suppose he's decided to distinguish himself and make an impression in Petersburg," the police commissioner thought. "Well, why not? I can gain something by it too."

I'm quite sure, though, that our poor governor would not have wished for a revolt even for the sake of an opportunity of distinguishing himself. He was a very conscientious executive who had been perfectly innocent of ambition right up to the time of his marriage. And was it really his fault if, instead of a nice soft post, a home kept snug and warm by some Gretchen, and a free supply of firewood, he had got himself entangled with a forty-year-old princess who wanted to raise him to her level? I can say with almost complete certainty that the symptoms of that state that landed the poor man in that institution in Switzerland, where he's now supposed to be resting, date from that fatal morning. But, as long as we agree that the symptoms of *something* became obvious that morning, we must assume that similar symptoms already existed, although in a less conspicuous form. I have it from the most intimate sources. (All right, let's say Mrs. von Lembke told me some of the story later, when she felt she was no longer at the peak of her glory and was *partly* regretful—inasmuch as a woman is never *altogether* regretful.) Anyway, I know that the previous night Lembke went to his wife's room at exactly three o'clock in the morning, woke her up, and demanded that she listen to his "ultimatum." He was, in fact, so insistent that she was forced to get out of bed, full of indignation and her hair festooned with curling rags, and sit up straight on the sofa to hear him out, although she did, it is true, twist her features into a sarcastic expression. It was then that she realized for the first time what a state her husband was in. She was quite horrified. This was, of course, the moment for her to come to her senses and adopt a mellower attitude toward life, but she kept the shock to herself and became more stubborn than ever. Like all wives, she had her own way of handling her husband and, in using it, she had often driven him to exasperation. Julie von Lembke's method consisted of a scornful silence that might last for one hour, two hours, a day, and sometimes as long as three days. She maintained this silence no matter what happened and regardless of what her husband did, even if he threatened to jump out of the third-floor window. It was enough to drive a sensitive man absolutely insane. Whether Julie was punishing her husband for his errors in judgment or for his jealousy of her administrative talents; or was indignant with him because of his disapproval of the way she behaved with the young set and in our society in general; or was irritated by his stupid jealousy over her and Peter Verkhovensky—she decided she wouldn't yield this time, despite the late hour and her husband's unusual agitation, just as she had never yielded before.

Walking feverishly up and down on the soft carpet of her boudoir, he told her everything, quite disconnectedly it's true, but *everything* that was bothering him, because, as he put it, "it was more than he could stand." He started by declaring that he was a general laughingstock and that he had allowed himself to be "led by the nose."

"I don't give a damn how I put it," he cried shrilly, his voice rising to a squeak when he noticed her sarcastic grin. "Yes, *by the nose*—it's a fact. No, ma'am," he went on, "this is no time for laughing or for airs and graces. This isn't a coy boudoir chat. We're like two human souls in a flying balloon obliged to face the truth!"

Of course, he got mixed up and couldn't find the right words to express his thoughts, correct though they might be.

"It was you, madam, who drove me out of my normal state of mind and forced this governorship on me to satisfy your ambitions. I see you're smiling sarcastically. Wait—don't look so pleased with yourself; let me tell you that I might easily have coped with this job, and ten more like it, because I have plenty of ability. But I can't handle it with you at my side, madam, because when you're near me, I lose all my ability. There's no room for two centers, madam, but you, you insisted on having two centers of authority:

one in my office and the other here in your boudoir. Well, I won't tolerate it any longer! In government, just as in marriage, only one center is possible—having two centers doesn't make any sense." Somewhat later he exclaimed, "And what have I gained from our marriage? It has consisted of your trying to prove to me at every moment of the day how insignificant I am, how stupid and even despicable, while I've tried to show you that I'm not really so insignificant, that I'm not stupid at all, and that everyone's impressed by my probity and high-mindedness. Don't you think it's rather humiliating for both of us?"

At this point he started to stamp both feet on the carpet, and she felt obliged to rise from the sofa with an air of severe and dignified disapproval. His flow of words dried up almost at once and was replaced by self-pity. He started to sob (yes, indeed, to sob), thumping his chest. And this went on for a full five minutes. The governor, driven into a real frenzy by his wife's obstinate silence, lost all control of himself and blurted out that he was jealous of her and Peter. Then, immediately realizing that he had made a terrible blunder, he became furious and shouted that he wasn't going to "stand by and watch them reject God"; that he was going to "scatter that unspeakable crowd in your drawing room"; that it was the duty of a Russian governor to believe in God and, therefore, his wife's duty too; that he wasn't going to tolerate "those young men" any longer. Finally, he said, reproachfully:

"And as to you, madam, your duties called upon you to stand by your husband and respect his intelligence and abilities even if those abilities were mediocre (and my abilities aren't at all mediocre, I'd like you to note). But instead, you bear the main responsibility for making them despise me here. You put them up to it!"

He shouted that he'd stop the agitation for women's rights, he'd smoke it out, he'd break up their idiotic party for the benefit of needy governesses (damn the governesses!), and that the first time he ever came across a governess, he'd have her driven out of the province by his Cossacks. "That'll show you! That'll show you!"

"And are you aware of the fact," he went on, shrilly and furiously, "that your thugs are agitating among the Shpigulin factory hands? Well, I'm very well informed on that subject! And do you know that they've been leaving their sub-versive leaflets all over the place? And may I tell you that I already know the names of four of those thugs? And, also, do you know that I'm going mad—yes, completely, hope-lessly, incurably mad?"

At last Julie von Lembke broke her silence. She told him in a severe, haughty tone that she had known of those criminal schemes all along, but that there was nothing to them; that, speaking of pranksters, she knew the names not only of four of them but of the whole lot (she was lying), but that she saw no reason to lose her sanity over it; that, on the contrary, it even gave her more confidence in her own judgment and in her ability to bring about a harmonious general under-standing: by giving hope to the young people, making them more reasonable, then suddenly revealing to them the fact that their plotting was no secret to her, and then directing them toward more sensible goals and more rewarding activities.

Ah, what her words did to her husband! Seeing that Peter had once again double-crossed him and made him look like an idiot and that, in reality, he had told Julie much more than he had told him, and much earlier, the thought flashed through his head that perhaps Peter himself was the main author of that criminal conspiracy, and he flew into an uncontrollable rage.

"I want you to know, you confused and venomous woman," he screamed, throwing aside all restraint, "I want you to know that I'll have your miserable lover arrested, put in chains, and locked up or—or I'll throw myself out of the window before your very eyes!"

Julie, who had turned green with fury, replied to this tirade with a long, resounding peal of laughter, larded with trills and tremolos, exactly as a Parisian actress performing in the French Theater under a hundred-thousand-ruble con-tract to play the *coquette* roles laughs in her husband's face because he has dared to be jealous over her flirtations.

Lembke ran toward the window, but stopped dead before he reached it, folded his arms on his chest, and pale as a corpse, stared ominously at the laughing woman.

"You know—you know, Julie," he finally managed to sputter gaspingly, in a beseeching tone, "I too, I can do something—"

But this was greeted by a fresh and even louder peal of laughter. The governor clenched his teeth and, moaning aloud, flung himself, not out of the window but at his wife, shaking his fist over her head. Of course, he never lowered it—never, never—but still that was the end of him, right there! Without knowing how he got there, he found himself in his study and, dressed as he was, threw himself face downward on the couch that had been made up into a bed for him, pulling the sheet over him. He remained this way, unsleeping, without thought and with a heavy load on his heart, and immersed in a blank, stagnant despair for two hours. Now and then a violent spasmodic shudder shook his whole body. Strange, incoherent images floated before his eyes: now it was the old wall clock with the broken minute hand he had had in Petersburg fifteen years before; now he remembered how he and a cheerful colleague called Milbois had once caught a sparrow in the Alexandrovsky Park and how, then, suddenly remembering that they had already attained quite solid positions, they had laughed so loudly that they could be heard all over the park. . . . It must have been at least seven in the morning when he finally slipped into sleep without noticing it; he slept pleasantly and had the most delightful dreams.

He awoke at ten, shot out of bed, remembered everything, and slapped his forehead violently with the palm of his hand.

He refused his breakfast, refused to see Blum, refused to receive the police commissioner, and sent packing an official who had come to announce the arrival of a committee from one of the outlying districts of the province. He refused to listen to anything; in fact, he couldn't really make out what they were talking about. He rushed madly to his wife's rooms. There, Sofia Anthropovna, an elderly gentlewoman who had lived with them for many years, explained that his wife had left at ten o'clock, setting out for Skvoreshniki with an entire party in three carriages. They had gone to inspect Mrs. Stavrogin's place, where the party to follow the benefit gala was to be held in two weeks. They had arranged this visit with Mrs. Stavrogin three days previously.

This news dumfounded Lembke. He returned to his study and ordered his carriage. He could hardly wait. His heart was thirsting for Julie—just to look at her, to stay with her for five minutes. She might even glance at him, notice him, smile her familiar smile, and, who knew, she might perhaps forgive him—ah!—

"How long does it take to get the horses ready!"

Without thinking, he opened a big book that lay on his

desk. He sometimes opened it like that at random and read the three first lines on the right-hand page. Now he read: *"Tout est pour le mieux dans le meilleur des mondes possibles. Voltaire, Candide."*

He shrugged and hurried off to the waiting carriage.

"To Skvoreshniki!"

The coachman said later that the governor kept urging him on all the way, but that just as they drove up to the Stavrogins' country house, he suddenly ordered him to turn around and drive back to town.

"And, please, hurry—hurry!"

Before they reached the town's ramparts, the coachman said later:

"The master ordered me to stop, stepped out of the carriage, crossed the road, and walked into a field. I thought the master wished to relieve himself, but then I saw that he was picking flowers and examining them and he went on doing that for a long time and I found it real strange—and I began to wonder. . . ."

That's what was learned from the coachman. I remember the weather that day: it was a clear, sunny September day, although rather windy and cold. Standing in that field by the road, Lembke was facing the bleak, stubble-covered land, over which the whistling wind was roughly swaying a few remaining, half-dead yellow flowers. Perhaps he felt a kinship between his destiny and that of those poor little yellow plants battered by the cold wind and stunted by the autumn frosts. But I don't think so. Indeed, I'm almost sure that was not the case; I think he was quite unaware of the flowers, in spite of what the coachman said, although his testimony was confirmed by the messenger who drove up at that moment in the police commissioner's carriage and who later asserted that he too had seen the governor standing with a bunch of yellow flowers in his hand.

This messenger, a police officer called Vasily Freebootin, was one of those enthusiastic officials; he was still a relative newcomer in our town, but he had already managed to earn himself great renown by his zeal, by the special zest with which he carried out his duties, and by his constant state of inebriation. Jumping down from his carriage and without showing the least surprise at seeing the governor standing rather strangely in the middle of a field, he reported to him in an insane but terribly convincing tone:

"Disturbances have broken out in town, Governor, sir!"

"Ah? What?" Lembke turned toward him, giving him a stern glance that, however, expressed neither surprise nor awareness of what was going on or of where he was. There's no way of telling, but perhaps he thought he was in his study.

"I'm Police Inspector Freebootin of the First District, sir. There's an uprising in the town, sir."

"Freebooters?" Lembke repeated, as if in a dream.

"Yes, sir. The workers at the Shpigulin factory are rioting!"

"Ah, the Shpigulin men!"

The name "Shpigulin" triggered something in the governor's mind. He started, touched his forehead with a finger, muttering "Shpigulin, Shpigulin . . ."

Still without answering the messenger, he walked unhurriedly toward his carriage, got into it, and ordered the coachman to drive to town. Messenger Freebootin followed in the police carriage.

I imagine many curious things must have flashed vaguely through his head while he was on his way, but it appears quite unlikely that he can have had a clear idea of what he was going to do as he drove up to the square facing the gubernatorial mansion. The orderly ranks of the "rioting mob" stood there, surrounded by a police cordon headed by the apparently helpless (perhaps deliberately helpless) police commissioner. And as soon as Lembke caught sight of them, as soon as he realized that everyone was waiting for him to decide something, the blood rushed to his heart. He looked terribly pale as he got out of his carriage.

"Off with your caps!" he said, addressing the "rioters" in a breathless, hardly audible voice. "Down on your knees!" he shrieked suddenly and was himself surprised at the shrill, squeaky notes in his voice. And perhaps it was this unexpected effect upon himself that determined subsequent developments. It was like a sled sliding down a snowy slope—Lembke couldn't stop any more than the sled can in the middle of the slope. Unfortunately for him, throughout his life, Lembke had been remarkable for never losing his temper, never indulging in foot stamping, never even raising his voice—and such people are more vulnerable once they find themselves suddenly launched downhill. The whole world went whirling before his eyes.

"Freebooters!" the governor screamed even more shrilly and

incongruously, his voice breaking. He stood there for a moment still not knowing what he was going to do next, but feeling with all his being that he was going to do something.

"God save us!" a voice came from the crowd.

A young fellow began to cross himself. Three or four men were really about to get down on their knees, but the bulk of the crowd moved three steps forward and then, all of a sudden, they were all shouting at once:

"Governor! Sir! Your Excellency! They never paid us for our time. . . . The manager—he wouldn't listen to us. . . ." And so on, without making much sense.

Lembke, alas, grasped even less of it than anyone else: he was still holding the bunch of yellow flowers in his hand. Riot and violence seemed just as imminent to him as arrest and Siberia had seemed to Stepan Verkhovensky a little earlier. Also, in his mind's eye he kept seeing the figure of Peter Verkhovensky among the "rioting mob," inciting them to violence—the hated figure that had been dancing in his head since the day before without giving him a moment's rest.

"Birch rods!" he yelled all of a sudden, again taking himself by surprise.

A dead silence followed.

That is how it all started, according to the most reliable accounts, which I have filled in with my own conjectures. As to what happened later, the reports become less accurate and my conjectures are consequently more tentative. Some facts, however, are available.

In the first place, birch rods did materialize and, it seems, somewhat hurriedly, as though they had been prepared in advance by the provident police commissioner. However, only two men were flogged—just two, not three, a point upon which I must insist. It is sheer fabrication to say that all the Shpigulin men or half of them were subjected to punishment. Nor is there any truth whatever in the story about an impoverished gentlewoman who happened to be standing innocently by somehow being seized and flogged too. Nevertheless, I later saw such an incident reported in the Petersburg papers as having happened. I've also heard many people talk about a woman named Avdotia Tarapigin who lived in an old-people's home near the cemetery. She was on her way back home after visiting some friends in town and, passing through the town square, elbowed her way through the crowd, prompted by a natural curiosity. When she saw what was happening, she cried, "Damn shame!" and spat, for which she's supposed to have been seized and also "dealt with" accordingly. This incident was reported in the press; also, on the spur of the moment, people of our town organized a subscription for her benefit. I myself subscribed twenty kopecks. And what do you think happened? It turned out that no one by the name of Tarapigin was listed in the town's old-people's home. I even went especially to the establishment by the cemetery where she was supposed to live, but they had never heard of any such person. Indeed, they looked rather offended when I told them about the rumor that was circulating concerning one of their inmates.

But I've mentioned Avdotia Tarapigin because something similar to what happened to her (if it really happened and if she even existed) almost happened to Mr. Verkhovensky. It is even possible that the whole absurd story about the woman originated with him—I mean that, as the gossip developed, Stepan Verkhovensky finally was metamorphosed into an unknown woman called Avdotia Tarapigin.

It is really beyond me how he managed to slip away from me as soon as we got to the square. Full of forebodings, I had attempted to lead him around the square to the gate of the governor's mansion. On the way, though, I was myself overcome by curiosity and stopped to ask someone what was going on, and when I looked around for Mr. Verkhovensky again he had disappeared. Following my intuition, I rushed over to the most dangerous spot to look for him, because for some reason I felt that his sled too had been started down a snowy slope. And, indeed, he was in the very center of events. I remember seizing him by the arm; but he gave me a quiet, proud look, with what was, for him, unusual composure.

"*Cher*," he said in a voice in which I heard a string vibrating that was about to snap, "if they all act so unabashedly here in the square, before our very eyes, what can we expect from *that man*, if he decides to act on his own authority?" Trembling with indignation and full of an immense desire to challenge them, Mr. Verkhovensky thrust an accusing index finger at Police Inspector Freebootin, who was standing nearby and staring at us with his eyes popping out.

"What do you mean by *that man?*" the policeman shouted in a frenzy, clenching his fists. "Which *man* is that? And who are you, anyway?" he roared insanely, straining his vocal cords.

I must add parenthetically that Freebootin knew Stepan Verkhovensky by sight perfectly well.

Another moment and he would've grabbed Mr. Verkhovensky by the collar. Luckily, Lembke turned his head in our direction just then and looked blankly but intently at Mr. Verkhovensky, as though trying to remember something. Suddenly he waved his hand impatiently. Freebootin stopped dead. I dragged Mr. Verkhovensky away, although I think that, by that time, he himself was rather anxious to retreat.

"Let's get out of here," I kept repeating, "let's go back home. It's certainly only thanks to Lembke that we didn't get a good beating."

"You go ahead, my friend. I mustn't expose you to such things—you're young and you have your career to think of, while I—*mon heure est sonnée.*"

And he walked determinedly into the governor's mansion. The porter knew me, and I told him we had both come to see Mrs. von Lembke. We installed ourselves in the reception room and waited. I didn't want to leave my friend, but I had nothing to say to him now. He made me think of a man about to give his life for his fatherland. We didn't sit next to each other but on opposite sides of the room: I near the entrance door, he facing me on the other side of the room. His head was lowered and he seemed deep in thought, one hand leaning lightly on his walking stick, the other holding his wide-brimmed hat. We sat there like that for ten minutes.

II

Lembke came in, walking quickly, with the police chief following close behind him. He gave us an absent-minded look and was about to turn to the right to go into his study without paying any further attention to us when Mr. Verkhovensky barred his way. This tall figure, so out of the ordinary, produced its effect. The governor stopped.

"Who's this?" he muttered, puzzled and apparently addressing the police chief, although he didn't turn toward him or take his gaze from Mr. Verkhovensky.

"Retired Collegiate Assessor Stepan Trofimovich Verkhovensky, Your Excellency," Mr. Verkhovensky answered, bowing with majestic poise.

The governor stared at him, still rather blankly.

"What is it?" he inquired in the laconic tone of a high official, turning his ear toward Mr. Verkhovensky with unconcealed impatience and distaste. He had evidently decided that he was dealing with an ordinary petitioner who was about to present some written request to him.

"I was subjected to a house search earlier today by an official acting in your name, sir, and I would like to—"

"What was that name? What name?" Lembke asked impatiently as though something had suddenly dawned on him.

Mr. Verkhovensky repeated his name with even greater poise.

"Aha! So that's it—the source of subversion. Let me tell you, sir, your activities—you're a professor, aren't you?"

"Once I did have the honor of offering a course of lectures to young university students."

"To young students!" The governor suddenly twitched, although I am sure he hardly knew what he was saying or even, perhaps, whom he was addressing. "Well, I won't tolerate that, sir!" he shouted, growing terribly angry all of a sudden. "I won't allow those young men—it's all those subversive leaflets! It's an attack on our institutions! It's a piracy, it's freebootery!—anyway, what was your request?"

"I have no request. On the contrary, your wife asked me to give a reading at her party tomorrow. I have come here now to claim my legal rights—"

"My wife's party? There will be no party! I won't allow any such party, sir! So you lecture? You lecture?" he repeated frantically.

"I would appreciate it very much if you would address me more civilly, Your Excellency, and if you would stop stamping your feet and shouting at me as though I were a small boy."

"Do you realize whom you're addressing?" Lembke said, turning purple.

"Yes, perfectly well, sir."

"I am here to protect our institutions, and you are trying to destroy them! Yes, des-troy! You! But I remember something about you now: you used to be employed as a tutor in Mrs. Stavrogin's house, isn't that right?"

"Yes, I used to be . . . employed as a tutor . . . in Mrs. Stavrogin's house."

"And for twenty years you've been sowing the seeds of all we are reaping now. It's all the fruit of your labor. Didn't I see you on the square just a moment ago? Well, you'd better watch out, sir, you'd just better, because I'm well aware of your views. Don't worry, I have my eye on you. I, sir, cannot allow you to go on giving lectures—I won't allow it! Don't come to me with such requests!" And he was about to walk on.

"I repeat: you are mistaken again, Your Excellency. Mrs. von Lembke asked me to give a literary reading at her party tomorrow, not a lecture. But I have come to decline her invitation. Now, I humbly beg you to explain to me, if you can, for what reason and on what grounds I was subjected to a house search today? They took some books and some private papers and letters that were of personal value to me, loaded them on a wheelbarrow, and wheeled them away through the town."

"Who was it searched you?" Lembke said with a start, suddenly realizing clearly what it was all about and blushing. He glanced quickly at the police chief. Just then Blum's clumsy, stooping, long-legged figure appeared in the doorway.

"Why, sir, that official over there," Mr. Verkhovensky said, pointing at Blum, who stepped forward with a guilty expression, but without appearing at all willing to give up the fight.

"*Vous ne faites que des bêtises,*" Lembke hissed at him exasperated. He seemed to have realized all at once what was going on. "I'm sorry," he muttered in a state of extreme embarrassment, turning as red as it was possible for him to turn, "it was all—it was obviously a mistake, a misunderstanding—just a misunderstanding."

"Your Excellency," Mr. Verkhovensky said, "once, when I was still a young man, I happened to witness a very revealing incident. Once, in a theater, someone rushed up to another man and publicly gave him a resounding slap. But when he looked at his victim and realized that he was not at all the person for whom the slap had been intended and only vaguely resembled him at best, the assailant—who seemed to be in a hurry and rather irritated—said, as you did just now, sir, 'It was a mistake; I'm sorry. It was simply a misunderstanding.' And finding the offended party was still full of resentment, th-offender repeated with audible annoyance, 'But since I've explained to you that it was a misunderstanding, why do you keep on protesting?' "

"That, of course, is very—very funny," Lembke said, smiling crookedly, "but—but can't you really see that I myself am very, very unhappy about it, most unhappy . . ."

He uttered these last words very shrilly, almost screaming them, giving the impression that he wanted to cover his face with his hands. This unexpected, agonized outcry, ending almost in a sob, was unbearable. That was probably the first moment that a complete realization of what had been happening since the day before came over him. And the realization was immediately followed by despair—unmitigated, humiliating, overwhelming despair. And, who knows, in another second, the reception room might have been filled with his sobs had not Mr. Verkhovensky, who at first had gaped at him in bewilderment, almost immediately bowed his head and said in a voice loaded with emotion:

"Please don't worry any more about my ill-tempered complaint, Your Excellency; just tell them to send me back my books and letters—"

He was unable to finish. At that moment, Julie von Lembke, accompanied by her friends, returned to the gubernatorial mansion. But I think I ought to describe what happened in considerable detail.

III

The whole company had arrived in the three carriages and now filed into the reception room. A special entrance to the left of the gate led directly to Mrs. von Lembke's rooms, but this time her friends had come in through the main entrance and the reception rooms, and I believe that Mr. Verkhovensky was the reason for this, because both what had happened to him and the incident with the Shpigulin workers had reached Julie's ears as she drove into town. She had been informed by Lyamshin, who, as a punishment for some misdemeanor, had not been taken along. Remaining in town, he was the first of the circle to hear about it. Full of spiteful glee, he hired a nag and galloped toward Skvoreshniki to meet the returning cavalcade and share the exciting news with them. I assume that,

despite her previous determination, Julie was somewhat overcome when she heard about these strange happenings, but, if
so, she immediately recovered. The political aspect of the
incident couldn't possibly have worried her—Peter Verkhovensky had repeated to her about four times that those
Shpigulin ruffians ought to be given a good flogging and,
indeed, for some time now, Peter had been a great authority
in her eyes. "But still," she must have said to herself, "I'll
make *him* pay for all this," and, by *him* she of course meant
her husband.

Let me say in passing that this time Peter hadn't taken part
in their expedition and that it happened that none of them had
seen him since the morning. I think it should also be mentioned that, having received these people at Skvoreshniki,
Mrs. Stavrogin, who wanted to be present at the final committee meeting concerning tomorrow's reception, had driven
to town in their company and, indeed, had shared Mrs. von
Lembke's carriage. She too, of course, couldn't fail to be
interested and even moved by Lyamshin's news concerning
the senior Verkhovensky.

Mrs. von Lembke settled accounts with her husband immediately. And he felt it coming too. Smiling disarmingly, she
walked rapidly over to Mr. Verkhovensky, gracefully held out
her elegantly gloved hand to him, and showered him with the
most flattering compliments, as though she had only been
waiting for this opportunity to convey to him her appreciation
for his coming to her house. She gave no hint that she had
already heard about the search to which he had been subjected
that morning.

She didn't say a word to her husband, never even looked
in his direction, and behaved as though he weren't there. She
went even further—she whisked Mr. Verkhovensky off to her
drawing room, either not noticing that he and the governor
were in the middle of an explanation of the matter or else
implying that, even if they were, the explanation had become
pointless now. Let me emphasize here that, in spite of her
refined, worldly ways, Julie von Lembke made a bad *gaffe* on
this particular occasion, a *gaffe* for which a considerable share
of the responsibility must be borne by Mr. Karmazinov.

Mr. Karmazinov had joined the expedition on Mrs. von
Lembke's special insistence and thus had finally paid a visit
to Mrs. Stavrogin, who was weak enough to be absolutely
delighted, even though it was an impersonal visit. Now he

entered the reception room after the others and, while still in the doorway, caught sight of Mr. Verkhovensky. He opened his arms wide for an embrace and, interrupting Mrs. von Lembke, shouted:

"Ah, my dear friend! Haven't seen you for ages and ages!"

He insisted on going through the kissing ceremony, starting of course by presenting his own cheek to be kissed. And, taken by surprise as he was, Mr. Verkhovensky did imprint a kiss on it.

Later in the evening, reviewing the events of that day, Mr. Verkhovensky said to me:

"Shall I tell you what I was thinking of at that moment, *cher*? Well, I was wondering which of the two of us was the most loathsome. Was it he hugging me just so that he could humble me then and there, or was it I, despising him and his cheek, and nevertheless kissing it instead of turning away. . . . Brrr!"

"Well, tell me—tell me everything about yourself," Karmazinov rattled on, lisping as he talked, as though it were really possible for Mr. Verkhovensky to reel off his whole life, just like that, in twenty-five minutes. But then, such silly, meaningless insistence was *chic* and in the best of taste.

Mr. Verkhovensky answered sensibly and therefore not in the best of taste.

"Surely you realize," he said, "that the last time we met was at a dinner in honor of Granovsky and that twenty-four years have elapsed since then—"

"*Ce cher homme!*" Karmazinov interrupted him shrilly, patting him rather too familiarly on the shoulder. "Please, Mrs. von Lembke, take us quickly to your drawing room, so he can sit down and tell us all about himself."

"And yet I was never a close friend of that peevish old woman's," Mr. Verkhovensky told me that evening, shaking with anger. "We met when we were still almost boys and, even then, I loathed him, and he, me, of course."

Julie von Lembke's drawing room filled quickly. Mrs. Stavrogin was very agitated, although she tried to look composed. I caught a couple of hate-filled glances she cast at Karmazinov and a few irate looks directed at Mr. Verkhovensky, irate in advance, irate out of jealousy and love: I think that if Mr. Verkhovensky had blundered this time and given Karmazinov an opportunity to slight him in front of everybody, she would have pounced on him and struck him.

Ah, I almost forgot to mention that Liza was there too and never before had I seen her looking so cheerful, so recklessly gay, so happy. And, of course, Maurice Drozdov had come along too. Finally, among the semidissolute young ladies and gentlemen who comprised Mrs. von Lembke's retinue (with whom dissoluteness passed for *joie de vivre* and cheap cynicism for intelligence), I noticed three new faces: a very obsequious Pole who was just passing through our town, a healthy-looking old German doctor who again and again burst into loud, delighted laughter at his own jokes, and some very youthful princeling from Petersburg, a real little manikin with the grand airs of a statesman and an incredibly high collar. Julie von Lembke obviously valued him very highly and was even worried that her *salon* might not make a favorable impression upon him.

"*Cher Monsieur* Karmazinov," Stepan Verkhovensky began, assuming a gracefully nonchalant pose on the divan and lisping so much that he almost outdid Karmazinov, "let me say this: the life story of a man of our generation who had certain intellectual leanings would sound rather dull, even if you took a whole twenty-five-year slice at a time—"

The German burst out into a loud, abrupt laugh, neighing as though he thought that that was a hilarious thing to say. Mr. Verkhovensky looked at him in surprise, but the German didn't even seem to notice. The princeling also turned toward the German, tall collar and all, put on his pince-nez, and looked the laughing man over, although without any apparent curiosity.

"Yes, it would sound quite dull," Mr. Verkhovensky repeated, drawling every word exaggeratedly. "Yes, and dull my life has been, indeed, during the past quarter century *et comme on trouve partout plus de moines que de raison*—a thought with which I am in full agreement—it follows that during the entire quarter century, I—"

"*C'est charmant,* the way he puts it about *les moines,*" Mrs. von Lembke whispered, turning toward Mrs. Stavrogin, who was sitting next to her.

Mrs. Stavrogin looked at her, full of pride. But Karmazinov resented Mr. Verkhovensky's success with the French saying and shrilly interrupted him.

"As far as I'm concerned, I've been living in Karlsruhe for over six years now, so I'm no longer bothered by such problems. When, last year, the town council decided to lay a water main, I felt deep in my heart that the Karlsruhe water main was dearer and more important to me than all the problems connected with so-called reforms in my beloved homeland."

"I can't help sympathizing, although it goes against my grain," Mr. Verkhovensky sighed.

Julie von Lembke was delighted: the conversation was becoming profound—and with political overtones.

"Did you say a main sewer?" the doctor asked loudly.

"No, Doctor, the water main. I even helped them to draft the bill at the time."

The doctor emitted a rattling laugh. Many others laughed too, openly amused at the doctor. But he didn't realize it and was very pleased that everyone else had laughed.

"I'm afraid I must disagree with you this time, Karmazinov," Julie von Lembke hastened to interpose. "The Karlsruhe water main is all very fine, but I still say that you just love to mystify people and in this particular instance I simply don't believe you. Tell me, of all Russian writers, who has created as many modern types and raised as many topical problems as you have? And who was it who pointed out the main characteristics of the modern statesman? You—you, and you alone! So how can you claim you're indifferent to your native land and completely absorbed in the Karlsruhe water mains? Ha-ha!"

"Yes, of course, of course," Karmazinov lisped, "in the character of Pogozhev I did show all the faults of the Slavophiles and in that of Nikodimov, all the faults of the Westerners—"

"*All* the faults? I wonder," Lyamshin muttered, almost under his breath.

"But I do that sort of thing *en passant*, just to kill time and to satisfy the insistent demands of my fellow countrymen."

"I suppose you've already heard, Mr. Verkhovensky," Julie von Lembke said enthusiastically, "that tomorrow we'll have the opportunity of listening to some charming lines. One of the latest of Mr. Karmazinov's exquisite literary inspirations. It's entitled *Merci*. He is announcing in the piece that he is giving up writing, that nothing will ever make him write again, that even if an angel, nay, the whole heavenly host, descended from the sky and begged him, he still wouldn't alter his resolution. Well, in a word, he is putting down his pen for good and this graceful *Merci* is addressed to the public, to thank them for their constant enthusiasm that, for so many years, has hailed his unswerving services to truly Russian thought."

Julie von Lembke felt she was in Seventh Heaven.

"Yes, I will take my leave, say my *Merci* to them, and depart. Then, over there, in Karlsruhe, I'll close my eyes and . . ." Karmazinov said, gradually filling up with self-pity.

Like so many of our great writers (and we do have a lot of them), Karmazinov couldn't resist praise; he melted under it immediately, despite his considerable sense of humor. But I think this is excusable. I've heard that one of our Shakespeares once even blurted out, in a private conversation, something to the effect that "we great men, we cannot help . . ." and so on, and didn't even notice it.

"Yes, there, far away, in Karlsruhe, I will close my eyes. We great men," Karmazinov, too, said now, "once we have accomplished our mission, must quickly close our eyes, without looking for rewards. And that's exactly what I intend to do."

"Give me the address and I'll come to Karlsruhe and visit your grave," the German said, laughing unabashedly.

"But nowadays they transport corpses by railroad," one of the inconsequential young men suddenly remarked.

Lyamshin squeaked with delight. Mrs. von Lembke frowned.

At that moment Nikolai Stavrogin walked into the drawing room. He walked straight up to Mr. Verkhovensky.

"But I was told they'd taken you to the police station," he said to him rather loudly.

"Well, I was lucky—a change of *policy* saved me from the *police* in the nick of time," Mr. Verkhovensky said, trying for a pun.

"But I do hope that this incident won't prevent you from accepting my invitation to read your piece tomorrow," Mrs. von Lembke quickly interposed. "I am certain that, despite this unfortunate occurrence—and this is the first I've heard of it—you won't disappoint us, you won't deprive us of the pleasure of hearing you read at my literary matinee."

"I'm not sure, you see; no, I am—"

"Really, Mrs. Stavrogin, I am so appallingly unlucky! Imagine, just when I am about to get to know one of the outstanding, independent Russian thinkers personally, he suddenly seems to want to keep his distance from us."

"That compliment was made too loudly for me to pretend

not to hear it," Mr. Verkhovensky said. "Nevertheless, I cannot believe that my poor personality can be so indispensable to your reception tomorrow. But since, after all—"

"Ah, but you spoil him too much!" shouted Peter Verkhovensky, bursting into the room. "I'd just taken him in hand and now, all of a sudden, in a single day, he is searched, arrested, collared by a policeman, and finally petted by ladies in the governor's own drawing room! I bet every cell in his body is swollen with rapture—he never even dreamed of such a moment! You'll see—any moment now he'll start writing secret denunciations of his socialist friends!"

"That's impossible, Peter; socialism is too great an idea for your father to ignore it!" Mrs. von Lembke said, coming energetically to the old man's defense.

"It is a great idea indeed, although those who advocate it are not necessarily always great people. Let's let it go at that, my boy," Mr. Verkhovensky said with finality, rising gracefully from his seat.

But here something unforeseen happened. For some time, Governor von Lembke had been in the drawing room. No one had paid any attention to him, although they had all noticed him come in. His wife had continued her policy of ignoring him. He had remained standing by the door, listening dejectedly to the conversation. When he heard the morning's incidents mentioned, he fidgeted uneasily and, for some reason, fixed his stare on the prince, struck, probably, by his stiff, starched collar. Then he heard Peter's voice and saw him run into the room. Before the senior Verkhovensky even had time to finish his sentence, Lembke started moving toward him. On his way, he brushed against Lyamshin, who jumped back with affected surprise, rubbing his shoulder and pretending to have been hurt in the collision with the governor.

"Enough!" von Lembke said, violently seizing the frightened Mr. Verkhovensky's hand and pressing it hard in his own. "Enough! the freebooters of our day have been unmasked. No more about it; all the necessary measures have been taken."

He said it with a great deal of conviction and in a loud voice that resounded all over the room. The general impression was quite painful. Everyone felt that something was wrong. I saw his wife go pale. And then this effect was topped by a silly incident: after announcing that all the necessary measures had been taken, Lembke turned around and walked briskly toward the door; however, a couple of steps short of it, he tripped over a rug, lurched forward, and almost fell. Regaining his balance, he stopped, stared for a second at the spot where he had tripped, muttered aloud, "It must be replaced!" and made his exit. Mrs. von Lembke rushed out after him.

When she had left, there was a general uproar in which it was very difficult to make out what was happening. Some said that he was just depressed, others that he was a bit "touched," others just pointed to their foreheads, while Lyamshin in his corner stuck two fingers above his forehead like a pair of horns. Some hints were made about family troubles. All this, of course, in whispers. No one seemed to think of grabbing his hat and leaving; they were all somehow waiting for something.

I have no idea what she could have accomplished in that time, but Mrs. von Lembke was back within five minutes, trying hard to look calm and composed. She said evasively that the governor was a little upset, that it was nothing important, that he had suffered from these spells since childhood, but that she knew better than to worry about them, and that, of course, her reception would take place the next day as scheduled. Then she paid a few more compliments to Mr. Verkhovensky, but only because she felt she had to, and suggested in a loud voice that the committee members should go ahead and hold their meeting. Only on that suggestion did those who were not members of the committee begin to take their leave. But this was still not the end of the painful events of that fatal day.

From the moment that Stavrogin had entered the drawing room, I had noticed that Liza was looking at him intently, never once taking her eyes off him, so that finally she began to attract attention. I saw Maurice Drozdov lean toward her from behind, apparently to whisper something into her ear, but he must have changed his mind because he straightened up again and looked around with a guilty expression. Stavrogin also aroused general curiosity. His face was paler than usual and he had an extremely absent-minded look about him. After his first remarks to Mr. Verkhovensky, Stavrogin seemed to forget about him completely. I don't think he even remembered to go and pay his compliments to the mistress of the house. He never once glanced at Liza and I am convinced that this was not deliberate but simply because he hadn't noticed her either. And now, immediately in the wake of Mrs.

von Lembke's invitation to the committee members to proceed with their meeting, Liza's purposely loud voice resounded in the drawing room, calling Stavrogin:

"I say, Nikolai, there's some captain who claims to be a relative of yours, a brother of your wife's or something—someone by the name of Lebyatkin who keeps writing me indecent letters in which he also complains about you and offers to reveal some secrets about you. If he really is a relative of yours, I would appreciate it if you'd tell him to stop bothering me and thus spare me so much unpleasantness."

There was a threatening challenge in those words, and everyone present heard it. The implication was obvious, although perhaps unexpected even to Liza herself. She was like a person jumping off a roof with her eyes half closed.

But Stavrogin's answer was even more surprising.

"Yes, I do have the misfortune to be related to that man," he said, "having been married to his sister, whose maiden name was Maria Lebyatkin, for five years now. Please rest assured, I will convey your demand to him and I promise he won't annoy you any more in the future."

I shall never forget the horror on Mrs. Stavrogin's face. She rose to her feet, a frenzied look on her face and her right hand raised as if to ward off a blow. Nikolai Stavrogin looked at his mother, at Liza, at the rest of the guests, smiled with unconveyable scorn, and casually walked out of the room.

We all saw Liza leap up from her seat as soon as Stavrogin turned to go, obviously on the point of rushing after him. However, she regained control of herself and, instead of dashing, also walked out very slowly, without saying a word to or looking at anyone. Maurice Drozdov, of course, followed her.

I shall say nothing about the uproar and the talk that this caused in town. Mrs. Stavrogin locked herself in her town house and it was said that Nikolai had gone straight to Skvoreshniki without seeing her. Mr. Verkhovensky sent me over to *cette chère amie* that night to plead with her to allow him to come to see her; but they didn't even let me in. He was terribly shocked and wept disconsolately, repeating over and over:

"Ah, what a marriage, what a *mésalliance;* how horrible for the family!"

Then, however, he remembered Karmazinov and began to abuse him. He also prepared energetically for his public appearance the next day and—ah, the artistic nature!—rehearsed before the mirror, trying to memorize some apt witticisms and puns from among those he had coined in his lifetime and written down in a special notebook to slip into his reading.

"My friend, I'm doing all this for the sake of the great idea," he said to me, as if justifying himself. "You see, *cher ami,* I've stood still for twenty-five years and now, suddenly, I'm on the move—I don't know where to, but I'm certainly on my way."

Part Three

chapter 1

<small>THE FESTIVITIES BEGIN</small>

I

The reception took place on schedule, despite the previous day's confusion involving the Shpigulin workers. I think that even if Lembke had died that night, the reception would have been held in the morning, because of the particular importance his wife attributed to it. She was, alas, blinded to reality and failed completely to perceive the prevailing mood. As the day approached, no one thought the event would pass off without the occurrence of something that would cause a colossal scandal—without things coming to a head, as some put it, rubbing their hands together in anticipation. Although many tried to look frowningly disapproving or diplomatically noncommittal, most looked forward to a public scandal, a thing in which Russians in general delight inordinately. There was, however, something more serious in it than a mere longing for a good row. There was a sort of general irritation, something implacably malevolent—everyone seemed suddenly disgusted with everything. The prevailing mood was one of mixed-up cynicism—a kind of forced, self-imposed cynicism. There was only one feeling about which there was no confusion, at least as far as the ladies were concerned, and that was relentless hatred for Julie von Lembke. All the feminine factions were agreed on this, but the poor woman didn't have the slightest inkling of it; to the very last minute she imagined that she was surrounded by followers who were "fanatically devoted" to her, as she liked to say.

I have mentioned before that various strange characters had appeared in our midst. In troubled, transitional times, all sorts of types crop up. I'm not talking here about the "progressive" elements who are always in a hurry and whose main concern (stupid though it may be) is to stay ahead of others in the pursuit of a more or less definite goal. No, here I have in mind just the scum. This scum, which exists in every society, comes to the surface during troubled times. They not only lack any particular ideological goals, they don't even have a single thought in their heads, their appearance being simply a symptom of the general unrest and impatience. Without realizing it themselves, they almost always become the instrument of small "progressive" cliques who are pursuing definite objectives and who channel this human flotsam into whatever direction they deem necessary—that is, unless the cliques themselves consist entirely of complete idiots, which, it must be said, often happens too.

In our town, now that everything is over, it is said that Peter Verkhovensky was controlled by the International, and he controlled Mrs. von Lembke, who, in her turn and under his directions, controlled the scum. The most highly reputed of our local brains are still wondering how they could have been taken in at the time. What caused our unrest and, if it was a period of transition, what it was a transition from and to—neither I nor, I believe, anyone could tell, except, perhaps, certain visitors from out of town. In any event, it happened—all sorts of insignificant, obscure characters, who before had never even dared open their mouths, suddenly gained the upper hand and started criticizing all our sacred institutions aloud and those who until then had occupied the leading positions started listening to them in silence, some among them even shamelessly tittering in approval.

The Lyamshins and Telyatnikovs of this world; types like Gogol's landowner, Tentetnikov; home-grown snivelers like Rodishchev; Jews with their sorrowful and arrogant smiles; guffawing passers-by; political poets from the capital; poets who made up for their lack of politics or, for that matter, of talent, by wearing peasant shirts and boots; army majors and colonels gleefully buzzing about the senselessness of their profession, who, if promised they would make an extra ruble, were ready to take off their swords and desert the army for a position as a railway clerk; generals turned lawyers; "progressive" arbitrators between landowners and peasants; merchants with a penchant for self-enlightenment; innumerable divinity students; women obsessed with feminism—all these suddenly gained the upper hand in our town. And over whom did they gain it? Over our club, over senior government officials, over generals with wooden legs, over our most strait-laced and unapproachable society ladies.

Since, for all practical purposes, even Mrs. Stavrogin was at the beck and call of this scum right up to the time of her son's catastrophe, attenuating circumstances may be invoked to explain the temporary aberrations of other local Minervas. Now, in retrospect, as I have already mentioned, the hand of the International is seen in everything. This notion became so deeply rooted that, on the basis of it, people made denunciations to the investigators from outside. Quite recently, a sixty-two-year-old councilor, wearing the order of St. Stanislav, came forth and testified voluntarily in emotional tones that, for three months, he himself had been strongly influenced by the International. When, however, with all due respect to his age and position, he was invited to be a little more specific, he had no evidence to offer, only insisting that he "felt it in his bones." And he refused so stubbornly to budge from this statement that it was decided that further cross-examination would serve no purpose.

As I have already said, there was among us a small group who remained aloof from the start and even, as it were, secluded themselves behind locked doors. But, let me ask you, what lock could ever hold against the laws of nature? Even the strictest families produce girls who feel an unconquerable urge to go dancing. And so all these careful people wound up by subscribing to the benefit for needy governesses.

The ball was expected to be an unprecedentedly brilliant affair. There were rumors that it would be attended by lorgnette-wearing princes from out of town; that ten handsome young bachelors with ribbons across their shoulders were to act as ushers; that some very important Petersburg figures were the prime movers of the whole affair; that, as an additional enticement to subscribers, Karmazinov had consented to read his piece, *Merci*, dressed as a governess of our province; that there was going to be a "literary quadrille," also in fancy dress, with each costume representing a literary movement. Finally, someone symbolizing something described as "Honest Russian

Thought," also appropriately attired, was to perform a dance
—which, of course, would be quite a novelty in itself. So how
could one resist? Everyone subscribed.

II

The festivities were divided into two parts: a literary matinee
from noon to four P.M. and then a ball from ten on, throughout the night. Now, this arrangement actually carried the germs
of trouble within it. To start with, the public somehow got the
impression that lunch was going to be served during a special
intermission in the literary entertainment—a complimentary
lunch, of course, and with champagne. The rather exorbitant
price of the tickets—three rubles—seemed to justify this impression. "They can't charge that much for nothing," people
reasoned, "and the program is scheduled to last almost twenty-
four hours, so they'll have to feed us: people are bound to get
hungry in that time."

It must be said that this disastrous expectation was due to
Mrs. von Lembke's own impulsiveness. A month earlier, when
she was still under the first spell of her great project, she had
gone around chattering about it to everyone she met and had
even sent a small item to a Petersburg paper in which she
mentioned that toasts would be offered in the course of her
reception. At that time she was more excited about those
toasts than anything else; she wanted to propose them herself and in preparation kept wording and rewording them.
These toasts were supposed to explain our main motto (what
this motto was to be I don't know; I'll bet the poor lady never
managed to compose a single toast), to be reported in the
national press, to delight and touch the high authorities, and to
spread to every province in the country, arousing surprise and
stimulating emulation.

But toasts cannot be proposed without champagne and since
champagne cannot be drunk on an empty stomach, the serving
of lunch to the guests became a necessity.

Later, however, when through Mrs. von Lembke's own efforts an organizing committee was formed and a more businesslike approach was adopted, it was pointed out to her that if
she was going to insist on having a whole banquet, very little
money would be left for the needy governesses, even if the sub-

scriptions surpassed all expectations. The committee presented her with the following alternatives: it was to be either a Belshazzar's feast with toasts and speeches which would leave perhaps ninety rubles for the governesses, or just a formal entertainment with an impressive sum left intact for the noble cause. But, of course, the committee presented Mrs. von Lembke with this dramatic choice only to impress the need to be practical upon her, for, in the end, it came up with a reasonable compromise itself: a fairly lavish reception in every respect, although without champagne, that would leave a substantial sum—in any case, much more than ninety rubles—for the governesses.

However, Julie von Lembke didn't agree. Her fiery nature scorned this vulgar, middle-of-the-road solution. She decided then and there that if the first way was impractical, they would go to the other extreme and raise such huge funds for the governesses that they would stir up envy in every other province.

"The public must realize after all," she concluded her fiery committee speech, "that the achievement of an objective that is of universal human concern is of an infinitely higher order of interest than the transient gratification of bodily appetites; that, in the final analysis, the purpose of our gathering is the proclamation of a great idea and that, therefore, we must be content with a frugal, German-style entertainment, offered simply as a symbol, since it seems we cannot do without the wretched ball altogether!"

That was the extent to which she had finally come to hate it.

But the others succeeded in moderating her resolve. It was at this juncture, for instance, that they came up with the idea of the "literary quadrille" and other aesthetic delights to make up for the lack of more carnal pleasures. And it was at this point, too, that Karmazinov definitely promised to read his piece, *Merci* (until then he had kept tantalizing the committee by shilly-shallying), supposedly obliterating the very thought of food from the minds of the incontinent public. Thus, the ball again became the brilliant gala that had been planned in the first place, although in a somewhat different style.

Finally, to prevent the affair from being too ethereal, it was decided that at the beginning of the reception the guests would be served tea with lemon and plain cookies, and later cool drinks such as lemonade, and perhaps even ice cream. But that was all they would get.

Now, for those afflicted with insatiable appetites, and, more particularly, thirst, a special buffet to be run by Prokhorich, the club's chef, was to be arranged. There, under the committee's strict supervision, of course, the guests could obtain whatever they wanted—for a price, a point that was to be made very clear by a notice near the ballroom door announcing that the buffet was not part of the program.

Later, however, it was decided to discard the idea of a buffet during the matinee altogether, for fear it might distract attention from the literary entertainment, although it would have been five rooms away from the White Hall in which Karmazinov had consented to read his *Merci*.

It is curious that even the practical members of the committee should have ascribed such significance to Karmazinov's appearance. At to the members with artistic aspirations—well, the head landowner's wife, for instance, declared that as soon as he had finished his reading, she would have a marble slab fixed to the wall with gold lettering informing posterity that on such and such a date a great Russian and European writer, who had decided to lay down his pen, had read his *Merci* there for the first time, thus saying farewell to the Russian public as represented by our town. This inscription was to be in place in time to be read during the evening ball—that is, only five hours after the reading of *Merci*.

I have it from unimpeachable sources that it was Karmazinov himself who categorically insisted that there should be no buffet under any pretext while he was reading, despite the objection of some committee members that this was not the way we usually did things in our town.

Such was the real situation, while the general public was expecting a Belshazzar's feast—that is, a complimentary buffet —right up to the very last moment. Even young girls dreamed of lots of sweets, jams, and all sorts of delicacies. It was common knowledge that the receipts were enormous, that the whole town was anxious to attend the festivities, that people were coming in from outlying districts especially for the event, and that there were not enough tickets to go around. People also knew that considerable voluntary contributions had been made above the price marked on the tickets. Thus, Mrs. Stavrogin had paid three hundred rubles for her ticket and was also contributing flowers from her hothouse to decorate the ballroom; the head landowner's wife contributed her house and the lighting; the club put an orchestra, servants, and the services of Prokhorich at the committee's disposal for the entire day. There were many more contributions that, although not as impressive, were nevertheless substantial enough to make the organizers consider, at one point, reducing the admission charge from three to two rubles. Indeed, the committee was at first afraid that young girls might stay home if they had to pay three rubles for admission and suggested that special family tickets be issued that would enable a family to bring ten girls free if they paid for one. But all these fears proved to be unfounded because the girls were the first to secure tickets. Even the poorest clerks brought their girls, and it was only too obvious that if they hadn't had young ladies in their families, the idea of buying a ticket would never even have occurred to them. One very hard-up petty employee brought his seven daughters, his wife, and also a niece; to see each of them holding a three-ruble admission ticket in her hand was an impressive sight.

Just imagine the agitation all this caused in town! Merely the division of the festivities into two parts implied that each lady had to have two different dresses—one for the literary matinee and another for the evening ball. Many people of moderate income, it was later discovered, pawned even the family linen and mattresses with our local Jews. (A number of Jews had settled in our town in the previous two years and more are still arriving.) Almost all the civil servants asked for advances on their salaries and many landowners sold some of their cattle, just to have their young ladies look like princesses and hold their own with the others. The magnificence of dress on this occasion reached an all-time high for our town. For a fortnight before the event, the town buzzed with revealing family stories that the gossips swarming around Mrs. von Lembke hastened to pass on to her. Witty caricatures depicting the predicaments of certain families were circulated from hand to hand, and I myself saw some such sketches in Mrs. von Lembke's scrapbook. Later, the victims of these jokes became aware of what was going on and I believe that this was one of the reasons for the sudden outburst of hatred for Julie von Lembke in some families. Now people abuse her and gnash their teeth when they remember what happened, but it was quite clear then that if the committee made the slightest mistake and displeased the public, there would be an unprecedented outburst of indignation. This is why everyone felt that a scandal

was imminent and, since they all expected it, how could it
fail to materialize?

At noon sharp the orchestra started to play. Since I was one
of the ushers described on the program as the "young
gentlemen with a ribbon across their left shoulders," I witnessed the opening of these festivities of deplorable memory.
It began with an incredible melee at the doors. From the
beginning, everything went wrong that day, starting with
the failure of the police to carry out their duties properly.
I'm not talking here about our ordinary townspeople: the
fathers of families didn't do any pushing. Indeed, none of
them even tried to take advantage of his social standing.
I am told that, on the contrary, they rather hung back while
still outside in the street, shocked by the sight of a crowd
such as had never been seen in our town before. It was
more like a mob besieging a fortress and trying to take it
by assault, than a group of ordinary people simply wishing
to enter a house.

Carriages kept driving up all the time, until finally the
whole street was blocked.

Now, as I write this, I have good grounds for asserting
that some of the lowest scum in our town were smuggled
in without tickets by Lyamshin and Liputin and probably
by some of the other ushers. And there were also people
no one had ever seen before who must have come from
out of town or even from outside our province. As soon as
these uncouth characters set foot in the house, as if by
prearranged plan, they asked the way to the buffet. And
then, when they were told that there was no buffet, they
became extremely abusive, using language to which we were
not at all accustomed. Some of them, it is true, were already
drunk when they arrived. Many of these savages, however,
seemed struck by the splendor of the head landowner's house,
having never seen anything approaching it before; they stared
with their mouths open and for the first few moments were
quiet and subdued.

It must be said that the great reception hall that so
overawed them, although a bit dilapidated and in need of
repair, was, indeed, rather impressive. It was huge, with two
rows of windows and an ancient ceiling with gilded moldings;
its walls were hung with mirrors and white draperies with
red designs; it had marble statues (whatever their artistic
merit, they were statues all the same) and heavy, white-

and-gold First Empire furniture, upholstered in red velvet. At one end of the hall, a platform had been set up for the occasion, from which the authors were to read their literary creations; while the rest of the great room was filled with rows of chairs divided by aisles, as in a theater.

But after they had recovered from their first surprise, the savages started asking the most nonsensical questions and making the most absurd declarations.

"Who says we want them to read their stuff? We've paid for our tickets! What are they trying to do, cheat us? Oh no! It's we who are giving the orders now and not the Lembkes!"

In fact, one might have thought they had been purposely smuggled in to cause trouble.

I particularly remember one incident involving the princeling in the incredibly high, stiff collar, who looked like a wooden doll and whom I'd met at Mrs. von Lembke's the previous day. At her ardent plea, he had consented to pass a ribbon over his left shoulder and join our ranks as an usher. And it soon became obvious that this speechless wax dummy, if he couldn't talk, could act, at least after a fashion. When a huge, pock-marked retired captain backed by a gang of hoodlums inquired which way the buffet was, the princeling motioned to a nearby policeman. The hint was immediately acted upon and, despite a stream of violent abuse, the drunken captain was ejected bodily.

In the meantime, the legitimate audience began to arrive, thronging in the three long aisles between the rows of seats. But even the genuine paying public wore perplexed and dissatisfied expressions, and some of the ladies even looked frightened.

At last everyone was seated and the orchestra stopped playing. People began looking around and blowing their noses. Their expectancy was too tense and solemn, which in itself boded no good. But the Lembkes hadn't yet arrived. Silks, velvets, and jewelry shimmered and glittered on every side and the air was filled with fragrant perfumes. The gentlemen were wearing all their decorations and some of the older ones even wore their dress uniforms. At last the head landowner's wife made her appearance, accompanied by Liza. Never had Liza looked so dazzlingly beautiful as then in her magnificent dress; her hair was curled, her eyes sparkled, a radiant smile played on her lips. The sight of her created a visible stir—people looked her over, whispered about her. Some said that her eyes searched for Stavrogin among the audience, but neither he nor his mother had arrived. At the time, I didn't understand why there should be so much happiness, joy, and liveliness in her expression, and when I remembered what had happened the day before, I was puzzled indeed.

And the Lembkes still hadn't arrived—it was a bad mistake. As I found out later, Julie von Lembke had waited till the last minute for Peter, without whom she had recently been unable to take a step, although she wouldn't admit this even to herself. I must also note here that, at the final committee meeting, Peter had refused to accept an usher's ribbon, and this had actually brought tears to Julie's eyes. Then, to her further surprise, which later turned into acute embarrassment (I am anticipating here), he never showed up during the entire literary matinee and no one saw him until much later in the evening.

In the end, the audience became openly restive. And still no one came out on the platform. Those in the back rows started clapping to express their impatience, as people do in theaters. Elderly ladies and gentlemen frowned—those Lembkes were really taking too much for granted, they thought. In the front rows, among the cream of the audience, an absurd notion was whispered back and forth that there probably weren't going to be any readings after all, that Governor von Lembke was really sick, and so on.

But, thank God, they finally arrived, the first lady on the governor's arm. I must say that I myself was very worried about what would happen when they appeared. However, it looked as though all the rumors had been unfounded and the truth had triumphed. The public seemed greatly relieved. As the governor came in, all eyes were fixed on him, and the general impression, as well as my own, was that he looked in excellent health. Very few among our higher society thought that there had really been anything wrong with the governor; on the whole, his actions were considered quite normal, and they even looked with approval on his stand in the square the day before.

"That's what should've been done in the first place," our prominent citizens felt. "Even if our high officials take office as humanitarians, they are bound to end up acting as he did because, in the final analysis, it is indispensable even from the humanitarian viewpoint." That was the general consensus of opinion at the club. If the governor was blamed at all, it was only for having lost his temper. "Such measures should be taken coolly and with deliberation," the old hands contended, "but, after all, the man is still new to the job."

There was the same eagerness in the eyes turned toward Julie von Lembke. Of course, no one can demand of me, as a narrator, too many details about what had gone on between them—we're dealing here with a mystery, a woman. However, I do know that she had remained locked in the study with her husband till well past midnight and that, having forgiven him, she had comforted him. The two had agreed on everything; every source of discord had been forgotten; and when, concluding his explanation, Lembke still had insisted on going down on his knees to atone for the main and final incident of the previous night, Julie's exquisite hand and then her lips had checked the passionate flow of penitent speeches from that knightly and gallant gentleman, weakened by emotion. Happiness was written on her face for everyone to see. She looked friendly and relaxed and was magnificently dressed. It looked as though all her wishes had come true: the festivities, the aim and crowning of her policy, had been realized. As they walked toward their seats, both the Lembkes bowed repeatedly, acknowledging greetings from the audience. Immediately a circle formed around them. The wife of the head landowner rose to welcome them.

But at that point there was a most unfortunate mix-up. For no apparent reason, the band suddenly struck up with a flourish—not a passage from a triumphal march but the kind of flourish that is usually played at the club when someone's health is drunk at a dinner. Later I found out that Lyamshin, who was one of the ushers, had had a hand in this. He had instructed the band to "greet" the governor and his lady in this fashion. And, of course, he could always offer as an excuse either that he had made a simple blunder or that he had acted out of excessive zeal. But then, alas, as I found out later, these people were no longer concerned with preparing excuses for themselves because they were sure things were going to be very different after that day.

And the flourish wasn't the end of it. While knowing smiles and perplexed looks were exchanged in the audience, loud cheers suddenly rose from the back rows and the galleries, also apparently addressed to the governor. Only a few people participated in this demonstration, but it lasted for quite a long time. Julie von Lembke turned blood-red and her eyes flashed. The governor stopped dead by his seat, turned his head toward the cheerers, and cast a severe gaze over the audience. The people around him quickly induced him to sit down. I noticed with apprehension that he again wore the ominous smile that had appeared on his face in his wife's drawing room, when he stood staring at Mr. Verkhovensky before walking over to him. I thought that now, too, there was an ominous expression on his face and, what is worse, it was at the same time comical, the expression of a man who had determined to immolate himself on the altar of his wife's higher aims.

Mrs. von Lembke hurriedly beckoned to me and asked me in a whisper to slip over to Karmazinov and beg him to start his reading immediately. But, as soon as I turned around to do as she asked, another disgraceful demonstration broke out, this one even more shocking than the first.

While the eyes and the expectations of the audience were fixed on the empty platform with its unoccupied chair and its table with a glass of water standing on a silver tray, the gigantic figure of Captain Lebyatkin, attired in tail coat and white tie, suddenly appeared on it. I couldn't believe my eyes. He seemed rather embarrassed and remained standing at the back of the platform. Then someone from the public shouted: "Hey, Lebyatkin, is that you?" and the captain's stupid, red face (he was very drunk) broke into a broad, vacuous grin. He raised a hand to his forehead, wiped his brow with it, threw back his shaggy head, and then, looking as though he were taking a plunge into an abyss, took a couple of steps forward and delivered a peal of laughter that, although it was not too loud, was very resounding, joyful, and protracted and made his whole bulk sway and his piggish little eyes close. At the sight of this, almost half the audience burst out laughing and a score or so among them clapped. The serious members of the audience exchanged gloomy glances. The entire scene lasted less than half a minute. Then Liputin, wearing his usher's ribbon and accompanied by two attendants, jumped onto the platform. The attendants took hold of the captain's arms, and Liputin whispered something in his ear. Lebyatkin frowned, muttered, "Well, if you insist," shrugged, turned his broad back to the audience and departed with his escort. But, a second later,

Liputin was back on the platform, his lips distended in his broadest sugar-and-vinegar grin. There was a sheet of note-paper in his hand and he walked to the edge of the platform, taking short, rapid steps.

"Ladies and gentlemen," he said, addressing the audience, "an amusing mix-up has just occurred through an oversight, and it has now been corrected. But now I have taken it upon myself to fulfill the request of a local poet, and I hope I'll be able to do so satisfactorily. Despite his appearance, our poet, moved by the humane and noble cause that has brought us all together here—that of drying the tears of the well-educated ladies of our province—the gentleman in question—I mean, the poet—who wishes to remain unnamed —very much wants to hear his poem read before the opening of our program. So, although this poem is not part of the program, having been handed to us only half an hour ago"— Liputin didn't make it clear whom he meant by "us"; I am simply reporting his rather incoherent speech here verbatim— "it seemed to us that, because of its striking freshness of feeling and the poet's cheerful outlook, the poem ought to be read, not as a serious work of art, of course, but as some-thing befitting this moving occasion—I mean, our Idea. And since it consists of only a few lines, I thought I would ask for the kind indulgence of the audience—"

"Read it!" a voice barked from somewhere in the rear of the hall.

"Shall I read it?"

"Read it, read it!" many voices cried.

"All right, I will read it, if the audience will allow me to," Liputin said, again displaying his sugar-and-vinegar smile. But he still hesitated, and I thought he looked rather worried. For all their arrogance, these people do hesitate sometimes, although I'm sure the divinity student would not have done so. But Liputin, in spite of everything, belonged to the older generation.

"I have the privilege to—that is, I must warn you that this poem is in no way an ode. It is nothing like the sort of thing that used to be written specially for such festive occasions. It is, in a way, more of a joke, although mixed in with its cheerful playfulness is indisputable emotion and, if I may say so, realistic truthfulness."

"Well, read it, read it!"

Liputin unfolded the sheet of notepaper. No one, of course,

had the presence of mind to stop him, especially since he was wearing his official usher's ribbon. So he declaimed in a clear and ringing voice:

"*To the National Governess, Native of This Part of Our Country*

Oh, needy governesses, hail!
Have a good time and stay up late.
Whether you follow George Sand's trail,
Or of reaction—celebrate!"

"But it must be Lebyatkin's! It certainly must be his!" several voices cried. Some, although not too many, laughed and cheered.

"With your snot-nosed charges poring
Over a dull French primer's line,
To escape that fate so boring
Even a sexton'd suit you fine!"

"Bravo! Bravo!"

"But in our progressive age
Even a sexton's not for free.
Better, Miss, his greed assuage,
Or else stick to ABC.

Follow George Sand or reaction,
Please yourself, your dot we'll bring,
No need now for drastic action,
Damn the world, just dance and sing!"

I couldn't believe my ears. The insolence of it was so obvious that it was impossible to ascribe it simply to Liputin's lack of judgment. The least that can be said about the man is that he was by no means a fool. The intent, to me at least, was quite clear: it was a deliberate attempt to cause trouble. The reading of certain verses in that idiotic poem could not be accounted for by stupidity alone.

And, indeed, Liputin appeared to feel that he had taken too much upon himself. He seemed to be a bit overcome by his own daring. Instead of leaving the platform, he remained standing there as though he wanted to explain something. Obviously he had expected a different reaction, for even the group of rowdies who had clapped and cheered during the reading now fell silent as if it were too much even for them. The most stupid aspect of the entire incident was that many of the audience, instead of dismissing the poem as the silly jingle it was, took it seriously as a satirical verse with an ideological purpose and a true statement about the position of our governesses. But finally, they too saw the vulgarity of its tone. As to the general reaction of the audience, it was both shocked and resentful. I am sure I am right in describing the general impression thus. Julie von Lembke said later that if it had gone on for another minute she would have fainted. One of the most respected elder citizens of our town pulled an old lady from her seat and they walked out, followed by many worried looks. And, who knows, perhaps many others would have followed them had it not been for Karmazinov, who at that moment appeared on the platform. He wore a frock coat and a white tie and held an exercise book under his arm. Julie von Lembke looked at him in rapture, as upon a deliverer—but then I rushed off behind the scenes, anxious to get at Liputin.

"You did it on purpose!" I said, seizing him by the arm in my indignation.

"No, no, I assure you; I never expected—" he said, immediately starting to lie. He pretended to be extremely unhappy about the whole thing. "I was simply handed the poem; I thought it would amuse the audience—"

"You didn't think anything of the sort! Anyway, how could a piece of junk like that amuse anyone?"

"Well, I find it amusing."

"You're lying. And it isn't true that they just handed it to you either. I say that you and Lebyatkin composed it together yesterday at the latest, precisely to cause a scandal. And I'm sure that bringing the sexton into it was your idea alone. And why did Lebyatkin come out dressed in a frock coat? Because you even intended him to read the piece, if he hadn't managed to get drunk beforehand."

Liputin gave me an icy, sarcastic look.

"And what business is all this of yours, anyway?" he asked me with strange indifference.

"Why, you and I are both wearing these ribbons, that's why it's my business. And tell me, where is Peter Verkhovensky?"

"No idea. I suppose he's somewhere around. Why?"

"Because I see it all clearly now: it's a conspiracy against Mrs. von Lembke—you're trying to spoil the festivities."

Liputin again looked at me with cold hostility.

"And what is that to you?" he hissed. Then he snorted, shrugged, and walked off.

I felt as though I'd been scorched. So all my suspicions were justified! To the last moment I had hoped I was wrong. Well, what was I supposed to do now? I thought of consulting Mr. Verkhovensky, but he was busy glancing at his notes and trying a variety of smiles in front of a mirror. He was scheduled to follow Karmazinov on the platform and he didn't have any attention to spare for me. Should I run to Mrs. von Lembke and warn her? She wouldn't have believed me; she needed much more tangible evidence to prove to her that her notion of having a following and being surrounded by "fanatically devoted" young people was just a delusion. She would have dismissed my warnings, sure that I was imagining things. Finally, I said to myself, "Damn it, it's none of my business after all, just as he said; and *when it starts,* all I'll have to do is remove my ribbon and go home." That's exactly the way I put it to myself—*when it starts*—I remember very well.

But now I simply had to go and listen to Karmazinov. I looked around once more and saw that there were many outsiders, including some unknown women even, coming and going backstage. This "backstage" was a rather narrow space completely screened off from the audience by a curtain and leading onto a corridor that led to other rooms. Those who were to read waited their turns here. Looking around me then, I was particularly struck by the man scheduled to follow Mr. Verkhovensky on the platform. He was also some sort of professor, who had resigned his post in some university after a scandal involving his students—to this day I don't know exactly who he was. He had arrived in our town only a few days before, on God knows what business, and had been recommended to Julie von Lembke, who received him with great respect. I only know that he had seen her only once before, on the previous evening, and that, on that occasion, he hadn't uttered a word; he had just smiled knowledgeably at the jokes and the tone of the conversation of the company surrounding her, producing an unpleasant impression on everyone because of his arrogant air combined with a morbid oversensitivity. Julie von Lembke herself asked him to read something at her reception. Now he was pacing up and down, whispering to himself like Mr. Verkhovensky but, unlike him, looking down at the ground rather than into a mirror. This one didn't bother to try out his smiles, although a carnivorous grin kept appearing on his face of its own accord. Obviously, it was impossible to talk to him either. He was about forty, short and bald; he had a small, graying beard and was decently dressed. But what struck me about him was that every time he turned around he raised his right fist above his head and then brought it down violently, as though to reduce an opponent to dust. As he went through this performance again and again, I began to feel uncomfortable. So I left and went to listen to Karmazinov.

III

Again something ominous seemed to hover over the audience. Let me be quite clear on this point: I venerate genius. What I cannot understand is why so many of our geniuses behave like little boys toward the end of their glorious careers. Couldn't he see that even if his name was Karmazinov and even if he swaggered onto the platform like five court chamberlains rolled into one, he still couldn't hold such an audience for a full hour by reading that one piece of his. In general, I've observed that even a supergenius cannot impose upon the public's attention for more than twenty minutes at a light literary reading without risking unpleasant consequences. True, the great man's appearance on the stage was greeted with considerable respect. The most severe old gentlemen displayed some curiosity and approval and their ladies even a certain enthusiasm. The clapping, however, was brief and somewhat discordant. But at least there was no demonstration from the back room until Mr. Karmazinov actually began to speak, and even then it was nothing particularly hostile, just a simple misunderstanding. As I have mentioned before, Karmazinov's voice was rather shrill, even slightly feminine, and on top of all that, the great poet spoke with a genuine, aristocratic lisp. So, as soon as he had said a few words, someone began to titter, probably some inexperienced fool, given to giggling, who had never come across anyone of such distinction before. But there was no heckling. Indeed, they shushed the fool and he fell silent, completely crushed.

But then, lisping and modulating his voice, Mr. Karmazinov declared that at first he "wouldn't hear of reading" here (why did he have to announce that?), that "there are certain lines that come from so deep in a singing heart that they cannot be uttered aloud and such sacred things really ought not to be offered to the public" (why was he "offering" them, then?). But "they pleaded with me so insistently that I decided to offer them," and since he was laying down his pen once and for all and had sworn never to write again, well, he had consented to write this very last piece; and since he had also sworn never to read anything again in public, well, he had consented to read this last piece publicly, and so on in that vein.

Even that wouldn't have mattered too much, because everyone knows what an author's introduction is like—although, considering our public's lack of education and the irritability of the back rows, it could have had an unfavorable effect. (Wouldn't he have done better to read us one of the short, very short, stories such as he used to write, somewhat overpolished and affected but still quite witty? It would have saved the day.) But that was not his idea at all; instead, he delivered a long moralizing oration. And what wasn't there in it! I am sure that even a Petersburg audience would have been reduced to a state of stupor, to say nothing of ours. Just imagine—ten thousand words of the most affected and vacuous chatter, and this gentleman reading it condescendingly with a sort of long-suffering expression that was rather insulting to his audience. As to his subject—but who on earth could tell what he was talking about? It was some sort of an account of some sort of impressions and reminiscences, but what actually had impressed him and what he was reminiscing about remained unclear. And knit though we might our provincial brows during the first half of his reading, we still couldn't make heads or tails of it, so during the second half we relaxed and just listened out of politeness. To be sure, there was a lot about love—the love of a man of genius for some lady or other—but I must say, if anything, it sounded rather embarrassing. The short, rotund figure of the great writer made the story of his first kiss a bit unconvincing, I felt. And what made it positively irritating was that his kisses were quite unlike those exchanged by the rest of humankind

—when the kissing took place, there were always gorse bushes growing nearby or some other outlandish plant that one would need a botanical atlas to identify. And the sky always had a peculiar violet highlight that no mortal had ever noticed before—that is, everyone had seen it, but no one had ever noticed it, until he, Karmazinov, saw it and described it to us, bunch of fools that we were, as if it were the most ordinary thing. The tree under which this fascinating couple elected to sit was unfailingly of some orangey color, and they sat under it somewhere in Germany. Suddenly they have a vision of Pompey or Cassius on the eve of battle and a chill of rapture runs down their backs. Some water fairy then squeaks in the bushes and, among the reeds, Glück strikes up his violin. The name of the piece he is playing is mentioned in full—*en toutes lettres*—but no one has ever heard of it and you'd have to go and look it up in a musical dictionary. In the meantime, mist begins billowing, and it billows and billows and finally looks more like a million pillows than mist. Suddenly all that vanishes and we are shown the great man of genius crossing a thawing Volga on a warm winter's day. The crossing covers two and a half pages, but he nevertheless manages to fall through a hole in the ice. And does the genius drown? Oh no, he hasn't the slightest intention of drowning; he has simply brought it in to tell you that when he was about to go under and was swallowing the cold water, he suddenly caught sight of a tiny, pea-sized ice floe, pure and transparent—"like a frozen tear"—and in that ice floe he saw the reflection of all Germany or, to be more accurate, of the German sky, and its iridescent glitter reminded him of the tear that, "don't you remember, rolled down your cheek when we sat under a turquoise tree and when you cried out in rapture: 'There is no crime!' to which, through my tears, I answered: 'Yes, but then there are no saints either.' Whereupon we burst into sobs and parted forever." She goes off to the seashore somewhere and he to some sort of caves. He goes down and down and down for three years—this happens in Moscow under the Sukharev Tower—then, suddenly, in a cavern in the bowels of the earth, he finds a sanctuary lamp and in front of that lamp a praying hermit. The man of genius presses his face to the bars of a little window and suddenly hears a sigh. Now you may think it is the hermit sighing? But why should he bother with the hermit? This sigh reminds him of *her* first sigh thirty-seven years ago when, "do you remember, we sat under an agate tree, in Germany, and you said to me: 'Why love? Look, the ruddle is blooming all around us and I love you, but when the ruddle ceases to bloom my love will be over.' " At this point the mist started billowing again, Hoffmann came on the scene, a mermaid whistled something by Chopin, and suddenly the laurel-crowned head of Ancus Marcius appeared out of the mist above the roofs of Rome. A shudder of exaltation seized them and they parted forever, and so on.

I haven't told it properly and cannot report it with great accuracy, but this was the gist of his chatter. And here I must also decry the unfortunate propensity some great intellects have for witticisms. Great European philosophers, famous scholars, inventors, martyrs, toilers—all of them are like mere flunkies in the pantry of the great Russian man of genius: he is the master; they report to him hat in hand when he summons them, and stand awaiting his orders. True, he scoffs scornfully at Russia too and is anxious to demonstrate her bankruptcy to the great European intellects. But when it comes to himself—oh no!—he puts himself incomparably above the greatest European intelligences, who, to him, are nothing but raw material for his witty observations. For that, he takes hold of someone else's idea, splices its antithesis onto it—and he has a witty paradox ready at his disposal: There is crime—there is no crime; there is no truth—there are no saints; atheism—Darwinism—the bells of Moscow. . . . Alas, although he no longer believes in Moscow's church bells, he needs Rome and laurels—but no, laurels won't do any more either, so he has a standard fit of Byronian torment, twists his face into Heine's grin, picks something out of Lermontov's Pechorin—and his engine is on its way, huffing, puffing, and whistling. "But, after all," he seems to hint, "please praise me, I get a terrific kick out of it; why, I'm just pretending to be putting down my pen. Just wait and see—I'll bore you three hundred times more and you'll get tired of reading me yet."

It goes without saying that it didn't go off too well. For a while there was some stamping of feet, blowing of noses, coughing, and all the noises that are heard at a literary reading if the literary gentleman, whoever he may be, holds the public for more than twenty minutes. But this writer of genius didn't notice a thing. He went on and on, rambling and lisping, completely ignoring the audience, which was growing bewildered and impatient. Then, suddenly, a single but very loud voice came from the back rows:

"Ah God, what bunk!"

This outcry, I'm sure, was quite involuntary and by no means part of any organized heckling. Someone had simply grown tired and couldn't stand it any more. But Mr. Karmazinov stopped, looked sarcastically and pityingly at the public with the air of an offended court chamberlain. Then he lisped:

"You seem to be frightfully bored with what I have to say, ladies and gentlemen, don't you?"

That's where he was responsible for what happened. He was the first to bring it up and, in asking that question, he gave the scum an opportunity to answer it, so to speak, legitimately. Had he abstained, they might have just blown their noses for a while and it would have passed off somehow. Perhaps he hoped that the answer to his question would come in the form of an ovation, but there was nothing like that. On the contrary, he seemed to have frightened them; they withdrew into themselves and fell quiet.

"And I say you've never even set eyes on Ancus Marcius. It's all a lot of pompous talk!" an irritated, almost exasperated voice came suddenly from the audience.

"Right!" another voice immediately chimed in. "There are no ghosts today, but there are the natural sciences. So perhaps you'd better check what you say with the natural sciences!"

"I must say, ladies and gentlemen, that I expected least of all to hear objections of that sort," cried the great genius, who, in Karlsruhe, had completely forgotten the mentality of his fellow countrymen.

"It is a disgrace to claim in our day and age that the world rests on three fishes," a girl suddenly rattled off. "You, Karmazinov, couldn't possibly have gone down into those caves of yours to see that hermit. And, anyway, who talks of hermits nowadays?"

"What depresses me most of all, ladies and gentlemen, is that you take it all so seriously. Although—although you are quite right—there is no one who has greater respect for the truth than I. . . ."

Although he was still smiling condescendingly, he had obviously been hurt. His face was trying to tell them, "I am not at all what you think. Can't you see I'm on your side and all I want is your praise? Please praise me, praise me as much as you can bear to. You'd never believe how much I love to be praised!"

"Ladies and gentlemen," he cried, really stung at last, "I realize now that my poor little prose poem is out of place here and I suppose that goes for me too—I also seem to be out of place here."

"You were aiming at a crow and you hit a cow instead!" some fool, who was probably drunk, shouted at the top of his voice.

Obviously, it would have been best to ignore that remark, although, it is true, there was some irreverent laughter from the audience.

"I hit a cow—is that what you said?" Karmazinov immediately retorted, in a voice that was growing ever shriller. "Well, as far as crows and cows are concerned, I'd better make no comment, ladies and gentlemen, because I have too much respect for people, whoever they may be, to indulge in comparisons, even the most innocent ones. I thought, however, that—"

"You'd better take it easy, mister!" someone shouted from the back rows.

"But I simply thought that, now that I am putting down my pen and saying farewell to the public, you would be willing to hear what I had to say—"

"Yes, yes, we want to hear, we want to hear!" a few, who had finally managed to muster up enough courage, cried from the front rows.

"Read! Read!" a few enthusiastic ladies' voices chimed in, and at last there was some meager clapping.

"Believe us, Mr. Karmazinov, it is a great honor for us," the head landowner's wife herself exclaimed, unable to restrain herself.

"Mr. Karmazinov!" a fresh young voice suddenly came from the middle of the hall. It belonged to a very young schoolteacher who had just recently arrived and had impressed us as a quiet and honorable young man. He even rose from his seat. "What I would like to say, Mr. Karmazinov, is that if I had had the luck to fall in love as you have described, I certainly would never have mentioned my love in a piece designed for a public reading." The schoolteacher was beet-red by the time he was through.

"I have finished, ladies and gentlemen!" Karmazinov shouted. "I am through. I will skip the ending and leave. Allow me just to read you the six concluding lines: 'Yes, my dear reader, farewell!' " he proceeded immediately, reading from his manuscript without sitting down again. " 'Adieu, my friend! In fact, I don't even insist very strongly that we part as friends, for why should I ask you to take the trouble? You may even abuse me—abuse me as much as you like, if that gives you any pleasure. The best thing would be if we forgot each other once and for all. And even if all of you, my readers, were so kind as to go down on your knees and beg me with tears rolling down your cheeks: "Write for us, Karmazinov, please, go on writing for Russia, for our descendants, for laurel wreaths!" well, even then, I would say to you—oh, of course, after thanking you with the utmost courtesy—"No! We have spent quite enough time together, my dear fellow countrymen, thank you—*merci!* It is time for our ways to part, *merci, merci, merci.*' " "

Karmazinov bowed ceremoniously and, as red as if he had been stewed, started walking toward the back of the stage.

"No one intends to go down on his knees. What a ridiculous notion!"

"What conceit!"

"He only meant it humorously," someone more sensible corrected them.

"You can keep his humor."

"But really, he has some nerve!"

"Well, at least we're rid of him now!"

"Ah, what a bore!"

All these discourteous remarks from the back rows (although by no means from the back rows only) floated among the cheers from the rest of the audience. There were calls for Karmazinov to come back and take a bow. A group of ladies, headed by Mrs. von Lembke and the head landowner's wife, crowded before the platform. Julie von Lembke produced a magnificent laurel wreath. It lay on a white velvet cushion inside a larger wreath of fresh roses.

"Laurels!" Karmazinov said with a subtle and slightly sarcastic smile. "I am touched, of course, and naturally I accept with great emotion this wreath that was prepared beforehand and has not yet had time to wither. But I assure you, ladies and gentlemen, that I have become so realistic in my outlook that I feel laurels would be more useful in the hands of a skillful cook than on my head."

"Yes, and we have more use for cooks!" shouted the divinity student who had attended the meeting at Virginsky's.

Some confusion followed. Many people had risen to their feet to watch the presentation of the laurel wreath.

"I'd rather pay three rubles for a cook than for him any time!" a voice chimed in so loudly that there was no doubt that it was deliberate heckling.

"Me too!"

"And me too!"

"And how come there's no bar?"

"I say it's nothing but an open deception!"

It must be noted, however, that all these disorderly elements were still very much intimidated by the presence of our high brass, especially the police commissioner, who was also in the audience. So, within ten minutes or so, they were all back in their seats. But the order that had prevailed at the start was never restored. And so poor Mr. Verkhovensky stumbled straight into impending chaos.

IV

I tried to ward off the trouble by rushing backstage to warn him. I told him that, in my opinion, the whole thing had fallen through, that the best thing would be for him to make any excuse, even an upset stomach, not to go out on the platform, and to go home. I told him I would discard my usher's ribbon and leave with him.

He was already on his way to the platform and he looked me up and down haughtily, then solemnly declared:

"I really can't understand why you should consider me capable of such a cowardly action."

I drew back. I was as certain as that twice two is four that if he went out to them there would be a catastrophe. As I stood there, full of these gloomy forebodings, I caught sight of the professor who was scheduled to follow Mr. Verkhovensky and whom I had seen earlier violently raising and lowering his fist again and again. He was still pacing up and down behind the stage, muttering something under his breath and smiling slyly and triumphantly. Unthinkingly, I can't explain why, I went up to him.

"You know," I told him, "I have observed many times that

if a lecturer goes on talking for more than twenty minutes, the audience ceases to listen to him. Even a celebrity cannot go on for more than half an hour—"

He stopped dead and started to shake with indignation. An infinite disdain appeared on his face.

"Don't let that worry you," he muttered scornfully and walked past me.

At that moment, I heard Mr. Verkhovensky's voice coming from the platform.

"Ah, damn the lot of them!" I thought and rushed back into the hall.

Mr. Verkhovensky had installed himself in the chair even before the disorder had died down. None-too-friendly looks greeted him from the front rows. Lately, he had become much less popular in the club and his prestige in general had declined considerably. Indeed, it was lucky, I felt, that they didn't hiss him as he came out. Since the day before I had been obsessed by the strange thought that they would boo him as soon as he appeared. In reality, however, his appearance went unnoticed in the wake of the previous excitement. But what could a man like him expect after the treatment Karmazinov himself had been given? Mr. Verkhovensky was pale—this was his first public appearance in ten years. From his agitation and his general attitude, I could guess, knowing him as I did, that he himself expected his appearance on that platform would somehow decide his fate. And that was just what I feared. This man was very dear to me, and I can hardly convey how I felt when he finally opened his mouth and I heard his first words:

"Ladies and gentlemen," he said abruptly, as though he had suddenly decided to go the whole way. His voice trembled as he spoke. "Only this morning there lay before me one of those subversive leaflets that have been distributed around here recently and, for the hundredth time, I asked myself, 'What is the secret behind it?' "

The audience immediately grew quiet and all eyes were fixed on him, some of them full of fear. There is no doubt that he had effectively captured their attention with his very first words. Even Liputin's and Lyamshin's heads appeared from behind the stage, and they both listened eagerly. Once again Mrs. von Lembke beckoned to me:

"Stop him, stop him—whatever you have to do, stop him!" she whispered in great alarm.

I just shrugged. How could one possibly stop a man who had decided to take the plunge? Alas, by now I understood Mr. Verkhovensky.

"Aha, he has something to say about those leaflets," whispers rolled through the public, and the entire audience stirred.

"Well, ladies and gentlemen, I have penetrated the secret of their effectiveness and the answer is human stupidity!" His eyes flashed. "Yes, ladies and gentlemen, if it were deliberate stupidity, feigned stupidity with an ulterior motive—it would be a stroke of sheer genius! But we must be fair to the authors of those leaflets: there is no counterfeit stupidity here. It is the most genuine, the most naïve imbecility, *c'est la bêtise dans son essence la plus pure*—it is something like a chemical element. If their formulation were just a tiny bit less inane, everyone would have seen immediately the bankruptcy of their idiotic contentions. But as they stand, everyone just stops perplexed, for no one ever dreams that they can be so completely senseless. 'Impossible,' people say to themselves, 'there must be something more to them!' And everyone assumes some mysterious meaning behind them and goes on trying to read between the lines. Thus the desired effect is achieved. Never in human experience has stupidity been so solemnly rewarded, although it may have deserved it often enough, Lord knows. And, allow me to add parenthetically—both stupidity and the greatest genius are equally useful in shaping the destiny of mankind."

"He is treating us to the old paradoxes of the eighteen forties!" a rather shy voice interjected, but it was a signal for a general uproar.

"Ladies and gentlemen, I propose a toast to stupidity!" Mr. Verkhovensky shouted, now completely beside himself and ready to take the audience on.

I ran up to him under the pretext of pouring some water into his glass.

"Mr. Verkhovensky, please—Mrs. von Lembke beseeches you to stop."

"No, you stop it yourself, young man!" he retorted at the top of his voice, so that the whole audience could hear, and I hurriedly took myself out of there. *"Messieurs,"* he went on, "why all this excitement and indignation? Why do I hear all this shouting when I have come to you with an olive branch? I have brought you the last word, for in this matter I happen to have the last word, and then we will make peace."

"Away with him!" shouted some.

"Quiet, let him have his say!" others cried.

I noticed that the young teacher who had interrupted Karmazinov earlier was particularly agitated. It seemed that, having dared to speak once before, he was now unable to restrain himself.

"Messieurs, the final word in this business must be general forgiveness," Mr. Verkhovensky continued. "I, an old man who has nothing more to expect from life, wish to declare solemnly that the life spirit is still present in us and that today's younger generation is still full of the life force. Its enthusiasm is just as pure and bright as ours was in the time of my own youth. All that has happened is a shift in goals—the substitution of one conception of beauty for another. The entire misunderstanding stems from different evaluations: what is more beautiful, Shakespeare or boots? Raphael or petroleum?"

"He's a police informer!"

"He's asking leading questions!"

"Agent provocateur!"

"And I declare," Mr. Verkhovensky squeaked, throwing himself unreservedly into the fray, "that, to me, Shakespeare and Raphael are of greater value than the emancipation of the serfs, than nationalism, than socialism, than the younger generation, than chemistry—and perhaps even than mankind itself! And it is this way because they represent the very highest human achievement, an achievement of beauty without which I wouldn't be willing to go on living.

"Oh Lord," he cried, throwing up his hands, "ten years ago I was shouting the same thing from a platform in Petersburg, using almost exactly these same words and, like you now, the people there didn't understand a thing; they snorted, laughed, and hissed. Ah, you poor, little people, there must be something missing in you if you can't understand these things! Let me tell you that mankind could survive without the English, without the Germans, and most certainly without the Russians; that it could subsist without science and even without bread. But it is impossible to do without beauty because then there would be nothing left for us to do in the world! And that's the whole mystery and the whole story! Science itself wouldn't last a minute without beauty—do you realize that, you who are laughing now? It would turn into black ignorance and it wouldn't be able to invent a nail for you. No, I won't give in!" he concluded shrilly and incongruously, bringing his fist down violently on the table.

And as he shouted on incoherently, the uproar in the audience increased: many were on their feet and some were moving forward, toward the platform. Indeed, all this happened much faster than I can describe it; there was no time to do anything about it even if anyone had contemplated any such action, and apparently nobody did.

"It's all very well for you to talk—you're given food and shelter for nothing; you're just a pampered pet!" the divinity student shouted from below the platform, grinning broadly at Mr. Verkhovensky and obviously relishing every second. Mr. Verkhovensky bounded to the very edge of the dais.

"Didn't I just say that the younger generation's enthusiasm is as pure and bright as ever, and that their only error is over the forms of the beautiful! Isn't that enough for you? And if you consider the fact that this statement is being made by a heartbroken and rejected father, then—you little people! —surely you can understand that it's impossible to be more objective and detached? How ungrateful and unfair can you be? Why, oh why, don't you want to make peace?"

And he burst into hysterical sobs. Tears poured from his eyes and he wiped them away with his fingers. His chest and shoulders were shaking spasmodically. He was no longer aware of what was going on around him.

The audience became really frightened. Now they were almost all on their feet, including Mrs. von Lembke, who caught her husband's arm and tried to pull him up too. The whole thing was turning into a full-fledged public row.

"Mr. Verkhovensky!" the divinity student roared happily. "An escaped convict called Fedka is roving around in the vicinity of this town. He holds people up, and recently he committed a new murder. Now let me ask you this: if fifteen years ago you hadn't forced him to join the army to raise a sum of money you needed to pay a gambling debt, or in other words, if you hadn't lost your serf Fedka at cards, isn't it possible that he would never have become a criminal in the first place? Perhaps he wouldn't have had to cut people's throats in his struggle for existence—what d'you think, Mr. Aesthete?"

I am unable to convey the scene that followed. First, there was some frantic cheering. Perhaps only one-fifth of the audience clapped, but they clapped frantically. The rest of the public moved toward the exit and, since those applauding were moving forward, toward the platform, general confusion ensued. Ladies screamed; some young girls started crying and demanded to be taken home; Lembke, still standing by his seat, looked around in bewilderment, while his wife lost her head completely for the first time during her stay in our town. As to Mr. Verkhovensky, at first he seemed completely crushed by the divinity student's words, but then he suddenly raised his arms, spreading them as it were over the audience, and screamed:

"I shake the dust from my feet and I curse you! This is the end—the end—"

And he turned around and ran backstage, waving his arms threateningly.

"He has insulted our society! Bring him here!" some desperadoes hollered, and they were even on the point of rushing in pursuit of him. It was impossible at that moment to reason with them. And then, a final catastrophe exploded over the meeting—the third reader, the maniac who had been waving his right fist backstage, appeared on the platform.

He looked completely mad. He examined the audience, which was in an uproar, with a wide, triumphant grin and seemed delighted at the chaos. The fact that he would have to read amid such a din didn't seem to bother him in the least. On the contrary, he seemed anxious to start. This was so striking that it attracted people's attention.

"And who's this one now?" they asked each other. "Where has *this one* come from? What does he want? Sh-sh-sh, let's hear what he has to say!"

"Ladies and gentlemen!" the maniac shouted in a voice that was almost as shrill as Karmazinov's, although it had no aristocratic lisp to it. "Twenty years ago, ladies and gentlemen, when Russia was at war with half of Europe, she was the ideal of all the state councilors and privy councilors too. The government controlled our literature, our universities taught military drill, our army was like a sumptuous ballet, and our common people paid their taxes without ever complaining, under the knout of the serf owners. Extorting bribes from the living and the dead had come to be considered patriotic; those who took bribes were branded rebels because they spoiled the general harmony. Whole birch groves were sacrificed in the name of order that needed the twigs for flogging. Europe trembled. But never before, in the thousand years of her stumbling existence, had Russia reached such a level of infamy. . . ."

He raised his right fist, waved it above his head with solemn enthusiasm, and then suddenly brought it down as if smashing his opponents to smithereens. An incredible howl greeted him, followed by some insane cheering, and now almost half the audience was clapping, even the most harmless people joining in. How could they refrain from howling with delight when all of Russia was being publicly insulted?

"Now this one really has something to say! That at least is to the point! Hear, hear! At least we are no longer chatting about aesthetics."

"Since then, twenty years have passed," the maniac continued in exaltation, "many new universities have been opened and now we have a multitude of them—but military drill is nothing but a memory and we are short thousands and thousands of army officers. Today, the railroads have eaten up all our capital and cover Russia like a spider's web, so there's a hope that, in fifteen years or so, we may really be able to use them to go somewhere or other. Our bridges burn down only rarely, while our towns have their fires regularly, in a well-established order, in turns, during the fire season. Our courts mete out Solomon's justice, and our juries only take bribes in their struggle for existence when they are threatened with starvation. The former serfs are free and they heartily whack at each other with cudgels instead of being flogged by the former serf owners. Oceans of government vodka are being soaked up to help balance the budget and, in Novgorod, facing the old and decaying St. Sophia Cathedral, a colossal brass sphere now commemorates our thousand years of chaos. Europe, beginning to frown at us again, is stirring uneasily. Fifteen years of reform! And yet, never before, even in her most ridiculous periods, has Russia sunk so low—"

These last words could not be heard—the roar of the crowd drowned them out. I saw him raise his fist once again and triumphantly bring it down. The enthusiasm of the public was now beyond anything one could imagine: they were hollering and clapping and some women were even screaming, "Enough! Stop there! It's impossible to improve on what you've said!" They all seemed drunk.

The speaker, whose gaze kept sliding over the crowd, seemed to be dissolving in his own triumph.

I noticed that Lembke, in a state of extreme agitation, was

pointing at something and that his wife, looking terribly pale, was hurriedly telling something to the princeling, who had run up to her side.

Then, half a dozen persons more or less connected with the organization of the festivities rushed onto the platform from behind the stage, grabbed the speaker, and dragged him away behind the scenes. I cannot imagine how he did it, but he got loose, ran up to the very edge of the platform, and frantically waving his fist, shouted at the top of his voice:

"No, never yet has Russia sunk so—"

But they dragged him away once again. Then I saw a group of fifteen men or so rush behind the stage to his rescue. They didn't go through the opening in the curtains at the back of the platform, but broke through the flimsy partition at one side. Then, hardly able to believe my eyes, I saw the girl student who was related to Virginsky standing on the platform. She was holding the same bundle of papers under her arm, was dressed exactly as she had been at Virginsky's, looked just as red and roly-poly. She was accompanied by two or three women and as many men and also by her deadly enemy, the schoolboy. Through the uproar I made out what she was shouting.

"Ladies and gentlemen, I have come to tell you about the sufferings of underprivileged students and to rally them to make a country-wide protest. . . ."

But I was in full flight now. I stuffed my usher's ribbon into my pocket and, using the back passages with which I had become familiar, I made my way out of the house and was soon in the street. Then, naturally, I ran to Mr. Verkhovensky's.

chapter 2

The End of the Festivities

I

He wouldn't see me. He had locked himself in and was writing something. As I persisted in knocking and calling him, he answered from behind the closed door:

"I'm through with everything now, my friend. Who can ask me to do more?"

"You aren't through with anything at all; you've simply helped to make a complete mess of things. So please unlock your door without any more dramatics. We must do something because they may yet come over here and insult you."

I somehow felt I had the right to be stern and demanding with him. I was afraid he might do something crazy. But, to my great surprise, I found him incredibly determined.

"So, don't be the first to insult me," he said. "Let me thank you now for everything you've done for me and repeat once again that I am through with everything and everyone, good and bad alike. I am writing a letter to Dasha, a thing that I have unforgivably neglected to do until now. I would appreciate it if you'd take it to her tomorrow, but in the meantime, thank you for having come—*merci*."

"Mark my words, Mr. Verkhovensky, this business is much more serious than you realize. If you think, for instance, that you demolished anyone over there, let me set you straight— you didn't. It was you who broke like an empty glass jar," I said, alas, rather rudely. "And you have absolutely nothing to write to Dasha about. And then, what will become of you now, impractical as you are, if I just walk off as you suggest? I'm sure you're up to something new. Aren't you now? And if you are, I'm sure it will only land you in trouble again."

He got up and I heard him come and stand right by the door.

"You haven't been exposed to their company very long, yet you have already been contaminated by their tone and language. *Dieu vous pardonne, mon ami, et Dieu vous garde!* I noticed from the start that you had the makings of a decent man and I hope that in time you'll come to your senses, just as all Russians will someday. Now, as to your comment about my impracticality, let me remind you of an old idea of mine: we have a lot of people whose main occupation is commenting upon everyone's lack of practical sense but their own, and they do it with the exasperating insistence of certain flies. Please, *cher*, consider the agitated state I'm in and stop tormenting me. Let me say *merci* once more to you and let's part like Karmazinov and the public, that is, let us forget each other as generously as possible. Although he was insincere when he beseeched his former readers to forget him, *quant à moi*, I am not so vain and I place my main hopes in the youthfulness of your uncorrupted heart: how would you manage to remember a useless old man for long? And I say to you, 'May you live to a ripe old age,' just as my Nastasya wished me on my last birthday. These humble people sometimes come up with *des mots charmants et pleins de philosophie*—so I won't wish you either too much happiness, for you'd get bored with it, or, of course, trouble. I will follow the wisdom of the common people and simply wish you a long life. And also, try not to get too bored —that unattainable wish I add from myself. So good-by then, good-by for good. And don't stay standing on my doorstep— I won't let you in anyway."

He walked away and I could get nothing more out of him. Despite his agitation he spoke smoothly, unhurriedly, and solemnly, apparently trying to impress me. He probably still resented the sarcastic remarks I had made the day before, when he had spoken of being whisked off to Siberia and those trap doors opening, and was making me pay indirectly for them now. On the other hand, shedding tears in public that morning had made him feel rather ridiculous despite his mild triumph, and I knew of no man more concerned with the aesthetic aspect of his relations with his friends than Mr. Verkhovensky. Oh, I couldn't really blame him! But the fact that he had retained his fastidiousness and sense of humor despite all the shocks he had received reassured me: a man who had changed so little from his usual self couldn't be contemplating anything tragic or extraordinary. That was the way I reasoned at the time, but alas, I couldn't have been more wrong! There were too many factors about which I didn't then know.

Anticipating a little, I shall quote the opening lines of the letter he was writing to Dasha Shatov, which she actually received the next day:

Mon enfant,
My hand is trembling, but I have done what I had to do. You did not witness my last clash with them; you did not attend that "literary matinee" and you were right not to come. But you will hear that in our Russia, which now suffers such a dearth of men of character, one at least got up and, ignoring the threats of death being showered on him from all sides, told those fools the truth to their faces, namely that they are nothing but poor fools. Oh, they are nothing but *petits vauriens et rien de plus, des petits* little fools— *voilà le mot!* The die is cast: I am leaving this town once and for all and I don't know where I am going. All those who loved me have turned their backs on me. But you,

Dasha—you are a pure and innocent creature whose life was nearly linked with mine as a result of the whim of a capricious and willful heart. You, who perhaps watched scornfully as I shed tears of weakness on the eve of our wedding that never took place; you who, however you look at it, cannot but regard me as a ridiculous personage— well, I have reserved for you my last *cri de coeur,* and I feel that I owe you my last thought! Why, I cannot leave you to remember me forever as an ungrateful fool, an igno- ramus, and an egoist—for that is the way, I am sure, that a certain hard and ungrateful person whom, alas, I cannot forget, keeps presenting me to you . . .

And it went on like that for four rather large, closely writ- ten pages.

Now, when he told me that he wasn't going to let me in, I banged three times on the door with my fist and shouted to him that I was certain he would send Nastasya for me at least three times that very day but that, this time, *I* wouldn't come. Then I left him and ran off to Julie von Lembke's.

II

There I had to witness an outrageous scene: the poor woman was being made a fool of to her face and I couldn't do anything about it. For really, what could I tell her? I had had time to calm down sufficiently to realize that I had noth- ing to go on except some vague suspicions and premonitions. I found her in tears, almost hysterical, with eau-de-cologne compresses on her head, trying to sip a little water from a glass. She was with Peter Verkhovensky, who never stopped talking, and the princeling, who never said a word, as though his lips had been padlocked. Julie von Lembke, shedding bitter tears, was bombarding Peter with reproachful ex- clamations about his "desertion" of her. What struck me was that she attributed the disgraceful fiasco at the literary matinee uniquely to Peter's failure to appear there.

And in him I found a noticeable change: something seemed to be worrying him very much this time—he looked almost grave. As a rule, he never looked serious, not even when he was irritated and angry, which he often was. Oh, he was angry now too and spoke rudely and condescendingly and with snappish annoyance. He assured Mrs. von Lembke that he had had a terrible headache and an attack of vomiting in the apartment of Gaganov, on whom he had dropped in early that morning. Alas, the poor woman was longing so terribly to be deceived! When I came in, they were debating whether the second installment of the festivities—that is, the ball—was to be or not to be. Julie wouldn't hear of appearing at the ball "after all those insults"—that is, she was longing desperately to be forced to appear there and by none other than Peter. He was a kind of oracle for her, and I felt that if he had walked out on her then, she would have fallen ill and taken to her bed. But he had not the slightest intention of leaving. He was absolutely determined that the ball should take place that night and that Julie von Lembke should be there.

"Well, what are you crying about? It seems you can't do without scenes. Do you really need someone to vent your rage on? All right, use me then, only hurry up because time is running out and you must decide. Whatever was messed up by that literary reading will be repaired by the ball. Look, the prince agrees with what I say! Yes, if we hadn't had the prince, God only knows how it would have ended!"

The prince had at first been opposed to the ball—that is, against Julie von Lembke's appearance there, for the ball had to be held anyway—but after Peter had referred to him two or three times as supporting his own views, the prince ended by mooing in consent.

I was struck by Peter's extraordinary rudeness. Oh, I reject with disgust the vile gossip that spread later about Peter and Julie being intimate—there was not and could not possibly be anything like that between them. He conquered her simply by frantically toadying, from the very beginning, to her dreams of gaining great influence over society and impressing high government circles. He became part of her schemes, even thinking some of them up for her himself, and he entangled her from head to foot in a web of the crudest flattery. Finally he became as indispensable to her as the air she breathed.

When she saw me, Julie von Lembke's eyes flashed and she exclaimed:

"Now you ask him, Peter! Like the prince, he never left my side all the time. Well, what is your opinion, sir? Isn't it obviously a plot, a cunning, disgraceful conspiracy to harm the governor and myself in any way possible? Oh, I'm certain they plotted the whole thing. They had a prearranged plan! It's a full-fledged political conspiracy!"

"Anything else? Your head is always stuffed with all sorts of fairy tales! Nevertheless, I'm very pleased to see . . ." he pretended to have forgotten my name. "Let's hear what he thinks of it now."

"What I think," I said hurriedly, "agrees very much with what Mrs. von Lembke thinks. There's a conspiracy, there can be no doubt about it. Here, ma'am, I am returning my official ribbon to you. Now, whether the ball takes place or not is none of my concern, because it is not up to me to decide, but I do know that my official participation in it as an usher is ended. I hope you will forgive my speaking so heatedly, but I cannot act against my convictions and my common sense."

"Did you hear that? Did you hear that?" she cried, throwing her hands in the air.

"I heard him all right," Peter said, and then turned toward me. "I'm sure you must have eaten something and that you're feverish and raving. I say nothing special has happened— in any case, nothing that couldn't have happened at any moment in this town. What conspiracy could there be here? Sure, the whole affair turned into a shameful, idiotic farce, but where does this conspiracy come in? Do you really want me to believe that it's a plot against Mrs. von Lembke here, who has coddled and spoiled them, forgiven them all their childish pranks and protected them? Now, you tell him yourself, ma'am, what I have been repeating to you constantly for a whole month! What have I been warning you about? Why, why did you need those people? Why did you have to get involved with that bunch of nonentities? What did you hope to achieve? To create a unified society? Did you really expect them to be united, for heaven's sake?"

"But when did you ever warn me? On the contrary, you always approved; you urged me on, in what I was trying to do. I'm really completely stunned by these words. Why, you yourself brought many of these strange characters to my house."

"You're wrong. I never approved and I tried to argue you out of it. And as to bringing those characters to your house— that's right, I did, but I did so only after dozens like them had started swarming through it anyway. And even then, it was only lately, to participate in that 'literary quadrille' of yours, because it couldn't be arranged without those uncouth types. But I'll bet you anything that, today, a score or so such brutes managed to smuggle themselves into the audience without tickets!"

"No doubt about that," I confirmed.

"So you see, we're in agreement already. Now remember the general tone that, for some time, has been adopted throughout this lousy little town. Why, we've seen nothing but shameless arrogance, nothing but an uninterrupted, ringing disgrace! And who encouraged them? Who used her authority to cover everything up? Who was it made them all lose their senses? Who would you say created all that resentment in the common little people? Why, open your scrapbook, ma'am, and you'll find all the secrets of the local families in it. Now tell me, did you or did you not pat those caricaturists and satirical poets of yours approvingly on the head? Didn't you allow that fellow Lyamshin to kiss your hand? Weren't you there when that divinity student insulted a state councilor and soiled his daughter's dress with his greasy boots? So why should you be so surprised if the public disapproves of you?"

"But you, yourself!—ah, my God, really—"

"No, ma'am, what I did was to warn you. We argued and quarreled; yes, d'you hear, we quarreled!"

"But you're lying to my face now!"

"Oh, it's very easy for you to say that. What you need now is a scapegoat, someone on whom to vent your rage; well, as I said, go ahead and use me for it. I'd better talk to you, Mr. —" He still seemed unable to remember my name. "Let's just get this straight now: I contend that, except for Liputin's little performance, nothing was planned or prearranged—nothing whatever! I'll prove my point, but let's first analyze the Liputin incident. All right, he came out with a poem by that imbecile Lebyatkin. But what makes it a conspiracy? Couldn't Liputin simply have thought it would be a funny thing to do? Couldn't he have come out and read that poem just to make the audience laugh and, above all, to amuse his patron, Mrs. von Lembke? You think it's unlikely, but tell me, isn't it really in keeping with the things that have been going on around here for a month at least? I even think that, under different circumstances, Liputin would've got away with it. Sure, I admit the joke was a bit crude, that it went a little too far, but it was funny all right. Don't you agree that it was funny?"

"What? You consider what Liputin did was funny!" Julie von Lembke cried with tremendous indignation. "It was so stupid! It was so tasteless, so low, so unspeakable! Ah, you must be saying that on purpose to irritate me unless—oh, you must be involved in the conspiracy with him yourself!"

"Oh sure, I was hidden behind the stage, pulling all the strings! Well, let me tell you something: if I had participated in a plot, you can be sure it wouldn't have ended with that prank of Liputin's. And then you must also assume that I had a secret agreement with my dear papa, for him to cause that row? Well, perhaps you can tell me whose idea it was to ask my papa to read his stuff? And who tried to stop you from inviting him, only yesterday? Yes, only yesterday!"

"Yes, but *hier il avait tant d'esprit,* I was so full of hope. And then, he has such nice manners and I thought that between him and Karmazinov . . . But then, alas—"

"Well, yes, just as you say: although he has *tant d'esprit,* my papa made a mess of things. Now, since I knew very well that he was bound to do so, if I'd had a part in that conspiracy, why should I have tried to dissuade you from letting the old goat into your vegetable garden? But I did try to dissuade you yesterday, didn't I? And I did so because I had a premonition that it wouldn't turn out well. Of course, I couldn't possibly know what would happen exactly. I doubt that he himself could have told a minute ahead of time what he was going to come out with, because these emotional oldsters aren't like other people! But you can still redeem the situation: to placate the public, have two doctors sent to his place by administrative order, let them politely inquire about his health and then send him off to an appropriate institution where he might be treated with cold compresses. I think you ought to do it today. Then, at least, they would all laugh and realize that there was nothing to get offended about. I could announce it myself at the ball tonight, since I happen to be his son. But Karmazinov, of course, is another matter: that slob went out there and rambled on and on with that piece of his for a full hour—of course, he must be part of my conspiracy against your literary matinee! We decided he'd make it so boring just to put one over on Julie von Lembke!"

"Oh, Karmazinov, *quelle honte!* I was so ashamed for our public that I was really burning up!"

"Well, I must say I would rather have fired him than burned up myself because, when one comes to think of it, the public was right. But anyway, who was responsible for Karmazinov? Was it my idea to invite him to read? Have I ever been among his admirers around here? Well, the hell with him. But that third madman now, the political one—he's a different matter. You all made a bad slip there and you can't really blame him on my plot."

"Ah, don't talk about that one, please, I'm solely responsible for him. Ah!"

"That's certainly true, but you needn't worry. I will explain to them in Petersburg that it wasn't really your fault. For who can keep a candid fool like that in check? Even in Petersburg they have trouble with that sort. Why, I understand he was recommended to you, and very highly at that. Well, in view of all this, you'll surely agree that you absolutely must appear at the ball, because you're faced with something serious here. You yourself gave that maniac an opportunity to speak in public, and so you yourself must announce publicly that you don't share his views, that the fellow is already in the hands of the police and that you've been used in some inexplicable way. You must declare indignantly that you were the victim of a madman, because that's certainly what he is and nothing more, and that's the way he must be referred to. I can't stand biting mad dogs of that type. And though I myself may say worse things, I don't do it from a platform. And it so happens that they're shouting like mad about that senator now—"

"What senator? Who's shouting?"

"Well, I don't understand much about it myself. But you, Mrs. von Lembke, haven't you heard anything about a senator?"

"Senator?"

"Why, there is persistent talk that they're sending a senator here and that Petersburg has decided to replace Governor von Lembke. I've heard many people say it."

"So have I," I said, confirming his words.

"Who's been saying that?" Mrs. von Lembke cried, flaring up indignantly.

"You mean who was the first to say it? Well, how on earth should I know? The ordinary people around are saying it and yesterday they repeated it persistently. And they seem to be very definite about it, although it's hard to understand how they can be so sure. Of course, the more intelligent of them, those who are better informed, don't talk, but even they seem to be paving serious attention to the rumors."

"How despicable all that is, how stupid—"

"Well, but it makes it even more essential for you to appear and show those fools what's what."

"I admit I myself feel duty-bound in a way, but—but suppose it only brings a new disgrace down upon us? And suppose the public refuses to come? Suppose no one—but no one— turns up?"

"What nonsense! How can you even think they won't come? Why do you think they had all those dresses made? Well, I'm absolutely flabbergasted to hear a woman make such a statement! Talk of insight into the human mind!"

"The head landowner's wife won't come, though. I'm sure!"

"But what do you think happened, anyway? Why do you insist they won't turn up?" Peter shouted angrily, becoming quite impatient.

"What do I think happened? It was a shameful, disgraceful flop, that's what! I don't know exactly how it happened, but I feel that, as things are now, it's impossible for me to appear there."

"But why? No, seriously—why is it your fault? Why do you insist on taking the blame for everything? I say that it's the fault of the public, the fault of all those local patriarchs, those fathers of families. It was up to them to stop those idlers and good-for-nothing troublemakers, for that's what those disrupters were and nothing more. There's nothing serious in it at all. There is no society in which the police by themselves are enough to maintain order, yet here they seem to demand a policeman to guard each of them when they attend a public gathering. And what action is taken under these circumstances by our patriarchs and dignitaries, our ladies, maiden and otherwise? Well, they just pout and say nothing. They don't even have enough social initiative to control childish mischief makers!"

"Ah, you're absolutely right there! They just sit there pouting and scowling and that's all—"

"Well, if that's the truth, you should state it aloud, proudly and severely. You must show those old fogies and all those mothers that you aren't beaten. Oh, I'm sure you'll succeed— you have a knack for handling them when your head is clear. You'll gather them around you and you'll tell them and tell them clearly! And then you'll send letters to the *Voice* and to the *Stock Exchange Herald*. Wait, I'll see to it myself. I promise you, I'll see that everything is taken care of. Of course, you must organize things more carefully, see that there is a well-supervised buffet, ask the prince and Mr. . . . Yes, you really can't abandon us, *Monsieur*, at a moment when we are trying to save everything," he said to me, and then, turning back to Mrs. von Lembke, he added, "And, finally, you'll appear on the governor's arm. How does he feel, by the way?"

"Oh, how unfair, how wrong, how offensive your attitude toward that angelic man has been!" Julie exclaimed with unexpected emotion, holding her handkerchief ready to catch the tears that seemed about to gush from her eyes.

Peter was rather taken aback at first and mumbled, "But why? When have I ever?—I always—"

"You've never, never rendered him his due or acknowledged anything he did!"

"Ah, try to understand a woman!" Peter grunted with a twisted grin.

"He's the most truthful, the most considerate, the most angelic man alive! He is the kindest person in the whole world!"

"But did I ever say he wasn't kind? I've always given him his due as far as kindness—"

"You never have! But let's drop the subject—I put it awkwardly. Ah, and then that Jesuitical head landowner's wife made several cracks about what happened yesterday."

"Ah her! Well, she has other worries now, besides dropping hints about yesterday. Anyway, why should you worry about her not coming to the ball? Of course she's not coming, since she got herself involved in that scandal. She may not even be guilty, but still, her reputation has suffered and her little hands have been sullied."

"What are you talking about? Why should her hands be sullied?" Julie looked at Peter in surprise.

"Well, I can't guarantee that it's so, but the town is buzzing with a rumor that she was the one who brought them together and arranged the whole thing—"

"Whom did she bring together? What did she arrange?"

"What, you don't know?" Peter exclaimed with very nicely feigned amazement. "Why, Nikolai Stavrogin and Liza, of course—"

"What did you say? What?" we all shouted.

"How can you possibly not have heard about it? Really! Why, Liza decided to transfer her person from the head landowner's carriage to Stavrogin's and to dash off to Skvoreshniki with that gentleman. It happened in full daylight, only an hour ago. In fact, less than an hour ago."

We were stunned. Of course, we started peppering him with questions, but although he had "by chance happened to witness" the scene, he proved incapable of giving us a proper account of what had actually taken place. Apparently, when the head landowner's wife took Liza and Maurice home in her carriage after the literary matinee (Liza's mother had stayed home because her legs were aching again), another carriage was waiting about twenty-five yards from the door of the Drozdovs' house. As soon as the first carriage stopped, Liza jumped out and rushed over to the other carriage, whose door opened to let her in. Before the door shut again, Liza just had time to shout to Maurice, "Spare me!" and then the vehicle drove off at full speed toward Skvoreshniki.

To our insistent questions, such as "Was it all prearranged?" and "Who exactly was in the carriage?" Peter replied that he didn't know anything more; oh, he was sure it had all been prearranged, but he hadn't seen Stavrogin himself in the waiting carriage—it could have been his old footman, Alexei.

When pressed with questions—"How did *you* happen to be there just then?" and "How can you tell for sure that it was to Skvoreshniki that they drove?"—he explained that he had simply been passing by when he saw Liza getting into the carriage; that he had even rushed toward it, but had been unable to make out who else was in it (very unlikely, in view of his notorious curiosity!) but he had seen that Maurice Drozdov neither rushed in pursuit of Liza nor even tried to stop her. Indeed, he even held back the head landowner's wife, who was screaming at the top of her voice as she pointed at Liza:

"She's run off with Stavrogin! She's run off with Stavrogin!"

At this point I lost patience and shouted at Peter:

"You arranged it all, you vicious beast! That's what kept you so busy all morning. You were working for Stavrogin, and it was you who drove up in that carriage and pulled her in. It's all you, you, you! Listen, Mrs. von Lembke, he is our enemy. He's trying to ruin you too, and you'd better watch out!"

And I rushed out of the house.

To this day I can't understand how I could have shouted those words at him. I'm still surprised at myself. But, as it turned out, I was absolutely correct in my accusation. His obviously contrived story about the Liza-Stavrogin scandal gave him away. He told it soon after he arrived, presenting it as the latest important piece of gossip and pretending he was certain we had already heard it without him, which, of course, he knew was impossible, since it had happened only about half an hour before. And then, even if we had heard it somehow, he surely couldn't imagine we would have kept it to ourselves until he felt like bringing it up. Nor could the whole town have been buzzing about the head landowner's wife, again because the event was so recent. Furthermore, while he was feeding us those fables, I noticed that a pleased and supercilious smirk appeared on his face a couple of times, as he felt, no doubt, the satisfaction of hoodwinking a bunch of credulous fools like us.

But I no longer concerned myself with him. I thought that, on the whole, the story about the scandalous incident must be true, and I left the governor's house quite beside myself. I felt this catastrophe as a personal blow. I was hurt almost to the point of tears; indeed, it is possible I actually wept. Instinctively, I ran to Mr. Verkhovensky's, but once again that impossible man wouldn't let me in. Nastasya assured me in respectful whispers that her master was asleep, but I didn't believe her. At the Drozdovs' house, I managed to talk to the servants; they had heard about Liza's elopement, but knew nothing firsthand. The house was in an uproar; its ailing mistress was having fainting spells and Maurice Drozdov was constantly at her side. I felt I couldn't very well ask to see Maurice. I asked the servants about Peter Verkhovensky and they told me that recently he had been popping in daily, sometimes even more than once a day. The servants were saddened by the scandal and they spoke of Liza with marked respect. Obviously, they all sincerely liked her.

So Liza was lost, I was sure about that. But I still couldn't understand the psychological aspect of her act, especially after the scene between her and Stavrogin the day before. Of course, I could have tried to get more information by running all over town and questioning gloating, ill-wishing acquaintances among whom the news must have spread by then, but the very idea filled me with aversion and I felt it would have been degrading for Liza. Strangely enough, I got a notion to go and see Dasha Shatov. She did not receive me; indeed, no one had been allowed to enter Mrs. Stavrogin's house since the day before. Anyway, I can't imagine what I would have said to her, if she had received me.

After that I tried her brother. Shatov heard me out in sullen silence. I noticed that he was in a particularly gloomy mood; he seemed preoccupied about something and had to make an effort to listen to me. When I finished, he got up without uttering a word and started pacing the room, stamping harder than usual with his boots. It was only when I was on my way downstairs that he shouted after me from the landing:

"Go and see Liputin. You'll find out everything there."

I didn't go to Liputin's though. Before I was halfway there, I turned back to Shatov's, pushed his door open a little way, and asked him abruptly and without explanation, "Why don't you go to see Maria Lebyatkin today?" Shatov just swore something in reply and I left. I note that down because, that same night, Shatov walked to the opposite end of town to see Maria, whom he hadn't visited for a very long time. He found her as well and as cheerful as ever. Lebyatkin was dead drunk and was sleeping it off in the next room. That was at exactly nine in the evening, as he told me himself when I met him in the street the next day. Before ten, I had already made up my mind to attend the ball, although not as an usher—I had turned in my ribbon to Mrs. von Lembke—but just out of insurmountable curiosity. I wanted to listen (but not to go around asking questions), to hear what people in our town were saying about all these events in general. And then, I wanted to have a look at Julie von Lembke too, even from a distance. I felt very guilty at having run out on her like that in the afternoon.

III

That entire night, with its absurd incidents and terrible dénouement toward morning, still lingers in my mind as a freak-haunted nightmare and, for me at least, this is the most painful part of the story. I arrived late at the ball, and since it was destined to end abruptly, I came just in time to witness the debacle.

It was between ten and eleven when I reached the head landowner's house. The White Hall in which the literary readings had taken place had been transformed in that short space of time and was ready for use as the main ballroom, where the whole town was expected to dance that night. Now, however much I had doubted the wisdom of holding the ball earlier, I had never expected things to be as bad as they actually were. Not a single family belonging to the upper crust of our society had shown up. No government employee holding a position of any consequence at all was present—and that was a very significant sign. As to the ladies and the daughters of families, Peter's recent calculations (we know now how perfidious they were) had proved completely wrong—very few of them turned up, so that, for every four gentlemen, there was, at most, only one lady and you should have seen what lady at that! Some were alleged to be the wives of some army officers or of post-office employees or other petty clerks; there were three village doctors' wives and two or three wives of the poorer landowners; there were the seven daughters and one niece of the pen-pusher I mentioned earlier and some merchants' wives. This was not at all the company Mrs. von Lembke had expected to find. Half the local shopkeepers even failed to turn up.

As to the men, despite the absence of the cream of our society, there was a fairly imposing number of them. However, the bulk of them produced a disquieting and unpleasant impression. Of course, there were some very quiet, well-behaved army officers with their spouses, and some very law-abiding fathers of families, such as the clerk with his seven daughters twice mentioned above. But these small fry came because of "the inevitability of circumstances" as one of the gentlemen described it himself. But there were also many tough characters, including many of the type whom both Peter and I suspected of not having had legitimate tickets at the matinee earlier that day, and their number seemed to have substantially increased since then. So far, they had all sat in the buffet, to which they had gone immediately upon their arrival as though it were a prearranged meeting place. That, at least, was my impression.

The buffet had been set up in a hall at the end of a long series of rooms. Prokhorich presided over an enticing array of drinks and the specialties of the club's kitchen. I found a number of characters there in almost threadbare suits—a rather disquieting-looking lot who were quite out of place at a ball. I found out later that many of them had had to be sobered up—no easy task—for the occasion and so, of course, were not likely to stay sober long. Most of them were not from our town, and I have no idea where they came from. I knew that

Mrs. von Lembke's original intention had been to keep the ball very democratic; that "even shopkeepers" would be allowed to attend "if any persons of that class presented a duly-purchased ticket." When she said that at a committee meeting, she felt sure that none of our local shopkeepers, most of whom were rather hard up, would think of buying a ticket. Still, I was doubtful whether this shabby and sinister crowd should have been allowed in, however democratic the ball was intended to be. And who could have let them in and what was his purpose in doing so? Liputin and Lyamshin had been deprived of their usher's ribbons, but they were present at the ball and were supposed to take part in the "literary quadrille." Liputin's place as an usher had been given, to my great surprise, to the divinity student whose heckling of Mr. Verkhovensky had made a considerable contribution to the ruining of the matinee performance, and Peter Verkhovensky himself was substituting for Lyamshin. So how could one expect any good to come of it?

I tried to listen to the conversation going on around me and was struck by the wildness of some opinions. I heard it said in one small group that the person who had organized Liza's elopement was none other than Julie von Lembke herself and that she had charged Stavrogin money for her services. They even mentioned the sum involved. They also claimed that these festivities had had the elopement as their main objective and, for that reason, half of the town had refused to appear when they found out about it. And as to the governor himself, he was so shocked that "he had gone off his head," and his wife was now "leading him around as though she had him on a leash."

There was much laughter too—coarse, raucous, wild, sly laughter. The ball was severely criticized and Julie von Lembke was berated without restraint. In general, people talked incoherently, drunkenly, and excitedly, and it was difficult to understand what they were saying or draw any reasonable conclusions from it. There were also some people in the buffet who were simply trying to have a good time, among them a few ladies of the type whom nothing could surprise or frighten, most of them army officers' wives accompanied by their husbands. They formed parties that occupied several separate tables and seemed very happy. The buffet had become a warm shelter where almost half of the public who had come to the ball were gathered. And yet all this crowd was soon bound to flood into the ballroom. It was a frightening thought.

In the White Hall, in the meantime, three meager quadrilles were organized, mostly through the efforts of the prince. The daughters danced while their parents watched them fondly. But even then, many of those parents were trying to think how they could let their daughters have a bit of a good time and then get out of there quickly, before *it* started.

I couldn't convey the state of mind of Mrs. von Lembke herself. I didn't speak to her, although I passed close to her several times. When I came in and bowed to her, she didn't acknowledge my greeting, having failed to notice it—I am sure she really hadn't noticed me. She looked pale and drawn and wore a haughty, scornful expression, but at the same time her eyes looked troubled and alarmed. It was obvious that she was making a violent effort to control herself and that it was causing her great pain, but why and in the name of what did she have to go through with it? She should have left immediately and, most important of all, she should have taken her husband away. But she stayed on. I could tell from her face alone that "her eyes had been opened at last" and that she knew that she had absolutely nothing to wait for any more. She didn't even call Peter over to talk to her, and he seemed to avoid her (I caught a glimpse of him at the bar in the buffet and he seemed extremely happy to me). But she wouldn't leave the ball and refused to let her husband move a step from her side. Oh, up to the last moment, she would have indignantly rejected the slightest hint that he was sick, although by now she really should have realized that he was. As to me, I thought Lembke looked worse than he had earlier. He seemed to be in a dazed state and not to realize very well where he was or what was going on around him. Now and then he looked around with unexpected sternness—twice, for instance, he looked at me like that. Once he began saying something very loudly, then cut himself short, but not before he had frightened a quiet, elderly government employee who had happened to be standing next to him at that moment.

Even the quiet section of the public present in the ballroom looked sullen and frightened from the moment of their arrival, and they shrank away from Mrs. von Lembke, at the same time casting at the governor curious glances that were so insistent they seemed strange coming from frightened people.

"It was the way they looked at him that stabbed me through

and through and made me begin to realize my husband's condition," Julie von Lembke herself told me later.

Yes, it was her fault again! Probably, after my hurried exit from her house earlier that day, she had finally made up her mind, prompted by Peter, that the ball would take place and that she would appear. And then she must have gone to her husband's study, where, using all her charms once again, she had swayed the poor governor, who had been completely shaken by the "literary matinee." But now, at the ball, she must have been suffering horribly, although she still refused to leave! I don't know whether it was the blow to her pride that caused her to stay and suffer or simply that she didn't know what to do next. Despite her haughtiness, she tried to smile ingratiatingly and say a few words to the women, who answered her in different monosyllables, "Yes'm," "No'm," and edged away.

The indisputable elite of our town had only one single representative at the ball—the important retired general whom we had already met at the head landowner's house after the Stavrogin-Gaganov duel and who, on that occasion, "opened the door to impatient public opinion." He walked from room to room with an air of great dignity, listened to conversations, and tried to give the impression that he had come to observe the local mores rather than for his personal enjoyment. Finally, he wound up at Mrs. von Lembke's side and from then on never left her, apparently trying to calm and reassure her. He was so distinguished, so kind, and so very old that anything could be borne from him, even his pity. However, she couldn't admit even to herself that this old gossip dared to pity her and was almost being patronizing in sticking close to her. She understood very well that he thought he was honoring her and she was very humiliated. But the general stuck around and never stopped chattering.

"They say a town can't exist without seven righteous men— is it seven? I can never remember the exact number. Well, I have no idea how many of those seven unquestionably righteous men from our town . . . have the honor of attending your ball, but despite their presence, I somehow feel less and less safe here. You will forgive me, my most enchanting lady, won't you? Actually I mean it allegorically, but still I feel very lucky to be safely back here after venturing to visit the buffet. I feel that our irreplaceable Prokhorich isn't quite in his proper place there, and I'm worried lest his stall be razed to the ground before morning. Oh, I'm just joking, of course.

I'm waiting to see the 'literary quadrille' and then I'm off to bed. I hope you'll forgive an old man who suffers from the gout—I always go to bed early and I'd advise you to turn in too. But, I must tell you, I came here in the first place for the sake of the young beauties whom I couldn't hope to find anywhere in greater numbers than here. Most of the pretty girls come from beyond the river and I never go there. There's the wife of an officer—an infantry officer, I believe—and she's not bad, not bad at all—and she knows it too. I spoke to the little rogue and, believe me, ma'am, she has a very sharp tongue. And there are a lot of fresh young things, also quite pretty, but I see nothing to them except their freshness. But, of course, I don't mind that—see what I mean? There are some delightful fresh buds, although their lips are a little thick. Generally speaking, among Russian beauties there are few who have regular features and, er—their faces often make me think of pancakes, if you don't mind my saying so, ma'am, *et si vous me pardonnez.* But I must say, I don't mind that as long as their eyes are pretty and full of laughter. Yes, these buds are ravishing in their youth, for two, perhaps three years—but then they open up once and for all, and that is what causes that sad indifference in their husbands that is such an important factor in the feminist movement, if, of course, I understand that movement correctly. Now let's see: the ballroom is good; the adjoining rooms are quite nicely decorated. Could be much worse. The band could be much worse too, although I don't say it should be worse. What produces a poor impression is the scarcity of ladies, not to mention the way these people are dressed. And that fellow over there is a disgrace—the one in the gray trousers who is dancing the cancan with such abandon. I could forgive him for behaving like that if he were a bit tight and because he's our local druggist, but it's not even eleven yet and that's much too early to be tight, even for a druggist. Ah yes, two fellows got into a fight by the bar, but they weren't thrown out. I think that before eleven all that sort should be thrown out, regardless of how the public feels about it. Around two or three in the morning, it's different, of course. Then allowances may be made for the prevailing mood. By the way, I wonder if this ball will last until two in the morning? I see that Mrs. Stavrogin didn't keep her word; she didn't send flowers as she promised. But I'll bet she has other things to think about, the *pauvre mère.* Ah, poor Liza! Have you heard the story?

They say there's some kind of a mystery behind it. . . . And Stavrogin is involved in it again! Hm, I suppose I'd better drive back home and turn in; my eyes just won't stay open. Ah, when is the 'literary quadrille' supposed to start?"

Finally, it did start. When people had mentioned the forthcoming ball, the main interest had always been focused on the "literary quadrille" and, since no one had any idea what it could be, everyone was fairly itching with curiosity. Nothing could have been more fatal to its success and, indeed, it turned out to be an unspeakable flop.

The side doors of the White Hall, which until that moment had been locked, were opened and a few masked figures emerged from them. The public eagerly gathered around them. To the last man, all those who had been in the buffet hurried to the White Hall. The masked figures prepared to start their quadrille. I elbowed my way to the front and found a spot just behind the von Lembkes and the general. At that moment, Peter, who until then had kept out of sight, suddenly appeared next to Julie.

"I've been keeping an eye on things in the buffet all the time," he whispered, looking at her with the expression of a guilty schoolboy, which he had obviously assumed just to irritate her even more.

Julie flared up angrily:

"You could at least stop lying to me now, you insolent man!"

The remark was torn from her and, coming out much too loudly, was overheard by a number of people.

Peter scurried off, looking extremely pleased with himself.

It would be difficult to imagine a more pitiful, vulgar, flat, and tasteless allegory than this "literary quadrille" turned out to be. It would have been hard to think up anything less suitable for our public, although, reputedly, it was Karmazinov himself who had contrived it. It is true that the performance was directed by Liputin in consultation with the lame teacher who had been at Virginsky's "birthday party." Nevertheless, it was Karmazinov's idea and, apparently, he originally even wanted to dress up and perform a solo number in the dance.

The quadrille comprised six pitifully disguised couples. Indeed, they could hardly be called disguised, for their attire was very similar to the rest of the public's. Thus, one medium-sized, middle-aged gentleman was wearing a frock coat—in fact, he was dressed very much as people generally dress—

and wore a flowing silver beard (a false beard, which was actually his only claim to disguise). He was shuffling his feet very quickly without moving from the spot and without altering his facial expression, which remained dignified and grave throughout. From time to time he emitted, in a quiet but husky voice, some extraordinary, low-keyed grunts, and these husky grunts were supposed to represent the voice of a famous national daily paper. Opposite this symbolic figure danced two frock-coated giants with the letters X and Z pinned on their coats, letters that were obviously meant to symbolize something—what exactly has never been made clear. "Honest Russian Thought" was incarnated in another middle-aged gentleman wearing a frock coat, glasses, gloves, and handcuffs—real handcuffs. Under his arm, Thought carried a briefcase containing the dossier of some case. An open envelope with a foreign postmark stuck out of his pocket and was supposed to contain a certificate of Honest Russian Thought's honesty. These details were, of course, filled in by the ushers since there was no making them out otherwise—for instance, there was no possible chance of reading the letter from abroad. In his raised right hand, Thought held a wineglass, apparently ready to propose a toast. On either side, he was flanked by two short-haired Nihilist females. Vis-à-vis this trio danced yet another elderly, frock-coated gentleman, but this one was wielding a heavy club. We were told that he symbolized a certain much-feared periodical published outside Petersburg and the gentleman's cudgel was meant to intimate: "If I let it come down on your head, there will be nothing but a grease spot left of you!" However, despite his weapon, the gentleman couldn't withstand the bespectacled gaze of Honest Russian Thought—he tried to look away, and while performing his *pas de deux,* he kept twisting about, apparently not knowing where to hide, so much did his conscience bother him.

I can't remember all the idiotic symbols they had contrived. They were all very much in the same vein, and after a while I began to feel acutely ashamed. A similar feeling was obviously reflected on the faces of the entire audience, including the unprepossessing physiognomies of those who had arrived from the buffet to watch the quadrille. For some time they watched in perplexed hostile silence. As a rule, a man gets angry when he is ashamed and tends to become cynical. Gradually a murmur began to rise from the audience.

"What's it all about?" muttered one of the men who had come from the buffet to the gang around him.

"Who knows, some damn nonsense."

"It's some literary stuff—they're criticizing the *Voice*—"

"What do I care about such bunk!"

From another group, someone shouted, "Ah, the fools!"

"Oh no! It's not them who are fools, it's us!"

"And why are you a fool?"

"No, I myself am no fool."

"Well, if you aren't, I'm certainly not."

In a third group someone suggested,

"We ought to give them a good pasting and then kick them the hell out of here."

From a fourth group a voice asked,

"How can the Lembkes stand by and watch all this? And they don't even look ashamed."

"And why should they be ashamed? What about you; are you ashamed?"

"Yes, even I'm ashamed, and he's the governor—"

"And you're a pig."

"Never in my life have I seen such a vulgar ball of such poor tone," a lady who stood only a few feet from Julie said venomously, obviously intending the remark to be heard.

She was fortyish, stocky, and rather heavily made-up. For this occasion she was wearing a very bright-colored silk dress. Almost everyone in town knew her, but no one received her. She was the widow of a state councilor who had left her a wooden house and a very small income. However, she managed to live well and even drove around in her own carriage. A couple of months earlier she had been among the first to pay a visit to the new governor's wife, but Julie hadn't received her.

"I knew it would turn out like this," she added, looking insolently straight into Julie's face.

"Well, if you knew in advance, why did you come?" Julie said, unable to restrain herself.

"Because I was too trusting," the rapier-tongued lady parried instantly, stepping forward eager for a scrap.

The old general stepped between the two.

"My dear lady," he said, bending toward Julie, "I honestly think that it would be best for us to leave now. I feel we're just in their way and that they'll have a much better time without us. You've done what you could; you've opened the ball and now why not leave them to their own devices? The governor doesn't seem to feel too well. We ought to do our best to see that nothing drastic happens."

But it was already too late.

During the "literary quadrille" the governor had been watching the dancers with an expression of angry perplexity, and when people had started making unpleasant comments, he had looked worriedly around him. That was when he first had become aware of the presence of the shady characters that had emerged from the bar. He had seemed amazed at what he saw.

Suddenly there was a loud burst of laughter. The man symbolizing the "much-feared periodical," the one who was dancing with the cudgel, at last decided that he could no longer bear the bespectacled glare of Honest Russian Thought and, in the last figure of the quadrille, he suddenly stood on his hands and, with his feet in the air, walked straight at the shining glasses, which feat, incidentally, was meant to convey the way common sense had been turned upside down in the periodical in question. Now, since Lyamshin was the only person around who knew how to walk on his hands, the role of the gentleman with the cudgel had been assigned to him. But Julie von Lembke had no idea that anyone had been asked to walk with his feet in the air.

"They concealed it from me entirely," she later told me emphatically, full of indignation and despair.

The crowd roared with laughter. Of course, they weren't reacting to the allegory, which didn't interest them in the least, but simply to the sight of a frock-coated gentleman, in tails and all, walking with his feet in the air. But Governor von Lembke shook with indignation.

"Get that thug!" he shouted, pointing at Lyamshin. "Get hold of him, turn him right side up . . . so that his feet . . . his head is on top . . . on top!"

Lyamshin jumped to his feet and the general laughter increased.

"Out with all the thugs who're laughing!" the governor suddenly ordered, and everything was at once in an uproar.

"That's not right, Your Excellency!"

"You'd better stop insulting the public, sir!"

"You're a big fool yourself!" a voice came from a corner.

"Freebooters!" another voice shouted from another corner.

Lembke quickly turned his head in the direction from which

that last cry had come, turning terribly pale. A stupid smile appeared on his lips, as if he had suddenly remembered something that made him understand what was going on.

"My friends," Julie von Lembke said, addressing the crowd that was advancing on them, "you must forgive the governor. . . ." As she spoke, she retreated, dragging her husband after her. "You see, Mr. von Lembke isn't well; please forgive him, ladies and gentlemen, please!"

I clearly heard her saying "please forgive him." The entire incident lasted only a short time, but I remember well that part of the audience rushed out of the ballroom at that moment, as though panicked by Julie's words. I can still hear one particular hysterical outcry from a woman in tears:

"Ah, it's the same thing as this morning all over again!"

Then suddenly it was as though another explosion had gone off in the middle of the melee—also rather like what had happened at the "literary matinee."

"Fire! The whole quarter beyond the river is on fire!"

I don't remember where that terrible cry originated, whether it came from the ballroom or from someone who had rushed upstairs from outside. But there followed a panic that I won't even try to describe. More than half the guests at the ball either lived in or owned wooden houses beyond the river. People pushed their way to the windows, pulled back the curtains, tore down the blinds. . . . The quarter beyond the river was aflame. True, the fire had only just started—in fact, there were three separate conflagrations, and it was this circumstance that frightened them.

"It's arson! It's the work of the Shpigulin workers!" people shouted.

I remember a few typical exclamations:

"I've felt in my heart that they were going to set something on fire! I've had a premonition about it for the last few days!"

"Yes, sure thing, it's the Shpigulin men! Who else could it be?"

"Yes, and they lured us here on purpose so they could set our houses on fire!"

This last shout, the most surprising of the lot, was the spontaneous, instinctive outcry of some woman whose worldly goods were on fire and who looked somewhat as I picture Gogol's Mother Korobochka.

They all rushed toward the exit. I will not try to describe the melee in the cloakroom, where people scrambled for their fur coats, shawls, and cloaks—the shrieks of the ladies and the tears of their daughters. I doubt that any deliberate thefts were committed at that point, but obviously, in the ensuing havoc, many had to leave furs and shawls that they couldn't find behind them. Afterward they kept talking about their losses all over town, gradually adding more and more embellishments and building up whole legends.

The Lembkes were almost smothered by the crowd in the doorway.

"Stop them all!" the governor shouted furiously, spreading out his arms. "I don't want a single one to escape! I want you to search the lot of them, one after the other, right away!"

A flood of abuse answered him from the ballroom.

"Andrei, please—Andrei!" Julie cried, desperately trying to calm him.

"Arrest her first!" Lembke shouted, pointing an accusing finger at his wife. "Search her first! This ball was organized with the object of abetting the arson!"

Julie let out a piercing cry and fainted (oh, there is not the slightest doubt that this fainting spell was a genuine one!). The general, the prince, I myself, and some others, even including some ladies, rushed to help her in this painful moment. We carried the poor woman out of that hell and placed her in her carriage. She didn't recover her senses until the carriage had almost reached the governor's mansion, and her first concern was again for her husband. Now that all her dreams had been shattered, there was nothing but her Andrei left in her life.

A doctor was sent for. I stayed there for a full hour, waiting. So did the prince. The general, in a fit of gallantry (although he had been rather frightened himself), insisted that he would remain at "the poor lady's bedside" until morning, but ten minutes later, while we were still waiting for the doctor, he fell asleep in an armchair in the drawing room, so we just left him there.

The police commissioner, who rushed straight from the ball to the burning suburb, succeeded in getting the governor out of the ballroom just behind us and urged him to get into the carriage with his wife, repeating that "His Excellency" needed a rest. But he wasn't firm enough with Lembke, who, of course, wouldn't listen to suggestions about taking a rest and was anxious to go to the fire. So the police commissioner took him across the river with him in his own carriage. Later, he reported that the governor was gesticulating violently all the way there and kept "shouting out orders that were impossible to carry out, owing to their strangeness." Later, it was officially announced that "His Excellency was already in a delirious condition at that time as a result of a sudden shock."

No need to dwell on the way the ball ended. A few score of the gentlemen and some ladies, who were having a good time, remained behind. With no police left, these people refused to let the band go, pummeling any musicians who tried to leave. By morning, "Prokhorich's stall" was razed to the ground. The rowdies drank themselves into a daze, danced wildly, and made a mess of the rooms. At dawn, some of them, completely drunk, arrived at the fire, where new trouble was brewing; and others collapsed on the carpets and velvet sofas, where they slept off their drunkenness, leaving the usual marks behind them.

Later, in the morning, they were dragged out by their feet by the servants and thrown into the street.

Thus ended the festivities organized in aid of the needy governesses of our province.

IV

The fire alarmed the inhabitants of the suburb across the river because it was so obviously a case of arson. It is worth noting that as soon as someone announced that the suburb was on fire, several people shouted that it was the "work of the Shpigulin workers." We now know for a fact that three workers from the Shpigulin plant did take part in setting the fire, but it was only those three, and the other workers were completely exonerated both officially and by public opinion. Besides the three thugs—one of whom was caught and confessed, while the two others are still at large—there is no doubt that Fedka the convict took part in setting the fire. That is all that is known for sure so far about the origins of the fires, although, of course, all sorts of guesses and theories exist. As to what motive the three thugs could have had and the question of whether or not they were acting on someone's orders—these are matters that are very difficult to decide even today.

Because of the strong wind and because almost all the houses across the river were wooden and, finally, because they had been set on fire in three places (actually only two, be-

cause they managed to get the third under control almost the
minute it flared up, as we shall see later), the fire spread with
extraordinary speed. Still, in the reports that appeared in the
Moscow and Petersburg press, our calamity was greatly exaggerated: actually at most a quarter, and probably less, of
the right-bank suburb of our town was burned out. Our fire
brigade, although rather small relative to the size and population of our town, was on this occasion very efficient, determined, and self-sacrificing. But, nevertheless, they wouldn't
have been very successful, even assuming they had received
great assistance from the citizens, had it not been for a change
in the wind, which suddenly dropped just before dawn.

When, about an hour after my flight from the ball, I reached
the burning suburb, the fire was at its height. The street that
ran along the riverbank was entirely ablaze. It was as bright
as day. I won't bother to depict the fire, for who isn't familiar
with such a sight in Russia? In the side streets leading onto
the burning avenue, there was a great deal of hustle and
bustle. The people living there were certain the fire would
reach them; they dragged their belongings outside, but remained near their doorsteps, sitting, in the meantime, on the
trunks and featherbeds they had tossed out of their windows.
Part of the male population was hard at work, ruthlessly chopping down fences and even razing to the ground the hovels
that were nearest to the fire and down wind from it. Small
children who had been awakened by the noise were crying,
and women who had had time to drag out their junk and now
had nothing to do were howling and wailing. Those who were
still bringing out their possessions were silent for the time
being. There were sparks and embers flying all over the place,
and people put them out as best they could. At the scene of the
fire itself, there were throngs of people who had come from all
sides of town. Some gave a hand in fighting the fire, others
just stared. A great fire at night always produces an exciting
and exhilarating effect—that is the main idea behind fireworks.
But then, fireworks create regular and eye-pleasing patterns
and, in view of their complete safety, their effect is light and
cheerful, similar in a way to the effect produced by a glass of
champagne. A real fire is quite a different matter: there's
horror in it, combined with a feeling of being personally
endangered, however slightly, and that is again combined with
the exhilarating effect a fire at night causes in the spectator
(though, of course, not in the inhabitants of the burning

house), a certain mental excitement, a kind of challenge to the destructive instincts that, alas, lie buried in the soul of the meekest, gentlest family man and humblest petty employee. This grim sensation is almost always overpowering.

"I really wonder if it is possible to watch a fire without deriving a certain fire from it!"

That is exactly what the elder Verkhovensky had said to me once, while he was still under the immediate impression of a night fire he had seen by chance.

Of course, even a lover of night fires can, on occasion, dive into the flames himself to save a child or an old woman, but that is quite another matter.

Following close behind a group of curious onlookers, I found myself, without having had to ask any questions, at the largest and most dangerous focus of the fire, where I caught sight of the governor, whom Mrs. von Lembke had asked me to find. He was in a strange and puzzling state. He was standing on a fallen and broken fence; thirty yards or so to his left rose the blackened skeleton of a gutted two-story wooden house with two horizontal rows of gaping holes in place of windows, a caved-in roof, and thinning tongues of flame still creeping along the charred beams. At the back of the courtyard behind the skeleton of the house, a small cottage, also two-storied, was beginning to blaze, and firemen were trying frantically to check the fire. To Lembke's right, firemen, assisted by the crowd, were dousing a large wooden building; they had succeeded thus far in keeping the fire under control, although it had flared up several times already and the building was bound to perish in the end. The governor, his face turned toward the cottage, was gesticulating and shouting out orders to which no one paid any attention. I thought at first that they had just left him there so he wouldn't get in the way. He was surrounded by a dense, motley crowd that, besides all sorts of common people, included some gentlemen and even the chief priest of our cathedral. Yet, though they listened to the governor's shouts with curiosity and amazement, no one tried to talk to him or take him away.

Governor von Lembke had lost his hat and stood there bareheaded and haggard, with his eyes glittering, making the most extraordinary statements.

"It's all the work of arsonists! It's sheer Nihilism! Whatever burns can be only the work of the Nihilists!" I heard him shouting, and although, from what I had seen before, it shouldn't have surprised me particularly, each actual contact with madness always has a shocking effect.

Finally, a policeman elbowed his way over to him and said:

"Your Excellency, perhaps you ought to go home and get some rest. Even just standing here is too dangerous for Your Excellency."

As I found out later, this officer had been specially detailed to watch over the governor, to try to convince him to go home, and in case of extreme emergency, even to use force—a task that was obviously beyond the power of this particular representative of the police.

"They'll dry the tears of the victims of the fires, but they'll see to it that the town is burned down! And all this is the work of four or, at most, four and a half thugs! Arrest him! It's all his work—he was just slandering the other four and a half. He sneaks into families and disgraces them! To set these houses on fire, they used the governesses! That's low and shameful! Ah, what's he trying to do?" he shrieked suddenly, seeing a fireman on the roof of the burning cottage, with flames leaping all around him. "Pull that man down! He'll fall through! He'll catch fire! Put that fire out! . . . What's he doing there anyway?"

"He's trying to put the fire out, Your Excellency."

"Nonsense! The fire is in the minds of people and not on the roofs of houses. Pull him down and leave those houses alone! Yes, it's better to give up putting out fires and then things will take care of themselves somehow. Oh, who's that crying in there? It's an old woman screaming! Why have they forgotten to pull her out?"

To be sure, the eighty-year-old aunt of the merchant who owned the burning cottage was still in her ground-floor room. But she hadn't really been forgotten—she had rushed back into the house with the insane notion of saving her featherbed before her corner room caught fire, and the fire had spread to it while she was in there. Now, choking with smoke and screaming with pain from her burns, the old woman was nevertheless pushing her featherbed through the broken windowpane with her wrinkled old hands.

Governor von Lembke rushed to her assistance. Everyone around saw him run up to the window, take hold of a corner of the featherbed, and pull at it as hard as he could. But at that moment a rafter fell from the roof, hitting the hapless man. He wasn't killed. But the end of the rafter that struck the back of his neck and felled him, unconscious, marked the end of Andrei von Lembke's career, at least as governor of our province.

At last day came and it was a gloomy and dismal one. The wind fell, the air grew suddenly still, and a drizzle started to fall as fine as though it were coming through a sieve. The fire abated.

I was in another part of the suburb, quite a distance from the spot where Lembke had fallen, and I heard all sorts of strange things said in the crowd around me. A very strange fact had come to light: just about the first house to catch fire was a newly built, isolated cottage standing at least fifty yards from the nearest house in an empty lot and separated from the rest of the suburb by vegetable patches. Now, even if that house had burned down completely, it couldn't possibly have set any other building on fire and vice versa—even if the whole suburb had burned down, that house could not have been affected, whatever the strength and direction of the wind. So it could only have caught fire independently, and therefore there was something suspicious about it. But the most remarkable part of it is that it never did burn down and strange things were discovered to have happened there. The owner of this house, an artisan who lived in a nearby settlement, caught sight of his new house on fire, rushed over there, and with the assistance of his neighbors, checked the fire by scattering logs that someone had piled against the wooden wall of the house and ignited. But then it was discovered that the tenants of the house, a retired captain, his sister, and their old maid, had been murdered during that night and apparently robbed. It was, by the way, to this spot that the police commissioner had gone while Lembke was trying to rescue the featherbed.

By morning this news had spread, and a huge crowd, including many who had been left homeless by the fire, rushed over to the isolated house. It was difficult to work one's way through the throng of people. I soon found out that the captain had been found lying fully dressed on a bench with his throat cut, that he had apparently been dead drunk and never knew what happened, and that he had "bled like an ox." On the other hand, his sister was all covered with knife wounds and was lying on the floor by the door, so she must have been awake and have attempted to fight off her assailant. The maid, who must also have been awake, had had her head cracked open. According to the landlord, the captain had come to see him earlier that day, already quite drunk, and had boastfully shown him all the money he had to spend— there was a lot of it, maybe as much as two hundred rubles. An old and battered wallet belonging to the captain was found empty on the floor. But his sister's trunk hadn't been touched, nor had the silver setting of the icon nor any of the clothes belonging to the captain. It was obvious that the murderer had been in a hurry to get out of there, that he was familiar with the captain's habits, and that he'd come specially for the money and knew where to find it. Had the owner of the house not rushed over there and scattered the logs, the house would have burned to the ground and it would have been hard to tell what had happened from the charred bodies.

This is how the story was given to me. Furthermore, I learned that the house had been rented for the captain and his sister by Mr. Nikolai Stavrogin, the son of Mrs. Varvara Stavrogin, the widow of General Vsevolod Stavrogin, and that he'd come in person and had even been quite insistent, since the landlord had had no intention of renting the house at all, having built it with the idea of making an inn out of it; he had finally accepted only when Mr. Stavrogin paid him for six months in advance.

"And the fire was no accident," people in the crowd kept repeating.

Most of the people were silent, sullen, and morose, but I didn't see any signs of great indignation. However, listening to the people around me. I heard still more about Nikolai Stavrogin: the murdered woman, it was said, was his wife; on the previous day, he had "disgracefully abducted" a young lady belonging to one of the foremost families of our town—the daughter of Mrs. Drozdov; a complaint had been made against him to the authorities in Petersburg; and it looked as if he had had his wife killed off so that he could marry the young lady.

Since Skvoreshniki was only a couple of miles away, I wondered whether I shouldn't go over there and warn them about it all. But then, I didn't feel that anyone was trying to incite the crowd to violence deliberately, although I did recognize a couple of the shady characters whom I had noticed in the bar at the ball. And I particularly noticed a thin, rather tall, pock-marked fellow, a locksmith by trade as I found out later, who was all grimy and covered with soot now. He was quite sober, I'm sure, but he seemed to be beside himself and stood out among the gloomy, sullen crowd. He kept addressing the people around him, but I couldn't make any sense from what he was saying. Indeed, I'm sure he said nothing more coherent than, "Well, pals, what's going on, after all? Is it really going to continue like this, with us just standing by?" and as he talked, he kept waving his arms.

chapter 3

THE END OF A ROMANCE

I

From the large drawing room at Skvoreshniki—the one where Mrs. Stavrogin and Mr. Verkhovensky had met for the last time—the fire could be seen as plainly as if it lay in the palm of one's hand. As it was dawning, around six in the morning, Liza stood by the corner window, her eyes fixed on the fading, reddish glow. She was all alone in the drawing room and wore the same beautiful dress she had had on at the "literary reading" the day before—a gorgeous light-green creation all covered with lace, but which was now crumpled and had obviously been put on carelessly and in a hurry. At one point she noticed that the front of her dress was not properly done up. She blushed, hurriedly fastened it, and picked up a red shawl she had thrown on a chair when she'd arrived the day before, and put it around her shoulders. Some locks of her beautiful hair that had come loose fell from under the shawl onto her right shoulder. Her face looked drawn and worried, but her eyes glowed from under her knitted brows. She returned to the window and pressed her burning forehead against the cold pane. The door opened and Stavrogin came in.

"I've sent a messenger on horseback," he said, "and in ten minutes we'll find out what's going on over there. In the meantime, I heard them say that the part of the suburb immediately by the embankment and to the right of the bridge has been all but burned out. It wasn't even midnight when the fire started. It's dying out now, though."

He walked toward the window where she stood, stopping three steps behind her. But she didn't turn toward him.

"According to the calendar," she said irritatedly, "the sun should've risen a full hour ago, but it looks like night outside."

"Never trust calendars," he said lightly and tried to smile, but somehow felt ashamed and added hurriedly: "It's so boring to live by the calendar, Liza."

He fell silent, annoyed with himself for uttering a new platitude.

"You're so depressed when you're with me," Liza said, with a little, twisted smile, "that you can't even find words. But please don't worry, you had a good point about the calendar—why, every step I take is calculated according to it, everything I do, in fact. . . . Does that surprise you?"

She turned away from the window and sat down in an armchair.

"Please, sit down too," she added. "We have only a little time to spend together and I'd like to say whatever comes into my head, and I wish you'd do the same."

Stavrogin sat down next to her and shyly, almost fearfully, took her hand.

"What sort of talk is this, Liza? What makes you say these things? Why do you say we have only a short time to spend together? That's the second puzzling statement you've made since you woke up half an hour ago."

"So now you've started counting my puzzling statements," Liza said, laughing nervously. "Don't you remember that when I arrived yesterday, I presented myself as a dead woman? Have you decided to forget that statement or did you simply pay no attention to it?"

"I don't remember, Liza. But why should you describe yourself as a dead woman? You must live. . . ."

"Now why have you fallen silent again? What's happened to your eloquence? I've had my time in this world—it's enough for me. Do you remember Christopher?"

"No, I don't," Stavrogin said, frowning.

"Why, Christopher—in Lausanne. You got terribly tired of him. He'd open your door and say, 'May I drop in for just a moment?'—and then stay the whole day. I don't want to be like Christopher and bore you all day."

A pained expression passed across his face.

"Liza, you hurt me when you say those twisted things, and

this pose of yours must hurt you too, I'm sure. Why do you have to do it? What's the point?"

Her eyes flashed.

"Liza," he said again, "I swear I love you more now than I did yesterday when you came to me!"

"What a strange statement! Why do you have to measure today by yesterday?"

"You won't leave me now, Liza, will you?" he said, almost in despair. "We'll go away together, today, won't we, Liza?"

"Ouch! Stop squeezing my hand like that! You're hurting me! Now, where do you think we could go 'today'? Somewhere, perhaps, where we could be 'resurrected'? No, I've tried that too many times—I can't make it; it's quite beyond my capacities. If we must go anywhere, let it be Moscow where we could visit people and receive visitors at home— that would be the ideal life for me—and, remember, even back in Switzerland I never tried to hide from you the kind of person I am. But since it's impossible for you to go to Moscow and visit people because you happen to be married, what is there to talk about?"

"But, Liza, what was it all about then, yesterday?"

"Yesterday was yesterday and it's gone."

"It's impossible! It's too cruel—"

"So what if it is cruel? You'll just have to put up with it."

"You're just trying to get back at me for your own whim of yesterday," he snorted spitefully.

"What a despicable thing to say!" she cried, flushing.

"Why then did you have to bestow 'this great happiness' on me? I have at least the right to an explanation, it seems to me—"

"I'm afraid you'll just have to forgo that right of yours. Now, don't make it worse: your supposition was despicable enough; you don't have to top it by stupidity. Nothing works for you today. By the way, perhaps you're afraid society will reproach you for accepting 'this great happiness'? If that's what's worrying you, for heaven's sake relax—you're in no way responsible for what happened and you need account to no one. Even when I opened your door yesterday, you had no idea who it was. It was nothing but a whim of mine, as you said yourself just now. So you see, you can look everyone straight in the eye and even like a sort of conqueror, if you wish."

"The things you say and the way you laugh, Liza, have

been horrifying me for perhaps an hour now. This 'happiness' you speak of so scornfully means everything to me. How can I lose you now? I swear I didn't love you this way yesterday. So why do you have to take it all away from me now? Do you know what this new hope has cost me? I've paid a life for it, Liza."

"What life? Yours or someone else's?"

He got up quickly.

"What do you mean by that?" he said, staring at her.

"Have you paid for it with your life or mine?—that's what I asked you. Why, you can't seem to understand what I say any more!" she said, flushing. "Why did you leap up so suddenly just now? And why are you staring at me with that expression? You frighten me! I noticed long ago that you're afraid of something—for instance, now, this very minute—ah God, why have you turned so pale?"

"If you know something, Liza, I swear, I don't—I wasn't thinking of *that* when I said that about paying a life—"

"I don't understand you at all," Liza said with hesitation, a note of fear in her voice.

After a while, a slow, faraway smile appeared on his lips. Unhurriedly, he sat down, put his elbows on his knees, and buried his face in his hands.

"A bad dream—a nightmare. We were talking about two different things."

"I have no idea what you were talking about—but didn't you know yesterday that I'd leave you today? Did you know it or didn't you? Now don't lie, did you really not know it?"

"I knew," he said in a very low voice.

"Well then—you knew it and you used the 'moment' at your discretion. What else is there left to say?"

"Now you tell me the truth," he said, and it was obvious that he was in great pain. "When you opened my door yesterday, did you know yourself that you were only going to stay an hour?"

She glared at him with hatred.

"Really, how can a sensible person ask such surprising questions! And anyway, why should it worry you so much? Can it be because a woman is walking out on you before you can walk out on her? Shall I tell you something, Nikolai? Well, while I've been here, I've found you very magnanimous toward me and that's something I can't stand from you."

She got up and took a few steps around the room.

"All right then, let's assume it must all end this way, but tell me—how could it have happened in the first place?"

"Don't you really have anything else to worry about? Anyway, you've worked it all out yourself. You understand what happened better than anyone, and you counted on it's happening. As for me, I am a young maiden brought up on opera, and that's how it all started."

"That's not true."

"There's nothing in that to injure your self-esteem, and it *is* the truth. It all started with a moment of great beauty that swept me off my feet. The other day, when I publicly insulted you and you answered me with such knightly gallantry, I realized, when I returned home, that you'd been avoiding me because you were married and not because you despised me, which, as a young society lady, was what I dreaded most. I understood that you were running away from me for my own salvation, fool that I was. So you see how subtly I discerned your chivalry! Then Peter came along and explained it all to me again. He also told me that you were driven by some idea, beside which he and I were nothing, but that I was in your way all the same. Then he managed to drag himself into it too. He insisted that the three of us were somehow bound together and kept saying the most fantastic things, something from some old Russian opera about a bark and oars made of maple wood. I complimented him and told him that he was a poet, and he took it at face value. And since I knew that I'd only last one moment anyway, I decided to do it. Well, so much for that—let's leave it there or we may quarrel again. But please don't let anyone intimidate you—I take the whole responsibility upon myself. I'm bad and whimsical and I fell for the lover's boat in the opera. I'm a well brought-up young lady —but, you know, I thought you loved me a great deal. So don't despise me too much, poor fool that I am, and don't laugh over that dainty little tear you may have seen falling just now. I adore crying out of self-pity. All right, that's enough now. I'm no good for anything and neither are you; we've dealt each other a couple of little slaps and that at least affords us the consolation of keeping our vanity intact."

"Nightmarish ravings!" Stavrogin cried, pacing the room and wringing his hands. "Liza, you poor girl, what have you done to yourself?"

"I've just burned my finger in a candle flame, that's all.

You're not crying, are you? Come on, behave—try to be a bit less sensitive."

"But what did you come for, why?"

"But, good Lord, can't you see what a ridiculous position you would place yourself in in the eyes of the world by asking such questions?"

"Why did you have to ruin your life so stupidly and in such an ugly way? And what is there to do now?"

"Is this Stavrogin speaking—Stavrogin the Bloodthirsty, as a certain lady around here who's in love with you calls you? Listen now, I made my calculations and compressed my whole life into one hour. I'm content. Why don't you do some calculating of your own? But, actually, why should you? You have plenty of 'hours' and 'moments' still coming to you."

"Just as many as you have. Take my word for it—not a single hour more than is coming to you."

He was still pacing the room and missed her quick, piercing glance that suddenly seemed to brighten with hope. A moment later, the brightness vanished.

"If only you knew the price I'm paying for my present impossible sincerity, Liza. If only I could explain to you—"

"Explain? You want to explain something to me? God save me from your explanations!" she interrupted him, almost in panic.

He stopped and looked at her in anguish.

"I must confess to you that even in Switzerland I was convinced that you had something horrible, disgusting, and murderous on your conscience—something that, at the same time, made you incredibly ridiculous. So you'd better be careful before you start revealing any secrets to me, for I'll laugh you off the face of the earth. Yes, I'll keep laughing at you as long as you live! Oh Lord, there you're turning pale again! All right, all right, I'll stop. I'm going now."

She rose from her chair with a gesture of scorn and distaste.

"Torment me, torture me, vent your spite on me," he cried in despair. "You have an absolute right. I knew I didn't love you and I've ruined you. Yes, I 'kept that moment for myself'; I had a hope—for a long time—one last hope. I couldn't resist the warmth that flooded my heart when you walked in yesterday, having come on your own initiative, yourself, alone. For a moment I believed it. . . . Perhaps I believe it now."

"Now I'll pay you back in kind for such noble sincerity:

I have not the slightest desire to be a sympathizing nurse to you. I may end up as a hospital nurse if I don't manage to die conveniently this very day, but I'll certainly not nurse you, although, of course, you're as badly off as any poor legless or armless creature. I've always imagined that you'd take me to some place where there lived a huge, vicious, man-sized spider and that we'd spend the rest of our lives staring at it in fear. And that's how we'd spend our days of mutual love. You'd better ask dear little Dasha, she'll go with you wherever you wish."

"Did you really have to bring her into it, even now?"

"Poor little lap dog! Give her my love when you see her. Did she know, even in Switzerland, that you had already allotted your old age to her? What admirable planning! Oh, who's that?"

At the far end of the drawing room a door opened slightly, a head popped in, then hurriedly withdrew.

"Is that you, Alexei?" Stavrogin asked.

"No, it's just little me," Peter Verkhovensky said, this time thrusting himself halfway in. "Hello, Liza, or should we say good morning, rather. I was sure I'd find you two together in this drawing room. Oh, I only dropped in for a second. I'm sorry, Stavrogin, but I must have two words with you; I simply must—but only two, I promise!"

Stavrogin moved toward him, but after three steps turned to Liza and said:

"If you hear something in a moment, Liza, you can be sure it's my doing."

She shuddered and looked at him fearfully, but he hurried away.

II

The room from which Peter had peeped was a large, oval vestibule. Alexei had been sitting there when Peter had arrived and Peter had sent him away. Stavrogin closed the drawing-room door behind him and stood waiting. Peter gave him a quick, searching look.

"Well?"

"Well, in case you already know," Peter said hurriedly, with a look in his eyes that seemed to want to probe into Stavrogin's soul, "then you must realize that none of us can be held the slightest bit responsible for what happened and you least of all, because it's such a—er—such a combination of circumstances—such a coincidence—well, in a word, they can't possibly hold anything against you, legally that is, and that's what I came here to tell you."

"Have they been burned? Murdered?"

"Murdered, but not burned, and that's just the trouble—but I swear to you that even this is not my fault, whatever you may suspect, and you do suspect me, don't you? Let me tell you the whole truth. It did actually occur to me—it was you yourself who gave me the idea, although you didn't mean it seriously—you were sort of teasing me, for you'd never say such a thing seriously—but I wasn't going to do it; I wouldn't have done it for anything, not even for a hundred rubles and so much the less as I had nothing to gain by it—that is, I personally," he rattled on in a great hurry. "But then there was the following combination of circumstances: I paid out of my own pocket—yes, out of my own money; there wasn't a single ruble belonging to you in it and you know it very well—I paid two hundred and thirty rubles to that drunken idiot Lebyatkin. I gave him the money two days ago, in the evening, and not yesterday after the 'literary matinee,' I'd like you to note—it's very important. It was a great coincidence, because I didn't know for sure then that Liza would come to you. Now, I paid my own money because you decided two days ago to tell everybody your secret. All right, all right, I'm not interfering—it's your private business. You're a gallant knight and all that, but I admit, I was stunned, as though someone had hit me on the head with a club. But since I was rather fed up with all these dramatics—and I mean it quite seriously, because they interfere with my plans—I decided that the Lebyatkins had better get the hell out of here and go to Petersburg without your knowledge and, I thought, that shouldn't be so difficult because he was very eager to get there himself. Now at this point I may have made a mistake: I gave him that money in your name. What do you say, was it a mistake or not? Maybe it wasn't. Now listen, listen how it all turned out—"

In his excitement, he advanced toward Stavrogin and reached out for his lapel—perhaps deliberately. Stavrogin struck a swift and powerful blow at his arm.

"Why, what's come over you—you could've broken my arm. . . . As I was saying, it was mainly the combination of circumstances," he rattled on again, apparently having forgotten the blow. "So I handed him the money in the evening on condition that he and his sister leave at daybreak, and I asked that crook Liputin to see that they did. But Liputin wished to play his schoolboy prank at that 'literary matinee'— I suppose you've heard about it? So listen, they sit and drink together and compose verses, with Liputin making up half of them himself. Then he stuffs Lebyatkin into a frock coat and, while assuring me he'd sent him off to Petersburg that morning, he hides him in a back room, ready to be pushed out onto the platform. But Lebyatkin somehow manages to get at the liquor and Liputin, to his surprise, finds him blind drunk. Then there's the row caused by their verses and they carry Lebyatkin off home, dead drunk—after Liputin has removed the two hundred rubles from his pocket, leaving him the change. Unfortunately, however, earlier in the morning Lebyatkin had gone around showing those two hundred rubles to the wrong people and bragging. Well, that was what Fedka the convict was waiting for. He'd overheard things at Kirilov's —remember the hint you dropped?—so he decided to make good on the opportunity. And that's the whole truth. I'm glad, at least, that Fedka didn't find the money, for originally he hoped to get a thousand out of it, the low schemer! He was in too much of a hurry, and it looks as though he got scared of the fire himself. Believe me, that fire was a terrible blow to me. No, but just think of it—it's absolute mob rule! You see, since I expect so much of you, I won't keep anything secret from you now: yes, I'd been toying with the idea of a fire for a long time, because it's so close to the people's hearts, so popular—but I was keeping it for the right moment, for that critical, precious moment when we would all rise and— but they decided on their own authority to start it now, without waiting for the 'go ahead' order, at a time when we were supposed to be lying low and holding our breath. It's sheer mob rule and indiscipline! I still don't know too much about how it happened. There's talk about two Shpigulin factory workers. But I can tell you that if I ever find out that one of *our* people had a hand in it, it'll be the end of him! Well, you see what happens when discipline is relaxed even the tiniest bit! Ah no, this democratic scum with their cells of five is absolutely unreliable. What we really need is one magnificent and despotic will, an idol resting on something unchangeable and standing aloof. Then even the Fives would cringe and put their tails between their legs and, once filled with awe, would be useful when the occasion arises. But in any case, although people are going around shouting at the top of their voices that Stavrogin needed to burn his wife to death and that's why the town has burned down, nevertheless—"

"So they're already shouting that?"

"Well, not really—at least I haven't heard anything like that myself. But you know how people are in general and people whose houses have just been burned down in particular: it's *vox populi vox Dei.* How long do you think it takes to spread an idiotic rumor? But what do you have to worry about? Legally, you're completely innocent—and morally too. You never wanted it to happen, there's no evidence against you whatsoever. It was all pure coincidence. Of course, Fedka could recall your careless hint at Kirilov's that time (it's a pity you had to say that!), but even that proves nothing; anyway, we'll see to it that Fedka keeps quiet. In fact, I'll see to it today."

"So the bodies weren't burned at all?"

"Not a bit. That animal didn't do anything properly. But I'm very pleased to see, at least, that you're taking it so calmly. Because, although you had nothing to do with it, not even in thought, still . . . And then, you must agree, this fixes things up very nicely for you: you're an unattached widower now and free to marry a beautiful maiden with a huge amount of capital who, by the way, is already at your beck and call, whenever you wish. You see what a simple, haphazard combination of circumstances can achieve! Great, don't you think?"

"Are you trying to threaten me, you damned fool?"

"Come on, come on, stop it! Why am I a damn fool now, and what kind of a way is that to talk anyway? You ought to rejoice and instead you—I hurried over here to let you in on the good news. And how could I possibly threaten you? And even if I could control you by threats, what good would it do me? I want you with me of your own free will, not out of fear. You're my light and my sun and it's I who am terribly afraid of you, not you of me. I'm no Maurice Drozdov, remember! And can you imagine—I came dashing over here in an open carriage, and I saw Drozdov standing by your garden fence. His coat was drenched through. I suppose he must have spent the whole night there. It's really amazing how crazy some people can be!"

"Really? Drozdov was there?"

"Sure he was. By the garden fence. I'd say he's about three hundred yards from here right now. I tried to slip by, but he saw me all right. So you didn't know he was here? In that case, I'm very glad I didn't forget to warn you. A man like that can be most dangerous, especially if he's carrying a gun. And then, he's bound to be irritated by a night spent in the mud and rain and all that. Anyone would get irritated under such circumstances, ha-ha-ha! And what do you think makes him stand there like that?"

"Obviously he's waiting for Liza."

"Some hope! Why on earth should she go out to him? Especially in this rain. Ah, the poor imbecile!"

"She'll go out to him in a moment."

"Aha! That's news! So it turns out after all that—but listen, I don't get it: now that the whole situation has changed, what does she need Drozdov for? You're a widower now and can marry her any moment—tomorrow if you wish. Isn't that right? She probably doesn't know what's happened yet. Well, let me take care of that—I'll arrange it all for you in a minute. Where is she? Let me tell her the good news and make her happy!"

"You think that'll make her happy?"

"I'm sure it will. Let's go."

"And you're also sure that she'll suspect nothing, with those bodies and all?" Stavrogin said, screwing up his eyes in a peculiar way.

"Of course she won't suspect anything!" Peter said in a light and deliberately stupid tone, "because, from the legal viewpoint—ah, you're funny! Suppose she did suspect something, what's the difference? Women are so good at ignoring things when it suits them. I can see that you still don't know women! Besides, she has every reason to marry you now, because she's involved herself in a scandalous situation. And then, I also spoke to her about that opera bark because I saw she'd go for that stuff. So I know what this girl is made of, and I assure you she'll step very daintily over those corpses, especially since you actually happen to be innocent of the crime. She won't even mention the corpses for at least a year of your married life and when she does bring them up, it will only be her way of giving you the needle. But then, every woman when she's walking to the altar gets hold of something from her husband's past that she'll be able to use against him one day. But who knows what'll happen in a year, anyway, ha-ha-ha!"

"Since you've a carriage by the door, I'd like you to take

her to Drozdov now. She's just told me she can't stand me and that she's leaving. So I'm sure she won't want to ride in my carriage."

"What? You can't mean it seriously? Why should she wish to leave? Whatever can have happened?" Peter asked, gaping stupidly at Stavrogin.

"She managed to guess somehow, last night, that I don't love her. Although I suppose she must've known it all along."

"But is it true, then, that you don't love her?" Peter exclaimed, looking flabbergasted. "If you don't love her, why did you allow her to stay with you overnight; an honorable man would have warned her as soon as she came in. You have acted disgracefully and I wonder whether you realize what an unpleasant position that leaves me in where she is concerned."

Suddenly Stavrogin began to laugh.

"I'm looking at my ape," he immediately explained.

"I see, you've guessed that I was playing the fool." Peter let out an extremely cheerful peal of laughter. "I did so to make you laugh and cheer you up because, as soon as I came in, I saw from your face that your amorous experience had been none too successful. Perhaps it was a complete flop? I'll bet," he suddenly shouted, almost choking with glee, "that you spent the night sitting next to each other on straight chairs in the drawing room and arguing on some lofty subject while the precious time slipped by. . . . Please, please don't mind my saying so—I was certain even yesterday that it would all end up in some such absurdity! Actually I only brought her here to amuse you and to prove to you that you won't be bored as long as I'm along. I'll render you three hundred more services like this because, in general, I like to oblige people. So now, if you have no further use for her, which is just what I was expecting on my way here, then—"

"So you brought her here just to amuse me?"

"Sure, why else?"

"And not to force me to kill my wife?"

"Wow! But since you didn't kill her! You really love to say dramatic things!"

"What's the difference. So it was you who killed her."

"But I didn't, you know, I had absolutely nothing to do with it, not the least tiny thing. However, you're beginning to worry me."

"Wait, I would like you to go on with what you started

telling me. You said that if I had no further use for Liza, then . . . What then?"

"Then, of course, you can leave me to deal with her. I'll have Maurice Drozdov marry her. By the way, it wasn't on my advice that he spent the night sitting by your garden fence. Don't get that idea into your head. Actually, I'm rather afraid of him. Now you're asking me to take her in my open carriage, but let me tell you, coming here, I didn't feel too happy as I dashed past him. Really, just suppose he'd had his revolver! A good thing I took mine along." He took his gun out of his pocket, showed it to Stavrogin, and put it back again. "I like to have it when I go on long trips. But I'm positive I can arrange things very quickly, because her heart must be longing for her Maurice now, or if it isn't, it ought to be. And you know what? I swear I'm really sorry for her! So I'll get them together, Maurice and her, and she'll immediately start abusing him to his face and praising you—ah, the heart of a woman! I see you're laughing again. I'm very happy that you feel cheered up. All right, let's go then. I'll start by talking to her about Maurice. As to the murder victims, I suppose it would be best not to say anything about them for the time being, don't you think? She'll find out about them soon enough herself."

"What is she supposed to find out? Who has been murdered? What did you say about Maurice Drozdov?"

The door had opened and Liza stood there.

"So you were eavesdropping?"

"What did you say about Maurice Drozdov? Has he been killed?"

"So you haven't heard. Rest assured, Mr. Drozdov is alive and kicking, and you can check it any time because he's outside by the garden fence and his coat is all soaked through because, I think, he spent the whole night there. He saw me as I came in."

"It's not true. I heard you say that someone had been murdered. Who was it then?" she insisted, still very worried and unwilling to trust Peter.

"It's my wife who has been murdered, and her brother, Lebyatkin, and their maid," Stavrogin said in a firm voice.

A shudder ran through Liza and she turned ashen.

"It was a strange, shocking murder, an incredibly absurd case of robbery," Peter started rattling hurriedly. "It was an attempt to take advantage of the fire and do some looting. It's the work of Fedka the convict and it was that fool Lebyatkin's fault; he went around bragging that he'd got hold of a sum of money. . . . That's why I came rushing over here. I felt I had to warn—it hit me like a bolt from the blue—and Stavrogin almost passed out when I told him. We were just discussing whether or not we should tell you about it."

"Is he telling the truth, Nikolai?" Liza managed to say.

"No, it's not the truth."

"What d'you mean it's not the truth? What's come over you?" Peter said with a start.

"Ah God, I'm going mad!" Liza cried.

"But please, try to understand, Liza; he's out of his mind now—after all, his wife has just been killed. Look how pale he is. Anyway, since you spent the whole night together and you know he never left you for a moment, you must know better than anyone that he didn't do it."

"Nikolai, tell me, as God is your witness, are you guilty of this murder or not? I swear I'll believe your word as though it were the word of God and I will follow you to the end of the world—oh, I'll follow you wherever you go, like a little dog—"

"Why do you torment her, you crazy man?" Peter cried frantically. "Listen, Liza, I swear to you—and you can crush me into powder if I'm lying—he is completely innocent! Indeed, it's practically killed him too and he's raving now. Can't you see that? He had nothing to do with it, not even in thought. It's all the work of bandits who, I'm sure, will be caught within a fortnight and will get what's coming to them. It's the work of Fedka and of some Shpigulin men. The whole town is talking about it and I'm just repeating what everybody knows."

"Is that true? Is it?" Liza mumbled, trembling all over, as though waiting for a verdict of life or death.

"I didn't kill them and I was against the killing, but I knew they were going to be killed and I didn't stop the killers. You'd better leave me, Liza," Stavrogin said and went back into the drawing room.

Liza covered her face with her hands and walked out of the house. Peter was on the point of rushing after her, but changed his mind and rejoined Stavrogin.

"So that's the way you act! That's your way! So I see, you're really afraid of nothing!" he pounced on Stavrogin, completely beside himself, growing incoherent and foaming at the mouth.

Stavrogin stood in the center of the drawing room. He didn't answer a word. Absent-mindedly, he tugged at a tuft of his hair with his left hand. A forlorn little smile played on his lips. Peter gave his sleeve a violent tug.

"Maybe now you feel you're lost, you've decided to inform on all the others and then get the hell out of the way yourself, retire to a monastery or something. But you can be sure I'll kill you before that, whether you're afraid of me or not!"

"Ah, you're still chattering on," Stavrogin said, at last noticing Peter's presence. "Get going now," he said, suddenly coming completely to his senses. "Order a carriage. Don't leave her! Well, run, run—hurry up! Take her home and don't let anyone know anything—and see that she doesn't go to look—to look at the corpses. Use force to get her into the carriage—Alexei! Alexei!"

"Stop shouting! It's too late. She must be in the arms of her Maurice already, and you surely don't expect Drozdov to accept a ride in your carriage? Wait—here's something better than a carriage!"

Peter's gun was out again. Stavrogin looked at him calmly.

"Well, why not? Go ahead—kill," he said quietly and almost peacefully.

"Ah, damn it, how can a man say such things about himself?" Peter started to shake with fury again. "Really, it wouldn't have been a bad idea to kill you! By God, she should've spat on you! What sort of opera boat are you! You're nothing but a leaky old wooden barge ready to be scrapped. You should come to your senses now, if only out of resentment, out of spite! And then, it must really all make damn little difference to you, since you're asking for a bullet between the eyes yourself."

Stavrogin emitted a strange laugh.

"If you weren't such a ridiculous fool, I'd perhaps have agreed with you. If only you were a little bit less stupid——"

"Maybe I'm a clown, but I don't want you—my better half —to be one. Don't you understand me?"

Stavrogin did understand. In fact, he was probably the only one who did. Shatov had been surprised when Stavrogin had told him that there was dedication in Peter Verkhovensky.

"Now get the hell out of here. By tomorrow I'll try to think something up. Come and see me tomorrow."

"Yes? You'll think up something?"

"We'll see—but to hell with you now; go to hell."

And he walked out of the drawing room.

"Well, perhaps it's all for the best," Peter muttered under his breath, putting away his gun.

III

Peter rushed out after Liza. She hadn't gone far from the house yet, for she had been detained by the butler Alexei, who, hatless and in his frock coat, had followed her, keeping discreetly one step behind and holding his head respectfully bowed. The old man, very frightened and apparently on the verge of tears, kept begging her to wait for a carriage.

"Go back home, Alexei," Peter said, shoving him aside and taking Liza's arm. "Your master's clamoring for tea and there's no one to get it for him."

Liza didn't pull her arm away, but then, she hadn't yet recovered from the shock and was in a sort of daze.

"To start with, Liza, you're going the wrong way," Peter chattered. "Come this way. We won't have to go through the garden. And then, let me tell you, you aren't dressed for walking the more than two miles to your house in this rain. If you'll only wait a few seconds, I'll get the carriage I came in— it's in the yard, over there—and I'll take you home and no one will see us."

"You're very kind," Liza said gently.

"It's nothing really. Any decent man would do the same in my place."

Liza suddenly glanced at him and was astonished.

"Good Lord, I thought it was still that old man—"

"Listen, I'm awfully glad that you're taking it so well because, really, it's nothing more than a stupid convention, and since that's the way it is, wouldn't it be better if I told the old man to get the carriage ready? It won't take ten minutes and we could wait for it under the porch, what do you say?"

"First, I want—where are those murdered people?"

"Any other fantastic ideas? That's just what I was afraid of! No, better leave that sort of nonsense alone. Besides, there's nothing there for you to see."

"I know where they are; I know the house."

"So you know! But for heaven's sake, it's raining and it's so foggy—ah, this is a task that requires the patience of a saint! Now listen here, Liza, one of two things: either you're coming with me in the open carriage, in which case, wait for me here and don't move one step further, because if you go another twenty steps or so, Maurice Drozdov is certain to catch sight of you—"

"Maurice! Where? Where is he?"

"Now if you wish to leave with him, I suppose I'll walk another few steps with you and show you where he is. But I myself don't feel like going over and saying hello to him. No, thank you very much!"

"Good God, he's waiting for me!"

She suddenly stopped and the color spread over her face.

"But surely, Liza, he's no slave to convention! Of course, it's none of my business and I have nothing at all to do with it, but, as you know, I only wish your good. Now, since that lovers' boat of ours didn't work out, since it turned out to be nothing but a leaky old tub—"

"Ah, it's wonderful—wonderful!" Liza cried.

"You say something's wonderful, but the tears are streaming down your cheeks! You must be brave. You must never give in to a man. In our age, when woman . . . Ah, to hell with it!" Peter almost spat with disgust. "But above all, there's nothing to regret and perhaps everything will end very nicely. Maurice Drozdov is a sensitive man, although he doesn't talk much, which is also an advantage as long as he has no stupid prejudices—"

"Wonderful! Wonderful!" Liza cried again, bursting into hysterical laughter.

"Ah, damn it all, finally!" Peter said, feeling suddenly offended. "After all, I'm here for your sake, because as far as I'm concerned, why should I care? I was doing you a favor yesterday, since you wanted to do it yourself, and if today you feel differently—all right, I can see Drozdov now. He's over there, see? Sitting there—that way. He hasn't seen us. Now tell me, Liza, have you ever read *Pauline Sachs?*"

"What?"

"It's a novel. I read it when I was still a student. It's about a prosperous civil servant called Sachs who catches his wife being unfaithful in their summerhouse. . . . But never mind—the hell with it. Anyway, you'll see—even before you get home, Drozdov will propose to you. Ah, he still hasn't seen us."

"I don't want him to see us!" Liza cried suddenly in a mad

voice. "Let's go away, into the fields, into the woods—" And she ran back.

"Well, that's sheer cowardice, Liza!" Peter shouted as he ran after her. "Why should you be afraid of his seeing you? On the contrary, you should look him proudly in the eye. You can't really feel like this because of *that*. All that stuff about virginity is nothing but a prejudice—an obsolete, meaningless convention. Wait, where are you going? Ah, the way she runs! Let's go back to Stavrogin. We'll take my carriage. Where are you going? There's nothing but fields that way. Ah, see, you've fallen—"

He stopped. Liza had been streaking ahead without looking where she was going, and Peter was already almost fifty yards behind when she stumbled over a hummock and fell. At that moment a loud and desperate shout came from the other direction: Drozdov had seen her flight and fall and was running across the field toward her. Peter beat a hasty retreat toward the gates of the Stavrogin courtyard, bent upon climbing into his carriage as quickly as possible and removing himself as far as he could from trouble.

Drozdov stood over Liza, who was now sitting up, in terrible anguish. He bent over her, holding her hand in both his. Seeing her under such incredible circumstances had given him a terrible shock, and tears were streaming down his cheeks. He had seen the woman he adored so unreservedly running madly across the field, at such an hour, in such weather, wearing only her party dress—the dress in which she looked so magnificent at the ball yesterday, but which was now all crumpled and covered with mud from her fall. He couldn't say a thing. He took off his overcoat and put it around her shoulders. Then suddenly he let out a frightened cry: he felt her lips against his hand.

"Liza," he mumbled, "I know I'm no use to you, but please, don't drive me away—"

"Come, let's go away from here. Don't leave me!" she cried, seizing him by the arm and pulling him behind her. "Maurice," she said suddenly in a very low voice, "I tried to put up a brave front over there, but here I'm afraid of dying. I'll die, I'll die very soon, I know it, but I'm afraid of death," she whispered, squeezing his hand desperately.

"Ah, if only there were someone here," he said in despair, looking around. "If only I could see a cart or a carriage. Your feet will get wet. You'll catch cold; you'll—you'll lose your reason—"

"Don't worry, don't worry," she comforted him. "I'm less afraid when I'm with you. Hold on to me and take me somewhere. Are we going home now? No, I want to see the bodies first. Everybody says *they* have murdered his wife, but he says he murdered her himself. It's not true, is it? It can't be true. I must see the bodies of those who have been murdered —because of me. Because of them, he didn't love me any more last night. When I see the bodies, I'll know everything. Come, let's hurry over there. I know the house—there was a fire there. My dear, dear Maurice, you mustn't forgive me— I've disgraced myself and there's no reason why you should forgive me. Why are you crying? Slap me rather and kill me here in this field, like a bitch!"

"No one may judge you now," he said with sudden firmness. "May God forgive you, but I have the right to judge you least of all."

They went on saying strange things to each other that would sound too incongruous if reported and, as they said them, they walked on quickly, hurrying like a couple of sleepwalkers, straight toward the fires. Maurice kept looking around in the hope that a cart might appear, but there was none to be seen. A fine drizzle permeated the whole landscape, absorbing all gloss, every shade, and turning everything into a smoky, leaden, undifferentiated mass. Day had replaced night a long time ago, but it was as though the sun hadn't yet risen. And suddenly, from the cold, smoky gloom, there emerged a strange, absurd figure, coming straight toward them.

As I visualize the scene now, I think that, if I had been in Liza's place, I wouldn't have believed my eyes. But she immediately recognized the figure and let out a joyful cry. It was Stepan Verkhovensky.

Why he was walking there, how his insane idea of flight had come to be realized, I'll get to later. For the time being, I'll only mention that that morning he was already feverish, but that the fever had not been enough to break his resolve. He was stepping firmly over the wet grass, and it was obvious that he had planned his action as thoroughly as an impractical, indoor man could without outside help. He was dressed "for travel"—that is, he was wearing an army overcoat, around which he had somehow buckled a shiny leather belt, and his trousers were tucked into kneeboots. Probably he had been imagining himself in the role of a traveler for a long

time and, to fit the image, had acquired the shiny leather belt
and the army officer's topboots, in which he was unaccustomed
to walking, a few days before. A broad-brimmed hat, a woolen
scarf tightly wrapped around his neck, a very small traveling bag packed to bursting in his left hand, and a walking
stick and an open umbrella in his right completed his traveling outfit. These three items—the bag, the stick, and the
umbrella—had proved rather cumbersome even during the
first mile of his journey, and now, during the second, they
were causing him real hardship.

"Can it really be you!" Liza cried, sorrowful surprise suc-
ceeding her first instinctive outburst of joy.

"Liza!" Mr. Verkhovensky exclaimed, rushing to her, also
almost delirious. *"Chère, chère,* so you're also out in this terrible fog! Did you see the fires? *Vous êtes malheureuse,
n'est-ce pas?* I see, I see, you don't have to say anything—but
don't ask me any questions either. *Nous sommes tous mal-
heureux, mais il faut les pardonner tous.* Let's forgive them,
Liza, and we shall be free forever and ever. To settle one's
accounts with the world and to become truly free—*il faut
pardonner, pardonner, et pardonner!"*

"But why are you kneeling?"

"Because in saying farewell to the world, I want to say farewell to all my past in your person!" He began to weep and
placed her hands on his tearstained eyes. "I'm kneeling before everything that was good and beautiful in my life. I kiss
it and I thank it! Now, I've cut myself in two: back there
is the madman who for *vingt-deux ans* dreamed of taking off
into the clouds; here is the broken, shivering old tutor in the
house of a merchant *s'il existe pourtant, ce marchand. . . .*
But you're drenched, Liza!" he cried, jumping up as he felt
his knees also getting soaked on the wet earth. "And why are
you outdoors in such a dress—and walking on foot over this
field—and crying? *Vous êtes malheureuse?* Yes, I think I
heard something. But where have you come from now?" He
seemed frightened and asked his questions more and more
hurriedly, casting puzzled side glances at Drozdov. "But do
you have any idea what time it is?"

"Tell me, Mr. Verkhovensky, have you heard anything
about the murder victims over there? Is it true? Is it?"

"Ah, those people! I saw the flames through the night and
they were their work. How else could they end up?" His eyes
flashed as of old. "I'm running away from a nightmare, from

a feverish dream. I'm running to try to find Russia! *Existe-t-elle la Russie?* Ah, it's you, Captain! I never doubted I'd find you performing a deed of great courage someday. Here, take my umbrella. But really, why must you go all the way there on foot? Take this umbrella, for heaven's sake. I'll take a carriage somewhere anyway. I'm walking now because my Nastasya would've started shouting and stirred up the whole street if she'd found out I was leaving for good. So I had to slip out as far as possible without being noticed. I know that the *Voice* keeps reporting robberies and assaults all over the place, but I don't think I'll stumble on a bandit just as I'm setting out on my journey. *Chère* Liza, I believe you mentioned that somebody had killed someone? *O mon Dieu,* you're ill!"

"Let's go, let's go!" Liza shouted hysterically, pulling Maurice behind her. "Wait, Mr. Verkhovensky!" She returned to him. "Let me make the sign of the cross over you. Perhaps it would be more appropriate to put you in a strait jacket, but I suppose I'd better just make the sign of the cross. You, too, pray sometime for your poor Liza. Oh, not too much; don't overwork yourself praying for me—just now and then, you know, a little. Hey, Maurice, give that child back his umbrella. Come on, give it to him immediately! Right. Now let's go—let's go!"

By the time Liza and Drozdov reached the house where the murders had taken place, the crowd thronging around it had heard plenty about how advantageous it was for Stavrogin to murder his wife. But I must say once again that the great majority just listened in sullen indifference. The only people who got excited were the noisy drunks and those who were somewhat off their heads to begin with, like that armwaving locksmith I mentioned before. He was usually a quiet man, but from time to time, when something shocked him enough, he would go off his head, like a bird taking off in flight. I didn't notice Liza and Maurice arrive and when I did finally catch sight of her, I was stupefied. At first I didn't see Drozdov—he must have been separated from her at that moment by the crowd, as she forced her way through it, oblivious to everything and everyone around her, like a delirious patient who has escaped from a hospital bed. And, as might well be expected, it didn't take long for her to attract the attention of the people around her. First they exchanged some remarks, then suddenly they were shouting,

"That's Stavrogin's sweetheart!"

"It's not enough for them to kill, they also want to have a good look at what they've done!"

Then I saw a hand rise and fall over her head and Liza went down. There was a mad howl and Drozdov, trying to go to her rescue, struck a man who was in his way with all his might. But at that very moment the arm-waving locksmith grabbed him from behind. For a while it was impossible to tell what was going on in the melee. Liza got up, but went down again under another blow. Then the crowd parted and a small empty circle formed around the prostrate Liza and Maurice Drozdov, who, covered with blood, was wringing his hands and shouting, while the tears streamed from his eyes. I don't remember exactly what happened after that, except that I saw them carry Liza away. I ran after them. She was still alive, perhaps even conscious. Of the crowd, they arrested the locksmith and three other men. These three fellows deny to this very day that they had anything to do with the mob killing and claim they were arrested by mistake. They may even be telling the truth. And, although there's no doubt about the locksmith's guilt, he is incapable to this day of accounting for what happened, having acted in a sort of trance. I was called to testify as a witness, though I was only a distant one. I declared that everything happened accidentally and that the culprits were people who, though perhaps bent on killing, actually hardly realized what they were doing; they were drunk and their thinking was already blurred. And that is still my opinion today.

chapter 4

THE FINAL DECISION

I

That morning all the people who saw Peter reported that he was in a very excitable state. At two in the afternoon he went to see Gaganov, who had arrived from his estate the day before. Gaganov's house was full of guests and they were excitedly discussing the recent events. Peter talked more than anyone, forcing the others to listen to him. He had always been considered rather a chatterbox with a screw loose in his head, but this time he was saying things about Julie von Lembke, and in the general uproar, she had become an absorbing subject. He spoke with the authority of one who had, until recently, been her most intimate confidant and disclosed many surprising details. Incidentally, and of course inadvertently, he repeated what she had said privately about some leading citizens of the town, which naturally wounded the vanity of some. The things he said were neither too clear nor too coherent. He sounded like a simple, straightforward man faced with the painful duty of explaining away a whole pile of misunderstandings, who in his simplicity and clumsiness didn't know where to begin or end. Quite carelessly he let slip the fact that Julie von Lembke had known of Stavrogin's secret and that, in fact, she had been behind the whole intrigue. She had lied to him too, though, because he, Peter Verkhovensky, was also in love with poor Liza—but then she'd manipulated him so adroitly that he had *almost* had to take Liza to Stavrogin in the carriage.

"Ah, I know, it's all very well for you to laugh at me, gentlemen, but you surely must realize that if I'd had any idea how it was going to end . . ." he concluded.

To the alarming questions about Stavrogin's possible connection with the Lebyatkin murder, Peter declared that, in his opinion, the timing of the murder was pure coincidence and it was Lebyatkin who had called it down upon himself by flashing the money around. On that point he was quite convincing.

One of the guests remarked that he didn't believe him and that he thought Peter was putting it all on. And that, anyway, he had eaten, drunk, and almost lived in Mrs. von Lembke's house and it wasn't right for him to talk like that about her now. But Peter immediately parried this attack by saying:

"I ate and drank there, not because I had no money to buy food and drink but because they insisted on inviting me, so it's not my fault. So please allow me to judge for myself how much gratitude I owe them."

On the whole, he created a favorable impression. The general consensus of opinion could be summed up thus:

"All right, even if he is an absurd and vacuous fellow, there's still no good reason to blame him for Julie von Lembke's stupidity. In fact, it appears he even tried to stop her."

Shortly after two o'clock, a rumor spread that Stavrogin, who was talked about so much that day, had taken the midday train for Petersburg. That caused a considerable stir. Many people frowned. Peter was so amazed that some say his face changed and he uttered a strange exclamation, "But who on earth could've let him go?" He immediately dashed out of Gaganov's house; however, he was later seen in two or three other houses.

Before dark that day, Peter even managed to get himself admitted to Mrs. von Lembke's house, although it wasn't easy, for she had steadfastly refused to see him. I found out about it only three weeks later, from Julie herself, just before her departure for the capital. She didn't go into detail, only saying that on this occasion "he amazed me beyond all measure." I gather that he warned her that if ever she decided to "talk," she herself would have to face the charge of being an accessory. He felt that he had to keep her quiet to prevent her from jeopardizing his plans, of which, of course, she knew nothing at the time. It was only five days later that she realized why he was so doubtful about her silence and so afraid of any new outburst of indignation that might come from her.

All five members of the local Five gathered after dark, around eight o'clock, in Second Lieutenant Erkel's room, which was in a small, tumble-down house on Fomin Street, at the very edge of town. The time of the meeting had been set by Peter Verkhovensky, but he was inexcusably late. The members of the Five had to wait a full hour for him.

Erkel was the officer from out of town who had sat throughout Virginsky's "birthday party" with a notebook and pencil in his hands. He had recently arrived in our town and taken lodgings in a house located in a remote district and belonging to two old working-class women. The meeting had obviously been arranged so as to attract the least possible attention. Erkel was a strange young man and an extraordinarily silent one; he could easily spend ten evenings in a row in noisy company, with the most peculiar conversations going on around him, without himself uttering a word, but simply listening and staring at the others with his childlike eyes. He had a pleasant face, which one might even have said looked intelligent. He did not belong to our local Five (whose members assumed he had some kind of special executive instructions that had been entrusted to him somewhere by somebody). We know now that he had no instructions and that he probably had no idea even of his own position. He simply had an unreserved admiration for Peter Verkhovensky, whom he had met only recently. If he had met some depraved monster who, under the romantic pretext of serving society, had persuaded him to form a mob and, to test him, had ordered him to see that they killed the first man they met, he would certainly have obeyed. He had an ailing mother somewhere to whom he sent half his meager army pay; I can imagine her kissing his fair head and constantly thinking and praying and worrying about him. The only reason I dwell on him so long is that I'm so terribly sorry for him.

The members of our local Five were very excited. The events of the past night had impressed them and I think they had got cold feet. The public scandal they had deliberately tried to provoke had suddenly taken a turn that had caught them by surprise. The fire of the previous night, the murder of the Lebyatkins, the mob violence against Liza—had come as so many unexpected shocks that had not been included in the program. They now angrily accused the hand that moved them of despotism and a lack of openness. And while they waited for Peter to arrive, they worked themselves into such a state that they determined to ask him for a formal account and, if he tried to dodge it once again, they were prepared to dissolve the Five and to organize a new secret society in its place for the "propaganda of ideas"—but this time to do it on their own and base it on the principles of democracy and equal rights. Liputin, Shigalov, and the expert on the people supported this course of action; Lyamshin said nothing, but wore an approving look; Virginsky hesitated and, in any case, wanted first to hear what Peter Verkhovensky had to say. So they decided to hear Peter out, but still he didn't come. Such disdain added to their rancor. Erkel maintained complete silence and went to order tea, which he brought back himself on a tray, already poured. He didn't let the maid into the room with the samovar.

Peter didn't arrive until half past eight. With small, quick steps, he walked up to the round table by the settee where the others were sitting. He kept his hat in his hand and declined tea. He looked irritated, stern, and haughty. He must have seen immediately from their faces that they were in a rebellious mood.

"Before I even open my mouth, I want you to come out with

it—I can see there's something troubling you," he said with a malicious grin, gazing at each of them in turn.

Liputin spoke "in the name of all" and, his voice trembling with resentment, said that "if we go on like this, we'll soon get bloody noses." Of course, they weren't afraid of getting bloody noses and didn't even mind it, but only as long as it furthered the Cause. (There was a general stir and sounds of approval.) Therefore, Peter should be more candid with them and let them know in advance what the next move was going to be, "for things can't go on like this." (Again a stir and a few guttural sounds.) His behavior up until now had been both dangerous and humiliating to them. "And it's not at all that we're afraid, but if only one man does the thinking and the rest are mere pawns, the chances are that he'll finally make a slip and then we'll all get caught." (Shouts of, "Hear, hear!" General approval.)

"So what the hell do you want?"

"To start with, what has Stavrogin's sordid private love affair to do with the goals of our movement?" Liputin hissed. "He may very well be connected with the central organization in some mysterious way—if any such organization really exists—but even so, we don't wish to have anything to do with his intrigues. In the meantime, a crime has been committed, the police alerted, and following from one clue to another, they're bound to come to us."

"If they get you with your Stavrogin, it won't take them very long to get to us," the expert on the people added.

"And it's not at all helpful to the Cause," Virginsky concluded gloomily.

"What nonsense! The murder was committed by Fedka and the motive was robbery."

"Hm, a rather strange coincidence, wasn't it?" Liputin remarked, grimacing.

"All right, if that's the way you want it, let me tell you that it was your fault that it happened."

"What do you mean our fault?"

"First of all, you, Liputin, took part in that intrigue and in the second place—and this is the main point—you were told to get Lebyatkin out of town and to pay him the money, but what did you do? If you had sent him away, nothing would've happened—"

"But wasn't it your own suggestion that it would be a good idea to let him come out and read that poem?"

"It was a suggestion, not an order. The order was to send him out of town."

"What's an order? It's a rather ambiguous word. But, anyway, you ordered me to delay his departure."

"You've got it wrong and you've displayed stupidity and lack of discipline. The murder *was* Fedka's doing and he was prompted only by robbery. But you've been listening to the trash that's been spread around, and you believed it. You got cold feet. Stavrogin isn't stupid enough to get involved in something like that, and the fact that he left by the twelve-o'clock train after an audience with the vice-governor proves it—they'd never have allowed him to leave for Petersburg in broad daylight if they'd had any doubts about him."

"But we never contended that Stavrogin had done the actual killing himself," Liputin hissed venomously, now quite unabashed. "In fact, he may not even have known anything, just as I knew nothing, a fact of which you're very well aware and which hasn't in any way prevented me from ending up like a chicken in a pot."

"Whom are you accusing, then?" Peter said, glaring at him grimly.

"Those who feel it necessary to set towns on fire."

"The worst thing about it is that you're trying to wriggle out of it now. But maybe you'll feel different when you've read this and shown it to the others. Mind you though, it's only for your information, of course." And Peter pulled Lebyatkin's anonymous letter to Lembke out of his pocket and handed it to Liputin.

Liputin read it with obvious surprise and, deep in thought, handed it to his neighbor. The letter quickly went the round of the table.

"Is this really Lebyatkin's handwriting?" Shigalov asked.

"It's his handwriting all right," Liputin said and Tolkachenko, the expert on the people, confirmed it.

"This is only to bring you up to date, because you all seem so sorry for Lebyatkin," Peter said, taking the letter back. "So, as you can see, gentlemen, Fedka, by sheer accident, has got rid of a man who was dangerous to us. You see what an accident can do for one sometimes! Wouldn't you say so?"

They exchanged glances with one another.

"And now, gentlemen, it's my turn to ask a few questions," Peter said, assuming a dignified air. "First, I would like to know what made you set fire to the town without permission?"

"So it's we who set those fires now! That's really shifting the blame! From the ogre to the babe!" several voices protested.

"I realize that you were somewhat carried away," Peter went on, ignoring their protests, "but you must understand that this fire can't be dismissed, like so many of the other pranks you played under Mrs. von Lembke's protection. I've summoned you here, gentlemen, to explain to you the dire danger to which you have exposed yourselves so stupidly and which places many other things besides your persons in jeopardy."

"Just a minute," Virginsky interjected almost indignantly; up to this point he had remained silent. "It was we who were on the point of protesting to you over the despotic and undemocratic methods that have made it possible for you to adopt a course of action so grave and at the same time so puzzling, without consulting the members of our group."

"So you're trying to deny it, are you? But I maintain that it was you and no one else who set fire to the suburb. Don't lie to me—I have indisputable information on the subject. By this breach of discipline, gentlemen, you've compromised our whole movement. Remember, you're nothing but one link in an endless chain and you owe unconditional obedience to the central organization. Disregarding that, three of you incited Shpigulin's men to arson without having been ordered to do so, and they lit the fires."

"Which three? Three of us? Who are they?"

"Two days ago, at about three o'clock in the morning, you, Tolkachenko, were inciting Fomka Zavyalov to arson in a dive called the Forget-Me-Not Bar."

"Good heavens!" Tolkachenko leaped from his seat. "I said just one word and even that without meaning it, just because the man had been flogged that morning. Anyway, I stopped talking to him almost immediately, because I realized he was completely drunk. In fact, until you mentioned it now, I'd completely forgotten about it. No, I don't believe that one word of mine could've lit those fires."

"You remind me of a man who's surprised that one tiny spark could blow up a whole gunpowder depot."

"Anyway, we were in a corner and I whispered it in his ear, so how can you know what I said to him?" Tolkachenko said, growing perplexed.

"I was sitting under the table. Anyway, you may rest assured that I know your every move. Why are you smiling so slyly, Mr. Liputin? Shall I tell you something? Well, I know that four days ago, around midnight, you pinched your ever-loving wife till she was all black and blue, in your bedroom immediately after the two of you had retired for the night."

Liputin opened his mouth and turned pale.

(Later it was discovered that he'd found it out from Liputin's maid, Agafia, who was in his pay and spying for him.)

"May I make a statement?" Shigalov said, rising suddenly.

"Go ahead."

Shigalov sat down, holding himself stiffly.

"As far as I was able to understand, and I hardly think I can have been mistaken, the picture you drew at first, and again later, with such eloquence, although it was rather too theoretical, was one of Russia covered with a tight network of cells. And, of these, each cell, while proselytizing and branching out indefinitely, was to engage in subversive propaganda against the local authorities, throw the population into confusion, create scandals, promote cynicism, undermine faith in anything and everything, agitate for better living conditions, and finally, at the desired time, use fires (as a device that greatly impresses the masses) to plunge the country into despair and confusion. I've tried to use your very words to describe your own picture. Now, is this the plan of action that you communicated to us on the orders of the central organization, of which, to this day, we know nothing and which, as far as we are concerned, may be a pure myth?"

"That's right, but why do you have to drag it out like this?"

"Everyone has the right to express himself in the way he thinks fit. Well then, when you led us to believe that the present network already extended over the whole of Russia and comprised hundreds of cells, you said that, if each of those cells did its work efficiently, at a set date, a prearranged signal would be given and then the entire country—"

"Ah, goddammit, we've plenty to do as it is, without having to listen to all this!" Peter grumbled, stirring in his chair.

"All right, I'll make it short and content myself with asking you one question: we've had scandals, we've witnessed popular discontent, we've contributed to the fall of the local administration, and finally, we've seen with our own eyes our town on fire—so why should you be displeased? Wasn't all that your own program? Of what can you accuse us?"

"Breach of discipline!" Peter shouted furiously. "As long

as I was here, you had no right to act without my permission. But that's enough. The informer has already prepared a denunciation and probably by tomorrow—possibly even tonight —you'll be arrested, the lot of you. Now you know. My information is absolutely certain."

Now they all gaped at him.

"They'll arrest you not only for abetting the arsonists but also as the local Five. The informer knows all the secrets of the network. That's the kind of mess you've got yourselves into!"

"I'll bet it's Stavrogin!" Liputin said.

"Stavrogin? Why? Why him?" Peter muttered, apparently taken aback, but he recovered immediately. "Ah hell," he said, "it's Shatov; the informer is Shatov. I suppose you all know that Shatov once belonged to our Movement. Now I must admit that, watching him through people he doesn't suspect, I've found out to my great surprise that he also knows certain secrets about the organization of our network and also—well, all sorts of things. So in order to obtain immunity for himself because of his former connection with the Movement, he's prepared to inform on us. Thus far he's still hesitated and I've tried to spare him. Now, tomorrow they'll arrest us as arsonists and political criminals."

"Is all this really true? How could Shatov know about it?" They were indescribably perturbed.

"It's absolutely true, although I'm not free to reveal my source of information to you. Still, here's what I can do for you: I can, acting through a certain person, force Shatov to delay his denunciation, but only for twenty-four hours. So then, you can consider yourselves safe for twenty-four hours —until the morning of the day after tomorrow. But that's all."

A silence followed.

"So let's get rid of him to hell!" Tolkachenko was the first to say.

"We ought to have done it long ago!" Lyamshin chimed in, viciously banging the table with his fist.

"But how are we going to do it?" Liputin mumbled.

Peter immediately pounced on that question and offered his plan of action. It consisted of luring Shatov to the place where the secret printing press that had been entrusted to him was buried, under the pretext that the organization wanted to turn it over to someone else. They could set a date "in the evening," Peter suggested, "and once he's there, he could be dealt with." He then went into many businesslike details that we shall skip here and explained Shatov's present ambiguous relations with the Movement, which I have mentioned earlier in my narrative.

"That's all very well," Liputin said hesitatingly, "but since it's another—er—adventure in the same style—well, it may set people's imaginations working."

"No doubt about that," Peter confirmed. "But there's a way to allay all suspicion."

And, in great detail, he told them about Kirilov's intention to shoot himself and of his promise to wait for a signal from the Movement before he went through with it and also to leave a note behind him in which he would take upon himself anything that Peter dictated to him, all of which we know already.

"His firm wish to end his life—which is of a philosophical nature and is, in my opinion, plain crazy—became known *over there,*" Peter explained. *"They* don't allow a loose hair or a speck of dust to go overlooked; they channel everything into the service of the Cause. Satisfied that they could rely on his intention and realizing that the Cause could benefit from it, *they* sent him the price of a ticket home (for some reason he'd decided he absolutely had to die in Russia), asking him to do an errand (which he did) and also making him promise not to kill himself before he was told to go ahead. He promised. Please note that he has certain special connections with the Movement upon which, however, I'm not free to elaborate. Tomorrow, after Shatov is done away with, I'll dictate a note to Kirilov that will say it was he who killed Shatov. That will sound very plausible because they used to be friends and went to America together, where, indeed, they quarreled— all that will be in the note. As a matter of fact, it occurs to me that, circumstances permitting, I might be able to dictate other things to Kirilov—about those subversive leaflets, for instance, maybe even about the fire. But I'll have to think that over. In any case, don't worry too much, he has no conventional prejudices. I think he'll sign anything."

Some were skeptical. The story seemed too fantastic. But they had all heard strange things about Kirilov, and Liputin more than any of them.

"But what if he changes his mind?" Shigalov said. "Being mad, he's bound to be unreliable."

"Don't worry, he won't change his mind," Peter said cuttingly. "According to the terms of our agreement, we must warn him twenty-four hours in advance—that's today. So I suggest that Liputin come with me to Kirilov's place and find out for himself whether I've told you the truth or not and then come back here and report to you. But do just as you please!" he suddenly said with infinite irritation, as if it had just occurred to him that he was honoring these nonentities too much and making too much fuss over them. "If you don't wish to go through with it, then all our connections are severed because of your insubordination and you may consider yourselves on your own. But remember—in that case, besides the Shatov trouble, you'll have to face another small inconvenience of which you were emphatically warned upon joining the Movement. As to me, gentlemen, believe me, I'm not at all afraid of you. And don't think that I'm that irrevocably tied to you. But it's up to you, after all."

"No, I think we'll go through with it."

"There's no other way out," Tolkachenko muttered, "and if Liputin comes back and confirms what you've told us about Kirilov—"

"I am against it! I protest most strongly against this murderous resolution. Everything in me revolts against it!" Virginsky declared, getting up.

"But what?" Peter asked him.

"What do you mean—but what?"

"Why, you said *but,* so I'm waiting."

"I don't believe I said *but* . . . I only wanted to say that if it's decided, then . . ."

"Then?"

Virginsky fell silent. Then Erkel suddenly decided to open his mouth.

"I believe that, in general, we may disregard the consideration of personal survival," he said, "but if the threat to our persons jeopardizes the safety of the Movement, we have a duty to protect them by every means at our disposal and may not disregard the danger. . . ." He became entangled in his words, blushed, and fell silent.

Erkel had spoken up so unexpectedly that, preoccupied though they were, each with his own worries, they all stared at him, surprised to find that he too could speak.

"I am for our common Cause!" Virginsky suddenly declared.

Everyone rose. It was decided that the final arrangements would be made by noon the next day and that they would communicate with each other, but without holding another general meeting. They were told the place where the printing press was buried and each was given his special assignment. Then Peter and Liputin left immediately to go and see Kirilov.

II

They were all convinced that Shatov was about to inform on them—and that Peter Verkhovensky was using them as mere pawns. So they all knew that they would be at the appointed place the following night and that Shatov was doomed. They felt like so many flies caught in the web of some huge spider—they were furious, but trembled with fear.

Peter had obviously rubbed them the wrong way. Everything could've been worked out more smoothly and easily if he had tried to make the reality appear a little less sordid. Instead of presenting what they had to do as a noble duty and themselves as some group of ancient Romans struggling for freedom, he played directly on their animal fear, on the threat that was hanging over their own hides, which was, after all, a very ungracious thing to do. Of course, the struggle for existence comes into every aspect of life and, as everyone knows, is its only guiding force, and so on; nevertheless . . .

But Peter was in no condition to try to move the Roman in them; he had been caught off balance himself. Stavrogin's flight was a great blow to him; he was utterly crushed by it. He had lied when he had said Stavrogin had had an interview with the vice-governor: what was most alarming was precisely the fact that Stavrogin hadn't spoken to anyone. He had left without even seeing his mother, and yet, strangely enough, he hadn't been bothered by the authorities. (Later, the authorities were asked for a particular explanation of this matter.) Peter had run around the whole day trying hard to find out what had happened, but he had learned nothing, so he was worried as never before. He couldn't give up Stavrogin so suddenly and for good! So it's not surprising that he wasn't too patient with the local members of the Movement, who, on top of everything, tied him down. He was longing to rush off in pursuit of Stavrogin, but he couldn't leave town before settling accounts with Shatov and cementing the local Five with blood, just in case. "I can't discard this cell just like that," I suppose he reasoned. "It may come in handy yet."

As to Shatov, Peter was absolutely convinced that the man was about to turn informer. He had lied when he told the others that he *knew* that Shatov had prepared a denunciation —he had never heard a word about it. It was just his private conviction that Shatov was about to inform, but he had no doubts. He thought Shatov would be unable to bear the deaths of Liza and Maria and that he would decide to talk. And who knows, perhaps he had good reason. I also know that he had a personal dislike for Shatov—they had had a quarrel once and Peter never forgot an offense. Personally, I'm convinced that this was the main reason for what happened.

The narrow sidewalks in our town are made of brick and, in some places, of wood. Peter walked in the middle of the sidewalk without bothering about Liputin, who was forced either to trot behind him or, if he wanted to be level with Peter when he talked, to walk in the mud of the street. Peter suddenly remembered how, a few days before, he himself had been forced to trot behind Stavrogin and to step into the mud, just as Liputin was now, because on that occasion Stavrogin had walked in the middle of the sidewalk without bothering to leave any room for Peter. He remembered that scene in every detail and rage made him gasp.

And Liputin, too, gasped with resentment. He didn't care how Verkhovensky treated the others, but what made Peter think that he could behave like this toward him? Liputin certainly *knew* much more than any of the others, and, although indirectly, was really closely connected with the Movement. Oh, he realized that, in case of *emergency,* Verkhovensky could still mean death to him; however, it wasn't that danger that made him hate him but the arrogant, condescending tone Peter used when talking to him. And now that they had determined to go into this venture, he was more furious with him than with all the others put together. But alas, he knew very well that tomorrow he'd be the first one there, "just like a slave," and that he'd even see to it that all the others were there too. He also knew that if he could have killed Peter Verkhovensky now without, of course, paying for it with his life, he certainly would have done it.

Deep in these reflections, he said nothing and just trotted along behind his tormentor. Peter himself seemed to have forgotten about Liputin, and only nudged him offhandedly out of his way with his elbow from time to time, when he came level with him. Suddenly, in the middle of our most populous street, Peter stopped and entered a restaurant.

"Where are you going?" Liputin cried out furiously. "This is a restaurant, you know!"

"I feel like having a good steak."

"But this place is always full!"

"So what?"

"But we'll be late. It's ten already."

"It's impossible to get there late enough."

"But I'll be late; they're expecting me back."

"Let 'em wait. Only, it would be stupid of you to go back to them, anyway. As for me, I missed my dinner, wasting all that time with you. And the later we get to Kirilov's, the surer we'll be of finding him home."

Peter ordered his meal served in a private booth. Liputin, angry and resentful, sat in an armchair in a corner of the booth and watched him eat. More than half an hour later, Peter was still at it. He seemed to be in no hurry, ate with great appetite, rang for the waiter and asked for a different kind of mustard, then rang again to order some beer. Not once did he say a word to Liputin. He seemed to be thinking very hard about something and one seldom sees a man do two things at the same time so thoroughly: think so hard and eat with such zest. Liputin worked himself up to such a pitch of hatred that he couldn't take his eyes off Peter; it was something akin to a fit of hatred. He counted the bits of steak Peter dispatched down his gullet, loathing him for the way he opened his mouth, for the way he chewed, for the way he smacked his lips over the tastier morsels. His hatred extended even to the steak itself. Finally, everything began to disintegrate and merge before his eyes, his head began to spin, and waves, alternately burning and icy, ran up and down his spine.

"Since you're not doing anything, read that!" Peter said suddenly, tossing a folded sheet of paper toward him.

Liputin took it and drew nearer to a candle. The sheet was covered with small, ugly handwriting, with corrections on practically every line. By the time Liputin had deciphered it, Peter had already settled the check and was leaving. Back on the sidewalk, Liputin handed him back the sheet.

"Keep it, I'll talk to you about it later—no, on second thought tell me what you think of it now."

Liputin shuddered.

"In my opinion a proclamation of that sort is simply ridiculous and absurd."

His fury had broken through and he felt as though hands had picked him up and he was being carried ahead.

"If we distribute such literature," he said, his voice shaken by his violent trembling, "the stupidity of it and its lack of grasp of the problems facing us will only make people despise us."

"I see. I happen to think differently, though," Peter said, setting out resolutely ahead.

"And I say you're wrong. Did you compose that yourself?"

"That's none of your business."

"And I also think that that pathetic little verse called 'A Noble Heart' is as trashy a piece as one could write—it could never have been written by Herzen."

"You don't know what you're talking about—it's a very good poem."

"What surprises me too," Liputin went on elatedly, his spirit still flying high, "is that we should be told to act in a way that is certain to bring about total collapse. It would make sense in Europe to wish for the existing order to collapse, because they have a proletariat there ready to take over. But in this country we are nothing but rank amateurs and it looks to me as if what we're doing here is just a lot of make-believe."

"But I thought you were a follower of Fourier?"

"Fourier doesn't say that—not that at all, I assure you."

"I know, it's nonsense."

"No, Fourier doesn't talk nonsense. I hope you'll excuse me, but I really cannot believe that there is going to be a revolution next May."

Liputin was so hot he had to unbutton his coat.

"All right, enough of that now," Peter said with frightening detachment. "You'll have to set the type and print this leaflet. You'll have to do it by yourself. When Shatov's printing press is dug up, you'll take it over. You'll produce as many copies of this leaflet as possible in the minimum time and then, throughout the winter, you'll see to their distribution. We'll advise you in time how to go about it. You must produce as many leaflets as possible because you'll be asked for them from other places."

"No, please leave me out of it. I can't take upon myself such a—I refuse."

"He did the right thing."

Peter's eyes flashed angrily, but he restrained himself.

"I don't care what you think as long as everyone keeps his word."

"I'll keep my word."

"Yes, I've always been convinced that you can be completely relied upon to do your duty because you are an independent and progressive man."

"And you're laughable."

"That's good. I'm delighted to make you laugh. I'm always anxious to be of service to people."

"You want me to shoot myself very much and you're afraid I might change my mind, aren't you?"

"You see, it was you yourself who linked your plan with our operation, so we have done things relying on your plan—you couldn't change your mind now without letting us down."

"You have no rights on me."

"I know, I know, it's all entirely your will and we're nothing. I only want to see to it that your free will is accomplished."

"And then I'll have to take all your filthy dealings upon myself?"

"Listen, Kirilov, you aren't getting cold feet by any chance? If you wish to give it up, say so immediately."

"I haven't got cold feet."

"I got that impression because you keep asking so many questions—"

"Will you leave soon now?"

"There, you're asking questions again, aren't you?"

Kirilov scornfully looked Peter up and down.

"You see," Peter went on, becoming more and more irritated and speaking hurriedly, unable to find a tone that seemed appropriate to him, "you would like me to leave so that you'd be left on your own and could give yourself over to your thoughts completely. But I say that all these are dangerous symptoms, dangerous for you more than anyone else. So you want to think. But I say it's better for you to do it without thinking too much. Really, I'm rather worried about you."

"The only thing that disturbs me, that bothers me, is that at that moment I will have a repulsive creature like you at my side."

"Well, that's nothing. I suppose I could go out for a minute and wait on the porch, say. What bothers me, though, is that you aren't indifferent enough to things, as you should be since you intend to die. That's a danger sign. So I'll go out and you can assume that I don't understand a thing and that I'm infinitely beneath you."

"No, not infinitely. You have abilities, but there are so many things you can't understand because you're such a despicable person."

"I'm delighted. I said before how glad I am to be able to provide you with distraction at such a moment."

"You don't understand a thing."

"That is I—anyway, I listen with respect to whatever you wish to say."

"You can't do anything. Even now, you can't hide your petty spite, although it would've been to your advantage not to show it. You'll irritate me and I may suddenly decide to live another six months."

Peter looked at his watch.

"I could never make heads or tails of your theory, but I know that you invented it without our help and that therefore you'll carry it out without our insistence. I also know that it's not you who controls that idea of yours but it that controls you, therefore you won't postpone the date."

"What? It's the idea that controls me?"

"That's right."

"So it's not me who controls it? Is that so? You have a tiny bit of understanding after all. Only you say that to tease me, while I'm quite proud of it."

"Very good then, that's just what I want. I want you to be proud."

"All right, that will do then. You've finished your tea, go away now."

"Ah, hell, I suppose I'll have to," Peter said, slowly getting up, "but it's still too early for me. Tell me, Kirilov, will I find that man, you know who I mean, over at the butcher's wife's, or did he lie to me too?"

"You won't find him there because he's here."

"Damn it, what do you mean he's here? Where is he?"

"He's sitting in the kitchen, eating and drinking."

"How dare he!" Peter went crimson with rage. "He was told to wait! It's idiotic. He has neither identity papers nor money!"

"I know nothing about it. He just came to say good-by. He's all dressed and ready to go. He won't come back. He said that you were a lousy crook and he didn't want to wait for your money."

"Aha! He's afraid that I— Well, I can do it even now if— Is he in the kitchen then?"

Kirilov opened a side door leading to a tiny, dark room. From this room three steps led down to a screened-off part of the kitchen where the cook's bed usually stood. It was there that Fedka was now sitting at a bare wooden table in the corner under the icons. There was a bottle of vodka before him and a plate with some bread on it and an earthenware dish containing a piece of cold beef and some potatoes. He was chewing lackadaisically and was obviously half drunk. He was dressed in a sheepskin jacket, as though ready to leave at any moment. Behind the screen a samovar was beginning to boil, but it was not for Fedka, who, every night for over a week, had lit it for Kirilov— "For Mr. Kirilov loves to have his tea at night, you know." And since there was no cook around now, Fedka's beef and potatoes had probably been prepared for him by Kirilov himself earlier in the day.

"What's the idea?" Peter shouted, sweeping down the three steps. "Why didn't you wait for me where you were told?" He banged his fist on the table.

Fedka straightened his back, looking at Peter with dignity.

"Wait, sir, wait—take it easy," Fedka said, enjoying the feeling of letting the words roll rakishly off his tongue. "First, you'd better remember you've the honor of being Mr. Kirilov's guest and that you're not even fit to polish his boots because he's a learned man and you're nothing but—foo!"

And turning aside cockily, he pretended to spit. There was unmistakable scorn and determination in Fedka's manner and it was obvious that his ominously calm way of talking might be swept away at any moment by an explosion of violence. But Peter had no time now to heed warning signs and anyway such a possibility didn't fit in with his conception of the way things should turn out. The events and failures of the day had completely befuddled him.

Remaining at the top of the three steps, Liputin viewed the scene with great interest.

"Do you or don't you want to have safe identity papers and a bundle of money that will take you where you were told to go?"

"Well, you see, Mister Peter, seeing as how you lied to me from the very beginning, the way I see it you're a no-good crook. To me you're some kind of a human louse—that's how much I respect you, mister. You promised me plenty of money to shed innocent blood and then you swore it was to be done for Mr. Stavrogin, and now it turns out it was all your nasty plan and nothing else. Myself, I got nothing out of the deal, let alone fifteen hundred, and Mr. Stavrogin slapped you around for that scheming of yours—we know that too. And now here you come again, threatening me and promising me money. You never explain what the deal is, but I've a notion you're trying to talk me into going to Petersburg to get you even with Mr. Stavrogin, because you're angry at him and you think you'll take advantage of my trusting nature again. And that'd make you the worst murderer yourself. And d'you know what you deserve for having stopped believing, in your black heart, in the true God and Creator? You're nothing but a pagan, no better than a Tartar or idol-worshiper. Mr. Kirilov's a real philosopher and he must've explained to you lotsa times about God and the true Creator, and told you about the creation of the world and what's to become of us and how every beast, every creature from the book of Revelations changes. . . . But you're dumb like a stupid idol and you've gone on being deaf and dumb and you've corrupted Lieutenant Erkel too and made him like you, an evil, godless tempter—"

"Ah, you drunken oaf! You rob churches and steal icons and then you dare go around preaching about God!"

"Let me tell you, Mister Peter, it's true I robbed them icons but what d'you know, perhaps just as I took out the pearls a tear of mine could've turned into a pearl in the Lord's furnace, because I'm just exactly like that orphan, you know, who had no proper shelter to go to. You know from the books perhaps about that merchant who, once upon a time, sighing and crying just like me, stole a pearl from the halo of the Blessed Virgin and then later how he went down on his knees and put all the money he got out of it at her feet with a whole crowd watching him. And then the Holy Mother covered him with her mantle to protect him from all them people so that, at that time already, they said it was a miracle and the authorities made 'em write down the incident just the way it happened. But you, you let a mouse in and that means you insulted the Lord! And if you wasn't my master by birth who I carried in my arms when I was still a young lad myself, I'd kill you here and now."

Peter was frantic with rage.

"Did you see Stavrogin today? Answer immediately!"

"Don't you dare question me like that! Mr. Stavrogin was very surprised at what happened and he had nothing to do with it at all. He never asked me to do it or offered me money. And what's more, I can tell you he didn't want it. It's you who pushed me into doing it, by tricking me."

"You'll get the money here. Then you'll get another two thousand in Petersburg, in cash and on the dot. And you'll get more later."

"Now you're lying, mister, and it makes me laugh to see you're so simple-minded. Why, it's like Mr. Stavrogin is standing on a tall, tall ladder above you and you're running around under it like a little dog and yapping, and he feels he'd be doing you too much honor spitting in your face."

"You know something?" Peter said, turning away. "I won't let you move a step away from here, you bastard. I'll turn you directly over to the police."

Fedka leaped to his feet, his eyes gleaming furiously. Peter's revolver flashed in his hand. There followed a short and revolting scene: before Peter could train his gun on Fedka, Fedka stepped sideways and hit him a powerful blow across the face. Then there was a second, a third, and a fourth terrifying thud, all of them landing on Peter's face. Peter was dazed, his eyes rolled, he mumbled something, then collapsed, stretching out full length on the ground.

"Here, he's all yours!" Fedka cried with a self-satisfied note in his voice.

Then he picked up his cap, took his bundle from under the seat, and was off.

Peter's breath gurgled in his throat as he lay unconscious. Liputin thought Fedka had killed him. Kirilov leaped down the three steps.

"Pour some water over him!" he shouted and, filling an iron jug from a pail, he threw it into Peter's face. Peter stirred, raised his head, and looked blankly around.

"Well, how do you feel?" Kirilov inquired.

Peter stared around him vaguely without apparently recognizing Kirilov. Then, suddenly, catching sight of Liputin standing at the top of the steps, a repulsive smile twisted his mouth and he grabbed his gun, which was lying near him on the floor, and leaped to his feet.

"If you get an idea to run away tomorrow like Stavrogin," he said suddenly, turning his full fury on Kirilov—he was pale and haggard, and stammered, garbling his words—"I'll get you—even on the other side of the world. I'll string you up, up—like a fly—I'll squash you—remember that!"

He pointed his gun straight at Kirilov's forehead, but almost immediately came to his senses, pulled his hand back, put the revolver in his pocket, and without saying another word, rushed out of the house. Liputin hurried after him. They crawled through the same gap and again had to hold onto the fence as they followed the edge of the ditch. In the street, Peter walked so fast that Liputin had great difficulty keeping up with him. At the first street corner, however, Peter suddenly stopped, turned toward Liputin, and asked in a challenging tone:

"So?"

Liputin, who was still trembling from the scene he had just witnessed, remembered the gun. But his answer somehow slipped from his tongue by itself.

"I think—it seems to me now that they can't be waiting all that impatiently *from Smolensk to Tashkent,* for *him* to come."

"And did you see what Fedka was drinking in the kitchen?"

"What he was drinking? Why, it was vodka, of course."

"In that case, for your information, that was the last time he will drink vodka. I advise you to remember that. And now, to hell with you. I won't need you until tomorrow. But I warn you, don't try to pull any funny stuff on me!"

Liputin ran home as fast as he could.

IV

He had long had a passport made out in a false name. It is extraordinary that this careful little man—a petty despot within his family, a government employee (although a follower of Fourier), and above all a capitalist and a moneylender—had long nursed the fantastic notion that he must have a false passport that he could use to escape abroad *if* . . . He envisaged the possibility of that *if!* True, he himself couldn't have formulated exactly what he expected might happen.

But now it formulated itself and in the most unexpected form. The desperate idea that had flashed through his head when Peter insulted him on the sidewalk was of dropping everything and fleeing abroad himself first thing in the morning. Those who cannot believe that such fantastic things are a daily occurrence in Russia should dig into the life histories of Russian émigrés living abroad. None of them had a better or more real reason to escape. They all had to flee from mad realms created in their own imaginations and peopled with phantoms of their own making.

The first thing Liputin did when he got home was to grab a suitcase and start packing. His main concern was about money—how much he'd be able to salvage and how. Yes, he actually viewed it all as an urgent salvage operation, because he felt there was not a moment to lose and that he must be on the road before daybreak. He didn't know how he was going to get onto the train—he decided to board it at the second or third stop from our town, trusting to luck to get him that far, if necessary, on foot. So, with all these plans whirling in his head, he was in the middle of packing his suitcase when suddenly he threw everything aside and lay down on his couch.

He had suddenly realized clearly that even if he ran away —and he felt that was the thing to do—he still had to decide whether he was going to flee *before* or *after* Shatov had been taken care of. He felt that there was no strength left in him, that he was now nothing but a crude, unfeeling body, an inert mass moved by a terrifying outside force, and that, although he had his passport ready and could very well run away *from* Shatov (for what could be the hurry otherwise?), that really he was escaping neither *before* Shatov nor *from* Shatov but precisely *after* Shatov, that it had already been decreed, decided, and settled. In unbearable anguish, bewildered, shuddering, alternately moaning and holding his breath, he managed to survive behind his locked door until eleven o'clock the next morning, when an unexpected shock abruptly determined his further course of action.

At eleven in the morning, just after he had unlocked the door of his room and shown himself to the members of his household, he learned from them that Fedka, the runaway convict who had been terrorizing the countryside and robbing churches and who had recently been involved in murder and arson—the man who had the entire police force after him, but on whom they had been unable to lay their hands—this man had been found dead that morning about five miles from town, at the point where the road leading to Zakharino crosses the highway. Now the whole town was talking about it. Liputin tore out of the house like a madman to try to find out more. He found out, in the first place, that Fedka had been found with his skull bashed in and had apparently been robbed. In the second place, he learned that the police had strong suspicions and even some sort of evidence that his murderer was the former Shpigulin man, Fomka, who was believed to have been Fedka's accomplice in the murder of the Lebyatkins and that their quarrel on the highway had been caused by Fedka's withholding Fomka's share of the money they had taken from Lebyatkin. Liputin raced over to Peter's place and, by making inquiries at the servants' entrance, managed to wheedle out of them the information that Peter had returned at about one in the morning, after which he had slept quietly at home until eight. Of course, there was nothing extraordinary about Fedka's death—careers like his usually end like that. But then there was Peter's promise about Fedka's having had his last drink of vodka and the fact that that prophecy had come true almost immediately. Liputin no longer hesitated; he had received his shock. It was as though a huge boulder had fallen on him and pinned him down once and for all. When he returned home, he morosely pushed his suitcase under his bed. That night, he was the first to arrive at the appointed place where they were to meet Shatov, although, it is true, his passport was still in his pocket.

A LADY TRAVELER   *chapter 5*

I

Liza's terrible end and the murder of Maria Lebyatkin really overwhelmed Shatov. As I mentioned before, I ran into him that morning and he didn't seem himself to me. By the way, he told me then that the evening before, around nine—that is, about three hours before the outbreak of the fires—he had been to see Maria Lebyatkin. In the morning he went to have a look at the bodies of the victims, but as far as I know he made no statement to the police then. By the end of the day, however, his soul was in turmoil, and I think I can safely say

that by dusk he was on the point of going and telling everything. He was the only one who could say what that "everything" was, but there is no doubt that he would have achieved
nothing beyond drawing suspicion down on himself. He had
no evidence that could have helped to solve the newly committed crime since he himself had only vague inklings about it
that added up to complete certainty to him alone. But he was
willing to give his life to see the "beasts crushed," as he put it
himself. Peter had been partly correct in predicting this impulse in Shatov, and he was aware of the great risk he was
taking in postponing his horrible new plan for a day. He displayed here his usual trust in his own ability to cope with any
situation and his infinite contempt for the bunch of "nonentities" with whom he was dealing, in general, and for Shatov in
particular. He had long despised Shatov for his "tearful imbecility," as he used to call it when the two of them were still
living abroad, and he was sure of his own ability to cope with
this guileless fellow, that is, never to let him out of his sight
and to intercept any dangerous moves he might make at their
first inception.

Actually, what saved—for a while at least—those whom
Shatov called the "beasts" and whom he was longing to crush,
was a circumstance that none of them had foreseen at all.

Between seven and eight that evening—at the time that the
worried members of our local Five were indignantly waiting
for Peter at Erkel's—Shatov, his head aching and slightly feverish, was stretched out on his bed in complete darkness. He
was tormented by rage and uncertainty about what to do. He
felt he was on the verge of deciding but couldn't and cursed
himself, at the same time feeling that nothing would come of
it anyway. Eventually, however, he slipped into a half sleep
and had a nightmare. He saw himself lying on his bed tied up
with ropes and unable to stir, while someone was pounding on
the fence, on the gate, at Kirilov's cottage in the courtyard,
and at his own door, shaking the whole house, and far away a
pained, familiar voice was calling out to him. Suddenly he
awoke and sat up. To his surprise the banging at the gate continued and, although it was not nearly as violent as it had been
in his dream, it was hard enough and persistent. He also heard
the familiar voice at the gate, although it wasn't plaintive as it
had been in his dream, but impatient and irritated, alternating
with someone else's more restrained voice. He got up, walked
over to the window, and opened it.

"Who's there?" he shouted, literally stiffening with fear.

"If that's you, Shatov," the answer came harsh and impatient from the gate below, "then do me a favor and state clearly and honestly whether you wish to receive me or not."

No doubt about it! He recognized the voice.

"Mary! Is that you?"

"Yes, of course it's me—Mary Shatov—and I assure you I can't keep the cabbie waiting one minute longer."

"Just a second—I'll get a candle," Shatov shouted weakly. He rushed to look for the matches. As usual in such cases, he couldn't find them. Instead he dropped his candlestick on the floor and at that moment the impatient voice came again from the gate. So he gave up the search and rushed downstairs like a madman to open the gate.

"Do me a favor and hold this suitcase while I deal with this idiot," Mrs. Shatov said as soon as he reached the gate, thrusting a light, cheap canvas suitcase studded with brass nails at him. Then she pounced angrily on the cabbie. "I tell you you're trying to overcharge me," she shouted at him. "If you dragged me through those filthy streets for an extra hour, it's your own fault—it was you who couldn't find this stupid street and this idiotic house. So you'd better take the thirty kopecks coming to you—you won't get a kopeck more."

"But, ma'am, you yourself kept saying 'Assumption Street' when we wanted Nativity Street. Assumption was miles out of our way. Look at my horse, he's steaming like anything and all for nothing."

"Assumption, Nativity—you should know more about those idiotic names than I do, because you happen to be a local cabbie. Besides, what you say is wrong: as soon as I hired you, I mentioned Filipov's house and you told me you knew it. Of course, you can lodge a complaint against me if you like, but meanwhile I demand that you leave me alone."

"Here—here's another five kopecks," Shatov said hurriedly, fishing a coin out of his pocket and handing it to the cabbie.

"Please, don't do that! Don't do that, I tell you!" Mrs. Shatov said, flaring up, but the cabbie touched his horse with the whip and moved off, while Shatov took her arm and drew her inside the gate.

"Come, Mary, hurry up; never mind the cabbie. Look—you're soaking wet! Careful here, there are stairs. I'm sorry I have no light. Watch out, the steps are steep; hold on to me, hold on . . . here's my room. I'm sorry there's no light. One moment!"

He picked up the candlestick he had dropped, but it took him a long time to find the matches. Mrs. Shatov waited, standing motionless in the middle of the room.

"Ah, thank God, here they are!" he cried joyfully, lighting the candle.

Mary looked quickly around the room.

"I'd been told you lived very poorly, but I never expected it to be *this* bad," she said with distaste, moving toward the bed. "Ah, I'm tired!" She sat down on the bed, looking completely exhausted. "Well, put my suitcase down and sit on that chair, please. All right, please yourself, but it tires my eyes to have you standing up like that. I'll have to stay with you here until I find a job because I know nothing about this town and have no money. But if my presence inconveniences you, please say so now—that's the only honest thing you can do. In fact, it's your duty. I suppose I could sell something tomorrow and pay for a hotel room. Only, in that case, I'll have to ask you to take me to the hotel. Oh, but I'm so tired."

Shatov began to tremble.

"No, Mary, why go to a hotel? What hotel? Why, why?"

His voice sounded imploring. His hands were clasped.

"If I don't go to a hotel, I'll have to explain a few things to you. I suppose you remember, Shatov, that you and I spent a little over two weeks as husband and wife in Geneva, after which we parted, without quarreling, however, roughly three years ago? Now, I don't want you to think that I've come back to resume our former stupid relationship. I've come here to look for a job, and if I picked this particular town, it was because it makes no difference to me where I live. I certainly haven't come to make up for anything, and you'll oblige me by not assuming any such nonsense."

"Oh, Mary, you don't have to say—you didn't have to . . ." Shatov mumbled indistinctly.

"Well, if that's the way you feel, if you happen to be sufficiently civilized to understand the situation, I'll take the liberty of adding that I turned to you in the first place and came directly to your address because I never considered you to be a despicable person—in fact, you're probably much better than those other good-for-nothings really."

Her eyes flashed. Probably she had suffered a great deal from those "other good-for-nothings."

"And please believe me, I wasn't laughing at you just now when I said I thought you were a decent fellow. I said plainly what I feel, without using big phrases, which I can't stand. But all that is neither here nor there. I was always sure that you'd be intelligent enough not to pester me. Ah, that's enough —I'm too tired really." She gave him a long, tired, harassed look.

Shatov stood by the wall opposite the bed, about five paces from her. He listened shyly as she spoke, but there was a perceptible change in his face, some new life, a strange sort of radiance. This strong, uncouth man, who usually presented a bristling exterior to the world, suddenly mellowed and lighted up. Something unusual and unexpected stirred in his heart. Three years of separation and a broken marriage hadn't displaced anything in his heart.

During those three years, he had probably thought constantly of the woman who had once said "I love you" to him and had remained dear to him ever since. He was ridiculously modest and chaste, considered himself incredibly ugly, hated his face and his character, and saw himself as a kind of freak who might have been taken around and exhibited at fairs. And because of all this, he valued honesty above all else, was fanatical in his convictions, sullen, proud, quarrelsome, and taciturn. And now, the only creature who had ever loved him (he'd always believed she had), even if it had been only for two weeks; the creature he had always considered immeasurably superior to him despite his quite sober appraisal of her errors; the creature he could forgive *anything* (there was no question about that and, in fact, in his eyes, it was always he who was guilty before her)—now this woman, Mary Shatov, was in his house again, with him again! He couldn't quite understand it or believe it. He was completely overcome—it was so terrifying and at the same time so elating! So naturally he couldn't—perhaps didn't even wish to, was afraid to—recover from the shock. It was a dream. But when she gave him that harassed, exhausted look, he suddenly grasped that the woman he loved was suffering, that perhaps she had been wronged. His heart stopped. With a feeling of pain, he examined her features: the glow of early youth had long ago vanished from her tired face. But she was still a handsome woman and, for him, she was as beautiful as ever.

In actual fact, she was now about twenty-five, powerfully built and rather tall (taller than Shatov), with thick, dark-blond hair, a pale oval face, and large dark eyes that, at this moment, were glittering with feverish brilliance. Her former lighthearted, naïve, good-natured exuberance had been superseded now by sullen irritability, bitterness, and a cynical attitude to which she hadn't yet accommodated herself and which still weighed on her. But, worst of all, she was a sick woman —he could see that. Despite his fear of her, he impulsively rushed up to the bed and seized her hands.

"Mary—you must be very tired—please don't be angry. Perhaps you'll have something—some tea at least? Tea is very invigorating, you know. Please try to drink some. Won't you accept some?"

"What's there to accept? Sure I'll accept. Ah, you're still just a child. If you can, get me some tea. But what a tiny, cold room you have!"

"Ah, just a minute . . . firewood, firewood, I have some logs . . ." Shatov became terribly agitated. "I have some logs, but—that is—one moment, I'll get everything and the tea too." He waved his hand with what looked like desperate determination and grabbed his cap.

"Where are you going? I gather, then, that there's no tea in this place?"

"There will be in a minute; there'll be everything. I—"

He took his revolver from the shelf.

"I'll sell this gun or pawn it—"

"Nonsense! It would take too long, anyway. Here, take my money if you don't have any. Here—there must be eighty kopecks in there. I believe that's all I have. Ah, it's like a madhouse here."

"No, no, keep your money. It won't take me a second. I can get some even without the gun."

He rushed off to see Kirilov. This was about two hours before Peter and Liputin arrived. Shatov and Kirilov, who lived in the same yard, hardly ever saw each other and when they did meet, they didn't talk or even say hello. They had really spent too long lying next to each other in America.

"Kirilov, there's always tea in your place. You do have tea and a samovar, don't you?"

Kirilov was pacing his room from corner to corner, as he did every night. He stopped and looked closely, though without seeming particularly surprised, at Shatov, who had burst in on him with these words.

"I've tea, sugar, and a samovar. But no need for the samovar—the tea is hot. Just sit down and help yourself."

"Kirilov, we lay next to each other in America. . . . My wife has come. I—let me have some tea—I need the samovar too."

"If your wife is here, you need the samovar all right. But come back for it. I have two. Take that teapot on the table for now—it's boiling hot. Take everything, take all the sugar, take plenty of bread—everything that's on the table. I have some veal too. I have one ruble in cash here."

"Let me have it, friend. I'll give it back tomorrow. Ah, Kirilov!"

"Is it the wife you had in Switzerland? That's very good. And it's very good that you rushed in this way too."

"Kirilov!" Shatov cried, tucking the teapot under his arm because his hands were loaded with sugar and bread, "ah, Kirilov, if only you could—if only you'd drop your crazy ideas and discard your godless ravings—ah, what a wonderful man you'd be, Kirilov!"

"I can see you still love your wife, even after what happened in Switzerland. It's very good after that Switzerland affair. Come again whenever you need tea. Come at any time of the night; I never go to bed. I'll have that samovar for you. Go on, take this ruble—take it. Go and join your wife and I'll be thinking about you and about her."

Mary Shatov seemed pleased to get tea so quickly and was eager to have some. But Shatov didn't have to go back for the samovar: she drank only half a cup, in sips, swallowing a tiny piece of bread, declining the veal with a disgusted and irritated air.

"You're not well, Mary, I can see that," Shatov said, waiting on her shyly.

"Of course I'm not well. Sit down, please. Where did you get the tea, since you obviously didn't have any?"

Shatov told her briefly about Kirilov. She had heard of him before.

"I know, he's mad. But please, enough about him—I know there are plenty of stupid fools in the world. So you went to America? Ah, yes, I know about it; you wrote to me."

"Yes, I wrote from Paris."

"Enough of that, please—let's talk of something else. Are you a Slavophile by conviction?"

"Me? Not really—but since it was impossible to be a Russian, I became a Slavophile," Shatov said with a forced grin.

feeling like a man who has tried to be witty at the wrong moment and on the wrong occasion.

"But aren't you a Russian?"

"No, I'm not."

"Ah, what nonsense. Sit down, please, for heaven's sake! Why do you keep tearing about the room? Do you think I'm delirious? It's quite possible. Did you say there were only the two of you living in this house?"

"Two of us, but downstairs—"

"And both of them so bright! But what did you mean about downstairs? You did say downstairs, didn't you?"

"No, nothing."

"Never mind 'no, nothing'; tell me. I want to know."

"I only wanted to say that now there are only the two of us, but the Lebyatkins used to live downstairs—"

"You mean the woman who was murdered last night?" She sat up suddenly. "That was the first thing I heard, as soon as I arrived in town. And you had fires here, didn't you?"

"Yes, Mary, we did and perhaps I'm acting very despicable in letting those beasts get away with it."

He got up and started pacing the room, throwing up his arms almost in a frenzy. But Mary had no idea what he was talking about. In general, she paid very little attention to what he said; she asked questions but was not really interested in his answers.

"Charming goings-on you have here! Ah, it's all so despicable! Everyone seems to be so low and contemptible. But will you *please* sit down—don't you realize how much you irritate me?"

She was utterly exhausted and her head fell limply on the pillow.

"I'm sorry, Mary; I'll keep still. But don't you think you ought to rest a little?"

She didn't answer. She was terribly weak and her eyes closed. With her ashen face, she looked exactly as though she were dead. She was asleep in one second. Shatov looked around, put the candle straight, once more glanced worriedly at the sleeping woman's face, holding his tightly clasped hands in front of him, then tiptoed out of his room onto the landing. There, he pressed his face against the wall in one corner and remained like that for ten minutes, soundless and motionless. He would've remained there even longer had he not heard someone walking cautiously up the stairs. Shatov remembered he had forgotten to lock the gate.

"Who's that?" he asked in a whisper.

The visitor didn't answer but continued climbing the stairs slowly. He stopped on the landing, but Shatov couldn't make him out in the darkness. Then suddenly the other asked carefully:

"Ivan Shatov?"

Shatov said yes and then stretched out his arm to bar the man's way, but the visitor caught his hand and Shatov shuddered as though he'd touched some revolting, slimy creature.

"Stop there," Shatov whispered hurriedly. "I can't let you in. My wife has come back to me. Wait, I'll bring the candle out."

When he came back with the candle he saw a very young army officer whom he thought he'd seen somewhere before but whose name he didn't know.

"Erkel," the officer introduced himself, "we met at Virginsky's."

"I remember—you sat and wrote all the time. Listen now," Shatov said with a sudden burst of anger, stepping forward, but still speaking in a whisper, "when you caught my hand just now, you made that recognition sign. Well, for your information, you can do you know what with all those signs of yours! I don't acknowledge that stuff; I don't want to have anything to do with it. And I could easily throw you downstairs if I felt like it—do you know that?"

"No, I know nothing of the sort—and I know even less what's made you lose your temper this way," Erkel said, without any apparent resentment, almost good-naturedly. "I have a message for you; that's why I came and my only wish is not to waste time. You have a printing press that doesn't belong to you and for which you're responsible, as you know very well yourself. I've been instructed to inform you that you must turn it over to Liputin tomorrow at seven P.M. sharp. I've been further instructed to tell you that once this is done, you'll never be bothered again."

"Never?"

"No, never—definitely. Your request has been granted and you have been released from the Movement once and for all. I was instructed to give you a positive assurance on this point."

"Who instructed you?"

"Those who gave me the recognition sign."

"Have you come from abroad?"

"That . . . I don't think that can be of any interest to you."

"But damn you—why the hell didn't you come sooner if you were told to tell me all that?"

"I was following certain instructions and I wasn't alone in—"

"I can well imagine you weren't alone. I know that. But why the hell didn't Liputin come himself?"

"I'll come for you here tomorrow at six, and we'll walk over there. Only the three of us will be present."

"What about Verkhovensky?"

"Verkhovensky won't be there. He's leaving town tomorrow morning at eleven."

"That's just what I thought," Shatov muttered furiously under his breath, banging his fist against his hip. "He's taking off, the bastard!"

He was greatly agitated. Erkel looked at him fixedly, waiting in silence.

"What will you do with it? You can't just pick it up and carry it away, you know."

"We won't have to do that. You just show us the place and we'll make sure that it's buried there. You know, we only know roughly where it is—we have no idea of the exact spot. Have you shown it to anyone else?"

Shatov gave him a funny look.

"But you—you're just a boy—and such a silly little boy; and, yet, you've stuck your head into it too, like a stupid sheep. Ah, but that's just what they need, young blood like yours! All right, off with you! Ah, and to think that that other swine has double-crossed the lot of you and taken off!"

Erkel looked at him quietly and composedly, but his face was blank.

"Verkhovensky has run away! Verkhovensky has left you holding the bag!" Shatov growled through clenched teeth.

"But he hasn't even left yet. He only intends to leave tomorrow," Erkel said softly and with quiet conviction. "I tried to insist that he come as a witness, because all my orders have been relayed through him," he blurted out, inexperienced boy that he was. "Unfortunately, he declined, explaining he had to leave, and I can well understand that he'd hardly have time."

Shatov once more looked pityingly at the simpleton, but

then he shrugged his shoulders with an expression that seemed to say, "Ah, what's the good?"

"All right, I'll come," he announced abruptly. "And now beat it—off with you!"

"I'll come for you at six sharp," Erkel said, bowing politely and starting unhurriedly down the stairs.

"Little fool!" Shatov shouted after him from the landing, unable to restrain himself.

"What?" Erkel shouted from below.

"No, nothing—go on."

"I thought you said something."

II

Erkel was the sort of "little fool" who lacked the real sense that should rule a man's head, but who had plenty of minor, subordinate sense, even to the point of cunning. He was fanatically and childishly devoted to the Movement—that is, essentially to Peter Verkhovensky, on whose instructions he was acting. These instructions had been given him at the meeting of our local Five, when the assignments for the next day were decided on and handed out. Peter Verkhovensky had given Erkel the job of messenger, taking him aside and talking to him privately for ten minutes or so. Carrying out orders was a vital need of Erkel's shallow, unthinking nature, which longed instinctively to be subordinated to another will. Oh, it goes without saying, it could only be in the name of some "great, common cause"—but what cause made no difference. Rank-and-file fanatics of Erkel's type cannot understand the idea they are supposed to serve without fusing it with the person who, in their opinion, expresses it. This sensitive, kind, gentle boy was perhaps the coldest of the killers set on Shatov. He was capable of participating in murder without any personal hatred, without batting an eye. In this instance, Erkel had been told to find out as much as possible about Shatov's habits while he was delivering the message and when Shatov received him on the landing and blurted out about his wife's having come back to him, he had shown sufficient sense not to evince any further interest in the subject, although it immediately occurred to him that the presence of Shatov's wife could vitally affect the success of their enterprise.

And indeed, it did affect it. Only Mary's return stopped Shatov from carrying out his intention. At the same time, it helped them to get rid of him. To start with, the presence of his wife flustered Shatov, threw him off guard, deprived him of his usual cautiousness and intuitive scent for danger. His head was too full of other things to think of his own safety. He was only too anxious to believe that Verkhovensky had decided to desert his puppets, because this fitted in with his long-held suspicions.

He returned to his room and sat down in a corner again, digging his elbows into his thighs and burying his face in his hands. Bitter thoughts buzzed in his head and tormented him.

Now and then he raised his head, stood up, tiptoed closer to the bed, and looked at her. "Oh God! She'll have a raging fever by tomorrow morning," he thought. "I think it's started already. I'm sure she must've caught cold. She's not accustomed to this terrible climate, and she had no warm clothes at all—nothing but that thin coat in the rain and wind. Ah, and on top of that she had to travel third class! How could anyone have left her, abandoned her like that, in all her helplessness? And what a tiny suitcase she has—ten pounds at most and all battered and wrinkled! Poor thing, she's so exhausted. She must have been through so much! But she's proud and doesn't complain. But she's very irritable. Well, that's the illness—even an angel is bound to be irritable when ill. I can imagine how dry and hot her forehead must be—and the rings under her eyes are so black and—and, how beautiful, despite everything, the delicate oval of her face is, her beautiful, thick hair, how—"

And he quickly looked away, quickly stepped back, apparently afraid of the mere thought of seeing in her anything but a poor, spent creature whom he must help. No, no, he had nothing to *hope* for from her—ah, what a vile and despicable animal a man is! And he returned to his chair in the corner, buried his face in his hands again, and again remembered and mused—and again *hopes* danced in his mind.

Her weak, broken voice telling him, "Ah, I'm so tired!" kept ringing in his ears. God, how could that man have left her! She has only eighty kopecks in that tiny old purse! She came to look for a job, but what does she know about jobs? What do they think Russia is? But they are all like innocent babes; they live in a world created by their own imaginations! And now, this poor thing is furious because Russia is so different from what, abroad, she dreamed it would be. Oh, the poor innocents! But I must say, it's really cold in here.

He remembered her complaining about the cold and that he had promised to light a fire. "The wood is right here in the house and I could get it, if only I can do it without waking her up. I think I can manage. And what shall I do about the veal? She'll wake up and she may want to eat. Well, I'll see about that later. Kirilov stays up all night. What can I cover her with? She's sleeping so deeply, but I'm sure she must be cold!"

And once more he went up close to the bed and looked at her. Her dress had got hitched up a little and her right leg was exposed to the knee. He quickly turned away, almost in terror, hurriedly removed the heavy overcoat he was wearing and, remaining in his threadbare jacket, covered her with it, trying to keep his eyes off her exposed flesh.

Lighting the fire, walking on tiptoe, looking at the sleeping woman, dreaming in the corner, looking at the sleeping woman again—all that took up quite a bit of time. Two or three hours slipped by, during which Verkhovensky and Liputin had time to come, see Kirilov, and leave. At last, when Shatov had finally dozed off in his corner, she let out a moan, woke up, and called him. He leaped up, feeling like a criminal.

"Mary, I'm awfully sorry. I dozed off—oh, I'm a real pig, Mary—"

She sat up and looked around in surprise, apparently trying to recall where she was. Then she suddenly became extremely indignant.

"I lay down on your bed and fell asleep because I was dead tired," she said, "but why on earth didn't you wake me up? How dare you think that I'd be willing to be a burden to you!"

"But I couldn't possibly wake you, Mary."

"You could have and should have! You have no other bed and I took yours. You had no right to put me in a false position. Do you think, by any chance, that I've come here to take advantage of your charity? I demand that you get into your bed immediately! I'll settle down on some chairs in the corner."

"But I haven't even got that many chairs, Mary, and then, I have nothing to put on them—"

"All right, there's the floor. If I don't sleep on the floor, you'll have to. I want to move onto the floor right now—now!"

She stood up and tried to take a step, but a violent spasm

of pain swept away her resolution and whatever strength there was left in her and, moaning painfully, she let herself fall back on the bed. Shatov hurried over to her. Mary hid her face in the pillow, took hold of his hand, and squeezed and twisted it desperately. This continued for about a minute.

"Mary dear, there's a doctor around here—Dr. Frantzel, a good, a very good friend of mine. Don't you think I'd better run over and fetch him?"

"Nonsense."

"Why nonsense? Tell me, Mary, where does it hurt? Don't you think a compress might help? Wouldn't you like a compress on your stomach? I could do that even without a doctor. Or what about a mustard plaster?"

"What's going on?" she asked strangely, lifting her head and staring at him.

"What, Mary? What are you asking about?" Shatov asked, puzzled. "Oh, Mary, I've completely lost my head; I can't understand a thing. I'm sorry, Mary."

"Oh, leave me alone. There's nothing for you to understand and it's none of your business anyway. In fact, it would be really funny . . ." She snorted bitterly. "Well, say something—walk up and down the room and talk; don't just stand there staring at me. This is the five-hundredth time I've asked you!"

Shatov started pacing the room, his eyes on the floor, forcing himself with a great effort not to look at her.

"There's some—please don't get angry, Mary, please—there's some veal and some tea—not far away. You ate so little before—"

She brushed him off with an irritated gesture of distaste and Shatov bit his lip despairingly.

"Listen, Shatov, I plan to open a bookbinding shop here based on fair, cooperative principles. Since you live here, what do you think—could it succeed?"

"Ah, Mary, they don't read much in this town. Besides there are hardly any books around. And even if they got hold of a book, why should they have it bound all of a sudden?"

"Who's 'they'?"

"The local readers—the inhabitants of the town in general."

"Well, express yourself clearly. How can I know who you mean by *they*? Can't you learn to talk properly?"

"It's the spirit of the language," Shatov mumbled.

"Ah, go to hell with your spirit; I'm tired of you. Now why shouldn't the local reader or inhabitant have his books bound?"

"Because reading books and having them bound are two different stages in cultural development, two strikingly distinct phases. At first, little by little, man acquires the reading habit. He does so very, very slowly. It may take centuries, and during that time, he throws his books around and tears them, refusing to grant them the status of a serious object. Now, binding a book is a sign that the book is respected, that man not only enjoys reading but now considers the book as a serious object. Well, Russia as a whole hasn't yet reached that second stage, but in Europe they've been binding books for a long time."

"Well, although you sound rather pedantic, what you say makes sense and it reminds me of you three years ago. You used to be quite witty, on occasion, then."

She paid him this compliment in the same disgusted tone in which she'd made her whimsical outbursts.

"Mary, Mary," Shatov said, deeply moved, "if you only knew, Mary, how much has happened and changed in those three years! I heard that you had come to despise me for changing my opinions. But whom have I deserted? Well, the enemies of everything that's really alive; the obsolete liberals afraid of independence; the slaves of some rigid idea or other; the enemies of individual freedom; the senile preachers of death and decay! What do they have to offer? Senility; the golden mean; the most Philistine, petty-bourgeois mediocrity; equality based on envy; and equality without personal pride, as it is conceived by a flunky, as the French conceived it in 1793. And the worst of it is that they're nothing but a bunch of pigs, the lot of them—nothing but vicious, nasty pigs!"

"Yes, certainly, there are plenty of vicious pigs around," she said, suddenly wincing with pain.

She lay stretched out and immobile, apparently afraid to move. Her head, thrown backward and slightly sideways, rested on the pillow. She stared at the ceiling with tired, feverish eyes. Her face was pale and her lips were parched.

"You recognize it then, Mary! You do!" Shatov cried.

She tried to shake her head in denial, but the attempt caused a spasm of pain to shoot through her. She again hid her face in the pillow and madly squeezed Shatov's hand for a full minute —he had rushed over to her in terror.

"But Mary, Mary, it may be quite serious!"

"Be quiet—I don't want, don't want!" she shouted, almost in a frenzy, turning her face toward him. "Stop staring at me with that stupid compassion of yours! Go on, walk up and down and talk!"

Completely at a loss, Shatov started muttering something.

"What do you do for a living here?" she interrupted him with impatient contempt.

"I help out a local merchant, in his office. And you know, Mary, if I'd set my mind to it, I could've been making quite good money even here."

"Good for you."

"I didn't mean anything, Mary. I just said it like that—"

"And what else do you do? What are you preaching now? I know you couldn't do without preaching. It's your nature."

"I'm preaching that there is God, Mary."

"In Whom you can't believe yourself. That's something I never could understand."

"Let's leave it for now, Mary. Later—"

"What was that woman Maria Lebyatkin like?"

"That too, we'll talk about some other time, Mary."

"Don't you dare brush me off like that! Tell me, is it true that these—these people must be held responsible for her death too?"

"No doubt about it," Shatov said through clenched teeth.

Mary suddenly raised her head and shouted at him hysterically:

"Don't you ever, ever dare to mention that to me, d'you hear?"

Pain shot through her again and her head fell back on the pillow. It was the third time it had happened and this time it was worse—her moans turned into a yell.

"Ah, you're unbearable! I can't stand you!" she said, twisting and tossing in the bed, no longer caring that this made the pain even worse, and pushing away Shatov, who stood by her.

"I'll do what you tell me, Mary—I'll walk and talk, shall I?"

"Ah, damn it, can't you see it's started?"

"What's started, Mary?"

"How the hell should I know? Do you think I know much about these things? Ah, damn it in advance, the stupid thing!"

"But you said it was beginning, Mary, so I suppose I'd better— What am I to make of it, Mary?"

"You're no use for anything but abstract chatter! The hell with everything in this damned world!"

"Mary—"

He seriously thought that she had gone mad.

"Can't you really see that I'm in labor?" She sat up, glaring at him, her features distorted with hatred. "May the damned child be cursed before it's even born!"

"Mary!" Shatov suddenly realized what it was all about. "But why didn't you tell me before?" He pulled himself together and took his cap with great determination.

"And how could I know when I came here? Do you really imagine I'd have come to you if I'd known? They assured me that it wasn't coming for at least ten days. But where do you think you're going? Don't you dare!"

"To get a midwife. I'll sell my gun. First I must get money—"

"No midwife, d'you hear! Just any woman—any old woman. There are eighty kopecks in my purse—take them. Peasant women manage to do without midwives, all right. Anyway, if I croaked, it'd be a damn good thing."

"I'll get a woman, an old woman—anyone you want, but how can I leave you alone, Mary?"

But he decided that it was better to leave her alone now, despite the state she was in, rather than have no one there when it came. So, ignoring her moans and her furious protests, he tore downstairs like a madman.

III

First he went to Kirilov's. It was around one A.M. Kirilov was standing in the middle of the room.

"Kirilov, my wife's having a baby."

"How do you mean?"

"She just—she's going to have a child."

"You sure?"

"Yes, yes, she's having those pains—you know. We need a woman, some old woman, and right away. Could you get one? You used to have a whole lot of old women—"

"It's a shame, I'm no good at childbearing," Kirilov said dreamily. "I mean not that I can't bear children but that I'm not good at helping to bear children—no, not that. I mean—no, I don't know how to explain."

"You mean you can't deliver a baby. But I wasn't asking that. I'm looking for an old woman, any woman, a nurse, a servant—anything!"

"I'll get you an old woman, but not right now. Perhaps in the meantime I could myself—"

"No, impossible. I must get Mrs. Virginsky, the midwife."

"She's a bitch."

"That's right, Kirilov, but she's the best midwife. Oh, I can see already what it's going to be like—she'll make a disgusted face and swear and blaspheme, and there'll be no reverence, no gladness at such a great, mysterious event—the appearance of a new human being! Oh, she's already been cursing the baby!"

"If you want I could—"

"No, no, but while I'm running around—oh, I'll drag that Virginsky woman here if I have to!—you could go to my door and listen. But don't go in, remember. You might scare her. Don't go in whatever happens. Just listen. Of course, in case of extreme emergency—in that case, better go in."

"I've got it. Here's another ruble. I wanted to buy a chicken tomorrow, but I've changed my mind. Run along now—run as fast as you can. My samovar will be going all night."

Kirilov knew nothing about the fate that was being prepared for Shatov; indeed, he'd never had the slightest idea of the man's danger. He knew that there were some unsettled accounts between Shatov and "those people" but, although he himself had been involved to a certain extent by the instructions sent him from abroad (they were rather vague at that, because he had never been too closely connected with anything), lately he had stopped carrying out any instructions and, retiring completely, especially from affairs connected with the common cause, had led a purely contemplative life.

Although, during the meeting at Erkel's, Peter Verkhovensky had decided to take Liputin along to Kirilov's to prove to him that when the moment came Kirilov would take the "Shatov affair" upon himself, Shatov's name had never come up during their talk. Apparently Peter hadn't thought it wise to bring the subject up, not being sure that Kirilov would accept the deal. So he had left it till the next day, after everything had been done and when Kirilov wouldn't really care one way or the other. At least that was Peter's reasoning. Liputin had noticed that, despite Peter's assurance, Shatov was never even mentioned, but by that time his nerves had been stretched to the breaking point and he was in no state to protest.

Shatov tore like a whirlwind up Ant Street, damning its length, wondering whether it would ever end. Then he had to knock for a long time at the midwife's house—all the Virginskys had been asleep for hours. Without hesitation, Shatov started pounding at the shutters with his fists. The watchdog in the yard pulled madly at his chain, filling the air with his furious, frantic barking. The dogs in the other yards down the street chimed in and a real canine bedlam started.

"Why are you knocking like that? What do you want?" Shatov at last heard Virginsky's voice from the window.

Its tone was strangely gentle for someone roused from his bed in the middle of the night. The shutter opened, then the upper part of the window.

"What swine's making all that noise!" a female voice squealed furiously, in a tone that was, after all, more to be expected on such an occasion. It was the maiden relative who lived at Virginsky's.

"It's me—Shatov. My wife's come back and she's about to give birth—"

"So let her! And you take yourself away from here!"

"I've come for Mrs. Virginsky. I won't leave without her."

"She can't attend to everyone. She doesn't practice at night. Go to the Mashkeev woman and stop that racket, I warn you!" the spiteful voice kept screeching.

Shatov could hear Virginsky trying to stop her, but in her rage the old spinster kept pushing him back.

"I won't leave!" Shatov shouted again.

"Wait—wait a minute, I demand it!" Virginsky said, finally deciding to raise his voice to his relative. "Please wait five minutes, Shatov. I'll wake up my wife, but please stop that banging and shouting. Oh, this is really terrible!"

After five endless minutes, Arina Virginsky finally appeared.

"So your wife's come to stay with you?" her voice came from the window and Shatov was surprised to hear that it wasn't unfriendly at all, just domineering. But then, Mrs. Virginsky didn't know how to communicate in any other way.

"Yes, and she's about to give birth."

"You mean Mary?"

"Of course it's Mary."

There was a brief silence. Shatov waited. He could hear them whispering among themselves inside the house.

"How long has she been here?" Mrs. Virginsky asked.

"Since eight this evening. Please hurry."

Again he heard them consulting in whispers.

"Say, are you sure? Did she send you for me herself?"

"She didn't send me for you; she wanted any woman, a peasant woman—anyone. She was afraid it would cost me too much money. But please don't worry; I'll pay."

"All right, I'll come, whether you pay or not. I've always respected Mary Shatov's independent way of thinking, although she may not even remember who I am. Do you have the most essential things?"

"I haven't got anything, but I'll get whatever's needed."

"Strange that that type of person can be generous," Shatov thought on his way to Lyamshin's. "The convictions he holds and the person himself are in many ways quite different. Perhaps I've wronged them considerably! Everyone is guilty— we all are and—ah, if only we were all convinced of that!"

At Lyamshin's he didn't have to wait long. To Shatov's surprise, Lyamshin jumped out of bed almost immediately and, barefoot, in nothing but his nightshirt, rushed to the window and opened it at the risk of catching cold. This was strange for a man who jealously looked after his health and tended to imagine himself afflicted with all sorts of diseases. But then, he had a special reason for such alertness and haste: Lyamshin's nerves were on edge and he'd been unable to sleep after the meeting at Erkel's; he was haunted by fear of certain unwanted and uninvited visitors. He had been terribly worried when he heard that Shatov intended to inform on him. And now, on top of all that, there was this horrible loud banging at his window.

He was so scared when he saw Shatov that he quickly slammed the window closed and took refuge in his bed. Shatov started shouting furiously and pounding at the window.

"How dare you come here, banging like that in the middle of the night?" Lyamshin shouted in a threatening tone, although his heart was missing beats from fear. It took him at least two minutes before he could make up his mind to open his window again, and he first made sure that Shatov was alone.

"Here's your revolver—give me back my fifteen rubles."

"Are you drunk? What is this, a robbery? You'll only make me catch cold. Wait, let me at least throw a blanket around my shoulders."

"Give me those fifteen rubles now or I'll stay here and shout and bang until morning. I'll smash your window."

"And I'll call for help and they'll lock you up."

"Do you think I'm mute myself or something? I can call the cops too, and who do you think should be more afraid of them, me or you?"

"What you're trying to do is contemptible! I know what you're hinting at. Stop it, stop it—don't bang, for God's sake! But where on earth do you expect me to get the money in the middle of the night? And what can you want it for at this hour, if you aren't drunk?"

"My wife's come back. I'm asking ten rubles less than what I paid you for it and I've never even fired it. Take the revolver—take it immediately."

Without thinking, Lyamshin stretched his hand out of the window and took the gun. He stood holding it for a second, then suddenly his head popped out and he spoke gaspingly, as if shivers were running up and down his spine:

"You're lying! It's not true that your wife has come back to you. You're simply trying to leave town."

"Where could I run to, you damn fool? I'll leave the running away to your Peter Verkhovensky. Let him take off—not me! I've just been to get the midwife, Mrs. Virginsky, and she's agreed to come. My wife's in agony; we need money. Give me those fifteen rubles."

A whole fireworks display of possibilities flashed through Lyamshin's shifty brain. He saw things differently now, but fear still paralyzed his reasoning somewhat.

"But how's that? You don't live with your wife, do you?"

"I could bash your head in for a question like that."

"Ah, good God, I'm sorry. I was just so flabbergasted—but I understand now; I see! But did Mrs. Virginsky really agree to come? You told me she was coming, didn't you? But you know very well it isn't true. So you see, you can't stop lying. You lie like you breathe."

"She's probably with my wife by now. Don't keep me waiting. It's not my fault that you're so stupid."

"That's not true, I'm not stupid. But you'll have to excuse me, I really—"

And once more, at a loss how to get rid of Shatov, he closed his window. But Shatov let out such a yell that Lyamshin's head immediately popped out again.

"But this is a scandalous infringement of my rights as a private citizen! Now, what are you demanding of me? Please formulate your demands. And I want you to note that you're presenting them in the middle of the night!"

"I'm demanding fifteen rubles, you fathead!"

"And what if I don't wish to take back this gun? You have no claims on me. You bought it and that's the end of it. Anyway, I can't produce the money just like that, in the middle of the night. Where do you expect me to get it from?"

"I know you always have money at home. And I'm even allowing you to keep ten rubles. Everyone knows what a miser you are."

"Come the day after tomorrow, you hear—the day after tomorrow, at twelve sharp and I'll pay you every kopeck, all right?"

Shatov pounded at the window again.

"Give me ten rubles now, and tomorrow, first thing in the morning, another five."

"I'll give you the five the day after tomorrow, I swear I can't have it by tomorrow. Better not come for it, better not—"

"Give me ten, you rat!"

"Why do you have to be so insulting? Wait, I must light a candle. Look, you've broken the glass! . . . Who ever heard of a man coming in the middle of the night and abusing people! Here!" Lyamshin handed a bill through the window.

Shatov grabbed it. It was five rubles.

"I swear that's all I have. You can kill me, I can't give you more. I'll pay you the rest on the dot the day after tomorrow, but I can't now."

"I won't leave!" Shatov roared.

"All right, here, take it. But that's all. Even if you split your throat hollering, that's all you'll get—that's all, that's all, that's all!"

Lyamshin was hysterical, desperate, sweating. The last bills he had handed Shatov were one-ruble bills. Shatov now had seven rubles in his hand.

"Well, the hell with it, I'll come for the rest tomorrow and I'll beat the guts out of you, Lyamshin, if you don't have eight rubles ready for me."

"But you won't find me home, you damn fool," Lyamshin muttered quickly under his breath. "Hey, wait! Stop!" he shouted after Shatov, who was already running. "Tell me the truth now—is your wife really back with you? Please, I'd like to know."

"Idiot!"

Shatov spat and ran all the way home as fast as his legs could carry him.

I must mention here that Mrs. Virginsky knew nothing about the resolution adopted at the meeting at Erkel's place. Her husband had returned home stunned and dejected and hadn't dared tell her about it. However, he couldn't refrain from mentioning Verkhovensky's warning about Shatov's intention of informing on them, although he added that he didn't quite trust Verkhovensky. Mrs. Virginsky was very frightened and that was why, when Shatov came for her, she had immediately agreed to go, although she was dead tired, having stayed up all the previous night attending a complicated delivery. She had always been convinced that "a piece of garbage like Shatov was capable of any antisocial act," but now Mary's arrival changed the whole picture. Shatov's fear, the desperate tone of his pleas for help indicated a change in the traitor's feelings: a man who was willing to bring about his own ruin in order to destroy others wouldn't look or sound like that. And so Arina Virginsky was determined to investigate the whole matter herself. Her husband was very happy about this determination—indeed, he felt as if a two-hundred-pound load had been lifted from his back. He even began to hope— Shatov's behavior wasn't compatible with what Verkhovensky had assumed.

As Shatov had expected, Mrs. Virginsky was already with Mary when he got home. She had just arrived and had scornfully dismissed Kirilov, who had been hanging around at the bottom of the stairs. She quickly introduced herself to Mary, who didn't remember having met her before, found she was "in the worst possible way," that is, irritated, dejected, and "in the most abject despair" and then spent five minutes or so overcoming the resistance the patient tried to put up.

"What's this stuff you keep repeating about not wanting an expensive midwife?" she was saying at the moment Shatov came through the door. "It's a lot of bunk—a collection of false notions owing to the abnormal situation you're in. An illiterate old woman has at least a fifty-fifty chance of landing you in serious trouble, and then you'll have more bother and expense than you would using the services of an expensive midwife. Anyway, what makes you think I'm expensive?

You can pay me later and I promise I won't overcharge you, while I guarantee success. With me, you won't die. I've seen much worse than this! As to the child, I can get him into the nursery tomorrow if you wish and after that get him adopted by some family in the countryside and that will be an end to the business. Later, you'll get back on your feet, get yourself a decent job, and in no time you'll be able to pay Shatov for board, lodging, and expenses, which won't be at all as much as you imagine—"

"That's not what I—I have no right to be a burden to him—"

"That's a very rational civic feeling, but let me assure you that Shatov will have hardly any expenses if he's only willing to give up his eccentric nonsense and be the least bit sensible. All he has to do is stop this crazy business of pounding on people's windows and trotting around the town with his tongue hanging out. If he's not restrained, he'll get all the local doctors out of their beds just as he woke up all the dogs in my street. No need for doctors—I can guarantee everything, as I said before. If you wish, though, you can hire some old woman to clean the place—that would cost practically nothing. And he himself could be of some assistance for once, instead of behaving like a fool. He has hands and feet and could run over to the druggist's, and I don't see why you should consider that as charity and be offended. How can it be a question of charity anyway, since it was he who put you in this state. Didn't he cause you to quarrel with the family where you were employed as a governess? Didn't he do it with the selfish motive of marrying you? We've heard the story, you know. Anyway, as I told you, he came clamoring for me like a madman and roused the whole street. I'm not trying to force my services on anyone, and I came here with the sole purpose of helping you, as a matter of principle, because we believe in solidarity as I told Shatov before even stepping out of my house. If, however, you feel you don't need me—good-by. I only hope there won't be any complications that otherwise would be so easy to avoid."

And she rose from her chair.

Mary was in such a helpless state, in such great pain, and, to tell the truth, so scared of the forthcoming delivery that she didn't have the courage to let her go. But suddenly she felt hatred for this woman: Mrs. Virginsky had completely misunderstood what Mary had said and the way she felt. Still, the possibility of dying at the hands of an inexperienced woman overcame Mary's antipathy. And to make up for it somehow, from that second on, she became even more demanding and more cruel to Shatov. She even went so far as to forbid him to look at her or even to turn his face in her direction. Her pains increased. Her swearing grew more frantic and even a few foul words were thrown in.

"I guess we'd better send him out," Arina Virginsky suddenly decided, glancing at Shatov. "He looks like nothing on earth and it's only scaring you—he's pale as a corpse! Why should it hurt you, you ridiculous crank? Ah, what a comedy!"

Shatov didn't answer—he had decided not to answer.

"I've seen plenty of stupid daddies going off their heads, but then they at least—"

"Stop it! I'd rather you left me to croak than said another word! I don't want to hear it—I don't, I don't!" Mary shouted.

"It's impossible not to say one word, and you'd know it if you hadn't gone off your head yourself. Because I think that's what's happened to you in your present condition. At least, I have to say things connected with the business at hand. I want to know whether you've prepared anything. You, Shatov —answer me; she's in no state to tell me."

"Tell me what you need."

"That means nothing's been prepared."

She told him all the things she had to have and, to do her justice, she asked only for what was absolutely indispensable, the very minimum. Shatov had some of them. Mary handed him the keys to her suitcase to get something out of it. His hands trembled so much that it took him a long time to unlock the unfamiliar catch. Mary became furious, but when Mrs. Virginsky hurried over to take the key away from him, Mary forbade her to touch the suitcase and, crying and shouting whimsically, insisted that Shatov do it himself.

For some of the items Shatov had to run down to Kirilov's, but as soon as he stepped out of the door Mary started calling him back hysterically and only after he had come back to her and explained that he was just leaving for a minute did she calm down.

"I must say, you're difficult to please, ma'am," Mrs. Virginsky said, laughing. "One minute he must face the wall and isn't allowed to look at you, and the next he can't leave you for a second without you dissolving into tears. He'll end up imagining all sorts of things this way, you'll see. All right, all right, take it easy; I was only joking."

"He won't dare imagine anything."

"Pooh-pooh-pooh—I'm telling you that if he weren't in love with you up to here, he wouldn't be running up and down the streets with a foot of his tongue hanging out, and he wouldn't be rousing all the dogs in town. And at my house, he even broke the frame of the window!"

V

Shatov found Kirilov still pacing his room from corner to corner. He was by now in such a distracted state that he had forgotten about Mary's arrival and listened to Shatov without understanding what it was all about.

"Ah yes, sure," he said, suddenly remembering and apparently making an effort to tear himself away for a second from the thoughts that absorbed him so completely. "Yes, that old woman. The wife or the old woman? Wait—both your wife and the old woman, right? I remember, I went to get her. The old woman will come, but a little later. Sure, take the pillow. Anything else? Yes, of course—wait, Shatov. Tell me—have you ever experienced moments of eternal harmony?"

"You know, Kirilov, you shouldn't go on staying up every night."

Kirilov suddenly stirred, woke up, as it were, and began to talk much more coherently than he usually did. Obviously he had thought it all out before and perhaps he had written it down too. "There are seconds—they come five or six at a time —when you suddenly feel the presence of eternal harmony in all its perfection. It's not of this earth; I don't mean by that that it's something heavenly but only that man, as he is constituted on earth, can't endure it. He must be either physically transformed or die. It is a clear, unmistakable sensation. It is as though you were suddenly in contact with the whole of nature, and you say, 'Yes, this is the truth.' When God was creating the world, He said, after each day of creation, 'Yes, this is the truth; it's good.' It's not elation really, it's simply joy. You forgive nothing because there's nothing to forgive. It's not that you love—there's something superior to love in it. The most terrifying part of it is that it is so terribly obvious and it's such a joy. If it lasted for more than five seconds, the soul wouldn't be able to stand it; it would have to disappear.

In those five seconds I experience a whole lifetime and I'd give my life for them—it'd be well worth it. To endure ten seconds of it, we would have to undergo a physical transformation. I think man must stop reproducing himself. What's the point of having children? Why strive for progress when the goal has already been achieved? It says in the gospel that in the resurrection they neither marry nor are given in marriage but are as the angels of God in heaven. That's a hint. Is your wife having a baby?"

"How often do you have this sensation, Kirilov?"

"Sometimes once in three days, sometimes once a week."

"Are you an epileptic?"

"No."

"Well, you're sure to become one. Watch out, Kirilov, I've heard that's how epilepsy begins. An epileptic described to me exactly what it feels like just before a fit. It's just like what you said: five seconds, and he felt it was impossible to endure it any longer. Remember Mohammed's pitcher from which not a drop was spilled while he flew around paradise on his steed. That pitcher—that's your five seconds. It's too much like that harmony of yours. And, you know, Mohammed was an epileptic. So watch out, Kirilov, it's epilepsy!"

"There won't be enough time for it," Kirilov said, laughing quietly.

VI

The night was coming to an end. Shatov was constantly called, sent on errands, abused. Mary reached rock bottom in her fear of death. She shouted that she wanted to live, "at all costs, at all costs" and that she was afraid to die. "No, no, not that!" she kept saying to Mrs. Virginsky. It was lucky it was Mrs. Virginsky attending her. Little by little she gained full control of the patient, and Mary now obeyed every word she said and tried not to incur her anger, like a child. Arina Virginsky believed in discipline rather than gentleness, but it must be said for her that she was wonderful at her trade.

Day began to break. Mrs. Virginsky pretended she thought Shatov kept running out onto the landing to rid himself of a prayer and laughed. Mary laughed too, spitefully and sarcastically, and this laughter seemed to make her feel easier. Finally, they chased Shatov away altogether. A raw, cold morning arrived. Shatov stood on the landing, his face to the corner, exactly as he'd stood when Erkel had come upstairs. He was trembling like a fall leaf in the wind. He was afraid to think, but his brain clung to every image that passed through it, as in a dream. Fancies entwined him, but they also broke apart like rotten thread. Then the moans that were coming from the room became horrible animal cries, unbearable, impossible. He wanted to stop his ears, but it didn't work and he fell on his knees saying, "Mary, Mary, Mary," without realizing it. Then there was a new, different cry. Shatov started and rose from his knees. It was a baby's cry, weak and discordant. He made the sign of the cross and rushed into the room. Mrs. Virginsky held in her hands a little, red, wrinkled creature that was crying and moving its minute arms and legs. It was terrifyingly helpless and, like a speck of dust, was at the mercy of the first puff of wind. But it was shouting and demanding attention as though it felt it had some special claims on life.

Mary seemed unconscious at first, but a minute later she opened her eyes and looked at Shatov in a very, very strange way. There was something completely new in that look of hers; it was something he couldn't put his finger on, but he was sure he'd never seen anything like it in her before.

"A boy? Is it a boy?" Mary asked Mrs. Virginsky in a voice weakened by pain.

"It sure is a male," the midwife answered, wrapping the boy up in a blanket.

At one point, when she'd already wrapped him up and was about to lay him down between two pillows, she asked Shatov to hold him for a moment. Mary winked at him discreetly, as if afraid Mrs. Virginsky might see. Shatov understood right away and immediately brought the baby close to the bed to show it to its mother.

"He's—pretty," Mary whispered with a smile.

"Brr, look at him staring!" Mrs. Virginsky laughed gaily, looking into Shatov's face. "What a funny face he has, this man!"

"Rejoice, Mrs. Virginsky—it's a great joy. . . ." Shatov mumbled with an idiotically blissful expression. His face had lighted up after Mary's remark about the child.

"Some joy!" Mrs. Virginsky said, still laughing as she busily cleared things up, working with great speed and efficiency.

"The mystery of the arrival of this new creature is a great and ungraspable one, Mrs. Virginsky, and it's very sad that you don't appreciate it." Shatov went on muttering incoherently, dazed and elated. He felt as if something were swaying inside his head and by itself, without his will being involved, pouring into his soul.

"There were two and now suddenly there's a third—a new human being, a new spirit, entire, complete, such as no human hands could fashion; a new thought, a new love. It's even frightening. There's nothing greater than this in the world!"

"The nonsense this man comes out with! It's simply a further development of the organism, and there's nothing at all mysterious about it," Arina Virginsky said, bursting into sincere and merry laughter. "The way you put it, every fly would be a mystery. But I can tell you one thing—there are useless people who should never have been brought into this world. First change the world so that they can be useful and then breed them. This one, for instance, will have to be taken away to a foundling home in a couple of days—but I suppose that's just the way it should be in this case."

"He's not going to any foundling home as long as I'm around," Shatov said firmly, staring at the floor.

"Are you adopting him then?"

"Don't have to. He's my son as it is."

"I know that legally his name is Shatov, but there's no need for you to pose as a benefactor to the human race. You can never manage without making high-sounding phrases. Well, that's all very fine and dandy, friends, but I suppose it's time for me to be going now," she said, as she finished tidying up. "I'll pop in sometime later this morning and then again in the evening if I'm needed. But now everything seems to have gone off very nicely and I must go and see some of my other patients. They've been waiting a long time for me by now. I understand you have an old woman somewhere around, Shatov, and it's a good thing you have, but you stick around too and don't leave Mary—you're her husband after all, so sit next to her and you can be helpful too. I don't think Mrs. Shatov will chase you away now— All right, all right, I was just joking. . . ."

She left very pleased. From the way Shatov looked and talked, it seemed as clear as daylight to her that "this fellow's a real doormat—he's got his head full of all that fatherhood stuff." And, instead of going directly to a patient who lived near Shatov, she rushed home first to impart this observation to her husband.

Back in his room, Shatov went up to Mary.

"She said you'd better stay awake for a while, Mary," he said timidly. "I know it's very hard for you. I'll sit by the window in case you need something, all right?"

And he sat down by the window, concealed from her sight by the back of the sofa. But before a minute had passed, she called him over and with an air of distaste asked him to plump up her pillow. As he did so, she turned away impatiently and stared at the wall.

"That's not the way, not like that! Ah, what clumsy hands!"

Shatov tried again.

"Bend over me," she said suddenly in a harsh, wild voice, trying not to look at him.

Shatov started, but bent down.

"Lower—not like that—lower—"

Suddenly her left arm shot up and coiled around his neck and he felt a firm, moist kiss on his forehead.

"Mary!"

Her lips quivered, for a while she tried to restrain herself, but then suddenly she sat up, her eyes flashing.

"Stavrogin's a beast!" she said.

And then, like a blade of grass cut down by a scythe, she collapsed, her face in the pillow, and squeezing Shatov's hand in hers, she burst into hysterical sobs.

After that, she wouldn't let him leave her side. He had to sit there, close by her, and although she couldn't talk much she kept looking at him with a blissful sort of smile. It was as though she had been suddenly transformed into a naïve, stupid little girl. It was like a regeneration. Shatov either cried like a small boy or kissed her hands, saying God knows what in a wild, entranced, and inspired tone. She listened to him with abandon and, although she may not have understood what he was saying, she kept passing her weak hand through his hair, smoothing it, admiring it. He spoke to her about Kirilov; about how they were going to live "from now on and forever"; about the existence of God; and about everybody's being so good. In their enthusiasm they wanted to have another look at the baby and Shatov picked him up.

"Mary," he said, holding the child in his arms, "we're through with the old nightmare, with the disgrace, with death and decay. We'll work and we'll open up a new path for the three of us. Yes, Mary, we will! But tell me, Mary, what shall we call him?"

"Him? What shall we call him?" she said, and a look of terrible bitterness came over her face.

She clasped her hands, looked bitterly at Shatov, then buried her head in the pillow.

"What's the matter, Mary?" Shatov cried with grief and anxiety.

"How could you, how could you—you're so ungrateful!"

"I'm sorry, Mary; I'm terribly sorry. I just asked what we should call—I didn't know—"

"Of course he'll be Ivan," she said, lifting her burning face wet with tears. "How could you think that we'd call him any other, *horrible* name?"

"Calm yourself, Mary, you're terribly overwrought."

"You're being insulting again in attributing my reaction to my being overwrought. I bet if I'd said I wanted to give him that other *horrible* name, you'd have approved—probably wouldn't have even noticed! Ah, you're an ungrateful, contemptible bunch, the lot of you!"

Within a minute, it goes without saying, they'd made it up. Shatov persuaded her to go to sleep and she slept without letting go of his hand. After that, she kept waking up, looking at him as though afraid that he might leave, and then going back to sleep.

Kirilov sent the old woman up with his "congratulations," hot tea, freshly fried beef cutlets, a jug of hot broth, and some white bread "for Mrs. Shatov." Mary drank the broth eagerly while the old woman changed the baby's diapers. Then Mary made Shatov eat the cutlets.

Time passed. Shatov was so exhausted that he fell asleep in his chair with his head on Mary's pillow. In that state, Mrs. Virginsky found them when she came in as she had promised. She woke them cheerfully, asked Mary the necessary questions, and gave her the appropriate instructions, examined the baby, and again told Shatov not to leave his wife's side. Then, after making a few rather scornful cracks about "the happy couple," she left, looking as satisfied as the last time.

It was dark when Shatov awoke. He hurriedly lit a candle and rushed to get the old woman. But the moment he stepped out onto the landing, he heard soft, unhurried footsteps that gave him a shock. Erkel came toward him.

"Don't come in!" Shatov whispered, seizing the man by the

arm and pulling him away. "Wait by the gate—I'll be there in a moment. I'd completely forgotten about you. Oh, you sure have a way of reminding me!"

He was in such a hurry that he just called the old woman without going in to see Kirilov. Mary was furious and in despair that he should even think of leaving her alone.

"But, Mary, this is the very last thing I must do," he said solemnly. "After this there'll be a new life and we'll never, never even mention that horrible nightmare."

He managed to persuade her somehow, promising to be back by nine. He kissed her tenderly, gave the baby a kiss, and scampered downstairs to join Erkel.

They then set out for the park of the Stavrogins' Skvoreshniki estate, where a year and a half earlier he had buried the printing press that had been entrusted to him by the Movement. It was buried at the very edge of the park where it merged into a pine forest. The spot was wild and deserted. It was quite a distance from the Skvoreshniki house and couldn't be seen from there; it was two and a half, perhaps three miles, from Shatov's house.

"Do you really mean to walk all the way? I'll pay for a cab."

"No—no cab, please," Erkel said.

They had insisted on that point—a cabbie is a witness, after all.

"Ah hell! Never mind then, I just want to get it over with as soon as possible."

They walked very fast.

"Hey, Erkel, you're still just a kid," Shatov said suddenly. "Tell me, have you ever been happy?"

"Well, you certainly seem rather happy just now," Erkel observed with curiosity.

chapter 6

AN EVENTFUL NIGHT

I

During the day, Virginsky spent at least two hours making the rounds of the conspirators to tell them that, in his opinion, Shatov wasn't going to inform on them, because his wife had returned to him and had given birth to a child. "If one has any understanding of the human heart," Virginsky declared, "one cannot possibly think he could be dangerous now." But to his disappointment, Virginsky found only Erkel and Lyamshin at home.

Erkel heard him out in silence, looking understandingly into his eyes, but when Virginsky asked him straight out whether he would go at six or not, Erkel smiled brightly and said, "Of course."

Lyamshin was in bed with the blanket pulled over his head, apparently seriously ill. He seemed terrified by Virginsky's arrival. As soon as Virginsky opened his mouth, he started waving his hands at him and whining that he wanted to be left in peace. Still, he listened to what Virginsky had to say about Shatov, and when he was told that none of the others except Erkel were at home, he seemed extremely surprised. It turned out that he had already heard from Liputin about Fedka's death, and he repeated what he knew, although quite incoherently, to Virginsky, who, in his turn, was very surprised. But when Virginsky finally asked him whether they had to go through with it or not, Lyamshin started waving his hands again, insisting that none of it really concerned him directly, that he knew nothing and wanted only one thing— to be left in peace.

Virginsky returned home deeply depressed and alarmed. What made it even worse was that, although he usually told his wife everything, he had to conceal this from his family. Had it not been for a new idea, a new, conciliating plan, that took hold of his feverish brain at that moment, the chances are he would have had to take to his bed like Lyamshin. But the new idea strengthened him, and he now began to wait impatiently for the fatal hour and actually left for the meeting place earlier than was necessary.

It was a very bleak spot on the boundary of the huge park of the Stavrogins' estate. Later, I went there especially to have a look at it. I can imagine how sinister it must have looked on that gloomy autumn evening. The ancient forest began there and the tall, century-old pines took on strange and threatening shapes in the darkness, which was so thick that it was difficult to see clearly for two paces. But Peter Verkhovensky, Liputin, and Erkel had brought lanterns with them.

For some unknown reason and at some unknown time, a rather absurd grotto had been built there of rough-hewn rocks.

Once there had been a table and benches in it, but by now the furniture had long crumbled into dust. A couple of hundred steps to the right, the third pond in the park ended. The three ponds stretched out, one after the other, in a line for a full mile, starting right near the house and ending at the outside edge of the park. It was highly improbable that any noise, shouting or even shooting, could have reached the ears of the Stavrogin household. Anyway, since Nikolai Stavrogin had left the day before and the footman Alexei was also away, there were only five or six very old, one might say, retired, servants left in the house. Even assuming that any of these isolated old people had heard shouts or appeals for help, they would've provoked nothing but fear and none of them would've stirred out of their cozy beds or away from their warm stoves.

By six twenty, all except Erkel, who'd been dispatched to bring Shatov, were there. This time Peter Verkhovensky was on time—he arrived with Tolkachenko. Tolkachenko was frowning and looked worried; his assumed boastful arrogance was gone. He stuck close by Peter's side all the time and seemed to have suddenly become infinitely devoted to him; he kept whispering things in Peter's ear, although Peter ignored these whisperings or just mumbled something to get rid of him.

Shigalov and Virginsky, who had arrived shortly before Peter, withdrew a few steps and maintained a complete, obviously deliberate silence. Peter raised his lantern and examined them with insulting persistence. "They must have something on their minds," he thought, and said to Virginsky:

"Isn't Lyamshin here? Who was it said he was ill?"

"I'm here!" Lyamshin said, stepping forward from behind a tree. He wore a thick overcoat and had a shawl over his head, so that it was difficult to see his face in the light of the lantern.

"So, only Liputin is still missing?"

Liputin stepped silently out of the grotto. Peter again raised his lantern.

"Why were you hiding in there? Why didn't you come out?"

"I assumed that we still had freedom of movement," Liputin mumbled, although he probably didn't know too well himself what he was trying to express with that remark.

"Gentlemen!" Peter said, for the first time speaking aloud, instead of in a half whisper. This produced a quite startling effect upon the others. "I'm sure you understand that we're not here to talk. Everything was chewed and digested yesterday, so now it's all clear. But I see from your faces that some of you may wish to say something—so hurry up and come out with it. Damn it, we don't have much time—Erkel may bring him at any moment."

"Oh, he's sure to bring him!" Tolkachenko for some reason felt it was necessary to add.

"If I'm not mistaken, he'll hand over the printing press first?" Liputin asked, once more sounding unsure of why he was asking the question.

"Of course," Peter said, again raising the lantern to Liputin's face, "we have no intention of losing the machinery. But then we decided yesterday that there was no need to take possession of it immediately—we just want him to show us the actual spot where it's buried and we'll pick it up later, at our convenience. I know it's somewhere ten steps from one of the corners of this grotto. But hell, Liputin, how can you have forgotten all that? It was agreed that you alone would meet him and that we would only appear later. So I wonder why you should be asking that—unless you're doing it on purpose."

Liputin looked at him gloomily and said nothing. For a while they were all silent. The tops of the pine trees swayed in the wind.

"I still hope, though, gentlemen, that each one of you will do his duty," Peter said in an impatient tone, breaking the silence.

"I know that Shatov's wife has returned to him and has had a baby. . . ." Virginsky spoke up suddenly and excitedly, gesticulating wildly and talking so rapidly that he hardly had time to form his words. "I know human hearts—I'm sure he won't inform now—because he's happy. I tried to tell this to every one of you, but I didn't find you home. . . . So perhaps we don't really have to do it now. . . ."

He stopped, quite out of breath.

"Suppose you, Mr. Virginsky, suddenly became happy," Peter said, stepping toward him, "would you postpone—oh, of course, I don't mean a betrayal; that's out of the question—but say, the performance of your duty as a citizen, which involved a certain risk but which you'd decided to go through with before gaining that happiness and which you considered your sacred obligation, whether or not it was dangerous and whether or not it was detrimental to your happiness?"

"No, I wouldn't! I wouldn't for anything in the world!" Virginsky said with absurd heat, his whole body jerking.

"Wouldn't you rather be unhappy again than be a despicable coward?"

"Certainly, certainly. Even, on the contrary—I'd prefer to be totally despicable—I mean, totally unhappy—rather than a despicable coward."

"Well, then you may as well know that Shatov considers it his duty as a citizen, his supreme obligation, to inform on us. And the proof is that he himself is compromised by this affair, although, of course, the authorities will be fairly lenient with him in exchange for his information. A man like Shatov will never give up. No amount of happiness will make him change his mind. In a day or so, he'll snap out of it, be furious with himself for having postponed it, and go ahead. Besides, I don't see why he should be so happy about his wife's coming back to him after three years and giving birth to Stavrogin's child."

"But no one's ever seen his report," Shigalov suddenly butted in with considerable determination.

"I've seen his report to the police," Peter shouted furiously. "It exists all right and you're acting very stupidly!"

"And I," Virginsky shrieked, losing his temper too, "I protest! I protest with all my strength. I demand—I demand that when he arrives, we all come out and ask him whether it's true. If it is, we'll make him change his mind and, if he does, ask for his word of honor not to— If he gives it to us, we ought to let him go. In any case, there ought to be at least a trial and then, according to the verdict . . . But we shouldn't lie in ambush and pounce on him as soon as he comes in sight."

"To stake our common cause on someone's word of honor is the height of stupidity! Ah, damn you, it's all so idiotic at this point! What a thing to do in a moment of danger, Virginsky!"

"I protest, I protest. . . ." Virginsky repeated stubbornly.

"At least stop yelling like that or we won't hear the signal. As I told you—ah, how absurd to waste time at this point— Shatov is a Slavophile—that is, he belongs to the stupidest crowd you can think of. But who the hell cares and what's the difference, anyway? You're only confusing me. What I really wanted to tell you is that Shatov is an embittered man and since so far, willy-nilly, he has still belonged to the Movement, I hoped till the last minute that we could make use of him, because our common cause could use such an embittered man. So I tried to spare him, despite the quite precise instructions I had received on the subject. In fact, in sparing him, I risked a hundred times more than he could possibly be worth to us! But finally he decided to inform on us. So, all right, that's enough now! I warn you, don't any of you try to go back on your obligations now! You can go and kiss him if you wish, but you have no right to stake the Movement on his word of honor! Only swine in the pay of the authorities would act like that!"

"And who's in the pay of the authorities here?" Liputin asked, forming every word precisely.

"You, perhaps. Yes, I'd advise you to shut up, Liputin. You've got too much into the habit of opening your trap this way. Now, gentlemen, to me, anyone who backs out in a moment of danger has as good as sold out. There are always fools whose fear makes them shout at the last moment, 'Forgive me, please, and I'll sell you the lot of them!' But let me tell you, friends, they won't forgive you any more, whether or not you inform on the rest of us. And even if they dropped one or two counts against you, you could still be sure of a good stretch in Siberia—each one of you. And remember, there is another avenging sword, and it is much sharper than the authorities'!"

Peter was in a terrible rage and had blurted out many things he shouldn't have said. Shigalov took three firm steps toward him.

"Since last night, I've given the matter a lot of thought," he started methodically and with his usual self-assurance. He gave the impression that, even if the earth had opened up in front of him, he wouldn't have changed his intonations or the elaborate order of his exposition, "and I have come to the conclusion that the contemplated murder is not only a waste of precious time that could be better used on more important and urgent business, but also represents a disastrous deviation from the regular course—the sort of deviation that has always hampered achievement of the goal, delaying it for decades and handing control of the Movement over to nonthinking politicians instead of pure socialists. I have come here with the sole objective of protesting against the contemplated act and of disassociating myself from it as of this moment—which, for some reason, you consider a 'moment of danger' to you. I am leaving not because I fear that 'danger' nor out of sentimental feeling for a man with whom I have no wish whatever to exchange kisses, but because this affair, from beginning to end, is harmful to my program. As to selling out to the authorities and informing, you may rest assured that I have no intention of informing on anyone."

He turned and started to walk away.

"Damn! He'll meet them and warn Shatov!" Peter shouted, pulling out his gun. They all heard the click as he removed the safety catch.

"You may rest assured," Shigalov said, turning his head, "that even if I meet Shatov coming here, although I may say good evening to him, I will not warn him."

"But do you know that you'll pay for this, Monsieur Fourier?"

"I would like to call your attention to the fact that I am not Fourier. The fact that you confuse me with that sentimental, syrupy, abstract mumbler only proves that, although you have had my manuscript between your hands, you're still completely unacquainted with it. As to your threats, I assure you that your removing the safety catch just now was an empty gesture because it wouldn't be at all to your advantage to use your gun now. Now, if you meant to threaten me for tomorrow or the day after, I repeat again that shooting me will only bring you more trouble: whether you kill me or not, sooner or later, you'll have to accept my system anyway. Good night."

At that moment, there was a whistle. It came from the park side, about two hundred yards away. As had been agreed the night before, Liputin immediately whistled back, using a toy whistle made of clay he had bought that morning for a kopeck, since he didn't want to rely on his rather toothless mouth. On their way, Erkel had warned Shatov about this exchange of whistles so as not to arouse his suspicions.

"Don't worry, I'll avoid meeting them; they won't even notice me," Shigalov said in a dignified whisper and left them, heading home through the dark park without hurrying and apparently without the slightest apprehension.

Now, we know down to the minutest detail all about this horrible affair. First Liputin met Erkel and Shatov by the grotto. Shatov didn't say hello to him, didn't offer him his hand, but said immediately in a loud, hurried voice:

"Well, where's the spade? And haven't you got another lantern? Well, what are you scared of? There's no one around and you could fire a cannon here without their hearing it in the Skvoreshniki house. It's here, right in this very spot, exactly here—"

He stamped his foot on a spot ten paces in the direction of the forest from the back corner of the grotto. At that second, Tolkachenko, who had been hiding behind a nearby tree, leaped at him, while Erkel caught him by the elbows from behind. Liputin rushed at him from the front, and the three of them knocked him off his feet and pinned him down to the ground. It was then that Peter came up with his gun. I've been told that Shatov managed to turn his head toward Verkhovensky and that he recognized him. Three lanterns lighted up the scene. Shatov suddenly let out a brief and desperate scream, but he wasn't given a chance to go on shouting. Peter Verkhovensky neatly and carefully placed the muzzle of his revolver against Shatov's forehead and pulled the trigger hard. The shot wasn't too loud—at least no one in the Skvoreshniki house heard it. Of course, Shigalov, who at that moment was hardly much more than three hundred yards away, heard both Shatov's scream and the shot, but according to his own testimony he didn't turn back and, indeed, didn't even stop. Death was almost instantaneous. Peter was the only one to keep his head, although I don't believe that even he remained cool. He squatted down by the murdered man and hurriedly went through his pockets. He found no money (it was under Mary's pillow) and the three scraps of paper he did find were of no interest: a note from the office Shatov worked for occasionally, the title of some book, and a bill from a restaurant abroad that had been preserved in this pocket, God knows how, for two whole years. Peter put these scraps into his own pocket and, suddenly realizing that the others were crowding around him and staring at the corpse without doing anything, began to swear furiously and viciously, ordering them to get busy. Tolkachenko and Erkel scampered to the grotto to fetch stones they had prepared there earlier in the day—two large, twenty-pound rocks with ropes tied securely to them. Since they planned to dump the body into the nearest pond (the furthermost from the house), they started tying one stone to the neck and the other to the feet. Peter did the actual tying of the stones to the body, while Tolkachenko and Erkel simply stood there, each holding a stone and handing them to him one after the other. Erkel gave him his first, and while Peter was tying it to Shatov's feet, swearing and grumbling, Tolkachenko spent those long minutes holding his stone in his arms, his torso bent forward to balance himself in what looked like a subservient posture, so as to be ready to hand over his load the second he was asked for it; he never even thought of putting it down in the interim. When the two rocks were finally tied to the body, Peter stood up. While he was examining the faces of the others, something quite unexpected happened that amazed everybody.

As we have seen, except for Tolkachenko and Erkel, the others had been standing around doing nothing in particular. Virginsky, who had rushed toward Shatov like the others, never actually laid a hand on him and didn't help to pin him down. And Lyamshin had only joined the struggle after the shot had been fired. After that, during the fuss over the body, which may have lasted ten minutes, all of them seem to have been partly unconscious. They crowded around the body, and before they began to feel worried and alarmed they felt nothing but a blank surprise. Liputin stood closer to the body than the rest. Virginsky was behind him, looking over his shoulder with strange curiosity, like an outsider, even raising himself on tiptoe to have a better look. Lyamshin hid behind Virginsky, only peeking diffidently at the body every so often, and then hiding behind him again. But when the stones had been tied and Peter rose, Virginsky began to tremble, threw up his arms, and shouted bitterly and unexpectedly loud:

"No, it wasn't right! It wasn't! It wasn't right at all!"

He might have added more to that belated exclamation, but Lyamshin grabbed him violently from behind, squeezing him in his grasp with all his strength and letting out the most extraordinary squeal. There are moments of great fright when a man begins to shout in a strange voice, a voice that no one suspected him of having and that can be very frightening in itself. Lyamshin's squeal was more animal than human. He kept squeezing Virginsky harder and harder and squealing uninterruptedly, his eyes staring at the others, his mouth wide open, and his feet stamping out a rapid tattoo on the ground. Virginsky was so frightened that he too began to scream madly and, with a ferocity that one would never have expected from him, began to scratch and punch at Lyamshin as far as he could with his hands behind his back, all the time trying to jerk himself free from his grip. Finally, with the assistance of Erkel, he managed to work himself free. But when, shaken by the shock, he jumped aside ten feet or so, Virginsky saw Lyamshin, who was now staring at Verkhovensky and had begun to squeal again, this time go straight for Peter. He tripped on the body and grabbed Peter as he fell over it, holding him in a grip so strong and pressing his head so savagely into the other's chest that Peter couldn't do anything at first even with the assistance of Tolkachenko and Liputin, who had rushed to his rescue. Peter shouted, swore, and hammered on Lyamshin's head with his fists for a long time before he got loose. Finally, he jumped aside, pulled out his gun, and put the muzzle straight into the mouth of the squealing Lyamshin, who was now being held by Tolkachenko, Erkel, and Liputin. But despite the gun, Lyamshin went on squealing and screaming until Erkel, making a ball of his handkerchief, managed somehow to stuff it into the man's mouth and stop his screams. In the meantime, Tolkachenko tied his hands behind his back with the remaining length of rope.

"Very strange . . ." Peter said, examining the madman with alarm.

He was obviously extremely surprised.

"I never expected that from this one," he said, deep in thought.

They left Erkel to guard Lyamshin. They were now in a hurry to dispose of the body, as they were afraid that someone might have heard all the shouting.

Peter and Tolkachenko, each holding a lantern in one hand, lifted the body, holding it under the head; Liputin and Virginsky held the feet, and the four of them carried it away. With the stones tied to it, the body was quite heavy, and they had to carry it for more than two hundred yards. Tolkachenko, the strongest of the lot, suggested they walk in step, but the others ignored him and each walked in his own way. Peter walked on the right side; he was leaning heavily forward, with the dead man's head resting on his shoulder, and supporting the stone from beneath with his left hand. Since it never occurred to Tolkachenko to help Peter carry the stone, Peter finally lost patience and started berating him. His shouted outburst was sudden and solitary, for the others carried their load in silence. It was only when they had almost reached the pond that Virginsky, stooping under the burden and obviously completely exhausted, cried out in the same loud, whining voice as before:

"No, it wasn't right—not the right thing to do at all!"

The spot to which they carried the body, the outer edge of the third pond, was one of the most desolate and deserted places in the park, particularly that late in the fall. Around there, the shore of the pond was overgrown with coarse grass.

They put the lanterns on the ground, swung the corpse, and hurled it into the water. There was a muffled, drawn-out splash. Peter lifted his lantern, and they all watched with curiosity as the body sank. There was nothing much to watch. The corpse, weighted down by the two stones, went down almost immediately and the big ripples that had spread over the surface of the water were soon smoothed out. It was all over.

"Gentlemen," Peter said, "the time has come for us to part. I'm sure each of you is experiencing at this moment the proud elation that always accompanies the discharge of a freely assumed obligation. Unfortunately, of course, some of you may still be too upset to experience such elation, but it'll come to you, no doubt by tomorrow—and if you don't feel it by then, you should really be ashamed of yourselves. I'm willing to dismiss Lyamshin's shocking behavior as the result of a high fever, especially as I understand he has been ill since this morning. As to you, Virginsky, a few minutes of serious thinking will convince you that we couldn't stake the Cause on a man's word of honor and that we had no choice but to do exactly what we did. I'm willing to overlook your exclamations; events will prove to your satisfaction that the written denunciation in question did exist. As to danger, I foresee none. It will never occur to anyone to suspect any of us—as long as you can control yourselves. Thus, everything depends on you and on your being fully convinced of the necessity of our action— which I hope you will be by tomorrow. This is just why, by the way, you've formed yourselves into this independent, voluntarily constituted group of people sharing the same opinions—to combine your energies at given moments and, if required, to keep an eye on each other. Each of you is bound to account for his actions with his life. Your mission is to instill new life into a senile cause that has begun to reek of stagnation—a fact you must always keep in mind. Now, your immediate aim must be to bring about the collapse both of the state and of the moral standards it represents. Then there will be no one left but us, and we will have been groomed in advance to take over power. We shall bring the smart ones to our side and ride on the backs of the fools. And there's no need for us to be ashamed of it. A generation must be re-educated to become worthy of freedom. We will have to face thousands and thousands of Shatovs still. We shall organize ourselves to take over control. It is shameful not to take advantage of something that is lying around idle and gaping at us. Now I'm going to see Kirilov, and by morning we will have the document in which, to explain his death to the authorities, he'll take everything upon himself. Nothing could be more plausible: in the first place, he had fallen out with Shatov; they used to live together in America and they had plenty of time to quarrel. It's common knowledge that Shatov's opinions changed—therefore their hatred could've been caused by their difference of opinion and by fear of betrayal, the most unforgiving hatred one can think of. That's exactly what he'll write. Finally, it will come up that, at one time, Fedka the convict spent his nights at Kirilov's. All this, as I'm sure you understand, will remove all suspicion from us and utterly bewilder all those blockheads. After today, you won't be seeing me for a while, gentlemen, because I have to leave on a short trip. But you'll hear from me in two days. As a matter of fact, gentlemen, I suggest that every one of you spend tomorrow at home. Now we'll leave two by two, taking different ways. Tolkachenko, I'll ask you to cope with Lyamshin and take him home. Perhaps you can calm him and explain to him how much trouble his lack of fortitude could bring down upon him. As to your brother-in-law, Shigalov, Mr. Virginsky, I'm not worried about him any more than I'm worried about you yourself—neither of you will go to the police. I can only regret his action. However, since he has never notified me of his wish to leave the Movement, I think it is still too early to bury him. Well then, hurry off, gentlemen, because although our opponents are a bunch of dumb oxen, caution is nevertheless always advisable."

Virginsky left with Erkel. Erkel, before turning Lyamshin over to Tolkachenko, brought him up to Peter and announced that the man had come to his senses, was sorry for what had happened, had asked to be forgiven, and couldn't understand what had come over him. After that, Peter left on his own, following the opposite shore of the three ponds, which was the longest possible detour. To his great surprise, when he was already halfway, Liputin caught up with him.

"Listen," Liputin said, "I'm sure Lyamshin will inform on us."

"No, he'll come to his senses and realize that if he did that, he'd be the first to go to Siberia. Nobody will inform now— not you, either."

"And what about you?"

"I'll certainly have the lot of you put out of the way if you show the slightest inclination to betray and you know it. But I know you won't betray us. Was it to hear that that you trotted after me for two miles?"

"Ah, Verkhovensky, just think, we may never meet again!"

"What makes you think that?"

"Will you tell me just one thing?"

"What is it now? Although I would really prefer you to get the hell out of my way."

"Just one answer, but the truth: are we the only Five in the whole world, or is it true that there are several hundred like ours? I ask this because I consider it of great ideological importance."

"I can see that by the state you're in, Liputin. And do you know what I think? Well, I think you're more dangerous than Lyamshin."

"I know, I know, but I want your answer!"

"You're really a very stupid man, Liputin, whatever else, but I don't see what difference it can make to you whether there's only one Five or thousands of them."

"That means there's only one! I knew it all along! I knew it—I knew it!"

And, without waiting for any further answer, he quickly turned around and dissolved in the darkness.

Peter became thoughtful for a moment.

"No, none of them will talk," he finally concluded, "but the group must remain a tight unit and obey or I'll teach them! Ah, but what scum, these people!"

II

First he went home and packed. He did so with unhurried efficiency. The train left at six in the morning. This express, which ran only once a week, had only recently been put into service on a trial basis. Although Peter had told his associates that he was only leaving on a short trip, it turned out later that his plans were quite different. When his suitcase was packed, he settled with his landlady, who had been notified of his intention to leave, and took a cab over to Erkel's—near the railroad station. Then, just before one in the morning, he went to see Kirilov, again entering through Fedka's secret entrance.

Peter was in a foul mood. Apart from the worries he already had—he still knew nothing of Stavrogin's where-abouts—he had received during the day a very confidential warning—probably from Petersburg—about danger threaten-ing him in the very near future. By now, of course, there are many legends about those particular days, but if anyone knows anything for certain, it can only be those directly concerned in the matter. I myself can only assume that Peter might have had connections outside our town and could very well have received such a warning. Personally, I'm convinced that, de-spite Liputin's hysterical denials, Peter may have organized another two or three Fives besides ours—for instance, in Moscow and Petersburg; but even if there were no actual Fives, he surely had connections in those towns, and I dare say some very curious ones at that.

In any case, about three days after his departure, our local authorities received a warrant for his arrest from the capital, although I can't tell for sure whether it was for his misdeeds in our town or elsewhere. The warrant came just in time to strengthen the devastating effect and the almost mystical fear produced among our local authorities and our hitherto frivo-lous society when the mysterious and most revealing murder of Shatov was discovered. This murder was the climax of the long series of apparently senseless acts that had been committed in our town. And in this case the circumstances were really mysterious.

But the warrant came too late—by that time, Peter Verkho-vensky was already in Petersburg under an assumed name, from where, having got wind of what was brewing, he quickly slipped across the border. . . . But I'm anticipating events.

When he walked in on Kirilov, Peter looked angry and aggressive. Apart from seeing that Kirilov made good on his promise, Peter seemed anxious to vent some private grudge, to avenge himself for something.

Kirilov seemed glad of this visit; he must have been expect-ing it for a long time with agonizing impatience. His face was paler than usual and the stare of his lusterless black eyes was heavy and dull.

"I thought you weren't coming," he said gruffly.

He was sitting on the corner of his couch and didn't stir to greet his visitor. Peter stopped in front of him, examining him lengthily before saying anything.

"So everything's in order and we're not going back on our word," Peter said at last, smiling with insulting condescension.

"I hope you're not really complaining at my being late," he added with tasteless jocularity. "You've gained three extra hours that way."

"I don't want any extra hours from you, and you are in no position to give them to me, you poor idiot!"

"What did you say?" Peter said, growing tense, but quickly controlling himself. "You're so terribly touchy! Ah, but I see we're furious tonight, aren't we?" he drawled with the same air of unbearable condescension. "I think that, for such a moment, calm detachment is much more suitable. The best thing for you would be to look upon yourself as Columbus and me as a mouse, and then you wouldn't resent anything I might say. I suggested that to you yesterday too."

"I don't want to consider you as a mouse."

"I trust you mean that as a compliment? Ah, but I see that even your tea is cold, which certainly shows that everything is topsy-turvy here. No, I'm afraid I don't like the state you're in tonight. But wait, I see something in the plate there by the window." He walked over to the window. "I see, boiled chicken with rice! But you haven't touched it! Does this indicate that we were in a mood when even chicken—"

"I did eat. Anyway, it's none of your business. Shut up."

"Oh, of course, it's none of my business; moreover, I really don't care. But it so happens that I missed my dinner, so—anyway, I don't suppose you'll have any use for this chicken now, will you!"

"Eat it if you can."

"Thank you very much. And do you think I could have some tea afterward?"

Peter immediately installed himself at the table and pounced with great appetite on the chicken, at the same time watching his victim every second. Kirilov looked at him fixedly with hostile disgust, unable to take his eyes off him.

"But we must attend to business," Peter said, straightening himself up, but still chewing. "So I gather we're not backing out, right? Well then, what about that note then?"

"As I said, it makes no difference to me. I'll write it. Is it about those leaflets?"

"Yes, leaflets among other things. But I'll dictate it, since it makes no difference to you. Why should what I ask you to write at this point worry you?"

"None of your business."

"Of course, it's none of my business. Anyway, it'll only be

a few lines to the effect that you and Shatov were distributing those leaflets with the assistance of Fedka, who, by the way, was hiding at your place. That last point about Fedka's staying here is very important—the most important of all perhaps. Now, you see, I'm being completely frank with you."

"But Shatov? Why bring in Shatov? No, not that."

"Well, why not? What difference can it make to you since now nothing can harm him anyway."

"His wife's returned to him. She woke up and sent the woman to ask me where he was."

"She sent her to you to ask where he was? Hm, that's bad. If she sends someone over again, I don't want them to know I'm here."

Peter became quite worried.

"She won't know. She went to sleep again. Arina Virginsky, the midwife, is with her."

"I hope she doesn't hear anything. How about locking the outside door?"

"She won't hear a thing. And if Shatov comes over, you can hide in the other room."

"Shatov won't come and you'll write in the note that you quarreled because of his betrayal of the Cause and because he intended to turn informer . . . and that you're the cause of his death . . . this evening."

"He's dead?" Kirilov shouted, leaping up from the couch.

"He died today, or to be more accurate, yesterday, at eight P.M., since it's almost one in the morning already."

"You killed him! I foresaw it yesterday!"

"So you foresaw it. Here, I killed him with this very gun." Peter pulled out his gun and held it in his right hand as though ready to use it again. "But you're a strange man, Kirilov, really. You knew very well that that fool was bound to end up this way. So what was there to foresee? I've spelled it out many times for you. Shatov was going to inform on us. I was watching him and I couldn't let him go through with it. You were also told to watch him and you yourself told me about three weeks ago—"

"Shut up! You were after him because he spat in your face in Geneva!"

"That and other things—many other things—although with no personal feelings involved. Well, what made you jump up like that? And why are you making such a face? Ah, so that's what you're trying to do!"

Peter jumped to his feet and raised the gun. The trouble was that Kiriov was now holding his own gun, which had been loaded since that morning. Peter trained his revolver on Kirilov. Kirilov let out an angry laugh.

"Admit, you rat, that you pulled out your gun because you were scared that I'd shoot you. But I won't shoot you, although—although . . ." he said.

And he pointed his gun at Peter, pretending to take careful aim and apparently finding it difficult to renounce the joy of shooting him. Peter stood ready to fire, forcing himself to wait until the last second before pressing the trigger, willing to take the risk of receiving a bullet in his head first—anything could be expected from this "maniac," he thought. But the "maniac" finally lowered the gun. He was trembling and gasping, quite unable to talk.

"All right then, we've had our little game and that's enough," Peter said, lowering his gun too. "I was sure you were just fooling. But let me tell you, you took quite a risk. I could've fired, you know."

And looking fairly calm, he sat down and poured himself some tea. However, his hand was still trembling slightly, Kirilov put his gun on the table and started pacing the room.

"I won't write that I killed Shatov—I won't write a thing now. No note."

"No note?"

"No note."

"What a dirty, stupid thing to do!" Peter hissed, turning green with fury. "And I felt it coming too! Let me tell you that you haven't caught me unprepared. Please yourself, however. Of course, if I could force you to write that note, I would. You're nothing but a cheap chiseler!" Peter said, working himself into a frenzy. "You kept asking us for money, promising us God knows what. But I can tell you, I won't leave here empty-handed, I'll watch you shooting your brains out at least."

"I want you to get out now," Kirilov said, stepping firmly in front of him.

"No, not that! Never!" Peter's revolver was in his hand again. "Now I suppose you'll decide to postpone it just out of pigheadedness or cowardice and tomorrow you'll run and tell the police and get some money from *them* this time. To hell with you—there are too many miserable little rats like you around as it is! But take my word, I've foreseen everything:

I won't leave before a bullet from this gun has smashed your skull just as that dog Shatov's was smashed, if you're too scared to do it now yourself and try to postpone it. Ah hell, I've had enough of you!"

"You really want to see my blood, don't you?"

"Yes, but you must understand, not out of hatred for you. I don't care one way or the other about you, but I must protect the Movement. As you must realize, it's impossible to trust anyone. I don't understand a thing about your fantastic notion of killing yourself. It wasn't my idea in the first place—you thought it up yourself. You mentioned it first, and not to me but to some members of our organization abroad. And please note, none of them tried to pry your secrets out of you—as a matter of fact, none of them had ever heard of you, and going to them and blurting out your feelings was sheer sentimentality on your part. Well, what can we do now if they decided then on a plan of action that was based on your promise and—please note carefully—on your own proposition, a plan that cannot be changed at this juncture. You've put yourself in a position in which you know too much. If you started talking or went to the police, it wouldn't be very helpful to us, would it? No sir, you promised; you gave your word, accepted our money. No one can deny that!"

Peter was extremely agitated now, but Kirilov had stopped listening to him long before. He was pacing the room, deep in his own thoughts.

"I feel sorry for Shatov," he said, stopping in front of Peter again.

"So do I, I suppose, but surely—"

"Shut up, you rat!" Kirilov roared, making an unmistakably threatening move. "I'll kill you!"

"All right, all right, I lied—I'm not sorry for him at all. But stop that, d'you hear me—stop that!" Peter mumbled, apprehensively raising his arm in front of his face in an instinctive gesture of defense.

Kirilov suddenly calmed down and resumed pacing the room.

"I won't postpone it. I want to kill myself right now. No one is any good."

"That's an excellent idea: no one is any good in this world and that makes it an impossible place for a decent man to live in. So—"

"I'm no better than the others. I'm not a decent man, you fool; there's never been a decent man in this world."

"At last you've got there too! I wondered how a man of your intelligence, Kirilov, could have failed to see until now that people are all the same, that none of them are better or worse than the rest, only smarter or dumber, and that they're all a bunch of villains—which, of course, is nonsense too—and that, therefore, there can't be any nonvillains."

"I believe you mean that seriously!" Kirilov said with a certain surprise. "You said that simply and with heat. Is it possible then that the likes of you can have convictions too?"

"Listen, Kirilov, I never could understand why you'd decided to kill yourself. All I know is you're doing it out of conviction—firm conviction. But if you feel the need of—of pouring your heart out, so to speak, please go ahead, I'm at your disposal. Only, we must keep in mind that time is running out."

"What's the time?"

"Hm, it's already two," Peter said and lit a cigarette, thinking that there still seemed to be a chance of reaching an agreement.

"I've nothing to say to you," Kirilov said through his teeth.

"I remember that God came into it somehow. In fact, you tried to explain it to me once—twice even, to be exact. If you shoot yourself, you'll become God—have I got it right?"

"Right, I'll become God."

Peter wasn't even smiling. He just waited. Kirilov glanced at him with subtle understanding.

"You're a political crook—a schemer. You're trying to change the conversation to philosophy, to make me feel emotional and make it up with you and then sign the paper saying I killed Shatov."

Peter answered with almost artless frankness:

"All right, let's assume I'm the kind of unscrupulous schemer you say I am—what difference can it make to you, Kirilov? Why do you have to bicker? Explain to me, please—you're one type of man and I'm another type, and so what? Besides, neither of us—"

"Is any good."

"Well, let's assume you're right. What's the difference since, as you know very well, those are just words."

"All my life I've wanted them to be more than just words. I

only went on living because I wanted it. And now, every day, I want it not to be just words."

"Why not? Everyone is looking for something that's better. A fish—I mean, everyone seeks his own comfort and that's all there is to it. That's all been known for ages."

"Did you say comfort?"

"Ah, why pick on words—"

"No, you put it very well—let it be 'comfort.' God is indispensable and therefore must exist."

"All right, I'm delighted."

"But I know there is no God and there can't be."

"That's more likely."

"Well, don't you really understand that a man cannot go on living if he believes both those things?"

"That's where the shooting comes in, I suppose?"

"Can't you really see that that alone is a sufficient reason to shoot oneself? Can't you understand that a man can exist—one out of your thousands of millions—who will refuse to endure it?"

"Oh, I do understand, but you seem to be hesitating and that's what worries me—"

"Stavrogin also got swallowed up by an idea," Kirilov continued, not paying any attention to Peter's remark and gloomily pacing the room.

"What idea?" Peter said, quickly pricking up his ears. "Did he mention anything about it to you?"

"Well, I guessed it myself. Stavrogin, if he believes in God, doesn't believe he believes. And if he doesn't believe, he doesn't believe that he doesn't."

"I must say, I'm sure there's something a little more intelligent than that to Stavrogin," Peter said in a quarrelsome tone, worried about the turn the conversation was taking and watching Kirilov's pale face closely.

"Damn it, he won't shoot himself after all this!" Peter thought. "I always felt something like this would crop up—the fellow's brain is twisted, that's all. Ah, what scum, these people!"

"You're the last person I'll see," Kirilov suddenly declared, "and I don't want to part on bad terms with you."

Peter didn't answer, immediately wondering, "What's he up to now?"

"Believe me, Kirilov," he said, "I've nothing against you personally. I've always considered you a—"

"You're a rat with a perverted mind. But I'm just as bad. Still, I'll shoot myself and you'll go on living."

Peter still couldn't make up his mind whether or not it was to his advantage to go on with this conversation; finally he decided to "leave it to circumstances." But Kirilov's air of superiority and his undisguised contempt for Peter had always irritated him and, for some reason, they did so now more than ever. Possibly Kirilov, who had perhaps only one hour to live at the most (Peter remembered that all the time), seemed to him a sort of half-man, something that was least of all entitled to be condescending and contemptuous.

"I believe you were boastfully declaring that you were about to shoot yourself?"

"It has always surprised me that everybody goes on living," Kirilov said, without hearing Peter's remark.

"Hm, you may be right there, but—"

"Ape, you'll just say anything as long as I get on with it. Shut up, since you understand nothing. If there's no God, then I'm God."

"That's a point in your reasoning I have never been able to understand—why should you be God?"

"If God exists, then the whole will is His and I can do nothing. If He doesn't exist, then all will is mine and I must exercise my own will, my free will."

"Free will? Why must you?"

"Because the whole will has become mine. I can't imagine that there's not one person on our whole planet who, having put an end to God and believing in his own free will, will dare to exercise that free will on the most important point. It would be like a pauper inheriting a bag full of money and not daring to put his hand into it, thinking himself too weak to own it. I wish to exercise my free will even if I am the only one to do so."

"Well, do so then."

"I have an obligation to shoot myself because the supreme gesture of free will is to kill oneself."

"But you aren't the only one to kill yourself; there are plenty of suicides."

"Yes, but they all have a reason. I'm the only one to do it without reason, just to establish my free will."

"He won't shoot himself," the thought flashed through Peter's head, and he said in an irritated tone:

"D'you know, in your place I'd have shot someone else rather than myself. You could be very useful that way. I'll tell you whom to kill, if you aren't afraid. Then, I suppose, you wouldn't have to shoot yourself tonight—we could change our agreement."

"Killing someone else would be the most despicable manifestation of free will. Only someone like you would suggest a thing like that. But I'm not you—I will express my free will in its highest manifestation. I'll kill myself."

"He worked it out all by himself," Peter muttered angrily under his breath.

"I must affirm my unbelief," Kirilov said, pacing the room again, "for there's nothing higher for me than the thought that there's no God. The history of mankind is on my side. Man kept inventing God in order to live, so as not to have to kill himself. To this day, the history of mankind consists of just that. I am the first man in history to refuse to invent God. I want it to be known always."

"He won't shoot himself, he won't. . . ." Peter thought worriedly. "But who'll know about it?" he said aloud. "There are only the two of us here. Perhaps Liputin?"

"Everybody will find out; they'll all know. There are no secrets that don't become known. It was He who said so."

And, with feverish excitement, Kirilov pointed to the icon of the Redeemer lighted by a little lamp. That made Peter lose his temper altogether.

"So in spite of everything you still believe in *Him* and you've even lighted that lamp *just in case,* right?" And as Kirilov didn't answer, Peter added, "I maintain that you believe more than any priest."

"Believe in what? In *Him?*" Kirilov stopped, staring ahead into emptiness with the expression of a visionary. "Listen, I'll tell you something great. Once three crosses stood in the center of the earth. One of the three of those crosses believed so completely that He said to another: 'Today you will be with me in paradise.' By the end of the day, both of them died. They went and they found nothing—no paradise, no resurrection—nothing. His words didn't come true. Listen now —that Man was the best on earth—He represented that which makes life worth living. The whole planet with everything on it is sheer insanity without that Man. There hadn't been anyone like Him before nor has there been since—never; and therein lies the miracle—that there never has been and never will be such a Man. Now, since the laws of nature didn't spare even Him, didn't spare even that miracle, and forced even Him to live among lies and to die for a lie—it proves that the whole planet is a lie and is based on a lie and an inane smirk. It proves too that the laws of nature are a pack of lies and a diabolical farce. So what's the point of living? Answer if you are a man."

"That's a different matter. I think you're mixing up two different reasons for killing yourself, and I don't think that's too safe. But, all right, let's assume you're God. That's the end of lies then because you've realized that lies were simply due to belief in the former god."

"Ah, at last you've understood!" Kirilov shouted ecstatically. "So it must be quite understandable if even you can see it! Now, if this thought can be proved to everybody, it will bring salvation for all. And who is to prove it but me? I don't understand why an atheist who is certain that God doesn't exist doesn't kill himself right away. To recognize that there's no God without recognizing at the same time that you yourself have become God makes no sense, for if it did, you'd have to kill yourself. On the other hand, if you do realize that you have become God yourself you are the king and don't have to kill yourself but can live in the greatest glory. Only one—the first one to realize it—must kill himself. And who else will begin and thereby prove it? So I'll kill myself to begin and to prove. Still, I'm a reluctant god—I'm unhappy because I must prove my free will. Up to now, man has been poor and unhappy because he has been afraid to exercise his free will on the crucial point and has only exercised it in marginal matters, like a schoolboy. I'm terribly unhappy because I'm terribly afraid. Fear is the curse of man. But I shall establish my free will. It is my duty to make myself believe that I do not believe in God. I'll be the first and last, and that will open the door. And I'll save them. That alone can save people, and the next generation will be transformed physically. Because the more I've thought about it, the more I've become convinced that, with his present physical make-up, man can never manage without the old God. For three years I've searched for the attribute of my divinity and I've found it—my free will! This is all I have at my disposal to show my independence and the terrifying new freedom I have gained. Because this freedom is terrifying all right, I'm killing myself to demonstrate my independence and my new, terrifying freedom."

Kirilov's face was unnaturally pale, his stare unbearably heavy; he looked feverish. Peter thought he was about to pass out.

"Give me a pen!" Kirilov shouted unexpectedly, as though something had suddenly inspired him. "Dictate. I'll sign anything. I'll sign that I killed Shatov too. Hurry—dictate while I still find it all quite funny. I'm not afraid of ideas created by pretentious slaves! You'll see for yourself that all the mysteries will become clear as day. And you—you will be crushed. I have faith! I have faith!"

Peter jumped up, instantly produced pen and ink, and started dictating, afraid to waste a second, trembling and overanxious to see the deal concluded.

"I, Alexei Kirilov," Peter dictated, "declare . . ."

"Wait! I don't want! To whom am I supposed to declare?"

Kirilov was shaking as if in a fever. The matter of declaring and some sudden idea connected with it seemed to have taken full possession of him, as though it were some nook where his exhausted spirit could take refuge, even if only for a moment.

"I declare to whom? I want to know!"

"No one in particular. To anyone who reads the note. Why do you insist on such precision? You're declaring to the world at large!"

"To the whole world? Bravo! And no need for regrets. I don't want to say I'm sorry about anything and I don't want to address myself to the authorities."

"All right, no need—to hell with the authorities!" Peter shouted hysterically. "Write down what I dictate, if you meant it seriously."

"Wait. I want to draw a face sticking out its tongue at the top."

"What rot!" Peter snarled. "You can manage without the drawing; the tone of the note should be enough to express the way you feel about it all."

"The tone? That's good. Yes, the tone, the tone—dictate in that tone."

"I, Alexei Kirilov," Peter dictated forcefully and sternly, bending over Kirilov's shoulder and watching each letter being traced by his trembling hand, "declare that on this —— day of October, between seven and eight P.M., I killed Ivan Shatov in the park for his betrayal and for informing the police about the leaflets and about Fedka, who hid in Filipov's house, in which we both lived, for ten days and nights. And if I'm shooting myself now with my own gun, it is not because I regret what I've done or am afraid, but because I decided to take my life long ago, when I was living abroad."

"Is that all?" Kirilov demanded indignantly.

"Not another word!" Peter stretched out his hand to get hold of the document.

"Nonsense!" Kirilov put his hand heavily on the sheet. "Wait—I want to say who else was in on the killing. Why did you bring Fedka into it? And what about the fire? I want to mention everything and then I want to tell them what I think of them, to abuse them and then, the tone, the tone!—"

"That'll do, Kirilov, believe me, that'll do now!" Peter said, almost beseechingly, terrified that the sheet might get torn. "It must remain obscure or they won't believe it. It must be just as we have it—no more than hints. You must let them see just a tiny corner of the truth, just to tease them. They can always be relied upon to hoodwink themselves better than we could hoodwink them, and there's no doubt that they'll trust themselves better than anyone else. Let me have it now. It's beautiful as it is. Come on, give it to me—let me have it!"

Peter tried to pull the note out from under Kirilov's hand. Kirilov had listened to him with his eyes popping out, looking as though he were trying to figure something out, but apparently unable to.

"God damn it!" Peter cried, losing patience. "You haven't even signed it yet! Stop goggling at me like that and sign it!"

"I want to abuse them," Kirilov muttered, nevertheless taking the pen and signing. "I want to abuse—"

"So write *Vive la République*. That should do."

"Bravo!" Kirilov almost roared with enthusiasm. "*Vive la république démocratique sociale et universelle—ou la mort!* No, no, no—better still: *Liberté, egalité, fraternité, ou la mort!* Now that's better, much better!" Delighted, he wrote it under his signature.

"That's enough now, that's enough. . . ." Peter kept saying.

"Wait, let me sign in French too: Kirilov, *gentilhomme russe et citoyen du monde.* Ha-ha-ha!" he burst into loud laughter, "I've thought up something even better! Eureka! Kirilov, *gentilhomme-théologien russe et citoyen du monde civilisé!* Yes, that's better than any of those—"

He suddenly leaped up from his seat, snatched the gun that

had been lying on the window sill, and rushed into the adjoining room, slamming the door shut behind him. Peter stood for a moment staring at the door, undecided.

"Unless he does it now, unless he fires now, he'll start thinking and then nothing will happen," Peter thought. He went over to the table, picked up the note, and reread it. He liked the composition of the announcement.

"What do I need now? I must confuse them completely and divert their attention elsewhere. It mentions the park. There is no park in town, so eventually they'll conclude that it means the Skvoreshniki park. But it'll take them time to think that one out; it'll take time to search for the body and time to find it. And, when they've found it, that'll prove to them that the note is telling the truth and therefore that everything in it is true, including what it says about Fedka. And what's Fedka? Fedka is the arsonist, the murderer of the Lebyatkins. Therefore, all the trouble really originated in Filipov's house. And they, the authorities, never suspected it and fumbled lamentably—that will confuse them completely! And they'll never even give a thought to my Five. There's only Shatov involved, and Kirilov, and Fedka, and Lebyatkin. As to why they went around killing one another—that's their business. But damn it, I still don't hear that shot!"

Although he had been busy reading and then admiring the wording, he had also been listening for a shot in painful anxiety. All at once he became furious. Worriedly he looked at his watch. It was getting late and at least ten minutes had gone by since Kirilov had left the room. Peter took the candle and walked toward the door through which Kirilov had disappeared. When he reached the door, it suddenly occurred to him that the candle was burning low, that in twenty minutes at the most it would be finished and he had no other. He took hold of the door handle and listened tensely. Not the slightest sound came from the other room. He opened the door and raised the candle above his head. There was a wild roar and something rushed at him. Peter slammed the door and held it closed with his shoulder. But all was quiet—nothing but dead silence again.

For a long time he stood there holding the candle and hesitating over what to do next. When he had opened the door before, he had been unable to see much, although he had caught a glimpse of Kirilov's face as he stood at the opposite end of the room, by the window, before throwing himself at

Peter with the fury of a savage beast. The thought of it made Peter shudder. He quickly put the candle down on the table, got out his gun, and retreated to the furthermost corner of the room so that if Kirilov opened the door and rushed toward the table with the gun in his hand, Peter could pull his trigger first.

By now Peter had completely given up hope that Kirilov would shoot himself. "He was standing there in the middle of the room and thinking—" he thought, his ideas flashing like a whirlwind through his mind. "What a horrible dark room — He roared and threw himself at me. There are two possibilities: either I disturbed him at the second he was about to pull the trigger or he was thinking how he could kill me—yes, that's it—he was thinking how to do it. He knows I won't leave without killing him if he gets cold feet. So obviously he must kill me before I kill him. Ah, that silence again! It's pretty scary: suppose he suddenly opens that door! And the most disgusting thing about him is that he really believes in God more surely than any priest. He'll never shoot himself! There are plenty around nowadays who think they've worked it all out by themselves. Damned scum! Ah, damn—the candle's getting low. It'll be burnt out in fifteen minutes for sure. I must finish this off—I absolutely must. Why not? I can kill him now—with this note, no one will suspect me. I could fix him up, arrange him on the floor with the unloaded gun in his hand, and they'd be sure to think he'd done it himself. But hell, how am I going to kill him? If I open that door, he'll rush out and fire first. Ah, damn it, I'm sure he'll miss."

He was trembling in agony—he had to act, but couldn't take the first step. At last he took the candle and walked toward the door with his gun ready. He carefully placed his left hand —in which he held the candle—on the knob. But he made a clumsy movement: the handle rattled and the door creaked. "He'll let go straight at me now," the thought flashed through Peter's mind. He pushed the door wide open with his foot, lifted the candle, and thrust the gun out in front of him. But there was neither shooting nor shouting—the room was empty.

Peter started. The room led nowhere. He lifted the candle higher and looked around: no one. In a hushed voice he called Kirilov's name—there was no answer. He called louder—still no answer. "Could he have escaped through the window by any chance?" A little ventilation pane at the top of the window was half open. "Nonsense, he couldn't have squeezed through that." Peter crossed the room to look at the window. "He couldn't possibly—"

Suddenly he turned around and received a terrible shock. Against the wall facing the window, to the right of the door, there stood a cupboard, and to the right of the cupboard stood Kirilov. He was standing there very strangely—motionless, completely straight, his arms stiff at his sides, the nape of his neck pressed hard against the corner of the wall, his face slightly raised—looking like a man trying to merge into the background and make himself invisible. Everything about him seemed to indicate that he was hiding, but somehow it wasn't that. From where he stood, Peter could only see the projecting parts of the figure and he hesitated to take a step to the left to get a full view of Kirilov and solve the riddle. The pounding of his heart increased. Then suddenly he flew into a mad rage. He literally leaped from where he stood and, shouting and stamping his feet, rushed toward the sinister corner.

But just before he was close enough to touch Kirilov, he again stopped dead, paralyzed by an even greater horror. What struck him most was that, despite his shouting and his mad rush, the figure hadn't budged, as though it were made of stone or wax. Its pallor was uncanny and its black eyes were gazing into some point in space. Peter lowered his candle, then lifted it again, lighting the figure from various angles, examining the face. He suddenly noticed that, although Kirilov was looking straight ahead somewhere, Peter was within his peripheral vision and, indeed, Kirilov was watching him. That gave Peter the idea of bringing his candle right up to "the dog's face, to burn it and see what he'll do." Suddenly Peter thought he saw Kirilov's chin twitch and his lips twist into a faint sarcastic smile, as though he had guessed his thought. He began to shiver and, beside himself, grabbed Kirilov by the shoulder.

At this point something so hideous happened so quickly that afterward Peter never had a clear idea of it. As soon as he touched Kirilov's shoulder, Kirilov lowered his head and knocked the candlestick from Peter's hand with it. The candlestick fell with a clang and the candle went out. That second Peter felt an excruciating pain in the little finger of his left hand. He let out a cry. Later he was only able to remember that, beside himself, he had hit Kirilov on the head as hard as he could with his gun, three times. Kirilov had Peter's finger between his teeth. Finally, he pulled his finger away and dashed madly out of the house, feeling his way in the dark and pursued by terrible cries:

"One moment! One moment! One moment! One moment! . . ."

The words were repeated about ten times as Peter fled; then, as he reached the outside door, he heard a loud shot. Peter stopped in the dark passage, hesitating there for five minutes. Then he went back inside. But he had to have a light. He could grope about in the dark for the bit of candle he had dropped, but how would he light it? Suddenly a faint recollection passed through his mind: last night, at the second when he'd rushed into the kitchen to get at Fedka, he had caught sight of a large red matchbox on a shelf in a corner. He found the kitchen door, went down the three steps, and in the very place on the shelf he had remembered found the matchbox, which was full and, in fact, still unopened. He didn't light a match immediately but hurried back to the place by the cupboard where he'd hit Kirilov on the head as Kirilov bit him, and at that moment he felt an almost unendurable pain in his finger. Clenching his teeth, he somehow managed to light the bit of candle and put it back in the candlestick. He looked around: Kirilov's body, the feet toward the right-hand corner of the room, was stretched out by the window with the open ventilation pane. He had fired with the pistol against his right temple and the bullet had come out above his left temple. Peter saw splashes of blood and brains. The gun was still in the suicide's hand. He must have died instantaneously.

Peter inspected everything thoroughly, then rose, picked up the candle, and tiptoed into the other room, closing the door behind him. He put the candlestick on the table in the first room, thought for a second, then left it burning because, he decided, it couldn't set the place on fire anyway. He glanced once more at the note that lay on the table, grinning unthinkingly. Then, still for some unknown reason on tiptoe, he walked out of the house. He slipped through Fedka's secret passage in the fence once more, carefully replacing the loose board behind him.

III

At exactly ten minutes to six in the morning, Peter Verkhovensky and Erkel were walking up and down the railroad platform by which a rather long train was standing. Peter was leaving and Erkel was seeing him off. Peter's luggage had been taken care of and his small suitcase was reserving his seat in a second-class compartment. The first bell had already rung, and they were waiting for the second. Peter seemed quite unworried as he watched passengers getting into the carriages. He saw no close acquaintances. Only twice did he have to acknowledge nods: once from a merchant whom he knew vaguely and once from a young priest who was leaving for his parish a couple of stops away from the town. Erkel seemed eager to have a serious talk during these last minutes, although he himself probably wouldn't have known exactly what about, but he didn't dare say anything because he thought that Peter was tired of him and was waiting impatiently for the final departure signal.

"You look at everyone so openly," Erkel said shyly, as though trying to remind Peter that it could be dangerous.

"Why shouldn't I? It's still too early for me to hide. Don't worry. I just hope that Liputin hasn't got wind of my leaving and won't come running over here."

"They're unreliable."

"You mean Liputin?"

"The lot of them."

"Nonsense. They're bound together now by what happened yesterday. None of them will betray. Who except a madman would deliberately doom himself?"

"But they'll go mad, all of them."

Obviously Peter had thought of that himself, so Erkel's words irritated him all the more.

"Perhaps you're getting scared yourself, Erkel? I was relying on you more than on the rest of them. Now I've found out what each of you is worth. Repeat my instructions to them today, orally. I put them all directly in your charge now. Make the rounds of their places first thing in the morning. But only read them my written instructions tomorrow or the day after, when they are in a state to hear them. Mark my words, they'll be ready tomorrow—they'll be terribly scared and malleable as wax. But above all, you yourself—never lose courage."

"Ah, I wish you didn't have to leave."

"But I'm only going for a few days. I'll be back in no time."

"Mr. Verkhovensky," Erkel said diffidently but firmly, "even if you were actually going to Petersburg, I would still know that you were doing the best thing for the common cause."

"I never expected less from you, Erkel. Since you've guessed that I'm leaving for Petersburg, you must also understand that I couldn't possibly have told them that yesterday, because it would've scared them. You saw yourself the state they were in. But you understand that I'm doing it because it's best for the common cause and not to save my hide, as a man like Liputin might assume."

"Sure, Mr. Verkhovensky, and even if they told me that you were going abroad, I would understand. I realize that you must watch out for your personal safety because you're everything and we're nothing. I understand that very well." The poor boy's voice was trembling.

"Thank you, Erkel—ouch!—you touched my sore finger!" Erkel had awkwardly pressed Peter's hand, forgetting about the sore finger, which was neatly covered with a black silk finger sheath. "But let me assure you positively that I'm going to Petersburg to see what's in the air and that I probably won't spend more than twenty-four hours there; then I'll take the train straight back. When I return, I'll stay at Gaganov's country house for appearances' sake. If they think there's any danger, I'll be here and I'll be the first to face it. If, however, it becomes necessary for me to stay there a bit longer, I'll let you know immediately through our special channels and you can pass it on to them."

The second bell rang.

"That leaves us five minutes. You know, I'd hate to see the Five in this town disintegrate. Not that I'm particularly worried about it—in any case, I have plenty of Fives in the general network and I can't attach too much importance to this particular one—but I feel that each group can be useful. Anyway, I'm not worried, with you here, although I'm leaving you alone with those freaks—they won't dare talk, don't worry. Ah, you're going today too!" he shouted suddenly in a completely different, cheerful voice, addressing a very young man who had come up to say hello to him. "So you're taking the express too? Where are you going? To see your mother?"

The young man, whose mother, a relative of Julie von Lembke's, was a very rich landowner of the neighboring province, had been spending a couple of weeks in our town.

"No, I'm going farther—all the way to R. I'll have to sit it out in the train for eight hours. And you, are you going to Petersburg?" the young man said, laughing.

"What makes you think I'm going to Petersburg?" Peter laughed even louder.

The young man wagged a gloved finger at him.

"Well yes, you've guessed it!" Peter whispered mysteriously. "I have some letters from Mrs. von Lembke and I'll have to call on three or four big shots for her. I can't stand the type, I must say. Ah, I'm damned if I like this sort of errand!"

"But can you explain to me why she should be so scared?" the young man whispered. "Yesterday she wouldn't even let me in to see her. I don't think she has any need to worry about the governor. He managed to fall so effectively by that burning house that it looked as though he were sacrificing his life to save someone."

"Well, there we have it," Peter said, laughing. "She's afraid that they may have written from here already—that is, some people. The main trouble here is Stavrogin—or rather Prince K. It's a long story and maybe I'll tell you part of it when we're on our way, limiting myself, of course, to what discretion will allow me to reveal. Have you met Lieutenant Erkel? He's a relative of mine, stationed in our district now."

The young gentleman, who had been squinting at Erkel, touched his hat. Erkel bowed.

"But you know, Verkhovensky, eight hours in a train will be a frightful strain. There's a certain Colonel Berestov taking this train with us. His estate is next to ours and he's married to one of the Garin girls. He's the right sort of fellow—great fun. He even has some ideas. He only spent two days here in your town. He's crazy about cards, so perhaps we could organize a little game, what do you say? I have my eye on a fourth already—one Pripukhlov, a bearded millionaire merchant from T.—and I mean a real millionaire, you can take my word for that. A wonderful old moneybag—we'll have great fun."

"I'm very partial to a little game and I'm sure it would've been great fun, but I happen to be traveling second class, so—"

"Ah, nonsense—never on your life! Get in with us and I'll tell them to transfer you to first class. The chief conductor eats out of my hand. What do you have in your compartment, a bag? A rug?"

"Fine then—let's go."

Peter picked up his bag, his rug, and his book and moved quite willingly into the first-class carriage. Erkel helped him. The third bell rang.

"Well, Erkel," Peter said hurriedly, shaking Erkel's hand through the carriage window for the last time, "they're waiting for me to start that game."

"You don't have to explain to me, Mr. Verkhovensky; I understand!"

"Well, in that case, I wish you all the best."

And Peter turned away from the window because the young gentleman was calling him, wanting to introduce him to the other two players. And that was the last Erkel saw of his Peter Verkhovensky.

He returned home quite depressed. It wasn't that he was frightened at Peter's leaving him so suddenly but—but Verkhovensky had so readily turned his back on him, as soon as that elegant young man had called to him. Hadn't he really had anything else to say to him, Erkel, besides "all the best?" Couldn't he at least have pressed his hand a bit harder?

It was the last that he felt most strongly. And something else was beginning to gnaw at his poor little heart, something that he himself didn't yet understand, something connected with the night before.

chapter 7

STEPAN VERKHOVENSKY'S LAST TRIP

I

There's no doubt in my mind that Mr. Verkhovensky was very much afraid as the day set for his crazy enterprise drew near. I'm convinced that fear tormented him most on the last night before he left—that horrible night. Later, Nastasya told me that he had gone to bed late, but that he had slept. However, that doesn't prove a thing. I've heard it said that convicts sentenced to death sleep very deeply even on the night preceding execution. And, although he left the house when it was already daylight, which usually has a calming effect upon nervous people (just as that major said at Virginsky's when he explained how he stopped believing in God as soon as night was over), yet I'm sure that, earlier, he couldn't have imagined himself walking along the highway all

alone like that without horror. Of course, his state of despera-
tion must have made it easier for him, at first, to bear his
terrible sense of utter loneliness when he left his warm corner
and his Nastasya for the first time in twenty years. Anyway,
it made no difference: even if he had clearly understood all
the horrors that awaited him, he still would have stepped out
of the house and taken to the road. He felt his was the right
gesture, a proud one; he was elated over it and didn't feel the
cost mattered. Of course he knew that if he had consented to
stay, Mrs. Stavrogin would have accepted him on the most
luxurious terms. But he couldn't possibly stay with her as a
humble dependent. No—he didn't want her charity, so he
didn't stay! He left her of his own free will and, carrying high
"the banner of the great idea," he was going to die for it on
the road! That is exactly how he must have felt and how his
action must have looked to him.

But I have often wondered why he actually had to set out
on foot instead of hiring a carriage. At first I put it down to
his fifty-year isolation from practical life and his tendency to
let his imagination run away with him when under emotional
stress. I thought that the picture of traveling by post chaise,
even if there were harness bells, must have seemed too ordinary, too everyday, to him, whereas a pilgrimage on foot,
even with an umbrella, was much more of a poetic gesture and
had something vengefully romantic about it. But now that all
the facts are in and it's all over, I believe the explanation is
really much simpler. In the first place, he was afraid to order
horses because Varvara Stavrogin would have found out and
forced him to stay—which she almost certainly would have
done—and he would have submitted, and that would have
been the end of the "great idea" once and for all. In the second
place, a person ordering post horses is at least supposed to
know where he wishes to go, and it was the fact that he had
no idea where he was going that worried him most. Because,
if he had picked on any town to go to, his venture would
immediately have become meaningless and absurd in his own
eyes. He felt that. Why should it be one particular town rather
than any other? Was he going to look for *ce marchand?* But
which *marchand?* Here again the second, more terrible question cropped up. As a matter of fact, there was nothing he
dreaded more than *ce marchand* he had so suddenly set out
after and he would have been really horrified if he had
actually found him. No thanks, he preferred just to hit the

road and walk and walk without thinking for as long as he could. The road is very, very long, and has no end to it; it is like a man's life, like a man's dream. There is a grand idea in the open road, but what kind of idea is there in ordering post horses? Ordering post horses is the end of an idea. So, *vive la grande route*—and then leave it to God.

After the unexpected encounter with Liza in the field, he walked on in an even deeper daze. The road passed within half a mile of Skvoreshniki, a fact that, strangely enough, had never even occurred to him when he took it. Reasoning or even realizing clearly what was going on was unbearable to him at that moment. The drizzle kept letting up, then starting again, but he didn't notice it. Neither did he notice that he'd slung his traveling bag over his shoulder and that this made it easier to walk. He had walked like that for perhaps a mile or so when he suddenly stopped and looked around. The old road, black and scarred with ruts and planted with willows on each side, uncoiled before him in an endless thread. To his right were stubble-covered fields, long since harvested; to his left, some bushes and beyond them a wood. And far, far away on the horizon, there was the hardly visible railroad running slantwise and, above it, the smoke of some departing train, the sound of which, however, didn't reach him.

Stepan Verkhovensky grew frightened, but only for a moment. He sighed without any particular reason, put his bag by a willow tree, and sat down to rest. He felt chilly and wrapped his rug around him. Then he noticed the drizzle, opened his umbrella, and held it above his head. He sat like that for quite a while, firmly holding the umbrella handle and now and then moving his lips. All sorts of images whirled past his eyes, bustling by and replacing each other. "Liza, Liza," he thought. "and *ce* Maurice with her— Strange people. What was that terrible fire they were talking about and who was it that was murdered? I don't think Nastasya has found out I've gone yet—she's waiting to bring me my coffee. . . . Why cards? When did I lose people at cards? Hm, in this country under serfdom—oh, God, and what about Fedka?" He started in terror and looked around. "Suppose that Fedka is sitting here behind some bush now? They say he has a whole gang on the road. Ah Lord, I'll tell him the whole truth. I'll admit that it was my fault, but that afterward I suffered more for him than he did himself in the army. And then—well, I'll give him my purse. I have forty rubles altogether—and *il prendra les rubles* and then he'll kill me all the same."

Fear somehow made him close his umbrella and put it next to him. In the distance he saw some sort of vehicle moving along the road. It was coming from town. He watched it uneasily.

"It's a peasant cart, thank God, and it's coming at a walking pace. It can't be dangerous—those are local, half-starved nags. I always spoke of breeding—although it wasn't I actually but Peter Ilyich who spoke of horse breeding and I just silenced him by saying—but what's that in the cart behind the driver? Looks like a peasant woman. A peasant and his woman, *cela commence à être très rassurant!* The woman behind, the man in front—very reassuring! There's a cow tied to the back of the cart, *c'est rassurant au plus haut degré.*"

The cart drew level with him; it turned out to be a good, solid peasant cart. The woman sat on a tightly stuffed sack and the man sat on the side of the cart facing Mr. Verkhovensky, with his feet dangling in the air. A reddish cow was jogging along behind, tied to the cart by her horns. The man and the woman gaped at Mr. Verkhovensky and he at them. But when the cart had passed him and was already at least twenty yards away, he hurriedly stood up and followed it. Naturally, he felt safer in the vicinity of the cart, but by the time he had overtaken it he had already forgotten everything and was again in a mist of fragmentary thoughts and images. He walked on, without of course suspecting that to the peasants in the cart he presented the most curious and mysterious object they could have met on the open road.

"What—what are you, sir, if you don't mind my asking?" the peasant woman said, unable to restrain herself, when Mr. Verkhovensky's absent glance slid over her. She must have been twenty-seven or so, buxom, dark-haired, rosy, with friendly, smiling red lips beneath which flashed even white teeth.

"Are you—are you addressing me?" Mr. Verkhovensky asked in mournful surprise.

"Must be a merchant," the peasant said with assurance. He was a big, tall man with a broad, rather intelligent face and a full, reddish beard.

"No, I'm not really a merchant, I'm—I'm—*moi, c'est autre chose,*" Mr. Verkhovensky managed to answer, taking the precaution of falling back a bit so that he was now walking roughly level with the cow.

"Must be from the gentry," the peasant concluded, hearing the foreign words, and he pulled at the reins.

"And we were looking at you, sir, puzzling our heads over whether you'd come out for a walk or what?" the woman said again, full of curiosity.

"Is it—are you asking me?"

"There are foreigners who come here by them trains, and your boots, sir, they don't look like local ones to me—"

"Army boots," the peasant said in an important, self-satisfied tone.

"No, no, I'm not really in the army, I—"

"What an impossibly nosey woman," Mr. Verkhovensky muttered irritatedly under his breath. "And the way she's examining me! *Enfin,* you'd think I'd done them some wrong, while I haven't done a thing really."

The man and woman exchanged whispers.

"Excuse me, sir, we'd be very glad to give you a lift, sir, if it pleases you."

Mr. Verkhovensky suddenly woke up as it were.

"Yes, yes, friends, please—I'd be very grateful, because I'm beginning to feel rather tired. But how can I get on?"

"Strange," he thought, "I've been walking level with the cow all this time and it never even occurred to me to ask them for a lift. *Real life* is really quite different."

The peasant, however, didn't stop his horse at once.

"Where is it you wish to go, sir?" he inquired with a certain diffidence.

Mr. Verkhovensky didn't understand at once.

"Is it Khatovo, sir?"

"Khatovo? No, not really. I don't know it, although I've heard it mentioned."

"Khatovo is about seven miles from here, sir; it's a village."

"A village? *C'est charmant!* Yes, I think I've heard of it."

Mr. Verkhovensky was still walking on foot and the cart still didn't stop for him to climb up. A brilliant idea flashed through his mind.

"You may perhaps imagine that I'm a—my papers are in order. I'm a professor, that is, a tutor, if you wish—but, a top one, a head tutor. *Oui, c'est comme ça qu'on peut traduire.* I would like very much to climb into your cart and sit down and I'll be very happy to buy you a quart of wine."

"I'll have to charge you half a ruble for it, sir. The road is real bad, you know."

"It wouldn't be fair otherwise, sir, would it?" the woman said, backing him up.

"Half a ruble? All right, so it'll be half a ruble. *C'est encore mieux. J'ai en tout quarante rubles mais . . .*"

The cart stopped and through the joint efforts of all three, Mr. Verkhovensky was hoisted into it and seated next to the woman on the sack. Thoughts never ceased whirling inside his head. From time to time, he himself realized what a distracted state he was in and that he couldn't think about the things he should've been thinking of, and he wondered why it was so. There were moments when he was painfully aware of his morbid inability to control his mind and it irritated and depressed him.

"Why is this—er, this cow tied behind like that?" he asked the woman.

"You never seen one before, sir?" The woman burst out laughing.

"We bought her in town," the man explained. "Our own cattle died back in the spring. In a plague. Around our village, it hit all the cattle and killed half of them—enough to make you howl!"

And he cracked the whip over the horse as the cart got stuck in a rut.

"Yes, that happens in Russia. And we Russians, in general . . . Yes, it certainly happens." Mr. Verkhovensky was unable to complete his thought.

"If you're a tutor, sir, what'll you do in Khatovo? Or are you going on further?"

"Me? Well, I don't really have to go any further, *c'est à dire,* I am going to a merchant's house."

"Must be in Spasov then?"

"Yes, yes, that's it—Spasov. Although it really makes no difference."

"Well, if you were heading for Spasov and walking on foot like that, and with those boots of yours, I'd say you'd have got there in a week or so," the woman laughed.

"Right, right, but that makes no difference either, *mes amis,*" Mr. Verkhovensky interrupted her impatiently.

"What terribly inquisitive people," he thought. "The woman speaks better than the man and I note that since the abolition of serfdom their syntax has changed somewhat. But what business is it of theirs whether I'm going to Spasov or not? I'm paying them, so why can't they leave me alone?"

"If you're going to Spasov, the best thing is to take the boat," the man continued to pester him.

"That's right," the woman chimed in, "because by cart along the lake shore, you're forced to go around and it's an extra thirty miles at least."

"Forty more likely," the man said.

"You can catch the two-o'clock steamer at Ustievo tomorrow," the woman said, settling the matter.

Mr. Verkhovensky firmly refused to go on with the discussion and remained silent, so his questioners left him alone for a while. The peasant sat there, occasionally urging on his horse with a flick of the reins and only from time to time exchanging some brief words with the woman. Mr. Verkhovensky dozed off. He was very surprised when the woman woke him up and he found himself in a rather large village and the cart standing by a wooden peasant house with three front windows.

"So you had a little nap, sir?"

"What is this? Where am I? Ah, well, what's the difference?" He sadly climbed down from the cart.

He looked around dejectedly. The sight of the village struck him as terribly alien and unfamiliar.

"Oh, I almost forgot about the half ruble!" he said to the peasant with an exaggeratedly anxious gesture. Apparently he was afraid they were already going to leave him.

"You can settle it inside the house, sir. Please come in," the peasant invited him.

"It's nice inside," the woman said enticingly.

He stepped onto a shaky front step.

"How is it possible?" he whispered in deep, frightened bewilderment, but he went in. *"Elle l'a voulu!"* The words stabbed at his heart and he suddenly forgot about everything, including the fact that he was now inside the peasant house.

It was a light, fairly clean, two-room house, not really an inn but just a place where outsiders who came regularly to the village could stop over. Quite at ease, Mr. Verkhovensky went straight to the corner of the room reserved for visitors, but he forgot to say hello, and sat down, sinking deep into thought. Soon a very pleasant warmth spread over him after the three hours spent out in the damp on the road. Even the chills that ran up and down his spine spasmodically—as always happens with particularly nervous people when they are feverish and pass suddenly from a cold place to a warm one—began to feel pleasant. He lifted his head and the delicious smell of hot pancakes, which the mistress of the house was busy making on the stove, tickled his nostrils. Smiling a childlike smile, he leaned toward the landlady and lisped.

"So I see there are pancakes going? *Mais c'est charmant!*"

"Would you like some, sir?" she said, offering him some politely.

"I would like some! I would like that very much indeed, and I would love to have some tea too," Mr. Verkhovensky said animatedly.

The famous, delicious, thin, peasant pancakes, dripping with melted butter, arrived on a large, blue-patterned dish. Mr. Verkhovensky tried one with relish.

"How gorgeous! How tasty! If only it were possible to get *un doigt d'eau de vie.*"

"Would it be vodka you have in mind by any chance, sir?"

"Yes, that's exactly what I had in mind—exactly, *un tout petit peu.*"

"Would you like a five-kopeck glass?"

"A five-kopeck one, a five-kopeck one, a five-kopeck one, *un petit rien.* . . ." Mr. Verkhovensky nodded approvingly with a blissful smile.

Ask someone from the simple people to do something for you and, if he is able and feels like it, he'll do it gladly and conscientiously; but ask him to get you some vodka and his usual quiet friendliness will be transformed into a great eagerness to please, almost a brotherly solicitude for you. As he goes for your vodka, although he's fully aware that you'll drink it alone and without his assistance, he nevertheless experiences your future enjoyment vicariously.

Within three or four minutes—the tavern was only a couple of houses away—a half bottle of vodka and a large, greenish glass stood on the table in front of Stepan Verkhovensky.

"And all this is for me!" he said with immense surprise. "I've always had vodka but I had no idea that one could get so much for five kopecks!"

He poured a glass, stood up, and rather solemnly crossed the room to the opposite corner where his traveling companion, the peasant woman who had shared the sack with him and had pestered him with all those questions, was now sitting. She was flustered and refused at first. Then, after refusing the required number of times, she finally stood up, drank politely in three swigs, the way women do, and, with her face conveying the scorching sensation in her throat, bowed to him and returned the glass. He returned the bow very solemnly and, looking very proud of himself, returned to his table.

He had done it all on the spur of the moment, having had no idea, even a second beforehand, that he was going to offer the woman a drink.

"I am very good at dealing with simple people, just as I always tried to tell them," he thought with self-satisfaction, pouring the remaining vodka into his glass, and although there was less than a full glass left, the liquor sent a warm wave through his body and even went to his head a bit.

"Je suis tout à fait malade, but it's not at all unpleasant to be ill—"

"Wouldn't you like to buy this, sir?" he heard a woman's quiet voice say next to him.

He raised his eyes and saw a lady—*une dame et elle en avait l'air.* She must have been past thirty and had a very modest look; she wore a dark town dress, with a gray kerchief around her shoulders. There was something very pleasant in her face that immediately attracted him. She had just come into the house, where she'd earlier left her things on a bench close to where he was sitting now, among them a brief case that he remembered having noticed on coming in and a small oilcloth traveling bag. From the bag she now produced two beautifully bound books with crosses engraved on their covers and held them before him.

"Eh—mais je crois que c'est l'Evangile. Yes, I'd be delighted to buy one. I gather you are *ce qu'on appelle* a gospel woman; well, of course, I've read it many times. Half a ruble?"

"Thirty-five kopecks each."

"Certainly, I'll be delighted, *je n'ai rien contre l'Evangile,* and I have been wanting to reread it once more for a long time."

It occurred to him at that moment that, actually, he hadn't read the gospel for at least thirty years, except for some passages he had reread about seven years ago when he'd been reading Renan's *La Vie de Jésus.*

He had no change on him, so he pulled out the four ten-ruble bills, all the money he had. The landlady went to get some change and only then did he notice that there were quite a few people in the room now and that they all seemed to be watching him and even talking about him. They were also talking about the outbreak of the fires, and the peasant with whom he had arrived was talking more than any of them, probably because he had just returned from town. They mentioned arson and the Shpigulin workers.

"Why didn't he mention the fire while we were on the road?" Mr. Verkhovensky thought suddenly. "He seems to have brought up everything else."

"Ah, Mr. Verkhovensky! Can it really be you, sir? I never expected to see *you* here! Don't you recognize me, sir?"

It was a middle-aged fellow who looked like some kind of servant—clean-shaven and dressed in a long coat with a wide collar. Mr. Verkhovensky became very worried when he heard his name pronounced.

"I'm sorry," he muttered, "I can't quite place you."

"Oh, I see, you've forgotten me, sir. I'm Anisim—Anisim Ivanov. I used to work in the house of the late Mr. Gaganov. I've seen you many times, when you visited him and the late Mrs. Gaganov. She even used to send me over to your house with books for you, sir, and twice she sent you some special Petersburg candy—".

"Ah yes, yes—Anisim, I remember very well," Mr. Verkhovensky said, smiling. "Do you live here now?"

"I live just outside Spasov, sir, in a village near the monastery, and I work in the house of the late Mrs. Gaganov's sister, who, you may remember, sir, broke her leg when she jumped out of her carriage on arriving at a ball. Now she's living near the monastery and I'm in her service. I've come to visit my relatives who live around here—"

"Yes, yes, I see—"

"I was so pleased when I saw you, sir. You used to be very kind to me," Anisim went on, smiling ecstatically. "But where is it you're going now, sir, all on your own? You never used to go around all alone like this."

Mr. Verkhovensky gave him a frightened look.

"You aren't, by chance, going to Spasov to pay us a visit, sir?"

"Yes, I'm going to Spasov, but then *il me semble que tout le monde va à* Spasov."

"Would it be Fedor Matveich you're going to see, sir? I can imagine how pleased he'll be to see you, sir. I remember how much he used to admire you, and even now he often mentions you."

"Yes, yes, I'll see him too."

"Well, to be sure, sir. And these peasants here almost burst with surprise because someone told them he'd seen you walking on foot on the road. Ah, they're a stupid bunch, sir."

"That's right, Anisim, it was I. I made a bet—you know, like the English do—that I could walk all the way on foot and I—"

Beads of sweat stood out on his forehead and temples.

"To be sure, to be sure, sir," Anisim said, lapping up every word with merciless curiosity.

Mr. Verkhovensky couldn't stand any more of it. He was so embarrassed that he felt like getting up and walking out of the house. But at that moment, they brought in the samovar, and the gospel woman, who had left the room for something, returned. Mr. Verkhovensky turned toward her and, sounding like a man trying desperately to save himself, invited her to have tea with him, whereupon Anisim gave up and walked away.

It was quite true that the peasants were greatly puzzled:

"What kind of a man is he? He was found on the road and he said he was a tutor. He's dressed like a foreigner and has no more brains than a baby. He gives answers and looks like he's running from someone. Yes, and he's carrying quite a lot of cash on him!"

Some wanted to alert the police, because "on top of all that, things had not been too quiet in town."

But Anisim immediately reassured them. Out in the passage, he informed everyone who was willing to listen to him that Mr. Verkhovensky wasn't really a tutor but "a great learned man himself and working on those great learned problems"; that he was a local landowner and had been living for twenty-two years at Mrs. Stavrogin's, the widow of the general; that "he was the most important person in her household, you see," and that everybody in town had the "greatest respect and admiration for him"; that he was the sort of man who'd get rid of fifty or even a hundred rubles at the gentlemen's club in one evening; that he had reached the rank of councilor in the government service, which is like lieutenant colonel in the army, "just one notch below a full colonel, you see"; and that obviously he had money because through "that general's widow, Mrs. Stavrogin, he has all the money he wants and don't have to count it ever," and so on.

"But she's a lady, indeed *une dame très comme il faut,*"

Mr. Verkhovensky thought, recovering from Anisim's siege and watching the gospel vendor with agreeable curiosity, undisturbed by her pouring the hot tea from her cup into the saucer and alternating sips with nibbles at a small lump of sugar. "Never mind this *petit morceau de sucre,* there's something distinguished and independent about her and at the same time so quiet. *Le comme-il-faut tout pur,* only in a slightly different sense."

He soon found out that her name was Sofia Ulitin and that she lived in K., where she had a sister, the widow of an artisan. She was also a widow; her husband had been killed in action at Sevastopol just after being promoted from sergeant to second lieutenant.

"But you're still so young—*vous n'avez même pas trente ans.*"

"Thirty-four," Mrs. Ulitin said with a smile.

"Why, I see you even understand French."

"A little. After I lost my husband, I spent four years in a wealthy family and I picked it up from the children."

And she told him how, left a widow at the age of eighteen, she had stayed for some time in Sevastopol working as a nurse, and then later had lived in various places and now was traveling around selling copies of the gospels.

"*Mais, mon Dieu,* could it be you then to whom that strange, that very strange adventure happened in our town?"

She blushed and it turned out that it was to her that it had happened.

"*Ces vauriens!* Those good-for-nothings!" he said, hatred beginning to stir within him as the loathsome memory tugged painfully at his heart. For a moment he stared absently around.

"But she's gone," he realized suddenly, seeing the empty chair next to him. "She keeps rushing out; she seems to be preoccupied with something. I think something must be worrying her. Bah, *je deviens égoiste.*"

He raised his eyes and again saw Anisim, but this time under the most threatening circumstances. The room was full of peasants and it was obvious that Anisim had brought them in. Among them there were the owner of the house, the peasant who'd given Mr. Verkhovensky a lift, two other men who turned out to be cab drivers, and a small half-drunk man dressed like a peasant but clean-shaven and with the air of a shopkeeper ruined by liquor, who did most of the talking. And all of them were speaking about Mr. Verkhovensky. The owner of the cart and the cow insisted that, if he went by land, the gentleman would have to make a detour and go an additional thirty miles, so he just had to take the steamer. But the half-drunk little man, backed up by the landlord, heatedly contested this point.

"It's because, you see, fellow, although it's right that it's nearer for the gentleman to go direct across the lake, the trouble is that at this time of year, the steamer just don't go there, see what I mean?"

"It does, it does—and it was running just a week ago," Anisim, who was the most excited of the lot, shouted.

"It runs perhaps, but it don't run regular in this season and there are times when it just sits in Ustievo for three days in a row, waiting like."

"It'll be here tomorrow at two sharp, you'll see—and I promise you, sir, you'll get to Spasov before evening even," Anisim insisted heatedly.

"Mais qu'est ce qu'il a, cet homme? What's come over him?" Mr. Verkhovensky said, trembling with fear as he waited to see where it would all lead.

Then the cabbies joined the fray and declared that they'd charge him three rubles to Ustievo; the others shouted that that was fair enough, just the right price in fact, and that it was exactly what they charged all summer long to take people to Ustievo.

"But I like it here—and I don't want—" Mr. Verkhovensky mumbled.

"You're right, sir, it's nice here, but it don't compare to Spasov," Anisim retorted, "and think how pleased Fedor Matveich will be to see you."

"Mon Dieu, mes amis, this is all so unexpected."

Finally the gospel woman came back. But she sat down looking sad and discouraged.

"It doesn't look as though I'll make it to Spasov," she told the landlady.

"Why, are you going to Spasov too?" Mr. Verkhovensky said, coming back to life.

It turned out that a Mrs. Svetlitsin, a landowner, had promised to pick the gospel woman up in Khatovo that evening and give her a lift to Spasov, but now it didn't look as if she would be coming.

"What am I supposed to do now?" the poor woman kept repeating.

"*Mais ma chère et nouvelle amie,* I can give you a lift to that village—what's its name?—just as well as that lady landowner, because I've hired a carriage to go there. So tomorrow we can go to Spasov together."

"Are you going to Spasov too?"

"Can I help going? *Mais je suis enchanté,* and I'll take you there with the greatest of pleasure. Here, you see, those men want—and I've already hired one of them. Which one of you have I hired?" Mr. Verkhovensky said, feeling a sudden urge to go to Spasov.

Within fifteen minutes they were getting into a covered cart, he very animated and pleased, she with her bag of Bibles and a grateful smile. They sat down next to each other, with Anisim helping them in.

"Good luck, sir," Anisim said, frantically busying himself around the cart. "It's been real good seeing you again, sir."

"Good-by, my friend, good-by."

"So you'll see Fedor Matveich—"

"Yes, yes, my friend, I'll see Fedor Petrovich, but good-by for now."

II

"So you see, my dear friend—for I do hope you'll allow me to call you that, ma'am," Mr. Verkhovensky began hurriedly as soon as the cart moved off, "you see *j'aime le peuple.* That is as it should be. But it seems to me now that I've never seen them at close quarters. Of course, my maid Nastasya, she's of the people, but *le vrai peuple*—those one meets on the open road—well, they seem to have only one concern and that is where *I* am going. But let's forget such vexations. You may think I'm talking a lot of nonsense, but I think it's just because I'm in such a hurry to say things—"

"I don't think you're very well, sir," she said, examining him closely but very discreetly.

"No, no—it's nothing. All I have to do is wrap myself up in the rug . . . although the wind is quite fresh—yes, very fresh indeed, but we'll forget about it. That's not what I was trying to say actually, *chère et incomparable amie.* I meant that I felt almost happy and that you are the reason for it. And being happy is not to my advantage at all because I immediately grow all soft and insist on forgiving all my enemies—"

"But that's a very good thing, sir."

"Not always, *chère innocente*. The gospel, *voyez-vous,* henceforward we're going to preach it together and I'll sell your beautiful books with pleasure. Yes, I think that's a great idea, *quelque chose de très nouveau dans ce genre.* The simple people are religious—that's an accepted fact, but they still don't know the gospels. I'll explain them to them. In an oral presentation, I'll be able to correct the mistakes contained in that remarkable book, for which, please believe me, I have the greatest respect. Thus, I could be useful on the open road too. I've always been useful and I've always tried to make *them* see it, particularly *cette chère ingrate.* Oh, but first let's forgive everyone for everything and let's hope they'll forgive us too, because we're all guilty toward one another, all of us. Everyone is guilty!"

"I think you put it very well, sir."

"Yes, yes, I think I'm speaking very well and I'll speak very well to them, but what was it I was trying to say? I keep losing track and forgetting what I was talking about. Will you allow me to stay with you? I realize you're looking at me and I'm quite puzzled by your ways: you're so straightforward and artless; you mispronounce certain words and keep calling me 'sir'; you drink your tea out of a saucer, nibbling at that horrible little lump of sugar; but there's something charming in you and I can see in your face—oh, please don't blush and don't be afraid of me as a man. Ah, my dear, incomparable friend, *pour moi, une femme c'est tout!* I cannot live without a woman near me—but only near me, nothing else. . . . I'm terribly mixed up, terribly. . . . I can't recall at all what I was trying to say. Ah, blessed is he to whom God sends a woman when he needs her. . . . I think I'm in a rapturous sort of state now. . . . There's a great idea about the open road, too! Yes, yes—that's what I wanted to tell you—about the idea, but, so far, I've kept missing the point. And why did they have to send us further, it was quite nice there, and here it's getting cold—*trop froid.* By the way, *j'ai en tout quarante* rubles, and here it is—take it, keep it. I always lose it or they take it away from me and—I feel terribly sleepy and something is going round and round and round inside my head—ah, how it spins! Oh, you're so kind. What's this you're wrapping me in?"

"You've got a high fever, sir, and I've put my blanket around you. But about the money, sir, I'd rather—"

"Ah, please, don't let's talk any more, *cela me fait mal.* You're really so terribly kind. . . ."

And he immediately plunged into a feverish, shivery sleep. The country road over which they had been driving for about fifteen miles was rough and the cart jolted badly. Now and then, Mr. Verkhovensky woke up, lifted his head from the little pillow she had placed under it, and inquired, "Are you here?" to make sure she hadn't vanished. He also informed her that he kept dreaming about a huge, open, toothy mouth and that it was making him feel quite sick. Mrs. Ulitin was very worried about him.

The cart stopped by a large, wooden, four-windowed hut. There was a courtyard behind it with some more smaller cottages standing around it. Mr. Verkhovensky, who had woken up, hurriedly entered the house, going straight through to the second room, the larger and better of the two. His sleepy face took on a very businesslike expression as he explained to the landlady—a tall, big-boned woman of forty or so, very dark-haired and with the rudiments of a mustache—that he wanted the entire room to himself and demanded that the door be bolted and no one allowed in *"parce que nous avons à parler. Oui,* I have so much to tell you, *chère amie.* Oh, I'll pay, I'll pay," he assured the landlady.

Although he spoke rapidly, he felt his tongue was stiff and hard to control. The landlady heard him out with a sour expression, but nodded consent, although there was something threatening even in that gesture. But he never noticed a thing and hurriedly—he was in a frantic hurry all the time—demanded that she go prepare their dinner immediately "without wasting time."

That was too much for the mustached landlady.

"We ain't no hotel, mister. We don't keep no dinners for travelers. You can have a samovar and I could maybe boil some crayfish, but that's about all we have. There won't be no fresh fish until tomorrow now."

But Mr. Verkhovensky waved his hands at her and just kept repeating, "Hurry up, hurry up, I'll pay. . . ." Finally they settled on fish soup, to be followed by roast chicken. The woman declared that there wasn't a chicken to be had in the whole village, but she agreed to go around and see what she could find for him, sounding as though she were doing him an immense favor.

As soon as she left, Mr. Verkhovensky sat down on the sofa and invited Mrs. Ulitin to sit next to him. The room contained this sofa and some armchairs, but they were very dilapidated. In general, the room was rather large (there was a partition and a bed behind it) and was papered with old, torn, yellow wallpaper covered with frightful mythological patterns, with a long row of icons hanging on it, in addition to the ones in folding brass frames in the corner near the door. All this, together with the odd assortment of furniture, presented an unsightly mixture of urban and peasant styles. But Mr. Verkhovensky didn't even notice that; he didn't even bother to glance through the window at the huge lake that wasn't a hundred feet away from them.

"At last we're by ourselves and we won't let anyone in," he said to her. "I want to tell you everything from the beginning."

Mrs. Ulitin stopped him, looking quite worried:

"Do you know, Mr. Verkhovensky—"

"How do you know my name already?" he asked with a radiant smile.

"I heard Anisim call you that when you were talking to him. But here's what I'd like to tell you."

And quickly, keeping her eye on the door all the time as though afraid that someone might be eavesdropping, she told him that this village wasn't at all safe. She explained that, although the local men were practically all fishermen, fishing being their main source of income, they didn't hesitate to charge travelers the most exorbitant prices in the summer, because the village wasn't on the main road but at a sort of dead end and people only came there because it was one of the stops the steamer made; and if the steamer didn't come— it didn't sail if the weather was in the least bad—then the whole place became terribly crowded in a few days. That was just what the landlords were waiting for because then they could charge three times as much for everything. As to the owner of the house they were in now, he was a very proud and arrogant man, being very rich by local standards—his fishing net alone was worth a good thousand at least. . . .

Mr. Verkhovensky looked at Mrs. Ulitin's flushed and animated face with something like a reproach and several times made a gesture to stop her. But she insisted on having her say, telling him that she'd come to this village last summer "with a very, very wealthy lady from town" and that they had had to spend two nights there because the steamer was two days late and that they had had such a terrible time that she was afraid to remember it.

"Now you, Mr. Verkhovensky, you've reserved this room for yourself—I'm just trying to warn you. In the other room there's already a middle-aged man, a young man, and a lady with her children, and by tomorrow, the house will be full until two o'clock, because the steamer has been due for two days and is just about certain to come in tomorrow. So, for reserving the room for yourself, and for the kind of dinner you ordered from her, and also for the vexation all this causes the other travelers—they'll charge you prices that would be unheard of even in Moscow and Petersburg."

Her talking like that caused him real suffering.

"*Assez, mon enfant!* Please! We have enough money with us and after that—*et après le bon Dieu* will take care of us. I'm surprised that you, a person so full of noble aspirations— That's enough, *assez, vous me tourmentez!*" he cried hysterically. "We have our future to consider—and you, you—well, you're making me uneasy about our future."

And he proceeded to tell her his story, hurrying so much that, at first, it was difficult to make out his words. He talked and talked for a long, long time. They were served the fish soup, then the chicken, and when the samovar arrived he was still talking. His story sounded a bit strange, a bit delirious, but then he was feverish. In the state he was in, all his mental faculties were exacerbated and this, as the worried Mrs. Ulitin foresaw, was bound to be succeeded by complete prostration.

He'd gone back almost to his boyhood when "my young chest heaving, I raced vigorously through the fields," and it took him the best part of an hour to reach his two marriages and his life in Berlin. However, I don't dare laugh at this, because there really was something in it that was sacred to him, something that could almost be described in modern jargon as "the struggle for existence." Now he was facing the woman whom he had chosen to accompany him in his future peregrinations and was, so to speak, initiating her. He felt that she should know he was a genius. Perhaps he had exaggerated ideas about Mrs. Ulitin, but he had already elected her. He couldn't live without a woman. He realized, seeing her expression, that she hardly understood what he was saying, even the most crucial points.

"Doesn't matter, *nous attendrons*, and in the meantime, she can understand me by intuition."

"My dear!" he exclaimed suddenly, interrupting his narrative, "all I really need is your heart and that charming, enchanting way in which you're looking at me now! Oh, please don't blush—I've explained already. . . ."

Much remained foggy to the poor entrapped lady, especially when his narrative switched to a dissertation on other people's constant inability to understand him and "talents being lost, thus, in our country." As she sadly described it later, "it was all so clever—quite over my head." At the time, she listened to him with an obviously painful effort, with her eyes popping slightly. And when he became sarcastic and made a few biting, witty remarks about our "leading progressives," she even tried, in her despair, to smile a couple of times in response to his sardonic laughter, but this turned out to be more painful than if she'd cried, and finally he himself became embarrassed. He tried to make up for it by attacking with even greater fury the "nihilists and the newcomers." This time she grew really frightened and she wasn't given a chance to recover until the moment when the actual romance began—and even then, it was only an apparent recovery. A woman is always a woman, even if she is a nunlike one. And now Mrs. Ulitin smiled, shook her head, blushed, lowered her eyes, all of which brought Mr. Verkhovensky to the verge of ecstasy and so inspired him that he even started embellishing his story with appropriately chosen lies. In his narrative, Varvara Stavrogin became a dark and sultry beauty who "caused a sensation in Petersburg and in many European capitals" and whose husband "was killed by a bullet at Sevastopol" only because he felt himself "unworthy of her love and wished thus to yield her to his rival," that is, of course, to him, Stepan Verkhovensky.

"Don't be embarrassed, my gentle little Christian!" he cried, looking fixedly at Mrs. Ulitin, almost convinced that it had really been just as he was telling her. "It was something ethereal, something infinitely subtle; we've never mentioned it, even once, to each other."

The reason for this state of affairs, he explained further along in his narrative, was another woman, this time a blond

(unless he meant Dasha, I can't imagine who she could be).
Anyway, this blond owed everything to the brunette and,
being remotely related to her, had been brought up in the
brunette's house. Then the brunette, noticing the blond's
love for Mr. Verkhovensky, locked her own secret in her
heart and the blond, also, noticing the brunette's love for
him, locked her secret in hers. And thus all three of them,
pining away in mutual abnegation, remained silent, each with
his private secret locked in his heart, and that for twenty
years.

"Oh, what passion—what passion!" he cried, sobbing in the
most sincere ecstasy. "I saw her—the brunette's—beauty reach
full bloom; I watched her walking by me every day with my
heart bleeding because I had the impression that she was
ashamed that she was such a beauty. . . ." (Once he made
a slip of the tongue and said, "such a fatty" instead.)

But finally he had fled, leaving behind him that feverish,
twenty-year dream—*un rêve de vingt ans!*—and that was why
he was on the open road now. Then, with his head burning,
he started explaining to Mrs. Ulitin the meaning of their
"accidental but fateful meeting and their union forever and
ever."

Finally, terribly embarrassed, Mrs. Ulitin stood up, at which
point he tried to go down on his knees before her, and that
made the poor woman cry. It was getting dark and the two
of them had now spent several hours in the locked room.

"You'd better let me go into the other room now," she
mumbled, "or what will people think?"

He finally let her go, promising that he would go to bed
immediately. As he said good night to her, he complained
of a very bad headache. Mrs. Ulitin had left her bag with
the landlady when they had first entered the house, intending
to ask the woman to accommodate her for the night. But
she didn't get a chance to rest.

During the night Mr. Verkhovensky, who, as all his friends
knew, suffered from chronic stomach trouble, had a violent
attack, the usual result of nervous tension and emotional shock
in his case. Poor Mrs. Ulitin spent a sleepless night. In looking
after the invalid, she constantly had to go in and out of
the house, which involved going through the other room;
the landlady and the other travelers grumbled at this and
even began swearing when, toward morning, she decided to
light the samovar. During the worst moments, Mr. Ver-

khovensky was in a semiconscious state; sometimes he fancied that someone was lighting a samovar and that he was being given tea with raspberry jam and that something warm was being applied to his chest and his stomach. But he felt all the time that *she* was there, by his side, that it was *her* coming and going, lifting him from the bed and putting him back into it. Around three in the morning, he felt better, sat up, put his feet down, and without thinking of anything in particular, fell flat on the floor at her feet. This time, it wasn't a dramatic attempt to kneel before her—he simply let himself fall at her feet and started kissing the hem of her dress.

"Please, don't do that—don't do that," she muttered. "There's no reason—"

"My savior!" he said with his hands clasped prayerfully before him. "*Vous êtes noble comme une marquise!* I, I am no good! I have been dishonest all my life."

"Please, please—calm yourself."

"What I told you before was all lies—out of vanity, pretentiousness—all lies. I'm nothing but a parasite, a nonentity!"

The stomach upset had turned into a new fit of hysterical self-condemnation. I have already mentioned these fits in speaking of his letters to Mrs. Stavrogin. Now he suddenly remembered his previous day's meeting with Liza in the field.

"It was terrible. Something must have happened to her, and I didn't even inquire! I was preoccupied with myself! Ah, what happened to her? Have you heard anything of her?" he kept asking Mrs. Ulitin.

Then he swore he would never "betray" *her* (meaning Mrs. Stavrogin), that he would go back to her. "We" (that is, he and Mrs. Ulitin) "will pass by her door every day as she is getting into her carriage for her morning drive and we'll admire her discreetly. Oh, I wish she'd slapped my other cheek —I would love it so! Yes, I'd have turned the other cheek just as in those books of yours. Only now do I understand what is meant by turning the other cheek. I never understood it before!"

For Mrs. Ulitin, the two days that followed were the most terrible days of her life, and, even now, she cannot think of them without a shudder. Mr. Verkhovensky became so seriously ill that he couldn't take the steamer that arrived that day punctually at two. So, since she couldn't leave him by himself, she stayed too. She told me that he was rather pleased when the steamer left without them.

"Well, wonderful," he muttered, lying in bed. "I was afraid we'd leave. It's so nice here, better than anywhere else. You won't leave me, will you? No, I know you won't leave me!"

Actually it wasn't at all "nice" where they were. He didn't want to hear about the difficulties she had to face. He was living in a world of fantasy. He thought his sickness was just a brief and passing interlude and busied himself with planning how they'd go around peddling "those books of yours." He asked her to read him the gospel.

"I haven't read it for a long time—except just extracts, I mean. Someone might ask me something about it and I might give him the wrong answer. That wouldn't sound right. I really ought to prepare myself."

She sat by his side and opened a Bible.

"You read beautifully," he said, interrupting her after the very first line. "I see I wasn't mistaken about you!" he added obscurely and enthusiastically.

In general, he was in a state of constant enthusiasm. She read the Sermon on the Mount.

"*Assez, assez, mon enfant*, enough. Don't you think that *that* is enough?"

And exhausted, he closed his eyes. Yet, although he was very weak, he remained awake. She stood up to leave, thinking he wanted to sleep, but he stopped her.

"My dear, I have lied all my life. I never spoke for the sake of truth, only for my own sake, and although I always knew it, I only really see it now. Ah, where are the friends on whom I have inflicted my insulting friendship all my life? Ah, and all the rest—*savez-vous*, it is possible that I'm lying even now; indeed, I'm quite sure I am. The main trouble is that I believe myself even while I'm lying. The most difficult thing in life is to live without lying and—and not to believe in one's own lies. Yes, yes, that's exactly it! But wait—we'll come back to all that later. Ah, we're together, together now!" he added rapturously.

"Mr. Verkhovensky," she said shyly, "shouldn't we send to town for a doctor?"

He was terribly surprised.

"What for? *Est-ce que je suis malade?* What do we need outsiders for anyway? What will happen to us if they find out? No, no, we don't want any outsiders, just the two of us are sufficient!" He remained silent for a while and then said: "You know what, read me a bit more, anything you like, the first thing your eye falls upon."

She opened the book and read:

" 'And unto the Angel of the church of the Laodiceans—' "

"What's that? What is it? Where is it from?"

"It's from the Revelation."

"Oh, je m'en souviens, oui, l'Apocalypse, lisez, lisez! You opened it at random and this passage will tell us about our future. I want to know what lot you've drawn. Read, read—starting from that angel."

" 'And unto the Angel of the church of the Laodiceans write: These things saith the Amen, the faithful and true witness, the beginning of the creation of God; I know thy works, that thou art neither cold nor hot; I would thou wert cold and hot. So then because thou art lukewarm, and neither cold nor hot, I will spew thee out of my mouth. Because thou sayest, I am rich, and increased with goods and have need of nothing: and thou knowest not that thou art wretched, and miserable, and poor, and blind, and naked.' "

"That—so that's what you've stumbled upon in your book!" he cried, sitting up, his eyes sparkling. "I didn't know that great passage! Did you hear that? Rather cold, rather cold than lukewarm, rather than *only* warm. Oh, I'll prove it to them! Only don't leave me—don't leave me all alone! We'll prove it, we'll prove it!"

"But I'm not leaving you, Mr. Verkhovensky, I'll never leave you, sir!" she said, taking his hands and pressing them against her heart as she looked at him with her eyes filled with tears.

His lips and chin began to twitch. "I was awfully sorry for him at that moment," she told me later.

"But still, Mr. Verkhovensky, what should we do now? Shouldn't I let some friend of yours know? Some relative maybe?"

But that scared him so much that she was sorry she'd brought it up. Trembling and shaking, he beseeched her not to call anyone, not to do anything. He made her promise him to send for "no one, but no one! Just the two of us. *Nous partirons ensemble.*"

She also had trouble from the landlords. They began to worry and grumble, pestering Mrs. Ulitin. She paid them and saw to it that they caught a glimpse of the bills she had. That mollified them temporarily, although the landlord demanded to see Mr. Verkhovensky's "document." The sick man, smiling condescendingly, pointed to his small bag in which Mrs. Ulitin found the certificate of his resignation from the university, which had served him as an identification paper for many, many years. However, even after that, the landlord kept repeating that "still the gentleman should be moved out of here somewhere, because this ain't no hospital and if he died we'd never hear the end of it." Mrs. Ulitin spoke to him about sending for a doctor, but it appeared that sending to town for one would be expensive and he suggested that the best thing would be to forget about a doctor once and for all. So she returned to her invalid rather dejected. Meanwhile, Mr. Verkhovensky was growing weaker and weaker.

"Now I want you to read me that passage about the swine," he said suddenly.

"What did you say, sir?" Mrs. Ulitin said. For some reason she was frightened by his request.

"About the swine—why, it's in this book all right—*les cochons*. I remember about the demons going into the pigs and getting drowned, the lot of them. Read me that passage, please. I'll tell you why later. I want to remember it verbatim. Yes, I want it word for word."

Mrs. Ulitin knew her gospels well and it took her no time to find what he wanted—the passage in St. Luke that I've used as an epigraph to my entire chronicle. I quote it here again:

" 'And there was there a herd of many swine feeding on the mountain: and they besought him that he would suffer them to enter into them. And he suffered them. Then went the devils out of the man, and entered into the swine; and the herd ran violently down a steep place into the lake, and were choked. When they that fed them saw what was done, they fled, and went and told it in the city and in the country. Then they went out to see what was done; and came to Jesus, and found the man, out of whom the devils were departed, sitting at the feet of Jesus, clothed, and in his right mind: and they were afraid.' "

"My dear," Mr. Verkhovensky said in great agitation, "*savez-vous*, this is a wonderful, an extraordinary passage and it has been a stumbling block to me *dans ce livre*, all my life . . . so I remember the passage from when I was a boy. But now, an idea has occurred to me, *une comparaison*. Ah, so *discussion of epigraph (Swines,*

many thoughts keep crowding into my head. You see, it is just like our Russia. Those devils or demons coming out of the sick and entering into the swine—they are all the festering sores, all the poisonous vapors, all the filth, all the demons and the petty devils accumulated for centuries and centuries in our great, dear, sick Russia, *cette Russie que j'aimais toujours!* But the Great Idea and the Great Will protects her from up above, just as it did that other madman possessed by demons; and all those demons, all that filth festering on the surface, will themselves beg to be allowed to enter the swine. Indeed, they may have entered them already! It's *us,* us and the others—my son Peter and those around him; and we'll hurl ourselves from the cliff into the sea and I'll be the first perhaps, and all of us, mad and raving, will drown and it will serve us right because that's all we're fit for. But the sick man will recover and will sit at the feet of Jesus and they will look at him in surprise. You'll understand it all in time, my dear, but it preoccupies me terribly now. *Vous comprendrez après— Nous comprendrons ensemble."*

He grew delirious and later became unconscious, and remained like that all the next day. Mrs. Ulitin sat by his side and cried. She had hardly slept for two nights and avoided coming within sight of the landlords. She had a feeling they were up to something. Deliverance came only on the third day. Mr. Verkhovensky recovered consciousness that morning and gave her his hand. She crossed herself as hope returned to her. He wanted to look out of the window.

"Tiens, un lac! Oh God, to think I hadn't noticed it!"

At that moment a carriage came rumbling along the road and stopped by the door. A frantic bustle started in the house.

III

Mrs. Stavrogin arrived in a four-seated carriage drawn by four horses, accompanied by Dasha Shatov and two footmen. This miracle is easily explained: the day after he met Mr. Verkhovensky, Anisim was in town. He dropped in to visit his friends in the Stavrogins' servants' quarters and told them that he'd met Mr. Verkhovensky all by himself in a village, that some peasants had seen him walking there on foot, that afterward he'd left for Spasov by way of Ustievo, this time in the company of Mrs. Ulitin. Since the servants knew that Mrs. Stavrogin was very worried and had been making all possible inquiries in trying to find her runaway friend, they immediately reported to her what Anisim had told them. She had him called in and listened to his story, paying special attention to the part about Mr. Verkhovensky's driving to Ustievo in the company of Mrs. Ulitin. After that, she immediately set out for Ustievo herself. She had no idea he was ill.

Her stern and imperious tone subdued even the landlords. She had only stopped to make inquiries, for she was convinced that by then Mr. Verkhovensky had been in Spasov for a long time; but when she learned that he hadn't left, she stepped into the house in great agitation.

"Well, where is he? Ah, there you are!" she shouted on catching sight of Mrs. Ulitin, who at that moment appeared in the doorway. "I see immediately by your shameless face that you are that woman! Get out of my sight, you dirty slut! I want you out of this house at once! I want her out of here. Mark my words, I'll have her locked up in jail for the rest of her life. In the meantime, I want her locked up in one of those cottages in the courtyard, until they move her to the town jail. And you, landlord—don't you dare let anyone in while I'm here. I'm Mrs. Stavrogin and I'm occupying the whole house. Just you wait, my beauty, you'll give me a full account of everything, yet!"

The familiar voice gave Mr. Verkhovensky a terrible shock. He began to tremble. But she had already stepped behind the partition and pulled up a chair with her foot. Leaning back in it, her eyes flashing angrily, she shouted to Dasha:

"I want you out of here for a moment. Go and wait in the other room. Why this curiosity? And close that door behind you!"

She remained silent for some time looking closely into his face with the expression of a bird of prey.

"Well, how are you, Stepan? Have you had a nice fling?" she suddenly threw at him with ferocious sarcasm.

"*Chère,*" he murmured helplessly, not realizing what he was saying, "I found what real life in Russia is like *et je prêcherai l'Evangile*—"

"Oh, how shameless and ungrateful can a man be!" she cried, clasping her hands. "It wasn't enough for you to disgrace me; you had to get involved with—oh, you dirty old libertine!"

"*Chère* . . ." His voice failed him and, unable to utter another sound, he just stared at her in terror.

"Who is *she*?"

"She's an angel—*c'était plus qu'un ange pour moi*. For the whole night, she—oh, please don't shout; don't frighten her, *chère, chère*—"

Mrs. Stavrogin suddenly leaped up noisily from her chair and let out a piercing cry.

"Water! Water!" she called in a terror-stricken voice.

He came to, but she was still trembling and pale as she looked into his distorted face. She had only then realized how sick he was.

"Dasha!" she called and then whispered to her, "Send immediately for a doctor—get Saltzfisch. Let Egörich set out at once. Tell him to order horses here and come back in one of our other carriages. Tell him I want him back here by tonight."

Dasha hurried off to do what she was told. Mr. Verkhovensky stared at Mrs. Stavrogin fixedly. He looked frightened. His lips were trembling.

"Wait, Stepan, wait, my dear," she said, trying to reassure him, as though he were a small child. "Wait, Dasha'll come back and—oh, my God! Hey, landlady. Well, come here then—hurry up, for heaven's sake!"

In her impatience she herself rushed off to find the landlady.

"I want *her* back! I mean *that* woman! I want her back here immediately!"

Luckily Mrs. Ulitin had only just left the house with her suitcase and her bag of gospels. They stopped her and sent her back. She was so scared that all her limbs were jerking. Mrs. Stavrogin took hold of her arm like a hawk grabbing a chick and dragged her violently toward Mr. Verkhovensky's bedside.

"Well, here she is—you can have her. I haven't eaten her, you know. I'm sure you thought I'd eaten her."

He seized Mrs. Stavrogin's hand, pressed it against his eyes, and cried. He cried and sobbed fitfully, hysterically.

"Well, well, calm yourself, calm yourself, my dear. Oh, my dear," she shouted furiously. "Ah, you, my tormentor, my eternal tormentor—"

"My dear," Mr. Verkhovensky managed to say at last, addressing Mrs. Ulitin, "would you please wait over there for a moment? I must say something here—"

Mrs. Ulitin hurriedly left the room.

"*Chère*, darling, darling—" he gasped.

"Wait, Stepan, wait—rest a bit. Here's some water for you. But wait, I tell you!"

She sat down on the chair again. He held her hand as tightly as he could. She wouldn't let him talk for a long time. He drew her hand to his lips and started kissing it. She clenched her teeth, looking away into a corner.

"I have loved you." The words finally burst from him, and she'd never heard him say anything like it, never heard him speak in that tone.

"Hm . . ." she growled in reply.

"I have loved you all my life, for *vingt ans*!"

She still said nothing. Two or three minutes went by.

"But that didn't stop you, when you were preparing to marry Dasha, from sprinkling yourself with perfume," she said suddenly, in a threatening whisper that caused Mr. Verkhovensky to stare at her in frightened amazement. "And do you remember that cigar?"

"Dear—" Mr. Verkhovensky lisped in terror.

"That cigar, in the evening, by the window, with the moon shining—after the summerhouse, in Skvoreshniki, don't you remember? Don't you? Don't you?" she shouted. Leaping up from her chair, she took hold of his pillow and shook it and his head, which was resting on it. "Do you remember now, you empty-headed, fickle, dishonorable creature? Always so horribly, horribly irresponsible!" she hissed furiously, just managing not to scream. At last she let go of the pillow and his head, covered her face with her hands, and sank into the chair. "Enough!" she said cuttingly, straightening herself up. "The twenty years that are gone cannot be brought back. I'm a fool myself."

"*Je vous aimais.*"

"How long will you go on repeating your *aimais, aimais, aimais?* Enough of that!" She jumped up again. "And if you don't go to sleep immediately, I—you need rest. I want you to go to sleep at once. Come, close your eyes. Ah God, maybe he wants his lunch? What can you eat? What does he eat? Ah God, where is that woman? Where's she disappeared to?"

She was about to start a commotion about feeding him, but

Mr. Verkhovensky murmured in a weak voice that he would indeed like to sleep for an hour or so and then—*"un bouillon, un thé—enfin, je suis si heureux."* He stretched himself out and it looked as though he'd really fallen asleep (probably he was faking). Mrs. Stavrogin waited for a while, then got up and tiptoed to the other side of the partition.

She installed herself in the landlords' room, chasing the landlords out, and told Dasha to call *that* woman. Then a stern interrogation began.

"Now tell me all about it, my good woman. All right, come—sit down here next to me."

"I met Mr. Verkhovensky—"

"Wait—be quiet. I warn you—if I find you've lied to me or even that you've tried to keep something to yourself, I'll dig you out of the earth, wherever you may be hiding, and make you pay for it. Well then?"

"I met Mr. Verkhovensky," Mrs. Ulitin said, gasping for breath, "well, just as soon as I got to Khatovo, ma'am—"

"Wait—shut up. Don't just rattle it all off like that. To start with, who on earth are you and where do you come from?"

Mrs. Ulitin told her very briefly about herself, starting from Sevastopol. Mrs. Stavrogin listened to her in silence, sitting stiffly in her chair and looking sternly and stubbornly into Mrs. Ulitin's eyes as she talked.

"Are you scared of me or something? Why do you keep looking at the floor all the time? I like people who look me straight in the face and aren't afraid to talk back to me. Well—go on."

Mrs. Ulitin told her about their meeting, about the gospels, about Mr. Verkhovensky's offering vodka to the peasant woman—

"That's right, that's right, don't leave anything out," Mrs. Stavrogin said to encourage her.

Finally Mrs. Ulitin told her how they had driven to this place and how Mr. Verkhovensky, who was quite ill even then, had kept talking and talking and how, upon their arrival at this place, he had told her "his life story, from the very start, you see, and he kept telling it for several hours without rest."

"What did he tell you about his life?"

Mrs. Ulitin's face went blank and she suddenly started stuttering.

"I couldn't repeat what he said, ma'am—I don't know how," she said, on the verge of tears. "Anyway, I hardly understood anything of it."

"You're lying. You must have understood something."

"He kept talking about some beautiful, black-haired lady, ma'am," Mrs. Ulitin said, blushing terribly as she looked at Mrs. Stavrogin's fairish hair and reflected that she couldn't possibly be Mr. Verkhovensky's sultry "brunette."

"Black-haired, eh? Well—what did he actually tell you?"

"That that lady, who was very wealthy and distinguished, was in love with him—Mr. Verkhovensky, I mean—all her life, for twenty whole years, but that she never dared to tell him and was ashamed, you see, because she was such a fatty."

"Ah, the idiot," Mrs. Stavrogin said, cutting her off firmly, although she was looking dreamily into space.

Mrs. Ulitin was really crying now.

"I can't tell it cleverly, ma'am, because I myself was very frightened for him and I couldn't understand because he's such an intelligent gentleman—"

"A goose like you is no judge of intelligence. Did he propose marriage to you?"

Mrs. Ulitin began to shake.

"Did he fall in love with you? Speak up! Did he offer to marry you?" Mrs. Stavrogin said, raising her voice.

"Yes, he almost did, ma'am—but I didn't take it seriously. It was just because he was ill, ma'am," Mrs. Ulitin said, looking with determination into Mrs. Stavrogin's face.

"What's your first name?"

"Sofia, ma'am."

"Well, Sofia, let me warn you, then, that he is the most despicable, the most irresponsible man in the world. Ah, dear God! You must think I'm a monster." The woman stared at her, her eyes popping out. "Yes, a monster and a tyrant who has poisoned his life, right?"

"How could I, ma'am, since you're crying yourself?"

It was true: tears actually stood in Mrs. Stavrogin's eyes.

"All right then, all right, sit down and don't be afraid. Look into my eyes again. Why are you blushing, woman? Hey, Dasha—come over here and have a look at her. Tell me, Dasha—do you think this woman has a pure heart?"

And to Mrs. Ulitin's surprise (and perhaps alarm), Mrs. Stavrogin suddenly patted her cheek.

"It's a pity you're such a fool. You're too old to be so foolish. Never mind, my dear, I'll take you in hand now. I can see it was all just nonsense. You can live in one of those huts in the courtyard in the meantime and I'll pay for everything—your meals too—and you wait there till I send for you."

Mrs. Ulitin shyly stammered something to the effect that she had to be somewhere soon and was in rather a hurry.

"You're in no hurry to get anywhere. I'll buy all your books, so you can just stay around here and relax. Don't argue. You know very well that if I hadn't come, you wouldn't have left him anyway—or would you?"

"I'd never have left Mr. Verkhovensky, not for anything in the world," Mrs. Ulitin said quietly but firmly, wiping her eyes.

Dr. Salzfisch was brought in late at night. He was a very respectable little old man and an experienced practitioner who had recently resigned his government post because he felt his superiors were thwarting his ambitions. Mrs. Stavrogin had immediately made him her protégé. He carefully examined Mr. Verkhovensky and asked him a lot of questions. Then he cautiously informed Mrs. Stavrogin that "the patient's state is critical as a result of complications" and that she should be prepared for anything, "including even the worst." Mrs. Stavrogin, who in twenty years had never thought that anything grave or decisive could be connected with Stepan Verkhovensky, was deeply shocked and turned pale.

"Is it possible that there's no hope?"

"I wouldn't say there was no hope at all, ma'am, however . . ."

She didn't go to bed at all that night, just sitting and waiting for the morning. As soon as the sick man opened his eyes—he had not so far lapsed into a coma, although he was growing weaker every hour—she told him in her most determined tone:

"Listen, Stepan, I think we must anticipate every possibility. I've sent for a priest."

Knowing his convictions, she was very much afraid he would refuse. He looked at her in great surprise.

"Rubbish, rubbish!" she cried, taking his surprised expression for a refusal. "We're not playing games now. We've fooled around long enough!"

"But—but is it that bad?"

Absently, he complied. In general, as I learned with amazement from Mrs. Stavrogin later, he was not in the least afraid of dying. Perhaps he simply didn't believe he was dying and considered his illness merely a minor complaint.

He confessed and took the last sacrament very readily. Everyone, including Mrs. Ulitin and the servants, came to visit his bedside now that he had received the sacrament. They all tried hard to hold back their tears as they looked at his drawn, exhausted, bloodless face and quivering lips.

"Oui, mes amis, I'm only surprised that you should take all this trouble for me. I'm sure I'll be up tomorrow and we'll be on our way. . . . *Toute cette cérémonie* to which, of course, I pay all due respect, was . . ."

"I'd like you to remain with the patient, Father," Mrs. Stavrogin said, stopping the priest as he was about to discard his surplice. "As soon as they bring in tea, I'd like you to talk to him about divine matters, to sustain his faith."

The priest talked. All the others sat or stood around the patient's bed.

"In our sinful times," the priest started smoothly, holding his teacup in his hand, "faith in the Almighty is the only refuge of the human race from all the vicissitudes and hardships of life, as well as its only hope of the eternal bliss promised to the righteous. . . ."

Mr. Verkhovensky suddenly became animated and a subtle smile appeared on his lips.

"Mon père, je vous remercie, vous êtes bien bon, mais . . ."

"There's no *mais,* no *mais* at all!" Mrs. Stavrogin cried, leaping up from her chair, "Ah, Father, he's the sort of . . . the sort of man that—you'll have to start all over again in an hour, confession and all. . . . That's the sort of man he is."

Mr. Verkhovensky suppressed a smile.

"Friends," he said, "I need God if only because He is the only Being who is capable of loving eternally. . . ."

Whether he had really found faith or whether the solemn rite of the sacrament had simply impressed him and touched his artistic nature, he uttered very firmly and, I understand, with great conviction, a few statements that directly contradicted his former convictions.

"My immortality is necessary if only because God would

not wish to do anything unjust and put out the flame of love once it was kindled in my heart. And what is more precious than love? Love is higher than existence—love is the crown of existence, so how can existence not be subordinate to love? Since I have come to love Him and am happy because of this love, how could He extinguish me and my happiness and turn me into a zero? If God exists, then I, too, am immortal! *Voilà ma profession de foi*—"

"There is God—believe me, Stepan, I know," Mrs. Stavrogin said beseechingly. "Forget about your silly games for this once!"

She apparently hadn't quite understood his *profession de foi*.

"My dear," he said, becoming more and more animated, although his voice kept breaking, "the moment I—I understood that—you know, about turning the other cheek, I—well, I understood something else at the same time. . . . *J'ai menti toute ma vie*, all, all my life! And I would've liked— But I'm sure that tomorrow we'll all be on our way."

Mrs. Stavrogin began to cry. His eyes were searching for someone.

"Here she is for you!" She seized Mrs. Ulitin by the arm and pulled her toward the bed. He smiled ecstatically.

"Oh, I would have liked so much to live my life over again!" he cried with a great influx of energy. "Each minute, each second of life must be bliss—must, yes, must! It's the duty of man himself to see that it is. This is the law—a hidden law, but it is certainly there. Oh, how I'd have liked to see my Peter and the rest of them, and Shatov!"

Let me note here that none of them, neither his sister Dasha nor Mrs. Stavrogin, nor even Dr. Salzfisch, the last to arrive from town, knew anything about what had happened to Shatov.

Mr. Verkhovensky was working himself up into a state of violent agitation that was too much for his waning strength.

"Just the constant realization that there exists something infinitely more just and happy than I is enough to fill me with a limitless joy and pride, whatever I may be and whatever I may have done! Much more than he needs happiness for himself, man needs to know and to believe at every moment of his life that somewhere there is an absolute and assured happiness for everyone, including himself. The law of human existence consists of man's always having something infinitely great to worship. If men were deprived of this idea of infinite greatness, they wouldn't want to live and would die of despair. The infinite and the limitless are just as necessary to man as is the little planet on which he lives. . . . Ah, my friends, hail the Great Idea, the eternal, limitless Great Idea! Every man, whoever he may be, needs to bow before the fact that the Great Idea exists. Even the most stupid man needs something great. Peter—oh, how much I want to see them all again! They don't know that the eternal Great Idea dwells in them too!"

Dr. Salzfisch, who had been out of the room, came in at this point and was horrified. He broke up the meeting, sent them all out, and insisted that the sick man should not be excited.

Three days later, Stepan Verkhovensky died. But he was completely unconscious. He went quietly, like a candle guttering out. Mrs. Stavrogin had a requiem sung, and then the body of her poor friend was transported to Skvoreshniki. He was buried in the churchyard there, and a marble slab already marks his grave. The inscription and the railing will be added next spring.

Mrs. Stavrogin stayed out of town eight days. She returned in her carriage with Mrs. Ulitin sitting next to her, and it seems she will remain with her indefinitely. I must note here that when Mr. Verkhovensky finally lost consciousness—which happened that same morning—Mrs. Stavrogin immediately sent Mrs. Ulitin out of the house again and insisted on nursing him herself until the very end. But she had her called as soon as he breathed his last. And she wouldn't listen to any protests from Mrs. Ulitin, who was extremely alarmed by her offer—or rather order—to come and settle in Skvoreshniki for good.

"Nonsense! I myself will go around with you selling the gospels. I don't have anyone left in the world now."

"But you have a son," Dr. Salzfisch remarked.

"I have no son," Mrs. Stavrogin said sharply. And that turned out to be a prophetic statement.

chapter 8

EPILOGUE

All the crimes and outrages came to light surprisingly quickly, much sooner than Peter Verkhovensky had expected.

To begin with, on the night her husband was killed the poor wretched Mary awoke just before dawn, found that he wasn't home, and became frantic. The woman who had been sent by Mrs. Virginsky and had spent the night there was unable to calm her and, as soon as it became light, ran over to get Mrs. Virginsky herself, having convinced Mary that the midwife knew where Shatov was and when he would return. By that time, Mrs. Virginsky was worried too: her husband had told her about the nocturnal party in Skvoreshniki.

Virginsky had returned home between ten and eleven at night, in a frightful state. He had immediately thrown himself on his bed, wringing his hands and muttering between convulsive sobs, "It wasn't right, it wasn't right, it wasn't right at all. . . ." Finally, of course, he told everything to his wife, who had pressed him hard on the subject. However, he told only her. She left him in bed, telling him sternly that, if he had to whimper, he should do it into the pillow so he wouldn't be heard, and that he'd be a real fool if he didn't manage to pull himself together by the next day and show no sign of what had happened. It made her think, however, and she started to prepare for an emergency: putting some papers, books, and leaflets in a safe place and destroying some others. Then she decided that she herself, her sister, her aunt, the roly-poly girl student, and even her long-eared brother, Shigalov, had really nothing much to fear. So when, in the morning, the woman from Mary's came for her, she went with her without hesitation. Anyway, she was eager to find out whether what her husband had told her in a feverish whisper last night had come about—that is, whether Peter's reliance on Kirilov's

681

suicide, which would benefit them all, had been justified.

But she arrived at Mary's too late. Having sent off the woman, Mary, left alone, had been unable to bear waiting. She slipped out of bed, pulled on the first piece of clothing she could find—it turned out to be something very light and quite unsuitable for the time of year—and went stumbling over to Kirilov's cottage, thinking that he might know more about Shatov's whereabouts than anyone else.

It is easy to imagine the effect on a woman who had just been through a difficult confinement of what she saw there. In her panic, she even failed to see Kirilov's suicide note, although it had been deliberately left in full view. She rushed back to Shatov's room, grabbed the baby, and went out into the street carrying him in her arms. It was a raw and misty morning. The street was completely deserted. She started running, her feet squishing in the deep, cold mud. Then, breathless, she began banging at the doors of houses. At the first house, they wouldn't open; in the second, it took them so long to answer that she gave up and rushed on to the third. This house belonged to a merchant called Titov. Here she caused quite an uproar by screaming, "They've just killed my husband!"

The Titovs knew Shatov and had heard something of his background, and they were horrified to see his wife running around in that weather just a few hours after her delivery, dressed like that and with a scantily covered newborn baby in her arms. At first they decided she must be delirious because they couldn't understand from what she said who had been killed—Kirilov or her husband. When Mary realized that they didn't believe her, she turned away and started to run farther. They had to hold her back by force, while she fought to get loose and shouted. Titov went over to Kirilov's cottage, and within a couple of hours Kirilov's suicide and his last note were known to the whole town.

The police tried to question Mary, who was still conscious, asking her how she could have known about Shatov's death without reading Kirilov's note, but they could make no headway with her. She only kept shouting, "Since that one's been killed, my husband has too—they were together, the two of them!"

By midday she lost consciousness and remained unconscious until her death three days later. The baby had caught a chill, too, and died even before she did.

Mrs. Virginsky, not finding Mary and the baby in Shatov's room, realized that things were not going well and was on the point of rushing back home. But she stopped at the gate and sent the woman to inquire from "the gentleman who lives in that cottage in the yard whether Mrs. Shatov wasn't there by any chance." The woman came back yelling like mad, her cries resounding all down the street. Mrs. Virginsky managed to quiet her down and convince her to keep what she had seen in the cottage to herself by using the classical argument, "Say nothing if you don't want them to suspect you and get you into trouble for nothing." Then she hurried back home.

Naturally, she was questioned that very morning, having attended Mrs. Shatov's confinement. But they didn't get very far with her. She reported to them very coolly and composedly everything she had seen and heard at Shatov's house. But she said she knew nothing about Kirilov or any other story and that, indeed, it made no sense to her at all.

The whole thing caused a fantastic commotion in our town. Another shocking murder! By now, it was becoming evident that a secret society of assassins, arsonists, revolutionaries, and mutineers existed in our midst. Liza's terrible death, the murder of Stavrogin's wife, the behavior of Stavrogin himself, the benefit performance for the needy governesses, the arson, the loose behavior of Mrs. von Lembke's entourage—they even insisted on seeing a mystery in the disappearance of old Stepan Verkhovensky. Rumors circulated about Nikolai Stavrogin. By the end of the day, Peter Verkhovensky's absence also became known, but strangely enough, he was spoken of least of all. The person mentioned most that day was "that Senator."

Throughout the morning a crowd gathered before Filipov's house, where Shatov and Kirilov had lived. The police were indeed misled by Kirilov's note—they believed that Shatov had been murdered by Kirilov, who then had committed suicide. But although the authorities were misguided, they weren't completely confused. The vagueness of the word "park," upon which Peter had relied so heavily to delay the investigation, didn't deceive anyone. The police thought of Skvoreshniki immediately, although not especially because of the word "park" in Kirilov's note nor because it was the only park in the vicinity of our town, but, by a sort of instinct, because many of the horrors that had occurred in the past few weeks were in one way or another connected with Skvor-eshniki. At least, that's the most likely explanation in my personal opinion. (Let me note here that early in the morning of the day after Shatov was killed, Mrs. Stavrogin, who hadn't heard a thing, left town in pursuit of Mr. Verkhovensky.)

Shatov's body was found in the pond in the evening of that same day, the police having been led to it by certain clues, including the discovery of Shatov's cap on the spot where the murder had taken place, a crude oversight on the part of the murderers. The autopsy and certain observations led to the conclusion that Kirilov couldn't possibly have done it without accomplices. It became clear then that there existed a political society of which both Shatov and Kirilov had been members and which was connected with the leaflets.

So who could the accomplices have been? That day no one even thought of our local Five. It was learned that Kirilov had kept to himself all the time, indeed, to such an extent that Fedka, for whom the police had been searching everywhere, had been able to spend his nights safely in his place. Everyone was quite frustrated because it seemed impossible at first to find any connecting link in all that terrible tangle.

It is really difficult to imagine what other conclusions, what new absurdities, our panic-stricken citizens might have thought up had the mystery not been completely solved by the next day, thanks to Lyamshin.

He broke down. Before he left, despite his reassurances to Erkel, Peter had been afraid that something like this would happen. Left to Tolkachenko's and later to Erkel's super-vision, Lyamshin spent all the following day in bed, com-pletely immobile, facing the wall, hardly answering when spoken to. Thus, he knew nothing about what was going on in town. But Tolkachenko, who was supposed to watch him, knew very well what was going on and by evening he de-cided to abandon the task entrusted to him by Peter and "absent himself briefly from the town and go to the country" —that is, to take to his heels. So he too lost his head, and it looked as if Erkel had been right when he had predicted that they all would. By the way, Liputin had also vanished, even before Tolkachenko—indeed, before midday—but the police didn't find out about his disappearance until the next evening when they arrived at his house and interrogated his family, who although worried by his absence had kept it secret.

But let's return to Lyamshin. As soon as he was left alone
—Erkel, relying upon Tolkachenko, had left even earlier—
he immediately rushed out of the house and of course heard
what was being said all over town. Without thinking any
further, he took to his heels, running straight ahead of him.
But the night was completely black and flight seemed so
difficult and frightening that, after he had gone two or three
blocks, he returned home and locked himself in for the night.
Apparently, at daybreak he attempted to kill himself, but
failed. After that he held out, sitting locked in his house until
noon or a little after. Then he suddenly jumped up and ran
off to the police.

They say that he fell to his knees, sobbed, squealed, and
kissed the ground, shouting that he was unworthy to kiss even
the boots of the public servants who stood there. They calmed
him and even treated him quite kindly. I understand that his
interrogation lasted about three hours. He told them everything he knew, every detail, volunteering information, anticipating, even telling them things in which they weren't
interested. It turned out that he knew plenty and was able
to give them an accurate picture of the whole business. It
came to light now that the tragedy involving Shatov and
Kirilov, the arson, the death of the Lebyatkins, and so on,
were all only subsidiary acts in the implementation of the
master plan. Behind it all stood Peter Verkhovensky with his
secret organization, the Movement, the mysterious network.
When asked what had been the point of all those crimes and
outrages, Lyamshin explained that they were trying "systematically to undermine the foundations of the existing order, to
bring about the disintegration of the social structure and the
collapse of all moral values, which would cause general
demoralization and confusion. Then the broken, decaying
society, sick and in full ferment, cynical and godless, but
thirsting for some guiding idea and for self-preservation,
could be taken over when the banner of revolution was raised,
making use of the vast network of Fives, which, in the meantime, would have recruited more and more new members
and probed the weak spots for their attacks." He said he
believed that, in our town, Peter Verkhovensky had only been
trying to test, for the first time, the ability of the organization to wreak havoc and that the results would indicate to him
what his further program should be and what plan of action
should be given the other Fives. That, Lyamshin pointed out,

was only his personal guess, of course, but they shouldn't fail to remember and take into consideration his frankness and his eagerness to expose the conspiracy and realize that he could be of service to them in the future too. When they asked him to give his estimate of the number of Fives in existence, he replied that there were very many of them— that indeed, the whole of Russia was crisscrossed by the network, and although he had nothing to support his estimate, I'm certain he was absolutely sincere in making it. He produced only a printed program of the Movement that had been published abroad and a rough draft of a plan for further action written in Peter Verkhovensky's own hand. It turned out that when he had spoken of "undermining the foundations" of society, Lyamshin had been quoting verbatim, almost pausing at the periods and commas, although he had asserted that he was just giving his personal conjectures. About Julie von Lembke, he rather ridiculously volunteered the opinion that "she was quite innocent—they just used her for their own purposes." What was more remarkable was that he insisted that Nikolai Stavrogin had no connection whatever with the Movement or with Peter Verkhovensky. (Lyamshin had no inkling of Verkhovensky's ridiculous plans for Stavrogin's future.) According to Lyamshin, the murder of the Lebyatkins had been organized by Verkhovensky without Stavrogin's knowledge because he wanted to compromise Stavrogin and thus gain control over him. But then, instead of the gratitude that Verkhovensky rather naïvely expected, he had met with nothing but indignation and despair from that highly honorable man. He ended his testimony by slipping in a hurried hint that Stavrogin was really a very important personage; that there was some mystery about the man; that he went around, one might say, incognito; that he was working for high government agencies; and that he would soon be back from Petersburg (Lyamshin had no doubt that Stavrogin was in Petersburg), but that, when he came, he would appear in a completely different light and under different circumstances and in the company of some very powerful people of whom they would hear soon enough. All that, he said, he had heard from Peter Verkhovensky himself, "the secret enemy of Nikolai Stavrogin."

It is well to note that, two months later, Lyamshin admitted that earlier he had deliberately tried to shield Stavrogin, counting on his protection and hoping that Stavrogin could get his sentence reduced a couple of notches and would provide him with money and a letter of recommendation when Lyamshin was sent to do his stretch in Siberia. From this admission we can gauge what a highly exaggerated idea of Nikolai Stavrogin's power he had.

That same day, of course, they also arrested Virginsky and, while they were at it, the rest of his household. (By now, Mrs. Virginsky, her sister, and the roly-poly girl student have long since been released; and I've heard that Shigalov, who doesn't fit into any category of political criminal, will also be released any day now, although this is still only a rumor.) Virginsky immediately confessed everything. When they came for him, he was in bed with a fever. I've been told he was almost relieved. "Ah, it's as if they'd lifted a weight from my heart!" he's supposed to have said. I hear that he is now cooperating with the authorities willingly, but with great dignity; that he refuses to give up his "bright hopes," but also rejects such means of reaching them as "the road of political action" as opposed to the road of social evolution into which he was drawn "by the whirl of an unfortunate combination of circumstances." In the part he played in the murder, certain circumstances mitigating his involvement have come to light, and apparently he can reckon on a lighter sentence. At least, that's the opinion prevalent in our town.

But it is unlikely that any leniency will be shown toward Erkel. From the moment of his arrest, Erkel was tight-lipped and, if he said anything at all, it was only to try and mislead the police. No one has ever heard a word of regret out of him. At the same time, however, even the severest investigators couldn't help feeling a certain sympathy for him, because of his youth and his helplessness and because he was so obviously nothing but a young fanatic used by a political manipulator. Most of all, they were touched by the fact that he was sending his mother more than half his scanty army pay. His mother is in town now. She's a sick woman, prematurely aged. She goes around crying and begging the authorities to spare her boy. Whatever one may say, many among us are very sorry for Erkel.

Liputin managed to get to Petersburg and was only picked up two weeks later. It is difficult to explain what happened to him. They say he had a passport in another name, an excellent opportunity to escape abroad, and was carrying a substantial sum of money. But for some reason he just stayed in Petersburg. He tried to trace Stavrogin and Peter Verkhovensky at first, but then gave up and suddenly took to the bottle. He drank without restraint and lost track of what was going on around him. He was picked up in a brothel in a state of complete stupor. There is a rumor that now he displays a lot of spirit at the questionings, lies to the authorities, and is preparing himself solemnly and hopefully (at least, so they say) for the trial, where he intends to deliver a speech.

Tolkachenko, caught somewhere in our district about ten days after he'd fled town, is much more cooperative with the authorities than Liputin. He doesn't lie or evade questions, tells everything he knows, doesn't try to exculpate himself, humbly acknowledges his guilt—and yet, he also exhibits a tendency to show off, and talks willingly and profusely when he has a chance to display his "understanding of the people" and of the revolutionary elements (whatever that may mean) among them. Like Liputin, he intends to make a speech at his trial. Indeed, strangely enough, neither he nor Liputin seems very frightened at the prospect before them.

I repeat, the case is not yet settled by any means. Now, three months later, our local society has rested and recuperated, and people have developed their own opinions. Some even go so far as to consider Peter Verkhovensky a kind of genius or at least "a man with certain traits of genius." As they say in the club, raising a finger toward the ceiling, "Ah, what an organizer!" But it is really quite harmless and, after all, only relatively few people say that sort of thing. Other people, on the contrary, without denying his sharpness, point out that it is combined with a complete lack of grasp of the actual situation, with a crippling predilection for abstract schemes, and with a freakishly lopsided mental development that results in shallowness of thought. And when it comes to his moral sense, people stop arguing—they all agree.

Whom else should I mention here? Maurice Drozdov soon left our town for some unknown destination. Old Mrs. Drozdov took refuge in a second childhood. And I suppose I must record another rather grim story. I will limit myself to the main facts.

Upon her return, Mrs. Stavrogin stopped at her town house. She was shocked when she heard everything that had been learned during her absence. That evening she locked herself in. Everyone in the household had retired to bed exhausted.

In the morning, a maid handed Dasha a letter. The maid wore a mysterious expression. She told Dasha that the letter had arrived late the night before, after Dasha had gone to bed, and that she hadn't dared to waken her. The letter had not come by mail—some unknown man had handed it to the footman Alexei at Skvoreshniki and he had driven to town and handed it to the maid, then had immediately driven back to Skvoreshniki.

For a long time, Dasha looked at the letter, not daring to unseal it. She knew it was from Nikolai Stavrogin. She read and reread what was written on the envelope: "For Miss Dasha Shatov, % Alexei—Secret."

Here is that letter. I quote it verbatim, without correcting any mistakes in the style of that Russian gentleman who had not quite mastered Russian letters, despite his European culture.

DEAR DASHA,

Once you said you'd like to be my "nurse" and made me promise to send for you. I'm leaving in two days and not coming back. Do you want to come?

Last year, just like Herzen, I registered as a citizen of the Canton of Uri and no one knows about it. I already have a small house there. I also have twenty thousand rubles. We can go and live there indefinitely. I would never want to leave there for anywhere else.

It's a very bleak place—a narrow gorge. Mountains all around restrict both view and thought. It's very dull. I bought the house because it was small and for sale. If you don't like it, I'll sell it and buy another one in some other place.

I am not well, but I hope the mountain air will help me get rid of my hallucinations. That takes care of the physical side; as for the mental side, you know everything. Although, do you really?

I've told you much about my life. Not everything, though. Not even you. By the way, I confirm to you that I do feel guilty for my wife's death, and it troubles my conscience. I haven't seen you since then, that is why I feel I must confirm it. I also feel guilty about Liza, but you know all about that. You predicted almost exactly the way it would happen.

It would be better if you didn't come. My calling you is very contemptible. Yes, and why should you bury yourself alive with me? I like you and, even in my grief, I feel good when you're around. You are the only person in whose presence I can speak aloud about myself. But that doesn't oblige you to anything. It was you who used the word "nurse," but why should you make such a great sacrifice? I want you also to understand that I am not sorry for you and that I have no respect for you either, since I am expecting you. In any case, I need a quick answer because I am leaving very soon.

About Uri, I have no illusions. I'm simply going there. I didn't choose such a dull place deliberately. There's nothing to tie me to Russia—everything here is as alien to me as anywhere else in the world. In fact, I've disliked living in Russia more than in any country, although, even in Russia, I could never manage to hate anything.

I've tried my strength in everything. You advised me to do that "to get to know myself." Testing it for myself, it seemed limitless to me, just as it had earlier in my life. You yourself saw me allow your brother to slap me in public; then I acknowledged my marriage publicly. But what was I supposed to *apply* my strength to? That I could never see and I still don't see it to this day, despite all the encouraging advice you gave me then in Switzerland, which I believed. Today as before, I'm still capable of wishing to do something decent and I derive some pleasure from this; but the next moment I want to do evil things and that also gives me pleasure. But neither of those wishes is strong enough to direct me: it is possible to cross a river on a log, but not on a splinter. I tell you all this so you won't think I'm leaving for Uri with any hope.

As before, I don't blame anyone. I had a go at wild debauchery and wasted my strength on it, but I don't like debauchery and didn't want it. Lately you have been watching me. You know, I even looked at our negators with hatred bred of my envy for their hopes! But your fears were unfounded; I couldn't be one of their brotherhood because I didn't share anything with them. I couldn't join them even for fun, and not because the ridiculous side of it stopped me—I'm not afraid of the ridiculous—but simply because, despite everything, I do have the habits of a decent man, and they disgusted me. But, possibly, if I had envied and hated them more, I might have joined them. You can see then how easy it all was for me and how I threw myself from one thing to another.

Oh my dear, you tender and generous creature whose heart I have divined! Perhaps you hope to give me so much love, to shower upon me so much beauty from your beautiful soul that finally there will be a goal in my life? No, I'd better warn you that my love will be just as shallow as I am myself and that you will be unhappy. Your brother said to me that a man who loses his links with his native land loses at the same time his gods and his life's goals. That, like everything, could be argued about indefinitely, but the only thing that has come out of me is negation without strength and without generosity. In fact, I didn't even have negation to offer, because everything in me was always shallow and apathetic. Kirilov was generous, and so he couldn't bear an idea and killed himself. But then, I can see that he was generous because he wasn't sane. I can never lose my reason and never believe in an idea the way he did. I cannot even get very deeply interested in an idea. Never, never will I be able to shoot myself!

I know that I ought to kill myself, to sweep myself off the earth like some pernicious insect. But I am afraid of suicide because I am afraid of showing generosity. I know that my suicide would be yet another hoax—a last hoax in an endless series of hoaxes. So what's the use of deceiving myself and pretending to act generously? I am incapable of shame or indignation and, therefore, I am also incapable of despair.

It has suddenly occurred to me that I'm writing at great length. Please forgive me. I could go on like this for a hundred pages, while ten lines should suffice. Ten lines should be sufficient to ask you to come and be my "nurse."

Since I left Skvoreshniki, I've been living at the stationmaster's at the sixth railroad stop from town. I met him during my drinking days in Petersburg five years ago. No one knows where I am. Write to me under his name. I enclose the address.

NIKOLAI STAVROGIN

Dasha immediately showed the letter to Mrs. Stavrogin, who read it and then asked Dasha to leave her because she wanted to reread it alone in her room. But only a few minutes later she called Dasha back.

"Are you going?" Mrs. Stavrogin asked almost shyly.

"Yes," Dasha said.

"Get ready—we'll go together."

Dasha looked at her in bewilderment.

"What else is there left for me to do? What difference does

it make now? I'll register in Uri too and live in that valley there. Don't worry, I won't be in your way."

They started to pack in a hurry, to catch the twelve-o'clock train. But before half an hour had passed, Alexei arrived from Skvoreshniki and announced that the young master had unexpectedly arrived on the morning train, but that he "didn't feel like answering questions" and just walked through the house and shut himself up in his suite.

"I came here without the master's orders, ma'am, to report it to you," Alexei said, looking very attentively at Mrs. Stavrogin.

She gave him one piercing look and didn't ask any questions. The carriage was ready in a matter of seconds. Dasha went along. On the way, I've been told, they kept crossing themselves. In Nikolai's rooms all the doors were open, but he couldn't be found anywhere.

"Could the master be in the attic?" a servant suggested.

Strangely enough, several servants had followed Mrs. Stavrogin to her son's suite, while the others waited in the big drawing room. Never before would they have allowed themselves such a breach. Mrs. Stavrogin noticed it, but said nothing.

They went upstairs. The attic consisted of three rooms. But he was in none of them.

"Would the master be there by any chance?" a servant said, pointing to the door of a tiny cubicle in the loft.

That door, usually kept locked, was now wide open. The cubicle was just under the roof and was reached by a long, steep, very narrow staircase.

"I don't want to go in. Why should he have climbed up there?"

Mrs. Stavrogin looked at the servants standing around her and turned terribly pale. They looked back at her in silence. Dasha was trembling.

Mrs. Stavrogin hurried up the narrow stairs with Dasha behind her. But when she stepped into the cubicle, she let out a scream and fainted.

The citizen of the Canton of Uri was dangling just by the door. On the table there was a scrap of paper with the words, "Accuse no one, I did it myself," written in pencil. Next to it on the table there was also a hammer, a piece of soap, and a large nail, apparently in case the other one hadn't held up. The strong silk cord on which Nikolai Stavrogin had

hanged himself was lavishly smeared with soap. All this indicated that to the last second he was in full possession of his
mental faculties and had acted with premeditation.

After the autopsy, all our medical experts rejected any
possibility of insanity.

Afterword

No other novel by Dostoyevsky provoked as much controversy as *The Possessed*. It was serialized in the *Russian Messenger*, a St. Petersburg monthly, between January 1871 and December 1872, and each new installment added fuel to the raging polemics. The indignant liberals saw in it a calumny on the Russian intelligentsia; radical critics found its characters utterly fantastic, on the borderline of madness, and considered their portrayal nothing more than a clinical diagnosis of pathological delusions. The conservatives, on the other hand, acclaimed the novel as a daring exposé of anarchistic nihilism, and praised its author as a defender of Monarchy and Church. Even after Dostoyevsky's death the argument went on with unabated vehemence. Any attempt to look at *The Possessed* dispassionately and to appraise it objectively was thwarted by political passion: the rightists were enthusiastic about it, and the leftists rejected it uncompromisingly. When the Moscow Art Theater decided in 1913 to adapt the novel for the stage, Gorky protested against the choice of such a "slanderous and sadistic work." Under the Soviets *The Possessed* became the emblem of reactionary ideology and was dubbed "socially obnoxious and detrimental to the cause of socialism." No separate editions of the novel were allowed to be printed in the USSR for almost forty years, and the Communist press never missed an opportunity of attacking it for political reasons while pointing out its purely literary defects. Critics in Europe and America have been less politically biased than their Russian colleagues but they disagree profoundly in their evaluation of the novel. Some of them include it in the list of "great books" and call it a most outstanding work of world literature; others deny its significance as a lasting creation of art, label it a melodramatic and inflated misfit, and attribute its popularity to obvious political factors.

Such a range of opinion, and the violence with which each faction sustains its thesis, can be partly explained by the complexity and unevenness of *The Possessed,* and by the singular circumstances in which the novel was conceived and written.

In the late eighteen sixties, while staying with his wife Anna in Dresden, Saxony, Dostoyevsky was making drafts for a new work and wavering between several projects. He was very attracted by the idea of a novel centered around the problem of atheism and the existence of God, and made extended notes for *The Life of a Great Sinner* (some of them served later for *The Brothers Karamazov*). On the other hand, he was greatly concerned with the issue of social revolution, and he felt a strong urge to write about the contemporary Russian scene. Critics had often pointed out that his novels, unlike those of Turgenev and Goncharov whom he considered his literary rivals, failed to depict Russian society and to reflect "the burning problems of the day." Dostoyevsky bitterly resented these reproaches and claimed that his *Notes from the Underground* and *Crime and Punishment,* for example, gave a more profound interpretation of nihilism than Turgenev's *Fathers and Sons*. Still, this time he was determined to produce some sort of social chronicle which would definitely refute his critics. He was well aware that events in his native land were approaching a decisive turn: after the emancipation of the serfs and the era of reforms in the early sixties, socialist and positivist ideas were becoming prevalent in educated society, particularly among university students; the increasing number of revolutionary groups and terrorist acts were signs of an imminent storm.

Dostoyevsky believed that bourgeois capitalism, the power-greedy Catholic Church, and Protestant rationalism were undermining the West, while the strengthening of socialism in Russia was a direct threat to the nation's future. He considered capitalism and socialism mortal enemies of Christianity. In his opinion, a truly topical and patriotic novel should unmask the demonic nature of the revolutionary forces, and by doing so would perform a civic and religious duty. Hence the sharp political edge of his new novel, which he conceived from its beginnings as a political pamphlet, an exposé of ideas and people that he considered subversive and dangerous for his country. A newspaper item helped him jell the plot of the novel which was later called *The Possessed*. A certain Ivanov, a student at the Agricultural Institute and a member of the People's Avengers, a secret revolutionary group, was murdered as a traitor to the cause. The crime had been instigated by Nechayev, the leader of the Avengers. He had spread the false rumor of Ivanov's betrayal because he had found the student a hindrance to his plans and wanted to liquidate him. A grim fanatic, Nechayev was ready to use blackmail, lies, and violence to attain his ends. His Jesuitical methods were condemned by Russian socialists of the seventies, but until his arrest he held a hypnotic power over his followers.

Ivanov's murder probably served as a catalyst to Dostoyevsky. He mentioned it in a letter written in October 1870: "One of the main events in my tale will be Ivanov's murder by Nechayev." He denied, however, having used Nechayev as the prototype of Peter Verkhovensky and Ivanov as that of Shatov, and although there are some similarities between the scenes in *The Possessed* and the actual events of the early seventies, it would be a gross error to take this highly exaggerated and polemical narrative as a precise rendering of social conditions. As was customary with Dostoyevsky, he did not simply represent reality but borrowed facts and occurrences from it which were then transformed in the laboratory of his creative imagination. Historical accuracy in *The Possessed* is sacrificed for the purpose of political denunciation and polemical intent. The latter is most evident in Dostoyevsky's representation of Stepan Trofimovich, with whom the story begins, and Karmazinov, a secondary character. He did give Stepan Trofimovich some traits of Timofey Granovsky, an idealistic historian and Moscow professor of history in the forties. But the inefficient parasite of Stavrogin's mother has little likeness to his alleged prototype and Dostoyevsky invented him for a double purpose; he wanted to laugh at the "beautiful souls" of useless liberals, and to prove that the progressive humanists of the forties were responsible for the socialist leanings of the following generation. Peter Verkhovensky is Stepan Trofimovich's son, and though he treats his father with contempt, the latter recognizes that his own negligence and vanity formed the mind and character of this monstrous young man. Thus Dostoyevsky tried to trace the origins of the "revolutionary disease" and to stress the role of heredity in its eruption. In the case of Karmazinov, he was simply giving vent to his hostility toward Turgenev, caricaturing the famous novelist in the figure of the pompous, vain, egocentric, and hypocritical writer who flirts with the revolutionaries and simply wants to be "in" on latest fashions.

Of course, Stepan Trofimovich and Karmazinov are fictional images distorted by sarcasm and anger. The same polemical passion guided Dostoyevsky's pen in the sketches of the individual "devils," as he called the members of the underground group led by Verkhovensky, the archvillain. They are freaks, demented visionaries, petty clerks gnawed by ambition, cowards spreading malicious gossip, potential criminals, jealous husbands and—at their best—naïve young men. Here again we have a collection of cartoons rather than a gallery of realistic portraits. But if Dostoyevsky failed in his immediate and topical purpose of drawing a picture of contemporary Russian society, he succeeded, in a most uncanny way, in making a prophecy. The people and situations he depicted might not have been typical of the seventies, but they did become extremely representative some fifty years later. He predicted the fanatical intransigence of the leaders, the justification of mass murder, the denial of individual freedom, and the replacement of religious precepts by a stricter revolutionary dogma. Peter Verkhovensky, who deals with human beings with utter cynicism, and is always plotting, intriguing, thriving on scandals, and taking advantage of the lower instincts in men, is a typical Communist politician of the Stalin era. Even more so is Shigalov, who foresees an earthly paradise in which one tenth of mankind will rule the remaining nine tenths with an iron hand; he accepts slavery as the price of equality and material well-being, and extols dictatorship as a prerequisite of a Communist regime. When *The Possessed* was published in book form, Dostoyevsky's contemporaries found it implausible, and now we agree that it was historically inexact. But as a foreboding of all the distortions of the Russian revolution it is frightening in its insight and accuracy.

For this alone *The Possessed* would still be an important novel today. Many observers of contemporary Russia believe that it offers a key to the psychological and political enigmas of Soviet society, and consider it a useful source book for the study of Communism. But, in fact, it is more than a piece of prophecy or a political exposé, despite Dostoyevsky's avowed intentions. He wrote in April 1870: "The novel I am working at is tendentious, I want to express myself with frenzy. They will all bark at me, all these Nihilists and Westernizers, they will call me a reactionary, but, what the hell, I will throw at them what I think." Yet the significance of what he created goes beyond the limits of an antirevolutionary challenge. In a strange and complex way it reflects the main themes he had pursued in his other novels and reveals the basic problems which, in his own terms, had "tormented" him all his life. The question most closely connected with his denunciation of socialists and revolutionaries was that of Russia's destiny. Dostoyevsky shared the Slavophiles' faith in Russia's special path of historical development determined by national character, the Greek Orthodox Church, and an autocratic regime. In the novel Shatov asserts a similar belief in the religious mission his country is bound to fulfill. False Westernizers murder him because he is a menace to their conspiracy—not materially but ideologically. Although Shatov recognizes that socialism is "healthier than Roman Catholicism," he sees it as a form of atheism because it dreams of a society based on science and reason and in this is opposed to the Russian spirit, which is linked to Orthodox Christianity. For him the problem of the revolution is essentially a question of God and religion, and man's place in the universe. In this the honest nationalist Shatov is akin to Kirilov, the half-mystical, half-crazy engineer who becomes a Christian atheist and preaches suicide as an act of will, asserting the potential greatness of man in his fight against fear. This generous and passionate epileptic, who would proclaim the death of the gods, is possessed by the idea of a man-god who will transform earth and history in his own image. Kirilov's theories and his manic suicide reflect Dostoyevsky's favorite themes of transgression and search *for* God which assumes the disguise of a struggle *against* God. In *The Possessed* militant atheism often is represented as the reverse of ardent religious faith. It leads to diabolical deceit, crime, evil, and degradation only if the atheist does not have a substitute for divine force, only if he does not believe in anything, not even in revolution. Thus the main hero of the novel is not Verkhovensky, this harlequin of the underground movement, an ambiguous and Mephistophelian apostle of destruction, but the handsome, elegant, and mysterious Stavrogin. Verkhovensky idolizes this former Guards officer and hopes to turn him into "the pretender," the dark prince of a revolutionary rebellion. But Stavrogin's force is only in negation. It is true that Kirilov, Shatov, and others got their ideas of atheism, nationalism, or socialism from Stavrogin, but their master is committed to none of these; for him theories are only a matter of intellectual exercise. This rich landowner married to a crippled and demented beggar, this sadist who pushes to suicide the girl-child he had raped, this aristocrat who plays with revolutionary machinations, is the embodiment of strength without direction. He may represent the symbol of Russia's latent forces which the "devils" try to harness for their nefarious ends. Stavrogin is equally capable of noble action and of beastly brutality, he is attracted both by vice and beauty, by degradation and sublimation. For him everything is permissible because he does not obey any moral code, and therefore he belongs in the company of Dostoyevsky's "transgressors," those who challenge God and society and their own conscience by willful actions "beyond good and evil." Whatever Stavrogin undertakes leads inevitably to disaster, and he becomes a tragic figure in the world of "little demons."

With the unpredictable Stavrogin as the main hero, and a revolutionary conspiracy as the vehicle of the plot, *The Possessed* is naturally filled with surprises and catastrophes. Its balance sheet of horrors is longer than in any other Dostoyevsky novel: six of the protagonists are murdered, three die a natural death, and two commit suicide, and all this is projected against the background of riots, arson, blackmail, secret marriage, duels, and intrigues. To all the paraphernalia of a mystery story must be added the rhythm of a narrative which constantly changes pace—from ironical exposition to philosophical dialogue, and from explanatory passages to melodramatic climaxes. Not only the principal actors in this drama-novel but also the secondary characters —drunken captains with a criminal record, prideful heiresses, plotting bureaucrats, dangerous convicts, verbose liberals— all move in an atmosphere of premonition, gloom, and the rise and fall of chance and bursts of passion. One can say that there is too much of everything in *The Possessed*, that the stage is overcrowded with actors and that the shifting of settings from students' garrets to sumptuous drawing rooms, or from the steps of a church to fashionable clubs, is too sudden—but all this dizzying saraband of incredible episodes is regulated by a unity of spirit and purpose, and each member of the cast has unforgettable individual characteristics. They all may talk or act in a most irrational, contradictory, romantic fashion, but we accept them more readily than the so-called "true to nature" literary snapshots. They are completely convincing because the hidden recesses of their mind and heart are revealed in the light of supreme insight and knowledge of human nature. Moreover, the inner fervor of the composition is so infectious, the building up of tension is done with such drive, the dynamism of this Russian fantasy is so powerful, that we forget all the formal shortcomings of the book and simply yield to its fascination. Repeatedly we are brought to the utmost peak of emotion, are given a few moments to relax, and then are launched again into a breath-taking flight. And to change the metaphor—the alternation of darkness and light, the intimation of mystery, the sense of foreboding that grips us, for example, in the description of Stavrogin's nocturnal wanderings, all this reminds us of Rembrandt, and leaves as lasting an impression as the paintings of the great Dutchman.

The Possessed is not only a novel about revolution, crime, atheism, religion, strong men, underground men, and the Russian past and present. It is, despite its dangerous closeness to melodrama and bad taste, one of the most captivating and thrilling tales of modern literature. And the story of extraordinary people, romantic adventures, and paradoxical ideas is told by a great builder of plots, a master psychologist and an artist-thinker who transforms abstract concepts into living realities, and turns symbolic, greater-than-life characters into believable and memorable representatives of humanity.

Selected Bibliography

Other Works by Dostoyevsky

Poor Folk, 1846   Novel

The Double, 1846   Novel

The Landlady, 1847   Story

An Honest Thief, 1848   Story

White Nights, 1848   Novel   (Signet CT300—75¢)

A Little Hero, 1849   Story

Uncle's Dream, 1859   Story

The Friend of the Family, 1859   Novel

The House of the Dead, 1859-1861   Stories and Essays

The Insulted and the Injured, 1862   Novel

Notes from Underground, 1864   Novel   (Signet CT300—75¢)

Crime and Punishment, 1866   Novel   (Signet CT362—75¢)

The Gambler, 1867   Novel

The Idiot, 1868-1869   Novel

The Eternal Husband, 1870   Novel

A Raw Youth, 1875   Novel

The Dream of a Ridiculous Man, 1877   Story   (Signet CT-300—75¢)

A Diary of a Writer, 1876-1877; 1880-1881

The Brothers Karamazov, 1880   Novel   (Signet CT33—75¢)

Selected Biography and Criticism

Berdyaev, Nicolas. *Dostoyevsky*. New York: Meridian Books, Inc., 1960.

Carr, Edward Hallett. *Dostoyevsky: 1821-1881*. New York: The Macmillan Company; London: George Allen & Unwin, Ltd., 1949.

Gide, André. *Dostoyevsky*. New York: New Directions, 1949.

Ivanov, Vyacheslav. *Freedom and the Tragic Life: A Study in Dostoyevsky*. New York: The Noonday Press, 1957.

Jackson, R. L. *Dostoyevsky's Underground Man in Russian Literature*. New York: Humanities Press, Inc., 1959.

Mirsky, Dmitrii S. *History of Russian Literature,* ed. by Francis J. Whitfield. New York: Alfred A. Knopf, Inc. (Vintage Books), 1949.

Seduro, Vladimir. *Dostoyevsky in Russian Literary Criticism: 1846-1956*. New York: Columbia University Press, 1957.

Simmons, E. J. *Dostoyevsky: The Making of a Novelist*. London: Oxford University Press, 1940.

Slonim, Marc. *The Epic of Russian Literature from Its Origins through Tolstoy*. New York: Oxford University Press, 1950.

Steiner, George. *Tolstoy or Dostoyevsky*. New York: Alfred A. Knopf, Inc., 1959.

Yarmolinsky, Avrahm. *Dostoyevsky. His Life and Art*. New York: Grove Press, Inc., 1960.

Zweig, Stefan. *Three Masters: Balzac, Dickens and Dostoyevsky*. New York: Viking Press, Inc.; London: George Allen & Unwin, Ltd., 1930.

SIGNET CLASSICS from Around the World

☐ **THE BROTHERS KARAMAZOV by Fyodor Dostoyevsky.**
Complete and unabridged, the great classic about a passionate and tragic Russian family. Translated by Constance Garnett. Revised, with a Foreword by Manuel Komroff. (#CT33—75¢)

☐ **NOTES FROM UNDERGROUND, WHITE NIGHTS, THE DREAM OF A RIDICULOUS MAN AND SELECTIONS FROM HOUSE OF THE DEAD by Fyodor Dostoyevsky.**
Selected writings by the great Russian author, newly translated with an Afterword by Andrew R. MacAndrew. (#CT300—75¢)

☐ **NIGHT FLIGHT by Antoine de St. Exupéry.** A novel of beauty and power about the intrepid flyers of the early, heroic age of aviation. Translated by Stuart Gilbert. Foreword by André Gide. (#CP309—60¢)

☐ **DEATH OF A NOBODY by Jules Romains.** This noted modern classic, by a novelist considered "the French Dos Passos," tells how the memory of an unimportant nobody survives in the minds of all who knew him. Translated by Desmond McCarthy and Sidney Waterlow. Foreword by Maurice Natanson. (#CD54—50¢)

☐ **DEIRDRE by James Stephens.** A haunting allegorical novel based on a violent, primordial Gaelic legend. Afterword by Walter Starkie. (#CP116—60¢)

☐ **THE STORY OF GOSTA BERLING by Selma Lagerlöf.**
An unfrocked minister's search for redemption amidst the farmlands and folk of 19th century Sweden. A new translation with an Afterword by Robert Bly.
(#CT125—75¢)

☐ **THE AMBASSADORS by Henry James.** A psychologically penetrating novel showing the conflicting cultures of Europe and America by the famous expatriate author. Afterword and note on the text by R. W. Stallman.
(#CP117—60¢)
